The Mammoth Book of

PARANORMAL
ROMANCE

Also available

The Mammoth Book of

PARANORMAL
ROMANCE

Edited and with an Introduction by

TRISHA TELEP

ROBINSON

RUNNING PRESS
PHILADELPHIA · LONDON

Constable & Robinson Ltd
3 The Lanchesters
162 Fulham Palace Road
London W6 9ER
www.constablerobinson.com

First published in the UK by Robinson,
an imprint of Constable & Robinson, 2009

A copy of the British Library Cataloguing in Publication
Data is available from the British Library

UK ISBN 978-1-84529-941-5

1 3 5 7 9 10 8 6 4 2

First published in the United States in 2009 by
Running Press Book Publishers

9 8 7 6 5 4 3 2 1
Digit on the right indicates the number of this printing

US Library of Congress number: 2008942197
US ISBN 978-7624-3651-4

Running Press Book Publishers
2300 Chestnut Street
Philadelphia, PA 19103-4371

Visit us on the web!
www.runningpress.com

Printed and bound in the EU

Contents

Acknowledgments

"The Temptation of Robin Green" © by Carrie Vaughn, LLC. First publication, original to this anthology. Printed by permission of the author.

"Succubus Seduction" © by Cheyenne McCray. First publication, original to this anthology. Printed by permission of the author.

"Paranormal Romance Blues" © by K.L.A Fricke Inc. First publication, original to this anthology. Printed by permission of the author.

"John Doe" © by Anna Windsor. First publication, original to this anthology. Printed by permission of the author.

"Taking Hold" © by Anya Bast. First publication, original to this anthology. Printed by permission of the author.

"How To Date a Superhero" © by Jean Johnson. First publication, original to this anthology. Printed by permission of the author.

"Daniel" © by C. T. Adams and Cathy Clamp. First publication, original to this anthology. Printed by permission of the authors.

"At Second Bite" © by Michelle Rowen. First publication, original to this anthology. Printed by permission of the author.

"Blue Crush" © by Roxanne Conrad. First publication, original to this anthology. Printed by permission of the author.

"The Wager" © by Sherrilyn Kenyon. First published in *Elemental: The Tsunami Relief Anthology*, May 2006. Printed by permission of the author.

"In Sheep's Clothing" © by Meljean Brook. First publication, original to this anthology. Printed by permission of the author.

"The Dream Catcher" © by Jennifer Ashley. First publication, original to this anthology. Printed by permission of the author.

Introduction

Demons are the new vampires, or so I'm told by reliable sources. The world of the paranormal has been blurring, blending with fantasy to a certain extent, to create a magical new partnership. There are now hundreds of blogs and websites devoted to different strands of the paranormal and to the authors who write it. All are full of lively discussions between writers, would-be writers, and devoted fans – the website *fangsfurandfey*, a LiveJournal community started by writers Jeaniene Frost, Caitlin Kittredge, and Melissa Marr, is just one fantastic example.

Such creative, energetic dialogue between readers and writers has given paranormal romance a fun, fast and furious buzz. Forget writers shuttered away writing with no connection to their fans; most paranormal romance authors are accessible and contactable, and are forever gracious with comments and questions. This is no ivory tower genre, but one with a very human face (albeit attached to a body with iridescent, fairy wings).

Put another way, paranormal writers quite simply have the best fans. These are readers who turn up to book signings bubbling over with enthusiasm, who get tattoos from their best-loved books (when Sherrilyn Kenyon's *Acheron* was published, one of my regulars showed up at the bookshop where I work one afternoon with a perfect replica of the Acheron symbol – "a yellow sun pierced by three white lightning bolts" – at the back of her neck), who don't say no to cupcakes because they are on some ridiculous Palm Beach diet, and who are passionate about the genre: what they like, they LOVE; what they don't, they LOATHE. How refreshing is that?

The authors in this new anthology have been drawn not only from the broad wealth of talent in the paranormal romance genre, but also from the world of fantasy. We haven't completely neglected our old friend the vampire (from the previous collection, *The Mammoth Book of Vampire Romance*) but he has been seriously overwhelmed by a magical collection of succubi, selkies, mermaids, werewolves, angels, ghosts, sorceresses, goddesses, gargoyles, fae princes and djinn, to name just a few.

This volume is the perfect opportunity to try out some new paranormal authors or curl up with the newest stories from your die-hard favourites. Where else are you going to find such a huge collection of bestselling, and critically acclaimed, authors in one place? Paranormal romance is blossoming.

The Temptation of Robin Green

Carrie Vaughn

The talking dog always whined when Robin fed the griffin.

"C'mon, Robin, please? The doc'll never know. I *never* get any treats."

"Sorry, Jones," Robin said to the dust-coloured mutt in the steel and acrylic-glass cell.

"Please? Please, please, *please*?" Jones' tail wagged the entire back end of his body.

"No, Jones. Sorry."

"But it's not fair. *Those* guys get fed late."

"They have bigger stomachs than you."

"Oh, please, just once, and I'll never ask again!"

But it was a lie, the whining would never stop, and giving in would make it worse. It turned out that a talking dog was even more endearing than the non-talking kind. It took all of Lieutenant Robin Green's army training to turn away from the mutt and move on to the rest of her rounds.

She hit a switch to illuminate a bank of lights in the second enclosure. The occupant had the thick, tawny-furred body of a lion, but its neck and head were those of an eagle: feathered, dark brown, with glaring eyes and a huge hooked bill. It opened its beak and called at her when the light came on, a sound somewhere between a screech and a roar.

A small door at the base of the acrylic glass allowed her to slide a tray of steaming meat into the cell. The griffin pounced on it, snarling and tearing at the meat, swallowing in gulps.

Robin jumped back. No matter how many times that happened, it always surprised her.

Next, she took a bundle of hay to a side door that allowed access to a third enclosure and went inside. Technically, entering the enclosures was against regulations, but she had asked for special permission in this case.

"Here you go, kid."

Hoofed footfalls shuffled towards her through the wood shavings that covered the floor. The animal stood about fifteen hands high, had a milk-white coat, cloven hooves, a tuft of hair under its chin and a silver, spiral horn between its eyes.

Robin spread out the hay, feeding some of it to the creature by hand. She and the unicorn got along well, though at twenty-three she didn't like to admit her virginity. She'd fallen back on excuses to explain why she'd never seemed to make time for dates, for getting to know the men around her, for simply having fun: too much to do, too much studying, too much work, too much at stake. She'd always thought there'd be time, eventually. But those old patterns died hard. Colleagues and friends paired off around her, and she'd started to feel left out.

All that aside, now she was glad about it. Otherwise, she'd never have had the chance to hold a unicorn's muzzle in her hands and stroke its silken cheek.

She'd graduated top of her class with a degree in biology and made no secret of her interest in some of the wilder branches of cryptozoology, however unfashionable. She'd gone through the university on an Army ROTC scholarship and accepted an active duty commission because she thought it would give her a chance to travel. Instead, she'd been offered a position in a shadowy military research project – covert, classified and very intriguing.

She'd had no idea what she was getting herself into when she accepted the research-assistant position.

After visiting with the unicorn for half an hour, Robin continued to the next level down. The Residence.

This level of the Center for the Study of Paranatural Biology made Lieutenant Green nervous. It seemed like a prison. Well, it was a prison, though the people incarcerated here weren't exactly criminals. Colonel Ottoman (PhD, MD, etc.) liked to say it didn't matter since they weren't really human. A lowly research assistant and low-ranking, newly minted officer like Robin was not supposed to question such a declaration. Still, she made an effort to treat the inhabitants of the Residence like people.

"Hello? Anyone home?" Colonel Ottoman and Doctor Lerna were supposed to be here, but Robin must have been the first in for the night shift. The day shift had already checked out.

Despite its clandestine military nature, the place was as cluttered as one would expect from any university laboratory. Paper-covered desks and crowded bookshelves lined one wall. Another wall boasted a row of heavy equipment: refrigeration units, incubators, oscillators. Several island worktables held sinks and faucets, microscopes, banks of test tubes and flasks.

One acrylic-glass wall revealed a pair of cells. The first cell was completely dark, its inhabitant asleep. Special features of this room included a silver-alloy lining and silver shavings embedded in the walls. The next cell had garlic extract mixed with the paint.

"How are you this evening, Lieutenant?" the occupant of the dimly-lit second cell greeted her.

"I'm fine, Rick. Where is everyone?"

"There's a note on your desk."

She went to her desk, the smallest of the group, and found a note in Dr Ottoman's jagged writing on her desk calendar:

Lt Green,
Sorry to leave you alone, special conference came up, Bob and I will be in DC all week. Hold down the fort. No special instructions regarding the new arrival, just leave it alone.
Col Ottoman.

Just like that. Gone. Leaving her alone on the night watch for a whole week. That meant she wouldn't actually have anything to do but feed everyone and keep an eye on the monitors.

"Bad news?" Rick said.

"Just inconvenient. Do you know anything about a new arrival?"

"In the aquatics lab."

She started for the next door.

"Ah, Lieutenant. Chores first?" Rick – short for Ricardo, surname unknown, date of birth unknown, place of birth unknown – slouched nonchalantly against the plastic window at the front of his cell. He didn't sound desperate – yet.

"Right."

From the incubator she removed the three pints of blood, "borrowed" from the base hospital, which had been warming since the last shift. She poured them into clean beakers, the only useful glassware at hand, and reached through the small panel to set the glasses of blood on a table inside Rick's cell. It wasn't really any different from feeding raw meat to the griffin.

Rick waited until the panel was closed before moving to the table. He looked composed, classic, like he should have been wearing a silk cravat and dinner jacket instead of jeans and a cotton shirt.

"Cheers." He drank down the first glass without pause.

She didn't watch him, not directly. The strange, hypnotic power of his gaze had been proven experimentally. So she watched his slender hands, the shoulder of his white shirt, the movement of his throat as he swallowed.

He lowered the beaker and sighed. "Ah. Four hours old. Fine vintage." His mouth puckered. A faint blush began to suffuse his face, which had been deathly pale.

Robin continued the last leg of her rounds. The next room contained aquariums, large dolphin tanks with steel catwalks ringing the edges. Bars reaching from the catwalks to the ceiling enclosed the tanks, forming cages around the water.

Robin retrieved a pail of fish – cut-up tuna, whole mackerel, a few abalone mixed with kelp leaves – from the refrigerator at the end of the workspace, and climbed the stairs to the top edge of the south tank.

"How are you, Marina?"

A woman lounged on an artificial rock which broke the surface of the water in the middle of the tank. She hugged a convenient outcrop of plaster and played with her bronze-coloured hair. Instead of legs she had a tail: long, covered in shimmering, blue-silver scales, ending in a broad fin which flapped the water lazily.

The mermaid covered her mouth with her pale hand and laughed. It was teasing, vicious laughter. Marina seldom spoke. "Here you are, when you're hungry." Robin nudged the pail to where the mermaid could reach it through the bars. Marina's laughter doubled. She arched her back, baring her small breasts, and pushed into the water. Diving under, she spun, her muscular tail pumping her in a fast loop around the rock's chain anchor. Bubbles streamed from her long hair, a silver trail.

Suddenly, she broke the surface and shook her hair, spraying water. Still laughing, her gaze darted across the catwalk to the north tank. Slyly, she looked back at Robin, writhed so she floated on her back, and splashed her tail.

Robin looked at the north tank, which until that night had been empty. A seal, torpedo-shaped, rubbery, its grey skin mottled with black, lay on the artificial rock and stared at her with black, shining eyes. The new arrival. A tag, sealed in a plastic, waterproof cover, hung from the rail by the cage. It read: "On loan from the British Alternative Biologies Laboratory. *HOMO PINNIPEDIA*. Common names: selkie (Scottish), silke (Irish)."

A selkie. It used its seal skin to travel through the water, but it could shed the skin to walk on land as a human. The creature raised itself on its flippers and looked at her with interest. Real, human interest shone in those round black eyes.

"Wow," Robin murmured. What were they going to do with a selkie?

She leaned on the railing, watching for a time, but the selkie didn't move. She kept a notebook, a journal for informal observations and such. She could write: "Seal, lounging."

She had to walk rounds every two hours, since many of the subjects didn't show up on the video monitors. She was supposed to conduct formal interviews with Rick, since he was obviously most active during the night watch. But Ottoman had collected all the arcane information he could from him – without going so far as staking and dissecting him – months ago, so they usually just chatted. Tonight though, she found herself leaning in the doorway to the aquatics lab. The lights in the lab were dim. The water seemed to glow with its own blue aura.

"It won't change form while you're staring at it," Rick said.

"I'm just curious."

The seal swam, fluidly circling, peering at her through the thick glass, disappearing regularly as it bobbed to the surface for air.

"It. Don't you even know what gender it is?" Bradley Njalson, the werewolf, had woken up. His deep voice echoed from his bed against the far wall of his cell.

"Yes, oh great biologist," Rick said, "have you sexed the specimen?"

She'd tried, but the seal had deftly managed to keep that part of its anatomy turned away from her.

"The tag didn't say," she said. She'd looked for the research files and the reports that had arrived with the selkie, but Ottoman had locked them up before rushing off to his conference.

For all she knew, it was just a seal.

The next night, she spent most of her shift sitting on the top step of the catwalk stairs, watching it.

She heard a splash from the south tank. Marina pulled herself to the bars and watched Robin watching the other tank.

"Marina, what do you know about selkies?"

The mermaid, who'd been caught in Dingle Bay in Ireland several years before, had been humming a song, an Irish-sounding jig. "A mermaid died to save a silke once."

"Can you tell me about it?"

"Ask 'im."

Robin turned to where the mermaid nodded, to where a man hung on to the bars of the selkie's cage, holding himself half out of the water, smiling. Surprised, Robin jumped to her feet.

He was lean, muscular. Slick with water, his pale skin shone. Black hair dripped past his shoulders. His face was solid, unblemished. He didn't grip the bars like a prisoner; he held them loosely, using them to balance as he treaded water. His smile was playful, like she was inside the cage and he was studying her.

Tentatively, she nodded a greeting. "Hello."

He pushed himself away from the bars and glided back through the water. He was naked and totally unselfconscious. His body was as sculptured and handsome as his face. He had the broad shoulders and muscular arms of an Olympic swimmer, powerful legs and every muscle in his torso was defined. She could have used his body for an anatomy lecture.

He swam to the artificial rock, climbed out of the water, and sat back, reclining. He spread his arms, exposing to best advantage his broad chest, toned abdomen and . . . *genitalia* was too clinical a word for what he displayed. He was posing for her.

Next to him lay a bundle of grey, rubbery skin.

Robin stood at the bars of his cage, looking through them for an unobstructed view. She didn't remember moving there. She took a deep, reflexive breath. Her heartbeat wouldn't slow down.

Marina laughed uncontrollably, both hands over her mouth, tail flapping. Her voice was musical, piercing.

Robin fled the room.

Back in the main lab, she stood with her back against the wall, eyes closed, gasping.

"Let me guess. The selkie – male?" Rick's tone was politely inquisitive.

The flush on Robin's face became one of embarrassment. So much for the biologist and her professional demeanour. "Yes. Yes, he is."

"They have a knack for that."

"A knack for what?"

"Flustering young women out of their wits. I'm sure you know the stories."

Since her posting to the Center, Robin had to question all the myths and ancient tales. They might be just stories, then again . . . She went to the bookshelves to look up "selkie" in Briggs' *Encyclopedia of Fairies*.

"How do you do it?" Rick asked, moving to the end of his window.

"Do what?"

"Remain so clinical. When confronted with so many contradictions to your assumptions about the world."

"I expand my assumptions," she said.

"What about the magic? Your inability to control your reaction to the selkie. You are so careful, Lieutenant, not to look into my eyes."

The impulse was, of course, to look at him. The voice hinted at rewards she would find when she did. Mystery. Power. She resisted, taking the book to her desk, passing Rick's cell on the way. She looked at the collar of his shirt. "Why are you all so damn seductive?"

"It's in the blood." He grinned. The allure disappeared. He could turn it on and off like a light switch.

Brad laughed, a sound like a growl.

Robin almost wished for the seal back. It had been much less distracting. For the rest of the night, the seal skin remained piled on the rock, and the man watched her. She turned her back on him to check off her rounds on the charts, and when she looked again he was right there, pressed against the bars. Sometimes, their faces were only inches apart. Sometimes, she didn't shy away, and she could feel his warm breath. He never said a word.

She was attracted to the selkie. That was a statement, an observation, something empirical with explanations having to do with the fact that she was a young woman and he was a young man. A very handsome young man. Hormones were identifiable. Controllable.

So why couldn't she seem to control the way her body flushed every time she entered the aquatics lab? Rick had mentioned magic. But the Center was here precisely because magic didn't exist, only biology that had not yet been explained.

Biology. She needed a cold shower.

Wednesday night.

She turned around after setting down Marina's supper and tripped on the catwalk. No, she didn't trip – Marina had reached through the bars, grabbed her ankle and tipped her over. The mermaid was stronger than she looked. Robin sprawled across the catwalk between the tanks, too surprised to move, lying with the meat of her palms digging into the steel treads.

The selkie was by the bars, right beside her. He touched her hand. Even though his hand was damp and cool, Robin thought her skin would catch fire. He took her hand, brought it through the bars and kissed it, touching each knuckle with his lips.

When she didn't pull away, he grew bold, turning her hand, kissing the inside of her wrist, tracing her thumb with his tongue, sucking on the tip of a finger. She hadn't imagined she could feel like this, all her nerves focused on what he was doing to her. She closed her eyes. Nothing existed in the world but her hand and his mouth.

She was on duty. This was not allowed. She should stand up and leave. Write a report about the cooperative behaviour of the selkie and the mermaid. Marina was laughing, quietly now, from behind her rock.

Gradually, Robin slid forwards so that her face was at the bars. She shouldn't be doing this. The security cameras recorded everything. The selkie kissed her. His lips moved slowly, carefully tasting every part of her mouth, letting her taste him. Then his hands cupped her face. If it hadn't been for the bars, she would have let him pull her into the water.

He drew away first. The bars kept her from reaching after him. He swam a few feet away, holding her gaze until he reached the door of the cage, where he lingered, waiting. The message: if she wanted to continue, she'd have to open the door.

Well then, that was it. She lay on the catwalk, her hand still thrust through the bars, dangling in the cool water.

She used the bars to pull herself to her feet. She trembled a little, her heart racing. Nerves, that was all. She couldn't take her eyes off him. She could still feel his lips.

She planned to go straight to the next room. The control box to deactivate the electronic locks on the cages was at the top of the stairs. A single move. That's all it would take. Marina made a sound, part-sympathetic, part-mocking.

She walked past the control box, into the next room. Her lips pursed, her blood rushed.

"Lieutenant?" Rick said.

Ignoring him, she continued to the side room which held the bank of a dozen TV monitors, showing the view from cameras focused on every enclosure in the Center. Jones the dog was gnawing on a rawhide bone. The griffin was scratching the steel wall of its cell. The unicorn stood with a foot cocked, nose to the floor, sleeping. In the aquatics lab, Marina was basking on her rock, brushing her hair with her fingers, probably singing as well. The selkie, still in human form, swam back and forth in front of the door, as if pacing. Like he was waiting.

She logged into the security computer and erased the evening's footage. Then she disabled the program. All the monitors went to static. She left a note for the day shift complaining that the security system was on the fritz, that she'd tried to fix it and failed.

On her way back to the aquatics lab, Rick called, his voice harsh. "Lieutenant Green, this isn't you. This is the magic. Selkie magic. Stop and think about what you're doing."

She paused at the door. She was sure she knew what she was doing. But she'd read the stories, and Rick was right. Male selkies had a predilection for seducing women. This wasn't her, it was the magic.

And she wanted it.

The hand that pressed the button for the lock to the north tank was not hers. Not really.

The door to the selkie's cage opened with a small noise. She kept her back to it. Her breath was short, her eyes closed with the realization of what she was doing. She'd worked so hard, stayed in control her whole life, and now she did nothing but wait. She gripped the railing by the stairs.

She heard dripping, water rushing off a body climbing onto the catwalk. Still, the touch on her shoulders came as a shock and made her flinch. He must have sensed her anxiety, because he brushed her arm gently, stroking lightly with fingertips until she relaxed. Letting her grow accustomed to him, as if he were taming a wild animal. Then both his hands touched her, moved along her arms to her shoulders. Her shirt grew damp with his touch.

He kissed the back of her neck at her hairline, below the twist she kept her hair up in. His breath was hot on her skin. Her body melted, slumping into his touch. He pulled her back, away from the stairs, slipped his body in front of hers, and pressed her against the cage. She was limp, unseeing. She let him guide her.

He nuzzled her neck. Her nerves tingled with every touch. Overwhelmed, she moaned softly. His hands moved to the buttons of her dress shirt. He had them open before she realized it, and his hands were inside, cupping her breasts, fingers slipping under her bra.

Instead of putting her hands on his shoulders to push him away, like she should have done, Robin clutched at him, her fingers slipping on his slick skin. She dug her nails in for a better grip.

"Hmm," he murmured and pinned her against the bars. It was the first sound she'd heard him make.

He pulled her arms away just long enough to take her shirt off. His hand slid easily over her skin, and her bra fell away. His kisses moved from her neck, down to her breasts. She wrapped her arms around his head, holding him close.

She bent, unconsciously trying to pull away from so much sensation, so much of him, but the bars kept her close. She couldn't get away. She didn't want to. Skilfully, more deftly than she could have thought from someone who lived in water and didn't wear clothes, he opened the zipper of her trousers, and slipped his hands into her panties. One hand caressed her backside, the other – played. Oh . . . She struggled to kick off her shoes, and get her pants off, to give him better access. He helped.

Her clothes gone, they were naked together, skin pressed against skin. His erection was hard against her thigh. He paid attention to nothing but her, and she was overwhelmed. Locking her against him, he pulled her down to the catwalk.

They were going to do it, right here on the catwalk, her clothes awkwardly spread out to protect her from the steel. Marina softly sang something in Irish that was no doubt very bawdy.

And Robin felt like she had saved herself just for this moment.

The next evening, she brought hay to the unicorn's cell.

"Here you go. Come on."

The unicorn stayed at the far end of the room, its head down, its ears laid back, its nostrils flaring angrily.

Robin stood, arms limp at her sides. Of course. She left the hay, closed the door, and continued her rounds.

She found a note in the lab from the day shift explaining that the problem with the security system had been fixed with a simple reboot, and if it happened again she should try it. The officer in charge sounded testy that they'd lost a whole evening's worth of surveillance. Not that anything around here ever changed.

Except that it had, everything had changed, and Robin didn't want anyone to know it. She shut down the recording program again, and removed fuses from half the monitors as well, blinding them.

"Lieutenant," Rick called to her as she removed his pints from the incubator and prepared his supper. "Look at yourself. This isn't like you. He has enchanted you."

"I don't want to hear it," she murmured, sliding his beakers of blood through the slot in the window.

Rick didn't look at them; instead, he pressed himself to the window, palms flat against the plastic, imploring. "He's using you. He doesn't care about you, he's only manipulating you."

She looked at him. Not his eyes, but his cheekbones, his ear, the dark fringe of his hair. Anything but his eyes. "Just like you would do, if I opened your door and let you seduce me?"

Which wasn't fair, because Rick had never tried to seduce her, never tried to take advantage of her. Not that she'd ever given him the opportunity. But he'd always spoken so kindly to her. He'd spoken *to* her. And until now, she had never thought of Rick as anything but the elegant man who was supposed to be a vampire, locked in a prison cell.

"I'd never hurt you, Robin."

Now when he looked at her, she flushed. Quickly, she turned towards the aquatics lab.

"Robin, stop," he implored. "Don't go in there. Don't let him use you like this."

She gripped the doorway so hard her fingers trembled. "I've never felt like this before," she murmured.

She hadn't meant for him to hear, but he was a vampire, with a vampire's hearing. He replied, "It's not real. Let it go."

"It feels . . . I can't," she said. Because she had never felt so good, so *much* before, it was like a drug that filled her up and pushed every other worry aside. A part of her knew Rick was right, that if this feeling was a drug, then she'd become an addict in a day and she should stop this.

The rest of her didn't care.

When she reached the aquatics lab, the selkie hung on to the door of the cage, his dark eyes shining in anticipation. As soon as she'd given Marina her supper, Robin pressed the button for the lock.

Friday night.

Colonel Ottoman left a message on voicemail saying he'd be back Saturday. So this was it, for her and the selkie.

She lay in his arms, on the rock in the aquarium. He played with her loose, damp hair, running his fingers through it. She held his other arm around her waist. He was strong, silent. He wrapped her up with himself when they were together.

She couldn't let it end.

"We'll go away, you and I."

He looked away and laughed silently. He kissed her hand and shook his head.

It was a game to him. She couldn't be sure what he thought; he never spoke. She didn't know if he couldn't or wouldn't.

"Why not?"

He traced his finger along her jaw, down her neck. Then he nestled against the rock and closed his eyes.

She couldn't hope to understand him. Colonel Ottoman was right, they weren't even human.

His seal skin lay nearby, on the rock where he had discarded it. She grabbed it, jumped into the water and swam to the door. He splashed, diving after her, but she climbed onto the catwalk and slammed the door shut before he reached her.

She stood, clutching the skin to her breast. Glaring at her, he gripped the bars of the locked door.

"Tell me why I shouldn't do this."

He pressed his lips into a line and rattled the door.

She put the skin out of reach of the cage and pulled on the slacks and shirt of her uniform. All expressions of playfulness, of seduction, had left the selkie. His jaw was tight, his brow furrowed.

Skin in hand, she ran to the main lab where she found a knapsack stashed under her desk. She needed clothes for him, maybe an extra lab coat . . .

"You know how all the selkie stories end, don't you?" Rick leaned on his window.

"They're just stories."

"*I'm* just a story."

She smirked. "You're no Dracula."

"You've never seen me outside this cage, my dear."

She stopped and looked at him. His eyes were blue.

"Robin, think carefully about what you're planning. He has enchanted you." The vampire's worried expression seemed almost fatherly.

"I – I can't give him up."

"Outside this room, you won't have a choice. You will throw away your career, your life, for that?"

The official acronym for it was AWOL, not to mention stealing from a government installation. Her career, as far as Robin could tell, amounted to studying people in cages. People who defied study, no matter how many cameras and electrodes were trained on them. The selkie had shown her something that couldn't be put in a cage, a range of emotions that escaped examination. He'd shown her passion, something she'd been missing without even knowing it. She wanted to take him away from the sterility of a filtered aquarium and a steel cage. She wanted to make love with him on a beach, with the sound of ocean waves behind them.

"I have this." She held up the knapsack in which she had stuffed the seal skin and left the lab to stash it in her car and find some clothes.

For all its wonder and secrecy, the Center was poorly funded – it didn't produce the results and military applications that the nearby bionic and psychic research branches did – and inadequately supervised.

She knew the building and video surveillance patterns well enough to be able to smuggle the selkie to her car without leaving evidence. Not that it mattered, when Rick would no doubt give Colonel Ottoman a full report. She waited until close to the end of the shift to retrieve the selkie. He came with her docilely, dressed in the spare sweats she gave him.

Marina sat on her rock and sang, her light voice echoing in the lab.

The selkie lingered for a moment until Marina waved goodbye. Robin pulled him to the next room.

"Sir," Rick, hands pressed to the plastic of his cell, called. The selkie met Rick's gaze, unflinching. "I know your kind. Treat her gently."

The selkie didn't react. He seemed to study the vampire, expressionless, and only looked away when Robin squeezed his hand.

Robin lingered a moment. "Goodbye," she said.

"Take care, Robin."

Impulse guided her again, and she went to the control box for the lock to Rick's cell. She pushed the button; the lock clicked open with the sound of a buzzer. The door opened a crack. Rick stared at the path to freedom for a long moment.

Not lingering to see what the vampire would do next, she gripped the selkie's hand and ran.

She smuggled him in the back seat of her car, making him crouch on the floorboard. Routine did her service now; the shift had ended, and the guard at the gate waved her through.

They'd be looking for her in a matter of hours. She had to get rid of the car, find a place to hide out. She stopped long enough to get to an ATM and empty her account. She could leave tracks now, then disappear.

Desperation made her a criminal. She ditched her car, swapping it for a sedan she hotwired. She kept the seal skin under her feet, where the selkie couldn't get to it.

Two more stolen cars, a thousand miles of highway, and some fast talking at the border, flashing her military ID and spouting some official nonsense, found her in Mexico, cruising down the coast of Baja.

She knew the stories. She should have driven inland.

They stayed in a fishing village. Robin's savings would hold out for a couple of months at least, so she rented a shack and they lived as hermits, making love, watching the sea.

Convinced that she was different, she was smarter than those women in the stories, she hid the seal skin – not in the house, but buried in the sand by a cliff. She wrestled a rock over the spot while the selkie slept.

He was no less passionate than before. He spent hours, though, staring out at the ocean.

She joined him one evening, sitting beside him on still-warm sand, curling her legs under her loose peasant skirt. Her shirt was too big, hanging off one shoulder, and she didn't wear a bra – it seemed useless, just one more piece of clothing they'd have to remove before making love. Nothing of the poised, put-together young army lieutenant remained. That person wouldn't have recognized her now.

He didn't turn his eyes from the waves, but moved a hand to her thigh and squeezed. The touch filled her with heat and lust, making her want to straddle him there and then. He never seemed to tire of her, nor she of him. Wasn't that close enough to love?

She kissed his shoulder and leaned against him. "I don't even know what your name is," she said.

The selkie smiled, chuckled to himself, and didn't seem to care that she didn't have a name for him.

He never spoke. He never said that he loved her, though his passion for her seemed endless. She touched his chin, turned his gaze from the ocean and made him look in her eyes. She only saw ocean there. She thought about the seal skin, buried in the sand a mile inland, and wondered – was he still a prisoner? Did he still see steel bars locking him in?

Holding his face in her hands, she kissed him. He wrapped his arms around her, kissing her in return. He tipped her back on the sand, trapped her with his arms, turned all his attention to her and her body, and she forgot her doubts.

One night, she felt the touch of a kiss by her ear. A soft voice whispered in a brogue, "Ye did well, lass. No hard feelings at all."

She thought it was a dream, so she didn't open her eyes. But she reached across the bed and found she was alone. Starting awake, she sat up. The selkie was gone. She ran out of the shack, out to the beach.

Seal skin in hand, he ran for the water, a pale body in the light of a full moon.

"No!" she screamed. How had he found it? How could he leave her? All of it was for nothing. Why had he waited until now to speak, when it didn't matter any more?

He never looked back, but dived into the waves, swam past the breakers and disappeared. She never saw him again. The next shape that appeared was the supple body of a grey seal breaking the surface, diving again, appearing further out, swimming far, far away.

She sat on the beach and cried, unable to think of anything but the square of sand where she sat and the patch of shining water where she saw him last. He'd taken her, drained her, she was empty now.

She stayed in Mexico, learning Spanish and working in the village cleaning fish. She treasured mundane moments these days. Nights, she let the water lull her to sleep.

The army never found her, but someone else did, a few months later.

That night, she sat on the beach, watching moon-silvered waves crash onto the white sand, like her selkie used to. Sitting back, she grunted at the weight of her belly. The selkie hadn't left her so empty after all. She stroked the roundness, felt the baby kick.

She didn't hear footsteps approach and gasped, startled, when a man sat down beside her.

Dark hair, an aristocratic face, permanently wry expression. He was even graceful sitting in the sand. He wore tailored black slacks and a silk shirt in a flattering shade of dark blue, with the cuffs unbuttoned and rolled up. He flashed a smile and looked out at the water.

"Rick! What are you doing here?"

"Besides watching the waves?"

"So you did it. You left." She was smiling. She couldn't remember the last time she'd smiled.

"Of course. I didn't want to stay to explain to Colonel Ottoman what you'd done. I brought Mr Njalson along with me."

"Brad's here?"

"He's hunting back on the mesa. Enjoying stretching all four legs."

Robin sighed, still smiling. Of course, Rick could have gotten *himself* out of there – just as soon as he convinced one of the doctors to look in his eyes in an unguarded moment. Now she wished she'd let them all out a long time before she did.

"When are you due?" Rick asked softly.

He startled her back to reality, and she swallowed the tightness in her throat. "In a month. It'll have webbed feet and hands. Like in the stories."

"And how are you?"

She took a breath, held it. She still cried every night. Not just from missing the selkie any more. She had another burden now, one she'd never considered, never even contemplated. The supernatural world, which she'd tried to treat so clinically, would be with her forever. She didn't know the first thing about raising a child. She didn't know how she was going to teach this one to swim.

She touched her face, which was wet with tears. When she tried to answer Rick, she choked. He put his arms around her and held her while she cried on his shoulder.

Succubus Seduction

Cheyenne McCray

One

Lilin opened and closed her wings, studying tonight's prey: Archer Dane.

As a Succubus, Lilin *usually* had her choice of *any* man. They were easy creatures. A naked woman and immediately a man hardened in greeting.

She would ride him, take his seed . . . and his soul.

But this male affected her in some strange way. After centuries of taking men to replenish herself she felt less and less pleasure. Most men proved to be little sport. She needed something *more*.

Unseelie Queen Rusalka insisted Lilin bring her Archer's soul. Odd. Normally, Lilin kept the male's soul to nourish her until she claimed her next prey.

For days she'd observed Archer. A powerful man with a muscular, hard body. Strong jaw, blue eyes, black hair and a rare smile that gave her tingles all over.

Lilin licked her lower lip. She gripped the corner bedpost as her wings created a draught, teasing his hair as he slept. In all her centuries of existence, no man had thrilled her so.

Stop thinking of Archer as if he's more than an assignment. I'll give his soul to Queen Rusalka and move to my next prey.

After making her wings disappear, and with unusual excitement in her belly, she stepped towards him.

Archer was being watched. He kept his breathing slow but slitted his eyes enough to see.

He almost opened his eyes as surprise arrowed through him.

A beautiful, petite naked woman.

With wings. She fucking had wings.

A breeze brushed his face every time she opened and closed those wings. The woman licked her bottom lip and looked at him like he was a treat. Her wings drew back and vanished.

What the—

Archer squeezed his eyes shut.

Dream. No other explanation.

He fully opened his eyes.

Nope. Still there.

The dream woman stopped. Blinked. Then smiled.

"Hello, Archer."

He frowned as he pushed himself up, swung his legs over the side of the bed and stood. He towered over the small woman.

Her gaze widened. "Why did you get up?"

Too real. Everything about this felt *real*.

"Who are you?" He slept in the nude, and he and his damned erection faced her.

"I'm Lilin." She tried to touch him, but he caught her wrist.

She moved close enough that her body heat burned into him, her bare breasts brushing his chest. The lower half of him was saying, "What are you waiting for?" But at the same time he was grinding his teeth.

This Lilin was gorgeous – long silvery-blonde hair and silver eyes glittering in the moonlight. Her scent was like a rain-washed spring night.

He hardened his grip. "I don't know what you want, lady," he growled, "but you'd better get your little ass out."

She gave a seductive smile. "I want *you*."

Even though his body was shouting otherwise, Archer said, "I don't do strange women. And I sure don't know you."

Lilin's lips curved into a wicked smile. "You will, Archer Dane."

She vanished.
He let his now empty hands drop away.

Lilin frowned as she sat on the bank of the River of Life in the moonlight. She wrapped her arms around her knees and held them close.

The human had rejected her. Rejected *her*!

She had wanted a challenge and apparently Archer was it. She would make good on her promise and the male would come to know her. Then she would bed him and drain him of his soul.

No one refused her.

Lilin rose, spread her wings, and flew. She enjoyed the sense of freedom that accompanied flight. As an air Succubus, she drank in the growing wind like an elixir.

Soon it would be daylight in Archer's world.

Soon she would begin her seduction.

Two

Archer Dane gripped a set of architectural plans as he strode into Dane Construction's headquarters and headed towards his office. When he reached his office door, Archer paused to speak to his assistant.

He almost dropped the plans he was carrying and he was certain his jaw fell to the floor.

The woman from last night's dream sat in Cammie's seat. The nameplate now read: LILIN NIGHT.

Lilin. From last night.

She looked up and smiled. "Good morning, Archer."

He growled. "What are you—"

"Your reports are on your desk, as well as the construction loan papers." She looked at the telephone and grabbed a stack of white notes. "Here are your messages."

Automatically, he took the notes but gave her a fierce glare. "Where's Cammie?"

Lilin looked at him with wide, innocent silvery eyes. "On vacation in the Florida Keys. You must have forgotten."

No. He remembered everything. Especially last night. He

hadn't been able to go back to sleep, his hallucination playing over and over in his mind.

But here sat his hallucination. At Cammie's desk.

He glanced to see if any employees noticed him and Lilin. Thank God everyone looked busy.

"In my office. *Now*," he said to Lilin in a low voice.

"Yes, Mr Dane." She picked up the compact laptop Cammie always used.

"Leave it," Archer said.

Lilin set it on the desk. "Yes, Mr Dane." The way she said "Mr Dane" in a slightly unusual accent was like a caress that made him so hard he had to grit his teeth.

Shit. He had to get into his office before any employees noticed how much Lilin affected him. He opened the door for her, then closed and locked it. Talking to this woman was *not* something he needed anyone to walk in on.

Archer turned from locking the door and froze. The architectural plans fell from one hand. His messages slipped from the other and scattered across the floor.

He was face to face with a very naked woman.

Before he had a chance to react Lilin had her arms around his neck and her body pressed to his. Her diamond-hard nipples rubbed him through his shirt and his erection pressed against her belly. She stood on her tiptoes and kissed him.

Ah, God. He almost dropped to his knees – they actually went weak. Lilin's kiss was like nothing he'd ever experienced. He couldn't begin to resist. His mind spun and all he could think about was laying her flat on his desk and driving deep inside her. His brain turned to mush and his body into one horny sex machine.

Damn, Lilin knew how to kiss. She tasted of woman and almonds, and her scent drove him crazy – the smell of rain after a thunderstorm.

She thrust her tongue into his mouth and made soft purring sounds. She nibbled his lower lip then teased his tongue with hers. As they kissed, she drew him with her so that they were moving backwards until she hit something hard. His desk. File folders crashed to the floor as she scooted onto the surface.

Lilin wrapped her arms around his neck again and brought him down with her as she continued the magic of her kiss. She pulled him closer until he stood between her thighs, his hardness pressed against her heat.

Archer placed one of his hands on her soft breast and pinched her nipple, causing her to purr louder. He moved the fingers of his other hand between their bodies and slipped them inside her core. She made small sounds of pleasure against his mouth as he rubbed her with his thumb.

He had to take her. And now. He braced one hand on the desk and reached to unfasten his jeans with the other.

Something knocked at the back of his mind as he continued kissing Lilin, the heat and fervour between them growing and growing.

He couldn't think clearly. The haze of lust was so strong.

The knocking in his head wouldn't stop.

Wait. It wasn't in his head. Someone was at his door.

The realization was enough to scatter the haze and bring him back to reality. He pushed away from the desk, away from Lilin, and shook his head to clear his mind.

The knocking grew louder.

"Mr Dane," came a muffled voice from the other side of the door. "Mr Garfield's here for his ten o'clock appointment. Is everything all right?" It was Molly's voice and she sounded both concerned and curious. She'd probably seen him walk in with Lilin.

Archer stepped back and nearly stumbled into one of the padded chairs in front of his desk. Lilin's beautiful breasts were pink from his caresses, her lips swollen from his kisses and her thighs wide, exposing her soft pink flesh. A wicked smile tilted the corners of her lips.

Another knock. Archer raised his voice. "I've been on an important call, Molly. Be right there.

"Get your clothes on," he ordered Lilin in a low growl. "However you were hired, you're now fired. Don't come back here."

She pouted. "Don't you want to take me?"

"Yes . . . No! Get your clothes on." He glanced around for her skirt and blouse. The only things on the floor were the scattered messages and architectural plans that he had to pick up in a hurry before Garfield came into the room. Archer turned back to his desk.

Lilin was gone.

Archer couldn't move. This woman – or whatever was happening to him – was driving him mad.

He hurried around his desk and checked under it. Nothing. There was no other possible place for her to hide in his office, which contained only his desk, chairs and a round conference table. She definitely wasn't under the table.

What was going on?

This took hallucinating to a whole new level.

He raised his fingers to his nose – the fingers that had just been inside her – and smelled Lilin's musk. He shook his head, trying to clear his mind.

Now his hallucinations included her smell?

Lilin grumbled as she walked in the Hall of the Lost. Her hair caressed her naked buttocks, the air felt cool against her breasts, and the marble floor smooth beneath her bare feet. She'd been summoned to Queen Rusalka of the Unseelie Court. No doubt because of her failure.

She'd almost had Archer. *Almost had him.*

There would be no resisting her tonight.

Her shoulders tensed and her skin tingled as the Unseelie Fae guards drew open the massive gold-leafed doors of Rusalka's receiving room. The guards were dark-green skinned with pointed ears and fierce expressions. They carried even fiercer weapons.

Lilin walked along the intricately carved footpath that led through the chamber to the Queen's throne. Walking into the chamber was like walking into the forest, complete with trees, fresh earth, and wildflower blooms.

Queen Rusalka was like all Fae: her features were ageless but she was centuries, if not millennia, old. She bore the darkness of the Unseelie.

A crown of white-gold thorns was perched upon her long ringlets and she wore a black gown as usual. Each gown was different and beautiful, but always black. Black gemstones sparkled on the bodice of her gown today, and a diaphanous skirt sheltered her small, always bare, feet.

Lilin knelt before the Queen and lowered her head.

"You have been unsuccessful." Queen Rusalka's sharp tone echoed through the trees in the chamber. "Twice. I commanded you to retrieve this mortal's soul and bring it to me. But you *failed*."

"Yes, my Queen." Lilin wanted to rush to explain what had happened this second time – the interruption that broke her hold on Archer – but she bit her tongue knowing that would gain her a worse punishment.

A dangerous growl rose within Rusalka's throat. "Fail again and I shall see you suffer a mortal's life."

Before Lilin could stop herself, her head shot up. "Mortal? As in human?"

Queen Rusalka narrowed her black eyes. "You dare to question me, Succubus?"

Lilin lowered her gaze. "Of course not, my Queen. I shall take Archer Dane's soul. Tonight."

Three

Archer stood at his wet bar with a shot of whiskey in one hand, the bottle in the other. What happened to him last night and this morning? The more he thought of it, the more absurd it seemed. Christ. Last night he had even imagined this Lilin woman had wings.

He swore he could still taste the sweetness of her mouth on his tongue, smell the rain-washed scent of her hair and her musk on his fingers.

In one swallow he downed the whiskey, then poured another shot as the drink burned his throat and warmed his chest. If he was going to lose his mind, he might as well do a good job of it.

He downed the second shot and turned towards his fireplace – and almost dropped the bottle.

Lilin stood inches from him, her wings slowly opening and closing. With his hands full, he had no chance to react as she reached up, wrapped her arms around his neck and pulled him to her for another earth-shattering kiss.

Something about her kiss drove all thought straight from his brain. She teased him with her tongue, darting it inside his

mouth and drawing it out again. She nibbled his lower lip and
he groaned. Then she pulled him down so that his knees landed
on a throw rug on the hardwood floor.

Damned if his knees hadn't been giving out on him anyway.
When they were kneeling, never breaking their kiss, Archer set
the shot glass and the bottle to either side of them. As soon as
his hands were free, he tried pushing her to the floor, but she
took control and rolled him onto his back so that she was on
top.

Her pelvis rubbed against the front of his jeans in a slow,
tantalizing movement. At the same time she purred and nibbled
his lower lip.

Archer groaned and cupped her breasts, perfect and soft with
large, hard nipples pressing against his palms. Lilin moaned
and rose up enough that Archer could suckle one breast then the
other. Her skin tasted unlike any woman he'd known. Just like
the exotic scent of her hair.

Definitely too many clothes on him. Lilin – she was perfect.
Perfectly naked.

The fact he was kissing a strange woman who'd appeared and
disappeared in and out of his life – and freaking had *wings* –
barely registered as she moved her mouth to his ear and darted
her tongue inside. "I want you, Archer."

He groaned, moved his hands from her breasts and felt for her
wings. They were gone. All he felt was the smooth skin of her
back. He continued on, skimming her flesh to her hips then
cupped her bottom.

Lilin licked a path from his ear, along his stubbled jaw, to the
base of his throat. She unbuttoned his shirt and tugged it out of
his waistband so that his chest was bare. Her hands never
stopped exploring him. Her touch – magic. Every place on
his skin that she caressed sparked as if a small electrical charge
ran through him.

Her mouth, her tongue . . . He wrapped his hands in her silky
hair and gripped it in his fists as she worked her way down his
chest, kissing, licking, nipping his skin. He hissed and she gave
a soft laugh. Like wind chimes.

Lilin continued, her tongue tracing a path from his abs to the
top button of his jeans. She unbuttoned them and tugged the

zipper. He didn't wear underwear and she made a sound of pleasure as she released him.

A growl rose in his chest as he clenched his hands in her hair as she took him in her mouth. God, he was flying. His body wasn't his own. It belonged to Lilin, a woman he didn't even know.

The thought jarred him a fraction of a second before she took even more of him inside her warm mouth.

She dug her fingers into the sides of his jeans and dragged them down. He reluctantly let go of her hair while she tugged off each of his boots then stripped off his socks and his jeans. He rose and ditched his shirt, leaving nothing but skin against skin as she crawled back up him.

Lilin's musk was strong as she rubbed herself against him, bracing her arms to either side of his head. "Do you want me, Archer?" she asked, her accent stronger.

Irish? What the hell. He didn't care who she was or where she came from. He just wanted to be inside her.

But they needed protection.

She gave a cry of surprise as he rolled her over so he was on top. God, she was beautiful. Her silver eyes were filled with desire. Her skin was so fair but pink wherever his hands touched her. Silvery-blonde hair surrounded her like a halo against the forest-green rug they were lying on.

Archer pressed himself against her – he was dying to be inside her. "Condom," he barely managed to get out as he pushed himself onto his haunches.

For a second, Lilin looked panicked, but the expression faded as she gave him a smile. "I *am* protected." She held her arms out to him. "I won't get pregnant."

Some of the haze in his mind started to wear off. "I don't have sex with a woman without a condom. Period."

"Come." She reached up to draw him to her but he pulled away.

Something wasn't right. Something about all of this was off. He blinked and shook his head. "What am I doing?"

She looked irritated. "You were about to make love to me."

"Like hell." He got to his feet and she stood too. "I don't trust a woman who argues against using condoms."

Lilin sounded sad as she said, "Goodbye, Archer."
She faded away.
"Shit." Archer pushed his hand through his hair.
His clothing was scattered across the hardwood floor. The bottle of whiskey lay on its side, a puddle of liquid surrounding it.
He swore he could smell her, and he was still moist where her mouth had touched him. And he was buck-naked.
He was losing his goddamned mind.

For the first time in longer than she could remember, Lilin was in tears. She hadn't remembered what it felt like to cry until this very moment.
She wiped her eyes before she passed through the doors into Queen Rusalka's chamber. Lilin found it difficult to walk under the Queen's disapproving glare.
The moment Lilin knelt before Rusalka, the Queen's harsh voice cut through her like a blade. "You failed, Lilin of the Succubae. You were given three opportunities, and you are found lacking."
Lilin hated the tears in her voice. "Please give me another chance, my Queen."
"My word is law." The Unseelie Queen's voice echoed in the chamber. "You are now mortal, Lilin, formerly of the air Succubae. Once you are on Earth, you shall have little time to arrange your affairs before I strip you of all memories of your former life. I will provide you with what humans require to live in their world – what they refer to as identification and the paper they use to trade for goods. I will give you new memories of living your life as a human."
Lilin looked at the Queen, fear punching her belly. "Please, my Queen. I will not fail if you give me another chance."
Rusalka scowled. "Do you dare contradict me? I demanded that you bleed Archer of his soul. As an Incubus he once disappointed me as you have. I will not tolerate such failures."
Lilin's eyes widened. Archer had been Incubae?
The Queen's face grew darker. "After giving him opportunity to adjust to his new mortal life, I stripped his memories. He remembers naught of being Incubae." Her lips twisted into a scowl. "Rise, Lilin, mortal."

All Lilin felt was numb as she obeyed. She didn't feel changed. Yet. But she was a mortal. A mere human now.

"I will send you to Archer." The Queen's expression became amused. "He may do with you what he will. Throw you out. Fuck you. It matters not." She gave a slight nod to her guards who stood to either side of Lilin. "Go."

Still stunned, Lilin stared at the Queen. She didn't move until the guards forced her to turn and walk out of the chamber and into the Hall of the Lost.

Four

So tired he could hardly see straight, Archer entered his sprawling mountainside home. He'd spent the day on a construction site and he was hungry and in need of a long hot shower.

He'd also spent the day thinking of the woman – whoever she was, whatever she was – who'd kept appearing and disappearing in and out of his life. What happened on his living room rug had been real. But the way she'd just faded away . . . He was going out of his freaking mind.

He tossed his keys on the entryway table then strode into the kitchen.

He came to a complete stop. *Again.*

Lilin. In his kitchen.

This time she had clothes on – jeans and a grey T-shirt with the Grateful Dead logo on it. She sat at the kitchen table, her elbows on the surface, chin in her palms, and a glum expression on her pretty face. Her silvery-blonde hair shone in the evening light coming through the bay window. Her eyes, though, looked more grey than silver as she looked at him. She didn't smile or get up.

He rubbed his hand over his stubbled jaw. "What are you doing here?"

Lilin gave a deep sigh. "No thanks to you I'm mortal now."

That made Archer pause. "Listen, lady. I don't know what planet you came from—"

"Otherworld. The Unseelie Court." She rose and draped her forearm on the table. Her Irish accent was stronger now than before. "I was a Succubus. I failed to get your soul for her so Queen Rusalka made me mortal and sent me to you to decide my fate."

Otherworld? Unseelie Court? Queen Rusalka? The names rang like bells in Archer's head, as if he should know them. They had to be from fairy tales read to him when he was a child.

Not that he remembered his childhood.

Lilin kicked at the table leg with her white tennis shoe. He saw a hint of her bare ankle. God, she had sexy ankles.

He shook his head to get the crazy thoughts out of his mind. "I'm tired, hungry, and I need a shower. You know your way out."

Lilin's eyes glistened and his gut ached at the sight of a tear rolling down her cheek.

"No crying," he growled. "That's not playing fair."

"I'm sorry." Her throat worked as she swallowed. "I have never been human before. I have no place to go, and I don't know what to do. There is only one thing I have ever been good at, and I won't lower myself to do it as a mortal. As a mortal I would be considered a prostitute, using my body to get what I need. I just won't do it."

Archer lifted a brow. "Sex?"

She sniffed and raised her chin. "If you could remember your past, you would know exactly what I'm talking about: sex and the taking of a human's soul. In your case, a female's soul."

He groaned and pinched the bridge of his nose with his thumb and forefinger before looking back at her. "Give me a break. I don't know what's going on and I want some answers."

Lilin stood and moved towards him. "Did you not wonder how I could appear and disappear? And wings – do you think mortals can grow them whenever they please?" Another tear rolled down her cheek. "I failed, damn you. Now I am as cursed as you are."

She was close enough that Archer reached up to cup her chin in his palm and rubbed away the tear with his thumb. "Why is it I want to believe you?" He continued to stroke her cheek. "What is it about the Unseelie Court and the name Queen Rusalka that makes me feel like someone punched me in the gut?"

Her grey eyes widened. "You remember?"

"Remember what?"

Lilin leaned into his touch. "You were once Incubae, as I was Succubae. But you displeased the Queen – I do not know why – and you were cast out and given a mortal's soul and a mortal's life. The fact you were an Incubus was probably why you were able to resist me."

Archer shook his head. "I should take you straight to the hospital and have you admitted to a psych ward."

Another tear rolled down her cheek, this one bigger. "I have no way to prove any of this. Queen Rusalka said I have little time to get my affairs in order before I will be as you and not able to remember my former life." She drew away from him and folded her arms beneath her breasts.

Those perfect breasts . . .

He snapped back to attention as she continued, more tears rolling down her cheeks. "If you do not help me, then I may as well be taken to a hospital. At least then I will have housing and food." She sighed. "I now know what hunger is. I have not had a meal all day and my stomach makes a funny rumbling, growling sound." She sniffled as a virtual flood of tears started.

Archer couldn't help himself. He was a sucker for crying females. He reached for her and brought her into his embrace. She buried her face against his shirt and sobbed.

"I don't know what to do," she whispered as she tilted her head up to face him. "Where does a Succubus go when she isn't immortal any more?"

He squeezed her tighter to him and couldn't believe the words that came out of his mouth. "You can stay here for now, OK?"

Five

Today was sunny and Lilin stood on the porch breathing in clean scents of pine and fresh earth. In the distance she heard the trickle of a creek, and it reminded her of something – something she couldn't quite remember. It had been nearly a month since she started living with Archer and already she had forgotten much of her life as Succubae. The more she struggled to remember, the harder it became.

It took a while before she and Archer fell into a routine. Lilin was so grateful to Archer she would have done anything for him, but he asked nothing of her. She had no skills – as an immortal she had even had to use magic to help at his office the day she replaced his assistant.

She would be a disaster as a human.

Archer took her step by step through small tasks. First teaching her how to cook, starting with how to boil water. That had nearly been a catastrophe when she knocked over the teakettle and water flooded the burner and snuffed the gas flame.

But she could now spread a substance called peanut butter on bread, although she had problems with jelly – wiggly, sticky stuff. She normally ended up with half on her shirt, but triumphant with the half that made it onto the other slice of bread. The taste was quite pleasant.

He was a patient teacher, but she knew when he was trying to hide a smile when she was mad enough to scream with frustration. The first time Archer grinned at one of her blunders, she had stomped on his foot. He kept his amusement to himself after that.

Wind stirred Lilin's hair, bringing with it the scent of an oncoming thunderstorm. She felt as if she could fly with the wind and soar through the trees.

What an odd thought.

It was difficult being around Archer and not sharing his bed. She was sure he felt the same, if the hardness in his jeans whenever he came near her was any indication. But he respected her clear desire not to use her body to gain favour. In contrast to her former life, she would no longer bed a man unless he cared for her, and she for him.

She wished to please him in other ways. For the time being. She was no longer Succubae and she would learn to live like a human. If it killed her.

Which it might if she didn't learn how to run that infernal washing machine. The first time she tried to wash a load of clothes herself, as a surprise for Archer, she'd put too much "detergent" into it. Bubbles had flowed out as if it was foaming at the mouth. In the beginning the bubbles were rather delightful, but it wasn't long before her delight turned to horror.

Her cheeks heated as she remembered how she had frantically used the "telephone", punching in the numbers Archer had left scribbled on a pad next to the phone. He'd hurried home to find her rushing around with towels to mop up the bubbles that kept pouring from the machine's mouth.

He'd turned it off and the soap bubbles stopped pouring out of it. She thought she heard him snort with laughter. The moment she shot her angry gaze at him, his features turned innocent.

Now Lilin shook her head and went into the house where she'd prepared a surprise dinner for Archer. She liked how predictable he was in coming home at the same time every day.

She'd set the table the way he'd taught her. In the centre she placed the mashed potatoes (so, they were a little lumpy and watery), peas (that were just a tad brown), and a beef roast she'd been cooking all day in the crockpot (it was on the overdone side, but never mind that). For dessert, she would grab the ice cream stashed in the freezer and the chocolate sauce from the refrigerator. She couldn't go wrong with that. She hoped.

On the table was the jelly jar filled with wildflower blooms he'd brought home yesterday.

Lilin wondered at the happiness expanding in her chest.

Thumping noises on the steps and porch. *Archer's home!*

A smile lit her face as she hurried to open the door. "I made dinner," she said as soon as he walked in. "By myself."

He gave her one of his sexy grins after he closed the door. To her surprise, he caught her by the waist, brought her to him, and brushed his lips over hers. "Thank you," he murmured against her mouth, and her knees nearly gave out on her.

Wow. If he did that each time she had dinner waiting for him, she was going to prepare a meal every day.

Archer drew away and she steadied herself by placing her palm on the entryway table. He took her free hand and led her to the kitchen where they sat at the table.

If Archer was unhappy with dinner, he didn't show it. He ate two big helpings of everything! She couldn't help grinning as he ate.

Later, when she started to prise spoonfuls of ice cream from the container into two dessert dishes, he didn't laugh when she flung a chunk of ice cream across the kitchen. However, she did see amusement in his eyes when she squirted chocolate sauce on her face and hands instead of on what ice cream had made it into the cups.

"Let me help." He took her in his arms and licked sauce from her nose and cheeks. She shivered with every touch, every kiss, as he continued on to her palms and wrists. When he had licked every bit of chocolate off her, he leaned his back against the kitchen counter and brought her fully into his embrace. She tilted her face and looked into his eyes before he moved his mouth to hers.

Six

Lilin sank against Archer and moaned as he devoured her. He tasted of chocolate and male. Better than anything she remembered tasting. His scent – Goddess, he smelled good. Testosterone, sawdust from the work site, pine and fresh air from the outdoors.

In all the time she'd lived with him, he hadn't kissed her. He'd taught her, taken care of her, bought her clothes, and had done so much for her. He'd never pressed her for anything.

In truth, she hadn't been ready. She, a former Succubus, was not ready for sex as a mortal. The thought was so absurd she would have laughed if she weren't so busy moaning at the things Archer was doing to her.

He kissed her thoroughly, like no human male should be able to. His big hands stroked her body as if she was fragile. He eased his hands further down until he cupped her buttocks, squeezing and massaging them.

His hardness pressed against her belly as she wrapped her arms around his neck. The ache between her thighs was fierce and her breasts felt heavy. She wanted him now, more than anything she had ever wanted before.

When he raised his head, his eyes were darker blue and his chest rose and fell faster than before. "I need a shower."

"I'm sticky from the chocolate." She bit his lower lip. "I'll join you."

"We'll save water." He slipped his tongue into her mouth then drew it out again. "Economical."

He picked her up and she wrapped her legs around his waist and kept her arms tight around his neck as he carried her into his bedroom.

Archer started the shower so the water would run warm. God, he'd wanted Lilin for so long. But he'd given her time to adjust and had given himself time to get to know her.

She *had* to be from another world. Or raised by wolves. She'd been like a child needing to be taught almost everything. He enjoyed her delight in simple things, like the time he brought wildflowers home for her. She'd been so disappointed when the first flowers had wilted that he brought her bouquets almost daily.

He finished adjusting the water's temperature and found Lilin naked. As magical as if she were still a Succubus. The idea still seemed unbelievable, but everything about Lilin was unusual.

She was so beautiful. Her silvery-blonde hair tumbled to her waist; her grey eyes were wide and innocent.

He took her into his arms and felt the softness of her body through his clothing. When he kissed her, he lost himself in the moment, never wanting it to end. Only the pounding of water against marble reminded him of their shower.

Archer stripped while she watched, and he tossed his clothing onto hers. Her eyes told him she wanted him, and that she was just as filled with desire as he.

He led her beneath the spray, shielding her from the brunt of the hard blast until they got used to it. She laughed and tilted her chin so that the water sprayed her face before she turned her back to it. He reached for shampoo and squirted some on his hand before starting to soap then rinse her hair.

When he finished he tilted her face so that their gazes met. He brushed his lips over hers before drawing back. "Everything about you is beautiful."

Lilin smiled, wrapped her arms around his neck, and kissed him again. "*You* are beautiful."

He released her, picked up a sponge and poured gel on it to wash her body. His body ached as he touched her.

Before soaping her breasts, he paused to suckle each of her nipples. Lilin moaned and gripped her hands in his hair.

God, she tasted sweet.

The crisp smell of soap didn't mask her scent of desire as he knelt. He used the sponge to pay close attention to her belly, thighs, legs, each delicate foot. He turned her to face the spray and wash the soap from her body.

Still on his knees, Archer nuzzled her soft mound. She fisted his hair tighter and cried out as he ran his tongue between her legs.

"Goddess. Archer." She pressed his face closer. Her legs trembled, her body tensed, and he knew she was close to flying towards the stars. A little more and she'd go supernova.

He bit her lightly and she screamed. Her whole body shook and her face flushed with the power of her orgasm. When her legs gave out and she dropped into his arms he felt somehow triumphant – that he had brought her to her knees.

He took her mouth in a fierce kiss, feeling a sense of ownership and protectiveness.

"I don't know if I can get up," she whispered when he moved his mouth from hers.

Archer smiled and kissed her lightly before drawing her up to stand. She pressed her face to his wet chest and gave a deep sigh. "I've never felt anything like that." She tilted her face up. "I have few memories left, but I know that no man ever made me feel the way you do."

The thought of any other man with Lilin sent a stab of jealousy through his chest. Maybe it shouldn't have, but he wanted her to think only of him, as if he was her first. His touch, his kiss, his hips between her thighs as he took her.

And God, he needed to be inside her now.

Even though she wanted to wash him as he had washed her, he refused and made short work of shampooing his hair and scrubbing his body with the sponge. After shutting off the water and climbing out of the shower, they dried off with a pair of towels.

Archer picked her up and she dropped her towel before she wrapped her legs around his hips and held on to his shoulders. She kissed him as he strode across the room and they tumbled

onto the bed. The need to be a part of her was so great he was in
a fog of lust.

Love.

The word came out of nowhere, pressing against his mind.
Could the feeling in his chest be love for Lilin?

He touched her, kissed her, slid his hips between her thighs.

"Wait," she said, her voice husky and her eyes heavy-lidded.

"What, baby?" he murmured as he nibbled at her ear.

She gave one of her sexy little moans. "The protection you
said you wanted to use the last time I came to you."

Stunned at himself and his forgetfulness, Archer rose and
looked down at Lilin, the first woman he wanted to take, screw
the protection. He brushed his lips over hers. "Thank you," he
murmured.

It took him all of ten seconds to reach into his nightstand
drawer and pull out a condom package.

When he was ready, he looked down at his Lilin. She was so
beautiful. And she was so very much his.

When he drove himself deep inside her, she cried out, "Oh,
Goddess!" with the sound of pain in her voice.

Archer went completely still. "You're a virgin?"

She looked as surprised as he did. "My memories aren't clear
any more."

He didn't move. "Are you all right?"

"I'm fine." She smiled. "The way you fill me is wonderful."

And she was so tight. Her velvet core gripped him like a fist
and he couldn't move for a moment or he'd come.

Slowly, he drew out, then slid back in. He didn't want to hurt
her.

She dug her fingernails into his biceps. "More, Archer."

He gritted his teeth as he withdrew, then drove himself back
inside her. Again he drew out slowly, then thrust into her. She
made small cries and he nearly growled with the feelings of
possessiveness that grabbed him.

As he took her, Lilin's body began to tremble, her thighs
shaking against his hips. Her lips were parted, her eyes glazed
and her moans louder.

While he continued to make love to her, he waited. Waited.
Waited. Holding back his own orgasm.

He drove in again. She arched her back and screamed. Her body rocked and writhed beneath him. Her core clamped so hard on him that he lost it. He shouted and pressed his hips tight against her as she continued to contract around him and his throbbing seemed to go on forever.

Finally he collapsed, barely rolling to the side in time to keep his weight from crushing her petite frame.

For a long time they held one another, her head against his chest, their breathing deep and ragged, him still inside her.

When he had the strength, he started kissing her forehead, inhaling her special scent and feeling incredible warmth deep in his heart and soul.

He brushed her wet hair away from her face with his fingertips. She lifted her head to look at him and smiled. Such an innocent, sweet, genuine smile. Nothing like the sultry, experienced look she'd given him when she'd been a Succubus.

Archer no longer doubted his sanity – or hers.

And now he'd lost his heart to this sweet woman in his arms. He wanted to show her the world and then give it to her.

Give everything to her.

The vision of a clear stone slipped through his mind. He drew away from Lilin and rolled out of bed.

"What's wrong?" she asked, sounding concerned. "Archer?"

Confusion clouded Archer's mind, but he knew he had to go to his drawer. "Wait."

He reached his bureau, opened his sock drawer, and dug through it. His fingers finally touched something round and hard, hidden in one of his socks. When he returned to the bed, he shook the sock out over the mattress. An enormous diamond slipped out of it. Archer's eyes widened, and so did Lilin's.

Where had it come from and why had he just remembered having it?

He grasped the stone in his hand – and everything came back in a rush so fast he nearly collapsed.

Every memory of being an Incubus, every woman he had ever taken. And Queen Rusalka with her fierce beauty and even fiercer temper. She'd been pissed with him when he'd said no to becoming one of her concubines. He'd never expected her to make him human.

The Queen had given him the stone so that every now and then he would remember what he had lost – an immortal life and the ability to bed any woman he wanted, every night if he chose to. But he had to be holding the diamond to remember. A little while after he parted with it, his memories would be gone again.

But with the stone he could also call to the Queen and beg to have his old life back.

He looked from the diamond to his beautiful Lilin. He would give her the stone, allowing her to remember her past – and return to the Unseelie Court.

His heart in his throat, he placed the diamond in her hand and folded her fingers around it. "My gift to you."

Immediately, shock registered on Lilin's features as she held the stone, and her eyes darted back and forth as if she was watching a ping-pong match.

"I could return," Lilin whispered. "The Queen would take me back."

It hit him like a blow to the chest. Lilin might leave. She would go back to the Queen and she would forget he existed.

And he would never forget her.

In that single crystal-clear moment he realized how much she had come to mean to him over the period of time he'd known her.

He didn't want to lose her.

Archer was on the verge of grabbing her, taking her into his arms and holding her tight so she could never leave him. Then she blinked as if coming back to reality and looked at him for a long moment.

His words and his breath caught in his throat as she took the sock he had hidden the diamond in, and slipped the stone inside so that it dropped to the toe.

Lilin handed it to Archer and smiled. "I choose to live a mortal life if it means I can be with you." She bit her lower lip before adding, "If you'll have me."

The relief was so great it stunned him.

"Will I have you?" Archer tossed the sock-covered diamond over his shoulder and it landed on the floor with a thump. "Does that answer your question?" He planned to take that damned stone and bury it in the landfill first thing in the morning.

She grinned and flung her arms around his neck. "I think I love you, Archer."

"I *know* I love you, Lilin." Archer couldn't keep the love out of his smile and voice as he looked down at her. "And I'm never letting you go."

Paranormal Romance Blues

Kelley Armstrong

"When I said I was in the mood for a meat market, I meant that metaphorically. I don't actually want to *be* anyone's dinner."

Tiffany rolled her eyes. "It's not that kind of vampire bar, Mel."

"What other kind is there? It's for vampires. What do they drink? Blood. And we're their primary suppliers of that beverage. Ergo . . ."

If she rolled her eyes any higher, they'd disappear into her skull. As I sipped my beer, I overheard a guy at the bar talking about women and not-so-discreetly jerking his chin our way. Cute guy, too. Hmm.

"I'll take the blonde," he said to his friend. "You can have the brunette."

"No, *I* want the blonde."

It was always nice to be argued over. Too bad I was the one they were arguing over *not* wanting. There are distinct disadvantages to being a half-demon with super-charged hearing.

"So this vampire bar," Tiffany tried again. "It's for dating. It's not easy being a vampire, you know. You think you have dating issues? Try being immortal."

"They are only *semi*-immortal. And why would I want to date one?"

"Uh, because they're hot."

Sure, if you went for tall, dark and parasitic. I gulped the rest of my beer. Sadly, it didn't make anyone in the bar look better.

And, considering the only guy glancing my way was at least sixty, apparently the booze wasn't doing the trick for them either.

I signalled the bartender for a refill. Even he ignored me.

"Hello?" Tiffany waved her hand in front of my face. "Earth to Melanie. Can we blow this joint please? The vampire bar is calling. Hot guys who've been waiting centuries to meet you."

I snorted.

"Oh, come on," she said. "Don't you find it the least bit romantic? A creature of the night, tormented by the emptiness of his life, searching for that one special woman, knowing if he doesn't find her in time, he'll be condemned to eternity as a soulless monster."

"That's a book."

She frowned. "Are you sure?"

"Yep."

"Fine, but they still need to find their true love, the one bright flame that will warm their cold existence."

"Book. More than one, I think."

"Forget romance. They need sex. It's like Red Bull for vampires, boosting their powers to unimaginable heights. They need lots of it, in every way, shape and form imaginable, including a few you haven't imagined."

"Book," I said. "I hope."

"Maybe, but they're still tormented creatures of the night—"

"They can walk around in daylight."

"No way."

"Yep. I'm not even all that sure about the tormented part. Sure, they have to drink blood and take one life a year, but once they work past that, they get a long life, eternal youth, near invulnerability and conga lines of swooning women fighting to get into their beds, eager to prove they'll be their 'one true love'. What's not to like?"

She slumped in her chair, a sigh whistling out.

"Maybe we can find you a tormented one," I said.

"How do you know so much about vampires anyway?"

"Wallace."

She winced. "Sorry."

Wallace was my latest ex, and the cause of the self-imposed celibacy I was now eager to break. Tall, dark and tormented fitted Wallace perfectly. He hadn't been a vampire, though not for lack of trying. A Vodoun priest with an inferiority complex, Wallace had been obsessed with the undead. Our relationship ended the day I walked in to find him shooting up with black market vampire blood.

I wish I could say Wallace had been a blip in an otherwise healthy love life, but he was only the latest in a string of losers. Dating fellow supernaturals solved a lot of problems, and opened up a whole bunch more.

"Forget the vamp bar then," Tiffany said. "Maybe there's someone here." She looked around. "Or maybe someplace else."

I sighed. I was being a bitch, really. This bar sucked. I didn't have another place in mind. And my friend *really* wanted to try this so-called vampire one. Was that too much to ask?

"All right," I said. "We'll check out this bar and find you a vampire. And if he's not tormented, I'm sure I can fix that."

A vampire bar. Now that we were on our way, I'd be lying if I said I wasn't just a little bit intrigued. And Tiffany wanted to go so badly that I could tell myself I was doing it for her sake . . . and almost believe it.

I'd met Tiffany three years ago in a support group for half-demons. As a rule, women don't hook up with demons willingly and bear their children. Our mothers have no idea that we're anything but human, and we don't either, until our powers start to kick in. That power depends on Daddy. In my case, it's enhanced hearing. Tiffany is a low-level ice demon. She can't freeze a guy in his tracks, though she has a glare that does the trick pretty well. Mostly she just turns water into ice. Useful at parties when the freezer is broken. Otherwise not so much. She's happy with it, though.

Not every half-demon is so content. Hence the support group. I'd first learned of my demon blood when I was "found" by a group that monitored medical channels and discovered I'd been trying to find an explanation for my super-hearing. They recommended the support group and I thought, Cool – I can meet others, then learn about my powers and how to improve them. Not exactly. As I discovered, it really was a support group – a place for half-demons to angst about the nasty blow life had dealt them.

Blow? Hello, super powers? They should have been celebrating winning the genetic lottery. Instead they whined about not fitting in, about having demon blood, about their slutty mothers screwing the forces of evil. I say, "Go for it, Mom." She'd been single and I'm sure the demon was damned hot – metaphorically speaking, I hope.

I didn't last long in the group, just long enough to meet Tiffany, who was every bit as puzzled by the "woe is me" sentiment. I also met Jason, my first supernatural boyfriend, who – as it turned out – wasn't even a half-demon, but a druid who infiltrated the group to pick up chicks. And so I was introduced to the wonderful world of paranormal romance.

"It must get lonely being a vampire," Tiffany mused as we walked down St James Street. "Just think of it. Centuries of watching everyone you love grow old without you, die before you."

"That's romantic?"

"Sure, don't you think so?"

I wasn't touching that one.

We passed a trio of wraithlike Goths, sticking to the shadowy edge of the sidewalks as if the streetlights would reduce them to dust motes. They took in our clubwear with sniffs of disdain. I returned the favour.

At least we seemed to be in the right neighbourhood. Which begged the question: how much of a secret was this place? Those kids were not supernaturals – we just don't call attention to ourselves like that. If everyone knew about the bar, that meant the chances of it really being what it claimed were next to nil. And just when I was starting to think this night might turn interesting. I swallowed a bitter shot of disappointment.

"Maybe the books are wrong," Tiffany piped up. "But I bet they got one thing right. What a vampire really needs is a mate. A life-mate. Someone he can turn. Someone to share eternity with." She gave a mooning sigh, as if being asked to join a life of blood-sucking was more romantic than being serenaded by the

Seine. "Can you imagine? Centuries together, bonded by love and—"

"Haemophilia? Please don't tell me you—"

"Oh, look. There it is!"

She pointed to a sign on the corner. A neon sign, flashing first VAMP, then changing to TRAMP. Vamp Tramp? Wasn't *that* from a book?

This did not bode well. Forget the unoriginal name. The flashing neon screamed "fake" even louder. In a world where supernaturals still hid their true nature with Inquisition-era fervour, neon-signed vampire bars were . . . unlikely.

Oh, who the hell was I kidding? This place was going to be as authentic as chicken balls. One double-shot of disappointment to go. And add a big chaser of head-slapping *duh*. There were maybe twenty vampires in the whole country. Did I really think they'd band together and open a bar in my home town?

It was then, when I'd fully convinced myself the place was a fake, that I saw the guy lying face down in the alley. A small crowd stood around him like a prayer circle.

When I started towards the man, Tiffany grabbed my hand. "For once, Mel, don't get involved. Let someone else handle it."

That's the problem, though, isn't it? Everyone thinks, Let someone else handle it, and no one does.

I shouldered past yet another Goth girl, this one so pale she lit up the alley like a flashlight.

"Has anyone called 911?" I asked.

Everyone looked at the person beside them, as if to say, "You called, didn't you?"

"I think some old dude went to call," said a kid so wasted he addressed the Goth girl behind me. "Or maybe he was just looking for another place to crash. I think this guy stole his spot."

I thought he was joking. One look at his face said he wasn't.

I turned to Tiffany. "Call 911." When she hesitated, I said, "Fine. I'll call and you can check him."

She pulled out her cell phone. I crouched beside the fallen man.

"You're not supposed to move him," said a middle-aged guy beside me.

Oh, sure, now he was Mr Helpful.

I tried to get a pulse at the man's wrist, but I'm an ad-copy writer, not a nurse, and I couldn't find the right spot. To get to his neck, though, I had to push aside his long, stringy hair, which was why I'd started with the wrist. But I'd never forgive myself if the man died because I got icky about touching his hair, so I pushed it back over his shoulder. Then I jerked back with an "Oh!"

"Holy shit," said the drunk kid. "Are those . . . ?"

"The kiss of the vampire," Goth girl whispered reverently.

On the side of his neck were two red puncture wounds and a small trickle of blood, still shiny. Too shiny, actually. I reached for the mark. Goth girl yelped. I peeled off the sticker and held it up.

"Performance art advertising. Everyone suitably impressed? Ready to go for drinks at Vamp Tramp? Buy two, get this free." I waved the "vampire bite" sticker, then nudged the fallen man. "Show's over. Get up."

He didn't move.

"Listen, asshole, my friend just called 911 for you. You're going to have some explaining to do, so get up and start now."

I booted him in the side. Still nothing.

"The bite marks are fake, but I don't think the lack of consciousness is," said a voice behind me, with a rapid-fire accent that reminded me of a recent trip to Northern Mexico.

I turned to see a man in a suit striding down the alley. Another man stayed on the sidewalk, eyeing the filthy alley as if hoping he wouldn't have to come any further.

"Miguel Carter," the first man said. "FBI."

He flashed a badge so fast all I saw was a blur. Nice try, buddy. I'd worked in advertising long enough to know a marketing ploy when I saw one. An elaborate and clever marketing ploy, but a ploy nonetheless.

"Can I see that?" I asked.

He handed me the badge. I inspected it, acting as if I had the foggiest clue what a real FBI badge looked like. I *did* know what an FBI agent looked like though, and whatever agency hired this guy had paid some serious bucks to get an actor who could play the part. He was in his thirties, dark hair and eyes, wide shoulders, square jaw. They'd added glasses, to give him that extra touch of intelligence, lift him above your average city cop. He wasn't a typical gorgeous actor, but he had that Clark Kent geek-cute thing, the kind that makes you think, "Hey, big boy, let me rip off those glasses and—."

Damn, it really had been too long.

I handed Carter back his badge. "So the FBI is taking 911 calls now?"

"No, I'm sure the local police and ambulance are on the way. I was in the area and heard there was a problem."

"In the area? Let me guess. At Vamp Tramp? Investigating, oh, let's see . . . A string of murders possibly related to the vampire subculture."

The surprise on his face looked almost genuine. The guy was good, I'd give him that. I knelt beside the "unconscious" man and touched the side of his neck.

"This one's still got a pulse, Agent. Seems you got to him in time. Good work." As I stood, I slipped a card from my wallet and pressed it against his palm, then lowered my voice. "It's a good guerilla marketing campaign, but the scenario needs work. Tell whoever's in charge to give me a call. I can help them smooth over the rough spots."

I walked back to Tiffany. As I approached, she shook her head. "Can't resist being a smartass, can you, Mel?"

"What? I offered my services. They do need to work out the scenario a little better. FBI has a certain cachet, but it would raise fewer questions if they just said they were city cops."

"But someone in the crowd might know the city cops."

"True."

"Also true that you were being a smartass, proving you saw through their act."

I glanced over my shoulder. Carter the FBI agent was still studying my card and frowning, trying to figure out where his performance had gone wrong. I smiled and continued walking.

We still went to the bar. My curiosity was re-piqued now. Would there be more of the show we'd just seen? A full viral performance-art campaign? Was it working? What were people saying?

I got the answer to question two as we reached the door, and found a line-up stretching around the corner. We got waved past it. OK, *Tiffany* got us waved past it. The bouncer took one look at her – blonde hair, high heels, low neckline and impressive cleavage – then he glanced at the line-up of middle-aged gawkers with cameras and teen goths with fake ID and frantically gestured us past the rope, as if terrified we'd see the line and keep walking.

Inside, it looked like a vampire bar. Or Hollywood's Eurotrash version of one. Lots of dark corners, blood-red velvet and lighting that lit nothing in particular. I suspect the decorator doubled as a set designer. I could imagine him directing the "shoot", placing the chaises longues in the dark corners, imagining a dilettante vampire gracefully sprawled on each one, surveying the eager crowd for their next meal, the sexual predator at its most predatory.

Unfortunately, this set was inhabited by real people. On the nearest chaise longue, two private school "Let's go Goth tonight!" girls were touching up each other's nail polish. Pink nail polish. A middle-aged couple sat erect on the next, staring around them, eyes wide with delicious "can you believe we're in a vampire bar, Frank?" horror. Chaise longue number three was occupied by a fifty-year-old platinum blonde. She looked suitably predatory, but her prey – every guy under thirty – was scampering the other way every time accidental eye contact occurred. And on the fourth chaise longue, a guy in his late thirties in full vampire gear, from the boots to the leather duster, lay with his eyes slitted, the tip of his tongue out, his expression rapturous as he stared at the frieze above his head – an erotic panorama of Dracula-style vampires invading the beds of virginal girls.

"One word," I said to Tiffany as we walked in. "Eww."

"That's not a word." She looked around. "But I second it. Damn." She sighed. "I guess we should get a drink. Too bad those chaises longues are all taken. They're kind of cool."

"You want one?" I started towards the guy enjoying the painted scenery.

She tried to grab my arm, but missed, managing only a chirped, "Don't!" that was almost drowned out by a bass-heavy blast of unintelligible punk rock.

As I approached the man, he froze, the sight of an actual woman inducing stark terror. He adjusted his overcoat, and slid his hand from . . . wherever it had been.

"Are you—?" I garbled a name, knowing the music would swallow it.

"Um, yes. Yes."

"Your wife is on the phone."

He shot from the lounge and disappeared into the crowd. Two nearby college girls sidled towards the vacated couch. A look from me stopped them cold.

"Your throne, madam," I said with a flourish.

Tiffany laughed and sat on one end, leaving the top for me. We lounged. It wasn't easy with two people and one chair, not without doing that fake lesbian-show thing that seems to attract guys even better than a free beer sign.

We still attracted plenty of attention. Guys looked, and looked some more, and kept looking. Not one took even a tentative step in our direction, all wary, as if certain the presence of actual twenty-something single women had to be a set-up.

Had they already gotten a taste of the performance-art advertising? As hard as I looked, I didn't see any other obvious scenes playing out around us. A few people were drinking fake-blood drinks, and a couple in a corner were going at it pretty good – neck nibbling included – but with the awkwardness of outsiders trying really, really hard to fit in.

"We have a contender," Tiffany whispered in my ear.

She directed my attention across the floor to a guy who was definitely checking me out. He stood with a small group of men hovering, obviously corporate types scoping out the alternate nightlife. My admirer quickly looked away when I glanced over. He shifted, then cast a surreptitious look my way. Hmm.

"Well?" Tiffany asked.

"A distinct possibility."

He was an average guy. Average height, average build, medium-brown hair. A pleasant face. Not someone who'd catch my eye, but when he caught mine, I took a closer look and saw nothing that quashed the deal.

"OK, he's playing shy," Tiffany said. "So I'm going to give him an opening. I'll go to the bar and take my time getting us drinks."

I watched Tiffany leave, the crowd parting for her, admiring looks following her ass as it swayed through. And when I turned back to my admirer, he was gone. His group was still there, but he was nowhere to be seen. I looked around, hoping he was making his way over to me. No sign of him. Great. Apparently I'd been hanging around Tiffany so long I'd learned her trick for freezing out guys with a single look. I considered going after Tiffany and switching my beer to a double Scotch, neat. Instead I curled up on the chaise longue and tried not to sulk.

A few minutes later, Tiffany returned, blue eyes wide. "There's a vampire here!" She plunked down beside me, setting the sofa rocking. "A real vampire!"

"Drinks?"

"He's bringing them."

"The vampire?"

She grinned. "Can you believe it? Probably one vampire in this whole place and I snagged him. I wasn't even looking for one. I was up there at the bar, and this guy brushes against my arm and his skin is cold." When I didn't react appropriately, she leaned into my face. "Cold skin? Vampire?"

"Um, air conditioning?" I held out my arm, goosebumps rising on cue.

"He's a vamp. Trust me. And when you think about it, it makes perfect sense, him being here."

"It does?"

"Sure. This place looks totally fake, so it'd be the ideal place for real vampires to hang out, undetected."

"Uh-huh."

"See him? Up there. Beside the urn."

I spotted the guy. Not too tall or too dark, but he did have that pretty-boy pout down pat. And while his clothing didn't scream "I've seen *Underworld* fifty times," it was suitably dark against his pale skin. "He definitely looks anaemic enough."

She followed my gaze. "No, not him." Gripping my chin, she redirected me. "Him."

I looked. I looked some more. "Holy shit."

I'm not usually one for gorgeous guys, but one glance at this one and my ovaries were doing the cha-cha. He was at least six foot two and built. God, was he built. Wide shoulders, muscular biceps, slim hips, perfect ass. With effort, I pulled my gaze back up to his face, which was a sculptor's dream. And, naturally, he was blond. And tanned. And *so* not a vampire.

When I said as much to Tiffany, she rolled her eyes. "Yes, he has a tan. So what? You said they can go out in sunlight."

"But . . . But that's . . ." I ogled some more. "As a man? Perfection. As a vampire? So wrong."

He still stood at the bar, his gaze fixed regretfully on a NO SMOKING sign. I glanced down at his hand to see him toying with an unlit cigarette. A smoker? Normally a deal breaker, but in this case, I could adjust.

I did direct Tiffany's attention to the cigarette though.

"And that proves what?" she said. "He's a vampire. No chance of lung cancer, emphysema, smoker's cough. I bet he doesn't even get nicotine stains. Why *not* smoke?"

Now the Nordic god was heading our way, three drinks effortlessly fitting into his big hands. Big square hands, workman's hands, the kind with old calluses that would scratch deliciously against the skin as he . . .

"He's mine," Tiffany said.

I shook off the lust attack and nodded. "I know, and I won't interfere." Like I could anyway, though Tiffany was kind enough not to point that out.

He handed us our drinks and Tiffany introduced me.

"Adrian," he said, then excused himself and scooped a nearby table and chair, and set them up for us. A gentleman too.

"I hope you don't mind me hiding out over here with you two," he said. "This place is—" an almost nervous glance over his shoulder "—not exactly my speed."

Tiffany shot me a knowing look, as if this proved he was indeed a creature of the night, desperately trying to convince us otherwise. When I asked whether he was local, he shook his head.

"I'm working with a construction crew on a big job up here. Just got in this morning, asked the motel clerk for a good place to grab a drink and he suggested here."

And so we started to talk. And the more we did, the more I really wished I'd taken my hairdresser's advice about that stylish new cut or splurged for that amazing dress I'd seen last week at the mall.

Adrian wasn't just gorgeous. He was a real sweetheart, the kind of guy that usually only comes in a much plainer package. Of course, the cynical part of me tried to insist he was an actor, part of the ad campaign we'd seen earlier, but I'd been around enough actors in my career to know Adrian was just what he seemed – a good-looking, small-town construction worker looking for some company in the big city. Unfortunately, I wasn't the one he'd chosen to play the role of "company".

We'd been talking for about a half-hour when Adrian took the cigarette from his pocket and rolled it between his fingers. He sheepishly joked about the bad habit, then asked Tiffany if she'd like to step outside for some air while he indulged. He was gentleman enough to extend the invitation to me, but in a way that said he was really hoping Tiffany would come alone. Naturally, I was gracious and said, "No, that's fine." He promised they'd only be a couple of minutes, and they left out the back hall.

Those couple of minutes turned into ten, then fifteen, then twenty. I tried not to think of how they might be filling those minutes, but of course I did, which only slid my mood dangerously close to self-pity territory.

I sipped the dregs of my beer, and eavesdropped on conversations that cheered me a little as they confirmed that at least I didn't have the most boring life in the room. Even surrounded by fantasy and opulence, people just chatted about nothing – work, kids, the in-laws, the mortgage payments.

Then I caught something worth perking up for. Two words: "body" and "alley", spoken in a male voice with a faint New Mexico accent. I rose from the lounge and followed it.

I tracked the voice into a back hall clearly marked NO ENTRY. I entered – and crashed into "Agent" Carter as he left a room. He blinked, then gave a slow, crooked smile.

"Ms . . ." He pulled my card from his pocket and looked at it. "Mancini. Our good Samaritan. You'll be happy to know the victim is recovering nicely." He winked. "Suffering only from the lingering after-effects of professional humiliation. I told him you're in the business." He waved my card. "But he still takes it personally."

"I take it that's the manager?" I pointed at the room he just left, where a gruff voice was on the phone, ordering beer. "I was just going to pop in and give him my card."

I tried to pass Carter, but he shifted, subtly blocking my path. "I'll do that for you. He's in a lousy mood."

In other words, his employer wouldn't want me going straight to the client. Understandable, and I didn't argue, just nodded and made a move to head back into the bar. Again, Carter did that subtle sidestep, not exactly blocking me, but making my exit a little more difficult.

"Do you come here often?" he asked. When I arched my brows, he gave a short laugh. "Sorry, I meant, is this your first visit? In other words, did our little performance work?"

"I was already heading here, but yes, it's my first time."

"No offence to my, um, employer, but—" he leaned closer, voice dropping "—there's a much better place a block over on South. Jazz, good drinks, great food."

"Sounds more my kind of place." I paused, then gathered the strength of three beers and asked, "Are you off-duty now?"

His eyes widened behind his glasses and he studied me, as if pretty sure I wasn't implying what he thought I was. The start of a slow smile, then it vanished in a frown. "If you're hoping for a job reference, I don't carry that kind of clout, Ms Mancini."

"Melanie." I plucked my card from his hand and tore it in two. "Better?"

His smile sparked. "All right, then. I'm not quite off-duty yet, but if you don't mind staying here for a drink."

I didn't mind at all. He shucked his jacket, loosened his tie and followed me into the bar. My chaise longue was, of course, occupied. Carter found us a table, and was about to head to the bar when he stopped and looked around.

"Weren't you with a friend? A blonde?"

Shit. Please tell me that wasn't why he agreed to the drink.

"She left," I said, then added, "With a guy." And for good measure: "I don't think she's coming back."

His chin jerked up, eyes filling with an alarm that doused my last fizzle of hope.

"Sorry," I said.

"No, I . . . Was it someone she knew?"

"Just met."

"What did he look like?"

What, was he trying to scope out the competition? I was tempted to turn and walk away, but couldn't resist dashing his hopes. Cruel, but he'd just accepted a drink invitation with me to meet my friend. He deserved cruel. I described Adrian in loving detail.

As I did, he fought to hide his reaction, but it seeped through – concern, sharpening to fear. I took some perverse pleasure in the concern, but when I saw that spark of fear, something in my gut said this wasn't right. Disappointment, I could understand, but not fear.

"Where'd they go?"

"Out back, I think. He wanted a cigarette. What—?"

"How long ago?"

"Maybe a half-hour." I took out my cell. "She hasn't texted to say she's going anywhere, so she must still be out—"

He was already on the move, heading towards the back door, hand pulling his own cell from his pocket. When I took a step towards him, he wheeled to face me, snapping out a brusque, "Stay here."

"But—"

"I mean it. Stay here. Get a drink. I'll be right back. I'm . . ." He hesitated. "I'm just going to check on her."

As he hurried off, I strained to hear what he was saying into his cell over the noise of the crowd.

"He's here," he said. "And he took a girl already."

Oh, shit.

There was no performance-art ad campaign. Carter *was* FBI. He *was* investigating crimes connected to Vamp Tramp. He'd played along with my misconception to keep a low profile while he stalked a killer. A killer who'd just taken my best friend into a dark alley.

I tried to tell myself I was leaping to conclusions. Maybe this was all part of the performance.

Right, a performance for one. A performance that barrelled through some serious ethical boundaries.

Maybe Carter really was just smitten with Tiffany and wanted to cut in before she got busy with another guy.

So, he's willing to make a fool of himself over a girl he's only glimpsed from afar? In a romance novel, maybe. But life, sadly, did not follow the rules of fictional romance.

I called Tiffany. Her phone rang twice, then came on with a message that implied she was out of range, which wasn't possible. I tried again. Same thing. As I was leaving a frantic message, I noticed my shy admirer from earlier, checking me out again. This time, when I caught his eye, he didn't look away.

Great timing, buddy.

I hung up and looked around. Admirer-guy had apparently consumed his share of liquid courage and was now lifting a glass and pointing at me, asking if he could buy me a round. Maybe the sane thing to do would be to accept – relax, have a drink, let the cops handle the situation. But if anything happened to Tiffany, I'd never forgive myself.

When my admirer started heading towards me, I held up a finger and pointed towards the hall leading to the ladies' room, telling him I'd be right back. Then I took off down that hall to the exit door at the other end.

I eased open the rear exit door and listened. That's become instinctive for me – listening where other people would look. The alley was dark and silent. Anyone else going out for a smoke must have heeded the FIRE ESCAPE ONLY sign and stepped out front.

I eased out. With no sounds to go by, I took a moment to let my eyes adjust. A scattering of stumpy white tubes, like garden grubs, littered the ground. Cigarette butts. I knelt and touched the ends. All cold.

When something rustled to my left, I peered down the dark alley. Another rustle, then a scratching noise. I started walking. The clicking of my heels echoed through the silence. I slid them off and tucked them behind a trash can, then took a few careful steps, getting used to the feel of cold pavement under my feet before setting out.

I followed the rustling to an alcove stuffed with boxes. It only took one rodent squeak to tell me I didn't need to investigate further.

As I pulled back, I noticed a scrap of blue fabric peeking between the boxes. It was a gorgeous deep blue shade that I'd been admiring all night on Tiffany. Her new dress.

I quickly moved the boxes, ignoring the outraged squeaks. There lay Tiffany, curled up on her side. Heart hammering, I dropped to my knees and checked for a pulse. It was there, and strong, just like the man in the alley. And, like him, she had two puncture wounds on her neck, one smeared with fresh blood. But when I touched hers, the blood came off. And the puncture wounds didn't.

I shot to my feet and fumbled for my phone. No signal. I was in the middle of the goddamned city. Why couldn't I get a signal?

I hurried down to the alley, waving my phone, desperately trying to get a connection. At the click of heels on pavement, I wheeled to see a woman walking out from another bar exit, an unlit cigarette dangling from her hand. She was about forty, with red hair and a sophisticated, feline sleekness that made me instinctively straighten and tuck my hair behind my ears.

Catching the movement, she turned and gave a brief nod. Then she glimpsed something behind me, her green eyes narrowing as she frowned. She glided over, saw Tiffany and whispered, "Dear God." Turning to me, she snapped, more than a little accusingly, "Have you called 911?"

"I—" I lifted my cell. "I can't get service. I was just going to head inside. Can you wait with her while I . . . ?"

She already had her cell out and was dialling, shooting me a look that called me an incompetent idiot.

"Yes, I'd like to report an emergency," she said into the phone.

She went through the process – explaining the situation, checking for a pulse, giving an address. But as hard as I strained to hear the operator on the other end, I couldn't.

As I walked to Tiffany, I brushed against the woman. She glared and pulled away, but not before I felt what I'd feared – cool skin against mine.

"They'll be here in ten minutes," she said as she hung up. "In the meantime, I'd suggest we—"

"No one's coming," I said, backing away slowly, like a postal worker facing a Doberman. "There wasn't anyone on the other end."

She frowned. Then, without even a ripple to her perfect composure, she nodded. "So your friend isn't the only half-demon. Auris or Exaudio? I suppose it hardly matters, though it does make this easier. My name is Cassandra DuCharme, and I'm a delegate—"

At a noise from down the alley, my chin jerked up and she stopped talking, her gaze following mine. Agent Carter stepped from a side alley. Seeing me, he pulled up short.

"Melanie?"

Cassandra smiled at him. "Ah, so you couldn't resist the bait after all. Excellent. This just keeps getting easier. Aaron?"

"Adrian" swung from a recessed doorway behind Carter, grabbed him and slammed him into the wall. Blood spurted. Aaron yanked Carter back, head lolling, nose streaming blood.

"Shit," Aaron said. "He's not—"

I bolted before he could finish. I reached the Vamp Tramp back exit. Closed. No handle. I was putting on the brakes, about to find another way, when the door opened and my shy admirer from earlier stuck his head out.

Seeing me, he smiled. "I *thought* you went out this way."

I wheeled in, shoving him back inside so hard he stumbled. As I quickly explained that my friend was hurt, I yanked the door shut and made sure it would stay that way.

I pulled out my cell phone. A drunken couple lurched into the hall, screaming the lyrics to "Sympathy for the Devil". My admirer pushed open the nearest door and motioned me into the supply closet, away from the noise.

I stepped in, my gaze fixed on the display screen on my phone. Full signal. Thank God. I started to dial. Then I heard the soft rustle of fabric right behind me. I turned to see my admirer in mid-pounce. I staggered back. He snarled, flashing razor-sharp canines.

I spun out of the way and slammed my elbow into his nose. A great self-defence move . . . if you aren't fighting a vampire. He only reeled back, then shook his head and lunged again. I feinted to the side, and grabbed an inventory pencil. I aimed for his eye. I missed, but rammed the pencil into his cheek with such force it broke when it hit bone and I was left holding a stub.

And the vampire? He just reached up, and plucked out the pencil. By the time it clattered to the floor, the bloodless wound was already closing.

I remembered Aaron throwing Carter against the wall, his oath of surprise at seeing blood streaming from his broken nose . . . because Carter wasn't a vampire, and that's what they'd expected.

The woman had introduced herself as Cassandra DuCharme. A delegate, she'd said. I now knew what she'd been about to say before I cut her short: delegate to the *interracial council*, a law-enforcement body for supernaturals. They'd been hunting one of their own – a killer. And I'd been the one to find him. Lucky me.

I'd taken enough self-defence classes to ward this monster off, but that was all I could do, considering the guy was impervious to injury.

My best bet was getting to the door. He knew that, which is why he stayed between it and me. Finally, he got tired of the dance and pounced. I waited until the last second, then spun out of the way. When he tried to check his charge and lost his balance, I grabbed him by the hair and slammed his face into a wooden crate. I did it again and again, until the wood cracked and split. Still he kept fighting.

I tried backing towards the door, but he grabbed my dress, holding me still. I was about to lunge, praying that the dress would rip, when the door flew open and a voice said, "I'll take that for you."

Aaron grabbed the vampire. I didn't wait to see what he did with him. I raced outside to check on Tiffany and Carter.

They were fine. Sedated, as it turned out. That's what a vampire's first bite does, as Cassandra explained while Aaron stashed their prisoner in a safe place. Aaron had bitten Tiffany just enough to put her to sleep, then Cassandra did the same for Carter. They'd wake up soon.

When Aaron returned, he filled me in on the rest as Cassandra waited impatiently.

Tiffany had been right about bars like this being the perfect way to "hide in plain sight" for vampires – at least for one who preferred leaving his dinner pulse free. This guy had apparently hit two other similar bars, the first in New Mexico, where Agent Carter presumably got involved. Aaron and Cassandra had caught up at the second bar. They hadn't seen their quarry, who was a new vampire, but they had seen Carter – both there and here – and presumed he was their killer.

One thing they did know about their target was that he had very specific taste in women.

"That's why you brought Tiffany out here," I said. "As bait."

"No, she wasn't the bait," Aaron said. "You were."

Great. I'm finally some guy's "type" . . . and he turns out to be a killer vampire. That's why Aaron lured Tiffany out, he explained. If I got worried and followed, so would the killer. And if I stayed inside, I'd be alone, giving him a chance to make his move.

"He'll be dealt with," Aaron said. "In the meantime, thank you. And Cassandra apologizes for startling you earlier and not explaining the situation before you took off."

Cassandra's perfect brows arched. "I do?"

"You do," he said. "Deep down, you're very apologetic."

She rolled her eyes and waved for him to wrap this up so they could be on their way. From the look and smile he gave her, I knew there was no use mooning over this vampire. He was taken, and probably had been for longer than I'd been alive. I wasn't too disappointed. Here was proof that really hot guys sometimes *do* go for bitchy women. So there was hope for me yet. Just not with this particular hot guy.

As a back-up, though, Agent Carter would do nicely. Very nicely, I decided as I sat in the back of the ambulance with him. He was still groggy, holding his glasses in one hand, his hair and shirt rumpled, looking very sexy, even if he probably felt like he'd been hit with a two-by-four.

He'd confirmed what I'd figured out – that he'd been following the case of a cross-country killer, starting in New Mexico.

Just as Aaron had noticed Carter in the last bar, Carter had spotted Aaron, and jumped to the same wrong conclusion – that the other must be the killer. Neither had noticed the relatively nondescript man who turned out to be the real culprit.

I couldn't tell Carter – apparently human – what really happened. But since he hadn't seen who'd assaulted him it was easy. When asked about his attacker, I described the real killer instead, knowing others in the bar could confirm his presence and disappearance. Earlier, when Tiffany had woken, I'd told her to do the same – say she had gone into the alley with the blond guy, then headed back in alone and been waylaid by the other man.

As for the unconscious guy in the alley? Carter suspected he really had been a bit of performance art, though the manager of Vamp Tramp had refused to confirm that.

In all this, though, no one mentioned the possibility that a real vampire was involved. To Carter, the explanation was obvious.

"It's some maniac who thinks he's a vampire or wants us to. He injects his victims with a sedative, then bleeds them to death. As for what he does with the blood, I don't really want to know. There are a lot of sick people out there."

"And now he got away. So what will you do?"

"Stick around the local office for a while, see if he tries again. And, in the meantime—" he gave me his lopsided smile "—I believe I owe you a drink. Are you free tomorrow? I'll throw in dinner. Least I can do after all this." When I didn't answer, the smile faded. "No?"

I met his gaze. "Does the phrase 'interracial council' mean anything to you?"

He frowned. "No, should it?"

"Cabal? Exaudio? Vodoun?"

"Is that Latin?"

His confusion convinced me. Agent Miguel Carter was, without a doubt, one hundred per cent human.

I smiled. "Pick me up at seven?"

John Doe

Anna Windsor

One

"Happy birthday to me." My voice didn't echo, but only because my office at Riverview Psychiatric Hospital was so small. I lifted my way-too-early-morning coffee to toast the institutional clock hanging opposite my only window, and wished the cinder-block walls weren't quite so blindingly white.

"The big three-oh," I said to nobody, and pretended like I was shaking a non-existent party noisemaker. The admissions nurse and aide were out with gastroenteritis, and the night-shift secretary was two months from retirement. She showed up only when it damn well pleased her to do so. Which was never.

So, here I was, Dutch Brennan, celebrating a milestone birthday in New York City, all by my lonesome.

Some things never changed.

In my opinion, *most* things never changed. My father taught me that, along with a lot of paranoid things about how dangerous the world could be.

Just when you think it's OK, baby girl – boom. Here come the monsters.

Then he'd put me through my paces. Sayokan: Turkish martial arts. I'd trained four days a week, almost every week of my life. If I ever met a monster, I was ready – but I guessed most monsters were scared of Riverview Psychiatric Hospital. I hadn't met any since I came to work here just after residency and fellowship. Hadn't met too many friends, either, which is why I was having a birthday at work.

My only gift to myself was a fresh-brewed pot of Starbucks Verona – brewed in the ancient pot down the hallway – mixed with a packet of no-fat cocoa. At least the fresh, nutty scent competed with the hazy stink of orange cleanser, bleach and old-stone-building mould. The rich perfection of chocolate-spiked coffee flooded my mouth and warmed my throat as I leaned back against my rattletrap wooden desk, careful not to bump my computer monitor or topple the stacks of last week's paperwork.

"Maybe I should buy myself a condo someplace warm, like Malibu," I told the clock, which silently informed me that it was 3 a.m., and I still had four boring hours to survive before I got to slog home through the snow. But the condo idea – maybe that did have some merit. After all, I *was* a doctor. And I had dark hair and kind of naturally tanned skin.

"But I'm too full-figured to fit in with the beach bunnies," I admitted to the clock. "I'd probably never score a date in Malibu."

Like I ever gave myself a chance to get a date in New York City, either.

How long had it been since I'd done something other than work the night shift, then hit the gym?

Four years?

Five?

The back buzzer blasted through the cool silence of the entire admissions area. I jumped so hard my coffee almost sloshed onto the sleeve of my lab coat.

Oh, great.

My heart thumped high in my chest, like it was thinking about making a break for my throat.

Nobody but the NYPD ever came to the back door, and they probably had a patient to drop off. I stepped out of my office and blinked at the darkened admission hallway. Even though there were five floors full of patients and nurses and aides above my head, ground level was totally deserted.

What if the cops had brought me Godzilla on Crack?

I glanced at the phone on my desk and reluctantly killed what was left of my coffee then threw the cup in the trash.

No big deal.

If I was uncomfortable with the patient, I could always ask the officers to stay for coffee while I completed my evaluation. If things got really hairy, I could call up to the patient floors and get some help.

For now, this was just more of the same. Probably nothing I couldn't handle on my own, like I did everything else.

I walked out of my office into the admissions hallway and covered the forty-foot distance to the back door as quickly as I could. Outside, I figured I'd find uniformed officers, and probably some poor homeless man or woman in handcuffs and blanket, sporting a wicked-evil case of frostbite on toes and fingers. Definitely the season for that. Had to expect it.

When I hit the intercom button, a gruff voice said, "NYPD. We got an evaluation for you, Doc."

The metal handle was ice cold when I gripped it and pulled open the door to reveal the two uniforms I expected, and—

Whoa.

OK, so *this*, I didn't expect.

"We found this guy wandering on the Triborough Bridge just before midnight." The officer's voice barely penetrated my consciousness as I stared at the "patient" standing between the two officers. "Central Emergency stitched him up – said it looks like he chopped himself up with a couple of Ginsu blades. Self-inflicted wounds. He hasn't said a word since the paramedics scooped him up."

I stood there, just as mute. Medical school, residency and five years of on-the-job experience at Riverview, and I'd never seen anything like this guy.

The man – John Doe for now – looked like a cross between an extreme bodybuilder and a knight from some book of medieval tales. He stood quietly, no cuffs or restraints, arms folded across his broad, bare chest. Silky black curls brushed the edges of his tanned face. He was barefoot and naked from the waist up, clad only in bloodied jeans that hung in tatters against long, powerful legs.

Way too long since I'd had a date. Yep. The flutters in my belly – definitely not OK. This was a patient, not some muscle hunk showing off in the gym.

Though if more muscle hunks at the gym looked like this . . .

Stop it.

My eyes travelled over each well-cut line and bulge.

John Doe's eyes, molten emeralds, fixed on me, and my pulse quickened. The air stirred, then hummed, and I could have sworn he was radiating some kind of . . . *power.* I could almost see it, like the moonlit darkness shimmering against the office's only window.

Good God, I'm as crazy as he is.

My heartbeat slowed, then revved again, this time with a funny, skippy, squeezing beat, and I couldn't seem to get a full breath.

No man could be this handsome.

The sight of him was actually rattling my senses.

And the power thing, that had to be in my head. In my imagination. John Doe was a patient. No supernatural abilities.

But if anyone on Earth really does have superhero powers, this *would be the guy.*

"Weird that he doesn't have any visible frostbite," the second officer was saying during my mute assessment. "Guess he got lucky."

Doing all I could to make myself be a doctor instead of a slack-jawed idiot, I inched back to allow the officers to escort the patient into Riverview's admissions hallway.

Those eyes.

I could barely look anywhere else.

I could dive into those eyes and swim for hours.

My fingers curled. I could not have thoughts like this about a patient. It wasn't ethical. It was downright slimy.

The man's lips parted, showing straight, white teeth. He smelled like cinnamon with a touch of cloves – fresh, but not overpowering. Delicious, actually.

Don't. Go. There.

"Tox screen was clear, labs were normal." The first cop patted the patient on the shoulder. "Hasn't given us any trouble."

John Doe kept staring at me, like he was trying to decide something. His beautiful mouth curved into something like a frown, and he lowered his hands to reveal the design carved into his Betadine-painted and stitched chest.

My eyes locked onto John Doe's cuts, and my brain seemed to make a whining noise. In fact, it seemed to short out completely. There wasn't enough room for me to assume a proper defensive stance to fight, but my muscles tightened from years of drilling and practice. I wanted a weapon. Felt like I *needed* a weapon. Riverview's admissions hallway became a twisting, bending rabbit hole, and I was Alice, falling forwards and backwards at the same time, exploding into some nightmare version of Wonderland.

"Doc?"

One of the policemen . . . but I couldn't shake off the five pounds of freak-out crawling up and down my spine.

"You OK, Doc?" The second officer sounded a little worried. "Want to come back to us here?"

But I don't like to go among mad people, Alice remarked. My thoughts chattered outside my control, and I barely kept my teeth from following suit. *Oh you can't help that, said the Cat: we're all mad here.*

John Doe's full attention remained on me, and those unbelievably deep eyes grew wider and softer with concern. I also saw him struggle for some sort of recognition, as if he thought he should know me, but didn't.

"Oh, my God." My voice didn't sound like my voice. I really couldn't breathe now. I barely kept myself upright. My vision blurred and swam, and all I could do was point at the cuts etched across John Doe's heart.

An odd arrangement of lines, like a phoenix in flight and on fire, burning to death as it screamed its fate to imaginary stars above.

I had seen it before.

I had seen it eighteen years ago in Armenia, when I was twelve, before my American soldier father brought me to the United States.

The same pattern had been carved into my mother's chest the day I found her dead in our living room.

Two

Run.

The urge was so strong I would have bolted down the admissions hallway and locked myself in my office if I hadn't had a shred of self-control left from years of martial arts training.

Run.

The cops were staring at me. I made myself breathe normally, but fought an urge to blast my fists into John Doe's gut and knock him away from me.

"It's OK," I told the officers, keeping my voice even and calm no matter how much I wanted to scream. Whatever was happening here, I had to find out what the hell it was – and without the audience. "I'll take it from here. You can go."

Both uniformed men regarded me like I might belong on a patient floor.

"Doc." One of the NYPD's finest looked hesitant. "Maybe we should cuff him for you. Leave you the key. The way he cut himself up, I'm not sure you'll be safe."

I waved them off. "I've got plenty of help. I'll just call a tech down here from the second floor." The lie came easily and I didn't know why I didn't take the officers up on the offer to cuff this Adonis when all of my instincts were saying, *Run.*

My frown must have let them know I was serious. "You have real sickos to go after and this guy doesn't look like a threat I can't handle."

After a pause they gave me nods and left without argument.

As the metal door swung closed behind them, leaving me in the dimly-lit hall facing a man carved up just like my murdered mother, I growled, "What's your name?"

John Doe kept looking at me. His lips didn't so much as twitch. Except for the cuts, the man was as perfect as an Italian Renaissance sculpture. I was caught between a desire to touch him or to slug him and get the hell away from those marks on his chest.

Was this it for me? Was I finally losing my mind?

That design on John Doe's chest. Right over his heart. Sweet Christ. How could it be there? *That* picture, in *that* exact place?

I was definitely losing my mind. This wasn't possible. This couldn't be happening.

But it was.

I picked at the edges of my lab coat to remind myself I was a doctor, and I did have a job to do.

"Come with me." I motioned towards my office, then took a few steps back down the admissions hallway and waited to see if John Doe would follow.

He did.

Slowly. Gracefully.

Which was a good thing, because even if I called every nurse in the hospital, shots and restraints notwithstanding, I doubted we could have moved that rock-hard body anywhere it didn't want to go.

At my office door, I glanced back again, and my senses catalogued every tiny detail about him: the black curls, the tanned face, the greener than green eyes. John Doe's muscles flexed as he followed me into the room and stood quietly on the polished tile floor.

I walked to my desk, then turned and leaned against the front. The clock on my right and the window on my left felt familiar. Normal. Some kind of balance when otherwise I might just tip over.

"What's your name?" I tried again, in the kindest, calmest voice I could muster.

Nothing.

I took a centring breath this time, and refused to let my annoyance rise. "Do you know what day it is?"

He didn't smile. He didn't frown. He didn't move at all, except for slow, even breathing. I kept trying not to appraise him like a piece of art, but I did it anyway. I couldn't stop myself. He was absolutely riveting.

"Do you know where you are?" I asked, my voice cracking as I stumbled through the last of my standard orientation questions. When John Doe didn't respond to that either, I shifted gears. "Why did you cut yourself?"

At this, John Doe glanced at his chest, then at me, snagging me once again with the power of his stare, of his presence. I left off the bigger questions about his wounds. *Why did you cut yourself like that? Why did you choose exactly that design?* But the brightness in his green eyes made me wonder if he didn't hear my unspoken words.

Long, heated seconds later, John Doe glanced at my office window and cocked his head, like he was listening to something other than me. His expression darkened, and his muscles bunched as he clenched his fists.

My chest tightened even as my heart sank, and my hand crept towards the phone on my desk.

Damn it, but this guy was probably hallucinating.

What was I thinking, bringing him back here alone?

Then, as I watched, John Doe's jeans just . . . changed.

I froze. Outwardly. Inwardly, I was falling back down that rabbit hole. My lips moved, but I didn't say anything. My pulse pounded so hard I could hear it in both ears.

Not my imagination. No.

One second those jeans were filthy and tattered.

The next, they were normal, clean and whole jeans.

John Doe was still barefoot and half-naked, but his chest – the phoenix wound – was healing before my eyes.

"What the—?"

It was all I had time to say before he vanished. More like moved so fast I couldn't really perceive it. I caught the flash of something silver, an image like a bird with bright wings outstretched. Then he was standing on my other side, by the door. The scent of cinnamon and cloves washed through my senses.

John Doe opened his perfect mouth and growled as he took hold of my arm, a grip as firm as a vice. He pulled me away from the window, almost against his hard, tanned chest.

I didn't fight.

Couldn't.

Thoughts barely formed in what was left of my mind, but I realized he was pushing me away from him now, away from the window and towards the office door.

At that moment, John Doe finally spoke, and his voice rumbled deep and low. Mountains might have mustered that resonance, if stone could find its own voice.

What he said was: "Run."

Three

Every nerve in my body fired, propelling me out of my office door into the admissions hallway.

For a split second my mind jerked back in time, to Armenia, to that awful sunlit day when I found my mother's body. I had run like this, crazy and unbalanced, into the streets, down the road until I made it to my father's base.

The memory made me stumble.

Fall to one knee.

A bolt of pain fractured the past and brought me back to the present.

Behind me, back in my office, glass crashed and shattered.

Concrete and mortar and plaster shot through my open office door, spraying across the tiles and stinging my calves.

I shoved myself back to my feet, throat closing, eyes tearing. Blood roared in my ears as I tried to move fast, but I felt my right knee give with a tearing agony.

Someone – or something – behind me let out a roar like a rabid bull.

"Shit. Shit. Shit!" I dragged my bad leg down the admissions hallway, past all the closed doors and darkened windows. My mind focused on the hospital's back door, on the cold metal handle that would let me out into the snowy night.

John Doe shouted something in a language I had known before, but didn't remember.

What the fuck is happening here? To me. To him!

I looked over my shoulder, and silvery light almost blinded me.

Fire poured out of my office door in sharp, massive jets, so big they almost reached me.

I barely got my face turned away before I almost lost my eyebrows. My skin ached from the heat as I fell forwards, one limping step at a time. I smelled burning hair. My own. Thick, sulphurous clouds made me choke as I tried to breathe, and each time my bad knee tried to flex, I let out a scream.

John Doe.

No way had he survived that explosion of fire.

But he had to.

I didn't want him to be dead.

I didn't want to die.

That friggin' door seemed like a mile away, even though it was less than ten feet now.

Fireballs streaked past me on both sides. Door facings splintered. Sprinklers went off, pulsing with the fast, hard beat of my heart.

I lurched forwards, slipped again, banged my hurt knee on the tile floor, and yelped.

Something huge and flaming and bellowing soared over my head and slammed to its feet right in front of me, blocking my path to the back door.

Oh God. It has gigantic, scaly feet.

Not real. I had to be hallucinating.

Boom, said my dead father's voice. *Here come the monsters.*

Claws the size of butcher knives gouged into the tiles, grating so loud they blotted out the hospital's fire alarm.

My heart stopped beating, and my breathing stopped too. My chest squeezed in on itself as I looked up into a tower of fire with scaly arms and clawed paws. Unnatural black-coal eyes burned with hungry hatred, and the thing grabbed for me.

I screamed, dropped, and rolled away from it.

Smoke choked me.

I couldn't see.

I used the hallway wall to pull myself up again and raised my arms in defensive posture.

No way out of the back door. If I ran the other way, there was only an elevator, and I might lead the thing to the patient floors.

That thought spiked some anger into my terror.

Not happening.

I'd die first.

The fire-thing hesitated, maybe confused – or amused – by my fighting stance.

My breathing and pulse picked up again. Like I was ready to fight. "Screw you!" I yelled at the creature.

I'm insane.

I'm going to die right here.

But I had to try.

And I had to protect the patients if I could.

It squared off with me and bellowed.

The sound rattled through my insides, ripping my courage to shreds. Somehow I kept my arms bent, fists raised, mind madly reeling through possible weaknesses I could exploit.

If I hit the fucking thing, I'll combust.

Silvery light flashed, and John Doe was suddenly standing between me and the creature.

Oh, thank God. Not dead. Barefoot and wearing only jeans – but he had a sword now. And wings.

Wings?

The feathers were singed. His shoulders were singed. His green eyes were wide, filled with fury, and he bared his teeth at the fire-thing. I wished I could build a wall around him, around us, to keep us safe from the flames, but John Doe never slowed as he swung his giant sword. The massive golden grip flashed, and the long, double-sharp blade whistled as it tore through the air.

The fire-thing lurched and banged against the firmly secured back door, barely keeping its big ugly head. Its black eyes literally spit sparks as it snarled. Fire blasted towards us, all around us, but something repelled it, as if we were standing inside a giant fireproof bubble.

Or behind a wall . . .

I gasped once, twice, finally getting enough air to still the spinning in my brain. My energy felt even more drained, like half my blood had just dumped onto the soot-streaked hospital floor.

"Run," John Doe told me again, but I felt melded to my spot against the wall, and to him.

"Can't," I said, and took a limping step backwards to prove it. The pain in my knee told me I'd never make it, and I absolutely couldn't leave him here to face this creature alone. I might not be much help, but even injured, I *could* fight.

John Doe swore and took another swing at the fire-monster. It jumped sideways, giving ground. Fire shot from its massive clawed hands, again streaming around us – but the air shimmered, seemed to bow inwards.

I felt so weak I could have collapsed, would have if I hadn't had my hand pressed against the wall.

A jet of flame broke through whatever had been protecting us and blasted into John Doe's bare chest.

"Damn it!" I shouted as he fell backwards and hit the tiles hard, feathery wings splaying outwards. The sword skittered out of his hand, spinning in my direction.

I jumped towards it.

Pain flared through my injured leg, and I crashed to the tiles as a blast of fire singed more of my long hair. No stopping. Couldn't stop. If I stopped, I'd be dead. John Doe would be dead – if he wasn't already.

Teeth clenched, I crawled forwards and snatched up the sword with both hands.

Fire-thing gave me another blast, but I rolled away from it and staggered to my feet – well, foot – lugging the sword, tip down. It would blast me. I'd be burned to ashes, just a lump of teeth for the Medical Examiner to identify.

"Come on!" I screamed at the thing, hoisting the sword. "What are you waiting for?"

It seemed to blink.

What *was* it waiting for?

Fuck it.

I roared at the thing, then managed to balance the sword's considerable weight with my shoulders and elbows. When I touched my right foot to the floor, I sucked in a breath. Rage powered my muscles as they strained from the effort, but the pain centred me. Freed me.

The world narrowed to just the hallway, and the freak-ass creature blocking the door.

It bellowed and lunged towards me.

I bellowed and lunged towards it.

Let myself fall, screaming as my knee gave.

I rolled under the horrible claws and arcs of fire, then came up on my ass, swinging the sword.

"Low man wins!" I shrieked as the blade made contact with the creature's blazing left ankle.

The impact made my teeth clamp together, but I kept hold of the sword, and sliced straight through the thing's big, thick leg.

My butt seemed to drive itself deeper into the floor as I made the cut, then I slid sideways as fire-beast howled and pitched towards the opposite wall.

Then the fucking monster blew up like a barrel of dynamite.

I felt the shock before I heard it, if I ever really heard it. Hot air slammed into me like a speeding train, shoving me hard and fast across the hall. My ears throbbed, then buzzed. My shoulder and head crushed against cinder block and the sword ripped free of my fingers. My vision dimmed, flickered. Darkness swept towards me, but powerful arms grabbed me and seemed to jerk me out of the abyss.

Moments later, I was cradled against a perfectly carved chest.

Smoke thinned, then swirled to nothing, and warmth – healing, not burning – poured through me. The mass of aches and pains in my body lessened, my knee straightened itself out and stopped throbbing, and the pressure on my ears eased. I could hear my own jerking breaths as I found myself looking into the liquid emerald eyes of John Doe.

Silver light outlined his dark curls, and the feathery arc of his wings rose above his well-defined shoulders.

Wings.

He really did have wings.

They were flapping slowly, almost gently, clearing River-view's hallway of the smoke and stink from . . . from whatever that fire-thing had been.

A shocked, almost dumbfounded expression had claimed John Doe's beyond-handsome face.

"You defeated a Raah," he said, his voice deep and smooth, but without the terrible, mountainous resonance I had heard before we fought the monster.

Raah.

That word stirred something in my memory, but I couldn't quite grasp the definition, or any image beyond the fiery beast that had invaded Riverview. I reached for my full awareness, the complete measure of my intelligence as a physician, philosopher, and devout practitioner of Sayokan – and the response I came up with was, "I defeated a what?"

From somewhere in the distance came the eerie moan of sirens, and I thought I heard voices and footsteps getting closer.

Probably rushing towards us from upstairs, and from the front
street entrance of the hospital.

John Doe held me tighter against him as he started walking,
so close I could feel his heart beating with mine. That strange
power I thought I had imagined earlier hummed between his
skin and mine, everywhere we made contact. It made me tingle
in ways I couldn't begin to describe. He carried me out of the
back door into the alley behind Riverview, but I didn't feel the
bite of the cold air, or even the wet kiss of the night's light snow.
I also didn't feel threatened, or that I should try to escape his
firm but tender grip. The terror I had felt when I met him had
been replaced by a feverish blend of curiosity and wonder.

Did this man, this being, hold the key to that door I had
locked on my past?

Do I want to open it?

Nothing ever changed. Nothing. No way.

*Because I won't let it? Because change scares me so badly I can't
even stand to consider it?*

John Doe was staring at me so intently I wondered if he could
see the blood pumping faster and faster through my veins.

He spread his wings.

I knew I should have been terrified, but there was no fear in
me at all. At that moment, I felt safer than I'd ever felt in my life
– and I couldn't stop looking at him.

After a moment, I lifted my arms and wrapped them around
his neck.

He took off, not in a brutal rush of speed, but in a quiet,
weightless whisper.

My heart gave a flip, like when I rode roller coasters or tried
to spar blindfolded in the gym. When I caught my breath, it
seemed easy, almost natural to be lifted so high, to be above
ground and flying.

We floated together towards the winter stars as moonlight
blended with his faint silver glow. All the while, he kept his eyes
on mine, like he was searching every inch of my soul. That
strange power he had, something almost magical, warmed me so
much I knew my cheeks had to be flushed. I wished I could see
into his essence, the depths of his being, so I could understand
him, and maybe understand myself.

As we drifted over the snow-capped roof of the hospital and the skyline of New York City spread beneath us, we spoke at the same time, and we asked the same question.

"What *are* you?"

Four

"I'm just Dutch Brennan." Lame answer, but the truth, which seemed like my only option, given that I was high above New York City, in the arms of a winged man who helped me fight some kind of ravening fire-monster. "I'm nothing. I'm nobody. I only killed that thing because I work out."

John Doe's jaw flexed. I wasn't certain, but he looked like he might be impressed. "With . . . weapons."

"Sayokan." I leaned into him, enjoying his warmth, his body, his unusual smell. "Martial arts, Turkish-style."

Another jaw flex.

His silence drove me to keep talking. "My father taught me, then found me other masters after he moved us to New York City. I live in SoHo now."

I rattled off the address, and John Doe made a slight course correction.

"Now it's your turn," I said as he descended slowly towards what I recognized as my neighbourhood, then my building.

A moment later, he rumbled, "I'm Shaddai."

The word gave me that sensation again, of things I should be remembering, but the meaning didn't come to me. I waited, assuming he would explain, but he didn't.

"What's your name?" I asked him as he touched down on my balcony and set me on my feet. "Can I at least know that much?"

I tested my knee and found I could walk with no pain at all, which only increased my wonder and confusion. I unlocked and opened the balcony doors of my third-floor apartment before I turned back to him. The ever-present glow of the city illuminated his look of contemplation, then decision. "Shant," he said, still using the deep, rich bass of a very big, very sexy man. "I come from Mount Aragats, and I have been on Earth three hundred and six of your years."

That made me freeze in the doorway, trapping him outside in the snowy night. Tiny white flakes brushed against his bare shoulders and wings, then melted to sparkling droplets. He didn't move or challenge me. He simply stood, wings folded against his muscled shoulders, and gazed at me with those green eyes, waiting.

For what?

My approval?

My belief?

Shant.

The name meant, roughly, "thunderbolt" in Armenian.

Fitting.

My insides shivered with my outsides. "Three hundred and six. OK." I managed to move enough to fold my arms. "We'll leave that alone for now. But Aragats? As in the mountain in Armenia?"

He nodded, his expression calm but solemn, as if he understood this might have meaning to me. Which, of course, it did. Mount Aragats was the only trip I remembered taking with my mother before she died. There was a special structure on those slopes – ruins of great stone towers joined together.

"Amberd," I said aloud, recalling the name of that place even as my mind translated its meaning: "fortress in the clouds".

I felt like my brain was creaking – or maybe it was just the hinges of that inner door I had slammed on my childhood.

My mother, standing beside me, dark hair billowing as she pointed to those rounded towers . . .

With a pained gulp of air, I shoved that image away from me, but I couldn't escape the vision taking up most of my little balcony. Shant filled the entire space except for where I was standing, and he moved even closer, so near I imagined the heat of his body forming a shield around me. "You have deeper injuries, older injuries that still need healing," he murmured. "Let me help you. Let me soothe your heart as I soothed your body."

I couldn't respond directly to that statement, or to him. I swallowed hard, trying to ignore the thready racing of my heart as I stared past Shant at SoHo. At the real world. At my present, not my strange, shrouded past. "Will that . . . fire-thing . . . show up again?"

"The Raah's essence returned to its maker." Shant's down-wards gesture was unmistakable. "But there will be others."

My brain really was starting to spin in my skull. I was sure of it. "You're trying to tell me that I sent whatever that thing was to Hell."

"Yes." Shant put his hands on my shoulders and moved me backwards. Carefully. Measuring out his strength so he didn't overpower me. In a smooth, balanced motion, he swept my balcony doors shut with his leg, cutting off the steady flow of snow and wind.

My cheekbones ached in the sudden warmth of my small, dark and sparsely furnished apartment. The main room was lit only by the city itself – and a slight but definite silver glow from Shant's skin. As for my skin, it seemed to hum where he was touching me. My body began to override my intellect, wanting more contact with him, leaning towards him even as I fought to force myself to step back.

"So, if that fire-thing – the Raah – if it was from Hell, then am I supposed to believe you're from Heaven?" I stared into Shant's eyes, his handsome face barely illuminated in the softer-than-soft light. "Does Shaddai mean some sort of an-gel?"

Shant's wings rustled, then slowly eased from view, as if he might be pulling them into his flesh. When he smiled, the curl of his lips made me want to stand on my toes and kiss him.

"I'm no angel," he assured me as he pulled me against him, then lifted one hand to brush my hair from my eyes.

I wrapped my arms around him, my palms pressing against his taut back, then the ridges of flesh where his wings had been.

His fingers lingered on my forehead, spreading tingly waves of heat through my temples, down the sides of my neck, and lower, through my whole body, especially the spot where his hard belly pressed into my ribs. I wanted to lean my head against the warm firmness of his chest, and I wondered if he was making me dizzy somehow, stealing my ability to reason, to be afraid, to even be cautious.

His face was lowering towards mine, his green eyes sizzling with light and life. I could almost taste his lips. His breath tickled against my chin and nose, and I realized he was doing it again, reading me somehow, and my heartbeat rushed, then slowed, rushed then slowed –

And he stopped.

Pulled back.

Let me go.

My chest tightened from the shock of the sudden abandonment. It felt wrong, being more than an arm's length away from Shant, and I wondered if I really had left my sanity back at Riverview.

His beautiful eyes had gone wide, and for a moment I worried that he'd turn, blast through my balcony doors, and vanish into the dark winter night.

Instead, the silver glow from his body increased, falling across me like a search beam. "It makes more sense now," he murmured. "It *was* you – the danger to you – that brought me here."

I saw him touch his chest, trace the spot where his phoenix wounds had been before they healed, but I didn't understand. I was still aching from wanting to kiss him, and my arms screamed to be around him again.

When I stepped towards him, he stepped back, and this time, he did bump into the balcony doors. He raised both hands as if to ward me off, then bowed his head.

"My apologies for my boldness," he said, his voice rough with shame. "Why didn't you tell me? If I had known, I would have never . . . Forgive me. Please. But how did you conceal yourself so perfectly?"

I rubbed one of my eyes to relieve the pressure building anew in my brain. "Shant, what are you talking about?"

And I just want to be kissing you, not figuring this out.

"I'm Shaddai," he said, as if that explained everything, then seemed to realize I truly didn't know what he meant – about himself, or about me.

"Shaddai," he said again, his voice rough with surprise and disbelief. "A protector, nothing more."

When I still looked clueless, he came towards me once more, but stopped well shy of grabbing me again, of pulling me against him like I so wanted him to do.

Shant's green eyes focused on me, and he folded his heavy arms across his chest. "I'm no angel, Dutch Brennan. But *you* are."

Five

God, but I liked hearing Shant use my name and call me an angel.

Then I processed what he meant.

"An angel. An actual angel. That's funny." I glared at him. And a heartbeat later . . . "You're serious."

I closed my eyes. Opened them. "And you're insane. *Damn* it. Look, today's my thirtieth birthday. If I was an angel, don't you think I'd . . . um, well, have figured that out by now?" I wiggled my fingers at him. "Look. No beautiful golden lights or heavenly music." I shrugged my shoulders. "And no wings. Wings are kind of standard issue for angels, wouldn't you say?"

Shant kept looking at me, as if puzzling through everything I was saying. I'd seen delusional people do this before, try to fit all the facts into their warped perception of the universe. I'd just never seen a delusional winged man do it before. A winged man who looked like a god and called me an angel.

"You're a half-blood. It's the only answer." He ran his hand through his hair. "And today, when you came of age, the Raah became aware of you."

This was getting worse.

What would it take to get a supernatural winged being back to Riverview's admission office? I rubbed the sides of my head with my fingers. Except, Riverview's first floor had been blasted to bits, I'd gone soppy over said supernatural winged being and let him fly me back to my apartment.

Greeeeaaat.

Even better – I still wanted to kiss the crazy son of a bitch. I so needed to lose my licence over this.

"You *are* an angel." Shant folded those sexy arms over his to-die-for chest. "Take me to your parents. I'll prove it to you."

"My parents are dead," I shot back, then clamped my mouth shut.

Oh.

Oh God.

The image of my mother's face hovered in my mind, as ethereal and beautiful as ever. And I saw Amberd, the fortress in the clouds, with its round, ruined stone towers.

Shaddai. That's what my mother had said on our journey up the mountain. *Come here to call them. They'll hear you if you truly need them.*

My legs instantly went rubbery, and I made my way to the couch and sat down, staring open-mouthed at Shant. My skin felt hot and cold at the same time, and my voice sounded shaky and weird when I found enough of my wits to speak.

"Amberd. I didn't . . . I didn't call you. My mother said I could go up the mountain, to the fortress in the clouds, but I didn't do it. So how did you find me?"

Shant touched his chest with his palm, and for a moment I saw the outline of the phoenix wounds that had so upset me when I first saw him at Riverview.

This time, the effect was different. It felt like some sort of answer, or maybe a clarification.

"I answered a debt of honour," Shant explained in a tone that suggested sorrow and new understanding. "When an angel dies on Earth, they can use their essence to send a message to us, their protectors who failed them, and we are bound to respect their dying request." He lowered his gorgeous head as I processed that my mother hadn't been killed by a knife-wielding maniac, but by some loony fire-demon instead. Those marks on her chest when I found her – she had carved them herself before she died.

The message.

A communique to the Shaddai.

That's why Shant had shown up in my admissions office, bearing the same marks, or, more accurately, the memory of them. Of that message. He must have submitted to the police and emergency room staff because he wasn't certain exactly who he was supposed to protect, only the general area where I was.

"Someone bound me to you long ago, Dutch Brennan." Shant's eyes were so intoxicating I could hardly stand to look at him. "Someone wished for you to be protected, should the Raah ever come to know of your existence, and your life on

Earth be threatened." He kept looking at me, those green eyes swimming with a thousand emotions I couldn't name. "Your birthday. When the Raah could sense you, so could we, and I answered the debt. Tell me – do you know who offered you such a gift?"

My throat clenched, and I had to rub my jaws to make them work enough to say, "My mother."

In the long, quiet moments that followed, I was able to tell Shant what she looked like, and the Armenian name she used – and how she died, beaten and bruised, neck broken, with the phoenix carved over her heart.

He nodded, eyes closed. "The Raah dispatched her many years ago. I remember the pain all Shaddai felt at her loss when we received her dying message. She had long been quiet on the face of Earth, and we had been wondering what became of her – then the tragedy."

I got to my feet, feeling unsteady, but I just couldn't sit still any longer. "But how could my mother be an angel? Did she die? Come back down from heaven?"

Shant's eyes caressed my face as if he wanted to offer me comfort and support as I struggled to understand all this. "Angels are not dead humans, Dutch. Angels are their own race, long-lived, even immortal, if not attacked or wounded too grievously."

I wished he would come closer to me, and he seemed to hear my thoughts. He took a step, lifted his arms as if to reach out, then caught himself and moved back. My insides actually ached from wanting to touch him, like that would make everything real and OK and sane, like anything in my life would ever be completely sane again.

"Many angels did not return to the sky in older days, when the world of men and the world of Heaven separated," he continued, gazing steadily at me and making heat rise all the way to my forehead. "We, my people, the Shaddai, it became our sacred duty to guard those gentle beings who remained on Earth, as best we could."

So far, so good. I was getting it, even if I wasn't having any success yet at understanding him, or luring him back into my arms. "Is it allowed, humans and angels, getting together?"

As soon as I asked the question, I realized how it sounded, then decided I didn't care. I was so far past coherent, rational thoughts and actions, it wasn't even funny.

"It's outside the natural order, but it happens." Shant's gaze heated up even more, burning me like he was secretly one of those fire-monsters. "Attraction and love can be unexpected – and sudden. Love at first sight, as humans would say."

No kidding.

He was coming towards me again, quietly closing in on me, and the glow from his skin eased to the brightness of a light, silvery candle flame. That stern-warrior persona slipped away, and I could see him as a man then.

A great big glowing man –

But a man.

God, what a man.

I had a sensation like melting into a puddle, but once more, he stopped, staying just out of my reach.

Is it OK to use God's name, if I'm actually part angel?

I really am losing my mind.

"Unlike Shaddai and other races, angels are not outcast if they intermingle," Shant said, as if suddenly remembering that little tidbit, and being pleased by it.

"And the fire-things?" I asked, more to keep myself from babbling or begging than anything else. "The Raah? What exactly are they?"

"The Raah: demons who once served the will of the creator, hunt angels for their own sport." The lines of his face tightened, and he shifted back towards stern-warrior mode so fast I wanted to scream. "Which is why, for your own safety, I must summon you another protector from Amberd, to serve you through your time on Earth."

My hands went to my hips, and I leaned forwards, not certain I heard him correctly. "Another protector? I thought *you* were the Shaddai bound to me."

"I . . . I cannot continue in that role." Shant looked away from me. I couldn't tell in the strange light rising off his skin, but I thought he might be blushing. "It wouldn't be proper."

"Why not?" I yelled, without feeling the least bit embarrassed.

My volume startled him, and he looked directly at me.

And I saw the answer in his face.

He wanted me.

My belly tied itself in a tight, hot knot.

For whatever reason, he thought his desire wasn't OK.

But he wanted me.

Maybe Shaddai had oaths and ethics, like psychiatrists had about patients. Maybe there was some other reason, something deep and mystical, or even scary.

Right that second, I didn't give a damn.

"I cannot stay with you, Dutch," he said, but I was moving towards him, and he wasn't backing away.

"To hell with that."

Before he could argue with me, I threw my arms around his neck, and I kissed him.

And kissed him.

And kept right on kissing him.

Now this –

Angel or no angel, 306-year-old winged guys, and all the demons in the universe aside –

This was Heaven.

He tasted like clean water, fresh air and toasted cinnamon. He felt like warmth and muscle and everything I had always wanted to touch, to stroke, to hold.

Shant kissed me back with a power and passion I had dreamed about, but never expected. The strength of his embrace, the way his mouth joined with mine as he tasted me right back, rumbling his pleasure so deeply I felt it in my throat, my chest. His hands caressed my waist, then my hips, then lower, pressing me against him, letting me feel exactly what he wanted, and how much he wanted it.

Every inch of my body responded to him, tingling, then burning, then throbbing with the force of my own need.

He pulled back long enough to press his lips to my ears and whisper, "You change everything."

I struggled to breathe, finally succeeded, and could think of nothing to say but, "I'm glad."

His smile was hungry and happy and sad all at the same time. My heart ached as I memorized each line and dimple on his face, and hoped I could remember that expression every minute of my life, forever.

When he picked me up, I felt like I was flying again, to my bedroom, to my bed.

Then we flew to places I never imagined I would go.

Six

Nothing. Ever. Changes.

I woke up alone.

Naked.

Sweetly sore.

Satisfied.

But alone.

Except for the tall, red-headed Amazonian-looking woman with the sword, sitting on a chair near my bedroom door. She was wearing jeans and a T-shirt and, when she turned away from me to sheath her blade, I could see the tall ridges of flesh on her back, outlined by the white cotton.

"I'm Houri," she said in a voice that sounded like a female Terminator from those Arnold Schwarzenegger movies. A bored female Terminator. "I've come to protect you. I'm—"

"Shaddai," I finished for her, then turned over and pulled the cover over my head.

Damn straight nothing ever changes – and crazy definitely doesn't change. I got cold all over and started to shake. Then I wanted to cry.

No. I wanted to scream. Demand that she take me to Shant.

But even as I pressed my face into my pillow and ground my teeth together, I worried.

What exactly would happen to him, for breaking the rules of his people? Had he said something about being an outcast? God, I really was a selfish bitch, wasn't I? A selfish bitch who was about to sob until she puked.

Stop it. Stop it, stop it.

My phone was ringing. Probably Riverview. Or the police. Or both. I ignored it, rolled over, and pushed myself into a sitting position, careful to keep my sheet under my chin. "Hey, robot girl. You up for a good fight?"

Houri blinked at me. Her android-ish expression said, *Does not compute.* Then she went back to looking bored.

I got up, pulled on a pair of jeans and my own T-shirt – this one black – and pushed past Houri into my sparse living room. I had gym mats on most of the floor instead of carpet, and I crossed to the centre of the padded blue vinyl. When I turned back to face Terminator Girl, I settled into a classic Sayokan stance, arms up, legs wide, and beckoned to her.

The edges of Houri's mouth curled into a smile. She stopped looking bored.

Then she kicked my ass all over the apartment.

Five or six times. Maybe seven.

I lost count somewhere between the separated shoulder and needing stitches in my chin because I wouldn't let her heal me.

She wasn't touching me.

Nobody was touching me again.

Except Shant.

If I ever saw him again.

And assuming I didn't kill him instantly for making me believe in love at first sight, then disappearing like a sweet dream before I woke.

Seven

My life became a blur of sparring with Houri (and trying to keep all my teeth) – my version of pining away for my lost love. The more bones I risked or broke, the better I felt. For about five minutes.

Then there were all the statements I had to give to the police, the FBI, the CIA, Homeland Security and a bunch of other alphabet acronyms I didn't know about the "terrorist bombing attack" on Riverview. Oh, and trying to convince the administration that the patient who had been present when the admissions office blew up had just run away, unharmed.

Yeah.

And *not* to my bed.

It took a month for the admissions office to get repaired and functional again, but when it was, I was stupid enough to go back to work even though my Shaddai protector assured me they could keep me in enough gold to rent a penthouse if I wanted one. Houri got passed off as a private bodyguard hired by my (non-existent) family following the terrorist attack.

To Terminator Girl's credit, she taught me about my angel abilities: enhanced fighting skills, the ability to briefly repel fire if I willed it, speed, empathy, insight and attracting demons. Woo-hoo. Not a great lot of powers to inherit from Mom, but I figured I should be grateful for whatever advantage I might have, should one of the Raah show up again.

"What are you thinking about?" Houri asked me as I drank my 3 a.m. Starbucks Verona one Wednesday night, about four months after my encounter with the Raah – and with Shant. She was ensconced in her usual seat just outside my office door, wearing her hospital-issued nametag, her jeans and a red T-shirt which almost matched her hair. The secretary had retired and not been replaced yet, and the night nurse and patient aide had been called upstairs for an emergency, so we were alone.

"What am I thinking about?" I tasted the delicious chocolate coffee and made myself look her in the eye. "I'm thinking about an asshole."

"A man," she said, sounding definite, a little more human, like she had learned to be in her weeks with me.

I glared at her and didn't answer.

"Was this man a boyfriend?" Houri looked almost amused, like we might be playing a game. "Did he tell you he loved you?"

My glare deepened, and I sank further into my creaky office chair. "No."

Houri shrugged. "Well, did he tell you that you were a good lover?"

I wanted to slap her, but that would just start a sparring match and get a lot of furniture broken. "No."

"What *did* he tell you then, to make you call him an asshole?"

I picked up my coffee again and sipped at it, letting the heavy chocolate flavour slide through my mouth, as in my mind I replayed as much of that night as I dared. Like I had done a thousand times. Maybe ten thousand. Every word. Every achingly hot, sensual movement.

When I thought I could speak, I looked her in the eye. "He said . . . He said I change everything."

Houri's expression shifted from amused to stunned. She got up from her chair, walked straight into my office, and put both hands on my desk, knocking papers in every direction.

"Shant," she whispered. Before I could deny it, she added, "You should have told me, Dutch."

I looked away from her. "There's nothing to tell."

"You're protecting him."

My turn to shrug.

"If you love him, you should tell him." Houri sounded definite and, when I glanced in her direction, she looked adamant too.

I wanted to beat her up again – only, I'd never quite succeeded in that pursuit. "I'm not protecting anything," I grumbled, going back to my paperwork. "It's wrong. Talking to him again would be crazy." Then, quieter, and definitely more honest: "I don't want anything bad to happen to him."

Houri cocked her head like she was trying to process information, which of course made her look totally like a robot Terminator all over again. "And being with you, Dutch Brennan – what makes you think that would be bad?"

Eight

"This is a rotten idea, Houri." I pulled the collar of my leather jacket tight against my neck and cheeks to fend off the major mountain breeze making my eyes water. "If he does this, he'll never be able to come here again. And I have no idea if things would even work out between us."

The wind didn't seem to be bothering Terminator Girl at all. She wasn't even wearing a coat over her sleeveless tank, and her biceps flexed when she crossed her arms. "There are worse fates than banishment. Like facing eternity without the one who has claimed your heart."

Even though my own heart did a little dance in response to what she said, I rolled my eyes. "We spent a night together. I haven't claimed anything."

Houri laughed at me.

I thought about throwing a punch, but decided if Shant really did come through the sanctuary portal that Houri assured me was located in the Amberd ruins, I'd rather not have a black eye.

The journey to Armenia had taken us almost a week, her flying me, us resting on various islands, then cities, then towns. It was a major feat that we hadn't killed each other.

Mount Aragats was much as I remembered from my childhood: volcanic and full of pits and pocks and craters. Vegetation was sparse this time of year, and a wicked cold breeze whistled between the flat stretch of rocks and grass where we stood and the ruins we had come to see. Sunlight flooded Amberd, and in the background clouds drifted against a crystalline sky. It really was a postcard-perfect scene, and my breath caught as I so clearly remembered standing in the same spot with my beautiful – my *angelic* – mother.

Shaddai. Come here to call them. They'll hear you if you truly need them.

"Shant," I whispered, heart aching so fiercely I had to fight sobs as I stared at the ruins of the rounded towers. Part of me wished he'd burst out of the tumbledown rocks and come striding towards me, but the better half of my soul hoped he wouldn't.

Houri said that, by coming, he'd be giving up the right to return to Amberd and to function as a protector – though I had no doubt he would protect me with every ounce of strength he possessed. But he'd be losing so much: his culture, his history, his identity. On just a chance, a whisper of possibility. Nothing was set between us, or definite. For all I knew, he'd take one look at me with morning bed head tomorrow morning and fly off into the sunrise screaming.

I shook my head, blinking to keep back the tears. "I'm not worth that kind of sacrifice."

"That, I believe, is Shant's decision." Houri sounded distant, almost distracted. "His sense of honour would have forced him to allow you to make the first move towards permanence, but now you have. You are half-angel, Dutch. You will have a very long life. You and Shant could share many, many beautiful years together."

"He won't come." I studied every nuance and crack in the fallen towers. "He shouldn't come."

When I couldn't stand the lump in my throat any longer, I turned away from Houri to cry in peace. She caught me by the waist, and I wheeled around, arm swinging to get in the first blow.

But it wasn't Houri who had hold of me.

It was Shant.

My heart throbbed so hard I almost shouted from the sensation.

He had caught my arm, mid-swing. He caught my other hand, too, as I raised it to slap him for leaving me without saying goodbye.

He held me there for an endless moment, his grip firm on my wrists, his green eyes dark with intensity. He still smelled like everything fresh and clean, mixed with cinnamon and a hint of cloves. He was wearing jeans again, no shoes, no shirt. His black hair rippled in the mountain wind, but I couldn't feel the cold any more, or the bite of the air on my ears and cheeks.

I couldn't feel anything but his hands on my arms.

So strong.

So warm.

He was here. He was actually here. He had come to me when I called. Even though I had only spent part of a day and night with him, he was so familiar, so right, like a piece fitting into the jigsaw puzzle of my existence with a tight, certain snap. How empty my old life would have been if I had tried to keep going without at least trying to get to know him. The ache of the truth struck me so deeply and suddenly that my chin trembled.

Shant pulled me forwards and we pressed against each other in the mountain sunlight.

Then, before I could start sobbing like a complete idiot, Shant let go of my wrists, wrapped me in his powerful arms, and kissed me.

The taste of him, the heat of him stole my breath and reason. I felt free and captured, safe and completely at risk. I was alive. I was eternal when he touched me. Everything in the world had to be as warm and bright as this moment, this place, and I didn't think I'd ever mind daytime again.

Shant nibbled at my bottom lip, then moved his mouth to my ear, my nape, then lower, to that perfect, sensitive spot between my neck and shoulder. Shivers and chills covered every inch of me, and I laughed as I ran my fingers through the black silk of his curls.

He lifted his head and gazed at me, searching my soul, asking a dozen questions without saying a word.

I had the answer, just one answer, to all of them.

I suppose I had known it the first time I saw him, or at least the moment he finally touched me in my apartment. I just hadn't admitted it to him, like he had been brave enough to admit it to me.

"You," I whispered, then kissed him again, and pulled back to gaze into his liquid emerald eyes. "You change everything."

Taking Hold

Anya Bast

She could lose this child. *Oh, please, God, no*. Not another one. Her heart wouldn't be able to stand it.

Lily stopped near a tree and inhaled the cold crispness of the early winter air. She didn't need a wolf's nose to know that snow was coming, a lot of it. Every step she took further up Elgonquinn Mountain ratcheted her panic skywards. So far she was doing a good job of using that reaction, instead of letting it use her, but it was close. There was nothing she hated more than not being able to control the circumstances affecting those she cared about . . . and she cared very much about this boy.

Deadfall rustled under the paws of the shifter accompanying her. Mac, a hulking silver-tipped wolf, came to stand beside her. He raised his nose to the wind to hunt beyond the scent of the impending storm for any trace of Casey, the lost boy they sought. Three days ago he'd just vanished into the forest. His parents were frantic, but had been commanded by the pack alpha to allow Mac to hunt for the child. The pack had only sent one lone wolf to search for Casey, which showed how much faith they had in the boy, or maybe it showed how little hope.

As a trained nurse, she'd volunteered to accompany him.

But she and Mac would have to find shelter soon or all three of them would be lost. Lily feared most for the child. He was fifteen, a man in the eyes of the pack and able to look after himself, but not from her all-too-human perspective. Or maybe it was her past that coloured her perspective and made her think of Casey as younger than he truly was.

Lily knew him. She did a lot of volunteer work for the Elgonquinn Mountain shifter school system. Casey was a solid beta, not particularly strong as wolves went, but not a weakling either. He loved music and girls, just like any other teenage boy. He liked to read too, something he didn't want his peers to know. Lily fed him fantasy novels on the sly. Of course, he especially liked books about vampires, werewolves and other paranormal entities. Every time she thought of that boy out there all alone her chest went tight with fear.

The one lone wolf they'd sent to search was a *true* lone wolf: Macmillan Hardy was the best tracker the Elgonquinn Mountain pack had to offer, and he was a telepath to boot, not a skill all shifters possessed. He worked often with the Elgonquinn Mountain forest wardens, an alliance that was rare in the chilly – no, *frigid* – relationship between human and shifter society. Lily had worked with him often and respected him greatly.

Mac looked tough and he was – broad-shouldered, brawny and intimidating from every angle. His face wasn't handsome, not by a long shot, yet there was some indefinable allure to him. His eyes, like his hair, were dark brown, and they were intelligent, full of depth and emotion. And for as much as his body contained strength, she'd seen a gentleness in him to sharply contrast it on more than one occasion. He cared every bit as much about Casey as she did – no matter that he lived apart from the pack.

The man was an enigma and Lily was fascinated by him, just as she was interested in shifters as a whole.

When Lily was a child, the shifters had been forced to make themselves known after a wolf was caught on video making the change (once video cameras became so readily available, it was inevitable). Humanity, predictably, had been shocked. But there were so few wolves, so few packs, that they'd been largely defenceless against this new human attention. The only thing that had stopped the pitchfork mob, and the scientists ready with their dissecting scalpels, was a small group of equal-rights activists. Her parents had been a part of the movement.

Paranormals had been popular in movies and books up to that point, but once werewolves were revealed to be real, all that changed. Some humans, like herself, were still fascinated by them, but the bulk of humanity feared them – as if the monster in their bedroom closet had suddenly turned out to be real.

But Lily had reason to think humans were more bloodthirsty than the wolves.

It was fortunate that the wolves had already cordoned themselves off from the greater human society, living in remote areas that allowed them the freedom to be who they were. They didn't interact with humans much and never had. Honestly, the shifters preferred it that way, anyway. Procreation between the species was impossible; it seemed they were biologically compatible enough for sex, but not for creating children. So the government had declared many of the lands where the wolves had already congregated to be federally protected, and the shifters lived on them in relative peace, for their own protection.

But it was really more to segregate them and everyone knew it.

"Anything?" she pushed out, her voice raw and filled with emotion – both for her safety and the boy's in the face of the impending storm.

Not yet.

Lily had been watching Mac and had noticed he was constantly scanning for any psychic traces of Casey. It would help their search a lot if Casey could tell them where he was . . . plus knowing if he was even alive would be nice. This mountain was unforgiving and had felled many an experienced hiker.

She closed her eyes for a moment, then swung her backpack down from her shoulder. She dug inside for a warmer pair of gloves, wishing for the hundredth time to have Mac's thick, warm fur.

Mac trotted into the clearing before them, headed in some direction unknown to her. Communication wasn't one of the man's strengths, but tracking was, so she'd trust him.

The wind gusted hard, stealing her breath. Mac disappeared over the ridge of a hill. "Hey," she yelled. "*Human* back here. I won't be able to survive the kind of storm brewing up on the horizon."

Mac looked at her, his handsome head tipped regally. Without a word, he sallied forth, further into the wilderness.

Great.

With a sigh, she followed him, her will to find the boy more powerful than her desire to protect herself. She headed into the wind. It was blowing hard now and slicing against her partially numb cheeks. Little bits of ice had started to pelt down on her, like tiny slivers of metal, and the cold scent of snow had grown heavier in the air. There was a point, when walking into a snowstorm, at which your vision became obscured from all the squinting you had to do. She'd surpassed that point long ago. Her head ached from having to trudge headlong into the wind.

Mac stayed ahead of her at all times, probably more to avoid her company than as a caring gesture. She didn't take it personally; Mac disdained everyone's companionship. And, hell, she was a human – beneath his notice completely, she was sure. Although there was a fierce note of protectiveness in him, if you knew where to look. It was in the little actions she'd noticed him make in Pack City, like accompanying an elder to the store and back, or defending one of the middle schoolers against a group of bullies. Right now he was all about finding the boy and that made her admire him – even more than she already did.

You had to be strong to be a lone wolf, to buck the pack. You had to be *stronger* than the alpha to stand on your own because standing on your own meant you were a threat to the larger social organization.

Kind of like herself.

Her friends and family would be shocked by just how much she knew about shifter society. Lily knew it was unacceptable, but she was fascinated. She always had been, ever since she'd been eight and the werewolves had announced themselves to the world. It was the reason she'd pursued a nursing career and ended up working with the Elgonquinn Mountain wardens and the local pack. She was one of the few human health care practitioners who would have anything to do with the shifters. It was she and her colleagues who worked closest with the seven wolf packs across the country, the Elgonquinn Mountain pack being the largest. That made her sort of an outcast in human society. At dinner parties – which she tried to avoid as much as possible – she received all kinds of odd looks and even odder questions and comments.

"Is it true the alpha has the right to any female in the pack?"

"I heard they'll eat human flesh given half a chance!"

"And when they shift from wolf to human they're naked as the day they were born . . . and they don't even care. Immodest beasts."

"They're all inbred, you know, won't touch a human . . . thank God!"

Most of their information was wrong, but she never bothered to correct them. People guarded their misconceptions of the shifters jealously. It gave them an excuse for their "justified" outrage.

Mac stopped and waited a beat or two for her to catch up and then continued on. It must have been difficult for him to keep her slow pace, but he never complained. Her boots snapped cold, dry twigs as she progressed, the smell of snow heavier in the air. Her coat rustled with every movement.

Suddenly, Mac stilled on the top of the hill, nose high.

Lily scrambled up to collapse next to the huge animal, kneeling on the frigid earth and breathing heavily. "Find something?"

Mac remained still and non-responsive.

I heard something.

He probably meant telepathically, Lily thought.

It's gone now. Come on, we need to get you to shelter.

He trotted forwards, following some wolfish instinct. Forcing herself to her feet, she tagged along, the cold wind biting her face, digging into her joints and invading her lungs.

The ice chips turned to snow and grew heavy fast. The world was only white, searing her eyes and melting pain into her head like thick acid.

Lily stopped at the edge of a frozen lake to rest, just for a moment, and watched Mac make his way across it, the snow swirling and billowing around his legs as he skated across the glassy surface. He was moving faster now and she had to concentrate on not falling too far behind. She pushed her exhaustion away as best she could and set off. Maybe the fact that Mac was moving more rapidly meant he'd caught some sign of the boy – a psychic or physical scent. Her steps quicker at the possibility, she shouldered the weight of her load and sped up, her boots crunching ice and the wind whooshing into the sides of her heavy hood. Every moment they didn't find the boy was another moment he might be lost forever.

Halfway across, the ice under her feet cracked.

Lily stilled, terror sending a jolt, colder than anything Mother Nature could create, through her veins. From a distance away, Mac also stopped, turned, stared.

Crack.

"Mac." Her voice came out a whisper. She was almost afraid her voice might weaken the ice further. *Stupid.* "Mac!" Damn it. She'd thought for certain the ice had been frozen all the way through. Hell, the possibility it wasn't frozen hadn't even crossed her mind.

Move. She had to move. Maybe she could progress past the weakness in this part of the ice. Carefully, she stepped forwards, inch by inch.

Crack. Crack. Craaaack.

Lily screamed. Plummeted. Frigid water closed over her head, stole her breath and heartbeat. She went motionless with shock for a moment before terror set her limbs to thrashing. Panic jolted through her veins. She couldn't even think. The cold drained everything away.

Weight. Dragging her under.

She struggled to get her pack off her back, then pushed herself up. Her head breached the surface and she took a ragged gulp of air, her lungs and major organs burning, *burning*.

Under again. Heavy coat pulling her down.

Quiet. So cold that the shock leached from her body, leaving numbness behind. The numbness was nice, almost warm. Silence. Stillness.

Floating. Would it be so bad just to let go?

Hands grasped her coat and yanked her up, the sweet tranquillity broken by a cold wind. She ate air in small, razor-sharp bites. The strong grip pulled her over the ice lip of the pool, dragged her across the frozen surface of the lake. Above her she saw only white. Pain had entered every molecule of her body. Her teeth chattered so hard, she was sure she'd break them.

A face entered her line of sight – eyes as light and icy as the frozen water, face as jagged and hard. Mac mouthed her name but she heard nothing.

Then she saw nothing.

Lily woke with a jolt, sitting up. "Casey!"

Mac sat beside a fireplace, poking a stick into the embers. His back was to her and he didn't turn. He wore only a pair of well-loved jeans, the muscles of his back working as he tended the blaze. Even his feet were bare.

The soft blankets shifted against her body and she realized she was naked. The bed was rough hewn from logs. In fact, she was in a log cabin and everything in it looked handmade. A small cooking area – not quite a kitchen – stood to her right. There was a couch and a chair, two hulking bookshelves stacked to bursting with books. There was Mac and the fireplace.

She hurt.

The memory of falling through the ice flooded her mind. Flailing against the weight of her clothing. The bitter cold. Giving in to the seductiveness of the water. Her nurse's mind flitted through the possibilities – hypothermia, frostbite? But she felt all right, if a bit chilled and sore.

"Where am I? How did you get me here?" She flipped the blankets back and her bare feet hit the wood floor with a slap. "We have to go. Casey—"

"Is safe," Mac said from the fireplace without turning around. "At least for now."

"What do you mean?" Pause. "Goddamn it, talk to me!"

He paused in his incessant jabbing at the fire and turned. "I found Casey. Telepathically." He paused in his incessant jabbing at the fire and turned. His gaze swept her. "Get back into bed." His voice had a rough edge that made her jerk away.

Remembering she was naked, she eased back under the blankets. Oh well, he'd been the one to undress her. He'd seen it before. Being a nurse, it wasn't like the naked body bothered her much. Mac needed to get a grip.

"Casey is in a cave. I think I know where he is, but he can't tell me for sure. He's lost." He paused. "He's being hunted."

"Explain."

Mac turned his head away from her. "He's being tracked by a

bunch of humans. They're hunting him like an animal. They intend to shoot him."

Lily's blood went almost as cold as when she'd fallen into the lake. "That's imposs—"

"No, not really. It wouldn't be the first time a group of shifter-hating humans has come up the mountain for a bit of sport. They always pick the young ones. They wouldn't dare try this on a mature member of the pack."

Lily stared at him for a long moment, letting his words sink in. He had no reason to lie, even if she desperately wanted this to be one. It made sense she'd never heard of it happening before. The pack wasn't exactly into information dissemination with humankind, not even with well-meaning, bleeding-heart nurses. "If that's true we need to get to him before the hunters do."

"Not that easy." Mac jerked his head towards the window. "Not even I can travel in this."

Beyond the window, it was white – a pure sheet of snow that looked like someone had taken a paintbrush to the glass. Every once in a while, the wind lulled and she glimpsed chaotic white swirling. It was a flat-out blizzard.

"Oh no." The panic welled and she forced it down with what she hoped was not a visible effort. "The boy . . ."

"Is safe, like I said, for now. He found a cave and he's in wolf form. Casey is a smart kid. He's warm and dry for the time being." Mac paused, his expression going tight. "Let's hope for less for the hunters."

"Where are we?"

"My home. I was leading us here when it became clear the storm was brewing. Luckily we weren't far when you fell through the ice. How are you feeling?"

She levered up a bit, covering her naked parts with the blankets and wincing. "Like I fell through the ice."

"I'll have food for us soon."

That was good since her stomach felt like it was going to gnaw through her spine.

"You didn't get frostbite, no hypothermia. It was close though."

"How do you know? You a doctor?"

"No." He stirred the fire. "I just have a sense for stuff like that."

She sneezed. "All I contracted is a cold, I guess. I can live with that. Thank you."

He inclined his head. "I thought the ice could hold you if it could hold a one-hundred-and-eighty-pound wolf."

She sniffled and raised a brow. "What exactly are you implying?" Well, at least her sense of humour wasn't totally lost.

He only stared blankly at her.

"Never mind." Apparently he didn't spend much time around women . . . or anyone, for that matter. "Please tell me you have a bathroom."

He looked pointedly at the back of the cabin. "Just like any other house."

Thank God. She went to flip the blankets back and was immediately hit in the face with a pair of grey sweats and a black sweater. "Hey, relax! I wasn't going to gross you out with my body again, don't worry about it."

"Wear those." He turned back to the fire. "Your clothes are still wet."

Fuming, she pulled on the too-big clothes, followed by a pair of thick wool socks that were lying on the bedside table. "I thought shifters weren't supposed to care about things like nudity."

He didn't answer her. Big surprise.

"Do you have running water?" she snapped, rising.

He was back to poking the stick into the fire. "Running water, heat, electricity. I equipped the place with solar collection panels."

Of course he was off the grid more than halfway up Elgonquinn Mountain, far from the pack and even farther from human civilization. Just the way he liked it, undoubtedly. She sneezed again, glowered at his back, then headed in to drive the residual chill from her bones with what she hoped was steaming hot water.

She entered the small bathroom and started the water in the shower. The wind whistled past the small oval window above the toilet, snow swirling. The boy was still out there somewhere in this.

Catching her reflection in the mirror over the sink, she pushed a hand through her short hair, letting the thick ends trail through her fingers. There were no tell-tale signs of injury as a result of her fall through the ice. Mac had rescued her from the water and managed to get her warm quickly enough. OK, maybe he did have a "sense for stuff like that".

She examined the skin around her eyes. Thirty-two years old and she was already getting wrinkles. Before this trek was over she'd probably end up with a few grey hairs to go with them.

Lily exited the bathroom rubbing a towel through her brown hair. Mac looked away from her, stirring the pot of stew on the stove.

It was strange to have a woman in his house, stranger that it was Lily. When he'd been paired with her to go after Casey, he'd been pleased. He was attracted to her, had been for a while.

Hell, it went past attraction.

But humans and shifters, it wasn't done. It was against federal law, in fact, not to mention every human or shifter societal norm. Not that he cared about norms, or laws for that matter.

He wasn't good at relating to people, but every time he was in her presence . . . he wanted to try. Really, he just wanted *her*.

She sneezed again.

"Come sit down. I have stew and some bread and butter." He glanced at her. "You need to eat something hot. The storm will have let up by tomorrow morning and we can hit the trail again."

She had less than twenty-four hours to kick the sickness trying to take hold in her body. Mac could sense a person's physical well-being and, while it was true she just had a cold, trudging through the snow could turn it into something much worse.

"Thanks." She settled into one of the set places at the table. He served a bowl and she dug in with the kind of appetite that Mac liked to see.

"The scars." He glanced at her. "On your thigh and sto-mach." He'd seen them when he had taken off her wet clothes. Long, wide slashes.

"I don't want to talk about it." She paused, softened. "If you don't mind."

He took a bite of bread.

"It's, uh—" She swallowed hard.

"You don't have to tell me."

"No, it's OK. I was married once and . . . he wasn't very nice."

"Oh." It came out a low wolf's growl. The bite of bread in his stomach turned to rock. Knowing someone had hurt her made his wolf hackles rise.

His father had been an abuser too. It was why, long ago, Mac had vowed he'd never hurt anyone else unless it was in self-defence or in defence of another. The Elgonquinn Mountain alpha had worried about Mac for a while, knowing he was strong enough to challenge his alpha position, but Mac didn't want it and wouldn't fight unless provoked first. Now the pack just left him alone.

"I was pregnant when he gave me the little love tokens you saw on my leg and stomach. I lost it." She paused. "The baby, I mean. It was a long time ago."

She couldn't have children any more, either. Mac could feel it. The bastard had really messed her up inside.

Lily stared at her stew for a long moment, then got up and paced to the window, wrapping her arms across her chest. "Looks like it's letting up a little."

"We won't lose the boy."

Her shoulders grew a degree tighter. "I hope not."

"He's not your baby."

She turned, dropping her hands to her sides and taking a step towards him. "How did you know to say that? How could you know that's what I was thinking?" Swift intake of breath. "I thought your telepathy only worked among shifters."

"It does, but that doesn't mean I'm not observant. You've committed your entire life to helping people, wildlife, the world, but especially children – shifter and human alike. After what you just told me about your miscarriage, it wasn't hard to make the jump."

She turned her face away. "It's dumb."

"It's human."

Her whole countenance darkened. "What's that supposed to mean?"

Damn it. He wasn't good at this. "I mean it's not dumb. It's a reaction to a disturbing event in your life. It might be irrational, but it's not *dumb*."

Lily studied him, licking her lower lip and then pulling it from under her upper teeth. It was a habitual gesture she displayed when she was deep in thought.

Mac had to look away, otherwise he'd get up and kiss her.

"How did you end up so emotionally intelligent?" she asked.

"You think because I live away from the pack that I don't have feelings?"

She regarded him for a long moment, eyes narrowed. "On the contrary. I'm starting to think that it's because you have strong feelings that you live away from the pack."

He turned away and spooned up more stew.

She sat back down. "Why *do* you live away from the pack anyway?"

"Most people irritate me."

"Join the club. Not that *you* would join a club." Pause. "So, do I irritate you?"

He set his spoon down and looked up at her. Mac made sure he had eye contact with her before he spoke. "You're one of the few people whose company I enjoy."

She blinked, then their gazes caught and held. "Really? I'm surprised you'd say that. After all, I'm a human and we really don't know each other very well."

"I'd like to fix that," he answered.

"The part where I'm human or the other thing?"

His mouth twitched. "I can't make you a shifter, you have to be born with the DNA, so I guess it's the other thing."

"Oh."

"You sound surprised."

"Well, I am."

He blew out a frustrated breath. "I live away from the pack because I don't want to be a part of the politics. I'd be expected to challenge Randall for position of alpha since I'm one of the stronger of the pack wolves, and I don't want it. I prefer to live here, away from the entanglements of other people."

"Away from responsibility."

"Sure, you could say that. I don't mind being alone. I'm not afraid of myself. Living this way suits me."

She studied him. "It does suit you." She took another bite. "So can I ask you a personal question? Since, you know, you're linking sentences together at the moment." She smiled a little.

He knew he wasn't the most verbose man in the world. "Sure. Ask me anything." He leaned back in his chair.

"Were you born as a human or a wolf?"

It was a common question. Some shifters were born wolf and then turned human when they reached maturity. Most shifters were born human though, and changed for the first time into wolf form when they hit adolescence.

Mac looked at her through half-lowered lashes, a secretive expression on his face. "I was born human. Would it make a difference if I'd been born a wolf?"

"No. I was only curious. I think shifters are fascinating. The ones born in wolf form especially fascinate me. They seem . . . wilder than the others. That's why I thought, er . . ." Way to put her foot in her mouth.

"So you thought maybe I'd been born wolf?"

"Maybe."

Mac leaned closer and Lily's breath caught. "Because I seem wilder than the others?"

"Uhm." A sneeze tickled her nose and she fought hard to suppress it. His eyes were like molten chocolate and his mouth was . . . lovely. Edible. She could probably sustain herself for days by nibbling on his full lower lip alone.

Was he going to kiss her? Her body tingled at the possibility of it, something in the centre of her warming in anticipation. Yes, she wanted him to kiss her. She'd fantasized about it more than once. She'd fantasized about more than just a kiss, too.

He stared at her for a moment, then eased back into his chair. "I'll take that as a compliment."

Disappointed, Lily let out the breath she'd been holding and sneezed.

Mac stood and took their bowls away. Outside the wind rushed around the cabin, whistling and rocking the shutters and doors. "I'll make you some tea, a Native American remedy. Hopefully it will help you kick the cold by morning."

She stared towards the window. "I just keep thinking of Casey. Not so much about the storm. I mean, if he's in a cave, he's sheltered enough. But to be out there, *hunted* . . ."

"If the storm has us holed up, you better believe the hunters aren't going anywhere either. Casey is safe enough for now, in all ways."

He made tea for her and they sat near the fire while she sipped, talking of their families until dark. Sue had a sister and her parents were still alive. He was an only child and his parents had passed away. Outside, the wind still blew furiously, dropping inches of snow on the cabin. Lily didn't want to think about how many.

"You know, you prefer to spend your life away from the pack, but I'm not much different than you, really."

Mac rolled his head towards her and asked lazily, "How's that?"

"I'll make a confession. I can't stand most people. Some are all right, a small minority, but most of the time I feel like I don't fit in."

"But you help to heal them."

She snorted. "Yes."

"So why don't you do what I do? How come you don't live apart from everyone else?"

Lily shrugged, studying her cup. "Maybe I just can't let go. Maybe I'm a little afraid too, afraid of being alone."

When she finally got up to go to sleep, Mac stood with her. He took the empty cup from her fingers and set it on a nearby table. He pulled her close and lowered his mouth close to hers. His breath warmed her lips, but he didn't touch her there, not yet.

Lily's heart tripped over itself for a moment. "But shifters and humans aren't supposed to—"

"Don't like rules. Don't like *supposed to*. How about you?"

"I, uh, don't right now, that's for sure."

"Give in to what exists between us, Lily." His gentle exhalation warmed her blood. "I know you can feel it, just like I can."

The press of his lips on hers drove away the rest of the cold from her centre. His lips skated over hers, nipping here and there until she was only a boneless mess of want.

"Wow," she whispered when the kiss finally broke.

Then he pulled her down to the bed and that was the very last thing she was able to articulate until morning.

Lily sneezed as she stared out the window at the winter wonderland before them. Mac handed her a tissue, then went back to securing his snowshoes.

He'd been correct about the storm ending by morning, but snow covered the ground in a good twelve inches that hadn't been there the day before. The cabin sat nestled, warm and cosy, in the middle of all the new snow and ice, but Lily couldn't wait to leave it. Casey needed them. It had taken a solid half an hour to even get the front door open, and snow had drifted clear over the roof on one side of the house.

Her body ached, not from her cold but from her night with Mac. She'd been right about his tender side. He'd shown it to her amply. It was hard to believe that such a muscular body could also hold so much tenderness, so much regard. He'd made her feel cherished, even loved – which was crazy. And yet . . .

Anyway, Mac was a multifaceted man. She wouldn't mind exploring those facets, if he'd let her. Screw what anyone thought about it, too.

"You ready?"

She turned towards him. He'd told her he'd travel in human form today to keep pace with her, and also because, even as a wolf, the snow pack would be hard to navigate.

Nodding, she followed him out of the door, shuffling awkwardly in the snowshoes and fifty-five layers Mac had insisted on dressing her in. She felt like the Pillsbury Doughboy. When the outside cold hit her, it stole her breath for a moment. The memory of falling through the ice the day before rushed back at her.

No crossing any lakes for her today.

He pulled her against him, his breath showing white in the wintery air. "I was glad when you volunteered to help me look for the kid," he murmured.

"I did it for Casey, but being with you is a definite perk."

He grinned, a quick flash of teeth, and they headed out, their snowshoes leaving round, criss-cross footprints leading away from the cabin.

Now that Mac had a bead on Casey's psychic signature, they went straight towards him. No more educated guesses. They went as fast as they could and Lily kept up well. Her cold remained mild. Perhaps the tea had helped, or maybe it had been Mac himself. She wouldn't mind a second helping of each, especially of Mac.

In early afternoon, Lily noticed Mac moving faster, perhaps sensing not only Casey but the hunters. They were well on the other side of the mountain now, not far from the cave where the child had weathered the blizzard. Her legs were tired and her ankles ached from trudging through the snow, but she pushed herself harder.

A crack sounded in the distance. Gunshot. Mac began to run as though he weren't wearing clunky snowshoes.

Lily tried to run too, but fell flat on her face. She pushed upwards. Someone grabbed her from behind before she could rise. She struggled hard and strong hands clamped down, hurting her even through the layers of winter clothing.

"Stop it, wolf lover," a deep voice growled in her ear.

She stilled, recognizing the owner. "Derrick?" He was one of the wardens. A big burly guy who liked . . . to *hunt*. Every fall he bragged to everyone about how many deer he'd bagged once the season opened.

"Damn it, I knew she'd recognize us," said a man to her left.

"Shut the fuck up, Steve."

Derrick swung her up and around. He wore a blue ski mask. "You just had to get in the way, didn't you? They were going to send the wolf alone for the boy, but you just had to fucking stick your nose in and volunteer to go too, didn't you? Not that we don't know why. You have a taste for fur, don't you?"

Was this a trap for Mac? Had they planned this all along?

"What the hell are you doing, Derrick? Mac's a werewolf. Do you really think you're going to live through this?"

God, she hoped not.

The blood chilling sound of a shotgun being loaded made her look to Steve, also wearing a ski mask. "He may have teeth, but we got bullets. Guess which one wins?"

Derrick yanked her forwards. She tripped on her snowshoes, but he pulled her up again before she could face-plant. "You should have stayed home, Lily. Now we have to kill you before we can hunt."

Oh, that was *great* news.

Mac leaped into the air and changed form. The extra clothing he wore, the snow shoes, everything down to the last fibre, was used up in the strange and mysterious magic that fuelled his transformation. It would make him appear heavier, give him more fur, longer, sharper teeth.

All the better to eat hunters with.

Paws made contact with the snow and he sank deep, struggling to jump through it, although he was still moving faster on four paws than he'd been doing on two feet. Muscles working, he made his way towards Casey's psychic signature, the same direction the gunshot had come from.

Up ahead, Mac saw a flash of black fur between the trees. In his mind, he could feel Casey close by.

The young, medium-sized wolf caught sight of him and stilled near a clearing. *Man, I'm so glad to see you.*

Mac bounded up to him and sniffed. *Are you all right?*

I want to go home. They keep following me. They've had chances to kill me, but they're just playing . . . chasing me around.

Bastards. They were hunting him for sport, just for kicks. *We'll get you back to Pack City and your parents as soon as we can.*

They flushed me out a couple of days ago. I was taking a run in the forest and they started chasing me. I wanted to lead them away from the others.

That was brave of you.

There are two hunters behind you, about a quarter of a mile. One is closer.

Yes, I can scent them now. The wind had changed direction, giving Mac some information on where the hunters were located. Damn it, he could smell Lily too. She was too damn close to the men.

It's impossible for me to lose them in this snow. They can track every move I make.

One of the hunters is coming closer. Get out of here now, Casey. I'll stop him from following you and catch up to you later.

But they've got guns. He'll kill you.

He won't kill me. Even in his mind, Mac's voice came out filled with low, cold fury. *Go!*

Casey hesitated a moment, then dashed off into the woods.

Moments later, the hunter entered the clearing. Mac lowered his head and laid his ears back, growling. Slowly, he circled the man, staring him down. The hunter was dressed in green snow gear, a brown ski mask covering his face.

"You're a big one. Derrick said you were. You'll make a nice addition to my wall."

Do you make a habit of hunting down unsuspecting teenage boys for sport? Do you murder kids often? Maybe pick off toddlers on the weekends?

The hunter was taken by surprise with the telepathy. "I don't consider that thing a boy or a child at all. It's an animal, like any other. Just like you."

We're all animals. Humans are animals too.

"You know what I mean. Don't start that bullshit equal-rights crap with me." He turned and spit into the snow. "Won't work."

Did you come alone? Mac let a long, thin growl trickle from between his lips. *You know that was stupid, right? Come alone and end up food for the scavengers.*

"You wouldn't eat me?"

I wouldn't touch your mangy hide even if I were starving. The vultures can have you.

The man repositioned the rifle in his gloved hands. He seemed to be stalling for some reason. "I didn't come alone. The others have the woman and are toying with her a bit before they kill her, that's all."

Mac lunged forwards, snarling, and the hunter raised the rifle with a jerk, betraying his nervousness. "Watch it or I'll shoot you now."

Why wait? Oh, I get it. You're under someone's authority. Did the boss tell you not to ruin his fun?

"I don't take orders from anyone."

I don't know. You look like the omega to me.

The omega was the whipping wolf in a pack – the one everyone else took their frustrations out on. It was a deceiving title, since it sounded like it would take a weak wolf to occupy such a position. In fact, it was a position of honour, held by one of the strongest members of the pack, a wolf able to withstand the beatings of the others. In fact, quite frequently the omega eventually became alpha. To a human, though, being called the omega was a high insult, since they lacked a finer understanding of shifter society.

"Shut up," the hunter snapped, the rifle shaking.

Oh, he'd hit a nerve.

Mac growled, hunkering down and ready to leap at the man. He needed to extricate himself from this and fast. This man lacked the *cojones* to pull the trigger without his boss's leave. Human pack behaviour wasn't all that much different from a wolf's. This man wasn't alpha material – not by a long shot.

"You seem antsy. Are you worried about the woman? Don't be. I'm sure she's dead by now." The hunter shrugged. "Nothing to be concerned about any more."

The hunter raised his rifle and sighted down the barrel at Mac. Mac balanced on his paws, ready to spring. Out of nowhere came a streak of black. The hunter went down with an anguished yelp of terror and the gun fired, shot going wide.

Somewhere in the distance, he heard a woman scream.

Mac bounded towards it, leaving behind him the sound of a growling Casey and an ever-widening red stain in the snow.

"What is it with you and the shifters, huh, Lily? What's with the fucking fascination?" Derrick shook her. "What's wrong with your own kind?"

"If we're using you as the model, Derrick, *lots*."

He pushed her down into the snow and pointed the rifle at her head. The sound of a bullet loading into the chamber made her shiver and her stomach go loose and nauseated with butterflies. Lily had never had a gun muzzle pressed to her forehead. She imagined she could even smell it – old blood and cold metal. The scent of her death.

She would like to be able to say she was fearless, but having a man so full of hate press a gun to her head made fear scream through her body and soul. She searched within for courage, scrabbling for every ounce she could find among the over-whelming flood of stark terror.

"I didn't want to have to do this. You weren't supposed to fucking be here and you weren't supposed to recognize my voice. All we wanted to do was draw Mac out here to an area he wasn't familiar with, so we could pick him off."

"Why Mac? Why do you care?"

"He's just good sport, Lily. Nothing personal."

Rage flared hot and hard in her. She kicked out with her snowshoe and caught Derrick in the shin. He stumbled, off balance.

She dived to the side to avoid the misfire of his weapon, snow cushioning her lunge. A ringing crack sounded in her ear and then all was silent in her head. She'd gone deaf from the close proximity of the fired weapon. There was a flash of a silver-tipped wolf, a splash of red. Derrick waved his rifle, fired it into the air, then turned to run, only to be pushed into the snow by Mac.

Lily turned her face away, melting into the welcome quiet where there was no violence.

Hands grasped her arms and turned her. She opened her eyes to see Mac's concerned face, his mouth moving. He'd shifted back to human form. Little by little, the sounds growing louder, his words became audible.

"I'm OK," she answered, then launched herself into his arms, not even caring about the blood that stained his chin, throat and the front of his coat.

Mac held her close, rubbing her back with strong hands. She melted against him, feeling for the first time in years – no, maybe for the first time – that the man who held her truly cared. In his arms, she was cherished. She shuddered against him, shaking off the sensation of the gun pressed to her skull, and the echo of her death she'd seen in Derrick's eyes.

A black wolf came bounding up to them and she recognized Casey. Lily knelt in the snow and wrapped her arms around him. With shaking hands, she explored the wolf's haunches, legs and stomach. He was uninjured. Lily had never been so happy not to have to act in her capacity as nurse.

She let out a pent-up breath and hugged him. Maybe she would never quite be able to let go of the child she'd once lost, but this one was going to be all right.

They made their way back to Pack City. Not far from town, Mac made a call to the proper authorities to let them know of Casey's well-being and where they could find the bodies of the hunters.

Lily and Mac stood at the top of the hill overlooking Pack City, watching Casey, still in wolf form, make his way down to the clutch of emergency vehicles at the base. Humanity and shifters alike swarmed the place. People everywhere. Just watching them all, anticipating their questions, made her tired.

"So, what are you planning to do now?" Mac asked.

"Now?" She sniffled. "I still have this cold, so I should probably get some rest."

"That's a good idea." Pause. "I've got some tea left."

"Is that an invitation?"

"It's an invitation for a whole lot more than tea, Lily." Mac's voice was low and husky.

She smiled, happy warmth suffusing her face and chest. "Consider it accepted. Can't think of anywhere I'd rather be. Can't think of anyone else I'd rather spend my time with."

In silence, they continued to watch the swarm of people. The news crews had arrived. One of the reporters spotted them on top of the hill and began to make his way up. *Ugh*.

"So, are you ready to let go a little?" Mac asked, watching the man scramble in the snow towards them.

She looked up at Mac, enveloping his hand in hers. "I'm not letting go, I'm taking hold."

Together they turned and walked back into the woods.

How to Date a Superhero

Jean Johnson

"Man, that was a great movie! Thank you again for inviting me this afternoon." Silver-gloved hands cut sharply through the air, wielded by blue-clad arms. "I didn't think an Ascendant could've survived that big an explosion at the end, let alone a normal citizen, but the way he did it . . . brilliant! Movie magic at its finest."

Red-and-silver limbs wrapped around the nearest blue arm, hanging – literally – on his every word. A female voice cooed, "Oh, I don't know; *I* think *you'd* have come out of it without a scratch."

The man's tanned mouth curved up in a wry smile below his blue-and-silver mask. "I may be a working Ascendant, a living, breathing superhero . . . but I'm no stunt-double. Those guys are *tough*. Besides, even if I did survive, the conflagration would've burned up my costume. I wouldn't be able to show my face afterwards, for fear of being recognized!"

"Believe me, if your costume burned off . . . who said we'd be looking at your *face?*" Laughter accompanied her words, as did the hint of a blush. Across the table, a body in orange-and-silver snorted with amusement, while the others around the briefing table smiled.

Carrie tried not to be sullen, but it was very difficult. She crossed her spandex-covered arms more tightly across her violet-and-silver chest. The only good thing about the rest of her night was that she wouldn't have to see the two lovebirds seated to her left interacting any more.

The door to the briefing room hissed open, giving her a respite from the flirting happening next to her. Sitting up a little more in her seat, showing respect for the silver-and-white uniform that had entered the room, she settled her mind firmly into her working persona.

It was time to stop being Carrie Vinson, part-time pottery artist, and time to start being Foresight, Ascendant superhero – defender of justice, peace and the citizens of Belle View City. Not everyone was born with the genetic potential to become an Ascendant. Not everyone who was born with the genes actually made the transition from normal to super. But whatever it was that turned a normal person into a real, live, spandex-outfitted superhero, she had it.

It also meant she had the responsibility – along with the seven other people in the briefing room – to use her abilities to protect and defend her fellow citizens from any number of extraordinary dangers. Sometimes it was an earthquake or a building fire; sometimes it was a bank robbery or a toxic chemical spill. Sometimes they had to fight a Rescindant: a former fellow Ascendant who had turned evil.

But nowhere in the Ascendant League's *Manual of Conduct* did it say she was allowed to wallow in sullen jealousy over the close camaraderie of two of her fellow teammates. Rather the opposite (even if fits of sullen jealousy weren't mentioned specifically). So she straightened up, pulled her mind into work mode, and gave her boss, Oversight, an attentive look. The fact that her arms were still jealously folded over the purple-and-silver plastron of her superhero suit was immaterial.

"Good afternoon, Ascendants," their supervisor greeted them. He started separating the stapled printouts stacked in his arms, handing them out to each of the team members. "I hope you all got a good night's rest, because it's Friday night, and the weekends are usually busy. League surveillance suggests that Rescindants Dr Mockery and the Pincushion might also be looking forward to this weekend. The Mayor's Educators' Ball is tomorrow night. I hope you got your ball gown and tuxedo dry-cleaned this last week, Foresight, Steelhand."

Carrie groaned. "Not again! We covered the Charity Ball *last* weekend. Why do we have to do it again?"

Oversight smirked. "Because both of you can do a decent foxtrot. Bomber never learned, Backhand is too big to blend into the crowd and Hindsight is even more touch-sensitive than Steelhand. And, as far as I know, the other ladies never even learned."

"Actually, that's not true," Farshot, a.k.a. Valerie Romano, interjected, her brown eyes flicking flirtatiously towards Steelhand. "I can do a passable foxtrot, and even a waltz or two."

"I'll keep that in mind for the next society ball," Oversight said. He gestured at the printouts he had passed around. "Let's focus on tonight's assignments, shall we? Farshot, Bomber, we need you to focus on the Eastside; rumour has it the Pincushion's minions have been nosing around the edge of town, somewhere between the industrial sector and the suburbs. It's an unconfirmed rumour, but it's all we have to go on right now. Nearsight, we still haven't found any concrete evidence of a Quad crime syndicate link to the Pearson Shipping Company on our end of things. You'll have to continue your undercover work a bit longer.

"Backhand . . ." Oversight paused, sighed heavily, and pinned the burly, black-clad Ascendant with a disappointed look. "You're lucky we're still short on replacement staff, because I'd put you on probation if I could. *Next* time you get into a street fight with a Rescindant, *don't* throw a car at them. There was a perfectly good – and considerably *cheaper* – street lamp you could've torn off and used. As it is, your wages are being garnished for the cost of the repairs to the citizen's SUV."

"*Citizen?*" Backhand protested, visibly affronted by the word. "He was one of Dr Mockery's minions! He was trying to get into his car and escape with the isotope last week. Just because I was *efficient* at ruining his escape method *and* in thwarting the Doctor from setting off his viral bomb . . . !"

"We have no concrete evidence that he was indeed a minion, so there's no way for the League to consider him anything but an innocent bystander." Oversight planted his silver-gloved palms on the table, facing down the younger man. "You have a very bad habit of overusing your super-strength, Backhand."

Backhand grumbled, folding his arms across his chest.

Oversight swept his gaze over the other young men and women in the briefing room. "The Police Forensics and Public Justice Departments have requested once again that Hindsight visit their evidence lockers to do a scan of all items picked up during the week."

"Once again, I'm stuck with the most boring, horrific job on the planet. Please tell me they didn't pick up any bloody murder-scene weapons this week?" Hindsight, team healer and touch-sensitive clairvoyant, muttered ruefully.

"Sorry. The City Morgue has an unidentified piece of human bone they want scanned," Oversight told him.

"At least *you* get hazardous duty pay," Backhand grumbled.

Oversight continued. "Foresight and Steelhand, obviously you're on Westside patrol. The League also wants you to stop by the ballpark tonight. The Belle View Batters are playing the Star City Novas. Don't disrupt the game – the Batters have a chance of getting into the division championship. Don't enter the stands; just do a couple of circuits of the concourses, meet and greet the citizens shortly after the game starts, then get on with your patrol."

Steelhand's blue-masked face twisted. "Ugh . . . photo-ops. Do I *have* to?"

Oversight sighed.

Steelhand wrinkled his lip. "Little kids are *always* trying to touch my mask. Why can't Backhand do it? Or Bomber?"

"Because you're partnered with Foresight, and because the two of you are very photogenic together."

Carrie heard Valerie's obvious sigh of disappointment.

Photogenic, sure . . . but not together, Carrie lamented. Out of the corner of her eye, she watched Valerie's silver hand slide under the table to sympathetically squeeze Steelhand's blue thigh. She was all over him. It made Carrie sick. She sighed heavily. Then a thought occurred to her. "Oversight . . . uh . . . why don't Farshot and I switch partners?"

"Because you're still mentoring Steelhand," her supervisor returned dryly.

"But it's been a month," she protested. "Surely he's got the hang of the city by now. At least enough to be switched to a new partner?"

"You don't want to be my partner any more?" Steelhand peered at her.

The disappointment in his voice made her want to squirm. Carrie didn't know how to answer without delving into her very personal problems to do with him; in specific, her problem with his lack of interest in her.

Tightening her arms across her chest, she shrugged uncomfortably. "I'm just saying . . . you know . . . you don't *have* to serve out the rest of your probation period with me. That's all."

Oversight studied her. "Foresight, do you have a problem with Steelhand? Is there something we should know, since you're his mentor?"

"What? No!" she quickly protested. Lies were firmly and officially discouraged among League members. As Steelhand's team mentor during his settling-in period, if her team supervisor asked her for an evaluation, she had to give an honest one. "Officially, as his mentor, I'm saying that he's smart, he's competent, he's good at the job and he's ethical as well as efficient. Overall, he's a great asset to the team. I'm just saying . . . that . . . you know . . . he's good enough. He *could* be paired with someone else . . . so why not pair him with someone else?"

From the way the others stared at her, she didn't think they were buying it.

"Foresight, did you foresee something?" the green-masked Hindsight asked her.

"Or is it . . . a personality conflict?" Farshot/ Valerie asked. It didn't help that the corner of her mouth curled up below the edge of her mask. It wasn't a big smirk, but it was definitely a smirk. Valerie *knew* damned well that Carrie was interested in Steelhand . . . and that he hadn't shown the slightest interest in return.

"It is *not* a personality conflict," Carrie stated crisply, losing her temper at the other woman. "Not with *his* personality. If anything, I'm tired of *your* constant innuendos, your monopolizations of his time and energy and attention outside of actual fieldwork. I don't even get any time during briefings and debriefings to discuss cases with him – you're always there! You know what? You want him? *Have* him.

Then maybe we can all get on with our work without further wasted time or effort.

"Just remember to *do it* where I don't have to see or hear it. And use protection – you'll have to retire if you get pregnant," she added tartly. "*Normally* your fieldwork is excellent, Farshot. I'd appreciate it if you stopped acting like a cat on heat!"

Shocked silence greeted her words. Carrie could feel her skin heating from forehead to chin. Farshot looked almost as red as her costume.

Oversight tightened his mouth for a moment, then let out a heavy breath. "Foresight, kindly leave your personal speculations out of the office environment. Please turn your attention to the future, the immediate future. Let's get started. What activities of importance will happen in the next twelve hours?"

Embarrassed, she set aside her feelings quickly and got to work. She unfocused her eyes, turning her attention inwards, then outwards again, in that strange mental flip that accessed her powers. She probed at the future. "Eastside . . . I see . . . a red gas pipe and valve wheel. Nothing about it seems to be important, but one of us will encounter it within an hour or so. After that . . . flashes of light . . . through a dirty set of windows . . . factory windows. Somewhere in the industrial centre. Workers . . . uh, 12th and . . . Olive Street? Oliver? Oldive? I'm not getting an impression of anything violent in the next five hours, just that you'll want to do some surveillance on the workers in the factory. And something about the gas valve."

"Maybe it's a potential gas leak?" Bomber offered.

Carrie turned her attention to the next sector. "Riverside . . . I see violence. Someone getting beaten up badly. Nearsight . . . you're there. You're watching."

"Can she interfere?" Oversight asked her. "Stop it somehow?"

Her ability to foresee alternate pathways took a lot of energy. Straining against the future, she examined that possibility. "No . . . No, it would ruin her current undercover work. The person . . . Pier 17, around ten thirty, eleven at night, I think. They're going to toss him off the dock. He's a citizen; he's hurt, he's weighted and he'll drown. But if Backhand saves him . . . he might turn and talk, maybe even stand witness against the syndicate."

"Probability?" Oversight asked.

Carrie shook her head. "I'd say . . . maybe 40 per cent. Can't guarantee anything; that's further ahead than I can foresee."

"We know. Nearsight," Oversight addressed the yellow-clothed female next to him, "if you can bring yourself to do a little participating in roughing up this fellow: curse him, kick him, whatever – nothing too harmful – it might strengthen your cover. Right, Foresight?"

Carrie nodded in confirmation. "It'll help, at least a little bit."

Oversight nodded to Carrie. "Do you see anything else?"

She shook her head, eyes still unfocused. The moment she turned her attention to the other side of town, however, she was struck by an immediate vision. Steelhand was planning on getting into a fight with her.

Grimacing, she shook it off, blinked and refocused her attention again, looking further ahead. Just because she *could* foresee the future didn't always make it a good idea to probe too deeply. At the moment, she really didn't want to sort through the argument she'd soon be having with her partner, not when she was still working.

"Uh . . . I see a random mugging . . . a stand-by call from the Fire Department that comes to nothing . . . Baseball game – we show up in the third inning, stay 'til the end of the fourth . . ."

"Who's up at the end of the fourth? I got a bet going with Stonewall from morning shift on the Batters beating the Novas tonight," Backhand joked.

Bomber reached over and whacked him on the back of the head. "You know she won't tell us. Now why didn't you let *me* in on this bet, huh?"

"Because you still owe me twenty bucks from the last one you lost?"

"Gentlemen . . . let the lady continue. What about after you leave the game?" their boss asked.

Carrie drifted into the future. She could see herself and Steelhand leaving the game. As with all her visions, she experienced a feeling of being both inside herself and seeing herself from the outside. She almost never got flashes of what her future self was thinking. This was no exception; all she could feel was how tense both she and her partner seemed.

"Steelhand and I get on our hover bikes, we ride off . . . we . . . get hit by some sort of . . . powder bomb?" Blinking, Carrie tried to focus on the details. The perpetrators were elusive. She shook her head. "Too many variables to foresee who did it. Just two figures. But we're dusted in some sort of powder."

"Skip ahead to the powder's effects. Is it a poison? Some sort of drug? A tracing agent?" Oversight prodded her. "Is there a good reason to avoid getting hit?"

She continued. "We're . . . We're . . ."

What the hell?

". . . we're showering in a rooftop garden somewhere. Hosing each other down."

Someone snickered, but with her attention turned inwards, Carrie didn't see who it was. She did hear a *thump* as that person was whapped, however.

"Uh . . . OK . . . now we're changing costumes, and changing locations. A more thorough shower in one of the hiding holes . . . now we're in civilians, it looks like we're changing locations again . . ."

She blinked, coming back to herself. A quick glance to her left saw Steelhand giving her a puzzled frown.

He's not at all interested to know what I look like outside of the anonymity of my costume. He will never even let me see his face. Sour grapes settled in her stomach.

Sure, he'll go to the movies as a civilian with her, *but he can't stand going out in public with* me. *Today is just getting better and better.*

"It sounds like a tracking powder then," Hindsight offered.

"We don't know that yet," Oversight cautioned him. "It could be some other sort of contaminant. It also sounds like a sensible precaution to put some distance between themselves and that powder, to limit any continuing contamination."

"I can try skipping ahead a bit more," Carrie offered, returning her attention to her power. "It'll tire me out faster, but . . . Wha—"

"What? What do you see?" Oversight demanded as her eyes widened in unfocused shock. "Foresight?"

She couldn't speak. What she saw was beyond her comprehension, beyond her belief. But . . . there was no mistaking what would happen, if none of them greatly changed the course of their plans for the evening. At some point, after relocating to yet another safe house, some point during the night – she and Steelhand would be . . . they would be . . .

Naked. Together. Bare hands roaming, naked limbs entwining, hungry mouths mating, supple hips flexing. *That* level of naked. Together.

She watched herself, as herself – as Carrie, not as Foresight – and him as . . . whatever his real name was, but not as the Ascendant hero, Steelhand. She watched him cradle her head in his palms, watched as he undulated over her in slow, strong strokes, watched their lips suckling and parting in devouring, deep—

Something hit her, jolting her out of her vision. Heart pounding, she blinked to clear her focus and realized someone had thrown a crumpled paper ball at her face. The rumpled sheet had landed on her purple-covered lap. Given the sardonic look of enquiry from the orange-clad hero opposite her, Bomber was the culprit.

"What did you see?" Oversight repeated.

She opened her mouth, but nothing came out.

"Was it something horrible?" Nearsight asked her. "It looked like something horrible."

"Or at least something shocking," Farshot added.

"Is it something we should try to avoid?" Steelhand asked her.

The concern in his voice pricked her out of her shock. Blinking again, Carrie cleared her throat. "Uh . . . I'm . . . not sure. It was such a *strong* vision."

She stopped and blushed so hot, she almost took off her mask to cool herself. Her silver gloved hands twitched; she wanted to fan herself, but she didn't dare. Not when she couldn't, *daren't* reveal the details of her vision.

"Um . . . it was such a *strong* vision, I, ah, don't think there's a way we *can* avoid it. I mean, I literally couldn't *see* anything else, when normally I'm at least peripherally aware of my real-time surroundings."

Not that there's any way that I would *want* to avoid it, she thought, still fighting the urge to fan herself with something. She did unfold one arm, but only long enough to pluck the crumpled paper ball from her lap.

"Well, that doesn't answer the question. *What* did you see?" Oversight asked her. "Was it the effects of the powder?"

Oh God . . .

The heat drained out of her face. *What if it's an aphrodisiac? What if the only reason that he makes love to me is because he has no choice in the matter?*

That was a horrible thought. Squirming uncomfortably in her chair, arms refolded tightly against her chest, she shrugged. "I don't know. But it could be. It, um, we look like we need to be isolated for a little while. A few hours. Maybe a full day. It's nothing really *harmful*. I doubt we'd need medical observation," she added quickly as Hindsight drew in a breath to speak. "It's just . . . potentially embarrassing, I guess you could say. The sort of embarrassing where observation would just be a bad idea all the way around."

"What, like you break out in massive pimples, or something?" Backhand asked, wrinkling his nose at the possibility.

"Uh . . . something like that," Carrie muttered.

"In that case, I think we should avoid it. If it's not harmful, but serves no purpose other than to isolate us for a while, we're not going to be free to do our jobs in patrolling the city," Steelhand pointed out. "And if it happens right after we leave the baseball game, then we should definitely *avoid* the baseball game."

"Nice try, Steelhand," their supervisor quipped, "but the two of you are still making a public appearance tonight. Be on the alert as you leave the ballpark though. Choose a different route, leave at a different time, but I do want you to go and make nice with the civilians. Try to ward off the powder and limit any direct vectors for contamination. Try to see who attacked you, Foresight."

Nodding, she unfocused her eyes, attempting to return to the point in time when they were assaulted with the powder. She focused on following *their* futures, and strained hard to follow the two men. She caught a glimpse of cement walls, metal shelving and glass instruments. "I'm seeing . . . a lab of some sort. Ah! Dr Mockery," she realized, catching a glimpse of the Rescindant. "I'm pretty sure it's him; he usually has those purple goggles of his and I can see them perched on his head. It's definitely his minions who are trying to dust us with the powder he's been making.

"He's . . . He's watching something on a monitor. He's yelling at them. He's *not* happy. Whatever the dust does to us . . . ow . . . I don't think it gives the results he was looking for. I'm sorry, I can't see any more right now." Closing her eyes, she rubbed gently at her temples, trying to ease the headache that came from pressing too hard against time.

"All right, you have your assignments. Do keep in mind that Foresight can't see *everything*, so stay sharp, keep your eyes open and be safe. There are old Ascendants, and there are bold Ascendants, but there aren't any old, bold Ascendants . . . except for Mr Invulnerable, of course," Oversight joked. No one laughed.

"Dismissed!"

Everyone gathered up their briefing reports and headed for the door. Carrie/Foresight turned to her partner. He looked like he was frowning behind his blue mask and, every once in a while, he glanced her way almost warily. She had no idea what he was thinking or why he was frowning. But she knew he was spoiling for a fight.

The door closed behind the others, leaving the two of them alone in the briefing room. She stood, but he didn't move. Clearing her throat in the awkward silence, she offered, "Well, just in case we *do* go through with what I foresaw, I think we should go grab a couple of old uniforms to stash somewhere in the city before we head for the ballpark. In case that powder *is* some sort of contaminant." When he just studied her, she prompted, "What do you think?"

Folding his arms across his chest in a pose reminiscent of her earlier one, he tilted his head a little. "*I* think you should tell me what you foresaw. The thing that requires 'isolation' and is 'potentially embarrassing' to both of us. As one of the potentially afflicted, I have a right to know."

And have you screaming and running for the hills at the mere thought of being intimate with me? The woman you cannot stand *outside of business hours?*

She shook her head. At least she had a better excuse to use than her fragile ego. "You know why I can't do that, Steelhand. Foreknowledge of an incompletely foreseen event can potentially lead to an even worse situation. League rules."

"Fine. Then let's talk about you trying to dump me as your partner. What is up with that?" he demanded, shifting in his seat to look at her. "I thought we were good together."

Good together . . . The words flashed through her, leaving behind an entirely different connotation than the one he meant. Once again, she could see their bodies intertwining, vulnerable and intimate, reducing her from Foresight, heroine of the city, to Carrie, lonely, longing woman. Flushing, she cleared her throat and dragged her mind back to the more neutral aspects of life.

"You and I *do* make a good team out in the field. I don't deny that, I have never denied that, and I swear that what I said just now in front of the others stands," Foresight repeated. "You are an excellent addition to the team. I just . . ."

His dark brown eyes had narrowed at her blush. They narrowed further now. "You just . . . what? You just want to get rid of me? You just want another partner? You just want to go solo? Is that it?"

I just want you to look at me like you look at Farshot! But that wasn't entirely accurate, so she bit back the words, frustrated. He was polite to their red-suited teammate, even flirted a little with her, but Foresight – Carrie – wanted more. She wanted more than he was giving her; she just didn't think there *was* anything more within him for her, and was afraid to find out for sure.

Aware of the passing minutes, she shook her head. "We don't have time for this argument right now. We'll talk later." Then swallowing the unpleasant lump of her discomfort, shoving it deep down where it wouldn't interfere with her job, she headed for the ladies' locker room.

It didn't look like Steelhand the Uninterested was going to try to get himself into her armour-reinforced stretch pants anytime soon. Shame.

"I'd be happy to. It's one of the few perks of the job," Foresight/Carrie said to yet another citizen wanting to have a picture taken with her and her partner.

Steelhand's smile was definitely looking strained, and hers was beginning to feel that way. She smiled a little more, posed with a giggling young woman between the two of them while the girl's eye-rolling boyfriend took the picture. Over Steelhand's shoulder, Carrie spotted a mother and a little boy coming out of one of the doors in the concrete-block wall. The moment the pictures were done, she gave the crowd around them an apologetic smile.

"Thank you all for your continuing support, but I see that the bathroom is now free, and even superheroes need to, well, you know. Steelhand? Shall we?" she asked, indicating the door behind him. The bathroom trick was really simply a ruse to get away from all the people. Sometimes it was the only thing that worked – the public could be so demanding.

"Please do excuse us," he said graciously, wading through the crowd with an eagerness that betrayed his dislike for the press of people. As he had explained during the interview process for this job, it was one thing if *he* initiated the contact and could brace himself against a person's thoughts, but an unexpected touch was unnerving and unwanted. She would've liked to believe that his disinterest in her was due solely to his dislike for inadvertently reading other people's minds, but he didn't seem to hesitate when it came to being close to Farshot. After all, today wasn't the *first* time they'd gone to the movies together.

Thankfully, the citizens parted way, and the pair made it to the bathroom door. As soon as the two of them were inside and Steelhand had thrown the lock, he faced her, guessing her intention. "You're going to read the future?"

She nodded. "It'll be easier now that we're closer to the events."

Leaning back against the wall next to the door, she stared across the room and unfocused her eyes. Her awareness of the crowds out on the mezzanine level faded as her attention twisted itself inside, then out, and she saw – *felt* – once again the scene of her and her partner being attacked. This time the image changed. They weren't ambushed unknowingly, and coated in the yellowish powder by surprise; this time, she watched herself fling up a protective bubble, then lash out telekinetically, capturing the two attackers as they tried to flee.

She saw Steelhand stripping off his gloves, saw him touching the face of one of the masked, struggling captives. But then the vision switched off without warning. That was the frustrating thing about her gift; she only ever saw in glimpses and snatches, incomplete pieces. It was like trying to grasp the image printed on a thousand-piece jigsaw puzzle with only a dozen pieces to go on. Sighing, she closed her eyes and shook her head.

"All I can see is the attack happening again. But I put up a shield bubble and we catch them. Nothing else."

"Well, what about the 'potentially embarrassing' stuff?" Steelhand asked. "If we aren't touched by the powder, thanks to your telekinesis, does the other stuff still happen?"

Paling a little at the thought of the two of them *not* . . . she quickly unfocused her eyes and returned her attention to the future.

"I see . . . us letting the minions go . . . We change clothes anyway? We're in street clothes . . . travelling . . . Oh! Oh God . . ."

Her power had hopped ahead, like a stone skipping across the surface of a lake. Now it plopped beneath the waters, dragging her down into the depths of her vision. Gone was the bathroom, gone was Steelhand's silver-and-blue masked face. All she could see was his real face, lips slack from panting, eyes shut, neck arched and muscles straining as he . . .

. . . as he invaded her vision? Sensations doubled, trebled abruptly, spiking desire sharply through all six of her senses. Bodies and minds collided, muscles flexed, pleasure seared. The image shifted without her conscious control; *he* shifted it, grabbing and lifting her thigh, tilting her hips just that little bit more for the perfect stroke, *exactly* what she craved most in her foresight-swamped thoughts . . .

Carrie gasped, jerking back from his touch. The back of her head thumped painfully into the wall, breaking up most of the lust clouding her senses. Blinking rapidly, panting for air, she found him staring at her with eyes so wide she could see the whites ringing the chocolate brown of his irises.

"What the . . . ?" he mumbled, still visibly stunned.

"What the *hell* do you think you were doing?" she hissed, barely remembering to keep her voice down. The last thing they needed was for any civilians to overhear the two of them arguing through the restroom door. "That was an invasion of my privacy. You are *not* supposed to scan your partners without their prior consent."

Her embarrassed anger snapped him out of his daze. Frowning, he focused on her. "I thought I had probable cause. At the last place I worked, my partner turned Rescindant. I thought he was acting strangely beforehand, secretive and not quite right, but I didn't exercise my right to scan him under probable cause. He nearly blew up half the team as he tried to make off with millions of dollars in bearer bonds. I *thought* it was happening with you. When you refused to say what you had foreseen, after acting like you didn't want me as your partner any more, I got a little suspicious."

Hands shifting to her hips, she gave him an annoyed look. "I am *not* turning Rescindant, Steelhand. And I didn't *tell* the others what I'd seen because it was none of their damned business!"

"Well, you could have told *me*!" he demanded, then winced, catching himself and lowering his voice as it started to echo off the hard cement blocks around them. "Dammit! This is *not* the best place for an argument."

"Well, we're *not* going to avoid it this time," she muttered. Somehow, she knew they would get through this misunderstanding; her vision had been too strong to suggest otherwise. She took a deep breath.

"I wasn't sure if that powder was an aphrodisiac. But if I keep it away with a shield bubble, and we *still* make love . . ." She stopped and trained her eyes on him. "Why the hell won't you flirt with me? Let's start with that, shall we? *Why* won't you flirt with me?"

He gave her a *duh* look. "Because you're my *partner*? League studies have proven that if two League members in the same city start dating each other, the partners become distracted whenever one or the other gets into danger. Because of that, I don't date fellow Ascendants."

"You *are* dating Farshot!" Carrie hissed, incensed.

"I am not! We're just friends," he whispered back defensively.

"Oh, *friends*, really? Then why is it she keeps coming on to you like a love-struck puppy? Or didn't you notice that, Mr Touch-Telepathic?"

"She's not in love with me. She's in love with Oversight. But he's gay!" Wincing, Steelhand covered his masked face with his bared hands. "Oh God, I did *not* mean to reveal that. God, this is another reason why I don't date people . . ." Dragging his hands free, he sighed. "Look . . . I *like* you. A lot. Too much to treat you as anything more than a colleague, because League policy prohibits partners from dating. I'm good at my job. I love my job. I will do whatever it takes to adhere to the rules."

She eyed him askance. "The League prohibits partners from dating? Since when? Where did you hear that piece of drivel?"

"When I first joined the League as an active-duty Ascendant, I was given the lecture that League members on the same team do not date each other," he explained patiently. "Adding a relationship to the situation is too much of a distraction, given the potential danger in our line of work. That means that, no matter how attractive, intelligent, funny or competent I find you – and you have no idea how much I do – I *cannot* date you. Statistically, it increases the danger on the job, and it puts a dual strain on the Ascendant in question, because if their date and their partner are ever both placed in peril, they'll be torn in two different directions as to who to go help first. The partnership has to come first!" Steelhand seemed to know the entire League manual by heart.

Memory of the study came back to her. Foresight rolled her eyes. "Did your superiors ever tell you about the *second* study they released? The one *encouraging* partners to date? Yes, to date someone who isn't your partner is a potential problem in an emergency, but if you're dating *your partner*, the study found that you tend to fight *harder* to protect them. The Spartans at Thermopylae were all lovers as well as partners, and they held off a massive invasion force for days back in ancient Greece – and I'll remind you that very few of them were Ascendant heroes! If it works for regular citizens, it'll definitely work for us.

"Look, why else would Oversight go to all the trouble of pairing us up male–female, if not to encourage dating opportunities? With your steel-skin ability, you'd actually be a better partner for Bomber, but he didn't pair you two together," she said. "That's because the League's policy is to *encourage* Ascendants to date, marry and produce more Ascendant-potential offspring. Stable families come from couples who have a long-term friendship and know how to work well together in times of adversity. Teammates who get along well fit that bill very nicely."

He frowned at her, confused. "If that were so, then why didn't I hear about this?"

"Maybe your former supervisor just didn't want to deal with the headache of couples dating and breaking up, and partnerships constantly having to be rearranged. Did you ever think of that?

"Backhand is patrolling the Riverside where Nearsight is working undercover. Between his super-strength and his ability to turn invisible, he can keep an eye on her at least part of the time. He wouldn't do any less for an assignment *because* they're dating each other. And Oversight knows it. That's why he has never reassigned Backhand to partner with anyone else."

Steelhand gave her a puzzled look. "Backhand and Nearsight are dating? Are you *sure*? They act so . . . professional around each other."

"You knew that Oversight is gay – which I didn't even know – but *didn't* know that Backhand and Nearsight were going out?" she asked.

A blush spread across his lightly tanned skin. Steelhand cleared his throat. "The only reason I know is because I caught him leering at me in his thoughts at my interview."

"Well, you *are* rather handsome," she told him. "And I have been flamingly jealous of Farshot because you've flirted with her, but not me. *That's* why I didn't want to be partnered with you any more. Because you weren't interested in me. And it's been killing me."

He moved closer to her, not quite bringing their bodies together, but close enough that she had to lean back against the wall. Not because he intimidated her, and not because she didn't want him to touch her, but because of the rising warmth in his dark eyes. "It's been killing me too. I didn't dare flirt with you, because I thought it was forbidden.

"When I date someone, it's very . . . intense for me. At least at first. I cannot touch someone without getting flashes of their thoughts. And when we make love—" his gaze drifted down to her mouth, and the corner of his lips curled up on one side "—everything feeds back on itself until I'm nearly mindless with our mutual pleasure. Of course, it does mean I'm a very good lover, because I'll know *exactly* what you're craving."

Carrie didn't have to focus her thoughts on the future to feel that same sharp spike of desire in the here and now.

Clearing her throat, she focused her thoughts. "Well. Now that we know that both of us are attracted to each other, and that the League policy doesn't forbid it, shall we finish meeting and greeting the populace, and then make our way out onto the streets to deal with the Doctor's minions and their mysterious powder? Since they *are* watching and waiting for us to exit the ballpark."

"And find a place to explore that . . . intense . . . future you foresaw?" he asked, touching her waist with his silver hand.

She started to say yes, then remembered an important detail. Tipping her head, she asked, "Do I at least get to know your real name before we make love? It might kill the mood a little if I shout out 'Steelhand' mid-lovemaking."

"It's Rio Sanchez." His smile turned into a smirk. "But don't worry, it won't kill the mood on my end if you call out my team name. I want you so much, I'm not going to give you time to think about anything once we're alone."

"Your name is Rio Sanchez?" she repeated sceptically, ignoring the promise in his words. She was still a professional, still an on-the-clock Ascendant at the moment . . . though she did plan on sticking to her "potentially embarrassing need for isolation" excuse to cover their abandoning of their patrol tonight. Sometimes it was good to be a precognitive, and protected by League policy from having to reveal the full truth of every little matter.

"I know I don't look it, but my father's Filipino and my mother's Korean," he stated with a grin. "You're not the first one to think the name doesn't match the face."

"No, I meant it sounded like a hokey sort of secret-identity alias. I'm Carrie Vinson," she introduced herself, holding up her gloved hand. "It's not much better as far as names go, but it's what I've got."

Steelhand/Rio clasped gloved hands with her, then leaned in close and kissed her. It wasn't exactly a brief kiss, but it wasn't a very passionate one either, just a gentle, warm salute of her lips. Mindful that he would be picking up snatches of her thoughts, Carrie carefully blanked out everything but the feel of his mouth pressing against hers and her enjoyment of it. He kissed her a little more firmly, then flicked the tip of his tongue along the seam of her lips. Before she could do more than inhale sharply in pleasure, he pulled back.

"We have to be professional," he muttered. "If I keep kissing you, I won't be able to go out in public. Not in spandex pants. Even if it *is* armoured down there. Foresight – Carrie," Rio corrected himself.

"Everything I know about you as a partner says I'll like you even more as a man, and I do want to find out all about you, if possible, she agreed."

Lifting his gloved fingers to her hair, Rio tucked a loose, light-brown curl behind her ear. "Everything I've learned about you as a partner makes me think I *definitely* want to get to know you as a woman."

Someone knocked on the door. Both of them jumped a little, then blushed. Carrie pulled her mind back into work mode – Foresight mode. "We need to get back on patrol. But I just want to tell you that I've never foreseen anything I've wanted to happen so badly before.

"By the way, what did you do for a living before you became a superhero?" She asked, stepping aside to let him check his mask in the mirror.

He gave her a smile. "Before I turned Ascendant, I worked as a translator, out of a tiny little apartment with a balcony barely big enough for a few tomatoes and a box of leaf lettuce. Now I work for the League and live in the suburbs on the Eastside, with a big backyard where I grow my own vegetables. I remember being very disappointed that I didn't get any green-thumb superpowers to deal with plants when I Ascended. But I suppose turning my body into living metal and reading minds aren't too bad as far as superpowers go. What about you? What does Carrie Vinson like to do?"

"Ceramic arts. It's extra easy, what with the telekinetic thing. I've even had a couple of pottery shows in local galleries," she confessed.

"Vinson . . . wait, Vinson Pottery? Isn't that the shop on the corner of Fourth and Stewart?"

"Yeah." She smiled. "It's a nice change from throwing around villains with my mind, or having to probe into the future. So you've seen my work, then?"

"I've *bought* your work. I bought one of the bamboo sculptures for my father's birthday—" Rio was interrupted by another knock on the door, cutting off their exchange of personal information. Sighing, they both squared their shoulders, preparing themselves mentally for the waiting public.

Carrie glanced at her partner as she reached for the door lock. "No rest for a superhero, and all that," she said. "Are you ready to face the public?"

"Not really. But now that I have tonight to look forward to, I can endure almost any torture," he quipped. "Bring on the crowd of adoring thousands, fellow Ascendant. The sooner we can get this over with, the sooner we can run away and be an adoring little crowd of two."

"I'm looking forward to that." In a much, much lighter mood than at the beginning of her evening, Carrie opened the door.

Daniel

C.T. Adams and Cathy Clamp

One

"Jenna! Ohmigod, Jenna Cooper! Is that you?" I made my voice a girlish squeal. Inwardly I was wincing, but I played the role to perfection, running up to the mark like a long-lost acquaintance, making sure everybody in the restaurant would be watching so that there'd be witnesses later if she tried to deny what was about to happen.

A gorgeous woman in a lavender silk suit and pearls the size of gumballs leaned back from her salad plate and eyed me suspiciously. But she didn't bolt or try to deny it, so I ploughed on.

"I'm not surprised you don't remember me. Nobody ever does. But it's you, isn't it? You *are* Jenna Cooper?"

She blinked a few times, and I could see her trying to match my face with a memory and failing. I mean, let's be honest, the Jennas of the world are beautiful, and popular enough that from the day they're born there are hangers-on and wannabes enough that they really *don't* remember. Was I that girl from high school or college? The quiet mousy one? Maybe from that office she worked in briefly before marrying well? The other woman at the table gave her a sympathetic look. It's always so embarrassing to be caught flat footed.

"Yes. I'm Jenna, but it's Jenna Ross now. I'm sorry, I really *don't* seem to remember you."

"That's all right," I assured her as I pulled a stack of folded papers from my fashionably large purse. "You wouldn't. We've never met." I dropped the pages onto the napkin in her lap. "My name is Karen James, and you've just been served."

I turned and walked away, my high heels clicking on the hardwood floor. All eyes were on me as I made my way through the restaurant. Not because I looked good – I did, but I will never be in the same league as the Jennas of the world. I'm short and stocky, rather than tall and elegant, my suit was black polyester, my necklace tiny seed pearls. But I'd done my job, and done it well. Mrs Ross had been served her divorce papers very, very publicly, just the way her husband wanted.

Nobody bothered me on my way out. Since I hadn't bothered with the valet, I waved him away when he started to approach, walking to the farthest end of the lot where the employees park. I'd left my car there, because my battered, twelve-year-old subcompact would've stuck out like a sore thumb among the shiny new BMWs and Mercedes.

I walked confidently up to my car, keys in hand. I'd parked directly under the street light. I could see every detail in that flat, orange light. He didn't step out of the shadows. There *were* no shadows. He simply *appeared*. Like smoke, in thin air.

I didn't scream. I've seen the show before. Only this wasn't Daniel. Which meant I was in trouble.

"That was cleverly done. A brilliant piece of acting work you pulled off in the restaurant, if I do say so myself." He was tall and slender, but well built. His hair was a natural silver-blond that looked perfectly in keeping with his marble-white skin. The voice was cultured too, as smooth as that same marble. Soothing. It was all part of the package. I didn't dare look into his eyes, but I had no doubt they were gorgeous – and utterly mesmerizing.

The stranger stood in quiet amusement as I took in every bit of his appearance.

"Thank you. I'm actually very good at my job."

"As am I."

I didn't doubt it. With those looks and attitude he probably had to beat off the prey with a stick. Sex is a powerful lure, and by God he was sexy. His whole body breathed pheromones. I felt my body tighten, and it wasn't from fear. Dammit.

"Look at me," he ordered.

"No." I fought the compulsion. It wasn't easy. But I'm as stubborn as hell and I've had lots of practice, so I managed.

"*Look at me*." There was a hint of a growl in the voice, and I felt my body give an involuntary jerk. But I closed my eyes and fought for all I was worth.

"You know our ways, how is that possible?" Hands like steel bands dug into my shoulders as he grabbed me, intending to drag me towards him. "I smell . . . Daniel."

He pulled harder, and the pain was blinding. I fought long enough for him to put some strength into it then surprised him by going utterly limp. When he bent over to catch me, I punched upwards as hard as I could, driving my car keys deep into his throat, my fist slamming against his windpipe.

He reared back, blood pouring from his neck in a wide spray. I'd caught an artery. His teeth bared, and I caught a glimpse of vicious fangs.

I started screaming bloody murder. The valet turned, as did the customers he was serving. They moved slowly, as if coming out of a trance. But they did move. Apparently I'd injured him badly enough that he couldn't heal and use his mojo. The men ran towards us. The woman pulled out a cell phone and began dialling 911.

"You'll pay for that, bitch." He spit the words out with a spray of blood, and vanished, like a puff of smoke.

"Are you all right? You're covered in blood! What happened? Where did he go?"

"I'm fine, I'm fine." I stood up and tried to brush the dirt and leaves from my torn stockings, which just smeared the blood around worse. My hands were covered in it. In fact, there was enough blood that if he'd been human I'd have worried about him bleeding to death. But he wasn't. Which meant that I'd just pissed him off. Of course, I couldn't tell my rescuers that. After all, vampires don't exist.

Yeah, right.

The police came, and there was an ambulance. It took hours to deal with all of the official crap. Other than bone-deep bruising on my shoulders, I didn't have any injuries, but the doctors were worried that I was going into shock. So I had to call my boss. His irritation at my being off duty for the rest of the night was only slightly mollified by the fact I'd gotten Mrs Ross. Knowing my luck, he'd dock me for the extra hours. Between the statements for the police and the emergency room rigmarole, it was 3 a.m. by the time I climbed out of the cab that dropped me off at my apartment door.

My eyes burned with exhaustion, my clothes and keys had been impounded for evidence, and I was out the cab fare home. If a particularly kindly ER nurse hadn't loaned me a spare set of scrubs, I don't know what I would have done. As it was, the thin cotton did nothing to cut the chill breeze blowing. I shuddered, shivering as I scrounged the last of the change from the bottom of my purse to come up with enough to pay the cabbie. No tip. But there you go.

A blast of cold wind plastered the thin green cotton of the borrowed scrubs against my skin. Swearing, I hurried across the short stretch of gravel that led to the back door of my apartment building.

Twitchy with nerves, I kept looking over my shoulder, my fingers trembling as I tried to punch in the access code for the door.

"What's happened to you?"

I screamed, not a full-throated shriek, but one of those sort of half-screams you give off when you're startled. I knew that voice. It was Daniel.

"Easy, easy." He started to reach for me, to pat my shoulder, but I flinched away in fear and pain.

"Karen, what happened?" He stood utterly still, perfect body outlined in the harsh shadows cast by the stark white light of the security bulb overhead. He sniffed, and a shudder ran through him. Even his eyes reacted, pupils expanding, moving more like the slitted eyes of a cat than a human.

"You smell of blood, and it isn't yours."

Another, longer, sniff, and he stepped closer, invading my personal space, but there was no threat to the motion. Nor was there any of the heat and sexual tension I'd come to expect.

He stepped back, his expression horrified. "Dear God, Karen. What have you done?"

I was shivering from the combination of cold and shock. My teeth weren't quite chattering, but that would probably be next.

"Let's get you inside."

"What do you think I'm trying to do?" I reached around his bulk to try to enter the numbers onto the keypad again, but he made a disgusted sound in the back of his throat. He placed a hand gently on my arm. I felt a rush of warmth, and I was suddenly standing in the middle of my living room.

"Lie down on the couch under the blankets. I'll run you a bath. You need to keep warm."

I didn't even bother converting the futon into the bed position, just curled up on it as it was. I wrapped myself up in the quilt my sister had made for me (as well as in every other blanket that I owned) and still I was shivering. Daniel moved with brisk efficiency, but none of his usual smooth elegance. He started a hot bath running before crossing the few steps into the kitchen to set a kettle on to boil.

I watched him because I couldn't not. Whenever he was near me, he had my full attention. He was so damned beautiful. His skin was the colour of caramel, smooth and creamy. The hair a mass of soft dark curls. Saying it was dark brown didn't do it justice. Every strand seemed a separate shade of brown, some with glossy highlights, others so dark they were almost black. Every time I looked at his hair I had a wild urge to run my fingers through it.

Tonight he was wearing new jeans in that deep shade of indigo that seems to fade after the first few washings. The collar of his navy silk shirt was unbuttoned, exposing his throat and giving just a glimpse of his smoothly muscled chest. I saw the pulse jumping in his throat and realized something completely unexpected.

"You're afraid."

He stopped, turning to face me. The movement was . . . odd, inhuman.

"You smell of blood and of Alexander. You haven't been bitten. I'd know if you had. Which means that you have somehow managed to hurt one of the most powerful of my kind. He won't let that stand. He *can't*. Yes, I'm afraid. And so should you be."

The phrasing struck me, as it sometimes did: "So should you be," not "You should be, too." How old was Daniel? I had no idea. He'd never say, just smile and change the subject.

"What do I do?"

The kettle began to whistle, and he moved into the kitchen. I heard him rummaging in the cabinets for a mug, heard him rip open one of the little metal packets of instant cocoa I drink. A few clinks of the spoon against china, and he reappeared, mug in hand. "Drink this, and tell me what happened."

I did as he said. It didn't take long. There wasn't much to it really, and I'd had lots of practice repeating the story to the police and the doctors.

He didn't interrupt. He just perched on the edge of my wooden rocking chair, sitting unnaturally still, barely seeming even to breathe until I finished. The stillness was odd, foreign. It wasn't like him. Normally he was animated, more *alive* than most of the people I know. Not tonight.

I was the one who got up and shambled into the kitchen to refill my cup, then into the bathroom to turn off the taps and strip for my bath. Daniel just sat. "Why me?" I muttered. It was meant to be a rhetorical question, but he answered.

"Because you were clever. It caught his attention. Alexander always says 'You are who you eat.'" He paused, his voice gaining a hint of dry sarcasm. "Of course, it didn't help that you parked in the farthest, most deserted part of the lot."

"There were people. It was well lit."

He let out a soft snort, but didn't argue.

I didn't hear him go – not that I would. But I'd been in the tub just long enough for the water to start to cool when he appeared in the bathroom doorway. In his hand he held what looked like a necklace of three charms strung on a black satin ribbon.

The warmth of the cocoa and the bath had helped. I felt better – good enough that I risked something I'd never done before.

I'd always been cautious around Daniel: kept my distance, carefully avoided looking him in the eye and never, ever, coming close enough to touch. It had become a game between us. We'd tease, play up the sexual tension, but we never stepped over the line. He'd moved slowly, allowing the friendship to develop. It had occurred to me more than once that he wanted – needed – that more than sex, more than blood.

I rose slowly and stepped out of the tub. I watched with satisfaction as his eyes followed the water that trailed down every curve of my body. His eyes darkened until they were almost black, and a bulge began to show beneath the tight denim of his jeans.

"Hunters are always alone."

"*Always?*" I put a teasing note in my voice and stepped up to him. Only a fraction of an inch separated us. Such a tiny distance. I could smell the hint of soap on his skin, feel actual heat radiating from his body.

"Karen . . ."

"Shush." I reached up and placed a finger against his lips. "We've known each other for months. If you were going to bite me, you would've done it by now."

"You don't know that." His whisper was as rough as the stubble that decorated his cheeks.

"Yes, I do."

He held his body stiff, motionless. He didn't move forwards, but he didn't resist as I moved my hand against his chest for balance and went up on tiptoe to kiss him.

It started as a gentle touch of the lips, my body barely brushing his. It didn't stay that way. He had me in his arms so suddenly it was startling, his hands sliding down my body until they reached my thighs. He grabbed me then, lifting me from the ground, pulling me tight against him, so that the rough denim ground against the most intimate parts of me as his tongue plunged into my mouth.

I whimpered, my hands tearing at the cloth of his shirt. I wanted, needed, to feel the warmth of his skin; needed to touch him, to have him touch me.

He groaned, pulling back from the kiss, but not putting me down or letting me go. Burying his face in my throat he spoke in a whisper that was hoarse with need. "We can't do this."

"Yes, we can."

I felt him gathering himself together, preparing to pull back. I couldn't stand it. Pride went out the window in the face of pure need. "Daniel, *please.*"

"You don't understand." He lifted his face and for the first time ever, I looked him straight in the eye.

"I don't *care*. I want you. Want *this*." I ground my body against his hardness.

He blinked, and I was caught in the magic of his gaze, a swirl of gold and copper, bronze and the rich brown of dark chocolate. I heard myself gasp, felt myself being carried into the living room.

He took his time, licking the water from every part of me, using teeth and tongue to tease as his hands explored. His shirt was gone. I writhed against him, shouting myself hoarse.

When we were done, he collapsed beside me, both of us sated and spent, the weight of his body pinning me to the futon mattress.

"When we can move, you need to put on the charm I made you. It'll make you harder to find and more difficult for Alexander to connect us. It'll let me know if you're in trouble."

"Harder to find?" I shifted my weight, rolling towards him, the fingers of my right hand tracing delicately over his sleekly muscled chest and six-pack abs.

"Alexander will be looking for you. He's going to want to kill you, as slowly and painfully as he can. I'm not going to let him."

"Can you stop him?"

"I have to."

Two

I rolled over and slapped my hand in the general direction of the alarm clock, hoping to hit the snooze button. The movement sent a wave of pain shooting through my shoulder and down my arm. The pain was a far more effective wake-up call than the buzzing of the clock. I gasped, my eyes going wide.

It took a second for my mind to click into gear, to remember last night. It hadn't been a dream. I had the bruises, and the charm necklace, to prove it. But Daniel was gone, and I had things to do before I went into work this evening.

I was sore and stiff, both from my injuries and from my amazing night with Daniel, so I set the shower massage on high, and turned the temperature up as hot as I could stand. By the time I had spent a few minutes under the spray, I was able to raise my arms above my head. Not without pain, mind you. The bruises were too deep for that. But at least I had full range of motion and was able to brush my teeth without screaming in agony.

I dressed simply: black jeans and a loose polo shirt. The bra straps hurt against the bruises, but I'm too busty to feel completely comfortable braless, so I wore it anyway. Dark socks and running shoes completed my outfit.

When I was dressed, I called in to the office. If anyone hadn't shown up there might be work available, and since I'd lost half of my shift to the hospital visit, I could use the money.

"Anderson Investigations and Process Service. This is Amber, may I help you?"

"Hey Amber, it's me."

"Karen! Ohmigod. Are you all right? I heard you were mugged and had to go to the ER last night."

"I'm a little banged up, but I'll be OK." Maybe. I hoped. Assuming Daniel and I could handle Alexander.

"Oh thank God. Well, look, there's nothing for you here until you come on shift, so take it easy and rest up. Good job on the Ross service by the way. The boss is pleased."

"Thanks." Glad he was pleased, but too bad there was no extra work. Oh well.

"See you when you come on shift."

"Right."

I hung up the phone feeling a little depressed. I needed to take my mind off of things, distract myself. So I flipped on the television and hooked up the game console. In minutes my mind was off in la-la land, chasing through dangerous mazes collecting weapons and killing aliens.

The more the day wore on, the more tense I became. I'd gotten lucky yesterday. Alexander had been expecting an easy kill and had been careless. Next time he'd be prepared.

I knew that Daniel wanted me to let him take care of it. Fine. I mean, let's face it, the "creatures of the night" have all sorts of advantages over the rest of us. First, nobody believes they exist; if I asked anyone but Daniel for help, they'd lock me up in the loony bin and throw away the key. Then they have that whole hypnotic-stare, super-strength, gotta-stake-me-and-cut-off-my-head-to-kill-me thing going.

Could I drive a stake through somebody's chest to save my own life?

Probably. But it wouldn't be easy. It takes a lot of strength, both of body and will to do that sort of thing.

Cut off the head?

Ewww. Um . . . maybe. But how do you explain it to the police after? "Gee, officer. I'm pretty sure the victim was a vampire . . ." Not so much. See previous comment re rubber room with padded walls.

But I'm not the type to just let the man take care of things. I'm not. So I needed to be prepared. I just wasn't sure *how*. Last night I hadn't taken the time to ask Daniel which of the myths about vampires were true and which were, well, myth. We hadn't spent much time talking.

Not that I regretted any of the not talking. That had been spectacularly wonderful, wonderfully spectacular, and I wanted more just as soon as I could get it, thank you very much. In fact, it had lived up to every single fantasy I'd had about him since our first meeting. But now I had a problem on my hands and I needed to figure out what to do about it.

I grabbed the spare set of keys from their hook and pulled on my jacket. It would take a little time to ride the bus out to the restaurant and pick up my car, but if I left now, I should still be able to get there before sundown. In fact, if I hurried, I might be able to run a few errands before it got dark and Alexander came a-calling.

I hurried.

"What *is* that smell?" The man changing the tyre was short and bulky, with the beginnings of a gut hanging over the top of his belt. His name was Jack Baker, and I was serving him with a restraining order. He apparently had a habit of beating up on his wife, to which she'd taken exception. I'd serve the papers. It's what I do. But I'd be careful doing it. Because, while Mr Baker looked innocuous enough, he was plenty dangerous.

I felt bad for his wife, and hoped she didn't believe that a simple piece of paper was going to keep him away from her. In my experience, most restraining orders didn't work. But if you're lucky – very, very lucky – they might result in the asshole going to jail long enough to give you a head start.

"Garlic," I answered him, because I was going to try to keep this friendly. It probably wouldn't work, but I was going to try. "I'm planning on making spaghetti when I get home."

"You cook? You don't look like the type." He raised his beady eyes from what he was doing to check me out, his hand clenching and unclenching on the tyre iron.

"I cook," I answered. "By the way, my name's Karen. Karen James. What's yours?" He was busy tightening the lug nuts, and didn't look up when he answered me.

"Jack Baker," he answered. Grunting, he finished tightening the last lug nut. "But make the cheque out to Baker Towing."

"Right." I dug in my purse, pulling out a stack of papers and setting them, along with my chequebook, onto the hood of the car. I made out the cheque, tearing it out and dropping the book back into the bag. Turning to Mr Baker, I thrust both the cheque and paperwork into his hand.

"What the *hell*?" He tried to shove the paperwork back at me, but I backed away.

"Mr Baker, you've been served."

I climbed into the car, slamming and locking the door before he could react. It was just as well that I did, because when he actually got a glance at the papers I'd handed him, he lost it completely. He swung the tyre iron in a wicked arc, smashing it into the car window, which cracked in a spiderweb pattern. Meanwhile I'd started the vehicle and threw it in gear. I was taking off, gravel spitting from my tyres when the second blow fell with the clang of metal on metal.

Crap. That had been close. *Damn it anyway!* My poor car. The clients were *definitely* getting the bill for this one.

I drove west, towards the last rays of the setting sun that were nearly blinding me, checking my rearview mirror every few seconds to make sure Mr Baker hadn't decided to follow. He might. He didn't seem like the type to let things go. But luck was with me; there was no sign of a tow truck.

My eyes were on the mirror when Daniel materialized on the seat beside me. I shrieked, and jerked, swerving across two lanes before I got the car back under control.

"Don't *do* that. Cripes! You scared me half to death."

"I scared *you*? What the hell are you doing out of your apartment? Damn it! Don't you realize how much danger you're in?" His handsome features twisted into a snarl. "And *what* is that smell?" He rolled down the window, letting fresh air into the car. I couldn't say I blamed him. In an enclosed space the smell was a little overpowering.

"Fresh cloves of garlic."

He sighed. "If you're thinking it will hurt him, it won't. Although the smell might just drive him off." He leaned towards the window, breathing deeply. "Tell me you're not wearing it in a necklace."

"No, but I've got some in my jacket pockets. The holy water is in a gun on the back seat."

He twisted around and peered over the top of the seat. I saw his eyebrows rise at the sight that greeted him. I'd gone to a toy store and bought *the* top-of-the-line squirt gun. It was made of neon plastic with no less than five tanks of assorted sizes, all of which I'd filled with holy water from the baptismal font at the Catholic cathedral, before having the gun itself blessed, along with a smaller one that was tucked in the inside pocket of my jacket. I was pretty sure the priest thought I was nuts. But he did as I asked.

"Does holy water work?"

"As a matter of fact, it does. So make sure you aim that thing carefully. Assuming, of course, you get a shot off." Shifting his weight, he pulled the briefcase I'd had on the seat out from beneath him. "I don't suppose I can talk you into staying home where you're relatively safe while I deal with this."

"No. Not really. I've got a job, bills to pay – a *life*. I refuse to cower in the corner."

Actually I'd thought about doing just that, but decided that the stress of worrying would probably do me in just as effectively as the monster hunting me. And then there was the worrying about Daniel. Because I did. Yes, he was a big, strong vampire, perfectly capable of taking care of himself. But I'd seen his expression in that fleeting instant when he'd realized I was up against Alexander. He'd been afraid.

"You do realize how stupid that is." He said it softly.

"Yes. But it doesn't matter." I took the 120th street exit, heading for my next assignment. This should be an easy one: little suburban housewife getting divorce papers. She was even expecting them.

"I could *make* you go home."

I thought about that for a moment. Maybe he could. I'd looked in his eyes last night, had felt the magic pulling me like an undertow. Could he use that same magic to bend me to his will? Probably. I just hoped he wouldn't.

"If you do, it's over. I won't be anybody's meat puppet. Not yours, not anyone's."

"Maybe I don't care. Maybe having you alive matters more than whether or not you hate me."

I wasn't sure how to answer that. So I didn't. The silence stretched uncomfortably. I pretended to concentrate on driving, turning left and slowing, my eyes scanning the row of split-level houses for the correct address. When I found it, I pulled the car to the kerb and shut off the engine. I grabbed my briefcase and climbed out of the car. Daniel did the same, following a few steps behind as I strode up the sidewalk to the front porch.

I rang the bell and Mrs West came to the door. She was pretty; a petite brunette that looked harried. In the background I could hear the sound of children fighting. She took the papers, thanked me and quickly closed the door.

It was only when I turned to go back to the car that I noticed Daniel wasn't behind me. Instead, he was standing in the middle of the Wests' manicured lawn. In front of him was the most striking woman I'd ever seen. She was tall, taller even than Daniel, with a muscular build and harsh features. I didn't know who she was, but I could guess *what* she was. And while she was distracting Daniel, Alexander was moving in from behind.

"I cannot *believe* you are sleeping with a *sheep*. God, Daniel. How can you?"

"Hey, you! Who are you calling a sheep?" I shouted the words as I reached into my jacket, my hand closing around the handle of the squirt gun.

I had expected her to react, to attack me. She did turn, and would've charged, if Alexander's magic hadn't struck out at her like a lash.

"The sheep is *mine*." His voice was a harsh caw. His throat might've looked whole, but either it hadn't healed completely, or there was permanent damage.

I didn't know what he was doing, but he somehow froze both the woman and Daniel in mid-motion. They stood, like statues, only their eyes moving. Those eyes followed Alexander's gliding steps as his stalked me across the grass. I kept my head down, and began edging towards the car.

"Stop right there."

I felt his power wash over me, felt him *willing* me to do as he said. But when the power hit the necklace Daniel had given me it scattered, leaving me in possession of my own mind, my own will.

It was then that I had a flash of insight. Daniel hadn't *made* the charm for me. There'd been no time. No, he'd given me *his* charm – the one thing that had protected him from Alexander's power. He'd left himself completely vulnerable to protect me. I knew, too, that if I didn't stop Alexander somehow, we'd both die.

Time seemed to slow. Everything was preternaturally clear. I would have to let Alexander get close enough to use the squirt gun. But if he got that close, with his speed and strength, I'd have almost no chance of survival. I might just be able to wound him, maybe even badly enough for Daniel to finish him off. There'd still be the woman to deal with, but there was nothing I could do about that.

I stayed utterly motionless, barely daring to breathe. He was close now. So close that I could see the glint of moonlight off the buttons of his shirt, smell the scent of old blood on his breath.

"Look at me," he ordered.

I turned, stepping forwards, lifting my head as though to comply, giving him exactly what he expected, right up until the last instant. When I pulled the gun from its hiding place, I aimed for the place where his heart should be, spraying holy water directly into his chest.

He screamed, an unearthly, high-pitched, keening wail that was nearly deafening. His body jerked back and flames erupted from a spreading hole the size of my fist, burning through his ribcage. I could see his lungs move as he tried to draw breath, then saw him raise his fist.

I knew that if that blow landed, I would be dead. But it didn't land. A last squeeze of the trigger took out what was left of his heart, and he collapsed. Flames leaped up from his corpse as though it had been doused in gasoline. The heat was horrendous, and I fell back from it, my arm thrown up to protect my eyes. The stench of burning flesh filled the night, gagging me. Dropping the empty squirt gun, I staggered back, horrified.

By the light of the flickering flames I saw a battle raging. Magic and blows fell like rain, too many, too fast for me to follow.

They were evenly matched – the perfect offence meeting an equally perfect defence. Neither had the upper hand.

In the distance I heard sirens. We were running out of time. I stumbled towards the car, intending to go for the large water pistol in the back seat.

The movement distracted her for barely an instant – just long enough for her to turn her head to make sure I wasn't a threat.

It was enough. Daniel used that moment to lunge forwards, claws extended. I heard the wet tearing of flesh, followed by her scream of rage and despair. She struggled, fought, as he tore the still-beating heart from her chest. She collapsed, like a puppet whose strings had been cut. With a roar of triumph, he threw it onto the still-burning thing that had been Alexander.

Bathed in blood, lit by firelight, the creature that stood before me was completely inhuman. It couldn't be Daniel. And yet, it was.

He turned to me then, slowly, his movements those of a predator that spots easy prey. He took that first step forwards, and a second, and I felt my pulse speed – primal fear making the blood thunder through my veins. I couldn't fight. I had no weapons. I couldn't flee either. All I could do was stand my ground, face the inevitable.

He stopped. I watched him swallow, saw him struggle against the beast that was so much a part of him. It wasn't easy. But slowly, the beast retreated and Daniel returned. When he was fully himself, he disappeared.

Three

I doused the woman's body with the holy water in the gun from the back seat. By the time the cops arrived, all that was left of the vampires was a pair of black burned spots on the grass. Normal human bodies do not burn that completely, nor that fast. But that didn't keep the police from investigating.

Eventually, I was cleared. But it took time: days and weeks. Long nights spent alone.

Daniel was gone. Vanished.

The sensible part of me knew it was for the best. The rest of me mourned his loss, hoped for him to return, if only to retrieve the charm necklace. I told myself I could go on without him – I didn't need him. But I did.

Nearly two months had passed. It was late. I was awake, staring out the window at the moonlight, unable to sleep. My mind was on the night I first met Daniel as I traced my hand absently over the charm I continued to wear around my neck.

"I came to say goodbye. It will never work." His voice was soft. "You're human. I feed on humans. I'm immortal. You're so terribly fragile. Anything could take you, at any time. If any of my kind find out, they'll kill us both. Alexander isn't the only hunter out there. I want you to live."

I turned slowly, letting him see the tears that coursed down my cheeks. "There's existing, and there's living. Without you I'll exist, but it won't be living."

He looked at me then, and I took a chance, met his gaze full on. If the eyes are the windows of the soul, I let him see mine, without any hiding or pretence. "I'd rather have a day with you, than a lifetime without. If time is so precious, do we even dare waste a second?"

It was a long time before he answered. Taking me into his arms, he pulled me close enough that his whisper was a breath of air against my hair. "No, we don't."

Light Through Fog

Holly Lisle

"Can he still see us, Mama? Does he still miss us?"

Sarah tried to keep breathing as she tucked the boys into bed. "Yes, Jim," she whispered. "He'll always be with us. I'll leave the light on," she added, and turned each of their nightstand lamps on low before she switched off the main light and stepped out into the hall. The feel of their hugs lingered around her neck.

She had lost so much – more than she thought she would ever be able to bear. But she still had the boys.

Sarah's mother stood waiting at the top of the stairs. "They're not ready. *You're* not ready. Bring the boys and come back to our house. At least for a few more nights."

Sarah hugged her. "Mom, we'll never be ready. But this is our life now. We have to start living it."

Her mother nodded. "I'm not sure how you're making it through the day. And you know whenever you need your father and me, we'll be there for you. We're . . . so proud of you."

Sarah watched her mother walk down the drive, get into her car, and back out. She stood in the doorway until the red glow of the tail lights faded away at the end of the block.

And then she shuddered and went inside, locking the door behind her.

She smelled flowers. Most of them would still be set out

under the tree, but the funeral director and his crew had carried the indoor arrangements and plants into the house.

Deepest Sympathies.

In Remembrance of Sam.

We love you, Sarah. You can count on us.

You're not alone.

She had never seen so many flowers. Everyone had loved Sam, everyone knew him. He'd been a light in the town, someone who did well at everything but who brought everyone else with him in his triumphs.

Including her.

Everyone had loved Sam.

She'd heard variations on the same theme from her friends and neighbours: as they put casseroles and baked goods into her fridge and her freezer; as they hugged her and wept; as they stood in the kitchen after the funeral and told stories about Sam and how wonderful he had been.

For those short hours while the house was full, while people lingered, she'd thought, "I'll be able to get through this."

But in the vacant rooms, the emptiness echoed. Sam was gone – he whom she had loved since the eighth grade – and this was her new life. She wanted to peek in on the boys. She wanted to cling to them. But Jim was twelve, almost as tall as Sam. Mike was ten, and already taller than her. Growing boys, soon to be grown. She had a few more years with them, and then they would move on to their own lives. She had friends; she had family. But she didn't have Sam.

She wished, when the drunk's car jumped the median and came at him, that she had been in the driver's seat. She could have been. She'd been going to pick up the boys from school and, at the last minute, he'd said he needed to run an errand so he would pick them up instead.

He never made it to the school.

She braved the living room and the flowers and plants, held her breath against the unwelcome sweetness in the air, and took Sam's urn from the mantel.

When darkness fell, when family and friends went home, when the boys went to sleep, the truth was that she was alone. But before she let herself sink back into the endless recrimination of how it *could* have been her and *should* have been her, she had a promise to keep.

Sarah walked out of the back door, carrying Sam's urn in her arms. She locked the door behind her, then walked through the tree-shadowed backyard, her arms dappled by the faint moonlight.

She crossed over the stream that bisected the yard on the little wooden bridge Sam had built for her, and stepped onto their island. The tiny island in the tiny stream had been the reason the two of them had bought this piece of land and eventually built their house on it. The north point of the island was covered with the rest of the flowers from the funeral.

On the island grew the tree under which they had first met, on an eighth-grade end-of-the-year picnic. It had to be 200 years old, a beautiful live oak with enormous spreading branches. Both had climbed the tree unaware of the other – they'd met in the upper branches.

They'd known they were supposed to be together the moment they met. When after getting their bachelors' degrees they got engaged, they bought the land and planned their future home there. They got married and moved into a tiny apartment, and Sam went on to graduate school in architecture. Sarah got a job as a draftsman for a local firm and supported the two of them.

Built into those branches was the tree house Sam had designed and built for her as a belated wedding present ("because you never had one and you always wanted one"). It was his first solo architecture project. He modelled it on the small but exquisite cabins you find on yachts. He'd had friends help him build it on evenings and weekends, but he'd done all the woodwork himself. The result was art.

They'd spent countless summer nights sleeping up there together, feeling the faint sway of the branches, hearing the rustle of the leaves. They'd played there, fought there, made love there. Mike and Jim had been conceived there, as well as the baby they'd lost.

If she'd been forced to choose between living in the house they'd built together later or living in the tree house he'd created for her, she'd have picked the tree house. They'd promised each other that when one of them died, the survivor would place the other's ashes beneath that tree. They'd thought they had another forty years before either of them would have to keep that promise.

She put the urn on the ground and leaned against the oak's rough bark. She'd cried when she identified him in the morgue, she'd cried when she met with the funeral director and she'd cried herself to sleep every night since his death. She had thought herself cried out.

But she hadn't been to the tree. Not until just that moment.

The weight of everything they'd been to each other since the eighth grade hit her with full force; her knees gave way, and she collapsed. Sam's death and her loss suddenly became terribly real. She sobbed and hugged herself. He was gone someplace where she couldn't reach him, couldn't find him, couldn't hold him, and all she had left was ashes.

"Oh, Sam," she whispered. "Oh, Sam, I still need you."

"Oh, Sarah," she heard Sam's voice ask, as if from the other side of the tree, "how could you leave me?"

She froze. A fog had come up and somehow she hadn't noticed. She rose on shaky legs and picked up the urn with Sam's ashes in it. Had she actually heard anything? Was she wishing Sam's voice into the air around her, or was her mind playing tricks on her? Or was someone there?

She gripped the urn tighter, grateful it had a screw-on cap rather than a lid. If someone *was* there, she didn't want to hit the trespasser and send Sam's ashes flying.

In the moon-illuminated fog, she could make out a shape kneeling by the tree. Familiar, that shape. She slipped closer, soundless. Or so she thought.

"Who's there?" He sounded exactly like Sam. He couldn't be Sam, but oh, God, she would have thought she could have recognized Sam's voice out of all the voices in the world. Was she just hearing what she wanted to hear?

"Who are you?" she asked. Her voice quavered.

The shape in the shadows froze. Like a deer in headlights, she thought.

"You . . . sound like Sarah," he said.

"That's because I *am* Sarah," she said, "and you're trespassing on private property. You need to leave. Now."

He stepped forwards, saying, "My wife died, and I don't know who you are."

They saw each other's faces at the same time as a gust of wind tattered the fog.

The urn slipped from Sarah's fingers and crashed to the ground. She heard the dull thud of something heavy hitting the ground by his feet too. She took a step towards him, not breathing – not *daring* to breathe – and reached out a hand to touch his cheek. It was warm. Rough with end-of-the-day stubble. Solid.

In all the world, in all her life, there had only ever been him. She knew what was happening was impossible, but she also knew that this was Sam. Her Sam. Somehow . . . and she didn't care how.

Nor did he.

He touched her hair, and his hand stroked it as it always had. She bowed her head and leaned into the pressure, willing the dream not to end, willing her confusion to stay because for that moment she had him again, even if she was hallucinating, even if she was going crazy.

When he pulled her close and kissed her, she didn't let herself ask questions. This was a gift. No matter how real it wasn't, it was a gift. It was the goodbye she hadn't got, the goodbye ripped from her by the telephone calls from the school where the boys wanted to know where she was, and from her RN friend Judy telling her that she needed to get to the hospital.

Sam kissed her, and she kissed him back. There were five days of hell and desperation and yearning and despair in that kiss.

"Oh, God," he whispered, and pulled away from her. But he wasn't leaving. He took her hand and led her towards the ladder up to the tree house, and she beat him to it. She launched herself up to the platform, through the door and onto the futon that had been there since he designed and built the place.

He was right behind her. They didn't talk. It was as if he knew he was a dream, as if he understood that this was all going to go away. For that moment, they were solid and real, and with only whispered "I love you"s, they undressed, and took each other – two starving people presented with one last banquet before a forced march into the desert of the rest of their lives.

Making love with him was what it had always been: wild, unexpected, an adventure. But this time, the desperation was so clear, the knowledge that it was the last time so poignant, that Sarah found herself weeping. When they were spent, she touched Sam's face again and felt his tears wet on his cheeks.

She lay beside him after, her hand on his belly, feeling him breathing. "It's hell without you," she said.

"You should have let me go get them," he whispered. "Then I would have died instead of you."

"I *did* let you," she told him. "That's why the boys and I are alone now. They would have been so much better off with you."

"The kids *are* with me. And they're falling apart without you."

They lay in the dark, now turned to face each other. She could barely make out the planes of his face. "Sam," she said carefully, "your funeral was today. I have your ashes in an urn at the base of our tree. You . . . aren't real."

"The urn is there," he said. "But the ashes are yours. I kept our promise. I brought you back here."

They sat up, and some stupid flicker of hope shivered to life in Sarah's chest. "What is this, Sam?"

"I don't know." He touched her shoulder, her breast, rubbed his thumb against her chin. "I don't know. But if it means I get to keep you, I don't care."

"How can it? How can it be anything but me losing my mind?"

"I'll *be* crazy if it means I get to keep you."

She smiled. It was the first time since the phone call from the hospital, and it was because that comment was so purely Sam.

She looked out the tree-house window. Fog blocked her view of the house. "You think they'll be all right?"

He hugged her. "The doors are locked. I have the keys. The kids will be fine."

Sarah had the keys, too. They were in the pocket of her blue jeans, lying crumpled on the floor next to his.

He was right. They would be fine.

So they lay in each other's arms, talking, laughing, happy, while the night passed them by.

Sarah woke to sunrise peeking through the tree house's east windows. Sam yawned and stretched. "I watched you sleeping for a while," he said. "Just because I could."

Sarah nuzzled his chest and laughed. "I didn't mean to fall asleep at all. But I haven't been sleeping well since . . ." She shook her head and touched him. "You're still here. How?"

He pressed a finger to her lips. "Don't ask. Just accept this, whatever it is."

"How do we explain this to everyone?"

"We'll think of something." He pulled her close. "I don't know what, but something. The kids and your parents and your friends will be happy to have you back. They were devastated."

Yours were, she thought, not mine, but she didn't say anything. It brought up events and images she needed to push from her mind.

"I love you," she told him. She was sombre again. She had sometimes taken him for granted. Had forgotten how wonderful he was. She had never realized how the world without him in it didn't hold enough air. She would never take him for granted again.

"They're going to be up soon," Sam said. "We should get back so they don't wake up to an empty house. They have no idea how things have changed."

She sighed. "You're right." They rose and dressed, slowed a little by the fact that neither of them could keep from touching the other.

When they climbed down the ladder, Sarah caught a glimpse of the urn on the ground, still half-hidden in fog.

"Don't look at that," Sam said. "That isn't us."

They turned towards the bridge, and the fog-wreathed shapes of the flowers on their many tripods confronted both of them, rows of monsters marching through the mist.

Sarah said, "We'll get rid of them."

Sam wrapped an arm around her shoulders. "The next few weeks are probably going to be rough," he told her.

She arched an eyebrow. "As rough as the next forty years would have been?"

He laughed and kissed her. "Nothing could be that rough."

They clasped hands and smiled at each other, and stepped onto the bridge together . . .

. . . and he was gone.

He did not gradually fade, he did not dim or slip away from her with a warning. His hand was warm and strong and callused in hers, and then it was gone.

Sarah faltered in mid-step, stumbled, and screamed, "Sam!"

She turned back to the island to discover no Sam. The floral arrangements on their stands now stood in crisp detail, the urn lay toppled on its side where she had dropped it the night before. "Sam!" she shouted again. She ran back to the tree house and climbed into it. The futon was folded up the way they'd left it, with no sign that anyone had spent the night there. The hand-rubbed oak floor bore no forgotten article of his clothing or hers. There was nothing that had fallen into a corner, no sign that anything had changed.

"Sam?" she whispered. "Come back."

But he did not.

Her hands started to shake.

She took a deep breath and forced herself to go back down the ladder, to walk across the bridge again, and to unlock the back door and let herself into the house. She kept her shoulders straight and her chin up. She forced herself to breathe in and out slowly.

One foot in front of the other. Up the stairs. Wake the boys. I can do this.

I have to do this.

I dreamed it. Or I hallucinated it.

The flowers in the living room are real. The ashes in the urn are real.

Last night wasn't real.

Sarah walked over the bridge every night for two months, knowing her one last perfect night with Sam had been a trick of her mind, but hoping against hope that it hadn't been. Hope died hard.

But it did die.

She marked the moment of its death in her memory.

"Up," she told Jim, who was curled under his blankets, his head under the pillow, just one bare foot hanging over the side of the bed.

Mike, who had been in the boys' bathroom, came out and said, "He doesn't want to go to school today. I don't either."

Sarah said, "You have to. You know your dad wouldn't have wanted the two of you to end up in trouble for skipping school."

And then Mike looked at her, eyes narrowed. "Are you all right?"

"I haven't been sleeping too well," she told him.

"You look . . . kind of sick, Mom. You need to eat more. And get some rest."

"I haven't been eating much, either."

But it was more than that. When she saw the boys onto the bus, she stepped on the scale again, wanting the news to be good. But she was down eighteen pounds from the day Sam died, and it wasn't just because she wasn't eating. She was dizzy all the time, weak and queasy. She couldn't eat: she could barely drink. She couldn't stay awake. Her lower abdomen hurt and it was bloated. Her back hurt. Everything hurt.

She'd tried to tell herself it was grief, but her symptoms kept getting worse.

So she made the appointment with Dr Gruber and kept it. He was a family friend, and had been her doctor since she was in her early teens. He'd watched her and Sam grow up. He'd attended the funeral. She had a pretty good idea what was going wrong, but he would help her figure out what to do.

Ben Gruber looked at her over the top of her chart and said, "You told Beth you're afraid you have ovarian cancer?" He studied her chart while she sat on the exam table.

She nodded, unable to say those words aloud to him.

"You've lost eighteen pounds in two months." He shook his head. "Not good. But not unheard of after the death of a loved one."

"I know. But I've been eating. It's just that everything comes back up. I can barely stomach broth."

"Sleeping?"

"All the time during the day. Not much at night, though I'm exhausted even then. It's just that . . . Sam's gone, and at night, I hear everything."

She lay on the bench while he listened to her heart and lungs with a stethoscope.

"You've been feeling like this for how long?"

"Since Sam died."

"The vomiting and abdominal pain, too? The bloating?"

"No, the vomiting and pain both started not long after the funeral. The bloating and the having to go to the bathroom all the time are more recent." She said "Ouch," as he pressed his fingers into her lower abdomen. "All the symptoms have been getting worse."

"You've already had blood drawn and we'll screen that for cancer markers. Your ovaries aren't enlarged," he told her, "but I want to do an ultrasound of your uterus. It's bigger than it should be. You might have fibroids. They're not that unusual for a woman your age who's had children. And you have no family history of cancer, Sarah." He gave her a reassuring smile. "So don't assume the worst.

She nodded. She'd spent time on the internet researching symptoms. The only things she could figure out that it might be were ovarian or uterine cancer. But Dr Gruber was right. It was easy to assume the worst when diagnosing yourself on the internet. She would let him tell her.

Beth, Dr Gruber's nurse, came in to be present while he did the ultrasound. Sarah winced at the cold gel, and watched his face when he turned the screen away from her.

Beth stood beside her. "Just relax," she said. "And breathe." Beth held Sarah's hand, but she didn't say, *Everything will be OK*.

Because, Sarah thought, it wouldn't. They could just look at her and see something was wrong, that she was dying.

Sarah couldn't see the screen, so she kept her eyes on Dr Gruber's face, which was why she saw his fleeting expression of shock and dismay before he schooled his expression to the careful neutrality she guessed doctors practised in front of mirrors when no one was looking.

"How bad is it?" she asked.

His eyes were fixed on the screen, while his hand moved the ultrasound probe over her lower abdomen in tiny, tiny circles.

"How bad?" she repeated.

He didn't look at her. "It's not cancer," he said softly. "And it's not fibroids."

"It's worse?" she whispered, still seeing that shocked expression that had flitted across his face, and wondering what could be worse than cancer.

He still wouldn't look at her, and her breath caught in her throat. Instead, he stared down at the floor. "You're pregnant, Sarah."

She was so startled, she laughed out loud, and he turned to stare at her. "Pregnant?" She shook her head. "Twenty years you've been my doctor, and that's the first funny thing I've ever heard you say."

But he didn't smile. His eyes didn't meet hers.

"Wait. You're serious? You think I'm pregnant?"

"I know you're pregnant," he told her. "I can see the heartbeat. I can see the baby. You're about two months pregnant."

Dr Gruber kept one hand fixed firmly on her abdomen, and carefully turned the ultrasound around so Sarah could see the screen. She knew what to look for, and she didn't need to have the baby pointed out to her. She could see the tiny heart beating, could see the blurry curved shape of the child within her.

She was pregnant.

He did a screen capture, took the ultrasound, and then handed her a towel to wipe the gel off her belly. "Thank you, Beth," he said.

Beth let go of Sarah's hand, nodded and left.

When the door closed behind her, Sarah stared at the picture Dr Gruber printed out, brow furrowed. "This is impossible. Sam had a vasectomy. And there has never been anyone but Sam."

She looked up to find him watching her, his expression distant. "I *did* the vasectomy," he said. She heard the coldness in his voice. "This happened right when he died, Sarah. Could have been a few days before, could have been a few days after."

She sat up and pulled the paper examination gown down, not liking the tone in his voice or the flat disbelief in his eyes. "There has never – not once – been anyone but Sam. Not for any reason, not for one minute."

Dr Gruber looked at her. "Then how do you explain the pregnancy?"

"You screwed up the vasectomy." She wasn't smiling when she said it.

"A vasectomy that worked just fine for you two for . . . what, ten years? Vasectomies have sometimes reversed themselves," he admitted. "But the odds of Sam's doing so and of you getting pregnant at the exact time that he died, when there are so many simpler explanations . . ."

Her hands knotted into fists. "There are *no* simpler explanations. There are *no other* explanations at all. I fell in love with Sam in eighth grade. I never dated anyone else, I never kissed anyone else and I sure as hell never slept with anyone else. So unless you're going to try to convince me that immaculate conception is more likely than a vasectomy reversal, or that people really do get pregnant off of public toilet seats, then we have one, and only one, theory to work with."

He dropped it, changed the subject. "Your third pregnancy was bad. It nearly killed you. This one could finish the job. You've had a recent trauma. You're not handling this pregnancy well. You need to consider terminating. For your sake, and for the boys' sake."

She slid carefully off the exam table, tucking the paper gown tight around her backside. "Thank you for letting me know that I'm not dying. And thank you for ruining the first good thing to happen to me since Sam died."

On the way home, she bought a pregnancy test, and she checked for herself. Yes, she had the ultrasound picture, but the blue stripe on the stick was the ritual. It was the way she should have found out.

She still had her stick from Mike, she still had her stick from Jim – both carefully labelled with the names she'd called them when they were still unknowns. Aloisius. Bob. She still had the stick from the miscarried baby, too. Sam.

She should never have put the baby's real name on the stick. But they had found out early she was going to be a girl. They had decided to name her Samantha. And Sarah hadn't been able to resist putting the real name on that stick.

Now Sarah had a fourth blue stripe, and the stripe on the stick made the pregnancy more real than the ultrasound had.

She was going to have a baby.

She had to sit down, and not because she was queasy, or because she was exhausted. She had to think.

There had never been anyone but Sam.

And Sam had a vasectomy after they lost Samantha, and after Sarah nearly died, too.

But . . .

But . . .

But . . .

She closed her eyes. She had one night she couldn't explain. One night out of an entire lifetime where she was not sure what had really happened. The night of the funeral, up in the tree house, with fog thick on the island and Sam holding her in his arms, they had made love.

She knew it hadn't been real, except she was pregnant.

And what if?

What if, the day he'd talked her into him going to pick up the boys, she had prevailed and *she* had gone? What if, in that moment, something had twisted in the universe, so that both possibilities actually happened? In one, Sam lived. In one, she lived.

It could have happened the same way after the miscarriage. In his "if", she'd had the surgery and had her tubes tied. In her "if", he'd had the vasectomy.

And when he had died in her world, and she had died in his, something connected them together again, out on the island, beneath the tree. Some need, some desperation, some call between them.

And now she faced being pregnant alone, knowing that the pregnancy could kill her. She was going to have to tell her mother and father, she was going to have to tell the boys, she was going to have to tell her friends. All of them were going to be horrified. They were going to point out that she had almost died last time.

Her parents and Sam's parents and her friends would worry about her, remembering the disaster of the last pregnancy. They would tell her to abort, to think of the boys and what would happen to them if they lost their mother too.

They would have a point.

But the baby was Sam's baby.

The last piece of him she had.

She was keeping the baby. She would take vitamins and eat plenty of fruit and rest whenever she needed it and she would take care of herself and not do too much. She would let her family and friends do things for her, and for once she would not try to be Superwoman.

Somewhere close enough that she had touched him, Sam was still alive. They were having a baby.

And, oh God, she needed him.

That night, she tucked the boys into bed and she locked up the house. She walked through the backyard, over the bridge and onto the island. The air was crisp with the first autumn chill, the flowers and their stands were gone, the urn sat at the base of the tree on the little pedestal she'd bought for it. She didn't do more than glance at it.

She leaned against the tree, her forehead to the rough bark, and she whispered, "Sam, I don't know if you can hear me. I don't know how to reach you. But I'm here, and I need you. I need you so much."

She waited, but he didn't come.

She felt sick. The pregnancy, her fear and her need for him all weighed on her. She'd promised herself that she would stay all night if she had to. But she didn't have the strength to spend all night leaning against a tree, and the cold was biting into her.

If she climbed into the tree house and he came, he wouldn't know she was there.

But they had the lanterns.

She climbed into the tree house, stopping twice to catch her breath, and made her way from the balcony into the interior. She went to the cabinet where they stored the lanterns, pulled one out and lit it, then hung it in the window that faced the house. He might see it if he looked out of the kitchen window; he might as he came over the bridge. If the magic let him.

She sat on the futon, a blanket wrapped around her and she rested her hands on her belly, on the baby. She prayed that he would see the lantern. And she waited.

"Who's up there?"

The voice sounded far away, but it was shouting and angry. Sarah woke and realized she'd fallen asleep. For a moment she was confused. She wasn't in her bed. She was in the tree house, the lantern was still burning and tendrils of fog were curling around the windows.

But her hands were still curved over her belly, and she remembered. Her breath caught in her throat. "Sam?" she shouted.

"Sarah?"

She heard feet on the ladder and, an instant later, he came through the door. Sam. Sam alive, with the fog swirling in behind him. They held each other, and wept, and kissed. But this time neither of them hurried to turn the futon into a bed. This time, they had to talk, and both of them knew it.

"I saw the light from the house, coming through fog on the island," he said. "But . . . it was real? You're real?"

"I don't think I can prove I'm real to you. I know you proved you're real to me. I'm pregnant."

He stared at her. "After Samantha, you had your tubes tied."

"Samantha?" she whispered. "We lost Samantha. She . . . I had a miscarriage almost five months in, and nearly died. She didn't make it. You had a vasectomy a month later."

He thought about that for a long time without saying anything. That was Sam. She watched his face, watched him working through the different connections, how all the pieces fitted, the same way he'd designed houses and office buildings. Carefully, methodically, he was putting things together, visualizing how they worked, seeing actions and consequences. She waited. As she'd always waited.

"So you're pregnant and I had a vasectomy. And there are going to be people who know you who know that."

She nodded. "Dr Gruber tested me today because I thought I

was dying: ovarian cancer, uterine cancer, something like that. He found out I was pregnant, and when I told him it could only have been you, he didn't believe me."

"He doesn't matter. How are you?"

"Lots of morning sickness and I've lost weight."

"I noticed. Let the kids . . . let the *boys* help you out." He rested his hand on her belly, and pressed his face against her hair. "We're still us, Sarah. You and me. But different. Slightly different pasts, very different futures. You're gone in my world, and the kids are lost without you. I'm lost without you."

"I know. I can't sleep at night."

"But . . . where you are . . . I left you taken care of?"

She nodded. "Everything's paid for. The investment accounts are still growing, the college trusts are fine, the passive income's fine. We'll be all right. But, Sam, it's like I can't breathe without you."

"How can I be here for you? I've tried to get back to you every night since that night. This is the first night I've made it. And I don't know why I made it, what I did, what you did, how to make it happen again." He took her hands in his and said, "If I could, I'd bring the kids here and hire someone to deliver food and I'd never leave this place again."

"I know. But could we bring the kids? Could they meet themselves?"

"I doubt it. I can't figure out how we can both be here. I can't figure out how this works."

"We're supposed to be together," she said. "We were always supposed to be together, and we both knew it."

"We still know it. Maybe that's the . . . the magic that makes this work." He closed his eyes. "Or maybe you were supposed to have Samantha, and you got this second chance, and once she's born you'll never be able to get back here again."

Sarah said, "I don't want to think of that."

He hugged her. "Sarah, know that whether I can touch you or not, whether you can see me or not, I am with you every minute of every day. And I can't leave the kids alone every night, but I'll come out here for a little while and light the lantern. Look for it at twilight. If you can see it, and if you can get out here, come."

She buried her head in his chest and he wrapped his arms around her. And finally they did fold down the futon and they made love.

The pale pink of dawn woke them both. He lay looking at her, tracing his finger along the tiny scar on her chin. "Where you fell off your bike," he said. "When you were twelve."

"Before we met." She ran her hand over the surgical scar on his left knee. "The end of your budding hockey career when you were seventeen."

"So much is the same," he said. "I know you. My heart and soul know you, and you're not some different Sarah. You're *you*. Only . . ."

"Only in your world I'm dead, so I can't really be your Sarah. And in my world you're dead, so you can't really be my Sam. I've been asking myself the same question you're asking yourself. Am I cheating on you with you? Is being here with you wrong?"

He touched the wedding band on her finger. "I gave you that ring," he said. "I promised to love and honour and cherish you until death parted us. And you're right here, not dead. So am I. I meant it then, Sarah, and I mean it now. *How* might matter to your family, or mine, or to our friends, but I don't give a damn about *how*. We found each other, we're together the way we should be and I'll do whatever I can to be with you as much as I can."

When, hand in hand, they stepped onto the bridge together, he vanished again, and again her heart cried out.

But this time was different. This time she knew he'd been real. And if she was alone in her world, she still had him in *their* world, tiny as it was.

Her mother said, "You're pregnant! How *could* you?" Her father turned away from her, shame and disgust on his face. Her friends, knowing about Sam's vasectomy, asked her, "Who's the father?" and eyed their own husbands with sudden distrust. She told them the truth and they didn't believe her. When she refused to have an abortion, her parents stopped speaking to her and her friends suddenly had their cell phones turned off.

The boys were supportive, if a little stunned, when she told them.

Every night for five months, Sarah looked for the light in the tree house window, and every night it wasn't there.

She took pictures of the boys, had them take pictures of her and her swelling belly, and she put the pictures into scrapbooks. She made no secret of the fact that she was storing the pictures in the tree house. "To keep them close to your dad," she told the boys. When Sam came again, she wanted to be able to show him.

She didn't tell them *that*.

She had a hard time with the pregnancy, but not as hard as she'd had with the baby she lost. She managed to gain a little weight.

She had never been so alone.

But she was sleeping nights. Sam was with her in spirit, and she went out to the tree and sat by the urn and talked to him. She told him about the boys. She knew that he was telling her about them and about Samantha, who in his world had lived.

Sometimes Mike and Jim went out and sat beside her while she talked. Sometimes one or the other would go out to the tree alone.

"He's always with us," she told them. "He will always love us."

Sarah made it through the long days and the lonely nights. He was out there. He was with her. She did not doubt him, and she did not lose faith.

She was standing sideways at the kitchen sink, washing the dishes around the huge obstacle of her belly, when she looked out the back window and saw the light in the tree house.

It was too early to send the boys to bed. It was, however, Friday night. She told them, "I'm going out to the tree house to talk to your dad for a while. You two can watch TV until midnight, and then go on to bed." She looked them in the eye. "I'm counting on both of you."

Mike hugged her. "We won't let you down. Or Dad. You're not alone, Mom."

Jim nodded agreement.

She hugged them. "Thank you. Thanks for being people your dad and I can both be proud of."

The boys locked up. She hurried out the door and across the bridge and into the fog. "Sam?" she called.

He burst out onto the balcony. "You're here!"

"I am. But I can't get up the ladder any more."

"I'll come down."

He touched her belly, and held her as close as he could. The baby kicked him, and he said, "I knew you'd see the light tonight."

"How?"

"I found all your scrapbooks. I was up there looking at pictures of you and the boys. They look just the same. But the hole where Samantha should be—" He pulled out his wallet and opened it and showed her pictures he had taken of the boys and Samantha. The boys were exactly the same. Samantha was beautiful.

"How are you holding up? Everyone helping you out?" he asked.

"Your parents and my parents aren't speaking to me because they think I cheated on you, my friends have dumped me because they think I cheated on you and they suspect their own husbands." She shrugged. "The boys have been wonderful though. And we're fine, all three of us. I come out to talk to you every day. I can feel you here."

"That's because I am here. I do the same thing."

She touched his arm. "Just knowing you're here, that you're alive, even if you can't be with me all the time, has been enough to keep me going." She laughed. "I sometimes wonder if we ever talk about the same things, or answer each other."

"Of course we do. Sometimes I can almost hear you. When you could still climb into the tree house, you sat on the futon and talked to me. You always sat on the left?"

"That's because you always sat on the right," Sarah told him, and they looked at each other and smiled.

He held her hand. "Sometimes, when we're sitting there, I reach out and take your hand," he said.

"I can feel you." She took a deep breath. "You know this is going to be the last night for a while," she said, suddenly realizing the truth of that. "I can't get into the tree house any more and, when the baby is born, I won't be able to come out at night at all."

"I'll still come," he said. "I'll still light a light every night. If you can slip away even for a few minutes, I'll be here."

Sarah made it through labour and delivered a healthy baby girl. She did not name the baby Samantha. Samantha was her daughter, and alive, if not with her. Instead, she named their daughter Magie, which was German for "magic".

Before she and the baby and the boys rode home in the taxi, she had the hospital do DNA tests on all three children. The results when she received them proved what she already knew: the baby was a full sibling to both boys – was hers and Sam's. She photocopied the results and mailed them to her friends, to her parents, to Sam's parents and to Dr Gruber, writing a note at the bottom of each: "DNA proof. The baby is mine and Sam's. Don't phone; don't drop by. I just wanted you to know I was telling the truth."

She raised her children, and loved them, and she watched every night for the light through fog.

When Magie was old enough, she took her and sat in the tree house while she fed her. And Sarah talked to Sam, and showed Magie pictures of the father who could not be with her, even though he loved her.

Magie grew, and the boys grew, and Sarah took pictures, and kept scrapbooks religiously. She shared them with Sam and, through his pictures, watched the Samantha she had yearned for and never known become a lovely woman.

When the boys went off to college and Magie was in school, Sarah took a painting course in watercolours and oils. She made a new friend, a woman a few years younger than her who hadn't grown up in the same town, hadn't gone to the same schools and didn't know all the same people. The two of them shared outsiders' lives, and enjoyed their camaraderie with each other. For Sarah, that one friendship, plus her children (and eventually her grandchildren) and Sam, made for a full life.

The children stayed in touch with both sets of grandparents, but there was no real closeness there. None of the four, her parents or Sam's, ever apologized for doubting her, and she could never forget how they had abandoned her when she and the children needed them.

Sometimes, for no reason either Sam or Sarah was able to discern, they both made it through whatever barrier it was that separated them, and they rejoiced in the few hours they stole from the universe.

So the years passed.

So a lifetime passed.

One day Mike, grown and with children and grandchildren of his own, stopped by the house because no one had answered the phone all day. In one universe he found his mother sitting on the left side of the futon she had refused to let him and his siblings replace, her right hand stretched out as if she had been holding someone's hand. She had taken her last breath some hours earlier. She was eighty-three. On the same day, behind a different door, in another "if", Mike found his father sitting on the right side of the futon, his left hand stretched out as if he had been holding someone's hand. He was eighty-four.

Mike called his brother and sister, and he called an ambulance.

On the day of the funeral, the children and grandchildren and the great-grandchildren gathered on the little island, and mixed Sam's and Sarah's ashes into the same urn. It seemed the only right thing to do. Neither of them had ever loved anyone but the other.

They were not alone. They had never been alone.

Sam and Sarah, young again, reunited, held hands and watched the families they had created and raised together and apart. And when the island emptied, they smiled at each other. "On that side, this moment seemed like such a long wait," Sarah said.

"I forgot how short that time truly is," Sam said, and pulled her into his arms. "I forgot you would be here when I got here."

"I forgot too," she said. "Everything there is like light through fog. You only see a little, you only understand a little, and it isn't until you cross the bridge that it all becomes clear."

They walked over the bridge of light, their hands clasped.

This time, nothing separated them.

The Tuesday Enchantress

A Guardian Story

Mary Jo Putney

It was just after 2 a.m. on a warm Tuesday morning when I stumbled into the corner deli and croaked, "Gimme a triple espresso mocha latte and make it fast!"

My pal and classmate Rajiv, who was minding the store for his grandparents, glanced up from his textbook. At this hour, he could get almost as much studying done in the deli as he would at home. "It might be malpractice to give you a triple when you already look like nine miles of bad road. Maybe you should try gettin' some sleep?"

Even after years of being friends, I smiled at the contrast between Rajiv's Indian face and his Texas accent. He'd saved my bacon when I returned to school after a couple of years of bumming around. I'd lost the habit of study, and it was Rajiv who helped whip my brain into academic shape again. "I'll sleep when finals are over."

He set aside his book and crossed to an espresso machine so big and fancy that it seemed like it should do more than just make coffee. "Don't worry, Charlie, you'll ace the exams. You always do."

"Only because I study so much I have no life." I waited impatiently until he gave me the tall, foaming cup. After slurping some whipped cream off the top, I started chugging the latte. Two swallows and I started to feel alive again. "Fat, chocolate and triple caffeine," I said contentedly. "What more can a desperate student want?"

Rajiv pulled a couple of hot samosas out of the warming case and handed them to me. "Some protein would be good. And then maybe a scone or three."

I thanked him through a mouthful of samosa. He made a cappuccino for himself – only a single shot, the wimp – and I decided I would survive this last exam after all. While I chewed, I surveyed the empty deli.

Spotlessly clean, the small place was jam-packed with corner-store staples, the espresso bar and a small but excellent selection of fresh edibles. This being New York City, there was every-thing from pastrami to burritos to stuffed grape leaves. The Guptas' deli had kept me from starving for years. "Sure is quiet tonight."

"It's Tuesday night. Nothing ever happens on Tuesday nights," Rajiv said authoritatively. "They're great for study-ing."

A chime rang as the door opened. I glanced over, then stopped in mid-bite. "That is the hottest chick I've ever seen," I said softly, speaking under my breath so she wouldn't come over and deck me for the sexist comment.

Rajiv studied her. "Nice looking, but not spectacular. Unless she has the keys to your DNA, and judging by your expression, she does." I could hear the grin in his voice.

She was tallish, with a nice figure, dark hair pulled back simply at her nape, a reserved expression, and a profile that belonged on an ancient coin. I couldn't see her eyes since she was frowning at the rack of packaged cookies. Technically, Rajiv was right. She looked damned good in jeans and a tweed blazer, but she wasn't a raging beauty. Nonetheless, she made me want to roll on my back and wave my paws in the air.

"OK, she's not exactly a hot chick," I conceded. "She's the kind of girl you want to take home to mother and, if you manage that, your mom says 'You finally did something right, Char-lie.'"

"Either you've gone nuts from studying and caffeine, or you'd better go over and introduce yourself right now," Rajiv remarked as he ambled back to the counter.

There was a mirror over the espresso machine. The reflection was discouraging. Tall and a little underfed, I'm average looking at best, and I wasn't at my best just now. My hair hadn't been cut in way too long, I hadn't shaved in a week and my mom would burn my battered sweats if I was ever fool enough to wear them home. The hot chick would probably call the cops if I tried to talk to her.

Tentatively I reached out with my power to see if I could get a reading on her. I was immediately slammed with a magical blow fiercer than a physical punch. I gasped. My God, the hot chick was a Guardian, like me!

Guardians are families where magic runs strong. The families have been around since time began, near as anyone knows. We're human, but with some special abilities. Our elders train us to use them conservatively, to help people, not just to accumulate wealth and power for ourselves. Most of us have regular jobs and regular lives. We're encouraged to marry other Guardians to keep the power strong, but I'd never met a female Guardian who made me think of orange blossoms and cottages with picket fences.

The hot chick whipped her head up when I tried to read her. Her quick scan of the store passed over Rajiv and landed on me with a scowl that would freeze the whiskers off a brass cat. So I walked over to her. "You're a Guardian," I said softly. "So am I."

Her expression chilled another couple of degrees. "Then you should know better than to probe someone without permission." Her voice was somewhere between whisky and velvet, her accent was educated British, and her eyes were a dazzling shade of honey gold. If she asked me to lie down so she could walk over me, I'd do it.

"I'm sorry. I didn't know you'd be able to sense that." I gave her my best, earnest nice-guy look. "You were so beautiful I had to know more."

You'd think a sincere compliment might soften her a bit, but no dice. She looked like she wanted to whack me with a package of cookies. "Good*night*, Mr Owens." She had a lot of power to be able to pick up my name when she zapped me.

"What's your name?" When her brows arched, I said reasonably, "I'm sure you don't want me to be thinking of you as the Hot Chick."

For an instant, I thought she'd crack a smile, but instead she said frostily, "Maggie Macrae. That's Ms Macrae to you."

A Guardian, all right. The Macraes were one of the best-known British families. As she brushed past me, I asked, "What's your strongest ability?"

"Shielding." She pivoted and crossed to the counter with long, graceful strides.

No kidding – her shields were blocking me cold. I sighed, regretful but not resigned. Now that I'd met her and knew she was a Guardian, I could find her again.

Maggie pulled out her wallet to pay for the cookies. "Do you ever have British biscuits like McVitie's chocolate digestives?" The smile she gave Rajiv was dazzling.

"No, but I could order some if you want to come back in a few days," Rajiv said enthusiastically. Though she might not have as much impact on him as she did on me, he wasn't immune to that killer smile.

She pursed her lips – her ripe, full, kissable lips – and said, "I shall be in New York for some time, so if you could order four boxes, I'd be most grateful. Will they be in by Monday?" I could listen to her gorgeous voice and accent all night. And if Rajiv put the moves on her, I'd *kill* him.

Before he could reply, three guys who looked like your worst nightmare came in waving guns. "This is a stick-up!" one yelled as he shot out the security camera in a blaze of bullets. As glass shards rained down, another snarled, "Give us the money!"

The robbers were young, and I could see from their wild eyes that they were sky-high on some kind of drug that made them hyper and stupid. A headline flashed through my mind: SHOP-KEEPER AND TWO CUSTOMERS MURDERED IN BURGLARY! Thank God I wasn't clairvoyant – that was fear talking, not a pre-monition.

The lead guy, a hulk with a tacky little goatee, spotted me and Maggie Macrae. "Put yer hands up and get over to the counter," he ordered with a wave of his gun: some kind of big, mean-looking semi-automatic.

I raised my hands and edged towards the counter very slowly.

I tried to look harmless, which wasn't much of a stretch. Maggie did the same.

"No problem, man," Rajiv said peacefully. "You can have all the money in the register. I'll open it for you."

He reached for the cash drawer. The robber who had shot out the camera, a short guy with bare, tattoo-covered arms, shouted, "He's going for a gun!"

The tallest guy fired a long blast of bullets, the noise ear-numbing in the small space. The slugs slammed into Rajiv. He pitched sideways, his glasses flying and gouts of blood spurting horribly over his yellow "Buddha Rocks!" T-shirt.

Maggie screamed, and three guns swivelled towards us. The barrels looked like the Grand Canyon. I dived for the floor, dragging her down and shielding her with my body as best I could. Guardian magic can do a lot of things, but it won't stop hot lead.

Maggie felt soft and indignant under me, but was smart enough not to struggle. Guardians have sometimes been persecuted as witches over the centuries, and the ones who survived long enough to procreate knew how to duck and cover.

A couple of bullets splintered the counter above my head before Goatee Guy growled, "Stop shooting, Shark! Someone will call the cops."

My guess was that Rajiv already had, using a foot switch under the counter. God, Rajiv! My stomach churned. He was an only child. His death would destroy his parents and grand-parents.

Maybe he wasn't dead yet. Keeping my voice soft and unthreatening, I raised my head. "I'm a doctor. Will you let me look at the clerk?"

Tattoo Man said incredulously, "This loser is a doctor?"

The third guy, Shark, said in a jittery voice, "We should shoot 'em all and get the hell out of here while we can."

Maggie said from her position flat on her stomach, "Charles won't cause any trouble." Her voice was as persuasive as honey poured over a bear. "If he can keep the clerk from bleeding to death, it's better for everyone."

Goatee Guy gestured towards Rajiv with his gun. "OK, but don't try nothin'! Shark, break open the cash register. When you've got the cash, we'll take what these two have." His gaze lingered on Maggie in a way that made me nervous.

I moved to Rajiv's side. Blood everywhere, but he was still breathing. I'd had my share of rotations in the ER, so I shut my mind to the knowledge that one of my best friends was bleeding out. This was just another crime victim. Start by figuring out how bad the damage was.

I ripped his T-shirt open from neck to waist. There were three bullet holes, one just a graze across the top of his shoulder, no big deal.

His eyes flickered open. "Don't get creeped out if you fail, Charlie," he whispered unsteadily. "Remember I'm Hindu. I get . . . to reincarnate." His eyes drifted shut again.

What kind of loon cracks jokes at a time like this?

The best kind.

Two of the bullets had gone into his chest. Either could kill him. I closed my eyes and skimmed my hands above the wounds, feeling the catastrophic damage to muscle, bone, nerves and blood vessels.

But the wounds weren't quite lethal, if I could repair the worst of the damage in time. "Maggie, get over here," I ordered. "I need help applying pressure."

She joined me in kneeling by Rajiv's side. After a wary glance at the thugs, she turned away and hunched over Rajiv. I felt the buzz as she generated a minor spell to reduce their interest in her.

"Do you have a clean handkerchief or anything like that?" I asked.

"Who carries handkerchiefs these days?" Looking a little green at the amount of gore splashed around, Maggie reached over to a rack of miscellaneous grooming and toiletry products to our left. It took her only a moment to crack open a package that contained a shoe polishing kit.

After handing me the folded polishing cloth, she opened a second package. A *smart*, hot chick. I really hoped we both survived this so I could persuade her that I was worth knowing. As I used the folded fabric to compress the worst of the bullet holes, I said, "Press on that other wound. And please don't faint."

She managed an uneven smile as she set the second polishing cloth on the other wound and leaned on it with the heel of her hand. "I won't."

As Shark noisily smashed the cash register, she breathed into my ear in a voice so soft only a Guardian could hear it, "You're really a doctor?"

"Yeah, if I pass the final exams I'm taking this week. I'm also a Guardian healer. But my specialty is disease and infection and that sort of thing, not surgery and trauma." I closed my eyes as I concentrated on Rajiv's torn vena cava, the most lethal of his injuries. When I had the structure clearly in my mind, I poured energy around the tear, pulling the ragged edges together . . .

Damn, I couldn't quite get it! The pieces slid out of my control.

I tried again, then again. Still couldn't repair the damage, and time – as well as Rajiv's blood – was running out fast. "I need more energy, Maggie. Drop those shields and touch my hand so I can borrow some power."

She started to protest, then shut up and spread her fingers so her right little finger touched the outside of my left hand. I could feel her shields go down, and also felt how much she hated doing it.

Sharing energy like this was usually done only between people who knew each other very well. Maggie and I were strangers, and she didn't even like me. But she was Guardian to the core – help was needed so she came through.

Any other time I wouldn't have been able to resist studying her mind and energy, but all I cared about now was channelling her magic. She had a hell of a lot of it, too. I felt a disorienting internal wrench as we connected, as if I was tumbling into free fall.

She gasped, and so did I. This was the Guardian equivalent of going skydiving with no training on how to open the parachute. After a couple of heartbeats, our energies began to adjust. It's hard to describe – sort of like the music of two different instruments swooping around each other while trying to find the exact same note.

Then we snapped into sync and her power began flowing through the link, smooth and rich and deep. I spent an instant

enjoying the sensation – she felt like the very best bittersweet
Belgian chocolate. Then I concentrated on focusing the blaze of
white light we had created.

When I'd mastered our combined energies, I channelled it
around the damaged vena cava and visualized wholeness. The
ragged edges slowly came together and began to meld until the
vessel was as good as new.

"Got it!" I said with quiet exultation. It was strange to be
saving a life while Shark was emptying the register a yard away
and the other two thugs were scarfing down hot food from the
case right behind Maggie. The deli looked even smaller from
the floor.

Maggie uttered a soft prayer of thanks. "Ready for the other
wound?"

"Yep." I took over the blood-saturated pad and did a detailed
scan of the damage. Besides blood vessels, some nerves needed
fixing. Bones were broken and that kind of repair would require
far more energy than Maggie and I could muster. But with her
help, I could manage the vessels and nerves.

As I worked on the second wound, I was dimly aware of
police sirens. I was just finishing the second repair when
suddenly sirens were screaming right outside the door. A gruff
voice yelled, "Police! Come out with your hands up!"

"Jesus, the cops are here!" Goatee Guy exclaimed. "We need
to get the hell out the back!"

I snapped in my ER voice, "There isn't a back way out!
Better to surrender before they shoot you down."

"If the guy's already dead, we should shoot you two as well so
there are no witnesses," Shark growled, his eyes crazed. I gave
him credit for the fact that he was trying to think. Can't say I
liked the murderous direction of his thoughts.

"Rajiv isn't going to die," I said swiftly. "Since you let me
work on him, he should pull through. You were smart. Be smart
again. Surrender to the police and you may serve a little time,
but you'll have a life ahead of you."

Tattoo Man scowled at Rajiv's limp body. "Ya shouldn't 've
shot him, Shark. Think the cops will negotiate if we take these
two hostage? Maybe we can use them to get away."

I was dizzy and light-headed from the energy I'd burned in

the healing, but I tried to find an argument that might work. "Rajiv is holding his own, but negotiations take time. He might not make it if you delay," I warned. "Rajiv's mom is a federal judge. If he dies, the cops will never stop hunting till they find you, and then they'll fry you for murder one."

"The smug bastard is lying to us," Shark said, voice panicky. "We gotta blow him away, too."

He was aiming his gun at me when Maggie Macrae said in a rich, soothing voice, "He's not lying. The clerk is going to be all right. You can be too."

Slowly she stood, uncoiling her long, lithe body. She'd shed her blazer and released her hair. Under the fluorescents, thick waves fell past her shoulders in a shimmering cascade of dark auburn. I stared, entranced. Ms Maggie Macrae was the most sensual woman I'd ever seen.

The thugs reacted the same way. Their gazes were riveted. Maggie took a step towards Goatee Guy, who was the closest. It was the bravest act I've ever seen.

"Jaybird, you've never done anything like this before," she said, her voice sultry. "Do you want to break your grand-mother's heart after all she's done for you?"

He gasped and his hand dropped until the barrel of his gun pointed towards the floor. She smiled and laid a hand on his shoulder. The weapon fell from his nerveless fingers and landed harmlessly on the floor as he stared at her like a stunned ox.

She turned to Tattoo Man with an enchanting smile. "Rocko, you've got a girl who loves you and a baby on the way. Why did you let yourself get talked into this?"

He looked as if he wanted to weep. His weapon also sagged towards the floor. Maggie patted his cheek and he beamed at her goofily as the gun slipped from his hand.

She turned to Shark, who backed away frantically, trying to steady his gun with two shaking hands as he aimed at her heart. "Jeez, what are you, some kind of witch?"

The spell she'd used on the others wasn't working on him, so I dragged myself out of my trance and hurled a can of tomato soup into Shark's throat. "Duck, Maggie!"

I was a pretty good pitcher in the days when I had time to play ball. Shark made a strangled sound and doubled over. I followed up the soup with a big, heavy can of garbanzos that hit him in the temple. He collapsed, loosing a shot as he fell, but Maggie had ducked and the bullet went over her head.

While she was bent over, she scooped the other two guns from the floor. By that time, I had collected Shark's weapon as well.

I yelled, "It's OK in here, officers! I'm one of two customers. The three robbers have surrendered and given us their guns. Call an ambulance! The clerk is badly hurt."

"Put your hands in the air!" the gruff cop voice called.

It wouldn't be good for the police to come in and see three guns, so I set Shark's way up on a shelf of canned goods. After I added Maggie's two weapons, I raised my hands and yelled, "Come on in!"

The two thugs who were still standing looked a little dopey from whatever Maggie had done. The police entered in a wary crouch, weapons at the ready. When they saw the threat was over, they relaxed and cuffed the robbers. I guess I still looked harmless because they didn't even suspect me of being one of the bad guys.

An ambulance arrived, and suddenly the deli was full of cops and EMTs looking to see if Rajiv was salvageable. One whistled softly as he checked Rajiv's heartbeat and blood pressure. "This guy's the luckiest man in New York City. He's lost a lot of blood, but the bullets seem to have missed the major blood vessels."

Fortunately, it wouldn't occur to them that Rajiv had been healed by magic. "I did what I could to slow the bleeding," I explained. "He and I are both fourth-year med students and his father is a surgeon. Take good care of him."

The EMT nodded as he and his mate stabilized Rajiv. Medical people look out for their own. "He'll make it. You do good work, doc." High praise.

As Rajiv was hoisted onto a gurney, he managed a crooked smile. "Don't let the grands get too freaked out, Charlie."

I patted his hand. "I'll tell them you'll be OK."

His grandparents would go straight to the hospital, I suspected. His parents, the judge and the surgeon, would grab the first available flight from Dallas. Thank God the news about Rajiv was good.

As the barely conscious Shark was wrestled to his feet, a policewoman said to Maggie and me, "Stay out of the way while we take care of the perps and victim. We'll need statements."

I nodded and moved to the back of the shop, Maggie following. She looked as drained as I felt. I asked, "Want a latte?"

She smiled crookedly. "You're a barista as well?"

"I helped out Rajiv sometimes when things got busy." I made two of my favourite mocha lattes, heavy on the cream and chocolate syrup, but only single shots of caffeine. I figured both of us had had enough stimulation for one night.

Maggie accepted the latte, took a swig, then slid down to the floor, her back against the cabinet. "That was an impressive job of healing, Dr Owens."

"Charlie." I heaped as much whipped cream on top of my latte as I could, then joined her on the floor, only a few inches between us as we leaned back against the coffee cabinet. Despite all the noise and activity – there were now TV cameras filming outside – we had our own private little space to talk. I'd brought a handful of cranberry scones down with me, and I offered one to Maggie.

Scones are first-class comfort food. She tried to be ladylike, but failed. After demolishing one in two bites, she said, "Remind me to never again go out for food at 2 a.m. in New York City."

"OK." I bit my scone in half, chewed and swallowed. "What you did was pretty amazing. How did you tame those two guys? What kind of spell were you using?"

She looked at me in surprise. Nice long lashes around those honey gold eyes. "Couldn't you tell?"

"You're an enchantress!" I exclaimed as I realized. One of the rarest kinds of mage, enchantresses were almost always female, and they could project allure so powerfully that a man's brain would turn to mush. The power has been studied in recent times and seems to be a matter of pheromones. An enchantress could turn hers on, calibrate the intensity, and focus them in an instant. Maggie Macrae could probably stun the whole male population of a New York borough if she wanted to. "I didn't realize."

Her brows arched. "I thought you knew as soon as I came in. I just arrived in New York, so I assumed jetlag had weakened my shielding."

I thought back, then shook my head. "You weren't sending out any enchantress vibes. If you had, I'd have passed out just looking at you."

"You thought I was that attractive even though I wasn't trying to attract?" Maggie said with interest as she nibbled more daintily at a second scone. This close, her lips looked even more kissable.

"I sure did!" Probably better if I didn't say that my reaction to her had been, "*This one! I want this one!*" The men in my family tend to fall in love at first sight and stay in love until they die, but no point to scaring her off now that she was talking to me. "Sorry about demanding your energy when we haven't even been properly introduced."

She made a dismissive gesture. "It was needful. I was able to follow you well enough to see what you were doing. He wouldn't have had a chance if you hadn't been right here and a superb healer."

Her admiring glance warmed me to my cockles, whatever cockles were. That wasn't covered in anatomy class. I matched my shrug to hers. "It was needful."

She closed her eyes, looking exhausted. "Enchantress magic doesn't always work. My thanks for your timely and well-placed tin of soup."

"Shark was so hopped up that nothing could get through to his addled brain, not even world-class pheromones like yours." I sighed, thinking of the work that needed to be done still. "Do you have enough energy left to help me put a spell of protection on the deli? I cast one here when I started at med school and until now it worked – no robberies, no violence. But something stronger is needed. This shouldn't happen again."

"Good idea. As I said before, I'm particularly good at shielding, so I'll take the lead." She cocked an eyebrow at me, clearly waiting to see if I was going to go gorilla on her and insist that I shape the spell.

"Good. I'm only middlin' at shielding and repulsion spells."

Maggie nodded approvingly. "Plus, you must be tired to the bone after that healing work." She took my hand, long cool fingers interlacing with mine.

I drew a shaky breath as lightning jolts of Maggie energy swept through me. I forced myself to relax and flow, putting my energy at her disposal. She wasn't kidding about being good at shielding. The protection she built was a thing of beauty, like the work of a first-class architect. No armed thugs would enter the deli any decade soon.

But she allowed nothing personal to show. I'm not as good at shielding, so she must have picked up some of my feelings. She gave me a spooked stare when we finished the spell work and released hands. I let go of her reluctantly, but figured I had to if she was going to believe that I wasn't a crazed stalker.

Before I could ask for her phone number, the cops came over and separated us to take statements. Yes, officer, there were three robbers. Shark was the one who shot Rajiv. They deserved some credit for allowing me to save his life. Yes, I'd put Shark out of commission with canned goods.

I was so tired I was weaving on my feet by the time they had finished with the questions. Mercifully, they said I could wait until later in the day to go to the station and sign my statement.

As soon as they finished with me, I looked around for Maggie. No enchantresses in sight. My pulse spiked with alarm as I asked the nearest policeman, "The woman, Maggie Macrae. Where is she?"

He shrugged, his attention elsewhere. "She left after giving her statement."

I wanted to howl that she couldn't leave, we had unfinished business. I was heading for the door when my brother David showed up, looking even scruffier than I did. He's an NYPD cop, the best detective in the city because he's a Guardian enforcer and not much gets by him. "Jesus, Charlie!" He gave me a bone-cracking hug. "I heard about this robbery on the radio and had a hunch you were here." Being Dave, it would have been more than a hunch. "Whose blood are you wearing?"

I stared down at my gory sweats. "Rajiv's. But he'll be OK, I think."

"Because of you?"

I nodded. Dave knew enough to guess the rest. I'd used my healing abilities on him often enough. He had a talent for getting banged up. "I need to get moving," I said numbly. "There was a woman here, Maggie Macrae, and I have to find her."

"Macrae?" He recognized the Guardian name, of course.

I nodded again. "She persuaded two of the yahoos to drop their guns. Now if you'll excuse me . . ."

Dave blocked my way. He can read me pretty well. "You liked her?"

"For me, she's why men fight," I said impatiently. "Now *get out of my way!*"

His hand locked onto my arm. "You're dead on your feet, little brother. And don't you have a final exam later today? Go home, get some sleep, take your exam, clean up so you don't look like a fugitive from a slasher flick, and *then* find her."

"I need to find her *now,* David," I growled. "Will you remove your hand before I break it?"

He looked startled – I don't lose my temper often – but let me go. "Want me to find her for you?"

Which he could easily, since enforcers are always brilliant finders. "Hell, no," I snapped. "Women are suckers for the tall, dark and dangerous thing you have down so well. I'll find her myself."

"Would that you were right about the tall, dark and dangerous thing," he said wryly. "Go left, then left again for half a block. And good luck."

As I said, he's a great finder, and I'll admit that it saved some time to have him point me in the right direction. But that still left a long avenue block of apartment buildings. I followed his directions. Left, then left again. My brain felt wrapped in cotton wool and I wanted nothing more than to collapse anywhere, a bed by preference though concrete would do. But I had to find Maggie Macrae before I could sleep.

Some senses operate better when you're tired. I closed my eyes and let my mind drift as I looked for Maggie's bittersweet Belgian chocolate energy signature. Chocolate and the smoothest Highland whisky, yesss . . .

I headed into the third apartment building on the right. A sleepy doorman was on duty. He came awake fast at the sight of my bloody self, and he was six and a half feet of frowning disapproval.

Before he could call 911, I said reassuringly, using all the persuasive magic I had, "Could you ring Ms Macrae in apartment 30D?"

Glad I'd been able to pull the apartment number out of the ether, I continued, "I'm respectable, really. Ms Macrae and I were both in a convenience-store robbery and I want to check that she's OK. Tell her it's Doctor Charles Owens."

It must have been the magic that persuaded him, because it sure wasn't my appearance. He rang up to her apartment. "I'm sorry to disturb you, Ms Macrae, but there's a fellow here who calls himself Doctor Owens. Shall I let him in?"

There was a long pause and my heart sank. If Maggie said no, I didn't have the energy to storm the building. Not tonight, anyhow.

But she must have said yes because the doorman grudgingly let me in. I don't even remember taking the elevator up, though when I exited on the thirtieth floor, I vaguely noticed I'd left bloody smudges on the wall where I'd leaned during the ascent.

Then I was at her door, knocking. Maggie opened it warily, her shields locked as tight as a bank vault. She'd discarded the jeans and blazer and wore a long monk's robe in gold velvet that matched her eyes. Every inch of skin below her neck was covered, and she was the sexiest woman I'd ever seen.

Maybe I'd gone nuts – entirely possible – but sexual tension crackled between us like heat lightning. I forgot about fatigue as every cell in my body went on alert.

Her gaze met mine then slid away. "No need to come by. I'm fine."

"*I'm* not. Can I come in?"

She stepped back and let me pass while I tried to figure out how to justify being here at 4 a.m. without admitting to crazed lust. Of course she wasn't worried that I'd attack her – the enchantress gift comes with a major talent for self-defence. But she was still way skittish.

The apartment was really nice. Glad to have a neutral topic, I said, "It looks like you're in New York for a while?"

"I was working in London in computers, and my company

just transferred me here." She crossed to a window and stared out at the lights of the city, her arms crossed tightly in front of her. The golden velvet robe might have been monkish, but the graceful body underneath sure wasn't.

"Of course, that's only my day job," she continued. "I imagine you've heard of the Protection Project? I'm also here to strengthen New York's shielding. "

I'd heard of the project, of course. Guardians around the world and across nations and ethnicities all worked to protect the great cities and historical sites from terrorism. We weren't always successful, but we'd prevented a whole lot of grief, especially in the Mideast. It made sense that someone as powerful at shielding as Maggie would be part of that. I guessed that this nice apartment came with the job. "As a resident of New York, I give you my thanks."

"I need to thank you as well." Her profile was as still and elegant as a Greek sculpture. "You saved me twice, and didn't even use magic to do it."

"Sometimes physical action beats magic." I really should go home, but I couldn't bear to leave. I needed something from her. A sign of interest maybe. Not easy to imagine when she was reacting to me like a porcupine.

Abruptly I realized why she was prickly. I said quietly, "It must be hard to be an enchantress and always have to be on your guard against men going crazy over you."

"You have no idea." Her laughter was brittle. "I had to learn shielding as soon as I could walk. That's why I usually react badly when men turn into idiots around me."

"I'd like to think I'm different." I was getting better at reading her for I caught a fleeting impression of an unhappy love affair in London. Guardian emotions run deep. Falling for some idiot who lusted after her body and didn't care about her brains and bravery and uniqueness had devastated her. That's why she'd taken the job in New York.

"Owenses mate for life," I continued. "As soon as you walked in the door, I knew. I don't expect you to feel the same way now, but I rather desperately want the chance to persuade you to take me seriously. Roses and canned soup and chess games in the park. Whatever you want."

She turned, startled. "How did you know about the chess? Of course, you're a Guardian. And a rather powerful one."

"The world always needs healers, and it's the main thing I'm good at." I dropped my internal shields so she could probe if she wanted to. "See for yourself."

I felt a light, hesitant brush on the edges of my energy field. Then a stronger touch as she began to relax. I felt like a cat being petted.

"My mother said it's best to find someone who thinks I look good even in the morning when my hair is wild and my eyes are half closed," she said thoughtfully.

"I'm entirely willing to find out." I looked into her honey brown eyes and felt myself falling, falling, falling. "But I already know the answer is yes. You'll look wonderful even then. Just like you do now."

She looked startled. "I've got my allure clamped down to zero. You shouldn't be able to pick up any enchantress magic at all."

"You're still the most attractive woman in Manhattan, and there's serious competition here." I stood very still as her energy reached deeper and deeper, as erotic as if she'd dropped her robe on the floor. Reaching out to her with my own energy, I said, "It's not just your looks. It's your brains and your courage in facing down those robbers. That was . . . amazing. Worthy of the most famous of your Macrae ancestors."

"You really know how to charm a woman, Dr Owens," she said with a slow, dazzling smile.

Her shields went down and she began to glow, her warmth and sensuality enfolding me even though we weren't touching. Her living room was full of swirling golden light as our energy fields danced and twined together. This was unleashed enchantress power, I realized. I felt like I'd died and gone to heaven.

"Not a doctor yet, but soon." Her openness produced a rush of relief so intense I felt downright giddy. To her inner sight, I probably sparkled like skyrockets. "I have no serious vices, I like kids and animals, and I clean up fairly well."

"You look rather fine now, in a downmarket sort of way." She frowned as she read me more deeply. "Heavens, you have your last exam in a few hours! You need to get beyond that before thinking about mating for life."

"You're right," I agreed. "Will you go out to dinner with me tonight, after the exam is over and I've showered and caught a few hours of sleep?"

"I have a better plan." Maggie crossed the room with gliding steps and reached up to rest her hands on my shoulders. Her burning, sexy hands. "You have a fine set of shoulders," she murmured as she skimmed her hands over them and down my arms.

"I'm supposed to be the healer," I said huskily. "But you could raise the dead."

Maggie laughed, not displeased. "Now you will go in my bathroom and take a shower while I throw those appalling garments into the wash." She kissed my left cheek. "Then we will both lie down on my bed and sleep." She kissed my right cheek. "Nothing else. But the energy exchange of being close will enable you to recover enough to pass your pharmacology exam so you needn't think more about that."

I slid my fingers into her shimmering hair. "Yes, ma'am. Whatever you say."

"Then you will come back here, and we shall not leave the apartment for the next week."

Her lips met mine, and we connected in a blaze of pure transformation. This, I realized hazily, was what the ancient Guardians called an alchemical marriage. Two souls bonding till death did us part. And it could happen in an instant.

I wrapped my arms around her slim, provocative body, and we fell into each other. "Are you sure nothing happens when we go to bed?" I breathed. "There is more than one way to share energy and be revitalized."

She laughed and stepped from the embrace. "You wish to play doctor? We'll see, Charles. We'll see."

I caught her hand and kissed it. She blushed adorably, heat radiating from her as she gave me a gentle push in the direction of the shower. I headed to the bathroom wearing a smile that could light up Manhattan.

Who said that nothing ever happened on Tuesdays?

Trinity Blue

Eve Silver

Prologue

Ten miles north of Fort Vancouver, Oregon Country, 1834.

Night settled, dark and wet, the air smelling of damp earth and blood and death. Daemon Alexander knelt in the dirt, a woman cradled in his arms. Her long hair fell across his sleeve and tumbled to the ground in a riot of guinea-gold waves. She shifted in his embrace as though trying to pull free of him, her breath rattling in her chest.

"Do you want to live for ever?" he whispered, wiping away the thin trickle of blood that slid from the corner of her mouth. *Say yes. Ask me. Only say the words.* He could do nothing if she did not say the words. Her gaze flicked to his, then away. He knew then that she could not bear to look at him now that she had seen the truth. Seen what he was. "Would you rather die?" Daemon rasped. He rested his fingers lightly on her throat and felt her pulse slow, the pace stuttering as her blood leaked out to pool beneath them.

"No . . . I do not want . . . to die," she whispered, a tear tracing a path along the pale skin of her cheek. "But . . . I cannot bear to live . . . not like . . . you."

Not like him. A monster. A dark creature that played host to even darker creatures. He had no reassurance for her because he had no reassurance for himself. There was no name for the vile thing he was, at least, none that he knew. Basking in the illusion of their life together, he had forgotten that for a brief time.

"I love you." His declaration hung in the air, pallid and weak. It meant nothing in the face of his betrayal. He had come to her as a man, made her believe he was a man. He had almost believed it himself. He had brought her here, to a place wild and untamed. Dangerous. The responsibility for the attack on her was his and his alone. "Let me save you, Alma. Only say it. Ask me. I beg you."

She turned her head and looked at him then.

"I love you," he whispered again, desperate.

"I despise you." Her words were so faint he might have made himself believe he had misheard. But no. He would not allow himself that reprieve. He deserved her hate.

"I—" His arguments, his pleas locked in his throat as her chest deflated on a final breath. Too late. She was gone. And he was left with her broken shell in his arms.

All around him the shadows shifted, dark forms rising from the bodies of the men who had come here to steal and rape and kill. They were dead. His will had seen them ripped limb from limb. But he had come too late. They had done their vile deeds before he arrived and so she was dead as well. His love, his wife. Dead.

His fault.

Rising, he held his arms wide, calling home the trinity. Again the shadows moved and three raced towards him, sleek in the night. They wound about him and through him, less than substance, more than shadow. He let his pain feed them, his rage and agony. Together, they burst into clear blue flames that spread and grew until every body, every drop of blood in the clearing was burned away in an icy inferno of smokeless blue fire.

One

Freetown, New York, present day.

Jen Cassaday pushed aside her grandmother's yellowed lace curtains and stared out at the stranger in her front yard. He stood, legs apart, arms hanging easy by his sides, head tipped back as he studied the house. Faded jeans, scuffed leather jacket over a dark brown T-shirt, dark hair, hanging in long, ragged layers. From this distance she could see great bone structure and a frown. Maybe it was the frown that kept him from being pretty. Or maybe it was the scar that ran across his chin, an angry white line against tanned skin. Either way, he was something to look at.

In one hand he held a newspaper, and the sight of it made Jen's pulse twitch. He was not at all what she'd meant to attract when she placed an ad for a handyman. And with any luck, he wasn't here about that.

"Make your own luck," she muttered, automatically quoting one of her mother's favourite phrases. Then she snorted. What else besides the promise of work would bring him all the way out here? She was miles from town.

Instinctively, she looked beyond him to the dark woods that flanked the field across the highway. Her skin tingled and her belly twisted in a tight little knot. The sensation had repeated itself over and over in the past few days, becoming stronger and more frequent. The sixth sense that was her legacy warned her: something bad was coming. She glanced back at the guy in her yard, watched him fold the newspaper and tuck it into his coat pocket, and wondered if he was the source of her unease.

With a sigh, she let the curtain fall back in place. Angling on her crutches, she headed down the stairs just as his knock sounded, hard and bold. She took her time. No sense rushing. It was haste that had landed her in this mess in the first place. She'd taken a tumble down the stairs and ended up with the terrible triad: two torn ligaments and a torn meniscus in her knee. And in Jen's opinion, they were taking their sweet time about healing, though her specialist disagreed.

"Your recovery is remarkable, Jen. I've never seen damage like this heal without surgery. Certainly not this quickly. It's something for the medical journals." His comments had made her laugh. Her capacity to heal was nothing compared to some of her relatives.

Setting the rubber tips of her crutches, she leaned her weight forwards and dragged open the front door. The sun was at her visitor's back, and for a second Jen blinked against the glare. Then her eyes adjusted and she raised her head to meet his gaze.

She was 5 feet 10 inches and she had to tip her head back to look in his face. It was an unfamiliar experience. Up close, she saw the dangerous edge to him. It was in the way he held himself, the tightness at the corners of his mouth, the way his eyes – a blue so clear and bright she'd never seen the like – took in every nuance of his surroundings in a glance.

"You here about the job?" she asked, wanting him to say no, knowing he'd say . . .

"Yes. Name's Daemon Alexander." He offered his hand.

"Jen Cassaday." She didn't see a way around it, so she shook briefly. His palm was callused, his grip pleasantly firm. Something inside her yawned and stretched, an unwanted awareness of him as a man. As though in silent response, his grip tightened ever so slightly. She pulled her hand away as quickly as she could without seeming rude.

For weeks she'd had that ad in the paper and he was the first person to apply. No surprise there. Everyone in town whispered about the haunted Cassaday place, and they were halfway right, only the elements that haunted these walls weren't the spirits of the dead, but a different power.

Daemon Alexander either hadn't heard the talk of hauntings, or he didn't care. He wasn't from town; she'd have recognized him if he was. In a place this small, you got to know faces if not names, particularly a face like his. He was a stranger passing through, most likely in need of cash. Her gaze slid to the rusted-out clunker in the driveway. Cars weren't her thing, but she guessed it for something American-built and decades old.

"You have painting experience?" she asked.

"I do."

"It's an old house. Some of the walls need repair and I'd like to go with plaster to match the original rather than drywall. I don't suppose you have experience with plastering old houses?"

"I do," he said again. "I like old things." He sounded amused.

She wasn't getting any sense that he was evil, and she knew that if he were she'd spot it. She always spotted it. Her built-in early warning system had never failed her.

"I have references," he offered, angling his body so that she'd catch his arm in the door if she decided to slam it, as though he sensed her hesitation and wanted to hedge his bets. But he didn't infringe on her space, didn't step inside. She caught the faint scents of leather and citrus shaving cream. They lured her to lean a little closer, breathe a little deeper. "I spruced up Mrs Bailey's porch last week. And Doc Hamilton had me paint his office the week before that. You can give them a call."

"How long have you been in town?"

"Two weeks."

"How long you planning to stay?"

His eyes narrowed. "Till the job's done."

For a second, she had the odd thought that he wasn't referring to a job working for her. He was talking about something else entirely. The air between them crackled, an electric sizzle, and she let her senses reach for him. Not sight or smell, but her inner senses, the ones that knew things most people didn't.

She came up empty. There was no good reason for her to turn him down. She wasn't getting any sort of bad vibe from him. He had references and she desperately needed the help, especially with her knee torn up. Still, she almost told him no.

"Eight tomorrow morning," she said at last. "If your references check out, you can start then. If not—" she shrugged "you can head back the way you came, Mr Alexander."

"Daemon," he said, softly. "Call me Daemon." He studied her with those clear, lake-blue eyes, and something hot flared in their depths. She felt the lure of that heat, and already regretted her offer. The last thing she needed was a to-die-for handyman hanging around and turning on the charm.

Either he sensed her preference that he not look at her like he wanted to take a taste, or he had similar thoughts to hers about mixing business with pleasure, because his gaze shuttered and he stepped away.

"See you at eight."

Jen hobbled out onto the porch as he walked to his car and drove away. Even then, she didn't go back inside. An odd sense of expectation held her in place. The air felt . . . wrong. Deep inside, restlessness stirred, an edginess that coiled tight and left her feeling that something was trying to crawl to the surface. Her every sense tingled as she looked again to the thick forest that banded the flat field across the road.

The sun was warm and bright, but a chill slithered through her. Because there was someone out there, in the woods. Watching.

Three days later, Daemon was up on a step stool in the parlour, putting blue paint up the wall to the ceiling, when the stumping of Jen's crutches announced her arrival. The air hummed with an electric charge, a zing of power that ramped up a notch the closer she got. He knew that hum. It heralded magic, and right now it was purring like a stroked cat.

Which made no sense, because Jen Cassaday wasn't a sorcerer or a demon or anything in between. She was a human woman. An incredibly attractive one with her long runner's legs and her pretty brown eyes, her sleek, dark hair that hung to her shoulders in a heavy curtain and the freckles that dusted across her pert nose. He had an urge to kiss those freckles, to peel her white T-shirt over her head to see if they sprinkled her chest and the tops of her breasts. And those thoughts were way off limits.

"Hey," she said. "Lunch is ready."

Then she headed for the kitchen, the air around her crackling. That was a mystery, because a human woman couldn't cause the slightest twitch in the current of magic that crossed dimensions. He knew that sorcerers called it the *continuum* or dragon current. Personally, he didn't bother to name it, though in the beginning, he'd called it his own personal hell.

His gaze slid to the window and the forest beyond. Maybe it wasn't Jen that affected the current. Maybe it was something else. A demon, here in this small, pretty town?

That was exactly what he was here to find out. He'd tracked the thing to Liberty and then lost it. His gut was telling him it had come here.

He wrapped his brushes to keep them from drying out and tidied his work area, then washed his hands and face before joining Jen in the kitchen. She'd made him a turkey sandwich on a bun with Boston lettuce and some sort of sprouts.

"Thank you," he said as he took a seat. He enjoyed having meals with her, talking to her. Hers was an easy sort of companionship.

"I didn't know if you preferred mayo or mustard, so I took a chance on both. I suppose I should have asked."

"I'm fine with both," he said, taking the top off the bun and carefully scraping the sprouts onto the plate. He looked up to find her watching him with a faint smile. He shrugged. "Some things a man—" or a creature that was more monster than man "—isn't meant to eat."

She laughed. "I feel that way about tomatoes."

"Do you? I have a fondness for tomatoes on a turkey sandwich."

"I'll remember that." She took a bite of her own sandwich. They chatted about easy things. Light things. The weather. The progress of his work for her. Then she mentioned that her grandmother had loved the wallpaper in the bedroom under the eaves, and she wished there was a way to save it.

"This house. It was your grandmother's?"

"And my mother's and mine."

The wistfulness in her voice reminded him just how short human lives could be.

"You miss them." He knew about that, knew what it was like to miss loved ones from his past. It was hard for an immortal to form friendships with humans, hard to watch them age or sicken and die. He almost asked her how they had died, but ancient, ingrained manners from a time long past prevented him from prying. Some instinct made him reach across and close his hand over hers. "They never leave us, the people we love. They come to us in dreams and memories that keep them alive as long as we're alive."

He let more pain leak into those words than he had meant to.

Her gaze shot to his and, for a frozen moment, they just stared at each other. Then she pulled her hand from beneath his and glanced at the window. "Looks like something's coming this way."

Following her eyes, he saw the storm clouds – the horizon. But it was something else that made him wary – a wrongness, a foulness that oozed towards them like an oil slick. Premonition slithered through his limbs and set the dark creatures that were part of him quivering with excitement. Beneath his skin, the trinity stirred, restless.

Yeah, something was coming – a storm that had nothing to do with the weather.

Two

Over the next two weeks, Jen watched her house bloom as Daemon worked at the repairs. Problem was, she hadn't expected to be so drawn to him. He was *there*, in her space, tall and broad and distracting. She caught herself glancing at him again and again, watching the play of muscle under smooth tanned skin, asking him questions just to hear him speak in that low, sexy voice.

She could hear him now, whistling as he worked in the bedroom under the eaves, the one that had been her grand-mother's favourite. The sun had set at least an hour past and creeping shadows darkened the hall. Pausing, she flipped the light switch, and gave a hiss of frustration as she realized the bulb must be burned out.

She made it to the base of the stairs when her insides knotted up tight. Breathing through the cramp, she rested her weight on the crutches, waiting for the twisting coil of pain to pass. Her body was changing, fighting for life. A new life. The one she needed to pass through an agony of fire to achieve. She sighed, wishing there was an easier way. For weeks, the pain inside her had flared and peaked at random times. She'd come to think that it was a good thing that she was on crutches. At least the sudden shards of agony didn't send her to her knees. But as the pain passed and she contemplated the darkened stairs, she decided that, at the moment, her crutches were a hindrance. They made climbing the steps to talk to Daemon a bother, so she called his name.

She waited, looking up, and frowned. An odd blue light shimmered from the room under the eaves, the one Daemon was working in today. A spotlight of some sort? She meant to ask him about it when he stepped onto the landing, but her words died in her throat. For a long moment, she simply stared. She still hadn't gotten used to the physical impact of seeing him in her home, especially not the way he looked right now. He was bathed in shadow, his dark hair tousled, his jeans slung low on his hips. A white tank top hugged his muscled torso, and she could see dark tattoos on his skin: a dragon on his left shoulder, another on his right biceps, the hint of a third on the bulge of his pectoral where the tank top dipped.

"You're working late today," she observed.

"Just want to finish this room."

Her gaze flicked beyond him to the dark hallway. There was no sign of the blue light now. Odd.

"I'm heading out to do some grocery shopping. I want to make it to the Shop Rite before they close at nine. If you're done before I get back, leave by the side door. It'll lock behind you." Turning away, she positioned her crutches to make her way to the door. "See you."

"Jen." His voice, low and rough, stopped her. The way he said her name made her shiver.

"Mm-hmm?" She glanced back over her shoulder. He'd hunkered down at the top of the stairs so he wouldn't lose sight of her. God, he was gorgeous. And he wasn't for her. No man was for her. Not right now. Not ever. A different future waited for her and it could never include a mortal man.

"It's dark out. Do you . . ." He raked his fingers through his hair. "Do you want me to take you to town?"

Wow. Chivalrous. "Not necessary. I'm a big girl, Dacmon. I've been taking care of myself for a long time. And, hey," she laughed, "it isn't as if I need to watch out for monsters."

She was almost at the door before she heard the creak of the floorboard behind her. The air hummed a second before she felt Daemon's hands on her, his long fingers closing around her upper arms. He steadied her, his body hard and hot at her back. Her pulse slammed into red line.

How had he made it down the stairs so quickly? How had she not heard his approach?

He stepped around to face her, his hands skimming the skin of her upper arms, as though he was loath to let her go. Her head fell back and she stared into his eyes, saw something there that made her shiver. Something primal.

"There are all sorts of monsters in this world, Jen," he murmured, "and you *do* need to watch for them."

Her breath came in a jagged gasp. She wet her lips, and his gaze dropped to her mouth, hot, intent. She thought he would kiss her. A part of her wanted him to, wanted to know the feel and taste of him.

He smiled, a dark, feral baring of white teeth. "You need to watch out for things inside your home, too."

For a second, she thought he meant *himself*, that he was telling her he was some sort of monster. Then he gestured to the ground and she looked over her shoulder at a dark lump: the rolled-up rug that usually ran the length of the hall. In the gloom, she hadn't noticed it there.

"I moved the rug so I could get my supplies in and out easier," he said. "You almost caught your crutches on it."

And he'd saved her. So she'd been wrong. His actions were chivalrous and *necessary*, otherwise she'd be on the floor in a pained heap right now.

"Thanks." She pressed her lips together, willed her pulse to settle. "My saviour." She laughed.

He didn't. "I'm no one's saviour, Jen." A heartbeat, two, then he brushed a strand of hair from her cheek. "Drive safe." His tone was nonchalant, as though he hadn't just moved faster than he ought to, hadn't held her close enough that she could smell the scent of his skin, hadn't made her ache for his kiss.

A half-hour later, Jen used her hip to bump her cart as she hobbled along the aisle of the Shop Rite on Route 52. Mrs Hambly – an old friend of her grandmother's – and the high school maths teacher, Gail Merchant, blocked the way.

"Terrible tragedy. Terrible. Things like that don't happen here," Mrs Hambly insisted. She plucked a grape from a bunch, popped it in her mouth, grimaced, then helped herself to another from a different bunch.

Jen wondered what tragedy had Mrs Hambly all worked up today. Last week it had been the kids lurking outside the variety store, and the week before that it was the lack of personal service at the ATM.

Planting her crutches, Jen added a head of lettuce and a couple of tomatoes to her cart. Ahead of her, Gail absently filled a bag with peaches, her attention on Mrs Hambly as she asked in hushed tones, "Does Sheriff Hale think she was killed there, or the body brought from somewhere else?"

"Didn't say," Mrs Hambly snorted. "Maybe he doesn't want to give anything away. Maybe that's part of the investigation."

Jen stared at the two women in shock. "Killed?" she echoed. "Who? Where?"

"Sheriff fished a woman – well, actually, parts of her – out of the stream that runs through the woods between your place and the Peteri's this morning," Mrs Hambly said bluntly. "Naked. Dead. You didn't know?"

"No." Jen shook her head, horrified. The forest between her place and the Peteri's stretched for miles, and somewhere in those miles a woman had died. *Parts of her. Which meant that parts were still missing.* She shuddered in horror, not willing to ask.

"He thinks she was in the water for about two weeks," Gail added.

Two weeks. Memories drifted like smoke, coalescing into solid recollection of the afternoon that Daemon had first turned up on her doorstep. After he'd left her that day, she'd sensed something in the woods, watching her. Something dark and frightening.

There are all sorts of monsters in this world, Jen. His words reeled through her thoughts. For an instant, she'd been so certain that Daemon was talking about himself. But had he known about the dead woman?

"You hate tomatoes, Jen Cassaday. What're you buying them for?" Mrs Hambly demanded, peering into Jen's cart.

"They're . . ." She shook her head, gathering her thoughts. "They're for the handyman. He mentioned he has a fondness for tomatoes on his turkey sandwich."

"Why doesn't your handyman bring his own lunch?" Mrs Hambly questioned at the same time that Gail asked, "You have a handyman working for you? Is it wise to have a stranger in the house with . . . well, with a woman dead and all?"

Jen shrugged with a nonchalance she didn't feel. "He works hard. And he seems to understand old houses."

"But you hired a stranger! You don't know anything about him," Gail exclaimed.

"He had references," Jen replied softly. For what that was worth. They dated back two weeks, which was about how long

Daemon Alexander had been working for her, the same amount
of time that the Sheriff was guessing the dead body had been in
the woods. What was she supposed to make of that?

The two women pegged her with identical "Are you crazy?"
looks. But Jen knew she wasn't. She'd had this built-in radar
detector for trouble all her life. It would uncoil and flare hard
and bright if ever she was in danger. It had never failed her, and
she was counting on that now, because the only vibe she got off
Daemon Alexander was a sizzle of hotter-than-hell chemistry.

And that was a whole other kind of dangerous.

Daemon moved through the dense woods, silent, quick. A little
moonlight filtered through the heavy canopy of branches and
leaves. That was fine. He didn't need light.

He stopped beside the rotting trunk of a fallen oak. Breathing
deeply, he closed his eyes and set the trinity free, sent the
shadows out into the darkness. The three misty shapes rose
from his skin, snaked around his limbs and through them,
blending, adapting, taking form then dissipating.

"Hunt," he said, sending them to their task. They darted
away into the night, unseen, unheard. But there. A silent
menace.

His resources no longer twined with theirs, he summoned his
stores of magic, a surge of bright power. He could see in the
dark. He could run for miles. He could hear the breath of the
smallest creatures in their burrows.

And he could sense dark magic. It made the *continuum* writhe
and twist at the insult.

Something other than him laid claim to these woods. And it
had killed. Recently. He could smell human blood and brim-
stone, feel the surge of demon power in the air.

Following instinct, he ran, skirting trees and vaulting logs,
his blood pumping through him, the wind clean and cold in his
face.

He hunted. And he found them.

Hybrids. Brutish creatures that had been human once, but
when faced with death, had chosen to allow demon will to
overtake their souls. They were human no longer, serving only
their own hungers and a monstrous master.

There were only two of them. A scouting party. Their hands were bloody which meant they had fed earlier. Daemon suppressed a shudder. Hybrids preferred their prey live, human and bloody.

The trinity sped to him, black shadows in the night.

"No," he said, wanting this fight to be his, needing to know he was the one keeping her safe. Jen. He *would* keep her safe.

They came at him, one from each side, claws raking his flesh. He welcomed the pain, welcomed the burn of cold fury that burst from deep inside. With a snarl, he lunged, speed and power. Sweat dripped from him, and blood. His – red, theirs – black.

In the end, he stood, breathing heavily as their remains bubbled and hissed and disintegrated into sludge.

At his call, the trinity came to him – sinuous smoke, dark shadow – and for a moment, the night flared bright with cold blue flame.

Three

The following morning, Jen sat in the kitchen with Sheriff Hale, answering a whole mess of questions. Actually, it was more like he asked and she sat silent and frustrated because she didn't have a shred of information to help him find that poor woman's killer. What was she supposed to say? That two weeks ago she'd looked out at the woods and had the ugly sensation that something watched her with inhuman eyes? Yeah, that'd be a good move. Hale would think she'd lost her mind, and it wouldn't bring him a step closer to the killer.

"So tell me about this handyman you have working for you," Hale prodded.

"His name's Daemon Alexander."

"Where's he from?"

Jen opened her mouth, then closed it. She had no idea.

"I'm from Oregon, originally."

She caught the look of surprise on Hale's face as they both turned. Daemon stood by the side door, leaning one shoulder against it. She hadn't heard him come in and, from Hale's sour expression, she gathered that neither had he.

"What about you, Sheriff Hale?" Daemon asked, his tone lazy and smooth. He shrugged out of his scuffed leather jacket and hung it on a peg behind the door. "Where're you from?"

Hale's face darkened to a dull red. "Right here. Born and bred."

"How fortunate for you." There was a wealth of the unspoken behind those words, an implication that strangers were a convenient scapegoat.

Jen watched Daemon cross the kitchen to the coffee pot and pour himself a cup. She frowned at the tattoo on his forearm. She could swear that it had been on his biceps last night.

"Jenny, you mind giving us a few minutes, man to man?" the sheriff asked.

For some inexplicable reason, she did mind, but had no reason to say so. Instead, she rose and collected her crutches. Daemon met her gaze and offered a tight smile. She realized that he wanted this, wanted to talk with Hale alone. She supposed he wanted to lay any suspicions to rest.

Seeing no option, she left them alone.

The sheriff's voice drifted to her. "So where were you last night, Mr Alexander?"

"Last night?" Daemon's tone was laced with perverse humour. "Why, I was right here, Sheriff. With Jen."

She froze. He didn't exactly lie. He *had* been here with her as night fell. But after that? Where had Daemon been then? And why did he only offer a partial truth?

"Why do you ask, Sheriff? Was there some problem last night?"

"Mrs Peteri says she saw someone lurking in the woods. Someone with a flashlight that has a blue bulb. A very powerful flashlight. That wouldn't have been you, would it, Mr Alexander?"

Daemon laughed. "Come outside and search my car if you feel compelled, Sheriff Hale."

"I just might do that," the sheriff said. "Might like to look at where you live, too. You rent a room at Maybelle Tewksbury's, don't you?"

"I do. You're welcome to look there, as well." Daemon paused. "I don't own a flashlight. Blue bulb or otherwise."

But he did. If not a flashlight, then some other type of light. Jen had seen it leaking through the door of the room Daemon had been working in last night.

Not bothering with stealth, because her crutches made that hopeless, she headed up the stairs to the room under the eaves. Heart racing, she pushed open the door. The walls that had been covered with her grandmother's floral paper were now a soft cappuccino colour. She hobbled into the room. Paint tins were neatly placed on a folded drop cloth, roller trays washed and stacked. And there was a high-power light in the corner, switched to "Off", but still plugged into the outlet. Plugged in. Which meant it needed electricity to work. This couldn't be the blue light Lina Peteri had seen in the woods.

With a sigh of relief, Jen turned back towards the bedroom door. Her heart twitched and stopped.

The wall was still covered in her grandmother's paper, but it looked fresh and new. No dirt, smears or tears. Somehow Daemon had cleaned and restored it. Moving closer, she placed her hand on the wall, feeling her world tip and tilt. What sort of man did something like this? Something so selflessly kind?

From outside came the slam of a car door, the roar of an engine, and a moment later Daemon was there, framed in the doorway, his dark hair falling across his brow. His lips curved in a small smile.

"Sheriff Hale left?" Jen asked, feeling inexplicably awkward.

"Yeah." Daemon closed the space between them. "Do you like it? The paper?"

"I love it." *I could love you, if I let myself.* Oh God, where had that thought come from? This man was not for her. He could never be for her. She had known for her whole life that she was different, that no man could be her future. And for the first time, that reality made her unbearably sad.

"I'm sorry I couldn't save it all, but I managed to strip away enough bits from the three most damaged walls and use them to patch the fourth. Then I restored it with an eraser and a little brush—" he gestured at a couple of small paint tins "—after I matched the colour of the flowers."

Again, her world tilted. The amount of work he'd done. For her. He'd done this for her.

"Thank you. You have no idea—"

"But I do. That's why I did it."

His blue eyes were bright and clear against the fringe of dark lashes. They were beautiful, deep, and glittering with something she was afraid to acknowledge. She felt the heat of him as he stepped closer. Catching her wrist, he drew her hand to his face, turning to rest his jaw against her palm. He drew a shallow breath and held very still, careful, cautious, as though it had been a long while since anyone had touched him this way.

The contact scorched her, made her ache and yearn.

Her crutches limited her movements and she cursed them silently. She wanted to rise up on her toes, press her mouth to his.

"Kiss me," she whispered. It was both an order and a plea.

He slid his fingers to the base of her skull, threading them through the strands of her hair. Her eyes flew open, then fluttered closed as he kissed her, lips hard on hers. He wanted her and he let her know that, his kiss spinning through her, touching every part of her like a live wire. With a moan, she arched into him, her crutches clattering to the floor, her weight held in his arms.

Heat and need spiralled through her. She wanted him, needed him, here, now. She opened beneath his kiss, tongues twining, teeth scraping. With one hand, he slammed the bedroom door shut, then pressed her back against it, his mouth hungry on hers. He bulged against his jeans as she fumbled with the zipper, freeing him, closing her hand around his hot skin. Desire scoured her, leaving her panting.

One hand slid under her buttocks, his other hand curving under the splint that guarded her injured knee. With a moan, she let her head fall back against the door, and she gave herself over to him, to the promise that his tightly corded muscles could hold her there.

He kissed her, open-mouthed, deep. Sensation spiked, her hips rocking in time with his, her moans and cries swallowed by his kiss. He made a raw sound: hard-edged pleasure and animal lust. She unravelled, her body clenched tight around him. Ecstasy rode her senses, blurring her thoughts, her awareness.

Finally, panting, he dropped his head, nuzzling the curve of her neck, still holding her up against the door. She felt weightless, boneless. Wonderfully alive. Then he shifted her so she was cradled in his arms and he carried her to her bed. There, he stripped off her clothes and kissed her – her neck, her belly, her breasts – taking his time, teasing her. He took her again, driving them both over the edge.

"Sleep," he whispered, cradling her in his arms. "Sleep, love."

And she did, her lids drifting shut, her body replete.

When she woke, he was gone.

Daemon was sanding the patch he'd put on the wall in the dining room when he heard Jen behind him. Schooling his features, he sent her a welcoming smile and felt a shimmer of the continuum, a hint of magic. Not sorcerer, not demon, but maybe she was a blighted seed, a human who had a magical progenitor somewhere in her past. Such mortals usually tapped their limited power to become psychics or healers or energy workers. But Jen was none of those. He was certain she had no clue that magic, both light and dark, existed at the edges of her world, no idea that there really were monsters in the closet. She was an accountant.

An incredibly beautiful, sexy accountant that he was willing to break all his self-imposed rules for.

"Hey," she said, sending him a glorious smile. No reservations. No regrets. Not his Jen. "Break time. I'll make lunch."

His Jen. What the hell was he thinking? That they'd set up house here in Freetown? Tend the garden? Walk in the park? And when he never got sick, never aged? When the trinity got restless and demanded release? What then? He knew how quickly love could shrivel in the face of the truth.

"Turkey sandwiches?" he asked, forcing a light tone.

She cocked her head to the side and studied him, a faint frown marking her brow, and he knew she sensed his tension. She saw too much, read him too well. It was like they'd known each other forever, rather than a few short weeks.

"Turkey it is. With tomatoes. And no sprouts," she said. "Give me five minutes."

He headed to his car and retrieved a package from the trunk. He left it in the front hallway and met her in the kitchen. "I, uh, bought you something."

She shot him a look of surprise. "What you did with my grandmother's wallpaper was more than enough. I don't want you to . . . that is . . . I just . . ."

Her voice trailed away, and he almost laughed, realizing that she was worried about him spending his money on her. If she only knew. Finances were not an issue for him. Looking down at her upturned face, at the sweet spray of freckles and her sparkling eyes, he had the crazy urge to tell all, to share with her the knowledge of what he was. Yeah, like that was a plan. She was a mortal woman. She would live and die. He had no business dreaming about a life with her, buying her gifts. He hadn't bought a gift for a woman in almost 200 years.

He led her into the hallway and gestured at the box.

She inhaled sharply and held her breath. "You bought me a motion-detector home alarm system?"

"With infra-red sensors."

"Why?"

Because the hybrids he'd taken down were only scouts. Something more powerful was out there. A killer. He needed to do everything he could to ensure Jen was safe, that the killer stalking the shadows could not harm her.

Not her. Not Jen. His Jen.

Four

Jen woke to afternoon sunlight peeking through the crack between her curtains. After lunch, Daemon had made love to her for hours, sweet and slow, taking his time, exploring every inch of her. But she was alone now and pain was tearing her in two. She breathed through the agony that swelled and ebbed. Bright shards spun through her, twisting her into a tight knot, doubling her over.

She had no idea how long she lay there, but when she came to herself, it was dark. Night had come. All around her, the air shimmered. Sparking filaments of light danced off her skin. Inside her, power uncoiled, stretched and laughed in delight.

Her time had come. The sorcerer magic that should have blossomed at puberty had burgeoned at last.

Reaching down, she freed the Velcro straps of her splint and pulled it from her leg. The pain in her knee was gone. She rolled from the bed and half skipped to the bathroom for a quick shower, then dressed and crossed to the window. Pulling back the curtain, she noticed that Daemon's car was gone. A flicker of disappointment touched her. She made her way downstairs and found a note in the kitchen.

> *Went to town to pick up dinner. Didn't want to disturb you.*
> *Back soon.*
> *—D.*

Smiling, she set the note back on the table, then froze, her head jerking up, her every sense on high alert. Tension coiled through her. There was something out there. Something dark. She could feel the power, the oily slide of demon magic tainting the air, making the continuum shiver and twitch.

She knew then who had killed the woman and left her remains in the woods. Not human. No. The killer was far more dangerous than any human could be. Calling her newly awakened power, she eased out of the back door into the night. Not that she meant to confront it. Her magic was too new to her. She didn't dare take on such a creature alone. No, she meant only to protect her property, to set wards and spells. To protect Daemon and keep him safe from the monsters in the night.

Daemon knew she was gone before he finished searching the house. The trinity twisted and writhed, feeling his fear, feeding on it and straining to tear free. Jen was out there somewhere. Alone. Unprotected. And the continuum writhed and twisted with dark magic, the aura of a powerful demon.

"Go," he snarled, and the trinity tore free, rising into the moonless night, wraiths in the shadows, leading him to the one he sought. Jen. He ran flat out for the woods, knowing she was there. In the woods. With a demon.

He needed to get to her, protect her. He couldn't lose her, not Jen. He couldn't be too late.

The air felt wrong. Tasted *wrong*. There was a demon out there, and something else. A sorcerer? Perhaps.

Trees flew past in a blur. Daemon tore full tilt towards the thick miasma of dark magic that oozed through the forest, foreign and vile. Then he saw Jen, backed up against a tree, her face pale, her eyes wide. He took in every part of her at a glance. She appeared unharmed, but her splint was off and her crutches nowhere to be seen.

Not ten feet from her was a demon – grey, cracked hide stretched over its meaty frame, blackened lips peeled back from row upon row of jagged yellow teeth.

Everything inside Daemon rebelled. He would lose her. Either way, he would lose her. She would die at the hands of this monstrous, foul beast, or Daemon would summon the trinity and save her and she would see him then for exactly what he was.

I despise you. A condemnation from centuries past. He couldn't bear to hear those words from Jen's lips. But the alternative was worse. She would die.

The beast stepped towards her, and she drew herself up, closed her eyes, as though she could not bear to see the promise of her death in its obsidian eyes.

Stepping forwards, Daemon snarled. "Come to me." His voice echoed through the trees, and the trinity came, swirling around him, through him, searing him to the bone and ramping his power to its highest level.

Jen's gaze shot to him and for an instant everything around them ceased to be. She saw him for all he was and all he could never be. Not human. Not mortal.

I'm sorry, Jen.

She held his gaze and drew a deep breath, casting her arms wide. Her body jerked and froze. Glittering, sharp-edged filaments of light swelled around her, swaying and weaving until they reached the demon, curling about its limbs as it lunged for her, claws bared. She yet held his gaze as he sent the trinity to their task, his light and theirs spilling through hers in a tumult of energy until the demon began to crackle and fizz, and finally burned away in a curl of smoke. Then she slumped against the tree as though their victory had drained her.

"You are a sorcerer," Daemon breathed as he caught her against him, holding her tight, desperate to feel the warmth of her skin, to know she lived and breathed still.

"With delayed maturity." She gave a rueful laugh. "What—" A thousand questions raced across her features then disappeared as she shook her head.

He knew what she wanted to ask, waited for her condemnation. Waited for her to demand explanations when he had none. She was a sorcerer, but what was he? He had no idea. He had never encountered another like himself.

Then she smiled, dragged his head down until their lips touched, and whispered, "What did you bring for dinner?"

Grace of Small Magics

Ilona Andrews

"Never look them in the eye," Uncle Gerald murmured.

Grace nodded. He'd calmed down some when they had boarded the plane, enough to offer her a reassuring smile, but now as they landed, he turned pale. Sweat gathered at his hairline. Gripping his cane, he scanned the human currents of the airport as they entered the terminal building. His fingers shook on the pewter wolf's head handle. She'd seen him take out a couple of men half his age with that cane, but she doubted it would do them any good now.

He cleared his throat, licking his dry lips. "Never contradict. Never ask questions. Don't speak until you're spoken to and then say as little as you can. If you're in trouble, bow. They consider it below them to strike a bowing servant."

Grace nodded again. This was the sixth time he had recited the instructions to her. She realized it calmed him down, like a prayer, but his trembling voice ratcheted her own anxiety until it threatened to burst into an overwhelming panic. The airport, the booming announcements spilling from the speaker, the crush of the crowd, all of it blended into a smudged mess of colours and noises. Her mouth tasted bitter. Deep inside her a small voice protested, "This is just crazy. This can't be real."

"It will be fine," Gerald muttered, hoarsely. "It will be fine."

They passed the gates into a long hallway. The bag slipped off her shoulder, and Grace pulled it back on. The simple action crested her panic. She stopped. Her heart hammered, a steady heavy pressure pushing on her chest from inside out. A soft dullness clogged her ears. She heard herself breathing.

Twelve hours ago she woke up four states away, ate her usual breakfast of an egg and a toasted English muffin, and got ready to go to work, just like she had done every day. Then the doorbell rang and Uncle Gerald was on her doorstep with a wild story.

Grace always knew her family was special. They had power. Small magic – insignificant even – but it was more than ordinary people had, and Grace had realized early on she had to hide it. She knew there were other magic users in the world, because her mother had told her so, but she had never met any of them. She'd thought they were like her, armed with minor powers, and rare.

According to Gerald, she was wrong. There were many other magic users in the world. Families, whole clans of them. They were dangerous, deadly and capable of terrible things. And one of these clans had their family in bonded service. They could call upon them at any time, and they had done so for years, demanding her mother's assistance whenever they needed it. Three days ago they requested Grace. Her mother had told her nothing; she simply went in her place. But Clan Dreoch called Gerald. They wanted Grace and only Grace. And so she flew to the Midwest, still dizzy from having her world turned upside down and listening to Gerald's shaky voice as he told stories of terrible magic.

Her instincts screamed to run away, back into the airport filled with people who had no concept of magic. It was just an animal reaction, Grace told herself. The Dreochs had her mother and if she did run, her mother would have to take her place. Grace was twenty-six years old. She knew her responsibilities. She had no doubt her mother wouldn't survive whatever they demanded, otherwise they wouldn't have re-quired her presence. Grace knew what she had to do, but her nerves had been rubbed raw, and she simply stood, unable to move, her muscles locked into a rigid knot. She willed her body to obey, but it refused.

The crowd of people parted. A man stood at the end of the hallway. He seemed too large somehow, too tall, too broad, and emanated power. He loomed, a spot of otherworldly magic among people who stubbornly ignored his existence. She saw him with preternatural clarity, from the ash-blond hair falling to his shoulders to the pale green eyes, brimming with mournful melancholy like the eyes of a Russian icon. His was the face of a brute: powerful, stubborn, aggressive, almost savage in its severity.

He looked straight at her and in the depths of those green irises she saw an unspoken confirmation: *he knew*. He knew who she was, why she was here, and, more, if she were to turn around and dash away, he wouldn't chase her. The choice was hers and he was content to let her decide.

The flow of people blocked him and she reeled, released from the spell of his eyes.

Uncle Gerald thrust into her view. "What is it? You have to come now, we can't keep them waiting, we—"

She looked at him, suddenly calm. Whatever would be would be. Her family owed a debt. Her mother had been paying it for years, carrying the burden alone. It was her turn. "Uncle," she said, holding on to her newfound peace.

"Yes?"

"You have to be quiet now. They're here."

He stared at her, stunned. Grace shouldered her bag and walked on.

They reached the end of the hallway. The man was gone, but Grace didn't worry about it. She headed to the twin slope of escalators. Behind her Gerald mumbled something to himself. They took the escalator down to the baggage claim.

"Grace!" The shot laced her ears. She wheeled about and saw her mother on the escalator rising in the opposite direction. Her mother stared at her, a horrified expression stamped on her face.

"Mom!"

"Grace! What are you doing here?"

Mother turned around and clutched the escalator handrail, trying to head down, but two people in grey blocked her. She pushed against them. "Let me through! Gerald, you old fool, what have you done? I've lived my life, she hasn't. She can't do this. Damn it, let me through!"

The escalators dragged them in opposite directions. Grace spun around to run up the moving steps and saw the man with green eyes blocking her way. He towered behind her uncle, immovable like a mountain. Green eyes greeted her again. Power coursed through them and vanished, a sword shown and thrust back into its scabbard. Uncle Gerald turned, saw him and went as white as a sheet.

They reached the bottom. Three people in grey waited for them, one woman and two men. Grace stepped onto the floor, light-headed as if in a dream.

"I've done . . . I've done the best I could," Gerald muttered. "The best. I—"

"You've done wonderfully," the woman said. "Nikita will escort you back to your plane."

One of the men stepped up and held out his hand, indicating the escalator heading up. "Please."

The green-eyed man stepped past them. His gaze paused on Grace's face. An unspoken command to follow. Grace clenched her teeth. They both knew she would obey, and they both realized she hated it.

He strode unhurriedly towards the glass doors. Grace matched her stride to his. She supposed she should have bowed and kept her mouth shut until she was spoken to, but she felt too hollow to care. "You robbed me of what might be my last moment with my mother," Grace said softly.

"It couldn't be helped," he answered, his voice quiet and deep.

They stepped into sunshine in unison. A black vehicle waited for them, sleek and stylish. The trunk clicked open. Grace deposited her backpack into it. The man held the rear door open for her. Grace took her seat on the leather.

The man slid next to her, filling the vehicle with his presence. She felt the warmth of his body and the almost imperceptible brush of his magic. That light touch betrayed him. She glimpsed power slumbering inside him, like an enormous bear ready to be roused and enraged in an instant. It sent shivers down her back, and it took all of her will to not wrench the car door open and run for her life. "You're him."

He inclined his head. "Yes."

The car pulled away from the kerb, carrying them off. Grace looked out of the window. She had made her choice. She was a servant of Clan Dreoch and there was no turning back.

The scenery rolled by, scrawny shrubs and flat land, its sparseness mirroring her bleak mood. Grace closed her eyes. A whisper of magic tugged on her. It was a polite touch, an equivalent to a bow. She glanced at him. Careful green eyes studied her. "What's your name?" he asked.

"Grace."

"It's a lovely name. You may call me Nassar."

Or "Master", she thought and bit the words before they had a chance to escape.

"How much do you know?" he asked.

"I know that my family owes your family a debt. One of you can call on one of us at any time and we must obey. If we break our oath, you'll murder all of us." She wished she had been told about it sooner, not that it would make any difference at the end.

His magic brushed her again and she edged away from it.

"What else?" Nassar asked.

Say as little as possible. "I know what you are."

"What am I?"

"A revenant."

"And what would that be?"

She looked him in the eye. "A man who died and robbed another of his body so he can continue to live." The cursed revenant, Gerald had called him. A bodysnatcher. An abomination. Monstrously powerful, clouded in vile magic, a beast more than a man.

Nassar showed no reaction, but a small ripple in his magic sent her further away from him. She bumped into the door.

"Any further and you'll fall out of the car," he said.

"Your magic . . . It's touching me."

"If all goes as planned, you and I will have to spend the next few days in close proximity. I need you to become accustomed to my power. Our survival will depend on it."

She sensed his magic halt a few inches from her, waiting tentatively. She was a servant; he could force her. At least he permitted her an illusion of free will. Grace swallowed and moved within its reach. His magic brushed her. She winced, expecting his power to mug her, but it simply touched her gently, as if her magic and his held hands.

"I won't hurt you," he said. "I know how people in your family see me. Body thief, aberration, murderer. The Cursed One. What I'm called doesn't concern me. Neither I nor my family will torture, rape or degrade you in any way. I simply have a specific task I need completed. I need you to want to succeed with me. What would make you want to help me?"

"Freedom," she said. "Let my family go, and I'll do whatever you ask."

He shook his head. "I can't give you permanent freedom. We need your services too much. But I can offer you a temporary reprieve. If you and I succeed, you can go home and I promise not to call on you and yours for six months."

"Ten years."

"A year."

"Eight."

"Five." The resolute tone of his voice told her it was his last offer.

"Deal," she said softly. "What happens if I fail?"

"We'll both die. But, our chances of success will be much better if you stop fearing me."

That was certainly true. "I'm not scared of you."

His lips curved slightly. "You're terrified."

She raised her chin. "The sooner we get done, the faster I can go home. What do you need me to do?"

Nassar reached into his jacket and took out a rolled-up piece of paper. "In our world disputes between the clans are resolved through war or by arbitration."

Grace arched her eyebrow. "How many clans are there?"

"Twelve. We're now in dispute with Clan Roar. War is bloody, costly and painful for everyone involved and neither of the families can afford it now. We've chosen arbitration. The issue is pressing and the dispute will be decided through a game."

He unrolled the picture and held it. She would have to move closer to him to see it. Grace sighed and moved another three inches to the right. Their thighs almost touched.

Nassar showed her the paper. It was an aerial photograph of a city.

"Milligan City," Nassar said. "Squarely in the middle of the rust belt. A couple of decades ago it was a busy town, a blue-collar haven. Good life, family values."

"Defined future," she said.

He nodded. "Yes. Then the conglomerates shifted their operations overseas. The jobs dried up, the real-estate values plummeted, and the residents fled. Now Milligan's population is down 42 per cent. It's a ghost city, with all the requisite ghost city problems: abandoned houses, squatters, fires and so on." He tapped the paper. "This particular neighbourhood is completely deserted. The city council's getting desperate. They relocated the last of the stragglers to the centre of the city and condemned this neighbourhood. In nine days, it will be bulldozed to make way for a park. The arbitration will take place here."

"When I think of arbitration, I think of lawyers," Grace said. "Both sides present their case and argue to a third party."

"Unfortunately this case isn't something that can be settled through litigation," Nassar answered. "Think of it in this way: instead of having a large war, we decided to have a very small one. The rules are simple. This area of the city was warded off from the rest, hidden in the cocoon of magic and altered. It's been officially condemned, so no others are allowed near it. Those who try are firmly discouraged, but if someone does make it through, to their eyes the area will appear as it always was."

She chewed on that "others". Normal, non-magical people. He said it in the way one might refer to foreigners.

"Arbitration by game is a big event. By last count, representatives of ten clans have shown up for the fun. Two weeks were allowed to each clan who so wished to dump whatever hazards they could manage into this space. It's full of things that go bump in the night."

"The other clans don't like you," she said.

"None of the clans like each other. We compete for territory and business. We have wars and bloody battles. And it will be up to you and me to help us avoid such a war this time." He touched the photograph. "Somewhere in the zone the arbi-traries have hidden a small flag. Two teams will enter the game zone to retrieve the flag, while the rest of the clansmen will bet on the outcome and enjoy their popcorn. Whoever touches the flag first will win and be ported out of the zone. Whether the flag is retrieved or not, in three days' time the wards will constrict, sweeping anything magic from the area into its centre. The pyromancers will destroy it in a preternaturally hot bon-fire, while the locals blissfully sleep."

"Are we one of the teams?"

"Yes."

Now she understood. Mother was almost fifty and over-weight. She wouldn't be able to move fast enough. They needed someone younger and she fitted the bill. "Will the rival team try to kill us?"

Another light smile touched his lips. "Most definitely."

"I don't have any offensive magic."

"I'm sure," he said. "You're entirely too polite for that."

It took her a moment to catch the pun. "I'm a dud. I sense magic and I can do small insignificant things, but I can't foretell the future like my mother and I haven't been trained as a fighter like Gerald. For all practical purposes, I'm the 'other', a com-pletely ordinary person. I've never fired a gun, I'm not excep-tionally athletic, and my strength and reflexes are average."

"I understand."

"Then why do you need—" Magic stabbed her, cold and sharp, wrenching a startled gasp from her. Her eyes watered from pain.

"Lilian!" Nassar barked.

"Go!" The chauffeur mashed a square button on her dash-board.

The roof of the vehicle slid aside. A dark sheath coated Nassar.

The pain pierced Grace's ribs, slicing its way inside.

Nassar jerked her to him. She collided with the hard wall of his chest, unable to breathe.

The dark sheath flared from him, filling the vehicle in long protrusions, shaping into a multitude of pale feathers.

"Hold on," Nassar snarled.

Grace threw her arms around his neck and they shot straight up, into the sky. Wind rushed at her. The pain vanished. She looked down and almost screamed – the car was far below.

"Don't panic."

The flesh of Nassar's neck crawled under her fingers, growing thicker. She turned to him and saw a sea of feathers and, high above, huge raptor jaws armed with crocodile teeth. Her arms shook with the strain of her dead weight.

"It's OK," the monster reassured her in Nassar's voice.

Her hold gave. For a precious second, Grace clung to the feathers, but her fingers slipped. She dropped like a stone. Her throat constricted. She cried out and choked as a huge claw snapped closed about her stomach.

"Grace?" The feathered monster bent his neck. A round green eye glared at her.

She sucked the air into her lungs and finally breathed. "Your definition of OK has problems." The wind muffled her voice.

"What?" he bellowed.

"I said, your definition of OK has problems!" The ground rolled past them, impossibly far. She clenched her hands on the enormous scaly talons gripping her. "Is there any chance that this could be a dream?"

"I'm afraid not."

Her heart hammered so hard, she was worried it would jump out of her chest. "What was it?"

"Clan Roar – our opponents in the game. Or one of their agents, to be exact. They're not dumb enough to attack you directly. Once the game is scheduled, all hostilities between the participants must cease. Interference of this sort is forbidden."

"What about Lilian?"

"She can take care of herself."

Grace shivered. "Why would they be attacking me in the first place?"

"You're my defence. If they kill you, I'll have to withdraw from the game."

"That sounds ridiculous! You're the revenant and I can't even defend myself."

"I'll explain everything later. We're beyond their range now and we'll arrive soon. Try to relax."

She was clutched in the talons of a monstrous creature, who was really a man trying to rescue her from a magical attack by flying hundreds of feet above solid ground. *Relax*. Right. "I serve a madman," she muttered.

Far beyond the fields, an empty piece of the horizon shimmered and drained down, revealing a dark spire. Tower Dreoch, Uncle Gerald had called it. He'd said the Dreochs lived in a castle. She thought he'd exaggerated.

Nassar careened, turning, and headed to the tower.

They circled the tower once before Nassar dived to a balcony and dropped her into a waiting group of people below. Hands caught her and she was gently lowered to the ground.

In the overcast sky, Nassar swung upwards and swooped down. The group parted. A dark-skinned woman grasped Grace by her waist and pulled her aside with the ease one picks up a child.

Nassar dived down. His huge talons skidded on the balcony and he tumbled into the room beyond. Feathers swirled. He staggered up. "Leave us."

People fled past her. In a moment the room was empty.

Grace hugged herself. Up there, in the evening sky, the cold air had chilled her so thoroughly, even her bones felt iced over. Her teeth still chattered. She stepped to the double doors and shut them, blocking off the balcony and the draught with it.

The large rectangular room was simply but elegantly furnished: a table with some chairs, a wide bed with a gauzy blue canopy, a bookcase, some old, solidly built chairs before the fireplace. A couple of electric table lamps radiated soft yellow light. An oriental silk rug covered the floor.

Nassar slumped in front of the fireplace. Bright orange flames threw highlights on his feathers, making them almost golden in the front. His feathers seemed shorter. His jaws no longer protruded quite as much.

Grace crossed the carpet and stood before the fire, soaking in the warmth. It all seemed so dreamlike. Unreal.

"This will be your room for the next couple of days," he said.

"You have no idea how strange this is to me," she murmured.

His smart eyes studied her. "Tell me about it?"

"In my world people don't turn into . . . into this." She indicated him with her hand. His feathers definitely were shorter now. He'd shrunk a little. "People don't fly unless they have a glider or some sort of metal contraption with an engine designed to help them. Nobody tries to murder someone through magic. Nobody has mysterious castles masquerading as empty fields."

A careful knock interrupted her.

"It's your room," Nassar murmured.

"Come in," she called.

A man entered, pushing a small trolley with a teakettle, two cups, a dish of sugar, a ewer of cream and a platter with assorted cookies. As he passed her, she saw a short sword in a sheath at his waist. "Your sister suggested tea, sir."

"Very thoughtful of her."

The man left the trolley, smiled at Grace, and departed.

Grace poured two cups of tea.

"I suppose in your world people don't drink tea either?" he asked.

"We drink tea," she said with a sigh. "We just don't always have servants armed with swords to bring it. Cream?"

"Sugar and lemon, please." Nassar had returned to his normal size. The feathers were mere fur now, and his face was bare and completely human.

"What's happening with your feathers?"

"I'm consuming them to replenish some of my energy. Transformations such as this are difficult even for me." He sank into a chair, took a cup from her with furry fingers, and sipped from it. "Perfect. Thank you."

"I live to serve."

His lips curved into a familiar half-smile. "Somehow I deeply doubt it."

Grace sank into the other chair and sipped shockingly hot tea, liberally whitened by cream. Liquid heat flowed through her. His magic brushed her again, but she had flown over miles bathed in it and she accepted his touch without protest. She was so very tired. "This is a dream. I'll wake up, and all of this will be gone. And I'll go back to my quiet little job."

"What is it you do?"

Grace shrugged. He knew, of course. His clan had been keeping tabs on her family for years. When you own something, you want to pay attention to its maintenance. He probably knew what size of underwear she wore and how she preferred her steak. "Why don't you tell me?"

"You're a headhunter. You find jobs for others. Do you like it?"

"Yes. It's boring at times and stressful, but I get to help people."

"You didn't know about your family's debt, did you?" he asked.

"No." She refilled her cup.

"When did you find out?"

"Three days ago."

"Was it sudden?"

"Yes," she admitted. "I always knew about magic. I was born able to feel it. At first I was told I was a very sensitive child, and then, once I was old enough to realize I needed to keep it to myself, more complicated explanations followed. I live in a world of very small magics. I can sense if I'll miss the bus. In school, I could usually foretell my grade on tests, but I could never predict anything else accurately. If I concentrate very hard, I can scare animals. A dog once tried to chase me, and I was frightened and sent it running."

She drank again. "Small things, mostly useless. I thought that all magic users were like me. Working their little powers in secret. I never imagined people could fly in the open. Or walk through crowded airports without being seen. My mother is a fabric buyer. My uncle's a mechanic who really likes weapons. My dad's normal in every way. My mother and he divorced when I was eighteen. He runs a shift at a tyre repair plant."

Grace drank more tea. Her head was fuzzy. She was so comfortable and warm in the soft chair. "When Uncle Gerald told me this half-baked story about blood debt, I didn't believe him at first."

"What convinced you?"

"He was terrified. Uncle Gerald is like a rock in the storm: always cool under pressure. I've never seen him so off balance."

She yawned. She was so drowsy. "I think my mother hoped I would never have to do this."

"I can see why," Nassar said softly. "We live in constant danger. I would think any mother would want to shield her child from us."

"I would." Drowsiness overtook her. Grace set the cup down and curled into a ball in the chair. "Even though your world is so . . ."

She vaguely saw him rise from his chair. He picked her up, his magic cloaking about her. She should have been alarmed, but she had no resolve left.

"So?"

"So magical."

He drew the canopy aside and lowered her onto the bed. Her head touched the pillow and reality faded.

Nassar stepped out of the room, gently closing the door behind him. Alasdair waited in the hallway, a lean sharp shadow, with a robe draped over his arm. Nassar took it from him and shrugged it on, absorbing the last of his feathers. His whole body hurt from too much magic expended too quickly. Walking was like stepping on crushed glass.

"Is she asleep?" Alasdair asked.

Nassar nodded. They walked down the hall together.

"She's pretty. Chestnut hair and chocolate eyes – a nice combination."

She was also calm under pressure, smart and wilful. When she looked at him with those dark eyes, Nassar felt the urge to say something intelligent and deeply impressive. Unfortunately, nothing of the kind came to mind. It seemed her eyes also had a way of muddling his thoughts. The last time he felt that dumb was about fourteen years ago. He'd been eighteen at the time.

"You like the girl," Alasdair offered.

Nassar levelled a heavy gaze at him.

"Lilian said you tried to be funny in the car. I told her it couldn't possibly be true. The moment you try to make a joke, the sky shall split and the Four Horsemen will ride out, heralding Apocalypse."

"How droll. Did you double the patrols?"

Alasdair nodded his dark head and stopped by the ladder. Nassar walked past him, heading to his rooms.

"Did you?" Alasdair called.

"Did I what?"

"Did you joke with the girl?"

Nassar kept walking.

"Did she laugh?" Alasdair called.

"No."

Nassar entered his room. He hadn't expected her to laugh. He was grateful she didn't collapse in a hysterical heap. Her uncle had been scared to within an inch of his life – fear had rolled off of him in waves. In Gerald's life of some fifty odd years his services had been requested only twice, but the second time had scarred him for life. In the zone he would be useless.

Grace's mother, Janet, was always meticulous and formal. She took no initiative. Working with her was like being in the presence of an automaton that obeyed his every order while being grimly determined to dislike it. Taking her into the zone, even if he could compensate for her age and health, would be suicide.

He was never comfortable with any of them. He was never comfortable with the whole idea of the bonded servant and took pains to avoid requesting their presence. But this time he had no choice.

Working with Grace presented its own set of difficulties. He could still remember her scent: the light clean fragrance of soap mixing with the faint rosemary from her dark hair. His memory conjured the feel of her body pressed against his and when he'd picked her up to place her on the bed, he hadn't wanted to let go. He wasn't an idiot. There was an attraction there, and he would have to manage it very carefully. The imbalance of power between the two of them was too pronounced: he was the master and she was the servant. Don't think about it, he told himself. Don't imagine what it would be like. Nothing can happen. Nothing is going to happen. She's off-limits.

Grace followed the servant into a spacious atrium. Morning sun shone through the glass panels in the ceiling. The stone path wound between lush greenery, parallel to a stream lined with smooth river pebbles. Spires of bamboo rose next to ficus and ferns. Delicate orchids in half-a-dozen shades dotted the moss-covered ground. Red Kaffir lilies bloomed along the stream's banks, echoed by paler blossoms of camellia bushes. The air smelled sweet.

The path turned, parting, and Grace saw the origin of the stream: a ten-foot waterfall at the far wall. The water cascaded over huge grey boulders into a tiny lake. Near the shore stood a low coffee table surrounded by benches. A dark-haired man lounged on the bench to the left, sipping tea from a large cup.

Nassar stood next to him, talking softly. He wore blue sweatpants and a light-grey T-shirt. A towel hung over his shoulder and his pale hair was wet and brushed back from his face. Poised like this, he appeared massive. Muscles bulged on his chest when he moved his arm to underscore a point. His biceps stretched the sleeves of his shirt. His legs were long. Everything about him, from the breadth of his shoulders to the way he carried himself – controlled and aware of his size – communicated raw physical power. His wasn't the static bulk of a power weightlifter, but rather the dangerous, honed build of a man who required muscle to survive. If a genius sculptor wished to carve a statue and name it *Strength*, Nassar would've made a perfect model.

He glanced at her. His green eyes arrested her and Grace halted, suddenly realizing she wanted to know what he would look like naked.

The thought shocked her.

Something in her face must've equally shocked him, because he fell silent.

A torturous second passed.

She forced herself to move. Nassar looked away, resuming his conversation.

I can't be attracted to him. He forced me to come here and risk my life and I don't even know why. I know nothing about him. He's a monster. That last thought sobered her up. She approached the benches.

"Grace," Nassar said. His magic brushed her. "This is Alasdair, my cousin."

Alasdair unfolded himself from the bench. "Charmed."

"Hello." Grace nodded at Alasdair, then turned to Nassar. "You drugged my drink."

"Actually I drugged the cream," he said, "and technically it was my sister who did it."

"Why?"

"You were in shock. I wanted to spare you the breakdown and anxiety when you came out of it."

Grace held herself straight. "I would appreciate it if you didn't do it again. We have a deal. I'll keep my part, but I can't do it if I have to watch what I eat and drink."

Nassar considered it for a long moment. "Agreed."

"A deal?" Alasdair's eyebrows crept up. He was lean and sharp, his movements quick. His stare had an edge. If Nassar was a sword, Alasdair was a dagger.

"I've agreed to do my best to help you and, in return, you'll leave my family alone for five years," Grace said.

Alasdair grimaced at Nassar. "That's incredibly generous, considering what they've done. We owe them nothing."

Nassar shrugged his massive shoulders. "It's worth the reward to have her full cooperation."

Grace took a seat on the bench. "What did we do exactly?"

"You don't know?" Alasdair passed her a plate of scones.

"No."

The dark-haired man glanced at Nassar, who shrugged. "You tell it," he said.

"At the end of the nineteenth century your family and our clan were in dispute," Alasdair said.

Grace was learning to decipher their code. "In other words, we were murdering each other."

"Precisely. The dispute grew out of control and so our families agreed to end it. The peace was to be sealed through a wedding. Jonathan Mailliard of your family was to marry Thea Dreoch."

"He was your great-grandfather's brother," Nassar supplied.

"The wedding went well," Alasdair continued. "There was a very nice reception in one of the Mailliard gathering halls, a beautiful old hotel. Everyone ate, drank and was merry. The couple went upstairs to their rooms, where Jonathan pulled out a knife and slit Thea's throat."

Grace froze with a scone halfway to her mouth. She had expected something of this sort. To force her family into indefinite servitude, the crime had to be horrible. But it still shocked her.

"He waited for almost two hours by her cooling corpse," Alasdair continued, "until the party died down. Then he and several Mailliard men and women went through the hotel door to door. They murdered Thea's sister, her husband and their twin daughters who were flower girls at the wedding. They killed Thea's parents and her two brothers, both minors, and would've slaughtered the entire party, but they were seen by a Dreoch retainer, who started screaming. Our offensive magic was always stronger and we were inside your family's defences. There was a bloodbath. Every member of the Mailliard family was killed, except Thomas Mailliard, who was fourteen at the time. He hid in a closet and wasn't discovered until later in the day, when the butchery had stopped. Because Thomas was a child and hadn't participated in the slaughter, he was given a choice: death or servitude for all of his descendants. And that's why you now serve us."

Grace sat in a sickened silence.

"Anything to say?" Alasdair asked.

"That's very horrible," she said.

"Yes, it is."

"However, I never knew Jonathan Mailliard. I didn't even know his name. I feel awful about the murder and I understand that my family bears responsibility, but *I* never killed anyone. I've never hurt you and neither has my mother, my uncle nor my great-grandfather, who hid in the closet." She tried to make her voice sound calm and reasonable. "I've done you no harm, yet you limit my freedom and force me to risk my life because of a crime perpetrated a century ago by someone I've never met. Our family has served yours for over a hundred years. At some point this debt will have been repaid. When do you think will that be?"

"Never," Alasdair said.

It felt like a slap. She looked to Nassar. "So this is how you do things? You dumped all of the blame for a bloody feud onto a fourteen-year-old child who hid in a closet, and because he failed to stop grown men from killing, you keep his descendants in perpetual servitude?"

"Hardly perpetual," Nassar corrected. "Since I assumed the responsibility for the clan fifteen years ago, I've called on your family only four times."

"But we know we can be called on at any point. We have to live with the knowledge that at a moment's notice we might be required to risk our life for a complete stranger for no reason and we might never see our loved ones again. We can't refuse. The terms are obedience or death. Would you want to live like this?"

"No," Nassar admitted.

"Can you tell me when the debt will be paid?" she asked.

"This arrangement is to our advantage," Nassar said. "It makes no sense for us to release you."

"I see. I'll have to release us then."

"Really?" Alasdair gave a short barking laugh. "How exactly are you planning on doing that?"

"My uncle has no offspring and I'm my mother's only child. To my knowledge, I'm the last of the Mailliards. I'll have to make sure that I don't continue the line." She rose. "I think I've seen the washroom on the way here. I really need to splash some water on my face."

"Second door on the right," Nassar told her.

"Excuse me."

Grace walked away. Her knees shook a little in her jeans. Her face burned.

Nassar watched Grace's figure retreat down the winding path.

"Wow," Alasdair offered.

"Yes."

"Think she'll do it?"

"She's a Mailliard."

He'd seen the same steely resolve in her mother's eyes, Nassar reflected. He suspected it was the same will that drove the wedding night atrocities a century ago. It enabled her mother, Janet, to grimly bear her service, and fuelled Grace's fight against it. He doubted she would ever go into outright rebellion, not while her mother and Gerald were alive, but he could tell by the way she held herself, by her face and her eyes and her voice, that she would rather give up her future children than bring them into the Dreochs' "service".

"You like her," Alasdair said.

"What of it?"

"Why don't you make a move?"

The imbalance of power between them was too great, and her antipathy and contempt for Clan Dreoch was painfully obvious. Nassar took the towel off his shoulder and sat on the bench. "Because she can't say no."

When Grace returned, Alasdair was gone; Nassar sat alone. It was easier if she simply admitted it, Grace decided. Sometimes you see another person in passing, your eyes meet, and you know by some instinct that there is something there. She felt that something for Nassar.

It was wrong on so many levels that her head reeled from simply contemplating it. He was a revenant, a creature more than a man. Her great-grandfather's brother slaughtered his relatives. His family held hers in bondage. If he really wanted her, he could simply order her to submit. Maybe it was some sort of twisted version of Stockholm syndrome. Or an animal attraction. He was . . . not handsome exactly, but very male. Powerful. Masculine. Strong. But there was more to it: the sadness in his eyes, the courteous way he managed himself, the feel of his magic. It pulled her to him and she would have to be very careful to keep her distance.

"You still haven't told me what you need me to do," she said.

He rose. "Walk with me, please."

Grace followed him down the path deeper into the atrium. Nassar led her out through an arched door and into a large round chamber. Bare, it was lit by sunlight spilling through a skylight very high above. A thick metal grate guarded the skylight. Plain concrete made up the floor, showing a complicated geometric pattern with a circle etched into its centre. Nassar stood on its edge.

"When a revenant takes a new body, he gains great power but he also inherits the weaknesses of that body. The body I took was cursed. After I transferred into it, I was able to heal the damage and break the curse. But all of my invulnerability to the curse is gone. I've used it all up."

"And the man who was born in this body? What happened to him when you took it?"

"He died," Nassar said.

She'd hoped he wouldn't say that.

A woman entered the chamber through the door in the opposite wall. A pale blonde like Nassar. She smiled at them. Nassar didn't quite smile back, but the melancholy of his face eased slightly.

"This is Elizavetta. My sister."

"Call me Liza," she said. "Everyone does."

"Grace," Grace said simply. "You're the one who drugged the cream."

Liza nodded. "Yes. Alasdair warned me I may have earned your undying hate for it. I sincerely hope we can put it past us. I didn't mean to hurt your feelings in any way."

"Given that I'm a servant, my feelings are hardly relevant, but I appreciate it," Grace said.

Liza blinked. An uncomfortable silence ensued. Nassar cleared his throat. "Liz?"

"Yes, right." Liza stepped inside the design.

"Every revenant has a fatal weakness," Nassar said, his gaze fixed on his sister. "This is mine."

Liza arched her back, spreading her arms. Her hands clawed the air. She spun in a place, twisting. Magic pulsed from her and filled the lines etched on the floor with pale yellow light. Liza brought her hands together, cried out and forced them apart with a pained grimace. A clump of mottled darkness appeared between her fingers. She stepped back.

The clump spun, growing, and ruptured, vomiting a creature into the circle. The beast was three-feet long and slender, shaped like a slug or a leech except for the fringe of carmine feathery hairs along its sides. A patina of grey and sickly yellow swirled over its dark hide, like an oil rainbow on the surface of a dark puddle.

The creature shivered. The red fringe trembled and it took to the air, sliding soundlessly a foot off the ground. A cold, foul magic emanated from it. It touched Grace. She jerked back and bumped into Nassar.

"What is that?"

He put his hand on her shoulder, steadying her. "A marrow worm. They live in dark places, where there is stagnant water and decay. They feed on small animals, fish and old magic."

The worm hovered behind the glowing outline of the circle. Its head was blunt and as it rose up, testing the boundaries of its invisible cage, Grace saw a slit of a mouth lined with sharp serrated teeth on its underside.

Liza approached the worm. The creature shied away, sliding as close to the glowing lines as it could.

"Think of them as germs. Most people have a natural resistance to them, an immunity. I don't. To me, they're fatal. We did our best to keep this fact to ourselves, but I have no doubt the Roars know it. They would be fools not to. Unfortunately, marrow worms are easy to summon."

He'd stepped behind her and she was painfully sensitive to the presence of his large body only an inch from her back. His magic touched her. Her every nerve shivered, hyperaware of his movements. She sensed him lean to her and almost jumped when his quiet voice spoke into her ear. "Do you remember when you sent that dog running? I want you to do that again."

Grace swallowed. "I don't remember what I did. It just happened."

His big hand pushed against her back gently, making her take a step towards the circle. "Try."

Grace took a deep breath and stepped over the glowing lines inside the circle. The worm jerked away from her like a wet ribbon. Grace glanced at Nassar.

"That's just normal resistance to humans. Keep trying."

Grace stared at the worm twisting. Go away, she thought. Gone. I want you gone.

The worm remained where it was.

Grace glanced at Liza. "Any idea what I'm supposed to be doing?"

Nassar's sister shook her blonde head. "None. Dreochs are aggressors. We have few defensive abilities and they're radically different from yours. Mostly our defences consist of Nassar hacking at things with something large and sharp."

"The magic you're trying to do is called the Barrier," Nassar said. "It's one of the natural Mailliards' magics. Very talented members of your family used it both as a defence and as a weapon. Your mother stated that it can't be taught. You simply do it or you don't."

Grace focused on the worm and tried to pretend it was a large, mean-looking German shepherd.

An hour later she sat exhausted on the floor. The worm floated at the edge of the design.

"It's useless." Liza unscrewed a cap from a fresh bottle of water. She had gotten a cooler with drinks, migrated to the wall, and now sat on the floor. "Why Janet didn't practise with Grace is beyond me, but she didn't. We'll have to change the plan. Instead of you and Grace, I'll go with Alasdair."

"No." Steel laced Nassar's voice. He leaned against the wall.

"You're being unreasonable."

Nassar's face was dark like a storm. "Both of you will die. I have resistances and power to counter Clan Roar's attacks. You don't."

"You can't counter this one."

He didn't answer.

"Why don't you just turn into a bird and fly through the zone?" Grace asked.

"Flight is forbidden in the game," Nassar answered.

Liza sighed. "Grace, would you like some water?"

"Yes."

Liza tossed her a new bottle.

"Thank you." Grace caught it. "Why are you fighting the Roars anyway? What's this dispute about?"

"It's about children," Nassar said. "And killing me."

"Our aunt married a member of Clan Roar," Liza said. "Arthur Roar. He turned out to be a wart on the ass of the human kind: abusive, violent, cruel. She left after eight years and took their three kids with her."

"Should've left sooner," Nassar said. His green eyes promised violence, the light irises so cold that Grace took a small step back.

"She had her reasons for staying," Liza said. "There was a large dowry involved and she didn't want us to have to pay restitution and interest. But in the end it was just too much. After Arthur broke his son's legs, she grabbed the kids and came home. Now, nine years later, Arthur suddenly wants his children back."

Liza took a drink from her bottle. "He's never shown any interest in them. No calls, no letters, not even a card. He's done nothing to support them. But Aunt Bella signed the wedding agreement that specified equal amount of time with the children for each parent in the event of separation. Arthur claims that since the kids were with her exclusively for nine years, now he has exclusive rights to them."

"He doesn't give a damn about the kids. It's an excuse for the Roars to test the waters," Nassar said. "They have a couple of strong people and they're thinking of moving in on our interests. Before they do it, they want to weaken us. They knew that if they challenged the clan, I would enter the game, and they believe they have a reasonable chance of killing me. They'll knock out the biggest power user of our clan and earn respect from other clans for killing a revenant, and they will do it all before the war ever starts."

He pushed from the wall. "It's almost time for lunch. Let's take a break."

Lunch was laid out on a long table in a vast dining hall. Nassar held out a chair for Grace and she sat down. He took a place to her right, while Liza sat down at her left, next to Alasdair. Other people came into the room – two men and three women. They took their seats, nodded and smiled, started conversations in calm voices. Alasdair said something and a woman laughed. They were so at ease and the warmth of their interaction began to thaw Grace's resolve.

The four chairs directly opposite her remained empty. She wondered who would sit there and a couple of minutes later she had her answer. Three children entered the room, followed by a pale woman. Of course. Nassar had arranged it so she would spend the meal looking at the faces of the children whose fate would be decided in the game.

They took their seats: the woman with careworn eyes, a young boy with a wild mass of dark hair, and two girls, one slender and blonde, and the other only about ten or so, with short dark hair and big blue eyes. The youngest girl saw Nassar and came grinning around the table. "Hug?" she asked him seriously.

"Hug," he agreed and put his massive arms around her.

"And no dying," she reminded him.

He let go and nodded.

The girl noticed her. "Hi. I'm Polina."

It was impossible not to smile back. "Hi. I'm Grace."

"You're supposed to protect Nassar," Polina said.

"That's what he tells me."

The child looked at her with her blue eyes. "Please don't let him die," she said softly. "I like him a lot."

"I'll try my best."

Polina went around the table to her seat. Grace leaned to Nassar and whispered, "Laying it on a little thick, don't you think?"

"I didn't put her up to it," he told her.

She glanced into his green eyes and believed him.

Lunch went on. Dishes were brought and passed around the table: roast beef and mashed potatoes, green beans, corn, iced tea and lemonade. The food was delicious, but Grace ate little. Mostly she watched the children. The boy leaned to his mother, making sure her cup was filled. The older girl seemed on the verge of tears. She became more and more agitated, until finally, just as peach cobbler made its way past Grace, the girl dropped her fork. Her voice rang out. "What if they win?"

The table fell quiet.

"They won't," Nassar said calmly.

"If Arthur touches us, I'll kill him." Steel vibrated in the boy's voice.

Their mother leaned her elbows on the table and rested her forehead on her hands. "No. You're not strong enough," she told him in a dull voice. "Not yet. You must do whatever it takes to survive."

"That's enough." Nassar's magic surged out, spreading behind him like invisible wings. It brushed against Grace. Breath caught in her throat. So much power . . .

Nassar fixed the children with his stare. "You're our kin. You belong to Clan Dreoch. Nobody will take you from us. Anyone who tries will have to go through me."

With his power rising above the table, the prospect of going through him seemed impossible. His magic was staggering. It would take an army.

The anxiety slowly melted from the children's faces.

"Let's try again," Nassar said, as the two of them strode back into the room.

The worm still floated in the circle. Grace stepped inside. It shied from her. "Why did you tell the children about the curse?"

"I won't lie to them. The possibility of defeat exists and they have to be prepared."

That defeat seemed very likely at the moment.

"But I will fight to the death to keep them safe. And even if I lose, the clan won't surrender them. We will go to war. We won't turn over children to a man who will break their bones."

Neither would she. It didn't matter who they were. A child was a child. She couldn't let them suffer, not after watching them near panic with the fear of having to leave their mother. Their family and their home, all would be ripped away if Nassar and she lost.

"Now do you understand why I fight?" he asked her softly.

She nodded.

"I need your help desperately. Please help me, Grace."

"I wish I could," she said, her voice filled with regret.

Nassar watched her for a long moment. "What do you remember about your encounter with the dog? What did you feel?"

Grace frowned. "It was twelve years ago. I remember being scared for myself. And for the dog. He was my friend's dog. I knew that if he bit me, he would be put down."

Nassar strode to her, a determined look on his face.

"What are you doing?"

Nassar kept coming.

She realized he was going to cross the line. "Liza isn't here to save you!"

"No." He gave her the familiar half-smile. "Only you can save me now."

Nassar stepped over the line. The worm streaked to him. It skimmed the surface of his magic and clamped onto his shoulder. Nassar's magic shrunk. He staggered and ripped the worm off. Grace cried out.

The worm flipped in the air and slid over him. Nassar tried to knock it off, but it slipped past his hands and leeched onto his side. Nassar gasped. His face went bloodlessly white. He spun, tripping over his feet, pulling at the writhing body, and stumbled to her. The worm slithered from his fingers and swooped down on him. Nassar fell.

Grace lunged forwards. She meant to thrust herself in front of it, but instead magic pulsed from her in a controlled, short burst. The worm hurtled back, swept aside.

She pushed harder and the worm convulsed, squeezed between the press of her power and the glowing lines. "Nassar?" She knelt by him. "Nassar, are you OK?"

Nassar's green eyes looked at her. His nose bled. He wiped away his blood with the back of his hand. "Protective instinct," he said. "You've done it."

It felt so right. As if the pressure straining at her from the inside suddenly found an outlet. So that's what she'd been missing. All these years, she had suspected there was something more to the magic coursing through her and now she finally found it.

"I guess I did," she murmured.

"Were you scared for me?"

"Yes. How could you have done that? That was so reckless. What if I couldn't save you?"

"I hoped you could," he said.

The way he looked at her made her want to kiss him.

"Your family is free," he said.

"What?"

"I've let Clan Mailliard go," he said. "I signed the order before lunch."

She sank to the floor. "Why?"

He sat up. "Because I decided that's not what I do. I don't force people to fight our battles. I don't want to be the man who blames children for their parents' mistakes. And I don't want you to be the last of the Mailliards. Whether you have children should be your choice alone. I don't want to take it away from you."

It slowly dawned on her. "So I'm free?"

"Yes."

She stared at him. "You don't even know me. I could just take off right now and leave you here to deal with the game on your own. Do you have any idea how scared I am? I don't want to die."

"Neither do I." He gave her another sad smile.

She hung her head, torn. She was deeply, deeply afraid. But walking away from the children wasn't in her. She wouldn't be able to look herself in the eye. It was as if they stood in the road with a semi hurtling at them at full speed. What kind of person wouldn't push them out of harm's way?

"I should practise more," she said.

"We're going to need another worm then," Nassar said.

She glanced at the beast. It lay dead, sliced in half.

"You killed it," he told her. "Sometimes the Barrier magic can also become a blade."

"But I don't even know how I've done it."

"We don't need to worry about that now," he said. "As long as you can defend me, we should be fine."

Three days later Grace stood in the middle of the street in Milligan City, hugging herself as the sun set slowly. Nassar loomed next to her. Behind them unfamiliar people moved, their magic shifting with them, their clothes colour-coded by their clan: grey and black for Dreoch, green for Roar, red for Madrid. Nassar had explained the rest of the colours, but she couldn't recall any of it. The anxiety pulsated through her with every heartbeat.

Ahead a seemingly empty stretch of a suburban street rolled into the sunset. The round, red sun hung low above the horizon, a glowing brand upon the clouds.

Familiar magic brushed her and a heavy hand touched her shoulder gently. Nassar. He wore grey pants tucked into military boots. A long-sleeved shirt hugged his arms and over it he wore a leather vest that wanted very much to be called armour. She wore the same outfit. The leather fitted her loosely enough not to be constricting, but tight enough not to get in the way.

"Don't worry," Nassar said.

Her gaze slid to the large axe strapped to his waist. She touched her own blade, a long, narrow combat knife. Gerald had taught her the basics of knife-fighting a long time ago but she'd never been in a real fight.

A male voice rose to the side. "Can he bring a servant into the game?"

It took a moment to sink in. Of course, her status would be public knowledge among them, but it still cut her like a knife. She turned. A group of people stood on the side. Five of them wore dark blue robes. The arbitrators, she remembered from Nassar's explanations. An older female in the arbitrator robe regarded her with serious grey eyes.

"If you want to withdraw, you may do so now," the woman said.

She could withdraw. She could simply refuse to go in. If she did, Nassar would be doomed. He had already committed to the game and she knew he couldn't simply substitute someone else in his place. He wouldn't.

Overnight, her fears had grown into near panic. Now she could walk away from them.

Grace looked at the gathering of the clansmen. Her family used to be a clan. Her people should have stood right here. Instead the clansmen viewed her as a servant. Pride spiked in her. She had as much right to be here as anybody else. The vague feeling of unease that had eaten at her ever since Nassar had transformed into a bird crystallized and she finally understood it: it was envy. Envy of the magic used freely. Envy of knowledge. Circumstances had jettisoned her out of this world, but she refused to stay locked out.

Grace drew herself to her full height. "Why in the world would I want to withdraw?"

A red-haired man in Clan Roar's green shook his head. "She can't refuse. She isn't even properly trained. She's a servant."

"Not any more," Nassar said softly behind her.

The gathering suddenly grew quiet.

The arbitrator surveyed them for a long moment. "Nassar, am I to understand that you've released Clan Mailliard from their service?"

"Yes," he answered.

The arbitrator looked at her. "You're here of your own free will?"

"Yes," Grace said.

The arbitrator glanced at the Roar clansman. "There is your answer. Let the record reflect that Clan Mailliard chose to assist Clan Dreoch. You have our leave to proceed."

They passed her. Grace let out her breath.

"Thank you," Nassar murmured.

"You're welcome."

Two young men in Clan Roar's green came to stand at the other end of the street. Both were lean, strong and hard, as if twisted from leather and twine. Both had long hair bound into horse tails: one red, one black.

Nassar leaned to her. "Conn and Sylvester Roar. Powerful, but they lack experience."

The arbitrators passed between them, blocking her vision. As the blue robes fluttered by, Grace saw Conn Roar turn to her. He grinned, his eyes alight with feral fire, and snapped his teeth.

Alarm dashed down her spine in a rush of cold. She raised her eyebrows. "Someone forgot his muzzle."

"See the pendant around Conn's neck?"

Grace glanced at a small black stone hanging on a long chain.

"That's a summoning stone. They'll use its power to manifest creatures."

Marrow worms. They'd use it to summon the marrow worms. Nassar had warned her that the Roars would try to kill them. Him, specifically. The game was only the opening salvo to the hostilities between the two clans, and the Roars wanted to land the first blow by taking out the Dreochs' best magic user.

The arbitrators raised their hands. A controlled surge of magic washed over the street. The reality drained down, as if it were a reflection in a melting mirror. A new street opened before them. Green and red lianas hung from the dark, sinister houses. Kudzu vines climbed in and out of windows. To the left a huge clump of yellow foam dripped rancid red juice onto the street. A puddle of brown slime slivered across the asphalt like an amoeba and slipped into the storm drain under the light of street lamps. Ahead something furry dashed across the intersection: a long, shaggy body with too many legs.

Somewhere in that zone a flag waited. Whoever touched the flag would be instantly transported out. They just had to survive long enough to reach it.

The woman arbitrator raised her hand, fist closed. Next to Grace, Nassar tensed.

"Let the game begin!" A white light pulsed from the arbitrator's fingers. The crowd erupted in a ragged cheer.

The two Roar clansmen screamed in unison. Flesh bulged out from under their skin. Their bodies contorted, their limbs thickened. Black fur sheathed their skin. Horns burst through their manes. Their eyes drowned in golden glow and an extra pair opened beside the first set. As one they raised monstrous faces up, the sharp fangs in their jaws silhouetted against the red sky. Eerie howls tore free from their throats, blending into a haunting song of hunt and murder.

The Roars dashed into the zone on all fours. Nassar watched them go, his face calm. Leaping and growling, they turned the corner and vanished behind the abandoned houses. The echoes of their snarls died. Nassar took his axe from its sheath, rested it on his shoulder, and strode into the zone, unhurried. Grace swallowed and followed in his footsteps.

The street lay quiet. They would be watched by magical means while in the zone, but for now the press of many stares bore directly into her back. Her nerves knotted into a clump.

They reached the intersection.

A hint of movement on the roof of a two-storey house made her turn. Grace frowned.

A flat, wide shape leaped off the roof, aiming at her. She caught a glimpse of a fang-studded mouth among bulging veins. Too stunned to move, she simply stared.

Nassar's huge back blocked the mouth. A hot whip of magic sprung from his hand, cleaving the creature in two. Twin halves of the beast fell to the ground, spilling steaming guts onto the asphalt.

"You're allowed to dodge," Nassar said.

★   ★   ★

The enormous blue beast bore on them. Grace watched it come. It thundered down the street, its six stumpy legs mashing potholes in the crumbling pavement.

In the past seven hours, she'd used her magic for defence countless times. Blood splattered her face, some dried to flecks, some still wet. Her side burned where a red, furry serpent had bitten her before Nassar chopped off both of its heads. A long rip split her left pant leg, exposing puckered flesh of the calf where a liana stung her with its suckers. It never ended. There was always a new horror waiting to pounce on them from some dark crevice. Grace clenched her teeth and watched the beast charge.

It brushed against a house, sending a shower of broken boards in the air, and kept coming, cavernous mouth gaping wide, the sound of its stomping like a cannon blast salute at a funeral. Boom-boom-boom.

Keep it together. Keep it steady.

Boom-boom-boom.

The beast was almost on her. Two bloodshot eyes glared. The black mouth opened, ready to devour her.

"Now!" Nassar barked.

She slammed her magic into it.

With a surprised roar, the beast rammed the invisible barrier. Her feet slid back from the pressure. The beast's momentum pitched it to the side. The mammoth body fell, paws in the air. Nassar leaped over it, a feral shadow caught in the moonlight. White light sliced like a huge blade from his hand and Nassar landed by her. Filthy and bloody, he looked demonic.

Behind him the beast lay split open, like a chicken with a cleaved breastbone. The soft, beach-ball-sized sac of its heart palpitated once, twice, and stopped,

Grace stared mutely at the carcass. She had never imagined the night could hide things like it – terrible, awful things. She felt like she had aged a lifetime.

A soft humming filled her skull. She shook her head.

"What is it?" Nassar grasped her face and turned it to him.

"Buzzing."

He raised his head, listened and grabbed her hand. "Run!"

She'd learned not to ask why. They sprinted, zigzagging through the labyrinthine streets, past overgrown lawns, past an abandoned playground, where small things with round red eyes clutched at the jungle gym with sharp claws, past office buildings, and burst into a park. In the middle of the park lay a pond, bordered by a row of street lamps spilling orange light. The moon slid from the clouds, illuminating the water's surface and the raised concrete basin of a dried fountain in the centre.

Nassar pulled her into the water and pointed to the fountain. "Go!"

She swam through the murky water without thinking. Something soft brushed her legs. She shied and squeezed a frantic burst of speed from her exhausted body. Dizziness came and then her hand hit the concrete base. She pulled herself up. Nassar climbed up next to her, grabbed her by her waist and hoisted her up into the seven-foot-wide basin. She fell on dried leaves and dirt.

The buzzing grew louder, steady and ominous like the hum of a giant engine.

An invisible whirlpool of magic built around Nassar. He stood cocooned in its fury, his axe held high. His body trembled under the pressure. The cuts and gashes on his arms reopened and bled.

The buzzing swelled like a tidal wave.

She saw the axe fall in an arc, its tip prickling the pond. The magic sucked itself into the axe handle and burst through its blade into the water. The pond became preternaturally calm, its surface smooth like glass. The buzzing vanished.

Nassar swayed. Grace grabbed his shoulders and pulled him against the lip of the basin, steadying him. His hand squeezed hers. He turned carefully, leaped up, and pulled himself into the basin next to her.

A swarm of insects spilled from the street. Green and segmented, like grasshoppers armed with enormous teeth, they were the size of a large cat. They streamed around the water in a mottled mass, bodies upon bodies, but none touching the pond.

"What are they?" Grace whispered hoarsely.

"Akora. The spell keeps them out of the water. As long as nothing disturbs the surface, they can't see or hear us. Don't worry. They can't survive the sun. They'll stay here entranced by the spell until morning." He lay on his back and closed his eyes.

Across the water the green insects crawled over the stone benches, perched on lamp posts, and combed the weeds of the once perfectly cut lawn. They had surrounded the pond. Everywhere Grace looked long segmented legs rubbed, sharp mandibles gnawed on random refuse and backs split to flutter pale wings.

There were too many of them.

She felt so hollow. The seven hours she had spent in this place had consumed her: there was nothing left inside her. "We'll die here," Grace whispered.

"No."

"They'll eat us, and I'll never see my mother again." What was the point of going on? They'd never make it out. She no longer cared if they would.

A warm hand grasped her and pulled her with irresistible strength snug against Nassar's chest. His arms closed about her, shielding her, shocking her cold body with their heat. His cheek rested against her hair. "I won't let you die, Grace," he whispered. "I promise I won't let you die."

She lay rigid against his chest, her face in his neck, listening to his strong, even heartbeat. His lips grazed her cheek. "I must be out of my mind," he whispered and his mouth closed on hers.

He kissed her, at first gently, then harder, as if he tried to breathe his life into her. She felt numb, but he persisted, his kiss passionate and searing. His arms caged her. His large hard body cradled hers, keeping her from slipping off into the empty deadness. His magic wrapped them both. He kissed her again and again, anchoring her, refusing to let her go. Caught on the threshold between complete numbness and painful awareness, Grace teetered, unsure. He pulled her back to life, back to the desperate reality. She didn't want to face it.

A shudder ran through her. She closed her eyes and let him part her lips with his tongue. He drank her in and finally she thawed. She wanted to live, to survive so she could feel this again. She wanted Nassar.

Tears wet her cheeks.

Nassar released her mouth and crushed her to him. "I want you so much," he whispered, his green eyes looking into the distance. "And I can't have you. I really must be cursed."

She lay in his arms for a long time.

The coal darkness of the sky faded to the pale grey of pre-dawn. Grace stirred. "Why did you do it?" she asked softly. "Why did you become a revenant?"

"I was dying," he answered, his voice hoarse. "We had a feud with the Garveys. They cornered my brother, John, and I went to get him. John didn't want to be taken alive. He didn't think help was coming, and he cursed himself and all those around him with a plague of marrow worms. A suicide curse is very potent. I brought him out of the trap, but the curse had caught me. We were both dying and the family could do nothing to keep us alive. I'd lost consciousness. John knew that if I took his body, I'd gain a temporary boost of power to break the curse. He made the family commence the ritual."

"He sacrificed himself?" she whispered.

"Yes. I remember there was a rush of red, like I was swimming through a sea of blood and drowning, and then I saw this shape floating in the depths. I thought it was my body and I knew if I wanted to survive, I had to get to it. I grabbed it, saw it was John . . . The pull to live was too strong. I awoke in my brother's body."

She put her arms around his neck and kissed his cheek.

"I killed my brother so I could live," he said. "It doesn't get any worse than that."

She simply held him.

A low growl froze both of them. Grace flipped onto her stomach and glanced over the lip of the basin. In the night, the insects had stopped moving. They lay still now, entranced by the spell, their chitin mirroring the grass and weeds around them so closely that if she didn't know they were there, she would've mistaken them for heaps of vegetation.

A lean muscled creature trotted along the edge of the pond. It gripped the ground with four oversized paws armed with sickle claws. Its serpentine tail lashed its dark pelt, which was spotted with flecks of red and yellow. The beast padded down the shore, its dragon-like jaws hanging open, showing off fangs the size of her fingers. Foamy spit leaked from between its teeth, staining the long tuft of red and yellow fur hanging from its chin. It halted, sniffed the air and turned to the basin. Four glowing amber eyes glared at her.

"Sylvester Roar," Nassar murmured.

Sylvester sniffed the water. His narrow muzzle wrinkled. He looked like he was grinning at them with his monstrous mouth.

Nassar growled. "No, you young idiot! Can't you see the spell on the water?"

Sylvester snapped his teeth and snarled in a feral glee. An eerie raspy growl came from between his teeth. "I see you, Nassar. You can't hide from me."

"Inexperienced fool." Nassar reached for his axe.

"I'm coming, Nassar. I'm coming for you." Sylvester gave a short ragged howl and splashed into the water. Little waves ran over the surface of the pond. Behind Sylvester the akora swarm swelled. Buzzing filled the air. Sylvester turned—

Nassar grabbed Grace and forced her to the floor of the basin, next to him.

A hoarse scream sliced through the morning, a terrible howl of a creature in impossible agony being torn to pieces. Grace squeezed her eyes shut. Sylvester screamed and screamed, the buzzing of the akora a morbid choir to his shrieks, until finally he fell silent.

Grace lay still, afraid to breathe. Slowly she opened her eyes.

An akora perched on the lip of the basin. It sighted her with dead black eyes. Its back split, releasing a pale gauze of wings.

Sun broke above horizon. Its rays struck the insect. Tiny cracks split its shiny thorax. The insect shrieked and fled, breaking apart over the pond. Grace rose. All around the pond the insect horde fractured and crumbled under the rays of the sun. The air smelled faintly of smoke. She looked beyond the heaps of melting insects and drew a sharp breath. Past the park, to the right, rose a tall heap of rubble that had been a multi-storey building in its former life. Atop the rubble a small white flag fluttered in the wind.

"The flag!"

Nassar had already seen it and jumped into the water. Together they swam across the pond. As she waded onto the solid ground, Grace passed a human skeleton, stripped bare of all flesh – all that remained of Sylvester.

Nassar moved cautiously along the sidewalk, jogging lightly on his feet, axe at the ready. She followed him, gripping her knife.

He wanted her and she wanted him. He'd forged a connection between them she couldn't ignore. The way he had held her, the way he'd touched her made her want to hold on to him. She had no idea what would come of their connection, but her instinct warned her she wouldn't get an opportunity to find out. Thinking of losing him now, before she had a chance to sort it out, terrified her.

They reached the rock pile. Nassar paused, measuring the height of the rubble with his gaze. It was almost three floors tall. He glanced at her. She saw the confirmation in his green eyes: it was too easy. He expected a trap.

"We go slowly," he said. "We must touch it together."

She nodded.

They climbed the pile of debris, making their way higher and higher. Soon they were level with the first floor of the neighbouring buildings, then the second. The flag was so close now, she could see the thread weave of its fabric.

The cold magic slammed her. Grace screamed. A lean shape burst over the top of the pile – half-man, half-demon, surrounded by marrow worms, the summoning stone on his chest glowing with white. The beast hit Nassar in the chest. Nassar reeled, the refuse slipped under him, and he plunged down, rolling as he fell, the dark worms swirling over him.

Grace ran after them. Below, the beast that was Conn Roar tore at Nassar, all but buried under the black ribbons of worm bodies.

She wouldn't get to him in time. Grace jumped.

For a moment she was airborne and falling and then her feet hit hard concrete midway down the slope. It gave under the impact, pitching her forwards. She fell and rolled down, trying to shield her head with her arms, banging against chunks of stone and wood. Pain kicked her stomach; she'd smashed into a section of a wall. Her head swam. Her eyes watered. Grace gasped and jerked upright.

Ten feet away the marrow worms were choking Nassar.

Magic surged from her in a sharp wave. The blast ripped the worms clear. They fled.

Nassar lay on his back, his eyes staring unseeing into the sky. *Oh no.*

She killed the panicked urge to run to him, crouched, and picked up his axe from where it had fallen. Her own knife was gone in her fall.

A dark shape launched itself at her from the pile. She whipped about, reacting on instinct. Nightmarish jaws snapped, her power pulsed, and Conn Roar bounced from the shield of her magic, knocked back. His paws barely touched the rubble before he sprung again. This time she was ready and knocked him down once more, deliberately.

Conn snarled.

She backed away towards Nassar's body.

"He killed my brother," the demonic beast said. His voice raised the small hairs on her neck. "Let me have Nassar and I'll let you live."

"No."

"You can't kill me." Conn circled her. He limped, favouring his left front paw, and a long gash split his side, bleeding. Nassar had got a piece of him before he went down.

"Of course, I can kill you," she told him, building up her magic. "I'm a Mailliard."

She only had one shot at this. If she failed, he'd rip her to pieces.

Conn tensed. The muscles in his powerful legs contracted. He leaped at her. She watched his furry body sail through the air, watched his jaws gape in joy when he realized her Barrier wasn't there, and then she sank everything she had into a single devastating pulse. Instead of a wide shield, she squeezed all her power into a narrow blade.

It sliced him in two. His body fell, spraying blood. His head flew by her, its four eyes dimming as it spun.

She didn't give it a second glance.

"Nassar?" She dropped the axe and pulled him up by his giant shoulders, sheltering a weak flutter of magic emanating from him with her own power. He was covered in blood. Her chest hurt as if she'd been stabbed. "Come back to me!"

He didn't answer.

No! Grace dropped and put her ear to his chest. A heartbeat, very weak, faltering, but a heartbeat.

She wiped a streak of blood from her eyes with her grimy hand so she could see. She couldn't help him. She didn't know how. But his family would.

Grace looked up at the pile of concrete and rubble, to the very top, where a white flag flailed in the breeze.

Nassar leaned against a tree across the street from a brick office building. Grace was inside. He couldn't sense her, not yet, but he knew she was inside.

He vividly remembered waking up to the familiar vaulted ceiling. He'd whispered her name and Liza's voice answered, "She's alive. She dragged you out, and I released her and her family, like you wanted."

He didn't believe her at first. He knew how much he weighed. No woman could have dragged his dead weight up that heap, but somehow Grace had done it.

She had left no note. No letter, no message, nothing to indicate that she didn't hate him for dragging her into the horror of the game. He thought of her every day while he lay in his bed waiting for his body to heal.

It took a month for him to recover. Three days ago he was finally able to walk. Yesterday he was able to make it down the stairs unassisted. Now, as he leaned against an old oak for support, his left arm still in a sling, he wondered what he would say if she told him to leave.

He would say nothing, he decided. He would turn around and go back to the airport and fly back to his life as the cursed revenant of Dreoch Tower. Nobody would ever know what it would cost him.

He wanted to hold her, to take her back with him, to have her in his bed, to taste her lips again, and to see the sly smile hidden in her eyes for him alone.

The door opened. Three women stepped out, but he saw only one.

Grace halted. Nassar held his breath.

She took a small step towards him, and then another, and

another, and then she was crossing the street, and coming near. He saw nothing except her face.

Her magic brushed him. She dropped her bag. Her hands went up to his shoulders. Her brown eyes smiled at him.

She kissed him.

Once a Demon

Dina James

Kyle tried to suppress a derisive smile at the monument that had been erected next to the one he was visiting. It was a large, weeping angel, prostrate over a fat marble block. A bouquet of faded flowers rested at the base. It hadn't been there the last time.

It almost matched the fountain monument on the opposite side in size. Truly, a working fountain. Who chose a fountain as a monument? Perhaps the departed had been fond of gardens. Even in death there was competition.

Let them compete with one another, Kyle thought as he laid his single, perfect, long-stemmed rose upon the ground below the monument that overwhelmed both the plot it sat upon and the markers on either side. It was a hulking stone dog with wings – a gargoyle most called it – with a bowed head. It was chained to the pedestal it sat upon with a thick, heavy chain attached to its metal spiked collar.

It was no average gargoyle. It was the Guardian of Hopes and Dreams, and when Kyle had seen it he knew exactly where it belonged and had it installed. Seven feet tall from the base to the tips of the wings, the monument dwarfed any other in the graveyard. Unless someone built a mausoleum, it would remain the most prominent.

Kyle kissed his fingertips and touched them gently to the petals of the rose before disappearing.

A reflection that had been shimmering in the water of the adjacent fountain smiled and disappeared also.

Red liquid swirled gently around the crystal wine glass held between his middle and fourth fingers.

Elegant.

That was the word for it.

Of course, the gesture was as purposeful as it was elegant, as were all of his gestures. It kept the liquid from congealing so that it was drinkable.

Cold, but drinkable.

If he could be bothered to drink it, that is.

His pale sea-green eyes were focused on the flames in the hearth, though his mind was elsewhere. Watching a fire flickering in the dark always brought him a modicum of comfort and helped him arrange his thoughts. It afforded him perspective.

Most of the time.

He smiled wryly as he sensed a presence, and though he didn't bother to lift his eyes to acknowledge it, he did greet it.

"Rude as ever, Destrati."

"Did you expect otherwise?" Nikolai countered as he all but swaggered to the mantelpiece to lean against it indolently. "The day you consider me polite is the day I cut that ridiculously long hair of yours, whether or not it would grow immediately back."

Kyle arched an eyebrow and his wry smile grew a bit wider as he reached to smooth his chestnut ponytail mockingly. Held in place by a strip of leather, it fell down his back to rest neatly between the blades of his shoulders. Long, perhaps, but well kept. Such had been the style back then.

"And what brings the Destrati Sovereign to breach the solace of my home *and* my dinner hour?" Kyle asked, eyeing Nikolai pointedly.

"I have a standing invitation," Nikolai defended with a smirk. "Or so it could be interpreted, no? I believe you said I could return anytime I wished, though I'm sure you meant in order to check on Trina while she was here. I merely took 'anytime' in the broader sense."

Kyle rolled his pale eyes. A human gesture, to be certain, but appropriate.

"You have learned much more than how to master your power," Kyle said dryly. "I didn't teach you to find loopholes."

"I was always good at interpreting things to my advantage," Nikolai said. "Besides, I knew you'd never invite me here. Invitations are an annoying necessity for everyone, even for a Sovereign. Besides, Trina wants to see you, and I said I would ask. You're welcome in our home, you know. Not that you would ever impose. Though, truly, it wouldn't be an imposition."

Kyle didn't reply as he contemplated his glass and the deep red liquid within.

Nikolai seated himself on one of the chairs facing the hearth and waited. After a long few moments of being completely ignored, he rose and spoke. "Well, I said I would tender the invitation, and so I have. After all, it's not like you have a postbox, nor would you give anyone the address even if you had. Trina is trying to bring Clan Destrati out of the Dark Ages. I'll remind her that her attempts should not extend to you."

With a bow he knew Kyle wouldn't see or acknowledge, Nikolai took his leave, vanishing as easily as he'd appeared.

Kyle brought his glass to his lips and drained the liquid within. Cattle blood never tasted the same as human, but it served a purpose, without the hunt. Hunting grew tiresome after a while, no matter the prey.

"Did you ask him?"

Katrina slid her arms around Nikolai's neck and kissed him deeply, welcoming her husband home.

Nikolai allowed himself to forget about everything except her touch for a moment and, when the kiss broke, he nodded. "What?" he asked in reply to Katrina's expectant look. "I tendered your invitation. I told you it wasn't likely he would accept."

Katrina sighed and scolded him in a mutter of her newly acquired Italian before she spoke again. "Send me there," she demanded. "I know you. You didn't even ask. You said something like 'come visit', didn't you?"

Nikolai looked guilty and didn't need to answer.

"Honestly, Nik, you and your 'doing without asking' thing! Now send me there. Kyle will send me back."

"Damned right he will," Nikolai said with a scowl, gesturing at his wife reluctantly.

Nikolai had made Katrina immortal when they'd married, but thankfully he hadn't made her a vampire or given her any ethereal powers. If he had, she'd be an even bigger force to be reckoned with.

Kyle smiled as his sanctuary was breached for the second time in less than an hour, and this time by a presence that was more human than ethereal. Immortal, yes, but human. Truly, one of the rarer of her kind. There were very few immortal humans, and Katrina was one of them.

"I'm sorry for Nik's likely rudeness," Katrina said as she appeared in Kyle's formal dining room. "And for mine, appearing unannounced like this, but you can't say you didn't expect me."

Kyle held up a hand as he continued gazing at the flames in the hearth at the end of the room. "He was not rude," he replied. He looked up at Katrina. "Well, not as rude as the Destrati have been known to be in the past. Your influence, I am sure."

Katrina blushed – an attractive feature vampires were incapable of – and stifled a giggle. "He's much better, really," she said, taking a step towards the very dangerous and formidable Kailkiril'ron. Kyle was known by many names, and though he preferred "Kyle Carillron" these days, he was known in legend among the vampire clans as "Kail the Betrayer".

She crossed the room slowly, giving him time to adjust to her presence. For everything he was to everyone else, he'd never been anything but kind, gentle and warm to her. But she didn't know how she hadn't felt the danger in his presence before, when she was still human.

"Because then you were under my protection," Kyle answered her thoughts aloud. He held her dark eyes. "Now you are not, and Nikolai sends you alone."

"I . . . I asked him to," Katrina said, though the defence in her tone didn't quite cover the slight tremor that his thinly veiled warning involuntarily elicited. Though she knew rationally he had protected her before, she was certain he could harm her with a thought if he were so inclined. "Well . . . 'asked' insistently."

The corners of Kyle's mouth twitched as he raised his glass, and Katrina knew she was responsible for his almost-smile. Kyle drained the glass and set it aside on the mantelpiece above the hearth.

"I never really got the chance to thank you for what you did for us," she continued. "And I don't quite trust that Nik expressed it the way he should have."

"No thanks are necessary," Kyle said.

Katrina laid a hand on Kyle's arm. He looked down at it and arched an eyebrow.

"Please come," she asked softly. "At least—" her eye caught the now empty glass, and she looked up at him meaningfully "—have a drink with us."

"You don't have to provide for me," Kyle said, wondering why the suggestion raised his ire. "I don't drink from men, and I don't want any of your willing blood slaves attending me."

"Don't be disgusting," Katrina said, scowling at him. "Clan Destrati doesn't do that any more. Everyone has their means, and it isn't as barbaric as you make it sound."

Katrina eyed him. Kyle was the epitome of tact, couth, civility and elegance. Something was bothering him if he was being anything but.

"And I wasn't offering any of that," she continued, meeting his pale eyes. "Just . . . company. An evening with friends. Everyone needs that now and again."

Kyle regarded her with a raised brow.

Katrina returned his look without flinching. She was serious. "If you don't want to come with me, then send me back alone," she said with a shrug. "Either way, I'm asking you to come and visit."

Kyle sighed. "I'm afraid I'm not very social, tonight or any night," he replied.

"Maybe that's because you haven't had anyone to socialize with," Katrina said, giving his arm a little shake. "Please? If you don't like the company you can leave any time you want and we won't question or pester, I promise. Please, Kyle? It's been months since we've seen you, and I can't bear the thought of you sitting here alone. We're not your enemies any more, though to hear Nikolai tell it, we never really should have been. The Destrati, I mean. No doubt you've done your share to alienate the rest of the clans."

Kyle threw his head back and laughed at her last half-teasing statement, then looked down at her with a smile. No one ever teased him. No one had the gall to. "My lady, I doubt in the whole of your existence that you have ever uttered so gross an understatement as that," he replied. "Though, as *I* cannot bear the thought of your very human worry over my happiness, I will accompany you on your return home and 'at least have a drink' with you."

Katrina smiled. "I'm ready when you are."

Within moments, they vanished together, materializing on a moonlit veranda where Nikolai stood next to a tabletop, filling three glasses.

Katrina had been right.

The company had been a welcome change, and the conversation had been more interesting than he'd considered it might be. As with the hunt, one also became bored with seeing paths and futures and with hearing the thoughts of others.

Though far from omnipotent, Kyle knew a great deal about a great many things – so much, in fact, that he sometimes forgot all he knew and understood until he had cause to remember it. What he didn't know immediately, he could easily learn through various means, but he tried to avoid infringing on the free will and privacy of others.

It was only polite; something many individuals, both ethereal and mortal, could do well to remember.

Nikolai had gone to oversee an issue in the Council chambers, though Katrina stayed behind to entertain their "guest".

"If the queen is needed . . ." Kyle said, offering Katrina a low bow.

Katrina blushed. "Stop that," she said nervously. "I don't feel like much of a queen, to be honest. I mean, just last year I was an American grad student on a spring break trip to London. Now I'm the wife . . . *wife* . . . of a gorgeous Russian guy who, as far as my mother knows, is some kind of banker, though

Mom is thoroughly convinced Nik is part of the Mafia, running guns or drugs or something. Getting her to accept that he's not only *not* any of those, but *only* a couple hundred years old and immortal – and oh, yeah, I am too, thanks to him – is hard enough without throwing some kind of pseudo-royalty into it."

Kyle was impressed. "My lady is displeased?"

Was that disdain she heard in his question? If it was, she ignored it. "No, not really," Katrina sighed. She turned, resting her hands on the balustrade as she looked out into the dark garden lit only by the three-quarter moon. "It just . . . gets a little hard sometimes, you know? And these people . . . um . . . well, they're not *people*, really, but they are . . ." Katrina put her face in her hands and sighed again.

Kyle waited a moment for her to collect her emotions. When she looked up at him, he returned her look just as frankly. He was so calm and collected all the time. Nothing seemed to bother him.

"Now, now," Kyle said softly. "Do not attempt to pry into my thoughts, my lady. You've learned much from Nikolai, but some things aren't for your knowledge. Not even if I were Destrati. Besides, it's impolite to enter without an invitation, and that doesn't extend solely to this realm."

"Who was she?" Katrina asked.

Kyle leaned forwards and pushed himself up from his chair.

She placed a quick hand on his arm as he began to bow and she tried not to flinch at the glare he gave her. "Tell me," she insisted, cutting off any farewell he'd been about to make. "Yes, I've learned a lot from Nik, but no one needs any kind of special reading ability to see that you're upset over something. That so doesn't mesh with everything I've been told about you."

"Perhaps what you've been told about me is not only the truth, but how it should be. Now, release me, Katrina," Kyle ordered.

Katrina ignored the warning in his tone and shook her head. "Uh-uh," she denied vocally. "Squirm all you want. Go 'poof' if you want to; it will just prove you're a wuss."

" 'Wuss'?" Kyle echoed.

"American slang for 'wimp'," Katrina clarified. "Coward, loser, chicken—"

"All right, I understand," Kyle said wryly. "I won't go 'poof'. And the correct term is 'shift', not 'poof'."

"Whatever," Katrina said, smiling up at him. She removed the gentle, restraining hand on his arm and sat back in her seat. "You're really tall. I thought Nik was tall, but you have him beat. But you're not big. Nik has muscles—"

"Please tell me I'm not being subjected to this to fulfil some strange comparison fantasy of yours," Kyle cut her off as he returned to the chair he'd been occupying. He reached for his glass. "Is Nikolai lacking in some way?"

Katrina shook her head.

"You're alone, and I know how lonely it gets," she said. "I mean, it's been less than a year for me, being . . . not like everyone else. Most days I'm OK with it, especially if Nik is around, but sometimes being 'alone' gets to me, even if I am something of a queen."

"I wouldn't downplay the importance of your role here, Katrina. You'd hurt Nikolai's feelings, not to mention those of the others," he said gently. "You're not 'something of a queen'. You *are* the queen of Clan Destrati, wife of Sovereign Nikolai Peityr. It pleases me to see that he hasn't gone the way of Dominic by having you sit as his right hand on the Council."

Katrina lowered her eyes and shook her head. "I thought everyone should get used to me being around before I try to change the way they govern themselves. But Nikolai is gone so often, attending things like that, and I can't help but feel lost and alone."

She looked back up at Kyle and shrugged a little, chagrined. "Though I'm sure that sounds pathetic, coming from me, considering how long . . . How long have you been alone?"

"I do not wish to have this discussion," Kyle said as he poured himself another glass of what Nikolai had informed him was goat's blood obtained from a local butcher. It certainly had the taste of livestock to it, and was unlike the cattle blood he was accustomed to.

It would not sustain him at all. Unlike the others of his supposed ilk, he needed human blood to maintain his form and powers. "To live off those he betrayed his Master for." That was the curse. Ironic and fitting.

Kyle often found a great deal of humour in irony.

"Kyle."

Katrina's voice recalled his attention.

"Yes? I'm sorry, my lady. I beg your forgiveness. My mind was elsewhere for a moment."

Katrina smiled. "I know," she said. "I asked you if there was anything else I could get for you, to make you more comfortable. You seem a little troubled."

"No, thank you, my lady," Kyle said, regaining his composure. "I should go. It has been a pleasant evening, and I thank you for your company and hospitality."

"Please, stay until Nikolai returns," she asked, putting her hand on his arm again. "He shouldn't be much longer. Keep me company."

Kyle looked uncomfortable, but nodded. He was losing himself in thoughts of *her* again. Why? Was it because no one had touched him as familiarly as Katrina had tonight since—? And Katrina had asked who "she" was. It was rude to ignore a question, though it was also rude to ask inappropriate ones. Katrina's question hadn't been entirely improper, just . . . one he'd never thought anyone would ask.

Four hundred years in the mortal plane and he still hadn't managed to rid himself of the compulsion to answer direct questions asked of him. He tried to reason with himself, telling himself he didn't have to reply to her, that curiosity was natural to humans. She was only being polite. He rationalized for a long moment, but he knew if he didn't answer her, the question would weigh on him until he did.

"Do you know what today is?" he asked softly.

"It's Thursday, the nineteenth," Katrina replied, confused. "Why?"

The nineteenth of March. Kyle's heart lurched in his chest as he remembered carefully choosing the rose he'd delivered that evening. It had to be perfect. Nothing less would do. When he'd found the perfect one, he'd used his power to make it as flawless as she had been. He could have used his power to manifest one in its entirety, but then it wouldn't be of this realm and would fade with the morning light. She deserved more.

"*La festa di San Giuseppe*," Kyle murmured. "The feast of Saint Joseph."

Katrina only looked more confused at his reply. He went on, clarifying.

"The Feast of Saint Joseph is a holy day in the Church, held every year on the nineteenth of March. Many years ago, on this day, I met her. Catrine."

The way he said the name sent an uncomfortable shiver down Katrina's spine, and she drew her wrap tighter around her shoulders to hide it.

"Yes," Kyle said, looking at her. "A name very similar – unnervingly similar – to your own."

Kyle reached for his glass and sat back, staring into the liquid as he gathered his thoughts. He contemplated where to begin, now that he'd decided to answer her.

"I am not Catholic, but tonight I will use you as my confessor, if the queen of the Destrati will consent to hear my confession, that is," he said. "They say confession lightens the soul, but as I no longer have one, I can only believe that it is so. Will you, Katrina, hear my confession?"

Katrina consented with a slow nod, wide-eyed, thinking it strange that he would ask her such a thing. Many vampires held to strange traditions, and permission was a big deal to ethereals. Nikolai had gone over and over that with her, teaching her how to construct her phrases, and the power of different word combinations that, if changed slightly, lost their magic completely. The fact that Kyle asked her for anything was enough to earn her consent, especially if all he wanted from her was a good listener.

Kyle smiled a little and continued, though he lowered his eyes again to study the liquid in his glass.

"She was beautiful. Not so tall, dark-haired, with deep brown eyes. Not attractive by modern standards, but beautiful nonetheless. Pure. Pure in all ways, down to her immortal soul. It radiated from her: an innocence so gentle it was almost brutal in its kindness. And strength. Not physical strength, though as far as that went in those days, she had that, too, but strength of spirit. Even mortals could almost feel it as they walked by her, not knowing what it was but yearning to be touched by it."

It was painful to hear Kyle talk this way. Katrina could hear the emptiness, the loneliness, the longing. The memory. But something told her he was far from finished, and she sat in rapt attention, listening to his melodic, hypnotic voice as he spoke. Truly, it was confessional.

"I had been sent to murder her."

Katrina gasped. Kyle could hear her thoughts. She was screaming with denial inside. Though she had been exposed to this new and violent world for nearly a year now, where such brutality was trivial and commonplace, it still shocked her to hear Kyle speak of taking a life so casually.

He continued, "But when I saw her, I could not fulfil my mission. I was struck by everything about her, and instead, I offered to walk her home, as her arms were laden with her morning shopping."

"Who sent you to kill her?" Katrina was pale.

"My father."

"Who is your father?"

"You need only repeat my true name and hear it for what it is to answer that, my lady," Kyle said quietly, meeting her eyes. "Speak it, and hear."

"Kailkiril'ron," Katrina obeyed, speaking the difficult Ancient name.

Ancient. But it was unlike any name of any Ancient she'd come across, and she'd been studying in earnest, trying to learn as much as she could about the new world she had become a part of when she took Nikolai as her husband.

"No, it's not the name of an Ancient," Kyle confirmed her thoughts. His pale eyes challenged hers. "Now, what am I called? Speak the whole of it."

"Kailkiril'ron the Be—," Katrina began. The word caught in her throat, but she swallowed and forced it out. "Betrayer."

Kyle nodded. He held Katrina's eyes and waited for the meaning to clarify itself to her.

It didn't take long. Kyle watched the realization cross her face and forced himself to endure it. He'd asked her to hear his confession, and he would endure the penance. It wasn't like he hadn't been exiled before.

Katrina rose from her chair and backed away instinctively. "You're a demon!"

"Former, please," Kyle said calmly, gesturing for her to sit down again in the chair she'd left. "Neither, thankfully, am I a true 'vampire'. I'm not like your Nikolai or any other Destrati, or any other in any clan. I did not choose this existence. I am a true lost soul. A consciousness in mortal form that must live off the blood of those I betrayed my father – my Master – for. And just to additionally clarify, as I don't wish to surprise you further, I am a former demon *lord*, not some common imp. There's a significant difference. Please."

Kyle gestured to the chair again.

Katrina slowly returned to it, looking at Kyle with new eyes. "I knew you were powerful," she said quietly, glancing around nervously though no one could have been watching. "They all say so, and those who don't speak of you with awe speak of you with contempt. I never understood why. But I didn't realize. I don't think any of them truly realize what you really are. You just toy with us, don't you?"

"Hardly," Kyle said dryly. "I spend most of my time avoiding you, or have you forgotten that? Wasn't it you that invited me here? Do you regret it now? Shall I go, now that you know the truth of what I am?"

"No." Katrina reached for his hand and covered it with her own, squeezing his gently. "And I'm sorry for my reaction. Demons . . . are frightening things, especially when the man you married has sworn himself to fight against them. I'm afraid I still think of myself as human, even though I'm not really. I saw *The Exorcist* when I was a kid and I haven't ever forgotten it."

Kyle smiled and brought her fingers to his lips to brush a reassuring kiss across them. She was at least trying to understand, and that hadn't happened in so very, very long.

"May you forget that vile film. It isn't remotely accurate where possession is concerned anyway. But always remember that you were once human," he said, lowering their hands. He released hers gently. "It is important to remember what you were, even if you might wish to forget at times. Now, I believe you asked a question, and though you may have already answered it for yourself, I shall continue, as there is more."

He took a sip from his glass and chose his words carefully.

"My father is, as you've no doubt surmised, the Fallen one named Lucifer."

"As in *the* Lucifer?" Katrina whispered. "As in, War Between The Sides, 'I will not serve', losing side, cast-down-into-Hell Lucifer?"

"The same," Kyle affirmed with a nod. "You know the tale. After angels, the Creator made humans, and a realm for them to live in. Man quickly became loved best above all things. One angel, the one who felt the most deposed, thought this unjust – this replacement – and formed a rebellion. He was met in battle by those loyal to their Father and lost. The rest you know. What you do not likely know, however, is that once cast down with those who had rebelled with him, Lucifer made new creations in *his* own image. Just as his Father had before him, he created beings to serve and worship him. I was one of the first among those creations. The only children Lucifer has are, as he so named us, *demons*, and we are all male, as he is. They do his bidding without question, out of blind loyalty, as I once did. Lucifer himself cannot leave the realm to which he is banished. He cannot leave Hell. However, he can send his children out for short periods for various purposes. There is far more to it than I've told you but, suffice to say, I was once first among Lucifer's children and in command of his legions of demons. But then one day he issued an order I could not obey, which brings us back to my 'betrayal'. My Catrine."

Katrina tried hard to grasp everything Kyle had said, but it didn't quite make sense. She had a lot of questions, but decided to wait and see if things would become clearer as he went on. She nodded for him to continue.

Kyle took a sip from his glass and spoke again.

"As I've said, I could not obey and take the life of this beautiful creature. I could not deprive the world of so wondrous a thing as she. I didn't even know at the time what 'beauty' was or even that I found her beautiful. All I knew was that I could not harm her. I didn't speak a word to her on the way to her home; I merely walked by her side."

Kyle laughed softly.

"I must have made quite the picture," he said, smiling at Katrina. "I was in this form, you see. It was slightly younger, but only slightly so, and easily inhabited. Demons, in case you don't know this already, have a form of their own within their own realm (or if they have been summoned into another), but in this case I was in possession of this mortal. He was the most despicable of mortals, truly wicked and corrupt, which is exactly the conduit needed for possession. When I think back on it now, I marvel at her grace. His name . . . I don't even remember what it was, for I gave my *true* name to her; an unthinkable thing for a demon to do, let alone the lord of demons. She made a wonderful effort to pronounce it, and asked if she could shorten it to simply 'Kail'. Of course I agreed. Words from her lips were unlike any I'd ever heard before. I have met many of the Host, and I can tell you now, no angel speaks as beautifully as she did."

Katrina smiled. "Love does things like that," she said. "She probably didn't sound angelic to anyone but you."

"Perhaps not," Kyle agreed, still lost in his memories. "Again, I didn't know anything about love, or beauty, or grace, but when I look back on it now, she was so gracious and polite that day. As I said, I was in possession of this form, inhabiting this body and sharing the corrupt soul within. It shames me now, knowing what she saw then, for this form was very dirty, with unwashed greasy hair infected with lice."

Kyle shuddered visibly.

"Despite all that, she allowed me to carry her burdens and walk by her side until she reached her home. When she tried to offer me recompense for my aid, I shook my head and bid her farewell. I ran as far and as fast as this mortal form would carry me, and then left it as immediately as I could. But even in my own realm, returned to Hell, I could not forget her. She had robbed me of every desire except the one to be at her side."

"I can't see you running from anything or any*one*," Katrina said, reaching for the bottle of diluted goat's blood. She offered to refill Kyle's drink, and he set his glass on the table for her to do so. "Especially a mortal. A mortal *woman*."

Kyle laughed a little before taking another sip from the freshened glass.

"Oh, believe me, nor could I. I had never returned from a mission unsuccessful, and that was the only fact that saved me further inquiry as to why I hadn't done my duty. After all, if Kailkiril'ron, Lord General could not fulfil the task, something must have gone terribly awry. Or so I let everyone believe. In truth, for days (and I mean 'days in Hell': time passes more quickly here compared to there) I was in agony. I paced and wondered and was generally more unpleasant than usual, even for those accustomed to my nature. My stoic composure would give way without reason to anger and annoyance, going instantly from one extreme to the other without provocation. I was truly more than a nightmare. I was dangerous and reckless, and it was noticed by others, but unquestioned, as one does not question the Lord General. Finally I realized I had no choice. I had to see her again. By the time I decided to return, nearly a year had passed in the mortal realm."

Katrina nodded. She sensed this wasn't a good time to interrupt.

"I knew what I was doing was strictly forbidden. I hadn't been given orders to inhabit anyone, nor had I been told to attempt to fulfil my mission again. I was rebelling against everything and I knew it. What's more, I didn't care. I had to see her. So I made my excuses and left, seeking out the form I had used previously. I found it, but it was in dismal shape, worse than before, and a great distance away from where I had first taken possession of it. Well, that wouldn't do."

"Why didn't you simply choose another form, closer to where she was?" Katrina asked, taking a sip from her own glass. Though Nikolai had made her immortal and she didn't need to eat or drink, she liked to keep up the semblance of normalcy. She couldn't taste the metallic oiliness of the goat's blood, but she drank it out of courtesy to their guest. She was proud of herself. A year ago she would have been utterly repulsed, but her husband drank blood to live. It was a lot like eating sushi, she supposed. Once you got over the realization of what you were putting in your mouth, it was easy to swallow.

"I blame my failure to do just that on being a complete, unthinking idiot. And on being slightly selfish," Kyle replied.

"You wanted her to remember you," Katrina accused, teasing him.

"I plead very, very, inexcusably guilty on that charge," Kyle said, laughing genuinely as he held up his hands in mock surrender.

Katrina laughed with him, and had the sudden thought that it had been a long time since she'd actually shared a teasing laugh with someone. Sometimes when she and Nikolai were alone she could get him to laugh, but laughing *with* someone was different. This was unique and special. She enjoyed it.

Kyle caught her thoughts without meaning to, effortless as always, and agreed that this was enjoyable. Nice.

"So," he continued, picking up the thread of his tale, "I set about cleaning up the mortal form I was 'borrowing', earning a little money, and generally trying to make myself presentable and somewhat respectable. After all, I wasn't your average, everyday demon, and if she was going to see me, I wanted her to actually see *me*, not simply the pitiful mortal I was using."

"From here it doesn't look like so pitiful a mortal," Katrina observed, deliberately eyeing him up and down before winking at him.

It had the desired effect, and Kyle smiled at her jesting.

"She must have thought the same, for when I finally presented myself to her, she remembered me, and greeted me with a smile, *by name*."

Katrina bit her bottom lip in a wistful grin, almost bursting. "Oh, that's wonderful!" She clapped her hands. "I was hoping she would remember you. She'd probably been waiting to see you again, all that time, wondering what had happened to you and what, if anything, she'd done to frighten you off." Katrina giggled.

"Indeed, she had," Kyle said with a nod. "Just as you say."

Katrina nearly spit out the drink she'd just taken. "I wasn't serious," she said, looking at him incredulously. "That's movie stuff. Not real life!"

"Regardless, it was so," Kyle said with a gentle smile. "Just as it is in fairy tales. It surprised me that she did remember, for time passes so quickly here. Nonetheless, she had been waiting, just as you say, to speak with me again. And all I could do was gaze at her. Every move she made was entrancement itself, from smoothing her dress to touching her hair."

His words faded as he lost himself in the memories of his Catrine. When he finally remembered himself, he apologized to his hostess for his inattention.

"Don't apologize," Katrina said. She reached to pat his hand lightly, ignoring his almost imperceptible look of disapproval at her touch. "I asked, and it's nice to hear you talk about her. Though I'm not sure I want to hear the end."

Kyle nodded and looked away. Yes, it ended. All things end. Even time itself would end one day. Some things simply ended before they should, or so he felt at times, even though he knew better.

"For months, mortal months, we carried on thusly," he went on, but his words had lost their enthusiasm. "I would visit and we would simply talk, or go for a walk, or I would carry her shopping from the market. I never entered her home."

Katrina nodded, indicating her continued attention and interest, but didn't interrupt.

"Catrine went every week to confession," he continued. "And I would wait outside for her. Outside the churchyard. It was consecrated ground, and I could not set foot on it, but she would come from it happier and smiling, so I was always content to wait on her. I would have waited on her until the end of time. Winter was slowly giving way to spring, but March was exceptionally cold that year. She was concerned that her offering to Saint Joseph for his feast day would be too meagre. I negated her concern. That led to a discussion of saints and souls and why I wouldn't come to confession with her.

" 'It's so cold out here, Kail,' she would say before going into the church. 'At least come in from the cold and warm yourself. Won't you please come in from the cold?' She said those words so often. I never understood what she was talking about, because I didn't feel the cold, or the warmth, or anything else like she did. And I told her so."

"Oh, Kyle," Katrina said, swallowing hard as tears prickled at her eyes. "What did she say?"

"I shouldn't have been surprised, but she told me that she already knew I was different. She just hadn't known how," he answered. "And so my explanation of who and what I was didn't surprise her exactly, but it distinctly unnerved her. All those months, unknowingly consorting with a demon. She accused me of befriending her so that I might take her soul. It was the one time I got angry with her. I told her that if I'd wanted that, I would have taken it already without having to spend so much time with her. She slapped me and refused to speak to me any more. But we had made plans for the Feast of Saint Joseph and I would not abandon her simply because she no longer wanted anything to do with me. At least, that's what I told myself. In truth, I just didn't want to be away from her, not even for a moment. I wanted her for myself, and I was unaccustomed to wanting for anything."

"How did she come back to you? Or did she?" Katrina asked, settling her nerves with another sip from her glass.

A half-smile touched Kyle's lips. "Demons are patient," he said. "And again, time passes differently in the mortal realm, and though it was only hours to me without her, it was days to her. But even a mortal hour can seem an eternity when your soul is cut to the core, and I knew I had hurt her deeply. Why that concerned me, I didn't know. I didn't know demons could love."

"Demons can love?" Katrina echoed, her brow furrowing.

Kyle nodded lightly, then shook his head. "Well, no, not truly," he clarified. "Our father made us in his image, as he had been made. Although he had been given a heart, his envy and hatred of Man twisted it. When he created his own children, he had to duplicate his own form, though he made the hearts he gave us small, hard and virtually useless so that we might never discover we had one. If we did, he feared we would begin to question him, as he had questioned his own Father. We would no longer truly be demons. We would become obsolete in a sense. I was the lord of his demons, and I had discovered my heart, though I did not know it yet."

Kyle took a sip from his glass and waited. He could sense her question, but let her phrase it for herself.

"So what did you do?" Katrina asked.

"The only thing I could think to do," Kyle replied. "I went to see her, one last time, to tell her she didn't have to worry about seeing me again, if that's what she wanted. I had no wish to harm her, or see her come to harm, or have her be afraid of me."

Kyle ran a finger absently around the rim of his crystal goblet.

"She was waiting for me, and chastised me for being late to accompany her to the church. She had to make her offering upon the altar to Saint Joseph," he said, his voice steady though it was clear the words hurt him to say as he relived the memory. "She thought I'd forgotten and, in truth, I had. But I went with her, and when we arrived, we stopped outside the churchyard.

"She told me everything she'd been thinking. Her thoughts had always been sacrosanct to me – I had never pried into them or allowed myself to hear them. I remember realizing that at that moment, as she spoke. She told me her feelings. All I could do was listen. I'd dropped to my knees when she reached to touch my face and, when I looked up at her, all I could do was apologize and beg her forgiveness for causing her grief."

Kyle hesitated then, but Katrina heard him force himself to continue.

"She asked me to please rise, as I was making her uncomfortable kneeling on the ground. I offered to come with her into the church, even knowing I could not, though for her I would try. If only she would forgive me for everything . . . for being what I was. I told her that I hadn't ever lied to her – as ridiculous as that sounds coming from a demon in a mortal body."

Kyle paused again, and Katrina could see him visibly struggling to maintain his composure. She waited patiently until he found it and continued.

"She kissed me then, leaning down to do so," he said softly. "Right there in front of anyone who cared to look. Her. An unmarried, pious woman, virtuous and sweet, kissing a son of the devil she spent her life avoiding. Oh, it was chaste, even for that time, but still. The bravery. The audacity. And the moment it ended, I heard inhuman laughter."

Katrina bit her lip again to keep from asking questions, but she had a fair idea as to what happened next. After all, Kyle was here, and his Catrine wasn't.

Kyle was silent as well, looking unseeingly into his glass. After a long moment, he looked up at Katrina. His pale, sea-green eyes were filled with obvious anguish, but no tears fell. None could. He didn't have any to shed.

"We had been found out, some time before. A young initiate, a low-ranking demon trying to earn a name for himself, had been spying on me – on us – and reporting back to my father. I hadn't had a clue about it. I'd been focused solely on my need of her, and not how reckless or careless I was being. I only cared about being with her." He sighed, then continued.

"Nothing happened immediately; nothing could at that moment. It was a holy day. That didn't change matters, however, only postponed how quickly my father could act. Still, we went on as if we hadn't a care in the world. We enjoyed the day together. Catrine made her offering, and we spent time talking about things no human should ever know about. There were things I was glad to tell her, and questions I was happy to answer. She spent the day with me as though I were a man. And when night fell, she spent that with me too, in her father's orchard with only a fire and her two dogs to chaperone us. I think she knew there would be literal Hell to pay for being with me, and had decided I was worth it. As I've said, she was a brave and unique woman."

"Was?" Katrina made herself say.

Kyle nodded stoically. "We talked long into the night, and she told me a great many things. She told me—" Kyle broke off, unable to continue. He closed his eyes and finished his drink before looking directly into Katrina's eyes.

"She told me she loved me," he said, his voice strong and firm. "Even knowing what I was and knowing that a life together was impossible in all ways. She let me hold her then. I never had, before that night. I'd never once tried to touch her, not even lightly. I was always content to just look at her, be in her presence and listen to her voice. Not once had I asked her for anything, but that night I did. I asked her to let me feel her in my arms, and she allowed me to hold her until midnight when the holy day was over. Then they came for me, and it all ended."

"Who came?" Katrina asked, wanting to hold his hand but not daring to. His demeanour had changed back to the dark and imposing one she knew. She didn't want to disturb him further. Kyle could be dangerous enough when he was calm, she'd been told.

"The one who had spied on us and others. With them they brought a severed human head that my father spoke through. I told you, he cannot leave physically, but there are ways he can enter the mortal realm briefly."

Kyle studied the golden ring he wore on his right little finger, twisting it absently.

"I was given a choice," he continued, his voice now devoid of any feeling or warmth. "Admit I loved her, or be ordered out of existence. There are very few things that can kill a demon, but one of them is being ordered out of existence by Lucifer. This is what we term 'The Annihilation'.

"I didn't understand at the time why they offered me such a seemingly easy choice – say I loved her or be ordered out of existence. I was suspicious. Nothing is ever as it appears, especially when offered by Lucifer. I took a moment to try to figure out what tricks my father could be up to. Catrine naturally took this for hesitation on my part – I was a demon after all – and she imagined I would betray her. She pleaded with me, and with my father. She just kept begging me to say that I loved her.

"My father offered to let her choose my fate instead of leaving it for me to choose. However, as brave as she was, she was not prepared to take on the Devil, whom she'd been brought up to fear her whole life. Staring a talking severed head straight in its dead eyes wasn't something she could do either, even if I could have prepared her for it. It had taken her long enough to decide she could live with loving a self-admitted, willing servant of Lucifer. But all this was too much for her. Or so I thought."

"What did she do?" Katrina prompted when Kyle lost himself again in his memories.

He got up from his chair and paced to the balustrade, looking out into the dark garden.

Katrina got up and went after him, sliding her arms around his lean waist. Kyle stiffened, but her embrace only tightened in spite of her fear. She leaned her head against his back and spoke, gentle but firm.

"Kyle, tell me. What did she do?"

"Release me and I will answer you," Kyle replied. It took more control than he wanted to admit not to shove her away. She was only trying to comfort him. But she was not his.

Though his tone was even, Katrina heard the dire warning in it and slowly let her arms drop from around his waist. She took a step back, horrified at her audacity but unwilling to draw attention to her mistake by apologizing for it. She was in a different world now, a dangerous world; she had to remember that.

Instead she offered him a nod, as he so often offered to her, and he continued.

"She confessed herself, to him and all present, unashamedly," Kyle said quietly. "And dared my father to fault her for it, for 'love is never wrong', she told him."

"She's right," Katrina said as she returned to her seat. "It isn't. It's the one thing that keeps me sane when Nikolai talks about things that just make my mind boggle. I don't suppose your father took too kindly to that."

The understatement made Kyle burst out in laughter.

"No," he admitted with a shake of his head though he kept his eyes on the dark of the garden. "No, he didn't. He killed her. Or rather, he had Kihirin do it. Right in front of me. I was held in my mortal form, trapped by a power greater than my own. It took the entire power of seven of them, plus what my father could spare, to restrain me and keep me in form. I couldn't even go to her as Kihirin drained her life. He was in mortal form and used a scythe to slit her throat. She kept her eyes on me as he prepared to do it, telling me the whole time that she loved me and it was worth it. When she was all but gone, they released me. I went immediately to her."

Kyle's voice had again lost some of its might, and Katrina wanted to embrace him again, but she didn't dare. Kyle wasn't like Nikolai at all, and neither could nor would be soothed by a hug and a kiss.

"She knew, though, didn't she? That you were with her?" Katrina asked in a whisper, knowing Kyle's keen ears would hear her.

"Yes," Kyle replied softly, "she knew. They never had any intention of letting us alone – letting us be with one another. They'd always planned to stop us in whatever way they could, and I was a fool to think I was indispensable. At that moment, I didn't care about any consequence that would come of the proclamation my father wanted me to make. I professed for her, and told her what I should have told her the moment I knew it. 'I love you,' I said. She smiled and made me promise to remember the day we had together, the holy day, and I promised her I would never forget. Then she died in my arms, and I could do nothing but watch.

"And as her soul left her body, I tried to stop it, even though my power had already been stripped. I was as powerless as a mortal, and I couldn't do anything to stop her death."

Katrina tried not to let her tears fall, but she couldn't help it.

Kyle turned around to regard her, and she hastily wiped her eyes. He crossed the veranda to the table she was again seated at, took a handkerchief from his breast pocket and offered it to her.

"Shh," he said as she accepted it hesitantly.

A fleeting thought of warning crossed her mind about accepting something offered by a demon, but it wasn't enough to dissuade her. Besides, he'd helped her and Nik before. But why? Demons never did anything selfless, did they?

She was so caught up in her own thoughts that she almost didn't hear what he was saying.

"If Nikolai returns to see you've wept, he'll never again allow me in your house, and you made such a fuss to have me here."

Katrina laughed as she dried her eyes and blew her nose. "So she died."

"Yes," Kyle said softly. "She died for love of me. Because she loved me. That is why, my lady Katrina, I choose to be 'alone', as you say."

"But you professed for her like they wanted," Katrina said to him with anguished eyes. She sniffed once more and dabbed at her nose with the handkerchief. "And . . . and . . . if you'd done that to begin with, she wouldn't have been killed!"

Kyle simply *looked* at her and Katrina cringed at the stupidity of what she'd just said. Now *that* was "movie stuff". It was Lucifer, after all, and he wasn't exactly an honest guy.

"What happened then?" she asked, mostly to cover up her silly accusation.

"I had become human," Kyle said with a shrug. "Though this was yet unknown to me and to the others who stood by. A demon cannot love, ever. If a demon finds his heart and professes love, he will become mortal. Human. Demons cannot love, therefore they become something else. When I professed for Catrine, I became human. The mortal I'd been in possession of, his soul and mine fused. Two souls cannot share one body without fusing. As the mortal's soul was already damned by his own hand, and mine was given to me by my father, Lucifer thought it his property and took it for his own, leaving me—"

"A body without a soul," Katrina said with him.

"Yes," Kyle affirmed. "In his words, 'forced to live off the blood of those I betrayed him for'. Worse, I betrayed him for love of a mortal – something he cannot abide. He took back what he'd given me, though he had no right to it. Looking back, I should have entrusted it to my Catrine. I should have given her my soul as well as my heart."

Kyle bent down to look Katrina firmly in the eye.

"Remember that, Katrina," he said gently. "When you're at your wits' end with Nikolai, and the Council and the Destrati, and immortals and souls. When you grow weary of the War Between the Sides, remember that it all comes down to one thing and that is love. It was love that began it, and someday, it will be love that ends it. Remember."

Katrina nodded and sniffed, wiping her eyes with the flat of her hand. She smiled, showing him she was all right.

Kyle reached for her hand and brought it to his lips. "My thanks for being my confessor," he said as he let her hand fall gently back to her side. "And I do offer my apologies that I cannot wait for Nikolai's return, but there are things I must see to."

He bowed to her and disappeared, and Katrina returned to her seat to wait for her husband.

She sat and thought deeply about all Kyle had said, and though she wouldn't share Kyle's confession with anyone else – confessors kept their confidences, no matter how horrible or terrifying – she could at least bring up the questions in her mind to Nikolai.

She had a lot of them.

Kyle smiled to feel the familiar presence arrive at his home.

"If I thought you were going to abuse the privilege of unrestricted entry into my home," he said as he turned to greet Katrina, "I would have rescinded it. How thoughtless of me."

"Then why haven't you corrected it by now?" Katrina asked innocently.

"Because I mistakenly had faith that Nikolai would have the very good sense to respect my preferences to be left in peace and *not* send you here whenever you grew bored of your role," Kyle replied as he took a sip from his glass. "You always seem to show up at my dinner hour as well. I do not think it coincidence that you disrupt my solitude *and* my sustenance.'

Katrina could hear the pleasure and teasing he was trying to keep from his tone and smiled at him.

"We expected you for Hallowe'en," she chided gently. "I mean, 'All Hallows' Eve', as Nik calls it. Should I have personally delivered an engraved invitation? With bows and ribbons on thick vellum with four envelopes?"

"Are you implying that I'm pretentious?" Kyle answered with a question of his own. "Or that I'm rude for not attending?"

Katrina let the silence and her innocent expression answer for her.

Kyle hid a smile. "Silly mortal holiday," he murmured. "Taken from origins long forgotten by nearly everyone. And I was not about to play 'vampire' to frighten children – if indeed they would be frightened of my 'real fangs' in this day and age – for your amusement."

"It was a party for charity, Kyle," Katrina reasoned.

"A charity to which I made a donation in your honour," Kyle replied, duplicating her tone. "I don't believe my presence is required for anything else."

"Well, I do," Katrina said flatly, but then paused. She bit her lip. "The church you told me about: Catrine's church. Is it still around?"

"Yes," Kyle confirmed. "Why?"

"Can we go? I mean, will you take me there?" Katrina asked.

"You wouldn't like it. It's nothing but an old churchyard now."

"Just take me, OK? I want to see it."

"No. I'm not Nikolai," he reminded her. "You can't just barge in here uninvited and order me about and expect to get your way. Nor can you ply me with your affections like you can him."

Katrina's scowl deepened.

Kyle returned her look with a bored, blank expression. Then sighed. "Humans. You have to see to believe, don't you? Very well then."

Before Katrina could answer him, they were there. It was dark and cold, and the wind, though gentle, blew through her. Immortal didn't mean that she didn't feel the cold, and it was bitter. She chided herself inwardly. What did she expect in November?

A light dusting of snow made the churchyard look like something Tim Burton would film.

"I told you that it was nothing but a churchyard now," Kyle said. His long chestnut ponytail was unruffled by the wind, as were his clothes. He, at least, looked somewhat dressed for the weather. Kyle manifested a long wool coat for Katrina, and she smiled in gratitude.

"You said 'churchyard', not 'graveyard'," she pointed out. "Where's the church?"

Kyle smiled. "Back then, the dead were all buried in churchyards," he said. "The church itself has long been demolished. I was very glad when it was deconsecrated. It meant that I could visit."

Katrina smiled too and cocked her head at the grave markers. "Let's go visit," she urged.

Kyle led her to the stone monument of the Guardian of Hopes and Dreams that watched eternally over Catrine's resting place.

"Nice," Katrina said quietly, gesturing to the huge gargoyle that served as a gravestone for Kyle's lost love. "Subtle."

"Sarcasm doesn't become you," Kyle said, also speaking in a low tone. "Besides, if you knew the purpose of a gargoyle, you wouldn't be surprised why I chose this one for her."

"They're said to scare off evil spirits," Katrina replied. "But I've never seen one like this. Why is it chained?"

"The Guardian of Hopes and Dreams is forever chained to the pedestal of destiny," Kyle replied softly. "Or so his description said when I found him. There's a lot of symbolism in this piece that speaks of what dreams we must hold on to, and which—" Kyle gestured to the ground below the monument "—we must let go."

Katrina put a comforting hand on Kyle's arm, but jerked it back when she heard laughter.

"For years," came a dark voice from beside the grave, "both mortal and in Hell, I have watched and waited for you to find another one, Kailkiril'ron."

A form appeared from behind the fountain.

"Still spying then, Kihirin," Kyle said in a bored tone. "I shouldn't be surprised. After all, thinking for yourself is such a hardship."

"Actually, this is 'for myself'," Kihirin answered darkly. "No one cares about you any more. You are a joke. No one here wants you either, I see, except . . . Who is that little thing you have there? Another one willing to die for you? You waste no time, Kailkiril'ron."

"And you're still inattentive," Kyle said with a menacing grin. "For all your spying, you haven't learned a thing."

"You have the Destrati sovereign's wife right there in your hands," Kihirin said. "Do you know what her soul is worth? You offer that and Father will give you back your own—"

Katrina watched in horror as Kyle grabbed Kihirin's mortal form by the throat. She stepped hurriedly backwards and fell hard against the base of the gargoyle monument. She yelped as the corner grazed her arm from wrist to elbow. She might be immortal, but that didn't mean things still didn't hurt like hell.

"You have no idea how badly Hell can hurt, little girl," Kihirin snarled at her, both his hands trying to free himself from Kyle's grip. "You have an idea, do you not, Betrayer? Forsake her, and you can have everything back. Remember who you were? Remember your legions? Remember your command? Andronicus leads now, and being under his command is nothing compared to what it was to serve under you. You were so much more *everything* than he is. Twenty thousand legions at your command, Lord General. Perfect obedience. And your masterful touch at soul-rending. No one could torture a soul, mortal or immortal, like you. Remember the sound of home? How often do you kill an innocent young one slowly just to hear that sound again? Remember your hound—"

"I remember," Kyle said darkly, "my service and blind obedience."

Kyle released Kihirin, tossing him dismissively towards the fountain without effort. The demon fell backwards, almost into the water.

"You can have it all back," Kihirin said again. "All you have to do—"

"Is give you what I don't have, and never will again," Kyle snapped. "You saw to that when you released her soul." He sniffed disdainfully. "I am . . . *was* . . . the Lord General. Firstborn. I do not just blindly follow orders like the rest of you.

"Father should have had more faith in me," Kyle added.

Kihirin laughed. "You imply that you would have given up her soul, if only you had been *asked* and not *ordered* to?"

Kihirin reached slowly into the pocket of the jacket he was wearing and brought something out of it. He opened his fingers and there, sitting in his palm, was a glittering ball of faint white light, marred by tendrils of black cracks manifested over its crystalline surface.

"No," Kyle protested, though it was little more than a whisper. He glared at Kihirin. "She was an innocent. Her soul ascended. Do not think I do not know the extent to which you will go for your amusement, Kihirin."

Katrina could only watch in horror. Was that really a soul she was seeing? It didn't look like she expected it to. It was quite small, and almost ordinary looking. It looked so sad and vulnerable all on its own.

"Well, it is not as pure as it once was after having been tortured for all this time. I can see why you wanted it for yourself," Kihirin said, laughing again. "Why you kept it from Father. You always did find it difficult to obey without proper motivation. When you came back unsuccessful . . . *you*, Lord General . . ." Kihirin tsked and shook his head, then held the ball of light out to Kyle. "I have kept her all this time for you, Lord General, so that when you regained your senses and remembered your loyalties you would have it to present to Father, so you could reclaim your place. I assure you, it is hers."

A mournful cry, like the screech of an improperly rosined bow over taut violin strings, reached Katrina's ears. The sound of it dropped Kyle to his knees.

"Catrine . . ." Kyle said, choking on the name.

Kihirin crouched down before him. "Return with me," Kihirin urged. "Present this to Father as you should have done before. Humble yourself before him, and he might even allow you to atone using her—"

Kyle flung Kihirin against the fountain monument with such force that the soul in Kihirin's hand fell to the ground at the base of Catrine's grave.

Kihirin's mortal eyes widened. Kyle stood over him, looking down mercilessly. Even as a lost soul, he was still more of a demon than Kihirin could ever hope to be.

Kyle roared an unintelligible word, banishing Kihirin from using the means to manifest here ever again. Then he knelt to look down at the abandoned soul Kihirin had left behind. But before he could touch it, the ball of light changed and took something of a transparent form before him.

It was fleeting, but Katrina saw the form reach to touch Kyle's face before disappearing entirely.

It was all Katrina could do to choke back the sob in her throat. It wasn't enough, however, and attracted Kyle's attention.

Kyle glanced at Katrina. Her cheeks were wet as he came to help her stand. He reached for her arm and righted her. She yelped again as his touch made her aware of her injury. Kyle held her wrist with one hand as he passed his other hand over her wound. It healed instantly.

"Are you all right?"

It was the first time in a long time that Katrina had felt gentleness and genuine warmth in Kyle's touch. She pulled back to look at him.

Even without a soul, Kyle's presence was formidable. What must it have been like when he was whole?

"That was her, wasn't it?" Katrina asked softly. "He wasn't lying to you. He had her, all this time."

Kyle nodded absently as his eyes strayed to the empty place where Catrine's soul had stood for a moment.

"Now that she's free, she can return to you," Katrina said, her eyes sparkling. "Sure, she'll have to be born again and you'll have to find her again and all that, but she'll come back to you, I know it! Don't look so unhappy. This is a wonderful thing!"

Kyle looked up at the heavens. Then he cocked his head to one side and slowly turned to gaze at Katrina. He could sense that she wanted to ask a question. He tried to hide his smile.

Katrina suddenly felt warm – too warm for the winter coat she had on.

"Kyle, um, you wouldn't really have—" she looked up at him, meeting his pale ethereal eyes "—given your dad Catrine's soul . . ."

Kyle lifted her chin with a crooked finger.

". . . if he'd *asked* for it . . ."

He smiled slightly.

". . . would you?"

The heat creeping up her neck was starting to become oppressive. She opened her coat and fanned the collar a moment, trying to cool herself slightly. She felt like she was being slowly strangled.

Kyle didn't reply. He simply studied her, looking deep into her eyes.

She smiled at him, waiting, but still he said nothing. Not even a hint of a wry smile, no arched, derisive eyebrow. It was a little . . . eerie, and she thought herself pretty well used to eerie by now.

But then Kyle smiled and offered her a graceful half-bow.

She knew it was the only answer he was going to give. She laughed to herself for thinking he *would* . . . thinking he *could* have.

Would he?

She met his eyes again, quickly. Pale and sea green. She could see more in them now.

"Once a thief, always a thief," her mother was fond of saying.

As Kyle gently took her arm, and shifted them both to her home, Katrina tried to silence her mother's warning in her head.

"Once a demon, always a demon?"

Night Vision

Maria V. Snyder

Sophia started the Honda 250X dirt bike. The roar of the engine cut through the quiet darkness. A perfect September night for a ride, she thought. The air smelled of living green. No moon. No wind.

She swung on her backpack, strapped on her helmet, and checked her safety gear before pulling on a pair of padded leather gloves. She straddled the bike.

Where to? Sophia glanced at the surrounding forest. She lived near the Great Smoky Mountains in North Carolina. Basically, the middle of nowhere with not a soul around for miles. Which suited her just fine. No neighbours. No annoying questions. No light.

She decided to ride over to Standing Indiana Mountain near Georgia's northern border. It had been a couple of months since she last visited. The old glider landing strip near the peak would be a nice place for a midnight snack.

The bike jumped to life as she feathered the clutch. Following the narrow trails, she rode hard. Low-hanging branches smacked against her chest protector. She ducked thicker limbs, navigated around trunks, splashed through streams and motored up inclines. Her heart raced with pure adrenaline as the bike chewed up the miles.

Sailing over the last mound, Sophia whooped in mid-air. The bike landed with a solid thud. She stopped at the edge of the airstrip and removed her helmet.

It took her a moment to realize that the long grass that had grown wild on the strip had been cut to stubble. Tyre tracks grooved the ground. The glider port was no longer abandoned, but no aircraft was in sight.

Curious to see if the farmhouse nearby was also in use, Sophia hiked to the dilapidated two-storey building. Sure enough, light gleamed from the windows despite the late hour. A blue Ford F150 pickup with Virginia licence plates rested in the weed-choked driveway.

Not a weekender – Virginia was too far. Perhaps the new owners were glider pilots.

The brightness from the house burned her eyes. She averted her gaze and headed to her bike. But the sound of tyres crunching over stones enticed her back. Crouching nearby, she vowed to leave as soon as she spotted the car's owner. After all, they were technically neighbours.

Face it, Sophia, it's the first bit of excitement you've had since Dad died.

A Land Rover bounced and bumped along the dirt . . . well, calling it a road would be an exaggeration. Clouds of dust followed in its wake. Keeping out of the headlights' beams, Sophia watched as the Land Rover stopped in front of the house with a squeal.

Two men stepped from the vehicle. A tank-sized, muscular man pounded on the front door. "Hey Rick, come out. We caught a big fish."

The driver unlocked the back gate. The door swung wide and Rick came out of the house to join his friends.

"Who the hell is that?" Rick demanded.

"He's a Fed, man," the Tank said. "Special Agent Mitchell Wolfe."

An icy chill crawled up Sophia's spine. The cliche about curiosity and dead cats churned in her mind.

"Shit. How much does he know?" Rick asked.

"He knows we've been collecting treasures, but he doesn't know the pick-up location," the driver said.

"Shit. What did you bring him here for?"

"He hasn't reported in yet. We didn't know what to do." Keys jangled as the driver gestured.

"How did you know he didn't talk to the Feds?"

"We threatened to harm *his* treasure. He blabbed like a baby."

"Did you get it?"

"Yep." The big man yanked a long mesh bag from the back seat of the Land Rover.

Rick jerked a thumb towards the house. "Inside. Wake Glenn. We're gonna need him." A resigned annoyance coloured his tone.

While living in the middle of nowhere had its benefits, it also had its drawbacks. No wireless signals. No authorities within fifty miles.

The two men discussed delivery times as they waited for Glenn. Sophia heard "4 a.m." and "three treasures" before Glenn slunk from the house.

"This better be good," Glenn said.

"We have a problem," Rick explained.

"No problem." Glenn gestured. "We're in the middle of bloody nowhere. Nobody'll find him." He pulled a gun from behind his back and aimed.

Sophia jumped to her feet. Ready to . . . what? Scream?

Rick shoved Glenn's arm down. "Not in the Rover, you idiot. Blood evidence stays behind even after you clean up. Don't you watch *CSI*?"

Glenn shrugged. "Whatever."

"Go ten miles and shoot him in the woods. Leave him for the cougars. Ed, you drive."

The driver closed the back. He slid behind the wheel. Glenn hopped in beside him.

Watching the Land Rover U-turn, Sophia's thoughts raced. There was no doubt she had to help, but Glenn was armed. She had a tool kit, but no weapons. Tonight had been a fun ride, not a hunting trip.

She had her Honda. The 250 cubic centimetre engine would keep up with the vehicle, and she had her . . . other talent, if desperate. Running to her bike, she jammed her helmet on, and kicked it into gear.

The beams of light from the Rover sliced the darkness, making it easy for Sophia to follow. Since she didn't need a headlight, the men should be unaware of her presence.

After bouncing and crashing along the tight trail for thirty minutes, the vehicle swung to the side, illuminating a thick patch of underbrush.

Sophia silenced her bike and coasted to a stop about a hundred feet up the trail. Propping the bike, she crept closer. The men stepped from the vehicle, leaving the engine running.

"Perfect spot," Glenn said. "He's starting to wake. Take him out to those briars." He checked his weapon.

Ed pulled the captive out. The man staggered. Ed steadied him. The agent's wrists were handcuffed behind him. Cuts lined his face and a purple bruise covered his swollen right eye. He looked groggy, but when Glenn flashed his gun, he snapped awake.

"Easy there, Mitch," Ed said. "We're just going to leave you here to find your own way home."

"Right." Mitch's voice rasped with sarcasm.

"Come on." Ed dragged him towards the briar patch.

With her heart doing gymnastics in her chest, Sophia bent the light around her, rendering herself invisible to the men. She reached the vehicle and crawled towards the front tyre, keeping her eyes on the men and away from the burning brightness. When the two men stepped into the Rover's headlights, they disappeared from her vision.

One chance. Sophia opened the driver's side door and switched the headlights off, plunging the three men into total darkness. Points scored for middle of nowhere.

Mitch used the sudden blackout to kick the side of Ed's knee. Ed crumbled to the ground in pain.

"Shoot him," Ed said.

"I can't see, you idiot!" Glenn shouted. He fumbled for the Rover's door handle.

The agent ducked and ran, but tripped and crashed. Without light to bend, Sophia became visible. She darted after the agent. He regained his feet as she caught up to him.

"I can help you," she whispered.

He jerked in surprise, but thankfully stayed quiet.

"Follow me. I have excellent night vision." She put a hand on his arm and guided him towards her bike. "Hurry."

They reached the bike as the Rover's headlights lit up the area. Silently thanking Honda for electric starters, she mounted.

"Over there!" Ed yelled. "What the hell?"

A gun fired.

"Jump on," she ordered. Panic threatened to scatter her senses, but she bit her lip.

The bike sank as Mitch's weight compressed the suspension. He wouldn't be able to hold on to her.

Another gunshot cracked through the air. Mitch grunted.

"Lean on me." She put the bike in gear, then took off down the road and away from the Rover. Mitch's stomach and chest pressed against her back.

Doors slammed and tyres spun on gravel.

"They're chasing us," Mitch said with urgency.

Great. Her heart dropped to her stomach to do a floor routine. Sophia reviewed her options. With his hands bound, she couldn't ride off-road with him. The Rover's headlights behind her caused sections of the road to disappear from her sight, making it difficult to navigate. She could bend the light around the bike, but if the headlights aimed directly at them, they would be suddenly visible.

She manoeuvred around a turn. Mitch leaned with her. *He's been on a bike before. Perhaps she could cut through the mountains and lose the Rover.* She searched for an appropriate path.

When she spotted a tight trail, she turned so Mitch could hear her. "I'm going off-road. Match my movements."

"Jesus, lady, you don't even have a headlight."

"Would you rather stay?"

"No."

Slowing to half-speed because of her passenger, she struggled to find a path that wouldn't unseat him. Curses, yells and a few more gunshots sounded. She concentrated on riding, pouring every ounce of energy into it.

"We lost them," Mitch said.

With her arms shaking from fatigue, she stopped. Mitch dismounted and dropped to the ground.

"That was close," he said. "You saved my life. Where the hell did you come from?"

She removed her helmet. Her long ponytail snagged in the strap. Sweat stung her eyes and soaked her shirt under the chest protector. "I was riding and saw you needed help."

"In the middle of the night *without* a headlight?" His tone implied disbelief. "It's pitch-black out here."

"I told you I have good night vision. Besides, I grew up around here. I know these hills like a bat knows its cave."

"What's your name – Bat Woman?"

"No. Wonder Woman. My invisible plane is in for repairs so I had to use my super bike."

His shoulders sagged. "Sorry. It's been a hell of a day. I'm Mitch Wolfe – a federal agent, and I'm going to need more of your help."

"Sophia Daniels. I'll do what I can."

"First, I need to get these cuffs off."

"My tool kit—"

"I have a key in the—" he cringed "—waistband of my underwear."

She couldn't suppress a chuckle. "Are they special spy underwear?"

"Yep. They're bulletproof, too. A man can't be too cautious when it comes to personal safety." He laughed with a deep, rich rumble that rolled right through her. "It's a master handcuff key. It's along my left side." He regained his feet.

His grey T-shirt was ripped and stained with blood. Too much blood. She gasped. "You've been shot."

"I felt a nick."

She pulled his shirt up. A deep gash oozed near his ribs on the left, cutting across the ripple of muscles along his abdomen. "It's more of a slice. You're going to need sutures."

"Sutures? Don't tell me my nocturnal rescuer is also a doctor because that would be another hell of a coincidence."

"My father was a paramedic. I have supplies—"

"Later. Key first."

Sophia tried pulling the waistband up past his jeans.

"You need to unbutton the pants," he said in a matter-of-fact tone.

She hesitated before fumbling at the button. Wonderful, Sophia, she chided. You're coordinated enough to jump a dirt bike over Ranger's Gap, but you can't undo one button. An eternity later, she ripped the key from his waistband and unlocked the cuffs.

He groaned with relief, rubbing his raw wrists. Sophia realized she stood rather close to him, and he was a stranger. He was about six inches taller than her own five foot eight, and had arms like a professional quarterback. He looked about thirty, a few years older than her. Mitch claimed to be a federal agent, but she didn't have any proof.

She remembered his injury and reached for the first-aid kit in her backpack but stopped. Her pack! She had left it by the airstrip. A quick mental scan of the contents made her relax. No personal information, but she didn't have the kit, food or water.

He tapped his pockets. "Shit. They took my wallet, phone and gun. Do you have a cell?" Mitch rebuttoned his jeans.

"No signals out here."

"Where then? I need to make a call. The sooner the better."

She sighed. No other choice. Her house was the closest. "I have a landline."

"Within walking distance?" A hopeful note crept into his voice.

"No. About twenty miles off-road."

"And on the road?"

"Fifty."

"Damn. I'm going to have to trust your night vision again, aren't I?"

"Yep." Buckling up the chest protector, she donned her helmet.

A queasy expression creased his sharp nose and he rubbed his hand along his five o'clock shadow. Long black eyelashes matched his almost military-style short black hair. His uninjured blue eye stared at her in concern.

"Relax, Mitch. I'll get us there in one piece. After we jump the chasm of death, we're home free."

"Funny," he deadpanned. "I don't suppose you have another helmet?"

"Nope. But if we do crash, I'll aim for the right side to even out your injuries."

He gave her a wry grin. "Enduring poor attempts at humour

is better than being dead. At least, you have a decent bike. My fragile male ego wouldn't be able to handle being rescued by a lady on a scooter."

With a passenger on board, the trip to her house lasted twice as long as normal. Mitch clutched her waist with a vice grip. He cursed and muttered under his breath, but matched the rhythm of the bike's motion.

When they arrived at her small log cabin, he slid off on unsteady legs. The bloodstain on his shirt had spread. Sophia tossed her helmet and gear into a pile. Leaving the bike next to her shed, she led him into the living room.

The place followed the standard mountain cabin decor – comfortable recliners, plaid-patterned couch, faux bear rug and animal paintings.

"Sit down before you fall down." Sophia guided Mitch to the couch.

"Are you going to turn on the lights or did you forget to pay your electric bill?" he asked with a nervous edge.

She closed her eyes for a moment, summoning the strength for a difficult explanation. If there had been a phone anywhere else, she would have avoided this.

Working up the nerve, she said, "I can't tolerate visible light."

"Can't tolerate light? Like a vampire?" His confusion turned into alarm.

She huffed with exasperation. "I wish! At least vampires can go to a movie."

Mitch gestured as if calming a crazy person. "Look, all I need is to use your phone."

She sighed. *Shouldn't have made that vampire crack.* "I'm sorry. I'm not explaining it well. I'm out of practice." Sophia drew in a breath. *Time for the standard spiel.* She would love to tell the truth, but who, except the wrong people, would believe her? So instead, she said, "I have a rare disease called erythropoietic protoporphyria or EEP for short. Light kills my red blood cells, so I have to avoid *all* visible light, which means I live in the middle of nowhere with no TV, computer or . . ." Human contact. But that sounded pathetic.

If anything, her story made him more uneasy. She wondered why.

"What do you do when the sun comes up?"

Retreat to my coffin. "I sleep during the day."

He had an odd . . . queasy expression. Perhaps he searched for words of regret or encouragement that she didn't deserve to hear. Before he could speak, she said, "There's a phone and a lamp in the guest room, and a light in the guest bath. You can make your call and at least clean that gash before it becomes infected."

"Phone call first." He surged to his feet, but paused. "Where are we?"

"North of Shooting Creek, North Carolina."

"North Carolina! I didn't realize . . ." He rubbed his hand on his swollen temple. "How far to Knoxville?"

"One hundred and thirty miles."

"Damn." He considered. "Do you have an address?"

"I have GPS coordinates. Will they work?"

"Yeah. I just wish I knew where *they* were heading," he muttered more to himself than to her.

"Your friends?" she asked.

"Yes."

Sophia realized he didn't know about the farmhouse. She explained. "It's isolated, but I can pull the GPS coordinates off a topographical map for you." Strangely, her offer increased his apprehension.

"Good." He seemed distracted. "Where . . . is the phone?"

She took his hand in the pitch-darkness and guided him to the guest room. The cabin's first floor contained a kitchen, living room, bedroom and bathroom. Her room and another bath were down in the basement.

Handing Mitch the cordless phone, she put his other hand on the lamp switch. "Wait until you hear the door close before turning the light on. I'll go pull the coordinates for you."

"Thanks," he said.

A strange hitch in his voice worried Sophia but, considering what the man had been through tonight, she didn't blame him. She was halfway to the door when he flicked the lamp on. Blinding whiteness obscured her vision. She stumbled and bumped into a chair.

"What did you do that for?" she demanded, fumbling

around. *Where was that door?* The light was too strong for her to bend.

Instead of answering, Mitch grabbed her wrists and pushed her against a wall.

"Let go!" Fear flushed through her. *Idiot.* Why hadn't she asked for identification?

She tried to kick him, but missed. He pressed his weight on her, pinning her legs.

"You can't see me, can you?" Accusation laced his voice.

"Turn off the light."

"You're working with Ed. What's the purpose of your mock rescue?"

"I'm not working with anybody. Get off!"

"Don't lie. I just have to look at your eyes to know you're one of *them*. I suspected, but when you said you were 'out of practice' I knew for sure."

"What are you talking about?"

"You're one of *those*. Who are you working for?"

Anger flared. "Guess I couldn't fool a *federal* agent. You're right, Sherlock. I saved you from those goons just so I could bring you back here and kill you." She tapped her head against the wall. "Oh damn! I left my Glock in the other room."

"You know what I mean," he said. "Your so-called night vision is physically impossible. I've trained for night ops. There's not enough light out here for night-vision goggles. You can see in the dark, but are blind in the light. So, who are you working for?"

She struggled to free herself, but his body trapped her. He wasn't buying her medical condition bullshit. He knew all about her. Not only could she even see colours in the dark, but read, too. The blacker the night, the better her vision. She had been born with a strange power and, as far as she knew, there weren't too many other people like her in the world.

"Tell me now or I'll take you into custody for questioning."

An image of being blind and helpless in an unknown place filled her with dread. Avoiding that situation had been the whole reason she lived here. She was out of options. *Shit.* "I'm not working for anybody. That's the whole point of living miles away from civilization."

That made him pause. "You're in hiding?"

"Give Mr Super Detective a gold star."

"From who?" The suspicion was back.

"Everyone!" Her father would be livid if he were alive. She had just undermined all his efforts to keep the government from knowing where she was hiding. Sophia would never forget the day the agents had visited them. They had called her special, and wanted her to train at an exclusive school to become an agent. Her father promised them he'd take her there. Instead of driving to the school, he headed for the hills. When she questioned him, he had explained that the government would train her to sneak around in the dark, stealing, spying and killing people for them.

"And you're the worst."

"Me?" Mitch balked.

"Yes. You said it yourself. The government wants to exploit people like me. We can see in the dark. That's a handy skill for an agent. The Federal Agency for Supernatural Security, my ass. You guys are the one group of people who give me *no* sense of security whatsoever. What is it you guys call us, again? The phrase is so hateful."

Mitch hesitated. "Blind assassins. But they do other . . . jobs as well."

"Do you think the members volunteer?"

"No. No, they don't," he said in a quiet voice. "In fact, for a long time I thought blind assassins were just an urban legend. Agents would blame them for unexplained events, things you would usually blame a ghost for, like rearranging your knick-knacks, or hiding your car keys. An agent even joked once that Bin Laden used a blind assassin to help him escape through the caves in Afghanistan. At least, I thought he was joking until . . ."

He released his hold. She didn't wait. Inching along the wall, she searched for the doorway with her hands. Was she even going the right way?

The lamp switched off, flooding the room with darkness. She sagged with relief. Mitch sat on the edge of the bed with his hand on the lamp.

She darted to the doorway, but paused at the threshold. "Until . . . what?"

"Until tonight," he said.

"Are you going—"

"No. I won't tell anyone about you." He gave her a sad smile. "But I might try to recruit you. *You* could find Bin Laden's hideout and—"

"Not interested."

He sighed. "Could you get the coordinates of the farmhouse for me?"

"Sure. There's a first-aid kit in the linen closet, clean T-shirts in the drawers. They're my father's, but . . . but he's dead. The shirts should fit you; he used to be a firefighter before he was a paramedic." She babbled, but couldn't stop herself. "There's food in the kitchen and flashlights in the closet. Help yourself."

Sophia ran downstairs to her bedroom. Embarrassed and upset, she had a whole gymnastic team of emotions doing twists and flips in her chest. He had attacked and threatened her and she had transformed into Miss Manners. She should have kicked him out. *One phone call, buddy and go.* Was she that desperate for company? *Yes, she was.*

Before tonight she thought she didn't need anyone. She had her books, her dirt bike, her pen pals, and was learning how to paint. *God, you are pathetic.*

She wanted to hide under the blankets, but she needed a shower and had promised Mitch those coordinates. Kicking off her motorcycle boots, she headed for the bathroom. She peeled off her long-sleeved riding shirt and padded bike pants. *Not very sexy.*

Her father had threatened to pull the spark plug from her bike if she didn't wear all the gear. Mr Safety. She missed him like crazy. He had changed his lifestyle for her, sleeping in the daytime so he could be with her at night. He taught her how to hunt and how to ride.

He saved her from being taken by the government or by one of those other agencies of questionable repute. *Someone with my skills can be beneficial to all types of organizations. Drug smugglers, weapons dealers, the military . . .*

Sophia shivered and jerked her thoughts to the present. She hesitated before removing her underwear. The idea of being naked with a strange man in the house unnerved her. She snorted. *Unnerved. Wonderful.* Considering how long ago it was that her last boyfriend declared he was too "freaked out" by her whole nocturnal existence and left, she should be seducing the handsome agent by now. She was pathetic and spouting cliches. *Handsome agent. Pah.*

After a quick shower, she changed into jeans and another long-sleeved shirt. Sophia combed her hair. With her pale skin, dark hair and silver eyes, no wonder he thought she was a vampire.

Her hair used to lighten in the sun. She had an almost normal childhood. That was the hardest part of her condition. Her eyesight had deteriorated as she aged. When she turned twelve, she was blind in bright light but, with a concentrated effort, she could bend the dim or indirect light rays around her body so she could see. But this had an unfortunate side effect; her father had jumped out of his skin the first time she had turned invisible. The appropriate name for someone with her talents was Light Bender.

Sophia rummaged through her desk for Standing Indiana Mountain's topographical map and pulled the coordinates of the farmhouse.

She crept up the stairs. A thin line of white shone under his door. The deep murmur of Mitch's voice sounded. She slid the paper underneath and retreated to the kitchen. One a.m. already. Her stomach grumbled. Slicing apples, she wondered if Mitch was hungry. Should she make him a sandwich? *No.* Miss Manners had told him to help himself.

Light illuminated the hallway as his door opened. He replaced the bright lamp with a flashlight's beam.

Not wanting to surprise him, she said, "I'm in the kitchen."

He stopped at the threshold, aiming the flashlight down. Water dripped from his wet hair onto his bare muscular chest. A whole new slew of cliches jumped up and down in Sophia's head. Her heart threatened to join in.

"Um. Could you help? I think it needs to be stitched." He held bandages and her father's fire department T-shirt. The gash below his ribs oozed. "Can you do that?" At least this time he tried to mask his suspicion.

She bit back a sarcastic reply. "As long as you're not allergic to lidocaine."

"And if I am?"

"Then I'll give you a shot of whiskey and a rolled-up washcloth to bite down on."

He laughed. "I'll pass on the washcloth, but the whiskey sounds good."

After she collected the supplies, she told him to sit sideways on the couch. He settled into position then doused the flashlight.

She crouched next to him, filling the syringe. "This is going to pinch, but it will numb the area." He smelled of soap and Old Spice – an intoxicating mix. To distract her senses, she asked him if he finished making phone calls.

"Yeah. My team will pick me up, but it'll take them a while to get here."

"How long?"

He squinted with suspicion. "Why do you want to know?"

"So I can tip Rick off." Sarcasm dripped, but his reaction surprised her.

He grabbed her arm. "How did you know Rick's name?"

"I overheard them talking."

"And you waited until *now* to tell me," he said with an outraged disbelief.

"Since we've just been sitting around doing nothing all night, I didn't want to ruin the mood." She knocked his hand away. Finishing the sutures, Sophia tied off the thread and bandaged his wound a little more harshly than necessary.

Mitch touched her shoulder. "Sorry." He pulled her beside him on the couch.

A strange tingling rushed through her as she realized his warm fingers still rested on her.

"It's disconcerting to hear your voice, but not be able to see you. I need a . . . physical connection. OK?"

"Sure." Her voice rasped. *How embarrassing!* But she relaxed and left his fingers on her arm.

"Could you please tell me everything you heard?" he asked.

As Sophia recited, Mitch stiffened. She felt his anxiety vibrate through his touch.

"A mesh bag? Are you sure?" he asked.

"Yes."

He swore. "And—" his voice cracked "—a 4 a.m. pick up tonight?"

"I don't know if they meant tonight."

He covered his eyes with his other hand. "My team won't be here in time. Maybe we can intercept the vehicle. Is there another road out?"

"The airstrip."

"What?"

"There's a landing strip next to the farmhouse."

Mitch shot to his feet. "I need to get there. Now!"

"What 'treasures' are worth risking your life for?"

"Classified. I need a ride—"

"Not until you tell me."

His hands balled into fists. She scrambled away as he stepped forwards. Mitch stopped and drew in a deep breath. "Those guys are kidnappers. They smuggle young girls to foreign countries. Young girls with special . . . talents. Some, like you, are blind assassins . . . I mean—" he quickly corrected himself "—light benders."

"I don't believe you. There aren't many people like me in the world."

"I think you'd be surprised. Hiding in your cabin all the time, you're a little out of touch with reality."

Emotion roughened his voice. "I sent my little sister to a special school after our mother died. She insisted she didn't belong in there because she could . . . *see* in the dark. I didn't believe her, of course. Your condition is rare—"

She interjected, "It's *not* a condition." Then she stopped herself as the picture became clearer. "Your sister is a light bender, isn't she?"

His fingers raked his damp hair. "The kidnappers think so. But I hadn't made the connection before meeting you. I was visiting her at the school last night when they jumped us. But I thought she had escaped. She disappeared while I was fighting with Ed's friend."

Mitch's sister was in the mesh bag. Sophia bolted from the couch. "Let's go."

Mitch donned the T-shirt and ran to the phone to update his team, careful to keep his flashlight out of her eyes. She dashed out the back to prep her bike. When Mitch joined her she said, "My father's helmet is in the shed."

"Any weapons?"

"Hunting rifles."

"Ammo?"

"In the cabinet in the living room. Take the thirty-thirty and my Winchester."

"Yours? Oh no. You're just giving me a ride. After you drop me off, you're coming back here."

"Don't be ridiculous. I can *see* in the dark."

Although unhappy, Mitch agreed, with conditions. "You are to do *exactly* what I say. No free styling. Understand?"

"Yes, sir."

Grumbling, Mitch used the flashlight to find the guns and helmet. He strapped the rifles on his back. The trip to the airstrip wasn't as exhausting as the ride home. Mitch's hold stayed loose. He moulded his body to her back. Although his warmth distracted her at times, the connection helped him match her movements faster. She realized he trusted her.

The Honda chugged up the mountain and crested on the far side of the runway. She cut the engine and coasted to a small dip. Mitch handed her the Winchester.

"Here's the plan," he said. "We'll approach the house from the east side. If they're still there, I'll get in close to see *who* is where. You stay put. You're my sniper. If the guys try to drive away, shoot out their tyres. *Only* if you have a clear shot."

"What are you going to do if they stay?"

"Wait. It's three thirty. If the plane comes at four, they'll leave the house with the girls and I'll surprise them. Otherwise, I'll wait for my team."

His plan sounded simple. The element of surprise combined with her night vision should work well together. Something about famous last words echoed in her mind, but she squashed all doubts. She remembered listening to her father lecture the rookies at the firehouse before the blindness forced her into isolation. He'd tell them to switch off their emotions, to think and act now, and leave the worries and the panic for later.

Good advice, Dad. But how do I get the rest of my body to comply? Her insides felt jittery and her palms left wet prints on her rifle.

Sophia led Mitch to the east side. Both vehicles were parked in the driveway and lights shone from the first-floor windows. The kidnappers hadn't left.

Mitch's relieved expression matched hers. He had enough light to navigate on his own. He pointed to the ground and mouthed the word "stay". She saluted. He flashed her a grin, turned away, then paused.

Something wrong?

Her heart decided to go for a gold medal in the hundred-yard dash. *I spent way too much time listening to the Olympics on the radio.*

Mitch moved to whisper in her ear. "Just in case I don't get a chance later, thank you for saving my life."

"Make sure you hold on to it. I doubt the next time you're in trouble that a blind assassin will ride to your rescue."

Another smile. She liked the way his eyes crinkled when he grinned.

He cupped her chin and peered at her. "A supernatural beauty." His gaze met hers.

Her body turned to stone as all her nerve endings rushed to where his fingers touched her jaw. He leaned in and kissed her. Sensation flared on her lips and she returned the kiss.

He pulled away. Sophia watched him for as long as he remained visible. Once he neared the house, she lost him in the light. She scanned the second-floor windows and thought she spotted movement, but couldn't be certain.

Glad the night air stayed calm, Sophia practised aiming at the tyres with her Winchester rifle. Scanning the black sky, she searched for signs of an approaching airplane. All quiet. After a few more minutes, she decided waiting sucked.

When the grunts and sounds of a scuffle reached her, she changed her mind. Waiting was better. A thud followed a curse and she heard voices, but not Mitch's.

"Told you the ambush would work," Ed said.

"Bring him inside," Rick said.

A door slammed. They had expected him. *How?* Didn't matter at this point. Mitch and the girls were in the brightly-lit house. Panic bubbled up her throat, but she gulped it down.

Think now, freak out later.

Option one: wait until they left the house to meet the plane at 4 a.m. She would play sniper, incapacitating them one by one. *Won't work. They would scatter at the sound of the first shot.*

Option two: hit the aeroplane when it landed. Unable to fly, they would be forced to drive out and, best-case scenario, run into Mitch's team. *No. They would kill Mitch. No reason for them to take him along.*

Option three: cut off the electricity and tip the playing field in her favour. Not the best plan, but she had a winner.

Sophia moved with care, circling the house. She searched for the electric box. The light from the windows made it impossible to find. She would have to crawl around the outside walls and explore with her hands. Approaching the house from the back side seemed logical; she held out a hand and entered the whiteness. She tried to avoid the direct light.

When her fingers touched the wood siding, she began the hunt. Two hands would be faster, but she wasn't stupid enough to put her weapon down.

On the west side of the house she heard loud voices through the window.

". . . your friend?" Rick asked.

"Dropped me off and went home," Mitch said.

He was conscious and alive. Sophia let out a quiet breath as relief washed through her. The feeling didn't last long.

A high-pitched squeal of pain sliced the air. "Mitch!"

His sister. Sophia wilted.

"Let's go over your story again," Rick said. "We know your biker friend was near the house and heard us talking about you because Ed found a backpack and tyre tracks nearby. Biker then follows the Rover and rescues you in a blaze of glory. Here's where *your* story gets . . . creative." He chuckled without humour. "You claim the biker took you to a rustic cabin with no electricity or phones, helped you clean up, and then brought you back here. Is this correct?"

"Yeah."

"Glenn," Rick said.

A heart-breaking scream erupted. Sophia rolled into a ball to keep from pounding on the window and surrendering.

"You won't hurt her," Mitch said in a flat, deadly tone.

"We already have," Glenn said.

"Surface bruises. You won't damage the merchandise or you'll lose thousands of dollars."

Mitch just bought her a few extra minutes. She hurried. She found the box and pulled out her Swiss Army knife. Silently thanking her father for teaching her another fireman's trick, she unlocked the box and turned off the electricity.

Her night vision returned as cries and curses sounded. She ran to the window and peered in. Ed and the Tank held Mitch tight. Glenn had one arm wrapped around a young girl. He had backed into a corner with his other hand pointing a gun. Rick told everyone to calm down.

"The biker only knows one trick," Rick said. "Stay put, I'll get the spotlight." He felt his way from the room.

Sophia aimed her rifle. A million worries and doubts boiled in her stomach. What if she missed? *Act now, agonize later.* She held her breath, braced for the recoil, and squeezed the trigger.

The window shattered, the noise ricocheted around the room, and Glenn slammed into the wall. The bullet pierced his shoulder right at the joint of his shooting arm. The force knocked him out. He slid to the floor with a thud.

Bingo! One down, three to go.

The girl yelled and threw herself flat, covering her head with her arms. Her brother had taught her well. Sophia swung the rifle towards the others. Ed dived into the hallway, but the Tank had his arm around Mitch's neck, pinning the agent in front of him as a shield.

"Shoot him," Mitch called.

Where? Mitch covered almost all of the Tank. And she wasn't a sharpshooter. Then she realized Mitch's hands weren't bound. One grasped the Tank's meaty forearm, but the other pointed down. The guy's knee poked out between Mitch's legs.

Oh shit. She aimed. *I bet Mitch is wishing for a real pair of bulletproof underwear*. She fired the gun and the bullet hit the

Tank's knee, obliterating it. *Yuck.* Mitch broke away as the Tank screamed.

"Jenna?" Mitch called, searching for his sister. They connected. The girl wrapped her arms around him and sobbed.

"It's OK," he said over and over.

I wish. She kept watch for the two men who escaped. The sound of an engine turning over came from the front of the house. Headlights stabbed the darkness.

"Mitch, they're in the Rover," she said.

The noise grew louder as the light brightened.

"Go!" Mitch ordered.

Sophia sprinted around the back of the house, hoping to loop behind them and shoot out their tyres. When she reached the front, light blinded her. She forgot about the pickup truck.

A shot boomed. Wood splintered. She dived to the ground, dropping her rifle, but kept moving, pulling herself along as if the air was filled with smoke. Gravel scraped her forearms as she sought the edge of light.

She bumped into a solid object. Please be a tree trunk, she prayed. But even blind there was no mistaking the touch of cold hard metal on her temple. A wave of terror swept through her.

"Stand up," Rick said.

She stood. The gun remained.

"Son of a bitch. No wonder you've been giving us such trouble. Are you working for the feds?" he asked.

"Yes, and my team will be here any minute."

He laughed. "Nice try." He shoved her forwards. "Up against the house."

Rick pushed her into the wood siding. The peeling paint chips scratched her cheek, a minor thing considering the gun's barrel now pressed on the back of her neck. She heard the Rover squeal to a stop.

"Did you get him?" Ed asked.

Rick snorted. "Our biker's a light bender."

Well, at least he used the right name . . .

"No shit!"

"Take the rifle and check the house. Let Mitch know we have his friend."

Rick must have turned the lights back on. Time flowed like sweet tea – the kind with so much sugar it had the consistency of syrup. Sweat collected and dripped down her back. *Why didn't I ride over to Nantahala Lake tonight?*

Finally, Ed returned. "Mitch and his sister have disappeared. Glenn's gun is gone and he and Max are in bad shape."

The tightness in her chest eased a bit. She hoped Mitch took his sister far away.

"The kids?"

"Gone too."

Rick cursed. "Get the spotlight and go find them," Rick ordered. "They couldn't have gone far." He grabbed Sophia's arm and propelled her into the house. "You saved his life and he left you behind. That's gotta hurt."

"I'm glad," she said. "I'd rather he save those girls than me." And she meant it. They could have full lives ahead of them – high school, graduation, college, romance, marriage and babies, if they weren't forced to become night-time operatives for some government. Her existence was just that, an existence. She had retreated from the world, but . . . she didn't have to. Suddenly a whole list of things she could do scrolled through her mind. If she had a second chance, she wouldn't hide any more. If not, then exchanging her life for four others would be consolation enough.

The fear left her, leaving behind a peaceful confidence.

Rick kept his hold and the gun on her. The hot scent of blood filled the air, gagging her. A man moaned in pain.

"Damn, lady. You sure did a number on them."

"They're survivable injuries," she said.

"But they're no good to me now. I can't take them with me and I can't leave them here."

The gun moved. "No!" she yelled. She spun, knocking his arm away as the gun fired. They fell together.

He rolled on top of her, pinning her down with his weight. Rick pressed the red-hot barrel into her neck. She cried out as the smell of burning flesh replaced the cloying blood scent.

"You're dead," he said.

She jerked as the gun roared. Pain blazed. Sophia struggled to draw breath as a heavy weight settled on her chest. Warm liquid soaked her shirt. *Can't breathe*. She felt light as her father called her name. Then he shook her shoulders . . . hard. When he slapped her, she tried to punch him, but he grabbed her wrist.

"Are you all right?" Mitch asked.

She felt her neck. Aside from the burn, it remained whole, but the metallic tang of blood dominated her senses. Her hands were sticky. "Rick?"

"Dead. Come on." Mitch pulled her to her feet.

She wobbled. "The girls? Ed?"

"Oldest trick in the book. I hid the girls in the basement, and left the back door wide open. Ed's out cold." He wrapped her in a hug. "I've done a number of stupid things today, but I wasn't going to leave you."

She clung to him, enjoying his warmth and strength. "Thanks for saving—"

He silenced her with a kiss. All too soon he broke away. "Just returning the favour."

Mitch kissed her again, but this one had a feeling of finality about it. He led her outside. The darkness embraced her and she fanned her blistered neck.

"My team will be here in an hour. You need to go." He was all business.

Despite the ache chewing holes in her heart Sophia understood he was protecting her.

Her moment of clarity had given her plenty of ideas of how to use her talent to help people. Even though she could see in the dark, it didn't mean she had to live there.

An icy chill gripped her. She slogged to her bike. The ride home blurred into one long endurance test, ending with a collapse on her bed.

Months passed. Sophia ventured back into society. The Association for the Blind taught her how to live in the light. She reconnected with the people at her father's firehouse. No longer afraid of being caught by the feds, Sophia explored the limits of her unique talent. She stopped hiding and rejoined the world. At night, her activities became more clandestine. She aided a search and rescue mission, helping to find a lost boy scout, and she followed a potential arsonist, stopping him before he set another barn fire.

Sophia was painting when headlights swept her cabin. The Association was delivering her guide dog tonight. Eager to meet her furry companion, she hurried outside. Caught in the headlights, she didn't need to act blind. She clutched a post on her porch to keep from tripping. When the lights extinguished, she saw a huge pickup truck with a Suzuki Z250 in the bed parked in her driveway. No dog.

Mitch hopped down from the driver's seat. She blinked, but he remained.

"What do you think?" He gestured to the bike.

"You should have bought a Honda instead of a Suck-zuki," she said.

"They're fighting words. You'll change your mind when you're eating my dust."

She laughed. "You think you can keep up with *me*?"

He reached into the cab and pulled out a helmet. "State-of-the-art night-vision visor." He glanced up. A waning half-moon hung in the sky. "Plenty of light. Want to go for a ride?"

"I can't. I'm waiting for a dog."

"A dog's more important?" he asked with a neutral tone.

"The dog's here to stay, and isn't just visiting for a joyride."

He set the helmet on the seat, and strode towards her. He wore her father's T-shirt. The bruises on his face were long gone, and her insides flipped when he reached her.

"I couldn't stop thinking about you. I've been keeping track of this area, reading the local papers and doing internet searches." He touched her neck, rubbing a thumb over her burn scar. "Seems a few unexplained, yet happy incidents have occurred in the Smoky Mountains these past three months." He dropped his hand. "Guess I was wrong about you."

"No. You were right. I've been hiding for a long time. Afraid to use my talents."

"And now you're not?"

"No. I'm still afraid, but I won't let it stop me."

"Admirable." He smiled. "Are you brave enough to expand your nocturnal activities, and work with a partner?"

"It depends."

His smile faltered. "On what?"

"On how close of a partnership you're talking about."

He pulled her towards him. Wrapping his arms around her, he kissed her. "Is this close enough?"

Instead of answering, she led him to her dark bedroom. "You can get closer. How's your night vision?"

Mitch grinned. "Excellent."

Pele's Tears

Catherine Mulvany

Dillon Makua stared glumly at the two empty bottles on the bar in front of him and contemplated the wisdom of ordering another beer. He was scheduled to meet with a new client in a few minutes. And dreading it.

Oh, hell. Reason enough. He rapped on the counter. "Hey, Keoni! How about a Primo over here when you get the time."

His cousin, Keoni O'Rourke, owner of the Shamrock Bar and Grill, plopped a paper parasol into the Mai Tai he'd just mixed and handed it to a waitress in a green-flowered *pareu* before glancing Dillon's way. "You sure? That makes three, brah."

"I can count."

"Well, excuse the hell out of me." Keoni set a beer on the counter in front of Dillon. "What's *your* problem?"

"My new case." Or more specifically, his new client.

Keoni raised a questioning eyebrow. "How bad can it be? Wait. Don't tell me you got conned into taking another dog-napping case. Not after the way that schnauzer you rescued chewed up your ankles."

"No canines involved this time."

"That's a plus." Keoni, the eternal optimist.

Dillon took a healthy pull on his beer. "The minus is I'm going to be stuck holding the hand of a spoiled little rich girl."

"Doesn't sound so bad to me," Keoni said.

Dillon was about to explain the downside when someone tapped him on the shoulder.

"Excuse me?"

Damn. Dillon swivelled around slowly. The beer hadn't helped. He still wasn't ready for this. For *her.* Noelani Crawford. First girl he'd ever kissed.

Only she wasn't a girl any more.

She still had the same long, glossy brown hair, big hazel eyes and kissable mouth he remembered, but her face was thinner, her cheekbones more defined. As for her body, gone was the coltish teenager. In her place stood a slim, elegant woman with curves in all the right places. Noelani Crawford had been a pretty girl; she was a gorgeous woman.

"Mr Makua?" A trace of impatience coloured her voice, but he couldn't find even the faintest glimmer of recognition in her expression.

Well, hell, what did he expect? It had been what? Sixteen years? And from her perspective maybe that kiss hadn't been as earth-shattering as he remembered it. Not to mention, he didn't look much like his scrawny fourteen-year-old self. And, thanks to Uncle Lopaka and his *Gunsmoke* obsession, Noelani had never known his real name. "Hey, Marshal!" Uncle Lopaka would yell. "Saddle a horse for Miss Crawford." "Hey, Marshal! Clean out the stalls in the east barn."

"Are you Mr Makua?" Noelani asked again.

"Yes." Dillon couldn't decide which was harder to swallow, the fact that she didn't recognize him or the fact that he cared.

She raised an eyebrow. "I'm the spoiled little rich girl, the one who needs her hand held."

Behind him, Keoni stifled a snort of laughter.

Noelani tilted her chin and narrowed her eyes. "If you don't want my business, just say so. I can take it elsewhere."

"Yes, I'd prefer that," he started to say, then realized it wasn't true. Noelani had broken his teenaged heart. This might be his chance to find out why. "Sorry if I sounded unprofessional. May I buy you a drink?"

"No thanks."

"I'm Dillon," he added. "Dillon Makua." He held out his hand and gave her his best lopsided grin, the one that generally scored big points with the ladies.

No reaction. At least not the expected one. Scowling, she

ignored his hand. "Yes and, as you've no doubt gathered, I'm Noelani Crawford. We need to talk, Mr Makua. In private," she added, glancing pointedly at Keoni.

Dillon led her to an empty booth, and she slid in across from him. But even though she was the one who'd insisted that she wanted to talk, Noelani just sat there, staring in silence at the green Formica tabletop.

Virtually everything in the Shamrock was green. Keoni could claim only a minuscule amount of Irish blood, but he liked to consider himself an exiled son of the Emerald Isle. He advertised the Shamrock as "a little corner of Ireland in the heart of Waikiki" and developed a thick brogue every year around St Patrick's Day. Fortunately, it was June now, so the "top of the mornings" and "begorrahs" were at a minimum. Unfortunately, the green decor was permanent.

Dillon leaned forwards. "Why don't you tell me what's bothering you?"

"Maybe this was a mistake."

Maybe it was, but . . . "Fill me in, Ms Crawford. If I don't think I can help, I'll say so, and no harm done. OK?"

"All right."

Catherine Zeta-Jones. That's who she sounded like. Looked a little like the actress, too, especially her lips.

"Mr Makua?" Noelani said, and he realized he'd been staring at her mouth. So maybe he ought to concentrate on her words, not her accent or her kissability potential.

He cleared his throat. "My secretary said you want me to look into your grandmother's suicide."

"If it *was* suicide."

"But the story made headlines last week. BIG ISLAND LAND-OWNER CASSANDRA CRAWFORD JUMPS FROM A HELICOPTER INTO KILAUEA VOLCANO. There were witnesses and, if memory serves, she left a suicide note."

Noelani frowned. "Someone could have forced her to write it."

"Why would anyone do that?"

"I don't know." She met his gaze again, and damned if his traitorous heart didn't kick into high gear. "I can't believe she'd kill herself though."

"What's your grandfather's take on it?"

"My grandfather was killed in the attack on Pearl Harbor eight months before my father was born."

"And your grandmother never remarried?" he asked in surprise.

"She was too much in love with my grandfather, kept pictures of him all over the house."

"So loneliness could have been a factor. Did she have other family nearby?"

"None," Noelani admitted. "I'm her only living relative, and I've been in the UK for the past few years. Her parents are long gone, of course, and she only had one sibling, a brother who died in his teens. Even my parents are gone, killed in a car crash when I was five. That's when I went to live with Grandmother." She paused before adding, "But to kill herself out of loneliness? That's absurd. Grandmother had friends. Lots of them." Noelani's inability to maintain eye contact told him she wasn't as convinced as she was trying to sound.

"What is it you want from me?" Dillon asked gently.

Noelani stared at the tabletop. "I need to know the truth. Was it truly suicide or merely an accident? I wonder if maybe she slipped when she leaned out to toss the tears into the crater."

Tears? "I don't follow."

She met his gaze, and his heart kicked into overdrive again. *God, how could she not remember?*

"You know the Pele legends, right?" she said.

"Sure. Pele's the temperamental Hawaiian volcano goddess. She likes to shake things up when she's ticked off – shoot out an ash cloud, spew a lava fountain or two. I don't understand the reference to tears, though."

"Pele's tears are what vulcanologists call fused droplets of volcanic glass."

"Obsidian?"

"Exactly. Naturally occurring obsidian teardrops. My grandmother started collecting them last year."

"I thought taking rocks from Pele was a big *kapu*," Dillon said.

"Oh, but she wasn't collecting the tears *from* Pele; she was collecting them *for* Pele. Grandmother bought tears wherever she could find them – in souvenir shops, from people who posted ads in the classified section of the paper, even on eBay. I suspect she believed returning them to the volcano would bring her good luck." Noelani quickly averted her gaze.

Dillon was fairly certain he hadn't imagined the catch in her voice or the glimmer of unshed tears in her eyes. "Then that's why she took the helicopter tour? To return the tears to Pele?"

"Yes, she arranged it all beforehand with the pilot. I know she meant to toss the tears into the crater, but I'm not convinced she meant to toss herself in as well."

"OK," Dillon said. "What are you suggesting? That Pele's responsible for your grandmother's death?"

"Don't be ridiculous!" Noelani glared. "What sort of super-stitious fool do you take me for?"

"I didn't mean—"

"No." She waved away his apology, her irritation vanishing as quickly as it had materialized. "I know suicide fits the facts, and I might have reconciled myself to it eventually, but then I got a call from Lily Yamaguchi, my grandmother's housekeeper. Lily was upset. She said she'd noticed something strange."

"What?"

Noelani hesitated. "On the wall of my grandmother's office at her place on the Big Island is a picture, an enlargement of an old black-and-white snapshot of my grandfather in his navy uni-form. He's leaning against a palm tree, grinning at the camera. His best friend snapped the photograph the week before the attack on Pearl Harbor." Noelani glanced up, and Dillon found himself mesmerized by her eyes – so sad, so vulnerable, so lovely. After a moment, she lowered her gaze, focusing in seeming fascination on a set of leprechaun salt and pepper shakers.

"I'm confused," Dillon said. *In more ways than one.* "What upset the housekeeper?"

"The picture," Noelani said. "It . . . had changed."

"What do you mean 'changed'? Was it ripped? Faded? What?"

"No damage." Noelani stared at her hands. "The change is, my grandmother's in the photograph now, standing beside my grandfather."

Silence filled the space between them for an endless moment.

Dillon was the first to speak. "Somebody obviously switched photographs without telling the housekeeper."

"There's nothing obvious about it," Noelani snapped. "With Grandmother gone, no one's living in the house. It's kept locked, and Lily's the only one with a key. No one else has been there."

No one she knew of.

"Besides, my grandmother wasn't on Oahu the day that picture was taken. She'd returned to the Big Island – to Hilo – the day before to bail her brother out of jail."

"So the photo was taken another time," Dillon said. "Mystery solved."

"That's the thing. It's not a different photograph. It's the same photograph. The only difference is that my grandmother's in it now."

Dillon took a deep breath. He'd seen it before. Grief made people – even sensible, intelligent people – gullible, willing to believe things they'd never accept under ordinary circumstances. "Could the housekeeper be mistaken?"

"That's what I assumed at first. What other rational explanation is there?" Noelani gave him a troubled look.

"So for the sake of argument, say I'm right. Say the photograph of your grandparents was taken at the same location on a different day. Maybe your grandmother swapped the pictures, but the housekeeper didn't notice until after your grandmother's death."

"If so," Noelani said, "there should still be some trace of the original photo, but there's not. Lily went through Grandmother's photo albums. There's no sign of it."

"Then maybe someone tampered with the original."

"Why would anyone do that?"

He shrugged. "People do all kinds of strange things."

"But if the picture had been altered, wouldn't the tampering be fairly easy to spot?"

"Not necessarily," he said. "Some of the new Photoshop programs can do incredible things. If you'd like, I could have a look at it."

"Does that mean you'll take the case?" She extended her right hand across the table.

"I guess it does." He took her hand in his to seal the deal. A mistake of mammoth proportions. Touching her – even in an impersonal handshake – served as a painful reminder of their past history.

"Thank you." Noelani smiled.

Common politeness dictated that he should smile back, but all he could think of were those 365 letters he'd written her, one a day for a whole year. She'd never answered a single one. Noelani Crawford was a cold-hearted bitch. He'd accepted that hard truth long ago. Only she didn't feel like a cold-hearted bitch. Didn't look like one, either. And that hurt even more.

"Jeez, look at this."

Noelani glanced across the crowded attic towards Dillon, who was holding up a pair of faded swimming trunks that must have belonged to her father back in grade school.

"I swear your grandmother saved everything."

Noelani shifted her gaze to the box of old magazines she'd been sorting through and heaved a sigh. "No kidding."

After an early flight to Hilo, she and Dillon had rented a Jeep for the drive north to her grandmother's macadamia nut plantation near Honoka'a. There, Lily Yamaguchi had been waiting for them. "About time you showed up, missy!" Lily had scolded before turning to Dillon. "Who's this?" she'd asked, sounding deceptively innocent, even though she must have been the one who'd set Noelani up by leaving Dillon's business card on the desk in Grandmother's office where Noelani was bound to see it.

"Marshal, of course," Noelani'd nearly blurted, though she'd managed to stop herself in time. Lily'd met her glare with a bewildered look, as if she hadn't a clue what Noelani's problem was.

Lily meant well, but Noelani didn't need her assistance in the romance department. She had a perfectly good almost-fiance waiting for her in London. OK, admittedly, almost-fiance was a bit premature since she and banker John Stoddard had only gone out once, a dead boring evening spent trying to make sense of an artsy French film about sex, blood and sunflowers. Still, better a boring banker than a heartless private investigator, even if said private investigator still looked like a cross between a cowboy and a surfer with broad shoulders, wavy dark hair and eyes the exact same shade of blue as the water in Kahaluu Bay.

OK, moron, she lectured herself. Focus on the goal. Only that was the problem. She upended the box, staring in despair at battered copies of *National Geographic* and *Scientific American*. She and Dillon had been at this for hours and were no closer now to solving the mystery of her grandmother's apparent suicide than they had been when they'd first started their search.

They'd begun with the office, which had taken all morning, though the rest of the house had gone more quickly. They were nearly done now, just this stuffed-to-the-rafters attic left to sift through. Although at the rate they were going, they'd be at it for a week.

Noelani carefully flipped through each magazine before stuffing it back in the box. With a heartfelt sigh, she repacked the last one, shoved the box aside, and reached for the next carton in the stack.

"Oh, my God," she whispered as she got a good look at the contents.

"Find something?" Dillon abandoned the battered chest of drawers he'd been riffling through and threaded his way towards her through haphazard stacks of boxes, crates and old furniture. "What is it?"

"Nothing." She tried ineffectually to replace the lid with hands that suddenly seemed to be all thumbs.

"Must be something, and something pretty shocking, too. You've gone as white as a ghost. Here. Let me." He took the box from her, tossed the lid aside, and pulled out an envelope, one of hundreds. He stared at it for a few seconds in silence. "What the hell?" He shot her a look that was two parts anger to one part hurt feelings. "You're a better actress than I gave you credit for, Noelani. I thought you didn't recognize me, but you've known who I was all along, haven't you?"

"I—"

"You deliberately brought me here on a trumped-up pretext."

"I didn't. I wouldn't. It was Lily. She knew I wanted to hire a private investigator to look into the circumstances of Grandmother's death. She deliberately left your card where—"

"The part I don't get is why you kept my letters all these years when you didn't even bother to open them."

"You wrote to me," she said, still not quite believing it.

His eyebrows slammed together. "Damned right I wrote to you. Every damn day for a whole damn year."

"I never got your letters," she said. "Grandmother must have . . ." She caught her breath on a sob as she realized the enormity of her grandmother's deception. But why? Why would she have done such a thing? Unless . . . "The kiss," she whispered. "She must have seen us that day at your uncle's stables."

He dropped the letter, grabbed her upper arms and dragged her upright. "What are you saying?"

"My grandmother must have intercepted your letters. I don't know why she would have kept them though."

He released her arms, but didn't say a word.

"In retrospect, I suppose I should have suspected something when Grandmother shipped me off to boarding school the week after our big kiss." She paused. "Good grief, we were thirteen and fourteen. What did she think we'd do? Elope?" She managed a shaky laugh.

But Dillon wasn't laughing.

She reached up to smooth the frown lines from his forehead. "I have a favour to ask?"

"What's that?" His voice sounded hoarse.

"Kiss me?" Because sixteen years was a long time, and maybe her memory was flawed. Dillon's kiss had seemed pretty special when she was thirteen, but she was more experienced now. More experienced and less impressionable.

Or then again, maybe her memory was right on the money, she decided a few seconds later when Dillon's lips met hers. Heat sizzled along her nerves. Pleasure flooded her body. "Wow," she said when he finally released her.

Breathing hard, Dillon propped his forehead against hers. "I see your 'wow' and raise you a 'hot damn'. But just to be absolutely certain we aren't overreacting, maybe we should put it to the test one more time."

"Try the kissing again, you mean?"

"Exactly." His smile turned her insides to mush.

"Why not?" Noelani spoke with a nonchalance she was far from feeling.

Dillon framed her face with his hands and pressed his lips to hers in a kiss, first soft and sensuous, then hard and demanding. He tasted of coffee and cinnamon, hot and sweet, wickedly delicious. Noelani let herself go, floating on a sea of sensation – boneless, mindless.

But when Dillon started to lower her to the threadbare rug, she pulled away. "This isn't a good idea. Not here. Not now."

He gave her a quizzical look. "But isn't that why . . .?"

"Why what?"

"Why you hired me in the first place."

She stared at him in disbelief.

He laughed. "You didn't think I bought that Lily-tricked-me excuse, did you?"

"Why not? It's the truth."

"Is it?"

The cockiness of Dillon's smile put her hackles up. "How was I to know private investigator Dillon Makua and Marshal, my teenage crush, were one and the same?"

"If you didn't know," he said, "then how would Lily have known?"

"I'm not sure. Maybe Grandmother told her, and . . ." She let her voice trail off, uncomfortably aware of just how implausible her explanation sounded.

"OK. If you say so. I just thought—"

"What?" she asked. "What did you think? That this so-called case was merely the spoiled little rich girl's ill-disguised ruse to get you into bed?"

"I'm not sure I'd word it quite that way, but yeah, something like that," he agreed.

"You egotistical jerk!"

"Jerk?" His eyes narrowed. "Me? I wrote you every day for a whole year. You're the one who didn't write back."

"Because I never saw your letters, not until now."

"Really?" He lifted one eyebrow in a sceptical look.

A chill wrapped itself around her heart. He didn't believe her.

"Let me be sure I have this straight. First, I'm a schemer, and now I'm a liar?"

"Don't forget a spoiled little rich girl," he said.

"Fine." Ice-cold fury stiffened her backbone. "If that's what you think, go. I don't need your help."

"I suspected as much." Dillon's smirk made her want to smack him, but she managed to maintain her dignity until he left the attic.

Then she promptly burst into tears.

Dillon paused halfway down the narrow staircase. Noelani's sobs pricked at his conscience. "You're a real jerk, Makua," he muttered under his breath. He should go and make sure she was all right.

Unless the waterworks were a deliberate ploy, a bid for sympathy.

Could Noelani cry on demand? How good an actress was she?

Not that good, he decided and was just about to head back up when he heard the first of several loud thuds, punctuated by some very creative profanity. Apparently, she'd progressed beyond the hurt feelings stage into the desire-to-cause-bodily-harm stage. Not the best time to apologize. He headed downstairs instead.

But the minute he stepped onto the moonlit verandah, he realized leaving wasn't an option either. Their only transportation was the four-wheel-drive Jeep Cherokee they'd rented at the Hilo Airport, and if he took off, Noelani would be stranded here alone until Lily Yamaguchi showed up tomorrow. *If* Lily Yamaguchi showed up tomorrow. Considering tomorrow was Sunday, that was a pretty big if.

Damn.

As he stood debating his next move, the porch light came on and the front door flew open. Noelani rushed out and grabbed his arm. "Wait!"

Very dramatic. Pretty damned effective, too, especially factoring in the entreaty in those big hazel eyes. "You just told me to go," he said.

"I know what I said, but please don't leave. Not until you see this." She held out a photograph.

Noelani wasn't trying to manipulate him, he realized, and felt like a bastard for suspecting otherwise. "You found it. The original."

"No, it's not the picture of my grandfather. It's a picture of my Great-uncle Thomas."

Dillon took the photograph from her trembling fingers.

"I dropped a box and this photo fell out of an old album. His name's on the back. There's no mistake. Besides, I recognize him from photos taken when he was younger."

"What's the big deal?" Dillon asked, then fell silent as he got a good look at the picture of a middle-aged man in a priest's cassock. "I thought you said your Great-uncle Thomas died when he was in his teens."

"He did," she said. "I've visited his grave. He's buried in the family plot in Hilo."

"There must be some explanation."

"Like what?" she said. "Great-uncle Thomas miraculously rose from the grave?"

"Maybe your great-uncle faked his death, then secretly ran off to become a priest."

"Great-uncle Thomas was knifed to death in a bar brawl. I've read the old newspaper clippings. Grandmother kept them in the top desk drawer in her office. I think she felt guilty, as if his death were her fault."

"How so?"

"Grandmother made a habit of rescuing her brother, but this time, she was too late."

"Knife wounds aren't necessarily fatal," Dillon pointed out. "Maybe the family just pretended he died. Maybe they were so embarrassed by the scandal that they forced him into the priesthood."

"That's ridiculous," Noelani said.

Dillon didn't argue. His suggestion had been pretty far-fetched. "OK then, what's your explanation?"

"I don't have one," she said. "I mean, say he faked his own death and ran off to become a priest. That doesn't explain how his photograph found its way into a dusty old album in Grand-mother's attic. No matter how I crunch the numbers, it doesn't add up."

Dillon studied the priest in the photograph. "You're right," he admitted. "Unfortunately, I'm too tired at the moment to do the maths. Why don't we call it a night? Tomorrow maybe we can visit your great-uncle's grave."

"So you aren't leaving?" Was that relief he saw in her expression?

"Not until we get to the bottom of this." He paused. "I owe you an apology, Noelani. I leaped to some unwarranted conclusions earlier. You didn't have any ulterior motives when you contacted my office, did you? You truly didn't realize who you were hiring."

"No," she said.

"And you never got my letters."

"No," she said again. "Grandmother's doing. I'm sure she meant it for the best, but . . . She was always trying to save people from the consequences of their own folly, you see. That's why she missed out on the last few days of my grandfather's life. She felt it was her duty to help Thomas." Noelani heaved a weary sigh. "Ironic, isn't it? Despite her well-meant intervention, Thomas continued down the same destructive path."

Noelani had already been up for an hour and a half by the time Dillon wandered into the kitchen looking for breakfast at a quarter to seven.

"You're up early," he said.

"I haven't adjusted yet to Hawaii time."

"Headache?" he asked.

"No. Why?"

"You're frowning," he said.

"I went out on the *lanai* to drink my hot chocolate a while ago, and I found this lying in the centre of the table."

"What is it?" He leaned closer to get a good look. "Obsidian? One of Pele's tears."

She nodded.

"What was it doing on the *lanai*?"

"I haven't a clue. Maybe it's a sign," she said lightly. "Maybe Pele's telling us we're on the right track." Then she frowned as another possibility occurred to her. "Or maybe she's warning us off."

*   *   *

Six stones marked the family plot, six stones but only five actual interments accorded her great-grandparents, her parents and her great-uncle. The remaining stone marked her grandfather's empty grave, empty since John Crawford lay entombed inside the USS *Arizona*.

"Grandmother's stone will go right there." Noelani pointed to a space next to her grandfather's memorial.

A shaft of sunlight sliced through the clouds as if to mark the spot. Dillon caught a flash as the beam glittered off something near John Crawford's headstone. He knelt to take a closer look. An obsidian teardrop glistened in the grass.

"Find something?" Noelani asked from behind him, then "Oh!" she cried when she realized what had captured his attention. "Another tear."

One might have been a coincidence, but two? Dillon didn't think so. He plucked the tear from the grass and stood. "Someone's playing games with us."

"But why?"

"Good question. Wish I had a good answer." He studied the little cluster of gravestones. One caught his attention. "What year did your great-uncle die?" he asked Noelani.

She gazed at him, obviously confused by the sudden turn in the conversation. "In the forties. The early forties."

"That's not what it says on his stone. Look."

She stooped to examine the grave marker. " 'Thomas Adam Ferguson,' " she read. " 'Born 6 May 1926. Died 3 June 1976. God was his salvation.' " She glanced up at Dillon, looking stunned. "But there must be some mistake. I've seen this headstone a dozen times or more, and I know it didn't say 1976 before or include that bit about God being his salvation. Someone's switched stones."

Dillon shrugged. "Maybe. The marker isn't new though. See the lichen growing along the edge?"

"But—"

He tugged her to her feet. "I don't know what's going on, Noelani, but I sure as hell intend to find out."

Noelani shot Dillon a furtive sideways glance. He hadn't said a word since they'd left the cemetery. His expression looked grim and more than a little angry, though she was fairly certain the anger wasn't directed towards her. Not this time.

Tropical vegetation – giant tree ferns, palms, bamboo and an occasional cluster of bright red anthuriums – encroached upon the narrow road and blocked much of the light. The humidity was so high that moisture dripped from the foliage and condensed in tiny droplets on the windshield.

"I don't recognize this road. Where are we going?" she asked as they splashed through a pothole bigger than the koi pond in her grandmother's garden.

Dillon's smile seemed forced. "Back to the plantation. I need time to mull things over though, which is why I opted for the scenic route."

Jungle route was more like it. Noelani half expected Tarzan to come swooping through the trees. What she didn't expect was the projectile that smacked the windshield. The glass cracked in a starburst pattern but didn't shatter.

Dillon hit the brakes.

"What was that?" she asked. "Did you see what hit us?"

"Chunk of loose rock, I think." He released his shoulder harness and climbed out of the vehicle to assess the damage.

Noelani followed more slowly. He was probably right about it being a rock, but her first thought had been that someone was shooting at them.

"Damn it to hell!" Dillon was swearing as she came around the front end of the vehicle.

"What is it?"

"Another of Pele's tears." He extended his hand to show her the obsidian teardrop he'd pulled from the cracked windshield.

"How is that possible?"

He shrugged. "I think someone's trying to tell us something. Your Grandmother maybe."

"Or Pele." Noelani shivered.

"Excuse me?"

Noelani, one hand pressed to her racing heart, spun around at the sound of a female voice.

A diminutive old woman in jeans, flip-flops, and a green-and-black University of Hawaii Warriors football jersey stood in the middle of the road, clutching an oversize purple handbag.

"Good heavens, you scared me to death," Noelani told her. "Where did you come from?"

The old woman set her handbag down with a sigh. "My car broke down, left me stranded back that way." She waved an arm to indicate the road behind them.

"That's strange," Dillon said. "I didn't see any cars off the road. Did you, Noelani?"

"Not on *this* highway." The old woman smiled, revealing a set of crooked teeth. "A secondary road halfway down Mauna Kea. I'm headed for my nephew's place in Honoka'a. I'd appreciate a lift."

"Of course," Noelani said quickly before Dillon could voice an objection. She could tell by the look on his face that he wasn't thrilled at the prospect of a hitch-hiker. "As it happens, we're headed for Honoka'a, too. I'm Noelani Crawford, by the way, and this is Dillon Makua."

The old woman gripped Noelani's hand with surprising strength, considering how frail she looked. "I'm Polly Ahiai-honua, but most people call me Auntie Polly."

"I'm pleased to meet you, Auntie Polly." Noelani accompanied her words with a smile, determined to make up for Dillon's stand-offish attitude.

"Watch your step," he said politely enough as he held the door open. He even offered Auntie Polly a hand climbing into the back seat and helped her get her seat belt fastened before handing her the purple bag she'd left sitting in the middle of the road. But he didn't look happy about the situation, and he left it to Noelani to make conversation with the old woman during the drive to Honoka'a.

Auntie Polly surprised Noelani with a hug when they left her at a small, seemingly deserted house on the outskirts of town.

"Are you sure you'll be all right?" Noelani asked. "I don't see anyone around. We can stay for a while, if you'd like."

"Chances are my nephew's off fishing. He'll be back before long. I'll be fine. Don't worry. And, Noelani?" As Noelani started to turn away, Auntie Polly took her arm in that surprisingly firm grasp. "Don't be angry with your grandmother. She meant well. She always meant well."

"You knew my grandmother?" Noelani asked, but Auntie Polly didn't answer. She just smiled, released Noelani's arm, then walked up the crushed-shell path towards her nephew's house without a backwards glance.

"How do you suppose Auntie Polly knew my grandmother?" Noelani asked Dillon as they headed for the plantation. More puzzling still, how had she known about the anger Noelani had been suppressing when Noelani herself hadn't even been aware of the feelings on a conscious level?

Dillon, who appeared to be wrestling with his own internal demons, didn't respond.

"Maybe she didn't actually know Grandmother," Noelani mused. "Maybe she just read about Grandmother's death in the paper and, when I mentioned my name, Auntie Polly made the connection." Though that didn't explain the old woman's parting comments.

They travelled another half-mile in silence. Then, just as they passed between the stone gateposts that marked the entrance to the plantation, Dillon spoke. "Did you notice what Auntie Polly had in that purple bag?"

"No," Noelani said, a little puzzled since she didn't see the relevance.

He pulled to a stop, shifted into park, then killed the engine. "Tears," he said. "The bag was full of them. I got a good look when I handed it to her after she climbed into the back seat."

"Pele's tears?"

He nodded.

"So if she's a collector, too, maybe she *did* know Grandmother." Noelani faltered to a stop. "Why are you looking at me that way?"

"Because you're ignoring cause and effect. An obsidian teardrop shatters our windshield. Moments later, when we stop to assess the damage, who shows up but a woman with a whole bag full of obsidian teardrops? Cause and effect."

"Are you suggesting Auntie Polly shattered our windshield? That she targeted us deliberately?"

"Makes sense."

"But why? Just so we'd stop and give her a ride?"

He shrugged, then released his shoulder harness and climbed
out of the Jeep. "I suppose we ought to finish searching the
attic," he said, not sounding overly enthusiastic.

"Go on up if you want," she said. "I'd like a few minutes to
think this through. If you need me, I'll be in the gazebo."

"There's a gazebo? Where?"

"Hidden among the trees on the other side of the koi pond off
the rear *lanai*."

"Would you like some company?" he asked, taking her hand.
She shot him a look.

"Not that kind of company," he said. "Unless, of course—" a
wicked smile curved his mouth"—you'd *like* that kind of
company."

"When you look at me like that, all I see is the boy I fell in
love with all those years ago."

He smiled again, and her heart beat a little faster. "Do you
remember when I told you about my dog getting run over?" he
asked.

She nodded. "I wanted to make you feel better, so I brought
you a pineapple shave ice."

"My favourite," he said.

"Only by the time I found you—"

"Uncle Lopaka had me cleaning out the loft."

"—the shave ice had melted into lukewarm pineapple slush."

"It's the thought that counts." His kiss started out sweet but
quickly morphed into wild and demanding.

When he finally released her, she gazed up at him, her body
buzzing, her mind in a whirl. "We're not teenagers any more."
But her protest was half-hearted, and Dillon knew it.

"The chemistry's the same," he said with another of those
wicked smiles. Then he tossed her over his shoulder and headed
for the gazebo.

"Hey! Put me down!"

"All in good time," he said and smacked her bottom. "Quit
squirming. I don't want to drop you on that pretty head."

No, getting dropped on her head didn't sound like much fun,
whereas . . . She tugged his shirt free of his jeans and splayed
her hands out over the warm skin of his back.

"What are you doing?" he asked.

"Just checking things out," she said.

"Then turnabout's—" he slid a hand between her thighs "—fair play."

Benches lined seven of the eight walls of the octagonal gazebo. Dillon deposited Noelani on the red-and-white flowered cushions of the bench opposite the entrance.

"Oh, right," she said in mock annoyance. "Get a girl all worked up, then just dump her."

He kicked off his shoes and stripped off his shirt and jeans.

Noelani gazed at him, her eyes huge and luminous. "We're really going to do this, aren't we?"

"We really are," he said, then sat down beside her and started to remove her clothes, a job that turned out to be more difficult than anticipated when her lacy pink bra got snagged on her necklace.

"Don't pull," she said. "You'll break it."

"The bra?" he asked, then realized what she was talking about when the pendant suddenly came free. A tiny horse's head carved from koa wood, dark against the skin of her breast, hung from a chain around her neck. "You kept that trinket? All these years?"

"You made it," she said. "It was all I had left of you."

"But you thought I'd forgotten you. You must have hated me."

She shook her head solemnly. "Never. Did you hate me?"

"I tried," he said honestly, "but the minute I laid eyes on you in the Shamrock, I knew I hadn't succeeded."

"Lucky for me."

"Lucky for us." He kissed her, tenderly at first, and then with increasing passion. They made love in a delicious tangle of limbs, playful and intense by turns, and when they were both sated, basking in the afterglow, he repeated, "Lucky for us."

Noelani studied Dillon's face in the flickering shade of swaying palms and royal poinciana trees, her expression solemn. "I love you."

"I love you, too." He brushed a thumb across her full lower lip. "So why so serious?"

"I don't understand why she did it. Grandmother, I mean.

She banished me to boarding school and confiscated your letters. She must have known the hell I was going through. I thought she loved me." She hesitated. "Do you think that's why she killed herself . . . to atone?"

"No." His heart clenched at the expression on her face. "I know what you're thinking, but it wasn't your fault."

"Then why? Why suicide?"

"I don't know," he admitted. "Maybe we never will, but—" he shoved himself to his feet "—we still have three-quarters of the attic to search. We may find a clue yet."

"Maybe." Noelani started to sit up. "Ouch!" She snatched back the hand she'd been using to lever herself up. A trickle of blood ran down her palm.

"What happened? Something bite you?"

"No. My hand slipped between the cushions. I must have dragged it across an exposed nail head."

"Move over and I'll have a look."

She inched sideways, nursing her injured hand, and he pushed the cushion aside to examine the bench. "Damn," he said. Another of Pele's tears, thin and razor sharp, had been wedged into the wood.

Noelani paled, and he thought for a second she was going to faint. "It . . . It m-must mean something," she stammered.

Anger flashed through him, fierce and hot. "Yeah, it means somebody's playing nasty tricks."

Noelani studied the obsidian teardrop, a frown creasing her forehead. "Or maybe it's a clue. Maybe we're supposed to look inside."

"What are you talking about?"

"Inside the bench. The tops are hinged," she explained, "so the cushions can be stored there during bad weather. But maybe there's something else inside. Maybe that's what the tear's trying to tell us."

She stood, tossed the cushions aside, and then lifted the top of the bench to reveal a storage compartment. Empty, Dillon thought, until he noticed the envelope tucked into one corner. He reached for it, but Noelani was closer and beat him to it. She turned the cream-coloured envelope over and over in her hands, oblivious to the blood she was smearing on it.

"Grandmother's stationery," she said. "And Grandmother's handwriting."

"Noelani" was scrawled across the front. Nothing else.

I spent my whole life trying to protect those I loved, and yet, one by one, I lost them all – except for you, my darling granddaughter, and even you have not escaped unscathed. Years ago when I saw you kissing that Makua boy, I panicked and sent you away. I was afraid he'd ruin you, break your heart. Instead, I was the one who managed that. You thought he'd forsaken you. He hadn't. I just made it seem that he had. Please don't hate me for my deception. At the time, I thought I was doing the right thing.

I tried to save my brother, too, with even more dreadful results. My efforts to control his behaviour drove him to greater folly. In the end, his recklessness cost him his life.

But my biggest mistake was leaving Honolulu – and John – in December of '41. Because I gave in to my well-intentioned – if futile – do-gooder tendencies, I missed out on the last days of my beloved husband's life.

Pele has offered me a second chance, an opportunity to relive those last few days with John. I'm not sure how she'll manage, but she's promised to grant you a second chance, too. Don't waste it.

Noelani set the letter aside.

"Well?" Dillon said.

"Do you believe the old gods and goddesses exist, Dillon?"

"If you'd asked me a week ago," he said, "I'd have laughed at the idea, but after our run-in with Auntie Polly . . ."

"What do you mean?"

"It was a classic encounter. Pele appears out of nowhere and asks for a lift."

"Pele? The Goddess Pele? You're saying that old lady in the football jersey was . . .?" Surely he didn't believe what he was suggesting.

"She told us her name was Polly Ahiaihonua, right? I'm pretty sure 'ahiaihonua' is Hawaiian for volcano. And isn't the name Polly suspiciously similar to Pele?"

Noelani considered his theory. It made sense . . . in a crazy sort of way. "According to Grandmother's letter, she struck a deal with Pele, returning the tears and sacrificing her own life so she could relive the last days of my grandfather's."

"The photograph was real then?"

She nodded, smiling as she remembered how happy her grandparents looked in the enlarged snapshot.

"And your great-uncle's altered headstone?"

"An unexpected side effect, I suspect. Because Grandmother didn't return to the Big Island to bail him out of trouble, he had to face the consequences of his actions. As a result, I'm guessing he straightened up his act and eventually became a priest."

"So," Dillon said, his voice carefully neutral, "that's it. Case closed. You won't be needing my services any longer."

"Think again." Noelani twined her arms around his neck and kissed him. Thoroughly.

"So . . ." He shot her a bemused look. "Am I to infer you *do* need my services?"

"Desperately," she told him.

Pack

Jeaniene Frost

One

I knew I was being hunted before I heard the growl. First there had been flashes of grey and black in the trees around me, too fast for me to make out. Then crackling of dried leaves and twigs as those forms came nearer. And that primal, icy feeling on the back of my neck that told me I'd just moved from top of the food chain to prey.

There was no one around to help me either. This was Yellowstone National Park, one of the last great American wildernesses. I hadn't seen another soul since my friends Brandy and Tom abandoned the hike three days ago, and I'd been lost for two days now. A wave of fear rolled over me, making my stomach clench in a nauseating way. Whatever had growled, it wasn't alone.

New growls emerged from behind the trees – low, guttural and more menacing than a mugger in a dark alley. I flicked my gaze around, trying to hone in on the source, while I drew my backpack off my shoulders. I had a gun in there which I'd brought along in what I'd thought was over-the-top paranoia. Now I wished I'd brought an Uzi and some grenades, too.

I had the backpack on the ground and was pulling the gun out when the animal struck. It came at me with incredible speed, ploughing right into me and knocking me over. Instinctively, I scrambled back, holding my hands out in defence, convinced I'd feel teeth tearing into me at any moment. The wolf – God, it was a huge *wolf*! – didn't lunge for my throat though. It stood a few feet away, mouth open in what seemed to me to be a sick caricature of a grin, with my gun on the ground between its paws.

I'd dropped the gun. How could I have been *so stupid* as to drop the gun?

That thought raced through my mind, followed by a slew of "if onlys". If only I hadn't gone on this camping trip. If only Brandy hadn't twisted her ankle, forcing her and Tom to leave early. If only I hadn't been so determined to continue the hike alone. If only the map hadn't gotten ruined. If only I'd had a satellite phone, instead of my useless, out-of-area cellular.

And if only I hadn't dropped the goddamn gun when an enormous wolf charged me. That would probably be the last regret I ever had.

Twigs snapped behind me. My head jerked back while I still tried to keep an eye on the wolf in front of me. Five more wolves cleared the trees, running around me with an easy, deadly grace. I started to scoot back more, but there was nowhere to go. My heart was pounding while my breath came in strange, jagged gasps. *You're lost out in the middle of nowhere, and these wolves are going to eat you. Oh God, no, please. I don't want to die . . .*

Only four days ago, I'd been laughing with my friends about how great it was to be outdoors, instead of trapped inside our stuffy offices. This was the vacation I'd been waiting years to take. How could this be happening?

One of the circling wolves broke from the ranks and charged me. I flung up my hands in useless defence when the huge grey wolf let out a growl that sounded like a word.

"Mine."

I gasped. That wolf did *not* just speak! But its yellow eyes gleamed with a savage intelligence and another rumbling, coherent growl came out of its throat.

"You. Dieee."

I abandoned all logic to scramble to my feet, running as fast as I could even while knowing it was futile. Scalding pain in my ankle had me stumbling, but I didn't stop. I lurched on, heart hammering and tears blurring my vision. Around me, the wolves gleefully yipped as they kept pace.

More pain seared my leg. I fell, panic urging me to get up even though both my legs felt like they were on fire. I tried to run again, but my left ankle buckled. The wolves' cries became more excited. They darted in, nipping me and drawing blood before bounding back and ducking out of the way of my wild punches. I couldn't run any more, but I staggered forwards, looking for anything that would help me. Maybe I could climb a tree. Maybe I could find a heavy branch to use as a weapon.

It's too late for that, Marlee, said an insidious voice in my head. Just give up. It'll be over soon.

The enormous grey wolf suddenly jumped in front of me. Its mouth was open, fangs gleaming in the late afternoon light. It let out a howl that stopped the other wolves in their tracks. Then they joined in, filling the air with their victorious cries.

The grey wolf became silent, coming closer while its companions continued their howls. I braced myself, images of my family and friends flashing in my mind. *They'll never know what happened to you. You'll just be another vanished hiker in the woods* . . .

Despite my overwhelming fear, anger also reared up in me. I looked at the grey wolf, only a foot away now. *You might kill me, but I'm going to hurt you before you do.*

When it lunged, I was ready. Its fangs sank into my right arm, which I'd thrown up to protect my throat. But even as I almost fainted at the agony of its teeth tearing my flesh, I didn't hesitate. My left thumb jammed into its eye, as deep as it could go.

Something like a scream came out of the wolf. Or maybe I was screaming. Either way, it took a second for the next, new sound to register, but when it did, I felt a surge of hope. It was the loud, unmistakable *boom* of a gunshot.

The grey wolf let go of me. I sagged back, clutching my torn arm to my chest. The wolf's right eye was bleeding and the animal was panting, but it didn't run. Neither did the other wolves. They crouched, staring over my shoulder, snarls coming from their throats.

"Leave," the grey wolf said, garbled but intelligible.

I'm hallucinating again, I thought. Maybe I've passed out. Maybe I'm being ripped to pieces right now.

Something brushed by me. I recoiled when I saw it was several more wolves. With my good arm, I began flailing at them in a pathetic attempt to keep them away, but they ignored me. Their attention seemed fixed on the other, snarling wolves.

When the naked man squatted down next to me, I *knew* I was hallucinating. I might have even let out a laugh. Maybe all of this was just a horrible dream, and I'd wake up safe in my tent.

"Are you all right?" the man asked, looking me over.

Now I was sure I laughed, but it had an edge of hysteria to it. "Never better."

I looked at his face – and gasped. His eyes were amber and slanted, just like the wolves' eyes, and the same wildness lurked in them.

God, please let this be a dream!

The man stood. He had a gun pointed at the grey wolf.

"You've gone too far, Gabriel," he said. "Hunting humans is forbidden. The Pack will judge you for this."

The wolf snarled. "They hunt us," it said.

"They don't know better," the man replied. "We do. Either you come with us, or I shoot you with her gun."

I was shaking my head from side to side, even though no one was paying attention to me any more, it seemed. Talking wolves didn't exist. Muscular men didn't walk around naked in the forest, chatting with non-existent talking wolves. Why couldn't I wake up? And what was that noise? It was getting louder, like a swarm of bees approaching.

When the grey wolf sat down, shuddered, and its fur began disappearing into its body, I didn't even blink. I was concentrating more on finding the source of that buzzing noise. It was almost deafening now.

The last thing I saw before the noise rose to a crescendo and my vision went black was the wolf's fur being replaced by skin . . . and the body of a naked man where the grey wolf had just been.

Two

Pain tugged on my leg. My eyes opened with a rush of terror as my last memory came roaring back. *The wolves. Attacking me.*

"No!" I screamed, trying to defend myself.

Something big held me down. I was so panicked, it took me a moment to realize that it wasn't biting me or covered in fur.

"You're all right, the doctor is just setting your ankle," said a deep voice.

My head felt cottony, but I tried to shake that off. I was in a bed. An older blonde woman was giving me a mildly irate look as she bent over my ankle. Someone held my upper body in an unyielding grip, and whoever it was didn't look like a nurse.

"Let go of me."

That grip didn't loosen. "Doc?"

"You can let her go, Daniel," the blonde woman said.

In my next blink, I was free, staring around the room with its wood walls, rustic interior and bloody bandages on the floor. Sure, I had healthcare, but unless medical standards had *really* dropped, this wasn't a hospital.

It took a second for me to recognize the tall, russet-haired man by the bed. "You're the naked guy," I blurted. He wasn't naked now, wearing a pair of loose-fitting denim jeans and a long-sleeved shirt.

He smiled, but it looked strained. "You remember."

Not all of it. I knew he'd stopped the wolves from attacking me, but I couldn't remember how exactly. Or why he'd been naked in the woods in the first place.

There was something about the wolves. Something really important that my groggy mind couldn't quite recall.

"The wolves—" I began.

"I need to finish this," the woman interrupted me. "Hold still. You'll feel some pressure."

She certainly *sounds* like a doctor, I thought. Professional, uncaring and using the word "pressure" to describe what would probably hurt like hell.

My premonition proved correct. A burning pain started in my ankle as she probed, muttering to herself while she shifted it a few times.

"Where am I?" I asked, biting back a yelp. "Is this a Ranger station or something?"

The man stared at me, his hazel eyes seeming to probe as much as the doctor's pitiless fingers.

"What's your name?"

"Marlee. Marlee Peters."

"The sedative shouldn't have worn off this quickly," the woman remarked when I couldn't help but yank back as she manipulated my ankle in a direction it didn't want to go. "You know that, Daniel."

"So give me another one," I said, clenching my teeth as the pain began to throb. "Pressure", my ass!

Daniel, as the doctor called him, let out a sigh. "Damn Gabriel," he muttered.

Gabriel.

The name conjured up an image of a huge grey wolf glaring at me, one eye bleeding. "They hunt us," it had said. Then it started writhing on the ground, its fur disappearing . . .

I tried to bolt out of bed, but Daniel had me pinned back before I'd even cleared the covers.

"It's all right, Marlee," he said.

"Like hell it is!" Whatever remained of the sedative they'd given me wore off in the flash of that memory. *Run*, my mind urged.

From over his shoulder, I could see the blonde woman sit back in disgust. "I can't work like this," she said.

"Get Joshua," Daniel told her, still holding me to the bed.

I screamed for help, which drowned out any reply the woman made. I kicked, too, even though that hurt my ankle like I'd set it on fire.

Daniel went from holding me down to flattening me on the bed with his body. It was like a ton of bricks just landed on me. He even had his legs tangled in mine so I couldn't kick.

I couldn't move, but I could keep screaming, which I did, long and loud.

He winced. "Stop that. You're hurting my ears."

His arms were pinning mine down, but his hands were loose near my face. He could have covered my mouth to shut me up, but he didn't. That meant he wasn't concerned about anyone overhearing, which meant there was no one near enough to help.

I stopped screaming and tried another tactic. "Let me go. I'll leave and you'll never see me again."

"Why were you in the woods alone, Marlee?" he asked. "That's not very safe."

Considering my current situation, the absurdity of that statement made me laugh. "You don't say?"

He ignored that. "You remember what you saw. That's why you smell like fear now."

"It wasn't real," I muttered. "I was tired, I'd been lost for days, and I panicked because of the attack."

"You know it's real," he cut me off. "Sorry, but you *know*, so we can't just let you go. Even if nothing comes of your bites."

That froze me more than the 200 pounds of muscle holding me down. I'd been bitten – several times, in fact. I'd seen the movies, knew enough of the folklore to know what happened to a person who'd been bitten by a . . .

"This can't be real," I whispered.

His gaze was grim. "It's as real as it gets."

I insisted on sitting in a chair to meet Joshua. Daniel stood next to me, his presence a silent threat that any attempts to leave would be quickly stopped. Still, when one met the leader of a pack of werewolves, one wanted *not* to be trapped under another werewolf in bed, right? Yeah, I thought so, too.

Of course, I was also still thinking – hoping – that I'd just eaten some bad mushrooms along the trail and none of this was real. Be careful what you wish for, ran through my mind. I'd wished for years to go to Yellowstone. My ex-boyfriend Paul and I had planned this trip, down to the places we'd hike and where we'd camp. We were thrilled when my best friend Brandy and her boyfriend agreed to come. The more the merrier, right?

But things changed. Paul moved to Manhattan, our relationship couldn't overcome the long-distance strain and, four months later, I ended up being a third wheel on this trip instead of it being a fun, couples' getaway. Add that to being overworked and underpaid as a paralegal, and my fervent wish for something new and exciting to come into my life.

Looks like I got that wish, though it might come with a set of claws. I waited, missing my small cubicle at the office more than I'd ever missed anything.

Ten minutes later, the blonde doctor returned with a man in his late forties. He had edges of grey on his temples, but the rest of his hair was thick and auburn – the same colour as Daniel's, actually. He also had a similar large, muscular build, albeit not quite as lean as Daniel's. He wore a tan jacket and vest over his collared shirt, with a pair of denim pants.

In short, he looked like your typical Yellowstone tourist, not the leader of a secret pack of monsters.

"I'm Joshua," he introduced himself, holding out a hand.

At a loss over what else to do, I shook it. Part of me wanted to run screaming out of the door, and the other part wanted to burst into tears. Surprisingly, this myriad of emotions left me feeling slightly numb, like I was running on autopilot.

"Marlee."

Joshua sat on the edge of the bed. His posture was casual, but there was nothing relaxed in his gaze. He looked me over as if I were a potentially contagious virus. I fought not to hold my breath.

"What happened yesterday was very unfortunate," Joshua began.

"Yesterday?" I couldn't help but exclaim, glancing at the window. It was nearly dusk. I'd thought it was the same day as the attack.

"Yesterday," Joshua repeated, giving me a frown that said he wasn't used to being interrupted. "A member of our pack was . . . distraught over his wife's death. He and a few others began hunting you. You were lucky Daniel found them when he did, but you'd been bitten, so we couldn't drop you off at the nearest hospital. You haven't heard of our kind before, Marlee, and there's a reason. We do whatever's necessary to protect our existence."

We'll kill for it was left unsaid, but I heard that loud and clear. I nodded, striving to hold on to my numbness. Hysteria wouldn't help me, no matter how tempting it was to give in to it.

"A person has to be bitten several times to be at risk of transforming, and half the people who've been bitten still don't shift," Joshua went on briskly. "We won't know whether you'll turn into one of us until the next full moon, two weeks away."

Two weeks? It would take that long for me to find out whether or not I'd become a monster? I'd go insane wondering until then. And if it did happen . . . well, suicide didn't sound like a bad idea all of a sudden.

"What happens if after the full moon, I'm not . . . ah . . . like the rest of you?" I couldn't bring myself to say "a werewolf". I just couldn't.

Joshua gave me a thin smile. "That depends on you. Either you stay with us, as a member of the skinwalker part of our pack, or . . ." He shrugged. That single gesture completed his sentence. *Or we kill you.*

One way or the other, I was screwed.

Three

"Hungry?"

I sat in the chair, my broken ankle finally in a cast, and glared at Daniel before replying. "Somewhere between the death threats and the thought of turning into a four-legged monster, I lost my appetite."

Part of me wondered why I dared to be so surly. The other part figured I was as good as dead anyway, so it didn't matter.

Daniel grunted. "Suit yourself, but I'm getting something." He stood, stretched, and then held out a hand.

I just stared at it. "What?"

"You're coming with me," he replied. "Who knows what kind of trouble you'd stir up if I left you alone?"

"And I suppose you'll just drag me along anyway if I refuse?"

A smile quirked his mouth. "You learn fast, don't you?"

I gave Daniel another withering look that didn't seem to faze him. He was extremely striking, in an outdoorsy-type of way. His hair was chin length and russet, and he had a faint weathering to his features that spoke of long days outside. Daniel only looked a couple of years older than me, which would put him at about thirty, but there was an air of command about him that made him seem older. None of the lawyers at my office had such a dominating presence, in fact.

But I wasn't about to let him know how much he intimidated me. Wasn't there a saying that showing fear in front of an animal made it more aggressive? "So, you're the group's babysitter, is that it?"

"I'm the Pack's enforcer, so it's my job to make sure anyone who's a danger to us – like you – doesn't get away. And I'm very good at my job, Marlee."

At over six feet tall with muscles bulging from every limb, yeah, Daniel looked like he did a good job of enforcing. He'd scare anyone with half a brain.

"What are you going to do with me for two weeks? You can't keep me tied to your hip." I didn't even want to think about after that, or what might happen on the full moon.

He rubbed a knuckle under his chin and considered me. "With your limp, you wouldn't get far even if you did manage to slip away from me – which you wouldn't. So, let's get some dinner, then you can wash up and begin plotting ways to outsmart us dumb animals."

Daniel said that last part with a challenging look that let me know he was both aware of my aversion to what they were *and* of my dreams of escape. I glanced away, gritting my teeth.

"Didn't you say you were hungry?"

He held out his hand again. "Come on. Let's eat."

I had to take Daniel's arm to avoid hopping on one leg to the dining lodge. They didn't give me any crutches, which I supposed was deliberate so as to keep me at a disadvantage. It looked like I was in some sort of tiny Wild West town, of all things. A narrow strip of street ran down between the twin rows of shops, lodgings, and . . . were those *saloons*? I half expected someone to gallop by on horseback, shooting at the moon.

"What is this place?" I asked.

Daniel grunted. "Not what you were expecting, right? Let me guess. You thought we'd live in a big den in the woods?"

From his expression, he was teasing, but I wasn't trying to make friends with my kidnapper.

"The 1800s called. They want their town back," I replied. Two could play at being a smart ass.

Daniel kept perfect pace with me. I was using his arm as a sort of brace. His reflexes were so fast that he counter-balanced my every step so I almost walked at my normal speed.

"You're not far off," he said, ignoring my sarcasm. "This was an old mining town back in the nineteenth century. It was empty for decades after the silver dried up, but then some of my relatives bought it and the surrounding land. We restored many of the original buildings and cabins, plus added upgrades. Now, we rent it out seasonally as a private resort area."

That brought me to a stop. "Werewolves running a *resort* town?" I asked incredulously.

He shrugged. "We have to make a living, just like everyone else."

This was like being in an episode of *The Twilight Zone*.

We passed several people on our way down the street. I was surprised at how normal they looked. There were men and women of varying ages, plus a couple of children, and everyone appeared to be minding their own business – aside from all the sideways glances I was getting.

"Are all of them like you?" I asked, keeping my voice calm. My heart had started to pound, however, and if the movies were right, they could hear it. *There were so many of them. How would I ever get away?*

"Most of them," Daniel said. "The others are skinwalkers – normal people to you. But you don't have to be afraid of anyone, Marlee. We're not what you think."

"I've already had some of your group try to kill me, and you and Joshua seem pretty open about how you'll finish the job," I replied shortly. "So you'll excuse me if I don't buy the whole 'we're misunderstood' speech."

Something flashed in Daniel's eyes. It made me back up a step, but his hand shot out and gripped my arm.

"Why'd you bring that gun camping with you?" he asked, his voice soft. "You brought it for protection, right? Because if anyone tried to hurt you, you'd hurt them, right? Well, now imagine someone's trying to hurt your entire family. How far would you go to stop that?"

Daniel leaned in, tightening his grip so I couldn't pull back. "I'd do anything to stop that," he whispered near my ear. "Including holding you hostage. If you got away, you'd tell people about us. People who would come and hurt my family. So yeah, I'm ruthless when it comes to protecting my pack. But

don't pretend you wouldn't be the same way, if the shoe were on
the other foot."

That gleam of wildness was in his eyes again. The *otherness*
that reminded me that an animal lurked inside him. I shivered.

"Let go of me."

He did, dropping my arm only to hold his out again. "We're
almost there," he said, nodding at the square building to the
left.

I balanced on his arm again. We didn't speak as we walked the
rest of the way to the dining lodge.

It looked like any normal, rustic restaurant inside, if a little
more upscale. Instead of smaller tables scattered throughout,
there were several long tables arranged in the room, each seating
over a dozen. The food seemed to be served family-style, with
large dishes placed in the middle of the tables from which
everyone took their servings. There was a moment of quiet as
Daniel and I walked in.

"This is Marlee," Daniel said to the room at large. "She's
joining us."

I didn't know if he meant for dinner, as a possible new
werewolf, or some other cryptic thing. I didn't argue though.
Not while feeling like a piece of meat dangled above a crocodile
pit.

"Hi," I said. God, that sounded stupid, but what else was I
supposed to say? *Somebody call 911* sounded tempting, but I
didn't think it would do any good.

An older woman bustled up to me, smiling. "Welcome, dear!
Aren't you pretty? Such beautiful brown hair."

I just wanted to sit, hide, and plot my escape, not exchange
pleasantries with Mrs Butterworth's version of a werewolf.

"Um, thanks."

"Let's set you up over here, it's quieter," she said, leading
Daniel and I to a table that only had four other people at it.

"Thanks, Mom," Daniel said.

I stopped so fast, I almost staggered. "*Mom?*"

A grin edged his mouth. "Everyone has one, after all."

"Quit teasing Marlee, she looks starved," his mother said to
Daniel, holding out a chair for me. "We have excellent venison

stew tonight. That should help put the colour back in your face."

I sat at the table, avoiding eye contact with the other four people, though I did notice one was a female. Daniel sat next to me, that half-smile still on his face.

"Not what you expected again?" he asked.

I glanced around the room once more. People were laughing, eating and chatting. Sure, I kept getting discreet looks, but no one was licking their chops in a menacing way at me. It all looked terribly . . . civilized.

"No," I replied, and left it at that. These people might look nice, but they were my kidnappers. My *executioners* if I refused to become one of their group. All the table manners in the world couldn't make up for that.

"Daniel," someone at the table said. "Introduce me."

I glanced up, meeting a pair of blue eyes on a smiling face. Black hair hung past his shoulders, untamed and playful, like his expression.

"Finn." There was a hint of a growl in Daniel's voice that hadn't been there before. "This is Marlee. Marlee, my younger brother, Finn."

Again I was surprised at the family connection, though I shouldn't have been. Why wouldn't all of their kind congregate together?

"Hi," I said in the same non-committal tone I'd used before.

"Charmed," Finn replied, grin widening.

"Cut her a break, she's had a bad day," the girl next to him muttered before giving me a sympathetic glance. "I'm Laurel, Daniel's cousin. Sorry about what happened."

"Which part?" I couldn't help but ask.

She sighed. "All of it."

There was no stopping my snort. "Yeah. Me, too."

Daniel cleared his throat. I returned my gaze to the table in front of me, tracing its edge. *It'll be another day or so before people even realize something's happened to me. How long after that before Brandy or my parents organize a search, if there is one? How many days will go by before they give me up for dead? How am I supposed to just sit here, surrounded by* werewolves, *and pretend nothing is wrong?*

A tear slid down my cheek. I sucked in my breath, aghast, but that only made it worse. Another one came down. Then another. I bent my head, hoping my hair would hide it, when a warm hand landed on my shoulders.

"Laurel, have the food sent to my cabin," Daniel said, then he scooped me up before I could even protest. We were out of the dining lodge and down the street in the next few heartbeats.

"God, you're so fast," I gasped in astonishment. Fresh tears spurted. How could I ever get away, if he moved this fast and there was a town full of more creatures like him?

"You're going to be OK, Marlee," he said.

No, I wasn't. I was trapped in a strange place surrounded by creatures that weren't supposed to exist. My old life might not have been all champagne and roses, but no one had the right to rip me away from it without my consent. The enormity of what I'd lost between yesterday and today slammed into me. I didn't care any more that the tears wouldn't stop, or that I started hitting Daniel. My grief was too sharp to worry about embarrassment or consequences.

Four

Wolves were chasing me, biting at my ankles, snarling as they crowded around me, letting out howls that made my blood turn to ice. I ran, twigs stinging me as I darted between the trees, gasping for breath, crying out with each new flash of pain in my legs. They were toying with me. My death was only a matter of time.

The full moon came into view between the trees, illuminating more wolves in my path. I screamed at them, but it came out as a howl. Horrified, I looked down to see that my feet had turned into paws. Fur slithered up my body, replacing my skin. I fell forwards, claws shooting out of my fingers . . .

"NO!"

I woke up screaming the word, flinging the sheets away like they were animals attacking me. It took me a second to orient myself. *Wood ceiling, wood walls, an antler chandelier above me.* Right. I was in Daniel's cabin. All the better to make sure I couldn't escape.

He sat in the reclining chair on the opposite side of the room, his eyes slitted. Watching me. He'd slept in the chair last night. I guess I should appreciate him giving me the bed, but my gratitude was in short supply.

"Another nightmare?" he asked quietly.

I'd had them all night. Either I was getting eaten by wolves, or I was turning into one. Terrifying no matter which way you sliced it.

Daniel stretched. The afghan he'd thrown over himself slipped, revealing that he'd taken off his shirt. Cords of muscles flexed beneath taut, tanned skin.

Despite everything, I looked. I'd never seen such a perfectly muscled body before – at least, one that wasn't on TV advertising gym equipment. Daniel didn't have the bloated look associated with steroid users, but he had a thick, brawny frame that usually spoke of many hours in a gym. Absurdly, the image of a werewolf bench-pressing flashed in my mind.

I glanced up to find Daniel staring at me. He didn't wink or make a comment, but there was no doubt he knew I'd been staring at his body.

I managed to shrug. "Stockholm syndrome," I said. "The whole 'bonding with your captor' thing. I've already cried in your arms, now I'm checking you out. Just ignore it. Of course, I can't be your first captive, so you're probably used to this."

A faint smile touched his mouth. "You're the first female I've had to quarantine, and none of the men looked at me the way you did."

There was something deeper in his voice with that last sentence. I shivered, both from unease and other things. Yes, Daniel was very attractive with his russet hair, thick brows, full mouth and piercing hazel eyes – not to mention that body. But this wasn't a first date. This was a hostage situation, and a macabre one at that.

"Don't let it go to your head. I'm scared to death and looking for any form of comfort," I said, regaining control. "Speaking of that, since a certain murderous grey wolf keeps appearing in my nightmares, I need to know. What happened to Gabriel?"

Daniel's face became shuttered. "He's under arrest. If you shift, he dies for infecting you against your will. If you don't turn, Joshua said Gabriel losing his eye was punishment enough. Joshua had liquid silver poured into Gabriel's eye so it wouldn't heal."

Their harshness apparently wasn't limited just to outsiders. I felt mildly sick over what I'd heard, but under the circumstances, pity for Gabriel was beyond me.

"And the others?" Gabriel hadn't been alone.

"They run the gauntlet."

Daniel said it lightly, but I swallowed. "As in, the thing Native Indians used to do with captives, where they line up on both sides and beat the shit out of the person as he tries to dash down the centre?"

There was that hint of wildness in Daniel's gaze again. A primal, untamed gleam I'd never seen except in the eyes of an animal. On a full-grown man, it was both mesmerizing and frightening.

"Something like that. Except we'll be in our fur, and they won't."

I couldn't help but gulp. That sounded barbaric, and it was on my account.

Something occurred to me. "But it isn't the full moon. How can you . . . you know?" In fact, how had any of the werewolves changed form the other day, if I had to wait until the full moon to see if I was infected?

"Once we're past the first year, we can shift at will. New pack members are dependent on the full moon to change though."

I digested this. "So, right now, you could turn into a—"

"Wolf," he finished for me. "Yes."

So many emotions crashed through me. Fear. Revulsion. Curiosity. Disbelief. What if all of this was a twisted farce, and I *hadn't* seen what I'd thought was a wolf turning into a man in the woods? What if this was just a town full of crazies who *thought* they were wolves, and in my stress, I'd bought into that?

"Show me."

The words were out of my mouth before I could form another thought. I had to see it. No matter what.

Daniel stood, the afghan falling to the floor. He met my eyes, and a ripple went through me. They were even wilder than before, starting to slant and gleam with amber. He undid his jeans, letting them drop to the floor. Nothing but bare skin underneath.

I might have made a sound. Seeing a magnificent naked male body only a few feet away is worth a sharp intake of breath, no matter the circumstances. But all my feminine appreciation fell away when he crouched on the floor and rivers of silvery hair began to replace the skin on his back.

There was a crunching sound. Bones curved, popped and formed where none had been before. It didn't look the same as in the movies. There was no screaming. No slow protracting of a muzzle replacing a face, blood spurting, or drawn-out writhing. Daniel had simply crouched on the floor and then, in about ten seconds, a wolf the size of a pony, covered in silver and charcoal fur, stared at me with bright yellow eyes.

"Marlee," it – *Daniel* – rumbled.

I felt light-headed. *Nope, you're not crazy, and neither are they. But that's the bad news.*

I had moved towards the door without even being aware of it. Daniel sat on his haunches in front of it, those golden eyes drilling into mine.

"Sit," he said.

A rather unhinged cackle came out of me. What looked like a huge dog was telling *me* to sit. How backwards was that?

"Woof," I replied in a shaky voice, but sat in the chair he'd recently vacated. The wolf's lips pulled back in a canine version of a grin.

"Stay."

I was about to say he was pushing it, when there was another ripple over his body. As seamlessly as water flowing on rocks, skin covered that thick silvery coat of hair, bones elongated, reformed, and in less time than it took me to get over the shock of seeing a wolf in the room, a naked man knelt on the floor. The only thing left over from the unbelievable transformation was a fine sheen of sweat on his skin.

"Does it hurt?"

Daniel sat back. "The first few times. Then you get used to it, and it feels . . . freeing."

He looked like a man. A beautiful, mouth-watering specimen of a man, in fact. But an enormous animal was inside him, and took up God only knew how much of his mind and conscience.

Daniel smiled slightly. "You smell like fear again, Marlee, but I've already told you – you have nothing to be afraid of."

"That's the scariest thing I've ever seen," I replied, glad my voice was steady even though I was shaking inside. "How do I even know I'm talking to you? It might just as well be the wolf."

"It's both," he said at once. "Always. And you still don't need to be afraid."

Yeah. Sure. Considering it might be *me* shifting into an animal in a couple weeks. From where I was sitting, I had plenty to be afraid of.

"I want to go home."

Even as I said it, I knew it was useless. But it was true – so true that the very words ached.

"I'm sorry for what brought you here. But even if you left and never told anyone about the Pack, think of your family. You'd hurt one of them, Marlee. You wouldn't mean to, but you'd do it."

Ice crept up my spine. "What are you talking about?"

He inclined his head. "Your ankle."

I looked at it. It was still wrapped in a cast, same as before. What . . . ?

It hit me. When I'd walked to the door from the bed minutes ago, I hadn't been limping, hadn't felt a twinge of pain. The ugly scratches and cuts were also gone.

"Your ankle isn't broken any more," Daniel confirmed, sympathy etched on his face. "And there isn't a mark on your skin, which would be impossible . . . unless you were one of us.'

Five

The lights from the street seemed to pale in comparison to the moon, which shone like an ominous bright hourglass in the sky. I looked up at it and shuddered. When it reached fullness, I would change into something not human. The thought was still as unbelievable as it was horrifying.

All the residents of the town were in the streets. I did a mental head count and came up with forty, maybe fifty people. The Pack, Daniel called them. My new family.

I thought I might throw up.

There was a slight commotion as a dozen people came from the far end of town. I recognized one of them and flinched, but Daniel laid a light hand on my arm.

Even though he was a virtual stranger, the gesture calmed me. It shouldn't, of course. Daniel was dangerous, but somehow I sensed he'd defend me against the man being led to the middle of the street.

I'd only glimpsed it right before passing out, but still, I'd know that face. When someone tries to murder you, it makes an impression. Not to mention that Gabriel was the only person here with one eye. His dark brown hair hung in strands around his face, and he was naked. What was it with these people and their lack of clothes?

Joshua stepped out from the crowd. At least *he* was still dressed. "Gabriel Thompson, you have been found guilty of infecting a human against their will."

"It's not the full moon," Gabriel snarled, trying to pull free of the two men who held him. "How do you know she will turn?"

Joshua looked my way. Daniel grasped my hand and led me forwards. I didn't want to get closer to Gabriel, but thankfully, Daniel stopped after a few feet. The blonde doctor stepped out of the crowd.

Gabriel shot me a look of pure hate. Instead of scaring me, it strengthened the momentary wobble I'd had in my knees. I'd never done anything to him, but he'd ruined my life. If anyone had a right to hatred, it was me.

I put my shoulders back and matched his glare. Daniel gave me an approving nod.

"Diana," Joshua addressed the blonde doctor. It was the first I'd heard her name. "You examined Marlee yesterday. What did you find?"

"Her right ankle was fractured," Diana recounted in a clinical voice. "She had multiple abrasions, contusions, lacerations and puncture wounds on both her legs, plus a deeper wound on her right arm."

Joshua swept out a hand to me. "Look at her now."

I could almost feel the eyes raking over me, taking in my skin revealed by the short sleeved shirt and rolled-up pants I was wearing. Both were too big, since they were Daniel's. My own clothes had been bloodied and ripped up in the attack, so they were no good. I didn't ask what had happened to my backpack. Seeing it again would remind me too much of everything I'd lost.

"She is completely healed. There is the proof," Joshua stated flatly. "Gabriel, your sentence is death."

Gabriel was released. He looked around in defiance, and I saw some people bow their heads, wiping at their eyes. Was his family here? I wondered. Daniel's was; I could see his mother on the opposite side of the street. How awful for Gabriel's family, even though I still didn't pity him.

"I die, but the rest of you will follow," Gabriel hissed. "I'm only giving out the same mercy our kind has been shown. I refuse to be ashamed to hunt those who kill us."

His words had barely died away when a shot rang out. I jumped, sucking in a breath as a gory crimson hole bloomed on Gabriel's chest. His eyes went wide, then he let out two harsh, laboured breaths before falling to the ground.

Somebody sobbed. Joshua's face was grim as he lowered the smoking rifle.

"We only hunt to eat what we need to survive. We will never be like them," he stated.

Seeing someone die from a gunshot wound was nothing like in the movies, either. No, it was horrible in ways I couldn't even begin to describe.

"Never be like who?" I asked Daniel. My voice was dull from shock.

He didn't look away from Gabriel's twitching, bleeding form. "Humans."

I didn't stay to watch the five men run the gauntlet. I'd already seen things that would be burned on my memory, no matter how I'd try to forget them. Daniel took me back to his cabin. He made coffee in silence and handed me a cup. It tasted like it was laced with something alcoholic, which I was grateful for.

Occasionally, I'd hear shouts coming from the direction of the town. The gauntlet was a noisy business, it seemed.

"Gabriel's wife," I said after the minutes stretched. "Joshua said a member of the Pack was upset because his wife had been killed. That was Gabriel, right? Did . . . Did hunters kill his wife?"

Daniel sat across from me, resting his elbows on the table as he drank from his own cup. The lighting in the kitchen reflected off his hair, making the russet colour look richer. "Yes."

"But why hurt me?" I wondered. "I was camping, not hunting wolves!"

A sigh rumbled out of Daniel. "Gabriel wasn't being logical. Neither were the others with him. The Pack has been going through a hard time since the laws were changed."

"What laws? No one even knows about werewolves; it's not like it's open season on them."

"Grey wolves were taken off the endangered species list a few months ago," Daniel said, his expression hooded. "The government did it knowing what would happen. Before the ink was dry, scores of wolves were killed. They're trying to eliminate all wolves again. What Gabriel did was wrong, but I know what drove him to it. You can't understand what it's like, having people try to wipe out your very existence."

His voice was bitter. I set my coffee cup down with a bang.

"I'm Jewish. Don't tell me I can't understand what that's like."

After a long moment, Daniel inclined his head. We sat in silence, but oddly, it wasn't tense silence. It was as if we'd come to an unspoken truce.

"So," I said at last, mythology and reality competing in my mind. "Gabriel's wife was shot while in wolf form. How would the hunters know to use silver bullets? Maybe you've been found out after all."

A bleak smile cracked his face. "The bullets don't have to be silver. No, Marlee, we can be killed in a lot of normal ways. But if the wound isn't mortal, and if it's not exposed to silver, we can usually heal it."

There was noise from the town again. Something like a cheer. Daniel nodded in its direction. "They must be finished."

What a strange, harsh society this was. Gauntlets. Executions. Shape-shifting. And me, stuck right in the middle of it.

"You know that soon my family will start a search for me," I said. "My parents will notice when I don't come back from vacation, not to mention that my employers will wonder what happened when I don't show up in the next few days."

He shook his head. "What were you thinking, hiking alone?"

His tone was so scolding that I stiffened. "I didn't start out alone. My friends came with me, but then Brandy twisted her ankle so she and Tom had to leave. I was going to leave, too, but . . ."

I stopped. Finishing that sentence would be too revealing. *But I was sick of putting my dreams on hold, waiting for the perfect situation.*

I'd put off so many things thinking I had to have my life set up *just perfectly* first. It's why I stayed at my job as a paralegal instead of continuing my education to be a lawyer (I wanted to decide on the perfect branch of law to practise before making that leap). It's why I'd waited so long to take this camping trip (I wanted to pay my car off before splurging on a vacation). It's also why I hadn't moved to Manhattan with Paul when he'd asked me. No, I'd wanted to be further along in my career before taking my relationship with him to the next level.

Staring at Brandy's twisted ankle that day, thinking that *again* I was going to have to put my plans on hold, had been the last straw. I'd decided to hell with waiting. Even if I was doing it alone, I was hiking through Yellowstone like I'd planned.

And look where that decision got me.

"You wouldn't understand," was all I said.

His gaze was steady. "I thought we'd just established that we're both capable of understanding a lot more than the other realizes."

I let out an impatient sigh. "All right, then how's this? I don't want to tell you. I don't know why I'm even talking to you. You're my kidnapper."

"Not really." Softly, but the words still resonated. "You're part of the Pack now. And as enforcer, I keep the Pack safe. Even if it's from themselves."

This wasn't a conversation I wanted to explore. I yawned, hoping he'd take the hint.

He did. Daniel pushed his chair back and stretched. "Are you going to give me trouble if I take a shower?"

I eyed him warily. "I won't throw a radio in with you, if that's what you're talking about."

He grinned. "Good to know, but I meant can I trust you not to run away while I'm in the shower? I don't want to have to tie you to a chair, but I also don't feel like chasing after you with soap in my eyes."

I looked away from his smile, which was charming, sexy and dangerous all at the same time. It wasn't the dangerous part that unnerved me; it was the other things.

"I'll stay put." *But only because you'd hear me if I didn't.*

Daniel went into the bathroom and I sat on the bed, debating whether to climb under the covers, since the room was chilly. Finally I decided to wait. I'd shower once Daniel was done, then I'd borrow one of his shirts to sleep in again. At least they were long enough that modesty wasn't an issue.

I cast one longing look at the window and the freedom that lay beyond it, but then sighed. Daniel *would* chase after me, stark naked and soapy, then he'd probably tie me to a chair after all. The thought of sleeping sitting up while duct-taped didn't appeal to me. No, I'd wait for another chance to escape. One had to come up.

After about ten minutes, Daniel appeared in the door frame. His hair looked darker wet, and drops of water still beaded his skin. All he had on was a towel slung low on his hips, the white colour emphasizing his tan. He ran a hand through his hair, flinging more droplets away. With that simple, muscle-rippling gesture, he made me forget everything for a moment and just stare.

No wonder he isn't human. No normal person could be this sculpted and gorgeous.

It occurred to me that I was still staring even though several seconds had ticked away. *Look away, stupid!* flashed through my mind. So I did, dragging my gaze up his chest to meet his face.

He wasn't smiling. He wasn't scowling. No, he was just

staring at me with such an open hunger that a painful clench grabbed me below the waist. All at once, I wasn't chilled. I was warm, bordering on sweating.

This is wrong. All wrong. Don't you dare! You need to snap out of this right now.

"Stockholm syndrome," I whispered. It could only be that. Who in their right mind got turned on by their kidnapper, no matter what he looked like?

"Or something else." Daniel's voice was equally soft, but it contained an undertone that sent a shiver through me. "Wolves can tell their intended mate by scent, sometimes before they've even sighted them. Once the two meet . . . things are inevitable from there."

That wildness was lurking in his eyes again. It made me twist the bed sheets with my fingers.

"I'm not a wolf."

Daniel just smiled, dark and sensual and promising. "You will be soon."

Six

There was a tentative knock on the door. "Can I come in?"

The voice was feminine. I would have said no, but as there was no lock, what was the point?

"Fine."

A girl with auburn hair came in. It took a moment, but then I recognized her from the other night. *Daniel's cousin.* Damned if I remembered her name.

"I brought you some clothes," she said. "Hope they fit, but if they don't, you can take them back. The store's right down the street."

The girl set a couple of bags on the bed. I'd barely left this room for two days since the night of the gauntlet. Confusion and uncertainty overwhelmed me. What had started out as a twisted hostage scenario had changed into something more: I could now sense the rain before it started, hear noises from further away than humanly possible, and had recurring dreams about turning into a wolf that had turned from terrifying to strangely exhilarating instead.

No, what had me hiding in my room at the moment was that I was increasingly drawn to Daniel. I craved his scent more than food, followed him with my gaze whenever he entered the room, and had to literally fight with myself not to touch him when he was near. It was unlike anything I'd ever experienced. The worst part was, I was pretty sure Daniel knew what I was going through.

He'd tried to talk to me for the past two days, but I refused to speak with him. I didn't trust myself. I should be focusing on the fact that I was changing into a *monster*, and not be secretly fascinated by my new senses, or lusting after the person who held me prisoner. The night of the full moon loomed in front of me like an executioner's axe. Whatever control I had over myself now, I knew it would be gone as soon as that ghostly orb rose in the sky. Some primal, burgeoning part of me was looking forward to that.

". . . thought we could have a soak," the girl was saying. "That always helps me when I'm upset."

"What?" I hadn't been paying attention to a word she was saying.

"The hot springs," she repeated. "We have indoor and outdoor ones. I bought you a swimsuit. Anything's got to be better than being cooped up in this room day and night."

Outside. With just her. I gave her a quick, cagey look. Maybe this was my chance. She was petite, looked about nineteen or twenty, and seemed nice. Let's hope she was gullible, too.

"Sure. Thanks," I added, smiling. "What's your name again? I'm sorry, I don't remember."

"Laurel," she said with an answering smile. "Here, I'll leave so you can change."

"Can we go to whichever spring has the least amount of people? I'm, ah, shy about being in a bathing suit around strangers."

Growing up spending my summers at Lake Michigan, that was a lie, but she didn't know that. She nodded. "Sure."

I lowered my voice. "*He* doesn't need to come, does he?" I asked, with a nod towards the rest of the cabin, where Daniel was. "I'm so tired of him shadowing my every move."

She lowered her voice as well. "I'll talk to him."

My smile widened. Nice *and* gullible. My luck was changing.

If circumstances were different, I would have been awed at how beautiful this place was. The cabins were set near the end of the mini-town and spaced well apart for privacy. The mountains loomed majestically around all of it. Forests bridged the bottom of the mountains, adding a more secluded feel, and the steam rising up from the rock-bed hot springs looked both soothing and inviting.

But, sinking into the warm mineral water, I was reminded of my tub at home in my apartment. A stab of longing went through me when I thought about my parents, who I'd meant to call before leaving on my camping trip; my older sister, Leigh; my nephew, who'd just turned one last month; my co-workers, who made the long hours from nine to five pass much more quickly; my best friend Brandy; her boyfriend Tom, who told me in confidence right before they left that he was going to pop the question. Would I see any of them again?

I will, I promised myself. I'll get away. I'll . . . I'll find a doctor to cure me. I just have to get away. No matter what.

"Feeling better?" Laurel asked. She leaned back, settling her arms around the edge of the rock lip.

"Yes." And I did. I'd committed myself to a course of action and I'd follow it through. No matter what.

"I don't know why you'd be embarrassed to be seen in a swimsuit, Marlee," she went on. "You're very pretty. Finn's already interested."

"Finn?" I asked blankly.

"My cousin. The guy with the long black hair. You met him the same night you met me."

Oh yeah. "He looked young," I said neutrally.

She laughed. "He's forty-two."

My jaw dropped as I remembered the smooth-skinned, flirty Finn. "Can't be."

Laurel gave me a slanted look. "There are advantages, you know," she said in a casual tone. "You know how one year equals seven in a dog's life? Well, we have the reverse of that. And you already know we heal a lot faster than normal people.

Plus, when we change, we experience the world in ways no one else can. I don't know how anyone would rather be just a human."

I gaped at her. Just when I thought things couldn't get any stranger. "How old are you?" I managed.

She settled back more comfortably. "Oh, I'm only twenty, but the good news is, I'll look like this for a long time. The age slowing doesn't happen until puberty's over, thank God. Imagine being a teenager for forty years?"

I couldn't. "And Daniel?"

"I'll let him tell you how old he is," Laurel replied. She had a little smirk that made me wary.

"What?"

"Nothing."

Like hell. She was obviously itching to say more. I scooted closer, lowering my voice.

"*What?*"

Laurel's smirk widened. "Normally, when someone's exposed to us like you were – which is very rare, by the way – Daniel is the one to bring them in, but he doesn't watch that person the whole time. He's big on privacy. He's never had someone stay at his cabin for four days straight, not even a girlfriend. Add his refusal to let Finn visit you and, well . . . he's acting possessive. Like a wolf with his future mate."

I was alternating between feeling shocked and triumphant. Daniel, seeing me as a future mate? So it wasn't just me who'd been so affected the past few days.

But that presented a whole new set of problems. It was one thing when I thought Daniel was just doing his job as the Pack's enforcer. Knowing he might be feeling the same thing towards me would decimate the slim hold I had on my control, and I still needed to get away. It complicated things to a fantastic degree.

Or, Laurel could be wrong. Daniel could be keeping me close because he knew I hadn't really accepted this as my new life. Either way, I had to take advantage of my chance, which brought me to why I'd agreed to this outing.

I hunched a little, letting an expression of pain spasm on my face.

"What's wrong?" Laurel asked.

"Cramps," I said with another grimace. "I'm getting my period. Could you do me a huge favour? I don't want to embarrass myself by springing a leak while walking back to town. Can you get me some tampons? I'll wait here."

I climbed out of the hot water and sat on one of the large rocks, wrapping a towel around me. Here's hoping the universal sympathy every woman had for that time of the month would result in Laurel doing something stupid.

She gave me such an odd look that I cursed myself for not coming up with a better reason for her to go away. Well, I didn't have much time to think up a clever ploy. But then she smiled. "Be right back."

Laurel got up, fastened a towel around herself, and walked away. I waited, barely breathing, until she rounded a cabin that took her out of sight, then I bounded up, running flat out towards the nearest line of trees.

Seven

I didn't have shoes on so rocks cut into my feet, but I ignored them. It would only take Laurel ten to fifteen minutes to return. That's all the time I had to get away.

I ran like I was on fire, noting with a growing sense of awareness that I was moving faster than I ever had before. Maybe it was the werewolf curse inside me that would help me get away. *Go faster. Head for the mountains. It'll be harder for them to track your scent over all the rock.*

The forest was alive with sounds; the cry of birds, the rustling of branches as they rubbed together in the wind, the thuds my feet made on the drying leaves strewn over the uneven ground. That feeling of fright began to lessen, replaced with an inexplicable joy over running as hard and as fast as I could. I might be running away from this life, but right now, I felt strong, free and wild, like the forest itself was spurring my steps. I went faster, forgetting the pain in my feet, until the trees were almost a blur around me. Giddiness bubbled inside me. This felt right. Like I'd been waiting my whole life to run this way.

Something hard collided with me, snatching me up. My heart was already pounding, but it kicked into another gear as I glimpsed who'd grabbed me. Daniel. He whirled me around to face him, those blazing hazel eyes pinning me as tightly as his grip did.

"What were you thinking?" he asked, giving me a shake. "You're in a bathing suit and a towel! I should have waited and gone after you tomorrow. Maybe spending the night freezing out here would have knocked some sense into you."

My emotions were on overload from the dizzying adrenaline rush of my escape, the frustration of being caught and the residual exhilaration of the run. I didn't feel like myself. I felt as if something hiding inside me had finally taken over.

I grabbed Daniel's hair and yanked his head down, slanting my mouth across his. There was a split second where he froze – then his mouth opened, his tongue twisting with mine. His hand tangled in my hair, jerking me closer, while the other hand moulded our bodies together. The heat coming from him made me gasp, but I pressed against him, wanting more of it. He growled, kissing me deeper, harder, unleashing a flood of lust even as it shook me from my earlier recklessness.

If you don't stop now, you'll end up having sex here on the ground just like the animal you're turning into . . .

"No!"

I wrenched away, panting. Daniel let me out of his arms, but his hand tightened on my wrist, not letting me get entirely free.

"What's wrong?"

I gave a bark of laughter. "You. Me. Everything."

He pushed his hair out of his face, staring at me with an intensity that made me shiver.

"It's right, even if you don't want to admit it."

My towel had fallen to the ground, leaving me in just the bathing suit. Daniel's eyes slid over me like a rough caress. A tremor ran through me and gooseflesh rippled, as if my skin were trying to arc towards him with a will of its own.

Daniel's grip on my wrist softened to a light stroke of his fingers. "You want me," he said in a low voice. "Why are you pushing me away?"

That stiffened my spine. "Because I can. You've stolen all my other choices, but this one's still mine. And I say no."

He let me go. That warm amber light in his eyes hardened to

something darker. He picked up my towel, handed it to me, and turned his back.

"I'm not the one who stole your choices. Gabriel did. If you stay in these woods, you'll probably die of exposure. If you don't, then in a week, you'll change, but you won't know how to change back. Eventually you'll go insane, trapped in your new form, controlled by urges you can't imagine. You'll end up mauling whoever you come across, be it man, woman or child. Then people will hunt you. They'll kill other wolves trying to get to you, but sooner or later, they'll find you. You'll get shot or caught in a trap, but either way, it will be horrible. Walk away now and people are guaranteed to die, including you. Come back with me and no one dies. There's your choice."

"I can get to a doctor, find a cure," I replied stubbornly.

Daniel laughed, but it was harsh. "We've had doctors within the Pack try to find a cure for decades. Not for ourselves, but to fix people who've been unwillingly infected, like you. There is no cure, Marlee. If there was, we'd have given it to you already."

Hopelessness crashed over me. "You're telling me I'll never see my family and friends again. You're so willing to do anything for your pack, but you expect me to just forget about anyone who's ever meant anything to me in my life!"

He still didn't turn around. "If you wouldn't have refused to speak to me for days, I'd have told you that you only need to be quarantined for a couple months. Once you've learned control, you can see your family and friends. They can come here, or you can move away. You'd need to live somewhere close to wolves, though, so when you change, you're not running on four legs down a city street attracting unwanted attention."

My brain whirled with this new information. *I didn't have to be trapped here forever. I could go home, see my parents, my sister, Brandy, even my nephew again. I could wait it out. Get control. Could I actually learn to live as both a woman and a wolf?*

Daniel started walking away, the dried leaves crunching under his feet. I stared after him, not moving. Was he really giving me a choice? If I walked the other way, would he truly not stop me?

I tested it. Turned and walked in the other direction. There wasn't the slightest hesitation in his steps as he kept going. *He's tricking you,* my cynicism whispered. *He'll come back.*

I kept walking. So did he. Soon the sounds of Daniel's footsteps began to lessen as we moved further away from each other. After ten minutes, I couldn't hear him at all.

Eight

Even with the moonlight illuminating the forest, I would have been lost without Daniel's scent. I wasn't used to relying on my sense of smell, but that's exactly what I was doing as I walked back through the woods towards what I thought was the town. In my peripheral vision, hazy flashes of maroon darted by. It had scared me the first few times I saw it, but then I realized what it was. I was seeing the heat living creatures gave off, just like I was looking through an infrared camera.

My sharpened senses made me feel more alive than I ever had. It seemed like I'd been sleepwalking the previous twenty-eight years of my life, numbed to all the brilliance of the world around me.

Of course, I knew what this was – the wolf in me, getting ready to be freed.

It was the main reason why, after sitting in the forest watching the sun fall and the moon rise, I was walking back to the town. Chosen or not, I was part wolf now. I couldn't go back to my family, friends or co-workers, not knowing what I was capable of, even if I did make it out of these woods. If the choice was sacrificing months of my life dealing with the strangest scenario imaginable, versus risking people I loved by hoping Daniel was wrong and I wouldn't one day eat them . . . well, there was no choice. Not in my opinion.

That wasn't the reason my heart started to beat faster when I recognized the man leaning against a tree just outside the limits of the town. All right, I'd had more motivation than just protecting my loved ones by returning. With every step I'd taken away from Daniel, something burning and heavy had settled in my heart. It was as unfamiliar, frightening and exciting as the other changes I'd experienced this week. How could I care so much after such a short period of time? I'd been with Paul for three years, but hadn't felt the crushing sense of loss at our break-up that I did walking away from Daniel. Was it some supernatural hormone gone haywire? I didn't know. I only knew it was the most real thing I'd ever felt.

"I thought you were letting me go," I said. "Yet here you are, still in the forest instead of in bed in your cabin."

Daniel turned. He was still too far away for me to see his expression, but his voice sounded raw. "I *was* letting you go, but no wolf can sleep while his mate is in danger."

Mate. Such a primitive word, and so possessive. All things considered, we barely knew each other. Why wasn't I uneasy at hearing it? Why did warmth spread over me, even as I was shivering in the cold night air?

I swallowed. "How can you be sure?"

He was at my side in the next heartbeat, enfolding me in his arms, his body heat almost searing my skin.

"I knew it as soon as I smelled your scent," he said, low and rough. "I told you, that's how it is with wolves. That day with Gabriel – I wasn't tracking him. He and the others had masked their scents so I wouldn't be able to trace them. But I found them anyway because I'd been tracking you."

This was overwhelming. I shuddered even as I leaned in closer to him. "Daniel, everything has happened so fast . . ."

He caressed my face. "Don't judge by that. Breathe me in. Tell me what you feel."

I inhaled near his neck, absorbing the mix of wood smoke, cinnamon and musk that made up his scent. Contentment battled with lust inside me. I wanted to throw Daniel to the forest floor, rub my body all over his, claim his flesh as my own, and then hold him and never let go.

"I feel more than I have a right to," was what I said, my voice shaky.

He bent so that his lips were almost brushing mine. "I give you the right. I want you to claim me as yours."

And I wanted to be claimed. That was the truth of it. Whether it was me or the wolf inside who'd made this decision, I didn't know. But I felt it through every fibre of me.

I'd asked Daniel days ago if it was him I was talking to or the wolf. *It's both*, he'd said. *Always*. I hadn't understood then, but

I did now. The wolf didn't feel like it was a separate entity from me any more; it *was* me, but without all my fears, doubts or hesitations. The wolf was me stripped of all my pretence, and it knew, unequivocally, that Daniel was mine.

And so did I.

"Take me home," I whispered. It was an invitation and a promise. I wasn't giving up my family or my friends, but I'd first learn to live in harmony with the wolf in me, and I'd do it here, with the help of my mate.

Daniel picked me up and carried me to his cabin. I was smiling the whole way.

When Gargoyles Fly

Lori Devoti

One

She touched him. Her fingers were warm, soft, undeniably human. Mord Gabion blinked, and his eyelids made slow painful movements. They creaked like stone scratching stone, like a gargoyle coming to life while its body was still frozen in its sleep – which it was.

He shouldn't be awake, shouldn't be aware of those supple fingers, or the scent of ginger and spice drifting towards him. Shouldn't be aware of anything, ever again – but he was.

Her fingers ran down the planes of his chest, traced the line of bone that formed the top of his wings, which were folded in sleep, but itching with the need to open, to take his body soaring through the night sky.

"Such detail," she murmured.

His eyes shifted in their sockets. He wanted to see her, needed to see her, but his body wasn't quite ready. It was still locked in its rocky state.

She edged closer, her feet scraping over the hard ledge on which he was perched. He could feel it too now, through the thin-soled shoes he'd worn when he'd agreed to the sorcerer's bargain, agreed to go to sleep for eternity so his enemies, the chimeras, would be put into the slumber too.

He and the others like him had given up their freedom, their lives, to save the world from the chimeras who would have enslaved humanity – but he was awake. He swallowed, or made the motion at the back of his throat; the action was uncomfortable, unnatural locked in this stony condition.

He tried again, managed to move his head to the side, but only an inch. The woman pressed against him, studying him, and didn't notice. But the movement was real. He was coming awake.

Were his enemies too?

Kami Machon clung to the gargoyle, kept herself from looking down by concentrating on the impossible detail of his wings, muscles, everything. How she wished she knew who had sculpted him, how the sculptor had put such strength and darkness into the white marble he'd used to carve the creature.

She'd been sculpting with clay for years, but had recently forked out the dollars for a block of alabaster. Her fingers itched to pick up that chisel, make the first chink in the stone. But she was afraid, wanted it to be perfect, beautiful, like this gargoyle.

She ran her hand lower, towards the strange kilt-like cloth that covered the gargoyle's lower body. The stone beneath her hand quivered. She jerked, then laughed at the flight of her imagination. Real as he might appear, this gargoyle (or grotesque, to use the more accurate term) was stone, cold and hard. He couldn't feel her hand moving over him, couldn't react to her touch.

She shook her head, forced her feet to inch further along the ledge. One hand gripping the gargoyle's for balance, she lowered her other to the flashlight that hung on a string from her neck. It was dark, past midnight – the only time she'd been sure no one would see her, try to stop her.

She'd tried going through regular routes, asked permission from the building's owner to view the statue up close, but her calls had been ignored. Then, miraculously, the temp agency she worked for part-time had offered a position with the building's cleaning service. The rest of the crew was gone now. She was left with free access to the outside ledge at the top of the building where the gargoyle perched, keeping watch over the city.

She flipped on the flashlight, directed its small beam onto the gargoyle's profile. His jaw was strong, firm. She laughed again –

of course it was. He was carved of stone. She lowered the light so she could feel the strength there, memorize it to replicate in her own work. The beam danced along the ledge and over her feet, drawing her gaze for just a second.

From the corner of her eye she saw movement, started to turn, but something hit her square in the back and knocked her off balance. She screamed, grabbed at the gargoyle's stone fingers, felt her own digits slip one by one until she fell free, and tumbled through the air towards the cement circle 200 feet below.

Mord heard the female scream, felt her fingers slip over his knuckles. His body tensed, vibrated with an uncontrollable need to save her. The stone encasing him cracked. His muscles flexed. His wings shook. He took a breath, forced it into his lungs. There was another crack – louder, like a cannon firing – and he was free. He shoved his body away from the wall, felt his feet break from the ledge beneath them. His wings expanded and he free-fell for a few seconds, revelling in the feel of the air rushing past him, of being alive again.

The night air was dark and cold, invigorating, just like in his memories. And the city below flickered at him like he remembered, but now with more lights: strange bright ones zigging along at impossible speeds.

The woman screamed again, pulling his mind back to her. Saving her was not his concern. People jumped from buildings. Before his forced sleep he'd seen plenty make that choice, hadn't tried to talk one out of it. He was a gargoyle, not a priest. His duty was to protect humans, but as a race, not individuals, and not from their own stupid choices. If the weak died, it made the whole stronger: part of the great formula that kept the world strong, vibrant.

Still . . . His gaze zoomed to the body falling beneath his. Her arms were flapping as if she thought she could take wing.

He shouldn't save her. He had issues of his own: finding out why he'd been awakened, and if others, allies and enemies, were awakening too.

The smell of ginger reached out to him as she screamed again, or tried to. Her voice was hoarse now, almost lost in the wind.

He gritted his teeth, started to turn away, to point his face towards the other buildings where gargoyles and chimeras had spent their nights before the freeze. But as quick as he did, as sure as he was that he was making the right choice, his body decided otherwise. His wings flexed, his shoulders shifted and he dived – straight down – towards the now silent woman plummeting to the earth below.

Air whooshed past her, tore at her clothes. Fear clutched at Kami's chest, made it impossible to breathe. She was falling . . . falling. Her brain screamed to reach out, grab for something to stop her descent, but there was nothing to grab, nothing around her but angry air. It roared in her ears. She was going to die. There was no way around it.

The thought echoed through her head, settled into her stomach. She was going to die, and it was her own fault. What idiot crawled onto a ledge to see a statue?

She screwed her eyes shut, tried to pull her arms in close but couldn't, the wind stopped her.

Tears ran down her cheeks, cold more than wet, and her world started to shift . . . fade.

She drifted for a second, forgot where she was, what was happening. Suddenly, something hit her, jarred her back awake. Despite her fear, her eyes flew open. The ground . . . had she hit? Survived?

She was still moving, fast, but sideways. Something . . . arms . . . held her. Her head fell backwards, over one of those arms, against a chest – solid, cool, bare. Her heart was beating. She could feel it, could feel air moving in and out of burning lungs. She'd been screaming. The thought seemed random, unattached to anything. Like her reality.

Nothing seemed real . . . She pressed trembling fingers to her cheeks. Felt that, felt everything.

She was alive. Impossibly someone had saved her. Finally, she forced her face to turn upwards, to see who held her.

A smooth, chiselled jaw. High cheekbones. Angled, strong features that should have been unattractive, but somehow, put together, were arresting, commanding and . . . familiar. She reached up, heard a whisper of movement and turned her gaze to the noise. Wings, six feet wide, glowed back at her – white as if carved from marble. Her eyes shot back to her saviour's face. He was looking at her now with features as strong as rock.

Rock, wings . . . the gargoyle.

Dear God. She'd been saved by the gargoyle. Her mouth opened, a scream ripped from her throat.

He ignored her, tightened his hold and dived forwards until air whooshed past her again to steal both her breath and the scream that had been flying from her throat.

Two

Mord angled his wings to slow their landing, let his feet skid across the roadway. The female in his arms lay limp, pale. She'd screamed as she was falling, and screamed again when he caught her.

He bent one knee and lowered her to the grass. They were in some kind of park. A statue of a man, dressed in a uniform unfamiliar to Mord, guarded the entrance. A large fountain that Mord remembered from when he had last been awake and flown over this city lay a few feet past that.

He stared at the statue for a moment. The date, 1944 – forty-six years after the gargoyles had agreed to the great sleep. He started to stand, to leave the female where she lay. He'd saved her. His job was done.

The wind shifted. The smell of ginger wove around him, halting his steps. He glanced back at the female. She was pale, too pale for a human. He knelt down and placed his hand next to her face. Her pallor almost matched his own, and he was still in his gargoyle form. He wasn't able yet to shift to his human shape.

He flexed and unflexed his wings, enjoyed the feel of them moving behind him. A breeze from his movement caught the female's hair and threw it across her face. The dark locks clung to her lips. He brushed them aside, or tried to. The tendrils wrapped around his hand, seemed to pull at him, refuse to let him go. He cursed. He couldn't leave her here, like this. He knew nothing of this time, the dangers that might lie in wait for an unprotected female.

He scooped her up. She weighed nothing, but was warm against his chest. Her arms fell at her sides, but this close, holding her, he could hear the even in and out of her breaths. She was alive, just passed out.

He exhaled, annoyed at his unexplainable need to care for her, to see she was OK before leaving to investigate whatever awaited him in this new time. He strode to the fountain. The water splattered onto a carved bowl then spilled into a bigger section at least twelve feet across. Kneeling, he opened his arms and let her roll into the water with a splash. As she sank below the surface, he bent his knees and propelled himself into the sky. The water would awaken her while allowing him to leave undetected. He couldn't risk staying by her side, revealing himself any more. Humans didn't know the gargoyles' secret. They couldn't.

His wings spread and he flattened them, allowed himself to glide for a second, silently, so he could hear her sputter back to life. He'd watch from up high as she pulled herself upright, then made her way back to wherever she called home.

Except she didn't. She sputtered and shook, rubbed her hands over her hair and face. Then she stood in the knee-high water, her thin shirt and obscenely short pants clinging to her breasts and buttocks. Water dripped from her hair. She shook her head again, then stared at the sky.

"Gargoyle," she whispered. "Where are you?"

Her voice was low, stunned, but sure. She'd seen him, and could somehow see him as he soared over her head. She was watching him.

He hesitated for a moment, then turned. She only thought she'd seen him, would easily convince herself otherwise soon. He'd been through this before. Humans were good at protecting their own realities. They believed what they had been trained from birth to believe.

And stone didn't come to life.

She'd forget him soon.

Water dripped from Kami's hair. She slicked her hands over it, sent a river running down her back, but kept her gaze on the sky. She wasn't crazy. The gargoyle was alive and had saved her.

Something moved above her, but high up – too high to make out in the darkness. She ran her hands over her arms, realized she was shaking. The wind whispered. She spun, hoped it was the gargoyle returning, but the grass beside her was empty.

She stepped from the fountain and wondered for a brief second how she'd landed there. Then another sound caught her attention, an engine turning over. She froze, prayed the driver wouldn't see her. She had no explanation for where she was or the state she was in.

She glanced up at the building she'd fallen from and the window she'd left open. She was sure of the last, but it was closed now. *Strange.* A memory tickled at the back of her mind. Something about her fall.

She frowned and stared at the ledge. The gargoyle? Her gaze darted to the right. Nothing. No statue, no sign one had ever perched there. Her heart jumped.

He was real.

For some reason the thought warmed her. With a smile she patted the keys in her pocket. Still there. She could drive herself home, or go back inside, see up close that he was really gone.

Knowing exactly what she was going to do, she stepped off the grass and into the road. She was halfway across when a motor roared behind her. She spun. Lights beamed at her, blinding her, freezing her steps.

For the second time in half an hour, she was facing a sure death.

Mord, clinging to a cold metal and glass building nearby, watched as the female stared up at the skyscraper he'd called home. Wonder, then joy, lit her face. She stepped off the kerb then moved with purpose towards the building.

He frowned. She was supposed to leave, to forget him. She looked up again, her gaze locked onto the spot where he'd been perched, frozen . . . for how long?

He was still staring at the ledge he'd vacated when he heard a strange, mechanical roar. Instinctively he jerked towards it, saw twin lights burning through the night, pointed at the little female. The machine rushed towards her and she stood frozen, staring at it.

Without thinking, he pushed away from the building, pointed his wings to the ground and the girl, and snatched her like a hawk capturing a rabbit from a field. The machine whizzed beneath them. He made out eyes, dark and intense, peering over the wheel.

Then his attention turned to the female. Her hands were wrapped around his neck, her cheek pressed against his chest. "You came back," she murmured. Her fingers stroked his neck, reminded him of how she'd touched him when he'd been locked in stone.

Who was she? And why couldn't he leave her to her fate?

Kami stared at the man settled on her couch. Mord. That was all she'd got out of him – his name. He'd given no reaction when she had supplied hers. She'd needed him to know it, hoped he would repeat it, like that would somehow make all this more real. But he'd done nothing, barely blinked or breathed.

Still, he was sitting on her couch, nothing could be more real than that.

His chest was bare. A cloth of some sort was wrapped around his hips. She'd mistaken it for a kilt before, but now could see it was less structured than that. It was more a strip of wool he'd knotted in place.

His wings had disappeared, and his skin was no longer marble pale, but she knew he was the gargoyle. Nothing he said would convince her otherwise. She'd traced his features with her fingers, memorized each chiselled inch of him.

A tingle ran through her. She clenched her fists and tried to ignore the need to run her hands over him again, to feel those same planes and angles, now warm and human. But male, still very male.

"What are you wearing?" she asked. It was an asinine question, but all she could think to say. Her mind seemed to have gone blank.

He glanced down, brows lifting. "A cloth."

Well, that explained it.

Mord stared at the female, struggled to make sense of why he was here, why he hadn't left before now. She stared back, her eyes huge in her heart-shaped face. Minutes ticked by with neither saying a word. Finally, unable to sit still, he stood, wandered to a far corner where a drop-sheet lay on the floor. Sealed buckets were stacked around its edges. In the centre sat a rectangular piece of stone. Alabaster. He moved towards it, bent to trace his finger over its top.

"You carve?" he asked. Perhaps this was the reason for his reluctance to leave. Perhaps she had a connection to the stone, thus a connection to gargoyles – to him.

She stepped closer, her gaze darting to the block of stone. "Not yet, but I want to. That's why I was on the ledge. I wanted to . . ." She raised her hand, held it up as if she were going to touch him, like she had when he was frozen in sleep.

Suddenly, he knew what kept him here, why he couldn't leave. He stood still, his heart thumping slowly in his chest. She took another step towards him. He could feel her warmth, smell her ginger scent. Her hand shaking, she reached closer, touched his shoulder first then ran her flat palm down his chest and over his abdomen.

He held perfectly still, used his gargoyle skills to keep from moving. Didn't even breathe.

"What happened to your wings?" she asked. She walked around him, her fingers still tracing his body, skimming his sides.

He didn't answer. She wasn't supposed to accept him so readily, believe the statue she'd seen would come to life. No human he'd encountered in his past ever had.

"They were here." She rose on her tiptoes, prodded his back where in his gargoyle form his wings appeared. "But I don't . . ." She paused, moved her fingers round and round then found the nub that hid his wings when human. "Here. Is this it? How?"

She continued her explorations. Mord's body tensed, tightened. He bit back a groan. Her touch was torture on this most sensitive part of him, but he couldn't tell her to stop, couldn't acknowledge what she was doing to him. That would give him away, be an admission that he was different. And, his mind whispered, he didn't want to, had been untouched for so long. Even gargoyles enjoyed being touched. They didn't *feel* like humans did, not emotions anyway, but they enjoyed physical sensations, and she was providing him with plenty.

She leaned closer. Her breath warmed his skin; her hair brushed against him.

He could stand it no longer. He was at risk of exploding, jerking her warm human form against his, showing her exactly what her innocent curiosity was doing to him.

"You're imagining things," he blurted, his voice rough.

Her hand paused in its movements, hovered above his skin. "Imagining?" She leaned forwards, spoke with her lips almost touching his skin. "My imagination isn't this good."

He took a step and turned. He needed to see her, decide what powers she held. She wasn't a simple human. He knew that. But what was she? And why had she come so close to death twice in their short acquaintance?

"Who wants you dead?" he asked.

She jerked, frowned. "I don't . . ." She shook her head. "I fell. It was stupid of me to climb out on the ledge, but I'd seen . . . I . . ." She closed her eyes. "I had to get closer." Her eyes opened, pinned him. "I had to see you. But I never imagined . . ." Her words drifted off. She curled her fingers into her palms and waited, like she expected him to say something more, to acknowledge that he was the gargoyle she'd sought out, or that he felt the strange pull between them, too.

He couldn't give her any answers. Secrecy was one of the gargoyles' greatest strengths. If humans learned the statues they walked by every day could come to life, that these statues had the strength and power to destroy mankind, fear would take over. His kind would be hunted. Attempts would be made to capture or kill them as they slept.

And the gargoyles would be forced to make a choice – destroy or be destroyed.

It was unthinkable.

As was admitting he felt the same pull she did. She was a human. Humans and gargoyles didn't mingle. And gargoyles didn't *feel*. Whatever was happening to him now was due to the sorcerer, and the wearing off of the spell, not her. It couldn't be her.

"Someone in the machine tried to run you down." He laid the words in front of her, stated them as the fact they were.

"Someone . . ." Her eyes widened and her fingers pressed against her lips. "Someone tried to run me down," she repeated. She caught his gaze. "And pushed me. Someone pushed me off that ledge. I remember now. I felt a hand." She pulled her shoulders back, as if the fingers still pressed against her skin. "Why?"

He waited, made sure her reality had sunk in, then headed towards the door. He'd done his part, made her aware of the danger she was in. Now he had a bigger threat to search out, one potentially disastrous to humanity as a whole – the chimeras.

"Wait!" She hurried after him, grabbed him by the arm.

A shock shot through him like a chisel hitting marble. He contracted his still-hidden wings, felt them reverberate in his back.

"You can't leave yet. You haven't told me anything, or explained who you are, *how* you are."

He gritted his teeth and took another step towards the door, but not far enough, not fast enough.

She moved with him, wrapped her hands around his biceps. "You can trust me," she murmured.

The one word that could stop him cold: trust. He'd believed in trust once, before he'd been betrayed by his brother . . . or the one being he'd let close enough to think of as a brother.

He turned. His shoulders pulled back and his eyes narrowed, he looked down at her. "Who can you trust? That's what you should be thinking about, not letting your mind run wild with some fantasy you created while you were falling."

She dropped her hand. He started to turn again, thought he'd shaken her, put her in her place.

Then she smiled. "So, I did fall. Over twenty floors? And what? That fountain saved me?" She laughed. "Now who has the imagination?"

He huffed. He wasn't used to humans – anyone – talking back to him. His wings tingled beneath his skin, screamed to be unfurled. That sight would overwhelm her, force her back into her place.

And it would reveal with absolutely no doubt that he was a gargoyle. A hiss escaped from between his closed teeth.

She placed her hand on his chest. "I know you were stone and somehow came to life. You flew. You saved me."

Her gaze was intense. It threatened to burn through him.

He wrapped his thumb and index finger around her wrist, plucked her hand from his chest. "Believe what you want. I can't stop you."

"Who . . ." Her hand shook. He could tell she wanted to touch him again, and damn everything, he wanted it too. She swallowed, glanced at the block of alabaster beside them then back. "Are you a man or a statue?"

He needed to leave.

"Did someone create you?"

He stopped at that. She was right; someone had created him, had created all of his kind. A sculptor turned sorcerer. He'd carved Mord, carved all of them, then infused them with life. He stared at the female with new interest.

Could she create more gargoyles? Did her touch awaken him? Could she awaken the others without awakening the chimeras?

"Touch me," he ordered.

Three

Touch him. She wanted to do nothing *but* touch him. Afraid he'd change his mind, continue on his trek out of her apartment, Kami placed both hands on his chest.

His skin was smooth and firm, colder than hers, but not as cold as the marble creature she'd touched on that ledge. And he was perfect, every inch of him. She ran her hands down his sides, let her fingers dip where his muscle dipped, rise where it rose. If he had been carved, his creator had been a master, better than she could ever dream of being.

She looked up at Mord, placed one hand on his chin. It was smooth too, no sign of stubble. There was a cleft in his chin. She hadn't noticed it before. Now she focused on it, ran the pad of one finger over it. What care had the sculptor used to perfect that?

Her heart was beating loud and fast, as if she'd sprinted up three flights of stairs. She exhaled. Her hand that had been resting on his chest moved upwards. He had inhaled.

She exhaled again. He inhaled.

She shifted her gaze to his eyes, wondered if he was playing with her. For a second he stared back, wonder and something close to fear reflecting back at her. Then he stepped backwards, breaking their connection and his gaze shuttered closed.

"Someone wants to kill you and I think I know why." The statement was low and earnest. The look on his face was startling, ferocious.

For the first time, she was unsure around him, scared. She glanced at the door, but he seemed to have forgotten it.

"When did these attempts on your life start?" he asked.

She stared at a bucket filled with clay, wondered what had possessed her to bring him here – to be here alone with him. "I . . . I don't know. Not until tonight on the ledge, I guess." Even after recognizing that she'd felt a hand press into her back, she still couldn't believe someone was trying to kill her, couldn't fathom the possibility. She was no one. It had to be a mistake, an accident.

"On the ledge. When you were next to me?"

His voice was so level . . . safe. She looked up and frowned. "Yes." She could see the truth in his eyes. He truly believed someone wanted to kill her. Yes, she'd felt a hand, but . . .

She thought back. Memories flooded her brain – little sounds as she was perched on the ledge, sounds she'd disregarded. Did someone lean through the window and reach towards her? If it had been an accident they would have screamed, right? Called someone? Done something? Reality hit.

Someone *had* pushed her, and on purpose. Someone wanted her dead.

His lips thinned. "I don't think this is about you. Not really."

"How can it not be about me?" she asked, her mind reeling. Someone tried to kill her. The thought shook her, more than anything that had happened that night. Meeting Mord, learning that gargoyles (whether he would admit it or not) weren't just the inanimate hunks of stone people thought – that hadn't surprised her at all. It had actually been reassuring.

Deep inside, she'd always known there was life inside stone. She'd felt it but been afraid to let the thoughts creep into her consciousness. Still, deep down, she'd *known*. Mord coming to life had been the evidence she'd always been lacking, the proof she needed. For the first time, everything made sense.

But a killer targeting her? *That* made no sense.

Mord held out his hand – large, square and reassuring. She slipped her fingers into his, let out a breath as his hand enclosed hers.

"I think I need to tell you a few things."

Kami's fingers were so small, so fragile, but they made Mord tingle with life.

How could he have missed it at first? Then doubted it? It was obvious she was no simple human. She held the secret to life in her touch. She was the reason he was awake, and he was the reason someone wanted her dead.

"Have you carved around anyone? Has anyone shown an interest in your work?"

She shook her head. "No, I . . ." Her words trailed off, her gaze shifted to the block of alabaster. "There was . . ." Her head tilted, her brows drew together. "No, that's silly. It wouldn't make sense."

"What?" The word came out more order than question.

She licked her lips, blew air out of her rounded mouth. He breathed in, couldn't stop himself. Pulling air into his body that had just left hers seemed to strengthen him, make him more alive than he'd ever been before.

She continued, "The man who sold me the alabaster. He called himself the Mason. He talked to me about what I was going to do. He had pictures of gargoyles, lots of them."

"He wanted you to carve a gargoyle?" Mord asked.

"Yes, but . . . not like you. All his pictures were of mixed animal grotesques – lions with wings, cat heads on eagle bodies. That kind of thing."

Chimeras. He had wanted her to create chimeras. Mord hid his shock, concentrated on getting Kami to talk. It wasn't hard. She almost bubbled over with information.

Within minutes she'd shared enough that Mord knew he had to find the man who'd sold her the stone, question him at least.

But the sun would rise soon and Mord would turn to stone. Hopefully, when night fell again, he would awake. Mord clenched his jaw – *hopefully*. There was no guarantee. He wasn't supposed to be awake now. Was supposed to still be under the sorcerer's spell. Once night fell, whatever magic had awakened him might disappear. He might go back into his rocky sleep never to wake again.

Kami's fingers flexed in his hand. She smiled up at him – trusting. And unexplainably, he wanted her to trust him. Wanted to wake the next night to be with her again.

But why? She offered only complications to his situation, kept him from travelling out and checking on the other gargoyles, the chimeras. He should want to be free from her.

What was happening to him? Some other piece to the spell?

He shoved the questions from his mind. Daylight was still a couple of hours or more off. He'd concentrate on Kami for now, then perhaps he'd be able to forget her.

Mord had been silent since they'd left her apartment. He was still human. There was no sign that he was in reality a gargoyle, except his perfect physique – a physique so well developed and balanced it had to have been crafted. No amount of training or special diets would have given those results.

And he was dressed as a human. Kami had gone next door and explained to her neighbour, who was just returning from a party, that her date had spilled marinara on himself at dinner. Luckily her neighbour was huge, although not in the same way as Mord, and generous. He'd supplied her with pants that managed to cover Mord's muscular thighs and a shirt that was able to close over his chest.

She'd sighed when Mord had pulled on the clothing. She missed being able to study him, press her fingers against his bare skin. He'd started to leave without her, but she'd insisted he take her, assured him she'd go alone to the Mason's if he didn't. Still, he'd only agreed when she pointed out that he couldn't know for sure where the Mason was – that he could be hiding nearby, to attack her as soon as Mord left.

She unlocked her car and waited outside the driver's door as Mord eyed the machine, then started to slip his massive body into the passenger seat. Her apartment was within walking distance of Mord's skyscraper. She'd walked by him every day for the past three years, but to get to the Mason's shop, they would have to drive – or fly. Although Mord had quit denying what he was, he had made no move to reveal his wings. She hoped he'd get past his hang-up and learn to trust her.

Lights came down the street, blinding her. She raised a hand to protect her eyes and fought the surge of panic that rose in her breast. It was just a car. Yes, someone had tried to run her down with one earlier, but she couldn't jump at every automobile that drove by. And last time she'd been alone. Now Mord was with her.

The car turned into a side street, an alley really, covered in gravel. She relaxed, laughed. See, silly.

She waved at Mord who was wedged into the passenger seat, looking crowded and tense. She laughed again and forced herself to find humour in his situation, to pretend all of this was normal.

She somehow dropped her keys in the process.

She bent to retrieve them and heard tyres crunching over gravel. Panic shot through her so quickly, she knew it had never really left her. She clawed at the ground.

An engine roared. She didn't have to look, she knew the car was speeding towards her.

Mord heard the auto turn. Kami had disappeared out of sight after bending to retrieve her dropped keys. Without seeing her, he didn't know if she sensed the danger, but it didn't matter. The human female had no hope of out-running the car. She was trapped between the one swinging towards her and her own. It had taken Mord a lifetime to wedge himself into Kami's tiny vehicle. He'd taken extra care so as not to damage the seat or frame as he shoved his too big body into the constraining space, but it took only seconds for him to free himself.

He thought of the danger approaching her. His anger rock hard, his body immediately shifted, grew even larger, more muscular. Wings sprouted from his back. Metal shrieked as they unfolded and ripped through the vehicle's roof. The door he'd just carefully pulled closed flew from its hinges; one strike of his elbow sent it sailing into the building Kami called home.

He sprang onto the street, didn't pause as he leaped again, his thighs propelling his body upwards, his wings, straight and strong, keeping him on track. He shot into the sky, saw the car – the same one that had tried to run her down earlier – hurtling down the road. Its lights were off this time, making the driver's intention all the more clear.

Kami. Where was she? An icy coldness wrapped around his chest, startled him. He'd heard humans describe the sensation. They called it fear. But gargoyles didn't fear, didn't feel any emotion. They did their job because they did – they got no joy from their acts, suffered no loss at their failures. They just "acted". Which is what he had to do now, if Kami were to survive.

He landed beside the car, facing the attacking vehicle. His feet crunched through the road's surface. He spun, ignoring the debris he'd created. "Kami," he called, intending to scoop her up, whisk her to safety.

"Here." Her voice was rough, afraid. She'd rolled under the car, lying with her face inches from the pavement; her keys were clasped in her hand. "Get out of here. The car – it's—" Her eyes widened.

Mord spun, faced the car. He could see the driver again – a man, small with a hat pulled low over his brow. The human grasped the car's wheel, his knuckles white. There was fear in his eyes. He knew he was going to die.

There was no time to stop the inevitable. Mord stood strong, let the man-made mass smash into him. The front of the car bowed inwards. Tyres squealed, metal screamed. White balloons of cloth billowed into the windows, muffling whatever noise the man emitted.

Mord thrust his fist through what remained of the car's windshield and grabbed the human by the front of his shirt. He hung there, limp.

"Is he . . . ?" Kami whispered from beneath her car. Her voice shook, but Mord could hear her scrambling beneath the vehicle, scooting her way to the other side. Within seconds she stood beside him.

He pulled the man who would have killed her close, stared into his blank face. "I don't know him," he muttered. He'd thought the man might be someone from his past.

"It's the Mason," Kami murmured. She stepped over mangled pieces of metal, didn't stop until she stood right next

to Mord. She lay her hand on his arm. "Put him down. Is he—"
she swallowed "—dead?"

"I—" Mord started to answer, but other voices cut him off.

"What's happening out there?"

"Dear God. Call 911."

Kami gripped his arm tighter. "The police, they'll be coming."

Sirens sounded in the distance. On the horizon the first pink
strip of the coming sun appeared.

Mord glanced back at the man in his grasp. Blood stained his
face, and his breathing was shallow – but it was there. He was
alive.

Kami saw it too. "Put him down." Her touch was warm and
insistent.

There were only minutes until Mord would turn to rock. If
he didn't leave, take his place back on the building, he'd be
found here. Then what? He didn't want to leave the man alive,
but he also wanted to question him, find out what he knew
about the gargoyles and their enemies, why he was hunting
Kami.

Kami pressed her fingers into Mord's skin, nodded towards
the ground. "Put him down. I'll be OK. I know now, and he's in
rough shape. He may not make it, and if he does it will be a long
time before he can try again."

She was right, but setting the human down, not crunching
her would-be killer's throat under his foot was one of the
hardest things Mord had ever had to do.

And he had to do it because Kami asked it of him. She'd
brought him back to life – he owed her, but it was more than
that. He wanted to do it because to do otherwise would cause
her pain.

He never wanted anything to cause her pain again.

He set the man down.

Relief washed over Kami's face, and she smiled. "It's right. I
couldn't . . . thanks." And she smiled again at him.

Then she leaned forwards and pressed a kiss to his lips. "Go
back to my apartment. I'll talk to the police, then later . . ." She
squeezed his arm again, her eyes glowing. "We'll talk." She ran
a finger along his chin. Mord's hands rose. He had to fight to

keep himself from gathering her to him. He could already feel his skin beginning to harden, his blood to slow. Her magic wasn't working, or had run out. With the sun, he would return to stone.

Would he wake again? Or was this it? His one chance outside the sorcerer's curse? He should be happy that he'd had this night with Kami. He could feel the sadness that leaving her was causing him.

Up on the building, perched on the ledge, he stared down at her as he began to lose feeling in his feet. All he could think of was how much it hurt to leave her, to know he might never see her again.

Kami had awakened him more deeply than he'd thought, changed not just his frozen state, but his heart – his soul.

Impossible as it seemed, he loved her.

And the next time he woke might be one hundred years in the future. Or perhaps, he'd never wake again.

Kami spent hours at the accident scene, telling her story over and over, or the one she'd made up. The bowed hood of her attacker's car was hard to explain, as was the passenger door that Mord had torn off her vehicle. By the time an officer discovered the footprints broken through the asphalt, they quit asking, just shook their heads and snapped photos.

It was almost ten the next morning when she was finally released. The Mason had been rushed off as soon as an ambulance arrived. She'd learned he was alive, but in critical condition. No one would say if they thought he would make it or not.

Kami wanted to get home, to be with Mord.

She hurried inside, but the place was empty. Belatedly, she realized she'd locked the door. He'd had no way in. He must have gone somewhere else to wait, but where?

Realizing exactly where he would go – the only other place he could go – she raced back out of the door without bothering to pull it closed behind her. She wanted to see him. Needed to see him.

Beneath his building, she paused, shielding her eyes from the bright light. He was there, right where he'd always been, in all his gargoyle glory. She smiled. All these people walking by and none of them realized he was alive.

She jumped up and waved to grab his attention.

He didn't move.

She jumped again.

Nothing.

He wasn't moving. He wasn't pretending. He was rock. Solid, hard rock. Just like the lump that had formed in her gut.

She raced towards the building, flew past the doorman who tried to stop her from entering and made it into the elevator. The other occupants stepped back, stared at her. She caught a glimpse of herself in the polished metal doors – hair tangled, eyes wild. She looked like someone who'd missed her meds, someone who believed in gargoyles.

She ignored the thought, darted from the elevator as soon as the doors opened. The room that led to Mord's ledge was empty. It was easy to get in, to slide up the window and crawl along the ledge.

He was there – beautiful, perfect. She whispered his name, reached out to touch him, and felt a hand wrap around her ankle. She heard a woman's voice shrieking, a man speaking softly as he pulled her in off the ledge. "You're fine now. Someone is coming."

But she wasn't fine. They didn't understand. She wasn't fine because Mord wasn't with her. She was alone. Again.

Months had passed. Months filled with medications and doctors, telling Kami gargoyles were just statues, that her vivid fantasies had caused her to somehow crash her car and cause a terrible accident that had almost killed a man.

She'd taken to walking the streets at night, staring up at the building, at Mord. He was always there, never moved.

The doctors were right. He wasn't alive, but it couldn't have all been a dream. It couldn't have.

The wind whistled past Mord's face. Another night, awake, alone. He'd travelled the city, searched to see if other gargoyles were awake, if the chimeras were awake. None were. He was alone.

His search for the sorcerer had also been futile.

Then he'd turned his attention to the Mason. The man had a warehouse full of statues, each intricately crafted, each a mix of man and beast. An army of chimeras, but locked in stone. Mord had walked among them in the deep of night. None had stirred. The Mason had to be building a force of chimeras, planning to use Kami to bring them to life. Was he alone? Or were there others in on his plan?

If Mord hadn't been so fixated on saving Kami, he might know the answer. But he'd reacted to the danger to Kami with no thought of saving the one man that might have the information he needed to keep the world safe – The Mason. He'd risked everything for one human: Kami. It couldn't happen again.

He gazed down, only his eyes lowering. Kami was below on the street, watching again. Every night she'd watched, appeared at erratic intervals. She needed to give up, move on. He couldn't be with her. A part of him said he couldn't even afford to allow her to live. Yes, she could bring the gargoyles back to life, but she could also be used against them. If she were dead, that risk would be gone.

At first he'd told himself he'd use her to awaken the gargoyles, then eliminate her once the job was done. But he knew that was a lie. He knew if he allowed himself to get that close to her, he'd weaken and think of another reason to spare her. But as long as the chimeras remained asleep, all would be well. Which brought him back to killing Kami.

But he was weak, couldn't bring himself to do it.

Night after night, she appeared, as if to torture him. And night after night he fought the same battle inside himself, between his head and his heart; the latter, an organ he hadn't had to deal with before meeting Kami. Which one would win?

"One last time," Kami told herself through her tears. She'd bribed a member of the cleaning crew, bought her way back into the building, and out onto the ledge. The crew was gone now, everyone was gone. Even the streets were empty.

There was no one here but her and Mord.

She inched forwards. Ran her hand down his arm. He was cold, still, stone.

*   *   *

She was here. Mord tried to stop his heart from beating, tried to stay in his stony state. If he revealed that he was alive, he'd have to make the choice. Do his duty and kill her? Or go with his heart and let her live?

Her hand grazed his arm, warm and supple. His body tingled, the feeling of life flowing into him almost painful. He gritted his teeth. Why wouldn't she give up?

"Mord?" Her voice caught. "Mord?" A whisper. Her fingers trailed down his side.

He kept his gaze firm – straight ahead.

"I love you." She pressed a kiss against his shoulder, started to move backwards, towards the window.

He'd won. She'd given up.

Then he heard it, a sob. He felt the moisture she'd left behind on his skin.

She was crying, over him.

He tried to resist, tried to stop himself, but couldn't. Couldn't deny any longer that the magic wasn't temporary. It had changed him. He loved this human, enough that he would risk anything, everything, to keep her safe.

He stepped forwards, off of the ledge. He spread his wings behind him and hovered behind Kami. "I love you too."

She froze, twisted too quickly, and fell. But Mord was there to catch her. Just like he would always be.

The Lighthouse Keeper and His Wife

Sara Mackenzie

She placed her hands on the man's face. He lay still, his flesh
cold, giving the impression of death. But the Sorceress knew
better. Beneath the chill flowed warm blood, just waiting for the
moment to spark into life. His eyelashes flickered. She began to
chant the words of waking, her voice soft at first and then rising,
growing louder and louder until it echoed about the high-
vaulted cathedral. The incense-laden air vibrated.

His eyes opened, one as dark and shining as jet, the other dull
and sightless. There was a scar running down his cheek where
the ship's wooden spar had caught him, blinding him and
tearing his flesh. He should have died in the storm that wrecked
his ship, rather than later, when he was the lighthouse keeper,
trying to save drowning passengers from a sinking steamer.

"Why have you woken me?" Zek asked, his voice ragged from
disuse.

"Because you have work to do," the Sorceress said sternly,
her blue eyes burning bright, her long red hair loose about her
face.

He struggled to sit up. His dark hair was tied back in a
seaman's pigtail, his skin tanned from all weathers. This was a
man who'd spent his life outside in the wind and the sun, and
who relished pitting himself against the elements.

He knew who she was: the Sorceress, the ruler of the between-worlds otherwise known as purgatory. It was her practice
to choose certain mortals, those she considered had not reached

their full potential during their original lifetime and, when the time was right, return them to the living world for a second chance.

"I am sending you back to the mortal world," she told him now. "You must put right the wrong. All those lives lost. You must save them and at the same time help me to capture the monster responsible."

He looked up at her, his one good eye glittering in the candlelight, the other dead and empty. She waited for him to argue with her, tell her he couldn't possibly do any such thing. But he surprised her.

"If I am to help you, I want something in return."

Anger flashed in her eyes. "I am giving you a second chance at life and you ask for more?"

"There is someone I have to find. My wife, Isabel. I long for her. I ache for her. Will you help me find her again?"

The Sorceress smiled. "Ah, you speak of love. Or is it lust?"

He smiled back, but she knew his heart was racing.

"She has been reborn into another time, into another body. Her life with you is over. There are some rules that even I cannot break, Zek."

"I don't care about the rules. I want my wife back again. I will only help you if you grant my wish."

"I could send you into the pit for eternity." Her voice was a growl. "Obey me, mortal."

Most men would have backed down, but not this one. "Not without her."

The Sorceress smiled; his reckless courage amused her. She had chosen well because he would need both those attributes to complete her task. "I will find your wife and you will help me capture the monster."

Zek knew he'd won. He bowed his head, relieved to take his gaze from the Sorceress' terrible beauty. When he looked again there was no one there. The flapping of wings made him look up. There was a large bird soaring into the shadows. A moment later the chapel was empty and he was alone.

Moving slowly, he swung his legs over the edge of the tomb and dropped to his feet on the marble floor. Memory was returning to him, slow and creaky, like a wheel that hasn't been used for a very long time. There had been a storm. No, two storms. One had taken his ship, and the second many, many lives. He died trying to save them, knowing it was his fault, the voice of the monster ringing in his ears.

The bird was back. He could hear the flapping of its wings getting louder, and just for a moment he saw the Sorceress' face where the bird's should have been – her blue eyes like daggers. There was a rush and groan of air, and then he was whirling and tumbling.

Back into the mortal world.

Back into his own past.

Izzy was dreaming again. The wind was blowing hard against her face, and she clung to the man beside her, afraid she'd fall. Below the lighthouse the waves were crashing against the cliffs, the spume flung high, wetting her skin and stinging her eyes.

"There!" he shouted, his arm pointing.

The lights of the passenger steamer were barely visible through the storm. Izzy imagined the rocks, sharp and murderous, waiting beneath the roiling sea. All those lives in danger, and it was only the lighthouse keeping them safe. Zek's lighthouse. She was so proud of him.

He turned to her as if she'd spoken aloud, and she pressed into his arms, feeling the wet warmth of his skin against hers, the sigh of his breath in her ear. "Isabel . . ."

Behind him something unimaginable was rising from the waves. Like a mountain it slid from the sea, water sloughing off slick, blue flesh, tangled white hair strewn with kelp, a face full of fury, broad shoulders, a barrel torso marked with strange designs and, instead of legs, a tail like a fish. A mythical monster from the deep. She had no words for it, but Zek did.

"Neptune."

The light from the lighthouse went out.

And that was when Izzy woke, lying dazed in her bed, reminding herself that the dream would pass. It always did.

A finger brushed her cheek, warm, gentle, the fingertip callused. Definitely male. "Isabel . . ."

Izzy froze. No one called her Isabel, not even her family or her ex-husband. Well, there was someone, but he was just a dream, a fantasy figure, he didn't exist.

The man who didn't exist touched her face again, this time with his lips. She felt him ease his body onto the bed beside her. Izzy told herself she should be afraid, she should scream for help, but she wasn't afraid. This was a man she knew as well as herself, and she didn't want to scream. In fact there was a humming of desire deep inside her that was growing by the second. Dreaming of making love was all very well, but it was nothing to the real thing.

"Isabel," he murmured.

She didn't open her eyes. Keeping them closed meant the fantasy was still that – a fantasy – and if she opened them and he wasn't really there at all, Izzy knew she'd be shattered. "Zek?" she breathed, reaching up. His face, dear God, she could feel his face. The patch over his eye, the thin line of his smiling mouth, the way his hair was tied back at the nape.

He kissed her fingers, then her lips, and the humming of desire turned into a roar. "Open your eyes," he commanded. "I'm here. I'm real."

Slowly, a little bit at a time, she did open them. He was looking down at her from the shadows, just as she knew he would be. "Zek?" His name was so dear, so familiar on her lips.

"I've found you. My love, my wife, my Isabel."

She wanted to say that no, she wasn't his wife, she wasn't *that* Isabel, and yet it felt as if she was. They were meant to be together. And just like that she was in his arms and their bodies moulded and moved, passion built and crested, and when it was over she drifted in the warm contentment of perfect sleep.

Zek stood in the shadows by the bed, watching her sleep. This was the woman he loved, and yet it wasn't. She was physically different with her fair hair and blue eyes and lithe body – reborn, the Sorceress had said – but he knew inside she was the same. Did she remember him? He thought that in some part of her mind and heart she did recognize him. Certainly she'd given herself to him willingly, eagerly. He'd found her, his Isabel, and if life was fair they could remain together forever.

But as he knew all too well, life wasn't fair. The Sorceress had kept her promise and now he must keep his, and it would more than likely end in his death. Only this time there would be no coming back.

By the time Izzy woke it was early afternoon. She was late. As she rushed about, showering and dressing, she tried to suspend her thoughts. Zek had come to her and she'd held him in her arms and loved him. Her dream man was real – or was he? Was the whole experience some sort of bizarre fantasy with a long medical name attached to it? There were so many unanswered questions in her head, but there was no time now to try to sort them out.

She had her job to go to and it was safer for her sanity to concentrate on that.

The job had been a real windfall for Izzy. There wasn't a great deal of employment to be found in a small town like Neptune's Bay – not out of the tourist season, anyway. Izzy had lived here for two years now, eighteen months on her own. Marriages didn't always work out, she knew that, but hers must have been one of the shortest in living history. Six months and he was gone, back to the city, and Izzy was left in the rundown weatherboard cottage in which, together, they'd planned to grow old.

When he left, Izzy had a choice: she could follow him back to the city, where her friends and family would have welcomed her warmly, or strike out on her own in Neptune's Bay. She'd chosen the latter option and, although since then there had been bad days, dark days, she'd never really regretted it. From the moment she saw this place she'd known she belonged here.

And soon after her husband had left, the dreams had begun. They weren't always exactly the same but they were always about the lighthouse and the storm, and Zek Cole and her need of him. It was as if she had been drawn to this little town for a reason.

Neptune's Bay was a holiday village, and in summer it swelled tenfold, only returning to normality when winter began to blast. The old lighthouse stood on the western point of the bay, high on the rocky cliffs that dropped dizzyingly to the heaving waters below. There was a new lighthouse now, further along the coast, its light automated but no less crucial to the well-being of ships passing out to sea. There had been a great many wrecks over the years.

The most infamous was in 1864. The *Maggie Mackenzie*, a steamship carrying nearly 200 passengers – emigrants from the Old World to the New – had been on her way around the point in a storm. She was seeking shelter in Neptune's Bay when she struck the jagged line of rocks beyond the point, and sank with the loss of all aboard.

Izzy knew the story well because she had to repeat it every Sunday as part of her new job as official tour guide. The old lighthouse and its adjacent buildings were retained under a heritage classification, and the tourists were lining up to visit the place. Izzy entertained them each Sunday, and she was good at it. Every time she told the dreadful tale of the *Maggie Mackenzie* she would find herself adding to it, embellishing the storm, the cries of the drowning, the horror of those who watched from the shore. It was so tangible it was almost as if she'd been there herself. Sometimes she felt as if she had, so often did she dream about that storm and the lighthouse and Zek Cole.

Captain Ezekiel Cole was the keeper of the lighthouse when the *Maggie Mackenzie* struck the rocks in 1864. Izzy knew what he looked like because there was a portrait of him, and because of her dreams – although she didn't know which had come first. The portrait hung inside the lighthouse, so that when she opened the door and walked into the chilly interior, there he was, staring straight at her.

The sight of his face took her breath away every time.

His black eyepatch made him look like a pirate, while his remaining eye stared out at her, dark and brooding. His mouth was a thin line, as if he was keeping whatever he wanted to say to himself, and there was a taut, anguished look to his face which made Izzy think he must be tormented by what had happened. And, of course, he had a reason to suffer. History had laid the tragedy at his door and made his name poison. When the steamer struck the rocks she had no warning, no chance of avoiding her watery fate, because the lantern in the lighthouse had been snuffed out.

Captain Zek had drowned that night, and his wife had never spoken of it, but everyone believed he had been drunk and failed to light the lantern. At least, they said, he'd tried to redeem himself by giving up his own life in his attempt to save those drowning, but it was a case of too little, too late in the eyes of the world.

And yet Izzy didn't believe it. What about her dreams and the sea monster from the deep? What about the sense, every time she saw his face, that he was trying to communicate with her? (Although it was difficult to know how she could help a man who'd been dead for over a century and a half.)

Izzy had been haunted by the handsome lighthouse keeper long before he had appeared in her bed.

Zek's head was spinning. He lowered it into his hands, as if that would ease the pain. He'd lost the sight in one eye sailing his ship from Nantucket to Sydney. There'd been an atrocious storm, and a broken spar hit him in the face. He'd fallen into the vast Pacific, half-conscious, tangled among torn sails and sodden ropes. He'd known he was going to die, but something inside him railed against his fate and that of his crew. He was a good captain and he didn't deserve this – it wasn't fair. He wasn't normally superstitious, but suddenly he'd felt the invisible presence of something far more powerful than he.

Neptune, god of the sea, was peering into his heart and brain. A desperate Zek made the mistake of bargaining with the monster.

"Let me live," he'd pleaded. *"Neptune, let me live and I will grant you whatever you ask of me."*

I will let you live. But when the time comes you will give me whatever I ask in return for your life. Remember this, mortal, for there is no changing your mind once our deal is struck.

The voice boomed in his head like waves in a sea cave. He told himself he had no choice but to agree. Flailing among the debris, struggling for the surface, he'd felt something cold and immense brush by him, and suddenly he was free.

He found a new strength and used the fallen mast to haul himself back on board his ship. He and his men fought on, until the storm had blown itself out and all was calm. But the ship was badly damaged and the cargo lost, and when they limped into port he'd seen the lighthouse. Then and there he'd decided to become the lighthouse keeper of Neptune's Bay. He told himself it was appropriate, since Neptune had saved his life. But deep in his heart he knew he was afraid of the bargain he'd made and what it might mean if he put to sea again.

Soon he'd met Isabel, and together they'd made their lives in the lighthouse. Zek forgot about Neptune's bargain – pushing it far back into his mind – and instead thought himself the luckiest man in the world; he'd survived a shipwreck and found love. But what he didn't realize was that it wasn't luck at all. Neptune was simply waiting until Zek had something in his possession that the god wanted for himself.

Now he lifted his head from his hands and tried to focus. The Sorceress had told him she would send him back, and he must save all those lost lives and capture the monster. But he'd failed once. How could he change the outcome this time?

He blinked again, and realized he was in the stairwell of the lighthouse, *his* lighthouse, gazing through the thick glass porthole. Outside it was a fine day, the sun shining like the blade of a sword through a gap in the clouds, and turning the dark seething seawater to brilliant emerald. Towards the horizon he could see rain approaching, the edge of a storm.

There was a sense of something else approaching, something as old as the ocean itself. Neptune knew he was back, and it wouldn't be long until the monster came calling.

Zek began to climb the stairs, around and up, until he reached the trapdoor. It was closed but not bolted from above, and when he heaved at it the door lifted. He climbed through and at last he was standing in the room that housed the very heart of the lighthouse – the lantern room.

It was like a living thing. The reflectors and the lamps revolved within their frame, flashing light that could be seen many miles out to sea. He had worked day and night to keep the oil up to the wicks, the wicks trimmed and the reflectors clean. He'd known how important his job was. At night, Isabel had come with him, sitting and watching, her face dreamy in the starlight. They'd talked about their plans, about their life together, never imagining it could end so soon.

Now, as he looked about the lantern room, everything appeared the same. When he peered through the windows towards Neptune's Bay, he saw that the rain had closed in. He started to pace around the light, as he used to, lost in his own thoughts.

Izzy unlocked the lighthouse door. The wood was thick and marked by time, and sometimes the damp warped it so that it stuck at the bottom. Today was one of those days, and she used her shoulder to force it open. The air inside was cool and still, and the portrait met her gaze from the opposite wall. As if he'd been waiting for her.

"Good morning, Zek," she said softly.

Good morning, Isabel.

"I dreamed about you again. At least, I think it was a dream."

Tell me about it.

"There was a storm and the steamer was heading for the rocks and then the sea monster came up out of the waves and I knew you were going to die. I didn't want you to die. I didn't want you to leave me."

The portrait seemed to understand.

"And then, this morning, it was as if you were there with me, in my bed. How can that be?"

He had no answer.

"I feel so lonely here without you," she whispered. "I don't care if you are a dream, I want you back."

There was a sound.

Startled, Isabel looked up.

There it was again – a thumping noise. The sound of the trapdoor into the lantern room closing! Even as Izzy began to move towards the stairs, she heard footsteps coming down. There was someone else in the lighthouse.

The hairs rose on her arms despite her warm sweater. She was unable to move, her feet rooted to the floor, as the steps came closer. A hand rested on the railing above her, a masculine hand. Suddenly, now she could move. Fear sent her stumbling towards the door, her hands grasping for the latch, but the warped wood was stuck fast. She heaved at it, gasping, making little sounds of terror. It wouldn't budge.

The man was coming closer, his steps echoing throughout the lighthouse like approaching thunder.

Izzy spun around, her back to the door, ready to fight for her life, just as he came around the last twist in the stairs. He was breathing quickly, his chest rising and falling. She saw it all: the eyepatch, the old-fashioned clothes, the so-familiar face.

"Isabel?" he said, and his voice was exactly as she heard it in her dreams.

Zek Cole was standing before her and he was smiling, his drawn face alight at the sight of her. He knew her, just as she knew him.

"How can this be?" she managed. "You're really here."

"I really am," he said softly, as if afraid he might send her running in terror. "The Sorceress is the queen of time and, if she wishes it, time can be made meaningless. She's brought us together again."

"Again? But I'm not your wife . . ." Then why did she feel as if she was?

"You *are* my wife." He said it fiercely. "The Sorceress told me you had been reborn, while I remained sleeping in the between-worlds, but it makes no difference. We were made to be together."

Too much information, she thought shakily, too much to take in. "The Sorceress?"

"I asked her to reunite us, and in return I must face the monster Neptune and help her to capture him."

Suddenly it was all too real. Izzy shook her head.

He was moving closer, and there was no humour in his dark eye, only love and longing. "I have been waiting to see you again."

"I've been waiting too," she said. "I'm so glad . . . so glad you're here at last."

Emotion overwhelmed her, and she pushed herself away from the door and ran on trembling legs into his arms. He was wiry and strong, his body hard from years of physical work, but he held her as if she were something very precious, and his breath against her cheek was warm and alive. Just as it always was in her dreams.

"You're mine," he said, "and I am yours."

She believed him. As fantastical as his words were, she felt their truth at her very core.

Izzy turned her face, her lips brushing his. He cupped the back of her head in his palm and began to kiss her. Deep, passionate, longing kisses.

"All the years alone," he murmured, pressing his face to her hair, kissing her temples, her cheeks. "Lying sleeping in the between-worlds, and waiting. And now I've found you again, Isabel."

Izzy lifted his face in her hands, feeling the rough stubble. As much as she wanted to lose herself in this remarkable moment she knew it couldn't be that simple. There was something poignant in his smile, a tragic edge.

"I remember . . . last time you faced Neptune you died. I stood safe in the lighthouse and saw it all. Please, I beg you, don't risk your life again."

Suddenly a squall hit the lighthouse, seeming to rock the very structure with its violence. Wind moaned up the stairs and rain lashed the porthole windows. It felt as if they were on a ship and under siege from the elements.

"He's coming," Zek said bleakly.

The memory was sharp in her brain – the cold blue skin rising from the sea, the dark predatory eyes that didn't blink, the dorsal fin stretching sharp along its spine. How could anyone fight such a creature and survive?

"We need to leave," she gasped, urgently pulling at his hand. "We must go. Now."

His face was calm, his gaze tender. "It's too late, Isabel. I've given my word and I can't go back on it."

"No." Izzy heard him but she refused to believe. She spun around towards the door and wrenched at the handle, tugging hard. To her surprise this time it came open a foot, and she squeezed through the narrow gap, shouting for him to follow.

Immediately her hair was tossed into her face, the salty air stinging her eyes. She took one step towards the paved path that led through the ticket office and into the restored keeper's residence.

And froze.

Her heart beat hard, the blood rushed in her ears, but she could hear neither above the whining of the wind and the crashing of the surf against the rocks below the lighthouse. The paved path was gone and in its place was a muddy track between tufts of grass. The residence was different too and, when she looked down over the wild waters of the bay, the town was not the one she knew at all. The houses were smaller, older, and smoke rose from the chimneys before being whipped into a frenzy by the gale.

She had been transported to another world: Zek Cole's world.

Izzy spun back towards the lighthouse, angry and frightened, and found the door shut against her. She began to pound her fists against the rough wood until it opened. He stood there. His chest was rising and falling quickly, his face coloured by the eerie light from the storm outside. A crackle of lightning tore through the sky, striking the ground behind her, and she screamed. He grabbed her and dragged her inside, and let the wild wind close the door behind them.

"Make it stop," Izzy shrieked. "Make it all go away."

"I can't stop it," he growled. "Not until it's finished. I told you. I have sworn to the Sorceress – I give her Neptune and she gives me you. I have to do what she wants. Only then can we be free to be together. I know last time Neptune won, but this time things will be different."

Izzy wiped the dripping rain from her eyes. "I can't remember everything that happened last time. My dreams are fragments . . . bits and pieces. Sometimes I think it's as if I can't bear to remember it all."

He gave her a long look. "Come with me," he said, "and I will tell you."

She didn't want to go; she didn't want to be here. Zek Cole was a man who'd been dead for over a century and a half, a man vilified by history, and yet he said she was his wife and he loved her. Madness, it was madness, she thought wildly, as for a brief moment commonsense reasserted itself.

And then he turned and looked at her and held out his hand. "Isabel?"

Izzy felt her feet moving, felt the warm strength of her hand in his, as she followed him up the steep staircase that twisted around and around to the top of the lighthouse.

*   *   *

Zek could hear her footsteps behind him. Her clothing was unfamiliar, the blue trousers and the knitted sweater manly, but there was certainly no way he could mistake her for anything other than a woman. The tight fit of her clothing around her curves, the soft line of her mouth, her long, curling fair hair were all very feminine.

In other ways, too, she was different to his Isabel – stronger, less inclined to obey him without question – and this worried him. Last time Isabel had stayed safe up in the lighthouse while he faced Neptune. Would she be so easily persuaded this time?

He had promised to do the Sorceress' bidding in return for finding Isabel, and now all he wanted was to keep her.

He stood on the landing and waited for her to catch up. By the time she reached his side he'd decided there was no right way to tell his story, so he simply began to speak. While he spoke, the images crowded in on him.

He explained to her about the bargain he'd made with Neptune on the voyage from Nantucket, and how in return his life and that of his crew was spared. "In time I forgot about it, or pretended I had. And then the storm came and the steamer was heading for the rocks."

That storm was like nothing he'd ever seen before, nothing he'd ever experienced. The wild tearing at the very fabric of the lighthouse, the pounding against the thick-glassed windows, as if the wind and rain wanted to come inside and attack him.

"We were up in the lantern room. I wanted to be sure all was well and that the lamps were burning bright. And that was when we saw him."

"I know," she whispered, "I remember that part." She shuddered. "The light went out."

"Yes," he said bleakly, "the light went out, and nothing I did would relight it. Without the light the only chance I had of warning the steamer about the rocks was to send off some rockets."

"You told me to wait here for you."

"I went out into the storm. It was so bad I could hardly see anything. I took the rockets out onto the edge of the cliffs . . ."

"He was waiting for you. Neptune."

She was shaking, and gripped her fingers together tightly. He could see her remembering the monster rising up through the waves, the seawater pouring from its blue skin, black eyes without any whites, unblinking and with nothing human about them. *Mortal,* it had said, its voice deep and hollow, *I am here to claim what is mine. We struck a deal and now it is time for you to honour it.*

"The steamer," Isabel murmured, her face chalky. "He'd come for the steamer and all those lives."

Zek didn't disillusion her. "I tried to light the rocket but I fumbled. Nothing was working and I understood then that Neptune was controlling matters. He could have squashed me flat with his hand, but that wasn't what he wanted."

"I know you did everything you could to save the steamer. You lost your life . . ."

She didn't understand; she didn't know the truth, and he wasn't going to tell her. Heart in his mouth, he remembered how he'd watched Neptune's black eyes peering into the lantern room. Isabel was standing, silhouetted against the faint light from the single lamp she was holding, and a smile curled the monster's lipless mouth. The unblinking gaze dropped to his again, and Zek saw the greed.

It was Isabel the monster wanted.

He had stood, frozen, and listened to the steamer's keel grinding against the rocks, and even though the wind was screaming he could hear the cries of the passengers and crew as they realized they were about to drown. And all the while the monster had stared back at him, enjoying his pain, and knowing there would come a point where he could no longer bear it.

I will give you my life, Neptune. Take me instead. Please . . .

No, mortal. I want Isabel. Give her to me.

The steamer was going down, the screams heart-wrenchingly desperate, more so because Zek knew it was impossible for him to save them. But it was equally impossible for him not to try, although he knew he would drown in the attempt. He'd turned to look up at Isabel, a final glance, thinking that at least she was safe. Then he'd dived from the cliff into the swirling, violent sea.

"Zek?"

Izzy felt another gust of wind strike the outside of the lighthouse, shaking it. Rain splattered. Lightning flashed, illuminating a violent world, before the thunder followed.

"This is the same storm, isn't it? The Sorceress has taken us back in time so that we can get it right."

"Yes."

"Well then, we *will* get it right. We have to. I can't live another 150 years without you, not again. We'll do whatever we have to."

He smiled, but it was a wary smile, and she almost laughed. It was becoming obvious to her that she was far more forceful and independent than the Isabel he'd known before. Just as well, considering what they had to do. She had no intention of waiting patiently in the lantern room while her man went out, alone, to save the world. This time her place would be right by his side.

They'd reached the trapdoor into the lantern room and climbed through. Time really had jumped backwards because the old, unused lamps were burning brightly and, as she stared, the lighthouse flashed out a warning over the waters below.

Zek was up and about, checking that all was in order, his movements full of confidence and long practice. This was his lighthouse, his job, and Izzy felt an ache in her heart as she remembered the way his name had been vilified all these years.

As he worked she stood, peering through the glass walls. The weather encircled them, pounding for entry, driving hail and spitting rain, as if it wanted to destroy them.

"Dear God," she whispered, as the lights of the steamer flickered out to sea.

And he was beside her, his face a peculiar shade of green in the storm's light. Once again he reached out for her hand. It seemed natural, and just as natural when she grasped his fingers, entangling them with hers, finding comfort in his touch.

"Neptune is an old god. He gains his power from the sea and those lost within it. The lighthouse is a bulwark against his storms and he'd like nothing better than to tear it down."

"So . . . what is the plan?" she said, taking a wobbly breath.

He looked at her and smiled. "I've come from the between-worlds, Isabel. I'm somewhere halfway between life and death, so I'm not entirely human either. That might give me the edge I didn't have when I faced him before."

As if in response to his words, the lantern room was plunged into darkness.

There was a tremendous roar from beyond the cliffs. Not thunder, not this time.

She'd dreamed about this, and now she wished it was still a dream. Neptune was coming up out of the waves, flesh shining an eerie blue, white hair long and wet and wriggling like a nest of sea serpents. It . . . he . . . was immense, a veritable monster, and as he rose to his full height he was as tall as the cliff and the lighthouse combined. His eyes had no white in them at all. They were shining like ebony as he gazed into the dark lantern room.

"Mortal!" he roared. "I have come."

Izzy was aware of Zek's arm tight around her. He was warm and strong, not like a dead man at all, and his breath stirred her hair as he spoke. "It is time for me to go down. Stay here."

"No! We go together."

He shook his head. "Stay here."

"I'm coming with you," she said stubbornly. "This time we'll face him together."

He opened his mouth again, but someone else spoke before he could get the words out.

"Tell her the truth, Zek. Tell her what Neptune really wants."

Izzy gasped, gaze flying to the opposite side of the lantern room. A woman in a long white dress stood there, her red hair loose, her eyes a brilliant blue. After one glance, she found she could not meet the woman's stare directly – the pain was too intense.

"No, Sorceress," her man said, "I will do this my way."

"Doing it your way wasn't so successful before," the Sorceress retorted with a nasty little smile. "Tell her. You say you love her. I believe you must do; you saved her last time at the cost of yourself and all those others. Trust her, let her stand with you. Learn from your mistakes, that's why you're here."

Then it suddenly all made sense. Neptune had saved Zek, and then he'd demanded Isabel in return. Not the steamer after all.

"It's me he wants," she whispered. "Isn't it? It was always me."

Neptune roared, his tail slammed down on the sea's surface and a huge wave of spume rose against the lighthouse. When the air cleared again, the nearing lights of the steamer were visible through the water running down the glass.

"Yes, Neptune wants you," he admitted. "He told me he would save the steamer if I gave you to him. I said no."

"But all those people . . . the passengers aboard the steamer . . ."

"I said no, Isabel."

Her mouth went stubborn and straight, and Zek watched it with fascination. It was Isabel's mouth and yet it wasn't. "This time he'll get what he wants."

"No!"

Tears drowned her eyes, overflowing. "Do you know what they've said about you all these years? How they've blamed you and blackened your name and destroyed your character? I won't let it happen this time. You don't deserve it. You saved my life and now it's in my power to put history right, and that's what I'm going to do."

She moved away, towards the trapdoor, but his quiet resigned words stopped her.

"We'll go together."

She felt a jumble of fear and relief, and the next moment they were through the trapdoor and running down the winding stairs. The wind dropped when they reached the door, and Zek was able to open it without too much of a struggle. She followed him out into the spitting rain, clinging to the wall of the lighthouse as they rounded it and made their way towards the cliff edge.

Before them, the massive form of Neptune was swaying in the storm and, behind him, Izzy could see the looming shape of the steamer approaching the rocks.

History must not be repeated, she told herself. If necessary she would give her life to save the others. To save her husband. An odd calmness came over her as she gazed over the dizzying drop to the water below, to where the god of the sea waited.

Zek stepped in front of her, spread his arms wide and threw back his head. "I'm here, my lord Neptune!" he shouted into the wind.

Neptune's oily eyes gleamed and his hair writhed. He swooped down, his face half fish and half man, and hovered over them. His mouth opened to show long sharp teeth. "I saved your life, now I'm here to collect on the deal, Captain Cole. The time has come to pay up."

"Tell me what you want," Zek said, but he was only playing for time.

"Isabel," the monster said, his voice hissing like spray against the rocks. He smiled as she stepped out from the shadows.

Zek wanted to turn her around and run with her back to the lighthouse, to safety, but he forced himself to remain still. The Sorceress was right, Isabel was right – they needed to face this together.

Izzy spoke calmly, as if she dealt with sea gods every day of the week. "I want you to bring back the light and save the passenger steamer."

The unblinking eyes fixed on her. "Why should I?"

"You said you wanted me. I'm here. Now do as I say."

Neptune laughed. Behind him they could see the steamer struggling in the storm, all those souls aboard.

"Come with me," Neptune hissed. "I command it, Isabel."

"Not until you turn the light back on," she shouted, angry and desperate.

But the monster just laughed, and suddenly they knew the truth. "You never meant to save the steamer, did you? If I hadn't died and negated our deal, you would have come back over and over again. Isabel was just an excuse to make me give you the steamer. There would have been another ship after that, and then another."

The monster's eyes were cold and pitiless. "Those who go to sea must pay a price. I only ask for what is fair."

"How is that fair?" Izzy cried.

"A life given for a life saved," he hissed. "This is my domain and I make the rules."

"But here's the thing, Neptune. The days of the old gods are past, and if anyone makes the rules, then it's me." The Sorceress was standing beside them on the cliff top, her long red hair streaming in the wind, her arms raised, the crackle of blue lightning flying from her fingers.

"No!" he roared, his tail thumping on the surface, sending water streaming into the air around him.

"Neptune, come with me," she shouted, her voice like a sonic boom.

"You cannot make me! I was in this world before you and your kind were even thought of. I belong here."

But the Sorceress had begun to sing, words with no meaning, weaving them into an achingly beautiful and yet terrifying song. The monster clasped his hands to his head and began to groan, and then he shook himself, trying to be rid of the sounds.

"You tricked me. This isn't fair . . ."

"I am the Sorceress and this isn't about being fair. I brought Zek back from the between-worlds so that he could redeem himself – become the hero he should have been. No, Neptune, I played you at your own game. You are a liar. You're not to be trusted. Isabel was willing to give up her life, but that wasn't enough for you. I knew you wouldn't stand by your word. You have no honour. Your time is over and you will leave here now."

Her words had hardly been spoken when Neptune began to vanish, fading like an old sepia photograph, until he was utterly gone.

Zek's hair was wet, plastered to his head, his clothes dripping, but he was alive. His eye glowed with passion as he drew Isabel into his arms, and they clung together as the storm began to wane.

"I have sent him somewhere he can do no more harm," the Sorceress said calmly, watching them. "When you called to him during the storm on your ship, you gave him the power to command you. If you'd let him, he would have sunk other ships and drowned many more people to satisfy his bloodlust."

"And now?" Izzy asked.

"See for yourself," the Sorceress said, looking up.

The lighthouse was shining out, warning of the rocks. The steamer was turning slowly but surely back to sea. The tragedy had been averted, the past was changed, and Zek had satisfied the Sorceress' commands.

The Sorceress met his gaze. "You want to know what will happen now."

He tightened his arm about Izzy. "I know what I *want* to happen now."

"A life together," Izzy said, pushing her dripping hair out of her eyes. "A long, happy, *uneventful* life together."

The Sorceress smiled. "Done."

A heartbeat later she was gone and they were alone on the cliff top. The storm was clearing and the sea growing calmer. It occurred to Izzy that she was now a resident in another time, but the lack of mod-cons was a small price to pay for all she'd gained.

"Will you be happy?" Zek asked, reading her mind.

"Yes." She cupped his face in her palms, kissing his cold lips to warmth. They turned back towards the lighthouse just as the sun came through the clouds, the rays weak at first but growing stronger, the lighthouse keeper and his wife.

Blood Song

Lynda Hilburn

"Are you sure you should walk home alone, Grace? Even in a small town like Boulder, women can't be too careful," a female voice called out.

Grace finished locking the door to her sound-healing studio and turned to the group of attendees still lingering on the sidewalk in front of the building. She looked into their sincere faces and smiled. It was the same every time. People got so energized after participating in the sound circle that they tried to stretch the evening out as long as possible. She, on the other hand, yearned for peace, quiet and a large glass of wine. After a session, she needed to be alone to recharge. Walking home through the quiet, tree-lined streets at the end of the evening had become a private pleasure.

Grinning, she reached into her shoulder bag and pulled out a small aerosol canister. "Don't worry about me." She raised the container. "I've got my trusty pepper spray. I'm armed and dangerous. Besides, my house is only a few blocks up the hill and, in all the years I've lived here, nobody's ever bothered me."

She almost mentioned she'd never even encountered a mountain lion, but decided not to broach the issue. It wouldn't be wise to give the group any more ideas about why she might need company – whether she wanted it or not. Nothing scary had ever happened to her – fanged predators or otherwise. Unfortunately, she thought, nothing exciting, either.

"I'll see you at the next sound circle." She waved and hurried down the street before the singers could foil her escape. She loved all her clients and circle members, but it had been a long week and it wasn't over yet.

Taking a couple of deep breaths, she felt herself begin to unwind. She walked until she came to a dead end, then turned towards the foothills, climbing the gentle trail that led to her house. She gazed up and smiled. The full moon illuminated the peaks of the Rocky Mountains, outlining them in breathtaking detail against the star-studded tapestry of the night sky. Lights from the houses sprinkled across the canyon glittered like suspended fireflies in the magical darkness.

The late summer air held a subtle hint of fall, her favourite season, and she fantasized about the autumn equinox sound ritual she'd be creating again this year. She had invited sound healers from all over the world to participate. Thinking about the event, she remembered the face of the handsome Brazilian musician she'd met at the summer solstice celebration in Rio.

He'd smiled at her with those amazing, full lips – displaying wicked dimples and beautiful white teeth – and she'd lost the ability to speak. His eyes were the colour of the Mediterranean Sea, and she'd longed to dive in. That memory caused heat to shimmer through her body, and she unbuttoned her jacket.

Of course, she hadn't had the courage to take him up on his unspoken offer. So, what else was new?

She'd mailed him an invitation to her equinox ritual, and she didn't know what worried her more – that he wouldn't attend, or that he would.

She shook her head, thinking how pitiful it was that even the thought of the musician caused her body to overheat. She was too old for that kind of reaction. She wanted to get over her dating anxiety and find a relationship – like a normal woman. How could she be so confident as a performer and healer, yet such a basket case about men? Why did she turn into a tongue-tied teenager every time a handsome guy came near?

A rustling sound a few feet away snapped her attention from the Brazilian. Startled, she stopped and raised the pepper spray, scanned the bushes and trees, and listened. Her heart pounded against her ribs, adrenaline shot through her system. That's what she got for being cavalier about mountain lions. She should know better. Simply because she'd never come across one of the beasts, didn't mean they weren't there. Her hands trembled so badly she almost lost her grip on the canister, and her knees threatened to fold. She'd heard that the deadly cats stalked their prey. Was one watching her now? Her mind spun as she tried to remember what the article in the newspaper said about the lions: try to look big and never run. Run? Even though that was what her brain demanded, she didn't think her legs could manage, since they seemed to be made of rubber.

She waited in the thick silence with her finger poised over the canister, her stomach tight. The seconds passed like hours. She finally let out a shuddering breath, relieved that her imagination had probably exaggerated the sound of a deer or a raccoon. She'd just relaxed her shoulders and taken a couple of shaky steps up the path, when something large burst out of the bushes.

Pivoting towards the movement, she screamed and pressed the spray button, sending a shower of the caustic substance into the eyes of a husky man who'd lunged at her, hands clutching, mouth gaping to reveal long, bloody fangs. He shrieked as the irritant coated his eyes and face, but still managed to tackle her ferociously, slamming her body down onto the asphalt path. Her canister bounced against the ground and rolled away.

The man – or whatever he was – had outrageous strength. He pressed against her like a concrete slab, easily holding her down, while madly swiping at his eyes with one of his hands. The treacherous, long, razor teeth she'd glimpsed as he'd leaped at her were poised over her neck, dripping saliva and blood. She could feel the slimy, wet substance oozing down her shirt as she choked on the hideous stench of his breath.

His long, dark hair hung filthy and stringy, his skin deathly pale, his clothing torn and foul.

She kicked and flailed, pushing against his powerful shoulder, trying to dislodge the unnatural, unbelievable beast. Her arms ached from the useless pounding, her throat went raw from screaming. His body weighed so heavy against her chest, she feared her ribs would snap any second. Her heart thundered in her ears as if about to explode from the terror.

He'd kept up a growling rumble, punctuated by yelps and

groans, as he frantically worked to clear his eyes and wipe his face.

Struggling for air, she made gasping noises, all the fight gone out of her limbs.

The tips of his pointed fangs broke through the skin of her neck, sending a wave of pain radiating down her body. *This is it!* As she braced for the expected horror, suddenly the monster was gone. His weight no longer pressed on her chest so she could breathe. Shocked, she blinked her eyes, realizing she must have closed them in her panic.

For a moment she felt certain she'd died – that the thing had torn out her throat or crushed her heart. She hadn't seen a white light or a tunnel. There were no idyllic scenes, no relatives coming to guide her to greener pastures. And it *was* strange that her body still hurt, but she had to be dead – there was simply no other possible explanation.

She'd looked up and seen the perfect face of an angel.

And then nothing.

"Shit!" Ethan yelled. He grabbed the back of the undead troublemaker's filthy shirt, jerked him off the woman and dangled him in the air. "Nelson! Come and take this disgusting specimen, would you?"

He turned his gaze to the frightened eyes of the beautiful woman sprawled on the path, gave her the command to "sleep", and watched her eyelids close.

Of all the rotten luck. He'd lost sight of the brainless newbie for one minute and look what happened? Of course there had to be a mortal walking around. Why didn't these humans stay in their houses at night, like they were supposed to?

Nelson crashed through the trees and retrieved the snarling bloodsucker from Ethan's grip. He locked eyes with the flailing fiend, gave him a suggestion to be still, then tossed the now quiet perpetrator across his shoulder. "Sneaky bastard almost got away, didn't he? I think we both need a vacation from this job."

Ethan snorted. "Yeah. That'll happen. Since Mordecai came to town and started turning out these mindless fools at an alarming rate, we're in greater demand than ever. There seems

to be no end to the number of these bloodsucking idiots we have
to track down and capture. Why does he only turn humans who
can't find their asses with a flashlight? Is stupidity the only
requirement for his recruits? If Alexander hadn't pissed off
Mordecai, and caused him to bring his grudge match to our
quiet little mountain town, we'd be dozing in our coffins and
watching reality TV right now."

"Yeah," Nelson laughed. "Fine way to talk about your lord
and master. Alexander's OK. He's just got a little bit of an
anger-control problem. And Mordecai knows exactly how to
push his buttons. But you know how it is with us vampires: one
drama after another. Angst is our middle name. If we weren't
focused on Mordecai's mindless minions, it would be something equally ridiculous. How else would we fill eternity?
Speaking of dramas – what are you going to do with the
delicious morsel our impolite friend intruded upon? You probably shouldn't leave her here. We aren't the only predators
prowling the area."

Ethan sighed and studied the woman. He had to admit she
was quite delectable. In the forty years he'd been undead, he'd
rarely paid more than passing attention to a mortal female. It
was simply too dangerous to be around most humans. The
bloodlust burned powerfully strong, and their fragile bodies
were no match for his hunger. He didn't have the age or ability
to ignore the urge to suck them dry. Every time he'd been
around humans he'd almost lost control of himself. Since he was
still sensitive enough to be bothered by useless slaughter, he
avoided temptation all together.

Of course, he had no problem drinking from the low-life drug
dealers, criminals and paedophiles who unknowingly volunteered to become his nightly entrees. Their blood tasted just as
sweet as any other, and he considered their executions to be acts
of public service. He'd even become remarkably talented at
disposing of the drained corpses, so he never broke the cardinal
rule of vampirism: remain hidden at all costs. In his world, it
was a true death sentence to betray the existence of the undead.

A slow smile spread his lips as he explored her body with his
gaze. This one was lovely. When she'd stared up at him with her
dark eyes, he'd had the odd notion that she was much older than

she appeared. But, strange ideas aside, Nelson was right. He couldn't just leave her as bait for the normal part of the animal kingdom.

"I'll carry her up to her house, wipe her memory of having crossed paths with our repulsive friend, and give her the suggestion that she'd merely arrived home and gone to bed. Go ahead and take your package back to Alexander's and dispose of him. I'll join you shortly."

Nelson smirked. "Why do you always get the good jobs?"

"Because I'm me and it sucks to be you," Ethan laughed. *Sucks to be all of us.*

Ethan heard Nelson tromp off through the bushes with his passenger, and he squatted down next to the woman. The scent of her blood enticed him – the pulsing vein in her exposed neck caused his fangs to descend. As his usual feeding trance threatened to enthral him, he argued with himself about whether or not to act on his immediate needs or take her home. His primal brain insisted he could simply drain her and dispose of the body – nobody would be the wiser. He was so hungry. But something about her gave him pause. An intriguing element he didn't want to destroy. In fact, the more he stared at her, the greater his curiosity about the pretty human. A faint voice in his head, a remnant of what he used to be, piped in to insist he wasn't an animal. He made the decision, willing himself to lock the bloodlust away.

He scooped her into his arms, scanned the area to make sure there weren't any other humans lurking about, and – satisfied they were alone – strode up the narrow path to the group of houses tucked away on the side of the mountain. It was pure luck, he thought, that nobody had heard the woman's screams. But he moved quickly, just in case rescuers were on their way.

Her scent loomed strong around her house. He decided she must walk the path often in order for the aroma to be so pervasive. The house smelled of herbs, coffee, flowers – and her.

She lived in a two-storey Victorian, the sleeping area upstairs. He carried her up to her bedroom, used one hand to pull the covers back on the bed, and settled her onto the soft mattress. Then he straightened, surveyed the area with his preternatural vision, and smiled.

Her room was colourful and feminine. He strolled around the
perimeter, studying the artwork, noting the musical instruments and appreciating the soft smells hovering around the
unlit scented candles. On a table in the corner, covered with a
vibrantly coloured cloth, lay a deck of tarot cards. He selected a
card and laughed: the devil. How appropriate. The walls were
adorned with photographs of the woman playing instruments in
various settings, along with diplomas from well-known uni-
versities. He read one of the diplomas. Grace Blackburn. *Her
name is Grace*. He paused in front of a framed newspaper article
about the opening of her sound studio on the Pearl Street Mall a
few years earlier. It didn't take a rocket scientist to figure out
she must be a musician.

I used to love music – a long time ago. In fact, I once hoped . . .
He immediately stomped on the useless thought, mentally
crushing it like a nasty bug. Nothing would be gained by
dwelling on the past. His existence had changed in the blink
of an eye and he had to face reality. Anything else was too
painful.

After exploring the human female's room, he found himself
strangely reluctant to leave. He tugged a wicker rocking chair
from the corner to the side of her bed and sat, watching her sleep.

If she knew what was in her room, she'd run screaming.
Something about this mortal woman made him feel oddly
peaceful. It was as if a relaxing energy emanated from her
person – like her actual physical body gave off a pleasant hum.
He imagined his skin warming from an invisible heat source. He
leaned in closer. Here he was, sitting beside a sleeping human
without drinking from her. What was wrong with him? Why
didn't he leave?

The expression on her face was sweet and innocent, like a
child's. He gazed down her curvy body and was reminded that
she definitely qualified as a grown-up woman. Her beautiful
blonde hair fanned out on the pillow, giving her an ethereal,
other-worldly appearance. Ivory skin shone translucent and
perfect. Full, soft-looking lips aroused his body. He wondered
how they'd taste.

That realization jolted him back to sanity and he leaped
quickly from the chair, then bent over the slumbering human.

"You will sleep through the night, experiencing only pleasant dreams, and will wake in the morning remembering an uneventful walk to your home the previous evening. You will feel relaxed and happy about your life."

Without thinking, he inhaled her aroma and pressed his lips to her forehead. "Goodnight, Grace."

What the hell, Ethan? You are so screwed up.

He bolted down the stairs, closed and locked her front door and ran with vampire speed back to the lair where his undead companions waited.

Grace woke to the sound of the telephone ringing.

She blinked her eyelids, which seemed overly heavy, and rolled towards the annoying noise coming from the bedside table.

"Hello?" she croaked.

"Grace? Is that you? What's wrong with your voice?"

"Uh-huh, it's me, Roz." She cleared her throat. "There's nothing wrong with my voice. I'm just groggy from sleeping."

"You're still sleeping? Are you sick?" her friend asked, anxiety elevating the pitch of her voice. "The only time I've ever known you sleep until noon is if you're too exhausted to get out of bed. Or you've sung yourself into a trance. Should I skip my yoga class and come over?"

Grace forced herself to sit up, which wasn't as easy as she would have expected. Maybe she *was* coming down with something. "Don't be silly, pal. I'm an adult woman who can take care of herself." She glanced at the clock, surprised. "You're right though. I don't usually sleep this late." She shook her head to clear away the strange mental cobwebs. "I had the most bizarre dream."

"Ah, a dream. Excellent. Right up my alley. What did you dream? Have you finally begun to explore your gift of prophecy? Roz sees all and knows all."

Grace chuckled. "I don't think so. Unless my future is filled with angels and vampires."

"Oh, yum! Angels and vampires. Maybe the dream represents the basic struggle between good and evil. You've always taken the high road, maybe you're ready to join me on the naughty side. Are you considering doing something wicked, my repressed friend?" She laughed.

"Not that I know of." *Yeah, as if the opportunity to make a wicked decision ever enters my life.* "Maybe I'm yearning for something unusual."

"Something unusual? Hmm. There's hope for you yet. What do you remember about the dream?"

"The strongest memory is the face of the angel who saved me from a fiend with fangs. My rescuer had long, dark hair, beautiful emerald eyes and pale skin. Hey! I just realized I dreamed in colour. That's weird for me. Even though the dream scene took place at night, I could still see the red blood dripping from the vampire's mouth and the green of the angel's eyes." She hooted out a laugh.

"What?"

"The angel wore a Rolling Stones T-shirt. The one with the big tongue. Not anyone's idea of standard celestial garb, I'd say."

"At least he had good taste. I'm encouraged that you're dreaming about a man. Remember what I told you . . ."

Grace snorted. "You mean your margarita-fuelled ramblings about my destiny? The man I'm supposed to meet? The one who'll rock my world?"

"Hey!" Roz pretended to be offended before assuming an obviously fake gypsy-fortune-teller accent. "You're trifling with an ancient prediction. Ignoring a prognostication passed down through the women of my family – the outcome of a revelation long awaited. Disregard at your own peril . . ."

"Chill, Madam Roz," Grace laughed. "Put away the crystal ball. I believe, I believe."

"OK then," Roz said, cheerfully speaking in her normal voice again. "Maybe your dream has deeper implications. I'll have to meditate on your symbols and see what I can conjure for you."

"Thanks," Grace sighed. "But I'm sure I can figure it out. I'll sing about it. Maybe I just watched too many horror movies as a kid."

Roz hesitated a few seconds. "You sound very serious this morning, Grace. Not yourself. Are you sure you don't want me to come over? I could cast a little healing spell – cook something chocolate in my cauldron. It's not a problem. I worry about you being alone so much."

Me too.

"You're sweet, Roz. I'm OK. I've got a busy afternoon with lessons and a recording session. Then tonight I have another sound circle. In fact, I'd better get to it. Thanks for calling. I probably would've slept all day if you hadn't."

"Well, if you're sure you're OK. I'm just a phone call away if you change your mind. Love you."

"You too."

Grace hung up.

She swung her legs over the side of the bed, still feeling slightly fuzzy. She hadn't felt so *off* since the last time she'd gotten carried away with champagne at a friend's wedding, and she was certain she hadn't consumed any alcohol in days. Unless she'd overindulged in her dream and had an imaginary hangover. Or maybe being in an angel's presence was intoxicating. She chuckled at the idea.

She shuffled into the bathroom, turned on the shower and stepped inside, thinking about the strange dream.

There was an air of mystery around the beautiful, phantom man with the green eyes. It was unusual for her to remember his face in such detail, after only a brief glimpse. She imagined herself running her fingers through his long silky hair and skimming her lips along the strong bones of his jaw. His features were almost too perfect, his body too buff. She laughed out loud.

Whoa! Get a hold of yourself, Grace! It was just a dream. A great dream, but all in your head.

The hot water felt wonderful against her bruised skin.

Wait a minute. Bruised skin? Why is my skin bruised? When did that happen?

She finished washing her body and hair, slashed the plastic curtain aside and angled over to the full-length mirror. Investigating all the tender spots, she discovered bruises on both elbows, her hips and an especially spectacular extravaganza near her tail bone.

As she pressed on the blue-purple skin of her hip she had a sudden memory flash of hitting the ground, hard.

What? I don't remember falling down. Did I roll out of bed onto the floor?

The pale face of the dream angel with the Rolling Stones T-shirt floated into her mind and she smiled, then shook her head.

How peculiar. She definitely didn't feel like herself today.

Ethan's eyes popped open the second the sun set.

Concentrating, he tried to understand the wispy, uncomfortable feeling he'd never had before. He couldn't shake the idea that he'd been . . . *interrupted*. Or something. Who knew what went on in his brain while he was dead during the daylight hours, but he had the craziest sense that he'd been *thinking* a few seconds ago when his life force (death force?) reanimated his body. His sire, Alexander, adamantly insisted vampires were simply empty shells while the sun ruled the sky, nothing but paralysed cadavers. But if that was true, Ethan must be losing his mind. Maybe he was. First he'd lurked around the human woman without fanging her and then he *dreamed*, of all damn things.

It was her. The mortal female. Grace. Her scent was all over him. She'd done something. He just knew it.

He sat up in one of the cardboard boxes that passed for coffins in the basement of the vampires' headquarters, gathered the bottom of his T-shirt under his nose so he could sniff it, and sighed. He flopped back, feeling suddenly as relaxed and limp as a drained meth addict. Even her smell melted his bones.

Compelled to see her, he quickly showered, changed into a fresh pair of jeans and a Jimi Hendrix T-shirt, ran a comb through his thick, dark hair and skulked out the hidden exit. It wouldn't do for Alexander to become too interested in his activities. The master had forbidden his offspring to take any action that wasn't a direct order or coven business. If the short-tempered vampire knew about Ethan's new obsession, there would be hell to pay.

Ethan wasn't an idiot. He usually gave every appearance of following the rules. But he couldn't seem to dampen his fascination with the blonde-haired human.

He knew what he intended to do was dangerous. Going to the human's – Grace's – studio meant being in the vicinity of other mortals. Other mortals with beating hearts and the pungent, intoxicating aroma of blood flowing just beneath the surface of their skin. He'd never been able to control himself before. Was he willing to go berserk and massacre an entire building full of people?

Apparently, he was.

On his walk downtown he practised saying her name out loud, "Grace, Grace, Grace . . ." The sound enchanted him. He'd gotten so caught up in his verbal trance that he missed all the reactions of the people he passed on the busy pedestrian mall.

When he arrived at her studio, he slipped around behind the building and leaned against the brick wall as a realization hit him. His knees went soft. Had he just walked along a street filled with his favourite food source without attacking anyone? The thought stunned him, then he laughed as he noticed he'd actually clutched his chest, making the familiar, mortal heart attack gesture. It had been a long time since he'd done anything like that. Something almost frighteningly freaky was happening. He hadn't felt this odd since becoming a vampire in the late 1960s. Almost *human*.

Beautiful chanting captured his attention.

He inched towards the music studio window and peeked in, expecting to see a roomful of mortals. The large space was empty. He took a step back and focused on listening to the sweet sounds still issuing from somewhere nearby. Lowering his gaze, he tracked along the foundation of the building until he came to an open window in the lower level. He stepped closer and squatted to investigate.

The basement of the building had been transformed into a sound chamber. Instead of muting the sounds, the acoustical structure of the room exaggerated the depth of the notes, causing the frequencies to reverberate in breathtaking ways.

He could literally feel the chanting in every cell of his body. Or whatever made up his body these days.

The chamber appeared much larger than he'd expected. At least fifty people sat in concentric circles on the marble floor. Grace knelt in the centre, next to a sobbing woman who lay prone on a body-size pad, clutching her stomach. Ethan's keen vampire nose told him the woman was sick. Not far from death. Why had she come to Grace's circle on her deathbed? Maybe she wanted to experience the same peaceful feeling he'd experienced at Grace's bedside. He knew from personal experience how horrible a painful death was.

The chanting was so powerful he felt his consciousness slipping away. He didn't know what would have happened if he hadn't suddenly been overwhelmed by the scent of blood – so many humans in one place – which immediately thrust him deep into his vampire nature. He growled and rose slowly to his full height, just in time to be surprised by a pair of mortals who turned the corner, heading towards his location. His mind spun as he thought of nothing but the aroma of the blood pulsing through the hapless mortals' veins. His fangs descended and he crouched, ready to spring.

"Hi! Are you here for the sound circle? We're late too. Why don't you come on in with us?" The female of the couple moved to the door of the underground area and stood, waiting, a smile on her friendly face. Her companion waved.

As if he hadn't just regressed into a snarling beast, he forced himself to straighten, then snapped his shoulders back and raised his chin. "Yeah, OK." He clenched his fists at his sides.

Yeah, OK? What the hell? Nobody ever told me vampires could have psychotic meltdowns. Maybe all the drugs I did in the 1960s have finally caught up with me. Did I just choose not to attack them because they were nice to me? Am I insane? Since when does my brain work when I'm near mortals?

He edged over to the door and held it open while the two humans entered and descended the staircase. He followed, already enraptured by the engulfing sound.

Can't these people sense me? Don't they realize a predator is behind them? What's happened to human instincts?

They entered the chant-filled sound chamber and quietly found places to sit in the outermost circle. He kept a distance between himself and the others seated nearby and scanned the room. It was incredible. Whatever Grace had done to the walls made the area seem as if they'd stepped inside an amethyst quartz crystal. The circle area consisted of gentle risers, so that people in each circle sat slightly elevated over the row before.

Scented candles burned atop tall, ornate holders, creating soft light and shadows. His vampire vision, especially attuned to the darkness, allowed him to see the blissful expressions on the faces of the participants. The sounds washed over and through him. Fifty voices chanted unfamiliar words, creating extraordinary harmonies. The vibrations lapped against his ears like the soothing waves of a vast sea. He imagined himself back in the womb.

His gaze finally locked on the only one who mattered, and he studied her as she sang, her face ecstatic. Grace's long, blonde hair flowed down the front of her body, hiding all but the sleeves of her shiny, white shirt. With his sensitive hearing, he was able to eliminate all the other voices and tune into hers. It was the most beautiful sound he'd ever heard. Her timbre caressed him like summer rain and he felt his heart sputter, then beat wildly, which startled him because he'd previously had no occasion to allow his cold, dead heart to mimic life.

He closed his eyes, lost in the pleasure of her vocalizations, and began chanting himself. Or, more accurately, the chant took control. The sound simply happened. He'd heard about the concept of channelling, but he thought it was a scam. He'd never have guessed what an amazing sensation it was to simply allow sound to flow from his body without any conscious direction. He hadn't sung in so many years, he was surprised by the power of his own tenor voice.

Suddenly, everyone in the room went silent. Everyone except Grace, that is. He'd stopped singing too, without even being aware of doing it. Had there been some imperceptible signal? Her glorious voice soared through the rarefied space as she leaned forwards, bringing her face near the woman on the floor, whose hands had relaxed at her sides. The sound was eerie and unearthly. Goosebumps rose on his arms – something that shouldn't have been able to happen.

After a few seconds, Grace stopped singing and eased back from the woman. Like releasing a taut rubber band, the formerly limp recipient sprang to her feet, thrust her arms into the air, threw her head back and laughed. "She did it! Grace did it! I'm pain free for the first time since my cancer was diagnosed. Thank you, Grace! Thank you!"

Grace stood, opened her arms, and the woman collapsed against her, sobbing.

Ethan sniffed in the woman's direction, expecting to recognize the familiar scent of impending death again and instead sensed . . . life. Shocked, he focused his full attention on the woman, scanning her body with his expanded perception, and was forced to acknowledge that he'd either been wrong when he declared her near death, or . . . no. That was impossible. Chanting couldn't have altered the woman's physical body. Grace couldn't possibly do anything so astounding. Impossible.

Then he frowned as it occurred to him that even if Grace *had* been able to do the impossible, the healing wasn't the most bizarre thing in the room. Erasing cancer with sound was nothing compared to rising from the dead and drinking human blood to survive. Would all these people who took Grace's miracle for granted be as open-minded about him? Yeah. He wouldn't hold his breath – so to speak.

Still hugging and patting the woman, Grace addressed her audience. "Thank you all for coming tonight and for lending your voices and your intentions to Mary's healing. We've shared something magical and special. It's been a wonderful night. I look forward to seeing you next time." At her words, everyone stood quietly and began moving towards the door, appearing to be in a light trance.

Grace hugged Mary again, and released her to her waiting friends. Ethan remained seated as the room emptied. He wasn't sure what he was going to do, but he felt driven to . . . what? He had no idea. His heart still pounded unnaturally.

He rose and moved quietly – with only human speed so as not to frighten her – to the centre of the circle where Grace had bent to retrieve the pad from the floor. As she straightened and saw him standing in front of her, she gasped.

"You're the angel in my dream." She backed away, let go of the pad and pressed her palms to her face. "I must be in an altered state. You're just a figment of my imagination. I've felt strange all day. This vision will pass any minute now. I'll just keep on talking to myself until you vanish."

"I'm sorry to startle you," Ethan said softly. "And to disappoint you. I'm afraid I'm no angel. And I probably could appear to vanish, but I'd rather not, if you don't mind." His gaze locked on her brown eyes and he had to force himself not to entrance her. For some reason it seemed important that she speak to him of her own accord. He struggled to control the urge to touch her.

Grace dropped her hands from her face and stared at Ethan. She reached out a finger and poked his chest. "You're real." She retreated another step, blinked a couple of times, and shook her head. "I'm so sorry. You must think I'm incredibly rude and very strange. I'm not myself immediately after a sound healing session. My brain waves don't return to normal right away. For a moment, you reminded me of . . . someone I've seen before. The resemblance is very strong." She stopped talking and stared again for a few seconds. "*Have* we met before? You really do seem very familiar." Anxiety shadowed her features.

He heard Grace's heart speed up, so he sent a light relaxation command. She inhaled a deep breath and released it. Her rhythm slowed. Deciding it might be wise to change the subject temporarily so as not to scare her – yet – he said, "I just wanted to tell you how moved I was by your session. I've never seen anyone heal with sound before. I'm impressed." He added another subtle, mental nudge, suggesting she would feel at ease with him. Trust him. He wasn't trying to manipulate her, only to allow a bond to form before he told the truth.

She gave a gentle nod and visibly calmed. "Thank you. I sometimes forget how unusual sound healing is to the rest of the world. I'm so used to doing it that it seems very normal to me." She offered her hand. "I'm Grace Blackburn." She cocked her head, inviting him to introduce himself.

Ethan grasped her hand. "Ethan . . ." He paused, unaccustomed to using his last name. In the vampire world nobody used surnames. "Ethan James." He hoped the last blood he'd taken had warmed his skin sufficiently so she wouldn't notice the coolness of his grip. He was relieved when she gave no indication of discomfort. It was so strange to be near a mortal without the bloodlust riding him. He was definitely in a parallel universe. "Do you have a few moments to talk? I'd really like to hear more about your healing techniques."

A beautiful smile spread her lips. "I'd love to talk to you . . . uh, about the sound healing. It isn't often I meet such a handsome man." She paused, her eyes wide. "Oh! Did I say that out loud? I'm sorry. I don't know what's wrong with me tonight. I don't usually connect with new people so easily. Especially men . . ."

Ethan laughed. "I'm happy to be the exception." *What am I doing, laughing like an idiot? She'll be disgusted and repelled as soon as she finds out what I am. What the hell is happening to me?*

Grace nodded towards a small couch against the wall. "Shall we be comfortable while we talk?"

Ethan grinned. His idea of being comfortable involved a lot less clothing, but sitting was a good start. It wasn't likely he'd be taking her home to his cardboard box. But who knew what would happen? He'd never been so attracted to a human before. He bowed. "Excellent idea. After you."

Keeping their gazes locked, they moved to the couch and sat close.

"What you did tonight was extraordinary," Ethan shared. "How can you be sure the woman's cancer is gone? Can you sense it?"

Grace smiled. "Gee, smart and gorgeous." She rolled her eyes. "Sorry, my mouth seems to have a mind of its own. I'll just go ahead and apologize in advance for anything else I might blurt out. But to answer your question, yes. I can sense it. Sort of. OK, this is going to sound weird, but it's as if I can feel the obstructions – or misalignments – in the body or the psyche as the sound flows around and interacts with them. Then, I imagine the disruption smoothed out by the vibrations and it seems to happen." She paused. "Now you probably think I'm a complete deviant! Not a normal person, right? You wouldn't be the first."

Ethan frowned. *She doesn't think she's normal?* "I think you're incredible. I wish I had your skills. I used to sing and play music years ago, but I never explored the healing aspects of music. Your talent fascinates me."

She shrugged. "I've just worked hard to build up my skills. I think anyone can heal with sound. It's natural. You can do it, too." She blinked a few times and stared at him, tilting her head. "I'm sorry. I don't remember if you ever answered my question about whether or not we've met before. I swear I know your face. In fact, I dreamed about it."

This was it. He'd run out of time to avoid the inevitable. He sighed, bracing for her horrified reaction. "What did you dream?"

She shifted her gaze to the centre of the room, ill at ease. "I dreamed I was attacked on the trail by my house. A monster with fangs pushed me down and was about to kill me, when you grabbed him and flung him aside. You stared down at me, and I thought I'd died – literally – and gone to heaven. You looked like a beautiful angel." She laughed. "An angel wearing a Rolling Stones T-shirt." She focused her gaze on his for a few eternal seconds, her expression serious. "That wasn't a dream, was it?"

"No. It wasn't a dream," Ethan whispered. He stroked his hand down the side of her face.

She leaned into his touch. "What was that thing you rescued me from? How were you able to control him?" She lifted a finger and slid it across his lower lip. "You told me you aren't an angel, but all I sense from you is good. What are you?"

He didn't want to answer. He knew his pleasant fantasy would end the moment he said the word. Her radar must be jammed, because he was far from good. He'd never killed anyone who didn't deserve it, but what could possibly be good about a walking corpse? He hesitated so long she cradled his face in her hands and began chanting. She closed her eyes and turned her head slightly from side to side, making glorious sounds for a moment. Suddenly her eyes flew open and she dropped her hands.

"There's no life force present. You aren't really here. I knew it was a dream . . ."

"This is no dream." Ethan leaned in, pressed his lips to hers and pulled her against him. Eagerly responding, she opened her mouth for him and moaned softly, as their tongues slid together in a sensuous dance.

"Well, well. What have we here?" A deep voice rumbled in the silence. "Ethan has been a very bad boy." Alexander – a dead ringer for a young Arnold Schwarzenegger – stood near the doorway, watching with amusement.

Ethan jerked back from Grace, his mind snapping to attention as he reacted to the sound of his master's voice. He cringed – prepared for the worst – as he waited for Alexander to take control of him. The master enjoyed treating his offspring like puppets who existed only to do his bidding, and he seemed particularly interested in dominating Ethan. Alexander's power was usually absolute.

"Who is this man, Ethan? Do you know him?" Grace clutched Ethan's arm, her voice trembling, her fear saturating the air.

Alexander narrowed his eyes and strode over to stand in front of Ethan. "What have you done? Why has my mental connection with you been weakened? I sensed the change and came to investigate because the only reason our bond would diminish is if you were truly dead. But you're not. Instead here you are, seducing your mortal pet. I'd say a little punishment is in order."

Ethan's mind reeled as he tried to grasp what Alexander said. How was it possible for their bond to be weakened? Alexander was his sire, his master. He couldn't exist without their connection. Could he? No. That wasn't possible.

Just as Ethan opened his mouth to speak, Alexander smiled, displaying long, sharp fangs, and pulled Grace off the couch. She whimpered before going limp and silent. Alexander had taken over her mind. Ethan had seen him control humans thousands of times. Bending her backwards, as if he were performing a sensual dance move, Alexander plunged his fangs into Grace's neck and began to suck greedily.

The sound enraged Ethan and he leaped off the couch. Grace wouldn't survive if he didn't act immediately.

He grabbed Alexander's collar with all his strength and pulled hard, forcing the master's mouth away from the ragged holes in Grace's neck. Alexander released her and Grace crumpled to the floor, boneless. Ethan expected Alexander to attack him, but to his shock, the huge vampire laughed. He wiped his hand across his bloody mouth and licked his fingers.

"So, you want to drink the leftovers? Be my guest. She's almost dead – you'd better hurry. I'll deal with you later." Alexander laughed again, turned and stalked out of the door.

Ethan dropped to his knees next to Grace. Her heartbeat was faint and crimson oozed from the torn vein. The rich smell of her blood caused his hunger to roar over him. His body shook with the struggle to resist draining her. If he used his saliva to close the wounds, he was terrified he'd lose control of himself and Grace would die. But if he didn't, she'd die anyway.

Her heart stuttered and, without thinking, he leaned down, ran his tongue over the gaping holes. The bleeding stopped. He gathered her into his arms and rocked her. He was astounded he could use his will force – that it still existed. He'd never been able to defy his master before. But it didn't matter. Grace had lost so much blood he couldn't see how she'd survive. He couldn't give her any of his because he refused to condemn her to his miserable existence.

As her heartbeat faltered, he cried. In his pain and frustration, he began keening and wailing, which started out ragged and broken, but soon grew powerful. As he reached the depths of his despair, all the sorrow of the last forty years poured out. The sound began to flow. He heard the sweet tone of his voice echoing through the sound chamber and he hugged her flaccid body tighter.

He would give anything to save her.

Mindless with grief, he felt the sound vibrations crash through him like a great ocean, reshaping his inner landscape, flooding his body with alien sensations. Waves of intense, unfamiliar emotions pounded his lifeless heart.

After his death, he'd shut down most of his human feelings. All that mattered was feeding and surviving. Existing. The undead have no use for sadness and regret, so why was he overwhelmed by those feelings now?

He shuddered as his body struggled to contain the onslaught, and was startled by the awareness of tears rolling down his cheeks.

Tears? Vampires can't cry. It's impossible. I must be dying.

In the midst of a soul-wrenching cry, the sound simply stopped. Without thought, his throat tightened and his mouth closed. He looked down to find Grace staring up at him, her heartbeat strong. The wounds on her neck had closed and were already healing.

"Grace! How . . . That's impossible. Your heart stopped."
Stunned, his voice cracked. Needing to assure himself that she
was really alive, he leaned down and brushed her lips with his.

"You saved me. Thank you," Grace whispered.

He shook his head, his tone knife-edged. "Don't thank me.
It's my fault you were attacked. I should never have come here.
I didn't mean to involve you in my horrible world. Aren't you
afraid of me?"

"Afraid? That's the last thing I feel about you. You've healed
more than my body."

"But . . . you know what I am."

"Yes, I do know." She stroked her hand down the side of his
face and met his eyes. "You're my angel."

He gave a disgusted laugh. "No chance of that."

"Then, what are you?"

"I'm a . . ." He stopped and stared off into the distance, his
head spinning. What was he exactly? He'd almost said he was a
vampire, but he'd been acting weird – like a mortal – ever since
his encounter with Grace the night before. Until then, his world
had been narrow and constricted, the rules clear. He drank
blood. His master controlled him. He died when the sun came
up. Now, nothing made sense. She'd changed him with her
voice, her very being. But what did that mean? Changed him
how? "It's impossible, but I don't know any more. I don't
understand what's happening to me."

"There's a legend," she said, drawing his attention back to
her.

He frowned. "A legend? About what?"

She smiled and snuggled closer. "Sound healing has existed
for millennia. For most of that time it was also used to raise the
dead – to restore the spark of life. Or so the story goes. History
tells of an actual sound ceremony used to reclaim the souls of
people possessed by demons."

"You're kidding, right? That's impossible." He laughed and
leaned back so he could see her face. "But, on the other hand,
I've said the word 'impossible' more times than I ever have
before, and I haven't been right yet."

She nodded. "Something is only impossible until we know
better."

Wait. Did she just say something about raising the dead and being possessed by demons? What's she trying to tell me? How could she know?

"So, what's that legend got to do with me? What are you saying?"

She gazed at him, her eyes soft and compassionate. "When I sang with you, I became a part of you. I sensed your mind – your soul. And now you're different – more. A mystical transformation occurred. But you had to desire the change before it could happen. You literally intended yourself into a new existence."

He shook his head. "That sounds crazy, Grace. That's imposs—"

She pressed a finger to his lips. "Impossible? Apparently not. And I was never afraid of you because I've been waiting for you."

"What?"

She grinned, then put on Roz's fake gypsy-fortune-teller accent. "You see, there's an ancient prediction, passed down by the gypsy women in my friend's family. It is foretold that I will meet an extraordinary man who will be reborn, and together we will do the impossible." She pressed her lips to his. "I think we've already begun."

"Yes, I guess that's possible. Tell me more about that extraordinary man . . ."

The Princess and the Peas

Alyssa Day

Once upon a time, in a land far, far away, there lived a princess in a tiny kingdom known as Elvania. The kingdom's exact location is long lost in the mists of time; some say it became part of France, while others claim it for Switzerland. The Swiss claim has more merit, perhaps, as the precedent of impartial and wintry-cold neutrality has sometimes been a guiding tenet of that people. All agree that the princess claimed a lovely view of the waters of what is now called Lake Geneva from her turret bedroom.

Not that she cared much for views. Or lakes. Or anything at all, in fact, other than her single-minded, unswerving quest for the perfect husband.

This is her story. (Except where it isn't.)

"Lucinda!" The dulcet shrieks of Her-Royal-Pain-In-The-Nether-Regions rang through Lucy's skull like a trumpet blown by a particularly incompetent musician. She shot up out of her narrow bed, clutching the threadbare quilt to her chest, blinking stupidly, wondering what was on fire.

With any luck, *she* was. *She* being Princess Margarita Gloriana Dolores Tresor Montague. "Glory" to her friends – not that she had any. Lady, mistress and personal hell to Lucinda since the two of them had been ten years old.

When the cry didn't repeat itself, Lucy closed her eyes and started to sink back into her lumpy mattress, hoping that it had been a nightmare. Maybe she could fall back into that inexplicably tingly dream, although it was curious that Ian, his dark eyes flashing, had been riding his horse through the main hall, coming to get her. Since when did she dream of Ian?

More to the point, since when did *any* dream leave her feeling quite so . . . breathless?

She repressed that line of enquiry and opened a single eye. The glimmers of pink light edging through her narrow window told her that it could be no more than an hour since the princess had finally (*finally!*) pronounced herself pleased enough with the preparations so that Lucy could crawl off to her room – the tiny chamber adjacent to Glory's own – and catch at least a few short hours of sleep before the guests arrived.

More stinking royalty.

If Lucy lived through the week, it would be a miracle. Why couldn't she be a cook or a scullery maid or even a laundress? Surely slaving away in the hot kitchens or over the clothes boiling away in the pots must be a stroll in the gardens compared to dancing attendance on the spoiled brat of a princess.

Never mind. It didn't matter. Sleep. Lovely, blessed sleep. Just a few hours, and then a strong mug or three of hot tea, and—

"Lucinda! Get in here right this minute, you lazy girl! We forgot the peas!"

Lucy startled awake with a jerk and slammed her head so hard into the stone wall that she was sure to have a goose egg on her skull in a matter of hours. Not to mention the headache. She gritted her teeth, threw her legs over the side of the bed and stood up, swaying a little with dizziness from the pain in her head.

"I. Am. Coming. You. Horrible. Monster," she gritted out under her breath. Then, louder: "Coming, my lady."

She didn't bother to put a sprightly tone in her voice. Glory wouldn't have believed it anyway. The last time Lucy had sounded sprightly was the day she'd left a very wet and slimy toad in Glory's bed. She grinned at the memory but then sighed.

It was sad to live on the memory of a childish rebellion that had happened nearly eleven years ago.

Lucy stumbled into Glory's room, taken aback as always at the virulent pinkness of it. Wall hangings, rugs, bed coverlets, and even Glory herself, were all a vision in nauseating pink. And rose. And red-tinged violet. It was like walking into the inside of a sow's stomach.

She rubbed her eyes again, hoping it would go away. It didn't. It never did.

"What are you talking about, Glory? What peas?"

"That's 'your Highness'," Glory snapped. "Or 'milady'. At least while our guests are here. I can't have it thought that I allow the serving wenches to address me with such familiarity."

"Serving wenches? *Serving wenches?* Whose shoulder have you cried on more times than either of us can count? Whose bed did you climb into for safety and comfort whenever there was a thunderstorm – and that up until you were fifteen years old?" Lucy asked with what she thought was admirable calm. "Mayhap you should rethink that term, or I'll find out if Magda can come help you this week."

Glory gasped at the idea of the pig keeper as her personal servant. "*Magda?* She hasn't bathed in months. You must be joking. Don't forget that you owe me—"

"I owe you nothing," Lucy said flatly. "I've spent the past eleven years working far and above the value of my keep, in spite of the promise your mother made to mine. I turn twenty-one in three days and am only staying this week as a favour to the Glory I once loved as a sister."

Glory had the grace to look abashed, but only for a span of seconds. "You know you cannot leave me, twenty-one or no. There is no place for you to go."

"There is the world, Glory. There is the world. Or do you forget?" Lucy waved her arm and the scattered pillows, clothes and assorted frippery covering every inch of Glory's floor flew gracefully to their assigned places in trunks and the wardrobe. "Now. What peas?"

"Oh, sure. You had to ask. 'What peas?' Addle-pated twit," Lucy muttered sourly as she slammed the final mattress down onto its gilded wooden frame with a thump. For the past hour and a half, she'd stomped up and down the corridor, crawling under mattresses in the guest chambers to deposit a single pea-sized iron pellet underneath each one. Finally she'd come to the royal chamber, kept free for visiting princes or Fae lords, and deposited the last pea. Now she was done.

Of course it had to be iron. Her magic didn't work on iron or the chore would have been done in a matter of moments. That was why she was here in the first place, according to Glory. To hide the tiny bits of iron that would block the Fae from working magic in their rooms during the treaty negotiations.

Fae magic did not work well in the presence of iron either. Still, something about Glory's reasoning seemed unsound to Lucy's exhausted mind. After all, iron's properties or no, Lucy knew there was no chance that she was even the slightest bit Fae. She repressed the desire to touch the very round, very non-pointed tip of her ear for reassurance. She claimed a bit of the old forest magic, mayhap, but never Fae.

She turned towards the door, longing for her bed more than ever, and attempted to brush some of the under-bed dust from her night shift. She needed to speak to the housekeeper about the lack of cleaning. No. It was no longer her concern.

"Like any of the elvish slugs are going to notice, anyway," she said to the empty room. "This is the stupidest idea—"

"Elvish slugs, hmm? I was unaware my race boasted that particular member." The voice was sensuality turned to music: teasing, hypnotic, and pitched exactly right to make Lucy feel warm in places a man's voice had no business warming.

Fortunately, such tricks had no effect on her.

She gave a slight effort to wiping the scowl from her face before she looked up, but the sight of him brought her scowl back in full measure. The Fae lord was beautiful, of course. They all were. A few inches taller than most human men. Silvery hair shimmering in a fall of moon-kissed silk to his waist. Long, lean muscles. Eyes the blue of the sky reflected in ice.

Ice to Ian's fire. Wait. What? Ian? She narrowed her eyes at the thought of the man who seemed to be popping into her mind with a growing frequency, and returned her attention to the man who was actually in the room with her.

Yep. He was an elf. She couldn't bear the sight of them. Pompous Fae with their overblown sense of importance. This one would be worse than most, since he wore the green and gold of the High House of the Seelie Court.

"Rugs. I said, 'Too bad we don't have any elvish rugs,' " she said quickly, although she didn't exactly add the "milord". It would be bad form to start a fight with one of the visiting princes on the very first day of the treaty renewal meetings, but truly a girl could only put up with so much.

He leaned against the doorway, effectively blocking her escape, and folded his arms across his chest. "Yes," he drawled, sweeping a leisurely glance from her head to her toes. "We of the Seelie Court are known for our . . . rugs."

"I—"

"Are you a gift to me? If so, I know not whether to be honoured by my host's graciousness at giving me such a beauty or insulted that he would send such a filthy hoyden to my bed."

Lucy gasped at his effrontery. "You *insufferable* . . . You . . . You . . . insufferable . . ."

"Yes, insufferable. I believe we've established that," he said dryly. "Or do you expect me to believe you have framed yourself before the fire in such a manner that your gown is nearly transparent merely by accident?"

Her face flushed so hot that she knew it must have turned bright red, which contrasted hideously with her dark red hair. Not that she cared what this pompous ass thought of her. She took a deep breath, twirled her hand in a semicircle, and the room was plunged into darkness as the fire extinguished itself.

"There. Now you can see nothing."

"Oh, so you wish to be alone in the dark with me?" Amusement shimmered in his voice as he took a step towards her.

"In your dreams, Milord Pointy Ears," she snapped. "Get out of my way or I'll make those flames spark to life again, but this time in your trousers."

He paused for a beat, probably thinking of ways to order her tortured in the palace dungeons, but he surprised her: he threw back his head and laughed. Still laughing, he bowed and moved away from the doorway. "As you wish, milady, in spite of your obvious fascination with my . . . trousers. But you will at least surrender your name to me for my trouble."

She raced past him, pausing only once she'd reached the safety of the corridor. "Of course. My name is Magda."

*   *   *

Rhys na Garanwyn, High Prince of the High House of the Seelie Court, stood staring after the lass as she raced down the corridor away from him. Human, surely. Perhaps with a touch of simple magic. But he'd sensed nothing in her that should have allowed her to resist him so defiantly. Humans were drawn to the Fae like dragons to jewels, irresistibly and inexorably.

Yet this one had scorned his attention, even when he'd opened his senses to her and infused his voice with a bit of enchantment. She should have been on her knees, begging for his touch. The idea, oddly, held a slight repugnance. She was beautiful and she'd been half-undressed, but there was no sexual appeal for him there. More an inexplicable fondness, which made him wonder if some previously unencountered spellcraft were involved.

The sound of tramping feet interrupted his mental wanderings and he took a deep breath, banishing all thoughts of the impudent Magda. He'd find her tomorrow perhaps. Or request her company as a guest-gift from his host. Entering his chamber and pushing the door closed behind him, he smiled.

This treaty renewal might prove to be far more fascinating than any in the past 600 years.

Evening, the next day.

Lucy trailed down the staircase behind Glory, muttering dire and mostly impotent threats under her breath as she tried not to trip over the gown she hadn't wanted to wear. Glory had decided that she needed a lady to serve her personally at all banquets during the week, since she'd heard that the elven ladies indulged themselves in such a manner. Of course, only Lucy would do.

She'd won the battle against the pink dress at least. After a long and painful argument (which had included much brush-hurling and foot-stomping on Glory's part), Lucy had come up with one perfect, irrefutable point: if she, Lucy, wore pink, it would take some of the focus away from Glory's own marvellously beautiful pink-clad self.

Glory's anger had transformed magically into an expression of thoughtful consideration. Then she'd turned towards her wardrobe, bent to yank something from the floor in the back, and pulled out one of the most beautiful gowns Lucy had ever seen. The emerald silk of the bodice and skirt draped richly over an underskirt of sheerest gold. Delicate golden beads – which appeared to be formed of actual gold – shimmered at the neckline and sleeves.

Lucy had caught her breath at the wave of utter longing that swept through her at the sight of it. Then she'd flatly refused to wear it.

"No. Not a chance. Those are the High House colours, so the gown must have been a gift. You know how political those elves are. If I wear it, it will send a very insulting message, and they probably invented the phrase 'kill the messenger'. No. Absolutely not."

Well. *That* had gone well. Now here she was, wearing the gown that would be the death of her, her hair done up in a ridiculous tangle of curls, and her mother's silver ring on a chain around her neck. Add in the oversized embroidered slippers (Glory's cast-offs) and she looked exactly like a child playing dress-up. She yanked the skirt up from around her toes and wondered how many bones she'd break when she went tumbling down the stairs, head over heels.

Without warning though, a surge of heat flashed through Lucy's nerve endings, shutting down her internal complaints and heightening her senses. The triple heralds of warning, danger and threat trumpeted through her mind. She snapped up her head and scanned the area, only to see Glory's profusion of pink ruffles blocking her view of all but the livery of one of the palace guards.

"Milady." The deep voice was respectful, as Ian – for surely it was he, no other mere human had that delicious voice – bowed to Glory. The princess ignored him completely, of course, and swept on down the stairs, leaving Lucy standing there staring at Ian like a fool, with a handful of skirt and a mind full of very naughty thoughts.

Ian's mouth curved in an admiring smile and heat flared in his dark eyes. "Lady Lucinda, you are more beautiful than a verdant summer day in that gown. It matches the emerald of your eyes," he said, his voice a little rougher than usual.

Lucy blushed, then scowled, then nearly tripped over the

hem of her dress. "Have you been at the ale already, Ian? This infernal gown will probably get me killed, when the house which gifted it to Glor . . . um, the *Princess* . . . sees me in it. Elves are not known for their tolerance." She blinked, suddenly remembering his words. "And since when do you call me anything but Lucy?"

Ian flattened his mouth into a thin line and a muscle clenched in his jaw. "I thought to compete with the damned Fae lords and their penchant for flattering words and poesy. Evidently a mere guardsman has no such hope. If you have need of me, send word. It will be no easy task to get through me to you, Fae or no."

His gaze dropped for an instant to her absurdly low bodice, then returned to her face. In that instant, Ian, whom she'd known for nearly all of her life, transformed into a stranger. A hard and dangerous stranger.

A faint, uncontrollable shudder ran through her as his eyes narrowed.

"If the princess or her father believe they will use you as a bargaining tool, they are sadly mistaken," he said flatly, menace icing his words.

Lucy gasped and scanned the stairs, relieved to find that Glory had moved much further ahead. "Watch what you say, Ian! You are dangerously near to speaking treason."

He stepped closer to her and caught her chin in his hand, tilting it up so that his face was mere inches from hers. "Treason is the very least of what I would dare to protect you, Lucy. Remember that. Two days until you are twenty-one, milady. Two days. And then I am coming for you, no matter how many elven princes stand in my way. You are mine."

Lucy stood, frozen in shock, as he pressed a brief kiss to her lips and then released her.

"Two days," he repeated, before bowing and resuming his journey up the stairs.

Lucy touched her lips with trembling fingers, wondering how such a slight touch could cause flame to sear through her body. She turned to watch his broad-shouldered, muscular form climbing the stairs and shivered.

Ian was King Padraic's captain of the guard, and all knew he had earned the post. He was easily the king's best warrior, best leader, best . . . everything. To hear him speak words of treason – *on her behalf* – was too much to comprehend.

But she could still taste his lips on her own.

"Lucinda!" Glory's shriek echoed off the stone walls and through Lucy's skull. "Get down here now!"

Grabbing a fistful of her skirt in either hand, Lucy took a deep breath and resumed her descent.

Two days, he'd said. Much could happen in two days. And, considering she'd be following Glory around the entire time, probably none of it would be good.

The dining hall was a scene of utter chaos, and Lucy nearly ran over Glory, who'd stopped dead at the threshold. Fae lords stood nearly nose to nose with the lords of the court and members of the palace guard, and all of them were engaged in shouting matches. At the high table, the king sat blinking in disbelief or – more likely at this late hour – sheer drunkenness.

"Glory, I think maybe we should return to our rooms. This looks as if it could go very badly, and I fear for your safety," Lucy said, speaking loudly so that Glory could hear her over the cacophony.

"Very good idea, your Highness," Ian said, suddenly appearing at their side. Only now he held a very sharp and deadly sword loose and ready in his hand. "I would feel much better if you were both to retire before these . . . debates . . . get further out of hand."

Glory tossed her head and flashed her most dazzling smile. Lucy had seen human lords, princes and kings hypnotized by that smile. Even the lesser Fae lords were not immune to Glory's beauty when she chose to employ it.

Ian, however, never even blinked. "*Now*, my ladies."

Glory somehow looked down her nose at him, though Ian stood several hand spans taller than she. "I recommend you consider to whom you are speaking, guardsman."

"If I had not considered that, Princess, I would have thrown you over my shoulder and carried you upstairs before you could endanger yourself and the Lady Lucinda," Ian said evenly.

Lucy's eyes widened, expecting Glory to throw one of her

legendary tantrums, but to her surprise the princess only laughed. "Oh, there is no danger to me. This is the night I am to be engaged to wed," Glory said, almost absently, her gaze sweeping the room.

"What?" Lucy caught Glory's arm. "What? You did not tell me. Who is it?"

Glory shook her arm free, then smoothed down her skirts. "I don't know yet, of course. Come help me find out who had the most difficult time sleeping last night on those horribly lumpy mattresses." Her laughter tinkling like the sound of tiny bells, Glory lifted her chin and floated into the room like the delicate flower she had never, ever been.

"Oh no," Lucy moaned. "The peas. This is going to be really, really bad." Casting an apologetic glance Ian's way, she raised the skirt of her dress and hurried after the princess.

Ian wanted to break something. Or someone. His eyes narrowed as he caught sight of one of the fanciest of the elven lords staring at Lucy. Oh, yeah. He definitely wanted to break some*one*.

The Fae prince was dressed all in green and gold, signifying that he was the highest of the treaty lords here to negotiate. Elvania's neutrality had long made it the perfect site for the renewal of treaty agreements between the various Fae factions. They came, they ate everything in sight, they ran through serving maids as if women existed only to give them pleasure, and then they departed for another year; if not pleased than at least content. From the look of things as they stood now, *pleased* wasn't on the table, and *content* wasn't looking very good, either. But if one of the lordlings thought he'd sample the pleasures Lucy might have to offer, Ian had a sharp objection to make. He grinned and glanced at the honed steel of his blade. A *very* sharp objection.

If he could keep his mind off how Lucy would look in his bed: that lush dark red hair spread across his pillow, those lovely breasts uncovered for his hands and mouth to touch and taste.

Or how she would look when he wed her, with flowers in her hair and his ring on her finger.

She was his, as he'd reminded her, and that meant his to protect in this madness. Ian tightened his grip on the sword and shouldered his way through the battling lordlings after Lucy.

Although she'd easily slipped through the crowd, he took a certain grim pleasure in shoving his way through to the king's table. One of the Fae lords Ian elbowed out of the way drew his dagger halfway out of its sheath, but a look at Ian's face seemed to give the elf pause. A true Fae would never back down from a fight, but of course a fight could be avoided. The lordling suddenly seemed to find something on the opposite side of the room to be fascinating.

Just as Ian reached the single step leading to the king's table, the princess' sharp, clear tone cut through the room. "I beg your pardon, my lords and ladies," she said with an arrogance that made it clear that – in spite of her words – she *would* never and *had* never begged anyone's pardon, ever. The room fell silent as everyone turned to face her. "I understand there was some problem with your rooms?"

Not without admiration, Rhys watched the deceitful little princess pose her deceitful little question. Some problem with the rooms indeed. Of course he'd found the iron pellet the moment he'd stepped into the very grand and overdone room assigned to him; of all the myths surrounding the Fae, *that* one was true. The higher-born the Fae, the more critically sensitive to iron.

Great power always seemed to come with great weaknesses, which seemed to Rhys itself to be a weakness in the basic ordering of things. Not that he'd ever voice such a supposition. To admit to even the slightest touch of philosophical thought would ruin his calculated image of languid boredom.

To that end, he adjusted one of his jade-green lapels, yawned and then raised one eyebrow. "Problem?"

A faint look of disgust moved across the princess' face so quickly that another, lesser being might have believed he'd imagined it. Rhys knew better. This reaction to his affected pose was exactly as it should be.

As the room erupted in complaint, all to do with the iron placed under the mattresses and accusations of conspiracy, he wondered why such a reaction bothered him for the first time in centuries. But he was far too brutally honest with himself to pretend he didn't know the answer. It was *her*. The wench from the night before, standing a step behind Princess Glory. Wearing his house colours, as though she belonged to him. He drew in a sharp breath as he realized the feeling he had at the thought was one of smug satisfaction. For a woman with such fire to belong to him . . . to be his friend.

Friend?

The wench – what was her name? Magda? – focused intently on an approaching guardsman, a man of prowess and sure strength, from the look of him.

Friend? What was happening to him?

He shook his head free of the unusual thoughts. It was irrelevant in any case. She was taken. Her heart was involved. Once that might have made it a challenge. Now he was merely resigned. What purpose to weave forgetfulness over true love for a brief time of . . . friendship?

He gave in to the impulse. Some mental imperative all but demanded he claim her friendship. Thus, he must destroy any possibility of it.

"Let us dispense with the charade, shall we, your Highness?" Rhys called to the king, his voice cutting easily through the bickering. "Your daughter has broken the treaty by her use of trickery as, no doubt, part of her childish quest to find a powerful Fae husband. The penalty is death or enslavement. I see no reason to execute such a lovely, if empty-headed, wench, so the princess will come to my bed until such time as I grow tired of her."

Glory shrieked and all of the colour drained out of her face as her drunken sop of a father tried to pull himself to his feet, spluttering and blustering. A shocked silence fell over the rest of the room. Idly, Rhys noticed that the warrior – the guardsman – held his blade at the ready as he stood at battle stance, protecting the princess.

But Rhys was uninterested in any of their reactions. He focused his attention on the only woman in the room who held the slightest interest for him.

Her face too was as pale as death, but her eyes flashed deadly defiance. "You will not have her, my lord," she said clearly. "At least not while I live."

As she lifted her hands into the air, preparing to work some form of magic to protect the princess, a flash of silver at her throat caught his attention. It couldn't be.

It *couldn't* be.

Quicker than thought, he was across the room and bending towards her, catching the silver ring she wore on a chain in his hand. "What is this? Where did you get it?" he demanded.

"Release her or die," the guardsman all but snarled at him, his sword raised in a lightning-quick motion to Rhys' neck. "In fact, I may kill you anyway, for daring to touch her."

Rhys knew a moment's amusement and looked into the man's furious grey eyes. "Negotiating, then, is not your skill, one can assume?"

"Release her or die," the man repeated, pressing harder.

The excruciating pain of steel cutting into his throat barely distracted Rhys as he lost interest in the mortal's nonsense and stared down at the girl again. "Where did you get it?" he asked, daring her to lie. Staring down into her dark green eyes.

Her oh-so-familiar dark green and slightly tilted eyes.

His own eyes. His sister's eyes.

"You're her child," he breathed. "My sister's child."

Her eyes widened, and she began to shake her head *no*, but he'd had enough of guesswork and supposition. He dropped the ring and caught her face in his hands, then touched his forehead to her own. The immediate family bond flared to life with almost painful intensity.

She *was* his own, and suddenly his aversion to anything but her friendship became poignantly clear.

"You're my niece," he said, almost laughing with the first unfettered joy he'd felt in the 300 years since his sister had disappeared. "You're my family."

She looked up at him, blinking. Dazed. "I . . . I know," she said. "Somehow, I know." She turned to glance at the guardsman who still held a sword to Rhys' throat. "Don't hurt him, Ian. He's my . . . uncle."

Ian slowly lowered his sword, clearly not understanding and just as clearly unwilling to trust the woman he loved to Rhys and his claims of family.

"Ah, and that is another matter," Rhys said, drawing himself up to his full and quite considerable height. "You are not nearly good enough for my niece."

In the space of a unicorn's heartbeat, the sword was at his throat again. "I'd suggest you rethink that statement, *Uncle*," Ian said grimly. "I'd hate our first outing as husband and wife to be attending your funeral."

Rhys' niece gasped. "Ian! He's my uncle – Wait. What? Husband and wife?"

Rhys looked from one to the other and began to laugh. Gently moving the sword to one side so the human male would not be threatened, Rhys bowed deeply to the king. "I return to you your daughter's life, though it were forfeit to me by right and by law. In exchange, I shall take this woman as my own. She is my kin, and it is my right. I hereby claim the Lady Magda."

Every single Fae in the room, silent and motionless throughout the encounter, dropped to their knees and proclaimed their fealty and accord. "*A Garanwyn!*"

The king dropped back down into his chair and stared at Rhys, befuddlement clear on his red face. "I don't understand. What on earth do you want with our pig keeper?"

Two days later.
"I still can't believe Glory wed that little round man," Lucy said, shaking her head in disbelief. "After all of her years of declaring that only a man whose beauty matched her own would do, she is overcome with joy to have secretly married a man who is a head shorter than her, at least five stone heavier and who has very little hair."

"Ah, but he loves her beyond distraction," Ian replied, putting his hands on her waist. "There is much to be said for that. Happy birthday, my love."

"I may become ill," Rhys pointed out as the annoying human kissed Lucy. Not that either of them could hear anything besides their own maudlin prattle. He held the reins of the silver mare he'd acquired for his niece and watched closely as Ian, after aiming a perfunctory glare Rhys' way, helped Lucinda into the saddle.

"Have a care as to how you lay your hands on a princess of the High House of the Seelie Court," Rhys snapped.

Ian smiled and deliberately raised Lucinda's hand to his lips. "My *future wife* and I will lay our hands on each other however we want, *Uncle*."

"Don't call me 'Uncle'," Rhys said between clenched teeth.

Lucinda arranged her divided skirt on the saddle, sighing in either dismay or resignation. "Is it going to be like this all the way across Elvania? Because if you two cannot manage to come to some form of accord, I may have to strike off on my own and abandon both of you."

"You can't—" Rhys began, offended.

"You would never—" Ian began.

"Watch me," Lucinda interrupted.

Rhys scowled fiercely at her, trying his best not to let his own smile escape. "You're my sister's daughter, all right," he admitted, swinging up onto his own horse. "The stories I could tell you . . ."

"Wonderful," Ian put in as he settled into his saddle and manoeuvred his horse closer to Lucinda. "Lucy and I will have no time to ourselves at all on this trip, will we?"

Rhys smiled as his expected companion stepped out from behind the stable door and stood waiting quietly, her arms held up to him. "Oh, I don't know about that," Rhys said, stopping to catch the beautifully voluptuous woman by the waist and lift her onto his horse in front of him. "I may be a little busy at times."

Ian blinked. "Who—?"

Rhys smiled again but said nothing, enjoying the smell of the lass' lavender-scented hair. She snuggled back between his thighs with a contented sound.

Lucy looked startled for an instant, but then slowly smiled. "Ian, meet Magda."

Ian's eyes widened. "Magda? The pig keeper?"

Magda smiled shyly and nodded. "I had a bath."

The End (In which they all lived happily ever after. Or at least for a very long while . . .)

At Second Bite

Michelle Rowen

"Do you know who I am?"

The handsome man's gaze searched hers so thoroughly she felt as though she was being strip-searched at the airport, not just propositioned at a singles bar called the Meet Market.

"That's an interesting line," she said.

"Pardon?"

"The 'do you know who I am' line. It's a bit of an alternative to the whole 'do you come here often' thing."

"My name is Evan Frost."

"Julia," she offered after a moment's hesitation. "Julia Donner."

He offered her his hand and she took it expecting a handshake. His warm fingers curled around hers and he brought her hand to his mouth to brush his warm lips against her skin.

"It is you," he said. "I know it truly."

"You know what truly?" She raised an eyebrow.

Was he going to buy her a drink? Should she buy *him* a drink? Damn, she hated getting dragged along to these kinds of bars with her desperate friends. It so wasn't her scene.

"She told me it was you, but I did not initially believe. Now I do."

"Who told you what?"

"The witch. The one who led me to you. I have searched 300 years and you are finally returned to me."

"What are you talking about?"

He looked at her very seriously. "You, Julia Donner, are the reincarnation of my beloved soulmate."

She actually laughed out loud at that. "You are kidding me, right?"

He frowned at her reaction. "I do not kid you."

She had to admit to being a little disappointed. At first glance the guy had potential – serious "introduction to her bedroom" potential. At second glance, he was just another loser. Pretty on the surface, but crazy underneath.

Julia sighed out loud. "Three hundred years? That's kind of a long time. What are you, a vampire, or something?" She was kidding of course, but the look on his face told her he wasn't.

"You sense what I am," he said with obvious approval. "You *know* me."

She tried not to laugh. "No, I don't. Besides, vampires are cold, undead creatures of darkness. And you're . . . well, you're—" *very hot* "—warm and breathing."

"Real vampires are not what you might expect. We are simply different than humans. We do live eternally. But when our soulmates are taken away before they are sired, we must try to find them in their next life. It has not been easy for me to locate you. I feared I would never find you again."

Right. "I think you should probably take off. My friend'll be back any minute."

Instead of departing, he took a step even closer to her. "It is I, dearest Julia. *Evan*. Search your heart. You know me. I know you do."

She leaned back from him. "I know you need to get away from me or we're going to have a big problem here."

He looked very confused. Either this guy was surprised that his whole reincarnation shtick didn't work on her or he was completely insane. She didn't know which. She didn't care. Either scenario creeped her out.

"I didn't mean to scare you," he said, with a deep frown creasing his forehead.

She slid off the bar stool. He put his arms on either side of her to block her from leaving.

"Please, stay and talk with me a while longer, Julia."

"I mean it," she said very firmly. "Get away from me now."

A small smile touched his lips. "I remember that fire, that spark of life inside you. There are many things that are so very, very different, but that remains. You are the one. The witch is not wrong. She guaranteed me that you are she."

"That I'm your reincarnated soulmate?"

"Yes." His smile widened. "You are beginning to believe. That is wonderful."

She tried to move away from him but he didn't budge. Was she going to have to call security? Not that anyone seemed like they were paying attention. A quick glance around the bar confirmed that several people were very close to each other getting to *know* each other much like she and Evan.

"What do you want?" she asked him warily.

"You, of course," he replied.

"Not interested." She eyed him. "Maybe you should go bite some necks somewhere else."

"I need to drink very little at my age."

"If you're a vampire, then how old are you?"

"I am nearly 400 years old."

He looked no more than thirty. A very hot, but creepy, thirty.

"I should be able to go wherever I want and not worry about getting harassed by some dead guy."

"I'm not dead."

"Undead, then."

He made a frustrated sound in his throat. "You don't believe me."

"Obviously not."

"The witch told me it shouldn't take long to convince you of my intentions."

"Which are?" Julia turned to face him again.

He stepped closer. "To woo you, to take you as my wife, to make love to you and worship your body until our desires are sated, and to sire you as a vampire so we will never have to be apart again."

That probably shouldn't have turned her on. This guy spoke like something out of a 1950s horror movie. But there was something about him . . .

Something familiar?

Nah.

"I don't believe in vampires," she told him, but her voice sounded a bit breathy now. "And I *don't* believe in soulmates."

He leaned closer and pushed her hair behind her ear so he could whisper, "Let me prove it to you."

It was working, damn it. Sad but true, she was starved for male attention. She'd put up her "girl power" front for years now, shunning relationships that didn't seem like they had the legs to go for . . .

To go for what? she thought. Eternity?

She didn't believe in true love. And she sure didn't believe in soulmates. Then why the hell was she letting this self-proclaimed warm-blooded vampire nibble on her ear?

And why was she letting him kiss her, there in the middle of the bar in front of everybody? That was something Julia's barhopping buddies did on their nightly hunt for masculine prey. Not her.

But soon enough she was kissing him back. So much for her half-hearted protests.

After a moment she felt a twinge of pain and pulled away. "What was that?" she asked.

"Sorry." Evan was frowning, his brow lowered. When he looked up at her she realized that his eyes were black. Like, black. Not darker, not shaded because it was low light in the club. But black, even the whites. "I didn't mean to taste you so soon."

She touched her tongue to realize that she'd cut it on something and was now bleeding. "What's wrong with your eyes?" she asked.

"It happened when I tasted your blood." He looked away. "I can control myself. You don't have to worry about your safety, I assure you."

She pushed at his upper lip, drawing it back from his teeth. "You have fangs," she stated.

"Yes. You may not have noticed them before. They are very small unless my hungers are triggered."

Her eyes widened as the slow, sick realization began to spread over her. "You're a *vampire*."

He nodded. "I don't normally share my secret for fear of attracting the wrong sort of attention – especially in a public area such as this. But I knew you had to know as soon as possible."

She just gawked at him.

His eyes slowly returned to their normal shade of blue. "So you see, I'm telling you the truth. You've witnessed it with your own eyes. I am immortal. You are my soulmate and we are finally reunited."

Julia slipped off the stool to stand in front of him on her high heels, which didn't even bring her close to looking directly into the tall man's eyes. He looked pretty happy actually. The long sharp fangs receded to become slightly pointy canines.

She put her hands on his chest and felt the warmth of his body, the muscles of his chest and abdomen beneath the thin black dress shirt he wore. His heart did beat, but she realized that it didn't beat very fast. Half as fast as hers did. Maybe less.

"Do you believe?" he asked.

She nodded. "I believe."

His pleased expression shattered as she kneed him in the groin, pushed away from him, and ran screaming out of the club.

Julia made a beeline for the subway entrance a block away, the gaping mouth in the sidewalk beckoning her back to normal life. But a moment before she reached it she found herself grabbed from behind in an iron vice of a grip. A hand clamped down over her mouth. She struggled but knew it was not going to be any use. Fear and panic fought for first place in her brain. It was a close race.

What was Evan Frost going to do now? Had she made him mad by running away? Obviously. Somebody didn't get grabbed and dragged into a dark alley if everything was peachy keen.

Fury then mixed with her other emotions. As soon as his hand left her mouth she was going to scream bloody murder. Her throat muscles tensed painfully in preparation.

She felt the brick wall slam against her back, knocking the breath out of her and suddenly there was a knife at her throat. A big one.

"Say one word and I'll remove your head," was the hard-edged threat that made her nod emphatically in agreement. The knife was sharp and she was very fond of her head exactly where it was.

Also, the guy who said it wasn't Evan. It was somebody else. Somebody she didn't recognize. He was tall, with shaggy dark brown hair. One eye was covered with a black patch. The other was dark blue, almost black and it glared at her. He wasn't smiling.

He slowly took his hand off her mouth.

The guy definitely didn't look happy. In fact, he looked pissed off beyond words.

"What's your name?" he growled.

Julia blinked, now confused. "I . . . I agreed not to t-talk, remember?"

"I'll only hurt you if you scream. Got it? I need some answers and I need them now."

"O-OK."

"Name."

"J-Julia." She bit her lip. She didn't want to give him her last name if she could avoid it. He didn't press for it, so that was one good thing. She clutched her purse against her chest.

He was eyeing her very intensely. "So you're Evan's soul-mate, huh? How sweet is that?"

"He's c-crazy."

"Tell me something I don't know."

"He . . . He's a v-vampire."

The man smiled at that, but it wasn't remotely friendly. Since she was now paying attention she saw the fangs immediately. The thought that this guy was also a vampire did nothing to help the panic situation. "I smell blood. You bleeding right now?"

She swallowed hard. "Evan bit my tongue."

"Such a charmer, isn't he? Can't even keep his fangs to himself during a good old-fashioned grope." He came closer to her and squeezed her chin enough to prompt her to open her mouth so he could see the small cut. His good eye turned to black and he grinned a little. "Probably shouldn't have done that. I'm really hungry right now myself. Haven't had a chance to feed lately. I've been too busy tracking Evan."

"T-tracking him?"

"He's been trying to lose me, strangely enough. Thinks I'm too overprotective. By the way, you can quit with the fake stutter now."

She frowned at him. "It's not fake. I typically s-stutter with fear when somebody has a knife to my throat."

He raised an eyebrow. "This little thing?" He lifted the huge machete-like blade so it glinted in the light of a nearby street lamp. "A guy has to protect himself against dangerous women like you in the big scary city, you know."

"Protect yourself. From me?"

His expression grew colder. "You'd be surprised." He drew closer to her so she could actually feel his warm breath on her face. "You're not as pretty as you were last time."

She glared at him. "Last time?"

"Last time you were with my little brother Evan 300 years ago. No, you were a major beauty back then. You know what they say about Helen of Troy? Well, you were even hotter."

In her current dire situation, she wasn't sure why his appraisal of her sub-par hotness pissed her off as much as it did. "For the record, you're not half as attractive as your brother either."

He grinned. "I guess I kind of deserved that."

"I'm not who you think I am."

"Yeah, right." He smiled, which helped to show his family resemblance to his handsome brother, but she couldn't really keep her eyes off that big old knife he held. "So you're Evan's reincarnated soulmate. And since I knew her – or rather *you* – I'm going to have to say that you should have stayed dead."

"You need to let me go now."

"Do I?" He eyed her. "You obviously have me confused with my brother. He'd do anything you wanted him to. You had him twisted around your little finger. That was not a good time in our lives. He may not have understood exactly what kind of woman you were, but I did."

"Oh yeah? And what kind of woman was that?"

"Evil," he said the word evenly. "Manipulative. Treacherous. Just because of how you looked, you could get away with anything. You nearly destroyed Evan. I won't let you do it again." He reached up to touch his eyepatch. "And I still remember when you did this to me. Just because we're immortal doesn't mean we can regenerate body parts. I do miss having two eyes."

She felt cold at that. "I never would have done anything like that." She took in a shaky breath. "Unless it was self-defence. A big, nasty thug like you probably deserved it."

He drew closer so that there were only inches separating their faces. "You did it when I was unconscious and tied up."

"Oh." Hard to claim self-defence when the other person was defenceless.

"You thought I was trying to get Evan to leave you and you were letting me know you didn't like me very much. It worked. I know Evan was shocked at what you did – hell, you almost killed me that night – but you'd already had your *soulmate-click* thing. If you hadn't fallen down that flight of stairs and broken your neck running away from me when I got loose of the ropes, he never would have been free of you."

She shivered at the vivid picture he'd painted in her mind. "*Soulmate-click* thing?"

He rolled his eye. "When soulmates find each other, this *click* thing happens. It's like their souls recognize each other and come together like magnets. Apparently it's impossible to ignore. Wouldn't know. It's never happened to me, happily enough."

"Are you going to kill me now?" she asked, her voice shaky.

"That was the original plan."

But he was frowning now, harder than before. He had a knife and he was going to kill her in cold blood but he was frowning. Hesitating. No one was around. If he wanted to cleanly and efficiently chop her up into little tiny pieces, then she knew this was his chance.

He breathed out through clenched teeth. "Dammit. This shouldn't be so hard. I know what you are. I know what you're capable of. But I do wish you looked more like you used to. This would be so much easier."

"Because that's what I want. For this to be easy for you."

He cleared his throat. "Why don't you tell me a little bit about yourself . . . *Julia*. A little small talk might be what I need right now."

"I'm a nun," she offered quickly, scrambling for anything that would make him not want to kill her. "I devoted my life to

God several years ago. A life of purity and giving to others. It's very rewarding."

He cocked his head to the side and damned if she didn't see a sliver of amusement slide through his one eye. "Nuns usually hang out at singles bars in this neighbourhood?"

"I'm trying to help others find their way. Lost souls and all that."

"Right. Sure, I believe it. So I guess as a woman of the Lord, you would think of vampires as demons, right? Evil incarnate?"

"Since I only realized that they were real about twenty minutes ago, I'd have to say that I have no defined judgments on vampires yet."

"What's it like to not believe something, to think it's only myth, and then to have it shoved in your face?"

"Jarring," she admitted. "Not as jarring as being threatened with a big knife, though – *by* a vampire."

"I can imagine that." He gave her a lopsided smile. "So, *Sister*, what are your defined judgments on me?"

"I don't even know you."

"You know I'm a vampire and that I obviously have murderous tendencies."

"You haven't killed me yet."

"Give me time."

She had no reason to doubt him, but there was something in the set of his mouth, and in the way he wouldn't look her in her eyes, which made her doubt him.

Why would she doubt him? She didn't know this guy. He even looked scary, although not as terrifying as he had a few minutes ago. Underneath his less-than-stylish black duster and eyepatch and days-growth of beard, was something that wasn't unattractive. Normally it was hard to judge somebody's physical appearance when they were threatening your life. Fear could be blinding.

He'd threatened her with a damn knife. She should be passing out from fear, screaming with terror, *not* appraising his hotness factor.

And yet . . . she was. Sort of. In fact, the longer their strange conversation continued, the more she didn't believe he was capable of murder, even though he was a vampire.

He was trying to help his stupid little brother from making a mistake. That was all. This guy *wasn't* a murderer. She knew it then. It was a gut thing.

And she'd reached this verdict, *why*? Because he had nice lips? Good cheekbones? A deep, sexy voice? A tall, muscular body?

No, it was something deeper than that, something she couldn't put her finger on. Besides, if he was a murderous vampire, then why wouldn't he bite her? He didn't even need an actual weapon since he already had sharp fangs. And her neck was as exposed as her cleavage in the tight black dress she'd chosen to wear to the club tonight.

She was going crazy. Possibly slipping into shock. It was the only explanation.

He was a vampire. A monster. And he had a big knife. Anything outside of that shouldn't have made one damn bit of difference to her.

"What's your name?" she asked.

He stared at her for a long moment, and then said: "Henry."

She was surprised that he'd actually answered. She was equally surprised that his name was Henry. He didn't look like a Henry. Maybe a Lucien. Or a Damian. Something dark and dangerous and sexy.

Wait, she thought. Why am I thinking that? No sense. I'm making zero sense.

Her head felt cloudy. She didn't know what it was about this guy that intrigued her so much. He was a vampire and he wanted to kill her. She had information overload. She must be in shock. That had to be the reason.

"Henry Frost," she said out loud, figuring he and Evan shared a last name.

"That's right."

"Have you always looked after your brother, Henry?"

He looked at her with a frown. "What?"

"What I said. I don't know you or your brother at all—"

"How can you say that?" His dark brows knitted together. "Are you trying to tell me you have no memory of your past life?"

She hissed out a breath. "Number one, I don't believe in reincarnation or soulmates. Number two . . . no, actually that's the only point I have. Of course I don't have any memories of it. I'm not the person you think I am. Trust me on that."

"The witch said it was you."

"Were you there? Did you hear this witch?"

"Yeah, I did. I wasn't in the room with Evan at the time but I was close."

She blinked. "Well, she was wrong."

"Of course you'd say that. You're just as manipulative as you've always been."

"We can discuss this until the cows come home, but it's not going to change things. I'm not your brother's reincarnated soulmate. I'm just somebody who works at the Clinique counter in Sears. And my room-mate who was in the bar with me is going to be looking for me. Any time now. And she's very mean."

"I thought you said you were a nun." Henry raised an eyebrow and his lips twitched with the barest glint of a smile. "And did you just use the expression 'until the cows come home'?"

"You need to let me leave now."

His expression tensed again. "I can't do that."

Frustration now mixed with fear. This man was unbelievably stubborn, but she wasn't giving up. She'd given up a lot of things in her life because they were too hard to get or maintain, but she was damned if she was going to give up her life now. Something about Henry made her want to keep talking, keep fighting, keep trying to convince him that he was wrong about her.

"Have you considered what will happen if you're wrong? If you kill me and I'm the wrong person? Like, oops, the witch made a mistake?"

"This witch doesn't make mistakes. It's what she does. She's a soulmate recovery expert. It's her specialty."

"Soulmate recovery," Julia repeated. "Maybe I'm dreaming. Maybe I didn't get up earlier. I did have an afternoon nap, after all. That would make much more sense than this."

Henry's frown was only deepening the longer she spoke. "The only strange thing is that normally a reincarnated soulmate will recognize their partner on sight. They might not remember every detail of their former lives, but they have that soul recognition and attraction which *clicks* for them. So either you're a very good actress, or something *did* go wrong."

She finally managed to breathe a little at that. "Well, there's your answer."

"That you're a very good actress?"

"I'm a terrible actress. The worst. I couldn't even get a part in the school play in grade six." She was grasping at straws but she had to. Her survival instincts had kicked into overdrive. "You don't want to kill me."

"I don't?"

She shook her head. "You're not a murderer."

His eye narrowed. "You don't know me."

"I'm a really good judge of character."

"That is debatable. So let me get this straight. I grab you, drag you into this alleyway with a knife to your throat, and now you're trying to tell me that you don't think I'm capable of murder? Maybe you want to reform me? You see past the rough exterior to the goodness in my heart, is that it?"

She swallowed. "OK, it does sound a bit naive."

"A lot naive." He shook his head. "You weren't naive in your previous life. You were a devious vixen who played men and got them to do whatever you wanted."

"Even you?"

His expression darkened. "You tried. But it didn't work. I was immune to your particular charms. A pretty face isn't enough to turn my head."

"Are you gay?"

That got a flash of shock on his face. "No."

"But you don't like women."

He made a low groan of annoyance deep in his throat. "I'm not gay. I do like women. But I didn't like you. I could see through to your dark deception in ways that Evan couldn't."

"So this woman. What was her name?"

"Katerina."

"So Katerina threw herself at you, even though she was already soulmated to Evan—"

"She was a whore."

Julia ignored that. "She threw herself at you and you weren't interested. Not even in a quickie? The woman was hot, wasn't she?"

"Like I said, her beauty was not enough to turn my head.

Besides, she . . . *you* . . ." He groaned with annoyance again. "You were involved with my brother. My bond with him prevented me from any disloyalty, even if there had been an attraction. Which there wasn't."

"She kissed you."

"She tried to do a lot more than that when she had me tied up. Before she took my eye." He shook his head and touched his patch again. "Her kiss disgusted me. And you know what they say about a woman scorned—"

Julia went up on her tiptoes and kissed him full on the mouth. She felt Henry's sharp intake of breath against her lips, his shock at what she was doing. Hell, *she* was shocked at what she was doing.

What the hell was *she doing?*

A moment later she heard a loud metallic clatter as the machete fell to the ground. She was a bit afraid at what would happen next, him being very anti-kissing and all. But for somebody who was repelled by Evan's previous soulmate macking on him, he didn't push her away and wipe away her lip cooties. Instead she felt his strong arms come around her waist to pull her closer to his very firm, very warm body. The kiss deepened and as his tongue swept across hers a strange and intense wave of desire nearly knocked her right off her feet.

The crazy, warm-blooded vampire could kiss. And he didn't seem to be stopping any time soon. She could feel his sharp fangs and was certain that they were bigger than they'd been a minute ago. Then again, his fangs weren't the only thing that had gotten bigger since their kiss began.

Guess he isn't gay after all. That was actually a relief.

Why? She realized how insane she sounded. *Why was that a relief?*

That was *two* crazy vampires she'd kissed this evening. And she hated to admit it, but she much preferred the one-eyed version.

"Wait—" Henry breathed and finally moved back a little from her. His eye was fully black again. "What the hell was that?"

Her mouth felt swollen and she bit her bottom lip. "Sorry, I must have slipped on something."

He was frowning so hard it had to be painful. "You disgust me."

"You have a funny way of showing disgust."

"Why did you kiss me?"

"Why did you kiss me back?"

He growled. "This isn't funny."

"I'm not laughing." She swallowed. "I was trying to prove to you that I'm not Evan's soulmate. You said you didn't like kissing Katerina."

"So you kissed me to prove I was wrong?" He shook his head, his good eye growing wider. "You are just as devious as you've always been."

His voice was harsh, but he wasn't pulling away from her or trying to retrieve his fallen weapon. She reached up to gently touch his eyepatch. "I'd never do something like this to you."

He flinched but still didn't pull away. "What the hell is happening to me?"

"First of all, I'm hoping that you don't want to kill me any more."

He sucked in a breath. "I don't."

"*That* is very good to hear."

He didn't say anything for a moment. "I don't understand what's going on. How can you not be her? You *must* be her. The witch is never wrong. Hasn't been for 1,000 years. Not once." He shook his head. "And yet, I feel that you are different from Katerina. When she kissed me, all I felt was coldness. Your kiss is pure heat."

She studied him for a moment. "Your eye is still black."

"Strong emotions will cause my hunger to increase. Like anger, or pain, or . . . or desire." His attention moved to her mouth. "I must never kiss you again. It's too dangerous."

"Too dangerous?"

He nodded. "Evan is your soulmate. Even if you have changed." He drew in a ragged breath. "Perhaps one is not doomed to be the same from lifetime to lifetime. In that case I am happy for him. My brother is a lucky man."

He seemed so sure that she was Evan's soulmate. Was it possible? If she pushed away her disbelief at the bizarre situation that had been thrust into her face that night, was she willing to consider believing it was true? After all, she didn't know vampires were real. But they were. She'd seen it now and she couldn't deny it even if she tried. Maybe the same was true of soulmates. Did the idea of having someone that you're destined to love throughout eternity appeal to her? Yes, it did. She'd never been in love before. She thought it would never happen to her. But maybe she'd kept finding fault in men, not letting herself get close to them, because she'd been waiting for that night. For her soulmate to finally find her.

If she was willing to believe that, then it meant that her soulmate was Evan.

But she didn't like Evan. He was attractive enough, but she hadn't felt any real, deep connection with him.

Like the connection you feel to Henry? she asked herself, knowing that she was making no sense.

Yeah, like that, she answered.

"So what do we do now?" she asked after a moment.

Henry still studied her intensely. "I'm sorry for what I said earlier."

"What was that?"

"That you weren't attractive. It was a lie. You're a very beautiful woman."

"Not compared to the original Katerina."

"Hers was a cold beauty. Untouchable. You—" he looked down to where he still held her "—are obviously very touchable." He swallowed. "Are you still afraid of me?"

"I probably should be, but I stopped being afraid around the time I attacked your lips."

"I see." His jaw tightened. "This will prove to be a very big problem for me. Seeing you with my brother. Knowing that you and he have found happiness together again." He shook his head as if trying to clear it. "I don't know what's wrong with me. I've never felt this way before."

"Me neither."

His gaze moved to hers again and locked. "No?"

She shook her head.

And it was at that moment that she felt something very strange – a *clicking* sensation deep inside of her.

"What just happened?" Henry's breathing increased. "That can't be what I think it is."

"The thing that felt like we're two Lego pieces that just got snapped together?"

"Yeah, that." He pulled away from her finally, releasing her completely to take a few steps backwards. "You are not mine. You belong to Evan."

"I don't belong to anyone."

Except you, she amended internally. Then she frowned.

What in the hell was happening to her? It wasn't right. She hadn't just *clicked* with Henry. She only recently met him, and under very unusual circumstances, to say the least. She didn't believe in love at first sight, especially when the subject was a centuries-old vampire carrying a big knife. And she *didn't* believe in soulmates.

Never had. Never would.

And yet . . .

No, she told herself sternly. *Just no.*

Or, well . . . *maybe.*

"Something has gone terribly wrong," Henry managed after a moment, his expression now giving way to a little of that panic she was very familiar with. "One cannot have *two* soulmates. It doesn't happen."

"Then I think we have a problem here, don't we?"

He nodded, his expression haunted. Then without another word spoken, he moved towards her and pulled her into his arms. "Tell me to stop. Tell me to go away and never come near you again."

"Kiss me," she said instead.

His eye widened. "That definitely isn't helpful."

"Sorry."

Then, just as she thought Henry was going to kiss her again, he stiffened. And not in a good way.

"Release her," Evan growled from behind him.

Henry moved his hands away from her and raised them up to his sides. He shuffled back a few steps so Julia could see that Evan had grabbed the machete from the ground and had it at Henry's back.

"This isn't what you think," Henry began.

"This is exactly what I think. You've always hated her. How could you do this to me after my long, difficult search? Do you deny that you planned to kill her?"

"I can't really deny that, actually. But—"

"Shut up," Evan snarled. "You always try to run my life, brother."

"What, by keeping you safe and alive?"

"I'm tired of it. Hundreds of years of being under your thumb. I wanted to escape you once and for all, and you follow me here?"

"You weren't that hard to follow." Henry shrugged. "You're kind of sloppy when it comes to travel arrangements. Always have been."

"How did you learn of her?" Evan flicked a glance in Julia's direction.

"I overheard you with the witch."

"I see. So you followed her from the club after I'd made contact with her. And you planned to use this—" Evan now pressed the sharp blade against Henry's throat "—to end her life over an old squabble."

"She took my eye. Not to mention that she was generally evil and liked killing people for fun and profit. Remember that?"

"She had her reasons. Just as I have my reasons for killing you now where you stand."

Julia watched them in horror. There was nothing friendly or brotherly about this confrontation. It looked as deadly as that machete. A fine line of red appeared at Henry's throat to prove just how sharp that blade was.

Evan turned to her. "Are you OK, my love?"

She held out her hands. "Put down the knife."

"I can't do that. I need to kill him once and for all. Now that I've found you again, I won't let you come to any harm." His expression softened. "I know you don't believe all of this yet. I know this has been a great shock. It will take my genitals some time to recover from what happened earlier—"

Henry raised an eyebrow at that.

Julia shrugged. "I kneed him in the balls when he got a bit frisky with me."

A small smile twitched at the corners of Henry's mouth. "See, I *knew* you were dangerous."

"Did I say you could speak?" Evan growled at his brother. "This must end tonight, Henry. I can't be constantly afraid that you will try to kill the woman I love for crimes that are now 300 years in the past. It ends here."

"You're really going to kill me?"

"I have to."

Julia knew in that moment that this wasn't fun and games. Evan was actually going to slit his brother's throat. She wasn't sure if that would be enough to kill a vampire, but she didn't want to take the risk.

"Wait," she said. "Please don't do it, Evan."

He turned to her. "You wish to wield the blade yourself?"

It took her a moment to figure out what he meant by that. Did she want to kill Henry? Definitely not. Sure they'd started off on the wrong foot, but something was there between them, something *major*, and whether or not it was magical or mystical or *whatever*, she didn't want it to end quite so quickly. She didn't want him to die before she figured out the tornado of strange feelings that whirled inside her.

"I'm your soulmate, right?" she said to Evan.

He nodded emphatically. "You believe it to be true?"

"Yes, of course," she lied. "You and me. Together for ever. It just took me by surprise, is all. Apparently I was kind of evil in the past." She and Henry exchanged a glance.

Evan frowned. "You mustn't listen to anything Henry says."

"Why? Was he wrong?"

Evan cringed. "Well, I wouldn't so much as use the word 'evil' to describe you. Challenging and exciting are better words."

"You have got to be joking," Henry said dryly.

"Shut your mouth," Evan hissed. "You mean to kill the woman I love and now you are smart-mouthing me? You are in no position to do anything but beg for mercy."

"Don't kill him," Julia said simply.

Evan frowned. "Why not?"

"Because . . ." She scrambled to come up with something that sounded like a reasonable excuse to prevent murder.

"Because I've changed. I'm not into evil things any more. I just want everyone to get along and be happy."

"That's wonderful, but I have no assurance that my brother feels the same way. He will never give up. He's relentless in his pursuit of what he wants. It's very annoying."

Julia looked at Henry, his head tilted back to avoid the blade Evan still held tightly against his throat. "Do you promise to not relentlessly pursue me?"

Their eyes locked and she only felt that *click* from earlier tighten up a notch.

"Not sure I can promise that," he managed. "I don't think I'll be able to stay away from you even if I wanted to."

She knew he didn't mean murder. But Evan didn't.

"Thank you for making this easier, brother." Evan pulled his arm back to prepare for the death blow.

Julia moved quickly, putting herself between Henry and Evan before he could bring the knife down across Henry's throat.

"Stop," she said. "Nobody has to die here. I'll go with you. Anywhere. We never have to see Henry again. Just don't hurt him. Please."

"You are acting very erratically," Evan said with a frown.

"It's been a strange evening."

Julia heard something then. A low buzzing sound.

Evan grimaced. "One moment, please." He pulled a cell phone out of his pocket and held it to his ear. "Evan Frost here." A pause. "Yes, that's right." Another pause and then he raised his gaze to look at both Julia and Henry in turn.

Julia could feel the heat from Henry's body behind her. She didn't want to turn. She didn't want to say anything else. She knew what would happen if she couldn't convince Evan to turn around and leave with her. He'd kill Henry with no more questions asked. It didn't matter how long they'd been brothers, how long they'd lived and survived. One would be dead. And she was sure that Henry wouldn't raise a finger to defend himself. He'd spent his existence trying to keep his younger brother out of trouble; he wouldn't fight to the death against him.

She knew it was impossible to have fallen in love with somebody in a matter of minutes – to love them so deeply that you'd be willing to change your life in order to save them. And yet, that's exactly what she was doing. She'd leave with Evan if it meant saving Henry's life.

It was crazy, but that didn't mean it wasn't true. She'd never felt so sure about anything before in her entire life. She loved Henry, and she didn't want him to die.

"Don't do this," Henry whispered into her hair. "Let him kill me. It'll be easier for everyone involved."

"Shut up," she told him.

Evan frowned as he continued to speak to whoever was on the phone. "I don't understand. Very well, if you insist." He looked again at Julia and Henry. "It's the witch who performed the soulmate recovery spell. She wants to be put on speakerphone." He pressed a button and held the phone out at arm's length.

"Hello, can you hear me?" the witch said.

"Uh . . . yes," Julia replied.

"Loud and clear," Henry said.

"Very good." The witch cleared her throat. "I'm afraid there's been an error and I'm not quite sure how it happened."

"An error?" Evan sounded disturbed. "What do you mean?"

"When you were here yesterday, Mr Frost, I felt as if there was something awry. The feeling has lasted until a moment ago when I got a surge of power here in my lair. My crystal ball lit up like a lantern. And I knew then, without a shadow of a doubt, that something was horribly, horribly wrong with the recovery I did for you yesterday."

Evan still clutched the machete as he gazed wistfully at Julia. "There is nothing wrong. I have found my true love with your help and I thank you from the bottom of my heart. Every penny of your fee was earned. She is mine for ever. Our souls reunited. I have never felt such deep love in my entire existence."

"Julia Donner is not your soulmate," the witch said simply.

"Excuse me?" Evan replied. "I don't think I heard you right."

"I know, it's very unusual. I found the wrong one. The energy I channelled yesterday pointed in the wrong direction but I don't understand why. No one else was with us. There was no other life essence that I could have drawn from. I can't understand this."

"Well, I was there." Henry's voice was soft.

"Pardon?" the witch said.

"I was there," Henry repeated. "I'd followed Evan. I wanted to find out the location of his soulmate so I could find her and murder her so she wouldn't exert her evil influence on my brother ever again."

There was a pause. "And is she dead?"

"No, still alive," Julia spoke up. "Very confused, freaked out and generally shaken, but alive."

"Then that must be the answer," the witch said. "OK, that totally makes more sense. I thought I'd screwed up and that never happens, thank you very much. Hello? We're talking a millennium of perfect soulmate recovery here. I have a very good rep. for this sort of thing, you know – the best in the biz, in fact. I didn't realize that there were two Frost brothers in attendance at the recovery yesterday. It's obvious to me now that I channelled the wrong essence and found your soulmate, Henry. Not Evan's."

Henry and Julia looked at each other. He swallowed. "That's impossible. I don't have a soulmate."

"You've never found her before probably because you didn't have my help, but there she is. Congrats. Live happily ever after. I'll send you my bill."

Julia was stunned. *More* stunned, that is. So it was true? That deep and nearly immediate connection she felt for Henry was because they were soulmates who'd just never connected before?

"Um," Evan said, the machete now lowered to his side. "*What the hell?*"

The witch cleared her throat nervously. "So very, very sorry about any inconvenience, Evan. If it helps, I did manage to locate your true soulmate, formerly known as Katerina."

Evan's previously dejected expression turned optimistic. "Where is my truest love?"

"It's a good news, bad news situation. She was reincarnated as a pit bull terrier. That's the bad news."

His shoulders slumped. "What's the good news?"

"She's in the same city you're in right now. If you want to see her again."

Evan chewed his bottom lip. "Yes, I'll be needing that address." He took the phone off speaker. "Henry," he said. "So sorry about the mix up. No hard feelings?"

"Consider it forgotten," Henry replied.

Evan wandered off with the phone pressed to his ear.

"So . . ." Julia began after a few moments of silence. "Strange night, huh?"

Henry swallowed hard. "I deeply apologize from the bottom of my heart for everything that has happened here."

She pressed her lips together. "You should probably know that I'm still not totally convinced about this whole soulmate thing."

"No?" He raised an eyebrow.

She shook her head. "It's a bit outside my comfort zone of knowledge."

He nodded gravely. "I would assume so."

"However . . ."

"Yes?"

"I suppose I'd be OK with learning more about it." She grinned at him. "That is, if you wanted to teach me."

"I could easily be convinced." A smile touched his lips. "So you forgive me for trying to kill you?"

"No. But if we potentially have forever together then I'll probably get over it eventually." She reached down to take his hand in hers. "But how about we start with drinks back at the bar and take it from there?"

"I'd say that's an excellent start."

The world seemed much bigger than it had before. Full of strange things like handsome vampires and soulmate-recovering witches.

Was Henry the one-eyed vampire her soulmate? Was he the man she'd waited her whole life – possibly *several* lives – to find, only to have him fall into her arms at a most unusual moment?

She was definitely willing to find out.

Blue Crush

A Weather Warden story

Rachel Caine

I love the ocean. I love the pounding heartbeat of waves on shore. I love the way sunrise turns the endless glitter into a bowl of spilled jewels – rubies, sapphires, with glints of diamonds everywhere.

I love the ocean, but I don't swim in it.

This is the same reason that Weather Wardens – who have powers that can affect the air and water – don't like flying. You're suspended in an alien environment, one that is instinctually aware of you and the potential threat you pose. The air *always* fights back. The ocean chooses its moments, and in a way that's worse; you can trust it until you suddenly can't.

So, I don't swim. Instead, I put on my bikini of the season and lie out on the sand, and occasionally tickle my toes in the rushing cool surf when I get overheated. But sometimes, as I bake on the beach, I watch people playing in the waves, and I long to be having that much fun.

"We should go out there," David said. Reading my mind, as usual.

I turned my head and skinned my sunglasses down my nose to meet his eyes. My lover was lying in the sun in a pair of black swim trunks and nothing else – a very pleasant picture indeed, and not just for me. David is a Djinn, one of those old-time genies from the bottles; he can be anything he wants to be.

For me, he's always the same: tall, with the lean, sleek muscles of a runner. Defined, not bulked. His skin is this gorgeous tint somewhere between gold and bronze, a shade you'll never find in any tanning booth or bottle, no matter how hard you try. He was slightly turned towards me, raised up on one elbow. David likes to wear round, scholarly glasses, but he'd left them off today, and it raised his hotness alert level from *smoking* to *nuclear*. His hair was a little shaggy, and it caught the light in gleams of auburn and gold.

"Out where?" I asked, as I allowed my inspection to move from his gorgeous face to his strong neck, his firm chest, down to the ridges of his abdominal muscles. "Because you look good right there to me, mister."

David has the most sincerely dangerous smile I've ever seen – dangerous not because it is so lovely (although it is that) but because it just brims with possibilities begging to be explored. The first time I'd seen him, we'd been enemies; the second time, he'd been trying to help me, or I'd been trying to help him, however you score these things. But it had been that smile that had thrown me off balance, and made me vulnerable to him.

Still did.

"You never swim," he said. "You should. Seems like a waste to have all this ocean at your front door and never enjoy it to the fullest."

"I enjoy it academically," I said. "Besides, I need to work on my tan."

"Your tan is perfect," David said, and drew a gentle finger down my arm, soft as a feather. "I want you in the water."

The hot flash that washed over me had nothing to do with overheating. "Public beach," I said, but it was a weak defence, at best. His smile widened.

"We don't get many vacations," he said. "When we do, we should make the most of them. And you know I can keep us from being seen, no matter where we are." Two fingers this time, dragged slowly and provocatively down the tender inner aspect of my arm. "No matter what we do."

I was having trouble keeping my breath. "Man, you'd make a very dangerous criminal."

"So I have," he agreed. "From time to time."

Different masters holding his bottle, I thought, but I didn't say that. David wasn't in a bottle any more. David was the conduit, the power connection between the New Djinn – Djinn who'd once been human – and the sleeping power of Mother Earth herself.

In short, he was the boss.

On the other side of the organizational chart were the Old Djinn, or – as they liked to call themselves – the True Djinn, which tells you something about their arrogance. They had a conduit, too, his name was Ashan, and he was a right bastard who didn't like David, didn't like me and didn't like humanity in general cluttering up his planet.

Mutually assured destruction kept the peace between the Djinn.

"You're going to have to tell me a story sometime," I said. I rolled over on my side to face David and propped my head on my arm. My long, dark hair slithered over my shoulders and cascaded down, curling at the ends in the moist breeze. "About that part of your life."

"I'm not sure you want to know." He considered that for a moment, and from the wry twist of his lips, he knew how wrong that was. "All right, I'm not sure that I want to tell you."

"If we're together, we're together. Good times and bad."

"I've got plenty of bad," he said. "I'd rather make some new experiences with *you*. Pleasant ones."

"*After* you tell me a story."

He tried to suppress a smile. "Can it be a bedtime story?"

"You wish. Something personal. About your – criminal past."

I think he might have actually started to open up to me. His lips parted, and I saw the resignation on his face – and then a shadow fell across both of us. A *big* shadow, maybe twice as broad in the chest as David, with biceps as large as my thighs.

A bodybuilder. One with so much overdevelopment that you could almost smell steroids in his sweat. He'd adopted a stiff military-style haircut, and a lot of truly ugly tattoos.

And he had friends. Four of them. Although none of them was anywhere near his desperation-level of intimidation. Lots of tattooing and attitude. They weren't exactly fitting in, but then, they didn't intend to.

Muscles stared down at David with what I suppose he thought was ferocious menace. "Move," he barked.

David looked up at him, eyebrows arched, perfectly at ease. "Why?"

Apparently, Muscles wasn't prepared for anyone to ask a reasonable question. "Because I said so," he blurted back, and then pulled his face into a frown that looked very odd on a grown man's face. "Because you're in our spot, asswipe. Get your punk ass up."

Here's the problem with being supernaturally gifted: you really can't go around blowing away every goofball idiot who tries to make himself your problem, no matter how convenient it might be. Muscles might think he was badass, but he wasn't up to going one round with me, never mind David. It's always difficult to break that fact to them gently, without wounding their sensitive, macho feelings of inadequacy.

David was already moving forwards on that. "There's plenty of beach," he pointed out.

"I said this is *our* spot. Now get up and leave before we bury you in it."

David looked at me, and I saw the frustrated humour in his shrug. I sighed and started to gather up my things. It wasn't worth the fight.

At least it wasn't until Muscles said, "Not you, bitch. You, you stay. We need us some candy." He stuck out his tongue and fluttered it in the approved Gene Simmons manner, although he was nowhere near able to pull it off like His Rockness. Meanwhile, his friends spread out around us, trying to cut us off. I noticed that other people who'd parked their towels and coolers nearby were hustling away, sensibly thinking that maybe they had better places to be right now.

I sat up and pulled my knees together, wrapping my arms demurely around them. "Excuse me? Did you just call me 'bitch'? Because I've got a name. In fact, every girl you leer at has a name. Mine's Joanne. Hi, nice to meet you." I let a slow, wicked smile spread over my lips. "Now take your inked-up posse of posers and find another spot."

"Oh, here we go," David murmured. He flopped down on his back, hands crossed peacefully on his chest.

Muscles stared at me like I'd grown another set of breasts. "What? Bitch, did you just tell me to *move on*?"

"Wait, let me go to the instant replay – the judges say 'yes'. And congratulations on mastering listening for comprehension. Your mom must be so proud."

I lost him on that one, so he took the shortcut straight to the point. "Shut the fuck up, or I'll fuck you up, bitch!"

Muscles was waiting for David to leap to my defence. He kept glancing down at him. David responded by moving his hands from their resting position atop his chest to a more comfortable behind-the-head pillow.

"Don't look at him, look at me," I said, and shook my hair back from my face. "This is between the two of us, right?"

"Bullshit." Muscles decided to get proactive, since he really wasn't into fighting girls, at least as a first choice. He raised one massive foot and brought it down on David's stomach.

Well. He tried.

David didn't bother to so much as flinch, but then, he didn't need to.

I reacted for him.

Muscles let out a raw yelp of surprise, and his back foot disappeared into the sand to the depth of about three feet as I instantly pulverized and dried the sand underneath him, making it as fine as powder. He flailed, fell backwards, and *poof*, disappeared in a puff of dust. I let him drop about two more feet beneath the surface before I hardened the sand again, added a little water for thickness, and helpfully raised him until his mouth and nose were in the air, gasping for breath.

I left him there, buried to the chin.

His friends stared down at him, dumbstruck. Muscles let out an inarticulate yell of rage and fear. Under the coating of dust, his big domed head was turning brick red with fury. Well, he could flail all he wanted, he wasn't getting out of there. Not on his own. Amazing how heavy a little damp sand can be.

A couple of his friends looked at me and David, and at least one of them looked willing to take up Muscles' cause. I softened the sand under their feet just enough to let them sink in about a foot. "Whoops," I said. "Quicksand. Who knew that kind of thing was a beach hazard in Florida? Hey, dude, how you doing down there?"

Muscles yelled. I didn't listen. His lungs were fine.

"What do you think?" I asked David. "Maybe we should go get him some help? You know, eventually?"

"You mean *now* you want to go?"

"Well, he's very loud. It's harshing my calm."

David shook his head, but I could tell he was more amused than annoyed. I took my time gathering up my stuff, folding my towel, packing the lotion and water. Muscles continued to howl, mostly inarticulately, but sometimes treating me to whole new vistas of insults. His buddies had prudently backed off and were watching from a distance.

"What if they'd been armed?" David asked me, very quietly, as he leaned over me to pick up the picnic basket. I gave him a one-shoulder shrug.

"We'd handle it. But honestly, it's pretty tough to hide a gun in your swim trunks without getting rousted for lewd behaviour. Not that much of a risk."

"You were just looking for a fight."

"No, they brought me one. I just didn't walk away from it."

David looked at me from the distance of a vast ocean of years. There were times – rare, but striking – when I realized just how old he really was, how full of experiences. "Sometimes you should try walking away," he said. "In the old days, honour said no one could back down from a fight without bringing disgrace on themselves. Today, you have a choice. You should exercise it once in a while."

I kissed him. I couldn't help it; his lips were close, and parted, and warm. It was lingering and sweet and had the dark, yummy promise of a whole lot more yet to come. "How about over there?" I asked, and pointed down the beach, alluding to an area just around the bend, where it was deserted. "Out of sight, out of mind?"

"Seems prudent," he agreed. We set off across the hot, sparkling sands, dodging around a few blankets and beach umbrellas and people who were standing around, still watching the show. "Are you going to leave him there?"

"Oh, he's OK. I didn't squeeze him or anything. They can dig him out, if they want."

"Jo, you—" David stopped talking, and he also stopped walking. He turned to look out over the water. "Do you hear that?"

I concentrated. All I heard was the constant rushing roar of the surf, with the continued ranting of Muscles floating over the top. "Hear what?"

"Someone calling for help."

Even as David said it, I spotted a human shape stumbling out of the waves just a little further down the beach – a boy, maybe sixteen. He fell to his hands and knees in the hissing foam and vomited up an impressive fountain of water.

I grabbed a towel out of my bag and raced to him. "Hey! You OK?" I got the towel around his shaking shoulders and rubbed vigorously as he choked and coughed and got out the rest of the sea he'd swallowed. There was some white spittle around his mouth and nose. He'd come really close to drowning. "Here. Sit. David, help me with him."

We got the boy up the beach and settled on dry sand, covered in towels. He was still shaking. His skin – a light cocoa, normally – had an unhealthy ashen pallor to it, and his eyes were blank and traumatized.

I took his hands in mine and squeezed. Slowly, his gaze refocused away from whatever horrible memory he had been seeing in his mind's eye. "What's your name?" I asked, keeping my voice low and gentle. "I'm Joanne."

"Cal," he said. "Calvin Harper." As if that was some kind of key to the lock on his mind, his face suddenly filled with emotion. With *panic*. "Where's Parker? Did you get Parker?"

"Who's Parker?"

He didn't answer me. He tried to struggle to his feet, but I put my hands on his shoulders and pushed him back down. Skin-to-skin contact woke my Earth powers, which travelled up in a slow, warm pulse from the soles of my feet and out through my fingertips, ghosting through Cal's body in a golden wave. He was all right – exhausted from fighting the ocean, and he still had water and foam in his lungs, but I concentrated for a moment and cleared that out. Otherwise, he was just full of pure anxiety.

"Parker," I repeated. "Who's Parker?"

"My girl," Cal gasped. He rubbed his face and close-cut hair with both hands, trying to scrub off the feelings of misery and fear. "I left her. I couldn't get her. She's in trouble out there."

I turned and looked at the waves. I couldn't see anybody out there.

I turned on my heels to look at David, who dropped the picnic basket on the sand. "I guess we're going swimming," he said.

I didn't see any way around it.

The thing that surprised me was that swimming felt *good*. It had been a long, long time since I'd voluntarily waded into the ocean. The first cold splash of the water was a livid shock, but then my body adjusted and, by the time the surf was cradling my knees, I felt comfortable.

David, next to me, was scanning the horizon. His eyes had taken on a hot golden shine – a whole lot more than human just now. A shimmer of bronze crept over his skin, giving him the appearance of living metal.

"See anything?" I asked.

"She's there," he said, and pointed. "I'll bring her in. Wait here."

That wasn't the agreement, but *blip*, the next wave that crashed down erased him right out of the picture. David could go anywhere he liked at a whim, but he couldn't take me with him. I had to travel the old-fashioned way.

Which was why he'd told me to stay put. The problem was, David was going to have to bring the girl back the old-fashioned way, too – faster than a human could swim, granted, but he couldn't blip her from point A to point B without leaving pieces of her behind.

I hate to wait. I wasn't *intending* to swim out there, but I kept pushing forwards, and suddenly I was floating, so it seemed like the thing to do. The cool rush of water over my body was exhilarating, and the little-worked muscles on the insides of my arms began to burn in a pleasant kind of way. As each wave rose towards me I dived into it and came out a little further out, a little deeper. I still couldn't see David. White clouds drifted by overhead, a few scudding at the horizon like steam from the waves.

Pretty soon I was swimming steadily out in the direction David had indicated.

My awareness spread out around me, like sonar through the water – an instinctive kind of thing, nothing I planned to do. At first I was only aware of the darting shapes of fish near me that stayed well clear of both the roiling surf and my kicking feet; but then my sense of the ocean deepened, focused, and I felt the vast network solidifying around me. It was different than living in the air – closer somehow. More connected. I was an alien element in a world where I wasn't necessary, and it was a very odd feeling.

I felt the rushing heat of David's approach across the water, and adjusted my course to meet him. Something odd was happening near him – no, around him. He was slowing down.

David was slowing down. That didn't make much sense. I swam faster.

I caught a glimpse of him as I rode the next wave's crest. He was still making forward progress, and he had a young, limp-looking girl in a rescue hold.

As I watched, they both disappeared under the water as if yanked by an invisible cord.

Crap.

I dived.

I found the girl first, floating free in the water – a drifting ghost, peaceful and silent. I grabbed her and arrowed back for the surface, where I got her face into the air again. She wasn't breathing. I did a Heimlich to force water out of her lungs, and was rewarded with a sputtering, coughing eruption, and a gasping breath. She flailed wildly, but I managed to keep her above the surface.

Where the hell was David?

I extended my net of perception down instead of out, driving into the darkness and pressure where humans wouldn't normally be found. Lots of life down there – cold, odd life, with little in common to my own human condition.

David was down there, and he was fighting something big. Something *strong*, obviously, because you just don't manhandle a Djinn and get away with it. I could feel the shocks not just through the water, but up on the aetheric level as well – the level of reality above the one we inhabited. Energy was swirling, turning on itself in ugly and destructive ways.

And the ocean was reacting to the fight. I could feel the growing agitation as energy fed into what was essentially a closed system . . . and I didn't like where things were going.

"Hold on," I told the girl breathlessly. "You're going to be all right. Be calm, OK?" Then I formed a shell of air molecules around her, permeable enough to allow gas transfers, but solid enough to keep out the water. It was like a soap bubble, slightly tinted in the glimmer of the sunlight. I let go of her, and closed the bubble seamlessly behind me; she battered at the shell trying to reach me, but right now she was better off as she was. She'd calm down in a minute, once she realized that she was safe, dry and drifting towards shore (something I made sure of with an application of force in the right direction).

I sucked in a super-oxygenated breath and dived into the darkness.

The water was a chilly turquoise roof overhead, sparkling with glitter from the wavelets, but as I descended the blue deepened to twilight, then to darkness. Pressure increased, crushing in on me. I had several choices of how to handle it, but I went for the simplest; Earth powers allowed me to adjust my body chemistry to cope with the changes, and my ability to form complex chemical chains out of the air in my lungs and the water around me helped me come up with a kind of temporary rebreathing mixture, the kind deep-sea divers would use. Invisible shields helped my ears hold against the increasing stress; the last thing I needed was a punctured eardrum at this depth.

I adjusted the structure of my eyes, letting in more light, but even that failed as I descended. I had to rely on Oversight – a kind of overlay heads-up display that showed me the aetheric patterns of the world around me. It was unsettling how crowded this environment was, and how little of it I could see. Animals darted around me, mostly uninterested in something my size but a few clearly wondering if I could be a potential new protein source. I didn't like sharks. Not at *all*.

But the strangest predator was yet to come, because I found David locked in battle with something that I didn't recognize – and then, I did. Not from science, but from mythology.

A *mermaid*.

Well, to be fair, not so much a *maid* as a *man*. This creature had the upper-body structure of something like a human, although the muscles seemed to be moving in world-bendingly odd ways around bones that didn't quite look right. I couldn't see it clearly, and I instinctively wanted to. Needed to.

I called fire into a small, self-contained bubble between us, and lit up the sea.

The merman turned on me with the speed of a striking eel, and he'd have had me if David hadn't gotten in the way. Well, I'd wanted a look, and I got one – a terrifying one. That was no romantic, Byronic prince of the sea. That was what you might get if you blended the Creature from the Black Lagoon with an albino shark, and gave it the muscular, iron-grey tail of a dolphin. He shimmered with iridescent scales in the bottled firelight, and his eyes were huge, all dark except for white vertical slits for pupils.

He had a lot of teeth, and they were all pointed at me.

I found myself swimming backwards, trying to put water between us as quickly as possible. There was something so utterly wrong about this thing that I felt sick, as if my understanding of the world had been turned upside down. Odd, because I lived in a world most normal people would find upsetting in the extreme.

David slammed a fist into the merman's face with enough force to pulverize granite. The merman just hissed in fury and sank his teeth into David's wrist. He had claws too, long bony things that scraped at David's chest and opened pale gouges. No blood. David had changed his body structure far enough from human to prevent real damage.

"Get out of here!" he yelled at me. His words came loud and clear, if a bit oddly high-pitched. "Surface! Get to shore!"

He was right. If this creature was beyond David, it was beyond me too. I could feel the power inside of it radiating outwards; it was a match for the Djinn. The water-world equivalent, maybe; something Wardens rarely encountered, if ever – or survived, if they did.

I was going to follow David's advice – really, I was.

But just as I started to arrow for the distant blue world above, something caught me by the ankle in a crushing grip.

Bony, astonishingly strong fingers.

I looked down, and in the murky swirls of Oversight, saw a *second* merman. No . . . this one really did seem to be a mermaid, complete with small, protruding breasts.

She wasn't any prettier than the male of the species.

I'm not supernaturally muscular, but I have powers that your average mermaid might not expect, and I took full advantage of this. I sent a violent burst of energy crackling through my body, electrifying my skin and burning her hand where she gripped me. She let go and swiped at me with her claws. I mostly avoided the slice, but she drew shallow red stripes across the back of my right leg, just above the ankle. I responded by kicking her, hard, right in the bony part of her chest. She flipped her tail and righted herself almost instantly, and came for me with her shark-like jaws wide open.

I hardened the water between us to the consistency of gelatin. She tried to swim forwards, hit the wall and bounced, and I recognized the look of bafflement that sped across her fishy face. I was supposed to be easy prey, wasn't I?

Not hardly.

Oddly enough, that seemed funny, although it wasn't. I knew I should be afraid, but I was weirdly amused. In fact, I was choking back a manic attack of giggles, and losing my focus. The hardened water turned softer and she lunged for me again. I was able to hold her off, but the urge to laugh kept getting more and more insistent. I was breathing in and out way too fast to get the necessary benefit. Hyperventilating, I thought. My chest hurt. Nothing looked right.

David's warm hand closed around my wrist, and I realized that I'd forgotten to re-oxygenate my mixture; black dots were swimming in front of my eyes, and I was starting to lose it. I relaxed and let David's strength pull me towards the surface. My concentration had to be focused inwards, on adjusting my body to the changing pressure and closing up the wound on my leg. The last thing I wanted to do was attract sharks right now.

I saw the merman and his mate chasing us, rising out of the depths like pale fish, flickering in the twilight and struggling to adjust to the decompression as we neared the surface. They were deep-water creatures, and the female dropped off first, heading back to the safe, crushing darkness.

The merman's bony claws brushed my foot, but failed to grab hold, and I saw him give a pained hiss of frustration before flipping his muscular tail and diving, heading straight for the bottom.

We broke the surface with so much speed we literally rose into the air about four feet, and then we splashed back down. David's arms went around me, warm and real, and I dragged in breath after breath of moist, sweet air.

"I told you to get to the surface!" he said. "Do you *have* to fight with everything you see?"

I didn't bother to argue that I was, in fact, *trying* to flee at the time. "I'm OK," I said, which was the answer he was looking for even if he wasn't asking. "I'm OK, David."

He let out a breath, and I felt his arms tighten around me. "This time you are," he said. "No more games, Jo. Back to shore."

I didn't have to swim, only float; David towed me, making for shore with steady, tireless strokes. I caught sight of the bubble I'd formed around our rescued girl. She was almost to shore now, swept in on the waves. I popped the bubble as the final wave crested, and she toppled into the surf and ended up on the sand, caught up in Calvin Harper's arms.

A happy ending, after all.

"What are they?" I asked David. "Those . . . creatures?"

He said a word I couldn't understand, much less pronounce. It sounded like dolphin clicks. "They're powerful," he said. "Even for the Djinn, they're dangerous. To humans, even to Wardens—"

"Deadly. Got that part." I coughed out a stray mouthful of salty ocean and pushed streaming hair off my face. The surf was pounding now as we neared the shore. I could feel the ocean bottom rising to meet us, and the warmer waters felt welcoming. Almost safe. "What set them off?"

"Nothing. They hunt for prey. Sometimes it's humans," he said. "But once they realized I was in the water, and you were a Warden, they wanted us."

"To eat?"

"You, maybe. Me, to keep," he said. "They have Djinn trapped below, not many, but over the millennia there have been a few, here and there. We can't save them."

I imagined a zoo, far in the dark, crushing emptiness of the deep ocean – Djinn, held captive, unable to break free. I imagined that happening to David, and felt ill. "What do they want them for?"

David shook his head. "We don't know."

That was . . . unsettling.

David slowed our progress as our feet touched the sandy bottom. A wave crested and lifted, then lowered us gently down.

I turned into his embrace.

His lips tasted of salt, hot metal, urgency. His skin was warmer than it should have been, as warm as bronze left in the sun, and it felt so good against my chilled flesh. I shivered against him and held on as tides swept us towards land.

"Well," I whispered, as our lips parted for a breath, "you wanted me in the water. I'm here."

"So you are." His hands travelled over me, pouring heat into me with every brush of his fingers on my skin.

"We should check on the girl," I said – not really feeling the urgency though, because his touch was waking all kinds of other thoughts instead.

I saw it mirrored in his smile. "She's being well cared for," he said. And he was right, absolutely right. A small crowd of people had formed around Cal and his girl, and I saw the distant flashing of emergency lights heading in from the street.

I could even see that Muscles was out of any danger; his friends were digging him out of his hole. After that, and the arrival of police and paramedics, they'd be withdrawing from the field of battle as fast as their stumpy legs could carry them.

David recaptured my focus with a gentle kiss on my forehead. "I love you, Joanne."

It wasn't that he hadn't said it before, or that he hadn't meant it, it was the intensity with which he spoke that made me shiver down to my bones. I put my arms around his neck and stared into his eyes – hot copper, shimmering with passion and almost-alien power. "I know," I said. "I can feel it, every moment. And I love you, David. More than my life."

His thumbs smoothed wet hair back from my cheeks and lingered in a caress. "Then I'm very lucky," he said. "Luckier than I've ever been in all my lifetimes. And I'm going to make sure your life is long and rich, my love. Despite your willingness to throw it away."

He kissed me, and this time it was full of fire and need, and it melted me into a hot, glowing puddle inside. I hardly felt the waves lifting and rolling us; if the ocean chose to strike at us, it would find me entirely unaware.

But I surrendered to David, and I knew, in that moment, that he could protect me. He *would*. Not from the obvious threats I faced every day, by chance or choice, but from myself.

His hands dragged over me and, where they touched, my wet bikini faded away. Top first, and then bottom. He'd already disposed of his swim trunks.

I could feel how much he wanted me, and it took my breath away. He slid his fingers slowly from the notch of my collarbone, down between my breasts, gliding through the warm water all the way to the softness between my legs.

I bit my lip on a gasp and closed my eyes, giving myself up to the dizzying sensation of his hands, his fingers, his mouth waking sharp points of heat along my throat. The water warmed around us until the caress of the tides felt as overpowering as David's touch – a thousand individual whispers over my skin, shredding my focus into a gauzy mist of sheer pleasure.

I wrapped myself around him, guiding him into the core of me, and he cradled me in his arms – weightless in this beautiful and silent moment, as if we had left all bounds of earth behind. The lovemaking was slow, thorough, sweetly tense. His skin tasted of the sea, of life, of all the beauty in the world. I let myself drift with him, helpless on the currents, feeling the waves of pleasure crest even as the other waves, the ones fuelled by wind and water, pounded over us.

David wanted me in water. I wanted him forever.

There, off the beach, in one stolen afternoon, we both got our wish.

The Wager

A Lords of Avalon story

Sherrilyn Kenyon writing as Kinley MacGregor

It'd been a long, cold . . . *Millennium.*

Thomas paused as he penned those words. Surely it wasn't that long. Was it? Frowning, he looked at the calendar on his PDA that Merlin had brought to him from what future man would call the twenty-first century and gave a low whistle.

It hadn't been quite that long, even though he lived in a land where time had no real meaning. It only felt like it, and therefore he left the word on the paper. It sounded better than saying just a few centuries – and that was what writing was all about, he'd learned. The truth was important, but not so much as keeping his audience entertained. News bored people, but stories . . .

That was where the money was. At least for people other than him. There was no money here, nor much of anything else.

But he was digressing. Millennium or not, it had been way too long since he'd last been free.

He who bargains with the devil pays with eternity, his dear old mangled mother had been fond of saying. Too bad he hadn't been better at listening – but then that was the problem with "conversation". So many times even when you paused for a breath you weren't really listening to the other person so much as planning your next speech. Of course, he'd been a cocky youth.

What did some old crone know about anything anyway? he used to think. He was Thomas Malory. *Sir* Thomas Malory – couldn't forget the Sir part. That was all-important.

In his day that Sir had meant that he was a man with standing. A man with prospects.

A man with no friggin' clue (Thom really liked the vernacular Percival had taught him from other centuries. There was just such colour to some of the later phraseology . . . but now to return to what he'd been thinking).

Life had begun easy enough for him. He'd been born into a well-to-do family. A *nice* family . . . "Nice" incidentally was a four-lettered word. Look it up, it really was. It meant, "to be agreeable. Pleasant. Courteous."

Boring.

Like any good youth worth his salt, he'd run as far away from nice as he could. Nice was for the weak (another four-lettered word). It was for a doddering fool (see how everything vile led back to four letters [even vile was four letters]).

And Thomas was anything but a fool. Or so he'd thought.

Until the day he'd met *her* (please insert footnote here that in French, *la douleur* i.e. pain, is feminine). There was a reason for that. Women, not money, were the root of all evil (it was a trick of their gender that "woman" was five and not four letters, but then "girl" was four letters too. This was done to throw us poor men off so that we wouldn't realize just how corrupt and detrimental they were).

But back to the point of our story. Women were the root of all evil. No doubt. Or at the very least the fall of every good man.

And Thom should know. He'd been doing quite well for himself until that fateful day when *she* had shown herself to him. Like a vision of heaven, she'd been crossing the street wearing a gown of blue. Or maybe it was green. Hell, after all these centuries it could have been brown. The colour hadn't mattered at the time because in truth he'd been picturing her naked in his mind.

And he'd learned one very important lesson. Never picture a woman naked when she was capable of reading your mind. At least not unless you were seriously into masochism.

Thom wasn't. Then again, given his current predicament, perhaps he was.

Only a true masochist would dart across the street to meet and
fall in love with Merlin.

Thom paused in his writing. "Now, good reader, before you
think me odd. Let me explain. You see Merlin in ancient Britain
wasn't a name. It was a title and the one who bore that title
could be either male or female. And my Merlin was a beautiful
blonde angel who just happens to be a little less than forgiving.
How do I know? See first paragraph where I talk about being
imprisoned for a millennium . . . give or take a few centuries
which still doesn't sound quite as impressive as millennium."

Thom felt a little better after uttering that speech. Though
not much. How could any man feel better while stuck in a hole?

For it was true. Hell had no fury greater than a woman's
wrath.

"That's what having a beer with your buddies will get you."

Well, in his case it was more like a keg of ale. But that would
be jumping ahead of the story.

Sighing at himself, Thom dipped his quill in ink and returned
to his vellum sheet. It was true, he had other means of writing
things down, but since it all began with a quill and vellum, he
wanted this diatribe to be captured the same way. After all, this
was his version of the story. Or more simply, this was the truth
of the matter. While others only speculated, he knew the truth.

And no, the truth would not set him free. Only Merlin could
do that and well, that was an entirely different story from this
one.

This story began with a poor besotted man seeing his Aphrodite across the street. She had paused in her walk and was
looking about as if she'd lost something.

Me, he'd thought. *You have lost me and I am right here.*

With no thought except to hear the sound of his beloved's
voice before she started on her way again, he'd headed towards
her only to nearly die under the hooves of a horse as he stepped
out in front of a carter. Thom not-so-deftly dodged the carter
and landed extremely unceremoniously in a trough.

Drenched, but still besotted by Cupid's whim, Thom attempted to wring himself dry before he again headed towards
her . . . this time a bit more cautious of traffic.

He couldn't breathe. Couldn't think. Couldn't dry the damn

stench of the reeking water off his clothes. All he could do was watch his Calypso as she waited (he told himself) for him to claim her.

As he drew near her, a million clever thoughts and introductions popped eagerly into his mind. He was going to sweep her off her feet with witty repartee. She would be bedazzled by his nimble, elegant tongue (in more ways than one if everything went according to plan).

And then she had looked at him. Those brilliant blue . . . or maybe they were green . . . eyes had pierced him with curiosity.

Thom had drawn a deep breath, opened his mouth to speak, to woo her with his charm, when all of a sudden his cleverness abandoned him.

Nothing. His mind was blank. Worthless. Aggravating.

"Greetings." Even he cringed as that simple, stupid word had tumbled out of his lips.

"Greetings, good sir."

Her voice had been clear and soft. Like the song of an angel. She'd stood there for a moment, looking expectantly at him while his heart pounded, his forehead beaded with sweat.

Speak, Thom, speak.

"Nice day, eh?"

"Very nice."

Aye, he was a fool. One who no longer bore any trace of his shrivelled manhood. Wanting to save whatever dignity he possessed (which at this point was in the negative digits), Thom nodded. "I just thought I'd point it out to you, fair maiden. Good day."

Cringing even more, he'd started away from her only to pause as he caught sight of something strange.

Now, being a rational human being, he'd thought it an unusually large bird. Let's face it, in fifteenth-century England, everyone spoke of dragons, but no one had really thought to ever see one.

And yet there it was in the sky. Like a giant . . . dragon. Which it was. Large and black with big red bulbous eyes and gleaming scales, it had circled above them, blocking out the sun.

Thomas, being a coward, had wanted to run, but being a lusty man, he quickly saw an opportunity to woo his fair lady with dashing actions instead of a feeble tongue. After all, what woman wouldn't swoon over a dragonslayer?

That had been the idea.

At least until the dragon kicked his ass. With one swipe of a talon, the dragon had batted him into the building. Thom had fallen to the street and every part of his body had throbbed and ached.

It was awful. Or so he'd thought until the woman had placed her hand on his forehead. One minute he'd been lying on the street reeking of trough water, and in the next he'd found himself lying on a large, gilded bed.

"Where am I?"

"Shh," his angel had said. "You have been poisoned by the dragon. Lie still and give my touch time to heal you or you will surely die."

(Note to self. I should have started moving about, thrashing wildly.)

Not wanting to die (because I was stupid), Thom had done as she asked. He had lain there, looking up into her perfectly sculpted features. She was beauty and grace.

"Have you a name, my lady?"

"Merlin."

That had been the last name he would have ever attributed to a woman so comely. "Merlin?"

"Aye. Now be still."

For the first time in all of his life, Thom had obeyed. He'd closed his eyes and inhaled the fresh, sweet scent of lilac that clung to the bed he lay in. He wondered if this was Merlin's bed and then he wondered of other things that men and women could do in a bed . . . especially together.

"Stop that."

He opened his eyes at the reprimand from his Aphrodite. "Stop what?"

"Those thoughts," she'd said sharply. "I hear every one of them and they disturb me."

"Disturb you how?"

"I am the Penmerlin and I must remain chaste. Thoughts such as those do not belong in my head."

"They're not in your head, my lady, they're in mine and if they offend you, perhaps you should keep to yourself."

She'd gifted him with a dazzling smile. "You are a bold one, Thom. Perhaps I should have let the mandrake take you."

"Mandrake?" As in the root?

"The dragon," she'd explained. "His kind have the ability to take either the form of man or dragon, hence their name."

Well, that certainly explained that, however other matters had been rather vague in his mind. "But he wasn't after me. He was after you. Why?"

"Because I was on the trail of a very special Merlin and the mandrake sensed me. That is why I so seldom venture to the world of man. When one possesses as much magic as I do, it is too easy for other magical beasts to find you."

That made sense to him. "You are enemies."

She nodded. "He works for Morgan le Fey."

Thom'd had the audacity to laugh at that. "The sister of King Arthur."

Merlin hadn't joined in his laughter. "Aye, the very same."

The serious look on her face and the tone of her voice had instantly sobered him. "You're not jesting."

"Nay. The tales of Arthur are real, but they are not quite what the minstrels tell. Arthur's world was vast and his battles are still being waged, not only in this time, but in future ones as well."

In that moment, Thom wasn't sure what enraptured him most. The stunning creature he longed to bed or the idea that Camelot really had existed.

Over the course of the next few days while he healed from his attack, Thom had stayed in the fabled isle of Avalon and listened to Merlin's stories of Arthur and his knights.

But more than that, he'd seen them. At least those who still lived. There for a week, he'd walked amongst the legends and shaken the hands of fables. He'd learned that Merlin was only one of her kind. Others like her had been sent out into the world of man to be hidden from Morgan who wanted to use those Merlins, and the sacred objects they protected, for evil.

It was a frightening battle they waged. One that held no regard for time or beings. And in the end, the very fate of the world rested in the hands of the victor.

"I wish to be one of you," Thom had finally confessed to

Merlin on the evening of his eighth day. "I want to help save the world."

Her eyes had turned dull. "That isn't your destiny, Thom. You must return to the world of man and be as you were."

She made that sound simple enough, but he wasn't the same man who had come to Avalon. His time here had changed him. "How can I ever be as I was now that I know the truth?"

She'd stepped away from him. "You will be as you were, Thom . . . I promise."

And then everything had gone blurry. His eyesight had failed until he found himself encased in darkness.

Thom awakened the next morning to find himself back in England, in his own house . . . his own bed.

He'd tried desperately to return to Avalon, only to have everyone tell him that'd he'd dreamed it all.

"You've been here the whole time," his housekeeper had sworn.

But he hadn't believed it. How could he? This wasn't some illness that had befallen him. It wasn't.

It was real (another four-letter word that often led men to disaster).

Eventually Thom had convinced himself that they were right and he'd dreamed it all. The land of Merlins had only existed in his mind. Where else could it have been?

And so he'd returned to his old ways. He'd gambled, he'd fought, he'd wenched, and most of all he'd drunk and drunk and drunk.

Until *that* night.

It was a night (another noun that was five letters in English and four in French. There were times when the French were greatly astute). Thom had wandered off to his favourite tavern that was filled with many of his less than proper friends. As the night passed, and they'd fallen deep into their cups, Geoffrey or maybe it'd been Henry or Richard had begun to place a wager.

He who told the best tale would win a purse of coin (note the four letters here).

No one knew how much coin was in the purse because they were all too drunk to care. Instead they had begun with their stories before a small group of wenches who were their judges.

Thom, too drunk to notice that a man had drawn near their table, had fondled his wench while the others went on before him.

"That's all well and nice," he'd said as Richard finished up some retelling of one of Chaucer's tales (the man was far from original). "But I, Thomas Malory . . . *Sir* Thomas Malory can beat you all."

"Of course you can, Thom," Geoffrey had said with a laugh and a belch. "You always *think* you can."

"No, no, there is no think . . . I'm too drunk for that. This is all about doing." He'd held his cup out to be refilled before he'd started the story. At first he'd meant to tell the story of a farming mishap his father had told him of, but before he could think better of it (drinking usually had this effect), out had come the whole matter of the King Arthur that Merlin had told him about.

Or at least some of it. Being Thom, who liked to embellish all truth, he'd taken some liberties. He'd changed a few things, but basically he'd kept to the story. After all, what harm could come of it? He'd dreamed it all anyway, and it was an interesting tale.

And the next thing he'd known, he'd won that wager and taken home a purse which later proved to only contain two rocks and some lint. A paltry prize indeed.

Then, before he'd even known what had happened, people had starting coming up to him and speaking of a book he'd written. Thom, not being a fool to let such fame bypass him, had played along at first. Until he'd seen the book himself. There it was, in all its beautiful glory. His name.

No man had ever destroyed his life more quickly than Thom did the instant that book became commonly available.

One instant he'd been in his own bed and the next he'd been in a small, tiny, infinitesimal cell with an angry blonde angel glaring at him.

"Do I know you?" he'd asked her.

She'd glared at him. Out of nowhere, *the* book had appeared. "How could you do this?"

Now at this time, self-preservation had caused Thom to ask the one question that had been getting men into trouble for centuries. "Do what?"

And just like countless men before him (and after him, is this not true, men?) he learned too late that he should have remained completely silent.

"You have unleashed our secret, Thomas. Doom to you for it, because with this book you have exposed us to those who want us dead."

Suddenly, his dream returned to him and he remembered every bit of it. Most of all, he remembered that it wasn't a dream.

The Lords of Avalon were all real . . . just as Morgan was. And as Merlin led the remnants of the Knights of the Round Table, Morgan led her Cercle du Damne. Two halves fighting for the world.

But that left Thom with just one question. "If you had all that magic, Merlin, why didn't you know about the book that would be written if you returned me to the world?"

With those words uttered, he'd learned that there truly was a worse question to ask a woman than A) her age, B) her weight, and C) do what?

"Please note that here I rot and here I stay until Merlin cools down."

Thom looked down at the PDA and sighed. Time might not have any real meaning in Avalon, but it meant a whole hell of a lot to him.

In Sheep's Clothing

Meljean Brook

Five years ago, Emma Cooper would have thought a blown tyre in the middle of a blizzard was bad. But *bad* was the small, spiked metal ball her fingers found embedded in the rubber – and *worse* was the truck, its headlights on bright, pulling off the two-lane highway and onto the shoulder twenty yards behind her Jeep.

The tyre iron in her hands rattled against the one lug nut she'd had time to crack loose. She hadn't even raised the jack yet; it lay on the icy asphalt behind the flat front tyre.

No, not much time had passed at all. He must have been waiting off the road for her to drive by, his truck concealed by the dark and the snow.

Don't panic, Emma told herself, and pulled in a long breath between her chattering teeth. Now was definitely not the time to panic.

Still gripping the tyre iron, Emma rose from her crouch. The rattling rumble of his diesel motor cut off. The pounding of her heart filled the sudden, snow-muffled silence.

Stay calm. She tugged open the front door of her Jeep, slid into the driver's seat and hit the locks.

Emma had been living in Seattle the past five years, but she'd kept up on the local news. In the last eighteen months, four vehicles – each with flat tyres – had been found abandoned on this rural stretch of Oregon highway. Each time, searchers recovered the body of a woman from the surrounding woods. Each woman had been raped and strangled.

The truck door slammed shut. *Oh, God.* She squinted against the glare of headlights in the rear-view mirror, but couldn't see anything. With her right hand, she rummaged blindly through her purse on the passenger seat and found her cell phone.

It had been years since she'd dialled the number, but she still knew it by heart. Nathan Forrester answered on the third ring. She spoke over his sleep-roughened greeting.

"Hey, Sheriff Studly." Emma could see the dark figure in her side mirror now. The silhouetted shape was tall, and wearing a thick coat and a cowboy hat. She couldn't tell if he carried a gun. "I'm on the side of the highway with a flat tyre, and I could really, really use a lift."

"Emma? Oh, Christ. Emma, listen – *don't accept any help.*"

"I didn't plan on it." She stared at the mirror. He'd walked half the distance to her Jeep. Her fingers tightened on the tyre iron, her nails drawing blood from the heel of her palm. *Stay calm.* "But I think he plans to offer help anyway."

She heard Nathan swearing and running across a wooden floor. "Where are you? You still have your Jeep?"

"About ten miles before the Bluffs turn-off. And, yes, I still have it."

"OK, Emma, I'm on my way, but you've got to drive. Stay in low gear. The flat tyre will pull hard at your steering wheel, but your Jeep will go. So you start it now and get the hell out of there."

Emma jammed the phone between her cheek and shoulder, turned the ignition key. The engine fired up. A shadow darkened her window.

She looked over just as he swung her jack through the glass.

It was worse than the others had been – the window shattered, the door hanging open, blood splashed in the snow. Gun in hand, Nathan jumped from his Blazer, his unlaced boots skidding on the icy road. He slid into the side of the Jeep, glanced inside.

The seats were empty.

The breath he drew to roar her name felt like the first he'd pulled into his aching chest since he'd heard the breaking glass and her aborted shriek.

"Emma!"

The echo faded, leaving the whisper of falling snow and the low growl of his truck engine. A trail of blood and thrashed snow led behind the Jeep. Nathan followed it, the freezing air biting at his face, his uncovered ears.

From the pine trees alongside the road came the snap of a breaking branch. Nathan swung around, scanning the night. The light from the half-moon barely pierced the treeline, and the shadows between the pines danced in the flashing red and blue lights from his truck. His muscles tensed; something was moving through the woods, its eyes reflecting the strobe lights like a cat's. He aimed his flashlight, switched it on.

The high-powered light flooded Emma's pale face before her hand flew up, shielding her eyes.

Oh, thank God. Thank God. His knees almost gave out, but through some miracle, he remained standing. He skimmed the light down her body, and his heart lurched. Blood stained her sweater and jeans. He pushed into the snowdrift on the highway shoulder, began to wade towards her. "Are you hurt?"

"No." She lowered her hand. Her voice was steady. "He's gone. Towards Pine Bluffs."

And must have turned down a side road. Nathan hadn't met anyone on his way here. "Is that his blood or yours?"

"His. I panicked and bit him." Her head tilted back as he drew closer, and he could see the trail of blood under her jaw, the faint smear on her chin.

"Good," he murmured, and lifted his cold hand to her warm cheek, gently turning her face. A livid bump had formed beneath the short dark hair; the skin was broken.

"Biting him was *not* good, Nathan. Not good at all." She sighed, then winced when he brushed his thumb over the bump. "He whacked me with the jack."

Hit in the head with a jack, and she was still upright? There was no chance that that was going to last; she must be running on pure adrenaline. He slipped his arm around her shoulders, turned towards the road. "Let's get you back to town."

Back. Finally. But he hadn't imagined her return would be like this.

And God only knew why she'd left in the first place.

*   *   *

Emma waited in Nathan's truck while he spoke with the deputy who pulled in behind him a few minutes later. She warmed her hands in front of the heater as Nathan grabbed her suitcases from the back of her Jeep. Melting snow darkened his brown hair to black, and plastered the short strands to his forehead. He'd come without a hat, without tying his boots, without changing out of his chequered flannel pyjama pants. He'd remembered to button his sheepskin jacket over his bare chest only after Deputy Osborne had arrived.

"Once word of this gets out, your deputies are never going to let you live it down," she said when Nathan slid into his seat.

He glanced over towards Osborne. When he looked back at Emma, his broad grin kicked her heart against her ribs. "Word *isn't* getting out. Last year, I caught Osborne in the break room singing – and dancing – to Britney Spears."

"How'd you know it was Britney Spears?"

"It's a damn good thing *he* never asked me that, isn't it?" Nathan made a U-turn, lifting his hand as he drove past Osborne. "How's your head?"

She prodded the bump on her scalp and grimaced. "Not bad. It only hurts when I touch it."

"Then—"

"Don't touch it." She met his eyes. There was warmth and laughter there, just as there'd been six years ago when she'd fallen off one of his horses, bruising her pride and her elbow. Her Aunt Letty had given her the same advice then – don't touch it. "Yes, I know."

His smile faded as his gaze swept over her again. "We'll stop at Letty's, have her look at that bump. Then I'll take you both to my place."

Aunt Letty's old farmhouse shared a lane with the Forrester property. "Do you think that's necessary?"

"Yes." The instrument panel cast a faint green light over his hard profile and the grim set of his mouth. "We're pretty sure he's local. And even if we try to keep your identity quiet, word *will* get out."

And everyone knew where Aunt Letty lived, where Emma would be staying. "Will he come after me?"

"If he thinks you can identify him, yes. No one's gotten away from him before."

Nathan had already asked if she'd recognized her attacker. Emma hadn't. She'd know him if she saw him again though. Or smelled him.

With luck, however, she wouldn't have to taste him again. "I bit his hand pretty hard," she said.

"I can see that." His gaze dropped to her shoulder. The blood soaking her wool sweater overwhelmed almost every other odour in the Blazer, so that beneath its metallic scent she only detected a faint hint of coffee, vinyl seats, the earthiness of male skin and his lingering fear. "We'll keep a look out for any hand injuries. But this time of year, everyone's wearing gloves. Even if you took a good chunk, he could hide it."

More than a chunk. Nausea churned in her stomach. "His truck had a diesel engine. It was a pickup truck. I know it was one of the big ones, because the lights were high up."

"Good. That's good, Emma. That'll help us." He rubbed his hand over his face before flipping the windshield wipers to high, whipping away the heavy flakes. "What the hell were you thinking, driving through this mess in the middle of the night?"

She'd been thinking that even if her Jeep had gotten stuck, even if it had slid into a ditch, she'd be fine. Running the distance to Aunt Letty's would have been no effort. It would have been *fun*.

"Well, I wasn't thinking that a murderer would give me a flat tyre." She waited until he glanced over, met her eyes. "You're only pissed at me because you were scared. Believe me, I was scared too. Out of my freaking wits."

Nathan clenched his jaw, looked through the front windshield again. "You're calm enough now."

And barely holding on to that calm. Her senses were filled with blood, with Nathan. "Trust me," she said softly. "That's a good thing."

Even waking her at two in the morning didn't trip Aunt Letty up. Telling her about Emma's run-in with a serial killer didn't either, but Emma hadn't expected it to. No, not Aunt Letty. Her only reaction was one similar to the reaction she gave the first time Emma had changed into a wolf in front of her: she stared at Emma with eyes like steel, but with softly pursed lips.

Then she'd ordered Emma to sit at the kitchen table while she collected her first aid supplies from the pantry. Her white hair was braided for sleep; beneath the mint green terry-cloth robe, Emma knew there would be a sprigged flannel nightgown with a bit of lace at the hem. Her cool fingers were all wrinkles and knuckles, gentle as she cleaned the wound.

"So, young man," she said to Nathan as she unwrapped a bandage, "you're moving us to your place because you're worried he'll come after my Emma."

"Yes, Miss Letty," Nathan said from the kitchen entrance. If he'd had his hat, Emma thought, it'd have been between his hands. Before retiring last year, her aunt had been both teacher and nurse at the tiny Pine Bluffs high school. Emma hadn't met anyone in town below the age of fifty who didn't speak to Letty with the same deference that Nathan did.

"And what did Emma say to that?"

"She didn't argue."

Letty arched her white eyebrows. "Well, isn't that something?" she murmured. "I thought for sure Emma would have said she'd handle any threat on her own."

"I bit him," Emma said quietly, her gaze locked with her aunt's. "He's dangerous – and going to get worse."

"Then it seems to me that, before things get worse, you've got some explaining to do." Letty straightened up. "Maybe you can get started on that while I pack."

Emma sighed, and watched Nathan step aside to let her aunt pass into the hallway. Of course Letty was right. But knowing was easier than doing. Knowing was *always* easier than doing.

But that was why she'd come back, wasn't it? There were things to do, and to explain.

She just hadn't realized she'd be starting this early.

"You might as well change now too," Nathan said, his deference going as easily as it had come. His fear had passed too. And his anger. In their place was speculation. His eyes narrowed as he assessed her from head to toe. "I'll need your clothes as evidence. It's unlikely that you'll be getting them back."

"That's fine." Emma hooked her fingers beneath the hem of the blood-stained sweater, and paused. "You're going to watch?"

"I will if you take them off here where I can see you."

In answer, she pulled the sweater over her head. He'd been teasing her, she knew. But now his smile froze in place as Emma took off her T-shirt and threw it on top of her sweater. Then she began to shimmy out of her jeans.

She heard his approach, the racing of his heartbeat. His hands flattened on the table on either side of her hips, closing her in with his wide shoulders and tall frame. "Stop it, Emma."

The growl rumbling up from her chest stole her response. She kicked the jeans free of her feet, and stood in front of him in her bra and panties.

Nathan's face darkened; his breathing deepened. "We got along before, pretending we could just be friends. I can't do that now, not after that phone call, not after hearing you scream and not knowing—" He bit off his words. His throat worked and he leaned in, forcing her back against the table. "So you should think a little before stripping off in front of me."

Off balance, she grabbed onto his biceps to steady herself. "I've thought more than a little. I've been thinking about you for five years."

"Not hard enough, obviously." He backed out of her grip. "Because for five years, you've been up in Seattle."

She crossed her arms over the scratchy lace of her bra. "You haven't exactly been burning up the highway between here and there."

He stared at her for a long moment before he turned towards the door, shaking his head. "You always ask the one question I don't have an answer to."

"I didn't ask anything."

"Yes, you did. Which suitcase do you need?"

She blinked. "The small one."

She listened to the heavy tread of his footsteps on the front porch, then to the snow crunching beneath his boots as he walked to the truck.

Winter in Pine Bluffs. Emma knew the summers better. When she was sixteen, her mother had sent her to stay with

Letty over summer vacation, arguing that time away from the city would do her good. Emma had chosen to come the next six years. Nathan had only been part of the reason, because her mother had been right – time in Pine Bluffs *had* done her good. She loved the forests with their thick mats of pine needles over red earth, loved the town with its three stoplights and not a single chain restaurant.

So she'd visited, first in high school and then throughout college, fully intending to make it a permanent move after she'd earned her degree. But she'd changed her plans that last summer.

Apparently Nathan had been thinking of that summer too, and the hike they'd taken around the lake, the tension simmering between them. "Your leg didn't scar," he said, setting her case on the table.

Automatically, Emma glanced down at her right calf. Smooth skin stretched over muscle that, five years ago, had been mangled, bleeding. "It turned me into a werewolf. So I heal faster now."

His short burst of laughter was exactly what she'd expected. No, she couldn't tell him straight out. She'd have to prepare him, so that he could more easily accept the unbelievable. After dropping Aunt Letty and her at his house, Nathan would have to return to the highway and help Osborne go over the scene at the Jeep. It would be a simple thing to follow him in wolf form and offer help . . . and then hope he didn't shoot her, as he had the werewolf who'd attacked her.

A lead bullet between the eyes killed a werewolf just as easily as it did a man; unfortunately, death hadn't changed him back to his human form. If it had, she might have known what was happening to her. She might have known where the cravings came from, and why she'd woken up naked in the woods just outside Nathan's bedroom window.

But she'd probably have been just as frightened, and run just as fast.

"Your Jeep was packed full," he said, and she could feel his gaze on her as she unzipped her suitcase. "Are you staying a while?"

"Forever, probably."

"Why now?"

She stepped into her jeans. "Aunt Letty's getting older, there's an opening for a science teacher at the high school, and I need a place to run."

His eyebrows drew together. "Are you in trouble?"

"Not a place to run *to*, a place to run. The city isn't good for that."

His frown remained, but he only nodded. Emma pulled on a sweater as Letty came back into the kitchen, bundled in her coat and knitted cap. Daisy, the yellow Labrador who'd been Letty's companion for as long as Emma could remember, had ventured downstairs and now sat at Letty's heel. The dog's body was taut, shaking. That was another reason Emma had left. But she'd since learned that, with time, a dog would get over its instinctive fear of her. It just took a lot of dog biscuits.

Letty's steely gaze landed on Emma's face. Emma shook her head.

An aging aunt, a job, a place to run. All true. And Nathan was another reason – but she couldn't tell him that until after she showed him the rest.

The snow let up just before dawn. Nathan walked the highway shoulder, sweeping his flashlight over the ground, hoping for even a foot of tyre track that hadn't been filled in. Emma had helped narrow down the type of vehicle, but a matching tread would go further in court.

Two hundred yards from her Jeep, he gave up. Turning back, he saw Osborne standing beside the deputy vehicle, lifting his hand. Nathan waved him on. There was nothing left here. He'd have the Jeep towed into town, and the snow and the ploughs would erase the rest.

Then he'd spend a good portion of the morning bucking through the logging roads that turned off the main highway between here and Pine Bluffs, searching for the route Emma's attacker had used. Cold, boring work, which would give him too much time to spend in his head. This meant he'd probably spend a good portion of the morning obsessing over Emma.

And wishing that he were with her in his old bedroom, in that old double bed heaped high with blankets, instead of trudging through the freezing backwoods.

He glanced into her Jeep as he passed it. An inch of white snow covered the driver's seat, and the black powder from the fingerprinting kit dusted the door handles.

Not much hope there either. Emma had been certain her assailant had been wearing leather gloves.

Yet she'd still managed to bite through the gloves hard enough that his blood had splashed all over her. Terror lent her strength.

A hot ball of anger settled in his gut. Nathan looked away from the Jeep, staring blindly into the treeline. They were going to get the bastard this time. If the son of a bitch knew what was good for him, he'd walk into the sheriff's office now and turn himself in.

But Nathan hoped to God that when the time came, the bastard resisted arrest.

Of course, they had to identify him first. With a sigh, he banged his fist against the roof of the Jeep, turned back to his vehicle. And froze.

A wolf lay in front of his Blazer, like a dog stretched out before a fire, but twice the size of any dog Nathan had ever seen. He'd seen a wolf this large before, however; he'd killed a wolf this large after it had attacked Emma on a hiking trail.

But this wolf wasn't snarling, hackles raised and fangs bared. Its thick, dark fur lay flat over its back; its head was raised, amber eyes watching him steadily, pointed ears pricked forwards.

He rested his hand on his weapon, but didn't draw it. Not yet. He edged to the side, began making a wide arc that would take him to his vehicle without directly approaching the wolf. He stopped when the wolf cocked its head, rose to its feet and trotted towards the Jeep.

It sniffed at the snow by the flat tyre, then began to work its way back. Scenting the blood, Nathan assumed. The tension began to leave his shoulders, and he watched as it began to dig through the small drift that had piled beside the rear tyre.

Then it turned, looked at him and sat. When Nathan only stared back, the wolf made a chuffing sound, pushed its long nose back into the drift, and nudged.

Something small and black rolled out of the drift, leaving – Nathan realized with a strange, swooping sensation in his stomach – specks of pink ice in its wake.

The wolf backed up a few yards, then sat again.

Slowly, Nathan approached the Jeep. He kept his gaze on the wolf, then dared a glance at the object on the ground.

His stomach did another swoop, and for a second he thought his head was going to go with it. He crouched, sitting on his heels, waiting for the light-headedness to pass.

It was a thumb, still inside the leather of the glove.

He had a fingerprint. Holy shit. Disbelieving, he took off his hat, pushed his hand through his hair. He looked up at the wolf.

"What the hell are you?"

Its mouth stretched into what Nathan would have sworn was a grin. For an instant, he remembered Emma in Miss Letty's kitchen, joking about becoming a werewolf.

God. Was he actually entertaining the idea that this wolf was a human? That it was *Emma*?

He was obviously lacking sleep or caffeine. Shaking the ridiculous thought from his head, Nathan stood. The wolf trotted past him, its shoulder brushing his leg.

He watched it break into a lope down the highway, and turned back to the thumb on the ground. He could think about the wolf later. Now, he had a job to do.

Fifteen minutes later, Nathan slammed on his brakes when the wolf appeared on the highway shoulder. The Blazer fishtailed before the chains caught and gave him traction. It took a long time for his heart to stop pounding.

He climbed out of the truck, pointed at the wolf. "Do you know how dumb that was?"

Probably not any less dumb than talking to an animal. And definitely not as stupid as feeling chastised when it gave him a *look*, then trotted a few yards up the highway.

To a logging road. It sniffed at the snow, moved further off the highway, then looked back at Nathan expectantly.

"You're kidding me," he said.

The wolf shook its head. *Answering him.*

And there went reality. Nathan trudged forwards. "No jury is going to buy this story."

Emma was still half-asleep when she heard Nathan come home. She turned, buried her face in her pillow, and listened to Letty ask him about the investigation, the status of the Jeep, and whether he preferred rolls or biscuits with the beef stew she was making. Then she sent him from the kitchen with an instruction to wake the princess who'd slept the day away.

The princess thought she deserved all the sleep she'd had. Emma had run more than thirty miles that morning. After she'd left Nathan by the highway, she'd searched through a quarter of the town, trying to track down the murderer by scent.

Unfortunately, she hadn't found any sign of him.

Nathan didn't knock. She held her breath as he came inside the room, locked the door and moved to the bed. He pulled off his boots and slipped in next to her, drew her back tight against his chest.

"You're awake," he said, his voice low in her ear.

She nodded, fighting the sudden need that was tearing through her, the growl that came with it.

"We got closer to him today." Nathan shifted slightly, snuck his arm beneath her ribs, and hugged her to him. "We found where he pulled off the highway and waited, got the imprint from a tyre track. We even got a fingerprint, sent it in to the state lab. Hopefully they'll come up with a match. Any guy with a missing thumb is going to have some explaining to do."

Emma forced the need away, found her voice. "It won't be missing for long. It'll grow back. And that story will be a lot harder to sell to a jury than the one you have for this morning."

The silence that fell was heavy, painful. Nathan didn't move. She couldn't see him, had no idea what he was thinking. But at least he didn't let her go.

Finally, he pulled her closer. His jaw, rough with a day's growth of beard, scratched lightly over her cheek. "This morning I thought I was having some kind of spiritual experience. The kind people have a few weeks before they play naked chicken with a train. So if you're saying what I think you're saying, it's a lot less worrying than believing I've gone crazy."

Emma could only nod again, her relief a shuddery ache in her chest.

But Nathan didn't let her off the hook. "If you're saying it, Emma, then *say* it."

She swallowed past the tightness in her throat. "It was me. This morning, the wolf you saw was me. I showed you which logging road he drove down, and I dug his thumb out of the snow."

"Christ." He muffled a laugh against her neck. "You've got one hell of a bite."

"Yes. But it also means that he's going to become what I am. Just like I changed after I was bitten by that wolf five years ago."

His fingers drifted over the unblemished skin at her temple. "You do heal fast. Does it hurt now when I touch you here?"

"No." She caught his hand. "It would only hurt if you *didn't* touch me."

"There's no chance of that." His lips ghosted over her ear, her jaw, then her fingers, where she held his hand against her neck. His other arm tightened around her waist. "This is why, five years ago, you didn't come back."

"I was afraid," she admitted.

"General fear, or are there specifics I should know about?"

"There *were* specifics. I'd lose whole chunks of time, wake up outside. And it was harder to fight myself when I wanted something." Like Nathan. "And I didn't want to accidentally hurt anyone."

"But now?"

"I learned to control it better. And the more I let it – the wolf – out, the more control I have when I'm human." Unable to help herself, she arched a little, rubbed her bottom against him, then choked out an embarrassed laugh. "But my control still isn't perfect."

His hand moved down to her hip, stroked the length of her thigh. "That isn't exactly a turn-off."

From the evidence blatantly present, she'd already realized that. Emma let go of his hand, twisted her fingers in the sheets. She didn't have much practice at controlling arousal, but her nails didn't rip the cotton, thank God. Her hips worked back against him and she panted, "We can't."

Nathan stilled. "Now, or ever?"

"Now. I hear Aunt Letty coming up the stairs."

He groaned against her neck. Emma laughed, but it was cut short when he rolled her over and fastened his lips to hers.

Oh, God, he tasted so good. Smelled so good. *Felt* so good. She pushed her fingers into his hair, opened her mouth to the slick heat of his tongue. His hips pushed between her thighs and he rocked forwards once, twice; her breath caught on each movement, her body aching for completion.

But it wouldn't be now. With a growl that sounded as feral as hers, Nathan lifted himself away, and pushed off the bed. He stood in his khaki uniform pants and shirt, his hair dishevelled, his breathing ragged and heavy. Not even a werewolf and he had to fight himself as hard as she did.

Warmth swept through her, curved her lips. "Sheriff Studly." She turned onto her side, propped herself up on her elbow. "That does have a better ring to it than Deputy Studly."

A teasing nickname she'd given him her first summer here, when they'd met and had an instant, strong connection with each other. But at sixteen, she had been too young for anything except a platonic relationship with a man just out of college. No wonder they'd fallen into the "we're just friends" rut: both of them afraid to change and risk the friendship they'd formed that first year. And both of them longing for that change.

And they'd both gotten change in a big way.

Nathan dragged a hand over his face, finally looking away from her. "You knew to call me that last night. Letty told you about the election?"

"I kept up on the news here."

"Well, what they didn't mention was that most people voted me in on name recognition. They saw 'Forrester' and checked the ballot, forgetting that my dad was heading off to Arizona to retire, so they were actually getting Junior." His smile became wry. "The past eighteen months haven't been such a fine addition to his legacy, have they?"

Emma sat up. "What does that mean?"

"It means there are four women dead, and their murderer is still out there."

"So your dad just retired at the right time." She cocked her head, studying him. There was more than just anger and frustration in him, there was shame, too. "So is this why you weren't burning up the highway to Seattle?"

He stared back at her. "You tilted your head just like that this morning. Gave me the same damn look." When she didn't answer, he shoved his hands into his pockets. "All right. So I wanted to have something to offer you first."

If he'd just walked through her door that would have been enough. But she'd stayed away because she'd had her own demons to fight – demons that he'd easily accepted – and so she couldn't just tell him that his demons didn't matter.

She slipped off the bed, rose to her toes to press a quick kiss to his mouth. "So we find him."

"We?"

"Yes, we. And don't argue," she said when he looked ready to, "because I bit him. That means, right now, he's probably fighting himself. And the urges to do what he craves, what he enjoys – which is apparently raping and killing – will be hard to resist."

Nathan watched her, his expression dark. "He'd already been waiting less time between attacks."

"So it'll get worse. And then *worse*, because he'll be stronger, faster. And he'll have new ways of going after the women. And new ways of getting away."

"So what do you propose we do?"

Emma tapped her finger against her nose. "Sniff him out. I know what he smells like, and this is a small town. I can cover a lot of ground in a night."

"I bet." He paused, considering her. "How much did you cover this morning?"

She grinned. "Only the houses south of Walnut Street."

Of course, he didn't let her go alone. His Blazer moved slowly down the darkened streets and, from the driver's seat, Nathan watched her flit between the houses, sniffing walkways and doors. Her appearance was raising hell with the dogs in town, more than one running along a backyard fence, barking its head off. He'd have a bevy of noise complaints to deal with tomorrow.

He put in a call to Osborne, who he'd talked into staying at the house with a promise of a home-cooked stew. The deputy reported that Letty had already gone to bed and that he was working through his third bowl.

Nathan would probably be rolling him out of there come morning.

He watched Emma trot down a side street, staying in the shadows. Now and then she'd lift her nose, smelling the air before shaking her head and continuing on. Nathan sighed, took a swig of coffee. They'd likely be out here for hours. And even if Emma identified the bastard, bringing him in could be tricky. No judge would issue a warrant based on a wolf's sense of smell. With luck, the print from the thumb would do it. But if not, Nathan would have to work backwards, find a solid link in the evidence that could have led him to the murderer's front door.

He frowned. Bringing a werewolf in was going to be tricky, regardless.

It was just past two when Emma returned to the Blazer, her breath billowing in the freezing air. Nathan leaned over, opened the passenger door. She leaped onto the bench seat, and lay down with a heavy sigh.

"Done for the night?" That sense of unreality hit him again. Knowing this wolf was Emma was one thing, talking to her in this shape was another.

She looked up at him, turned onto her side. The whine that escaped her sent chills down his spine. Her jaw cracked and bulged.

Oh, Jesus. He cut the Blazer's headlights and pulled off to the deserted roadside. He slid towards her on the seat, but didn't touch her for fear that his hands would add to the pain of the transformation. The change took less than a minute but felt like for ever; an eternity filled with her whimpers, the groans of her flesh and his murmurs that he prayed were helping, soothing. Finally she lay naked on the seat, her short hair and skin glistening with sweat.

"It's not so bad," she panted. "Once the pain starts, you just ride with it."

Speechless, Nathan shook his head. He reached into the back seat for a blanket, tucked it around her shoulders.

"Thanks." She gratefully accepted the coffee he offered, raised it to her lips with shaking hands. "I just need another second."

She wasn't exaggerating; by the time she'd swallowed the lukewarm drink, her shivers had stopped. She stared unblinkingly out of the front windshield, her fingers tapping against the mug. "I get a whiff here and there, but it wasn't concentrated anywhere. I think he must move around the town. Maybe he does repairs, or some kind of work on call."

Work was a reality Nathan could get a grip on. "We covered most of the town tonight. It might be he's on one of the farms or rural properties outside of town, and just comes in . . . for whatever it is he does."

"I can start running those properties tomorrow night." Her lips curved. "I'd go during the day, but someone would probably shoot at me."

"It might be over by tomorrow anyway, if the state comes back with a name on that print."

Emma's nod wasn't too convincing. She was thinking, he imagined, exactly what he had been earlier: arresting a werewolf wasn't going to be easy.

She tilted her head back and finished off the coffee, then placed the mug carefully in the cup holder. "Did it help – to see me change? Or make it worse?"

He didn't even ask how she'd known he was having trouble reconciling his Emma with the wolf. "Helps. I'm not saying I've got my head around it yet. But it helps."

"The transformation is grotesque."

His gaze ran up her pale, perfectly human legs. "Maybe for a few seconds. What you've got on either end isn't."

Her eyes locked with his. "You were afraid to touch me."

"I didn't know if it would hurt you."

"Oh." Her mouth softened. Her fingers, which had been clutching the blanket at her neck, loosened. "I thought we'd established that it only hurts when you don't."

The slice of skin and the pale curves of her breasts showing between the edges of the blanket undid him. Nathan pulled her towards him; she came eagerly, straddling his lap. Her mouth found his, then moved to his jaw, his neck. Her skin was hot beneath his hands. Her fingers worked frantically down the buttons of his shirt.

He thought about putting a stop to it. Thought that he'd always intended a bed for her, roses and wine – not the front seat of his truck. But thought that he'd never heard anything sweeter than her soft gasps and moans, nothing sexier than her growl when he slid his fingers down her stomach.

Her hips rocked, her back arched, her hands gripping his shoulders. She cried out his name when he pushed inside her. He offered himself to her just as he was, and took her just as she was.

Running a hundred miles couldn't have wrung her out as completely. Emma hadn't moved since she'd collapsed against Nathan's chest, her body limp. Didn't want to move.

But knew she needed to. With a soft groan, she slid from his lap. Nathan smiled, but he looked as shaken as she felt. Emma reached over the back of the seat for the bag she'd stuffed there before they'd left his house, not even trying to suppress the swelling emotion that constricted her chest, her throat. It was a sweet pain, knowing that it came from the wonder of fitting so perfectly with him.

It had been good between them. Better than good. Amazing.

Nathan finished buttoning his shirt, shoved the tails into his trousers. "I'll call Osborne, let him know we're heading back. You think Letty will notice if you sleep in my room?"

"Yes." Emma fished out her panties and jeans. "But she'll get used to the idea."

Actually, Emma would have been surprised if her aunt didn't already think that she and Nathan had been together all those years ago. She listened idly as Nathan spoke with Osborne, to Daisy's faint bark in the background.

Emma hurriedly shoved her jeans back down to her ankles. "Oh, my God. Nathan. Get out to your place. As fast as you can. Tell Osborne to get to Letty's room, and take his gun."

He didn't ask; he swung the Blazer immediately onto the road, repeated her instructions to Osborne.

As she removed her clothes again, she explained. "I can hear Daisy barking. She doesn't do that – she *never* does that. Except the night after I was bitten. She barked like crazy the first night."

Nathan nodded, his lips tight. Despite the two inches of snow that had fallen, a fresh set of tyre tracks led down the lane that her aunt shared with the Forresters.

"Oh, shit," Emma whispered, then turned to Nathan. His gaze was fixed on the road. "I'm going to change. I'm faster that way, quieter. He's probably still in human shape."

"And he might have a gun," Nathan said grimly. "So don't you think you're going anywhere yet. Emma! Dammit."

She heard his curse, the slam of his fist against the steering wheel, then the agonizing crack of her joints as she began her change.

Letty's place rose up out of the darkness like a gingerbread house frosted with white icing. Nathan glanced over at Emma, sitting up with her ears pricked forwards. "OK, I agree. You're safer in that form. Harder to argue with too – which I'm sure you love."

Emma turned her head and grinned at him before facing forwards again.

"There's his truck," he said, unsure if Emma's wolf eyesight had picked out the extended cab pickup parked just off the lane. "He drove past the house. Then did he walk back to Letty's or head out on foot to my place?"

Emma gave an uncertain whine. Nathan pulled up behind the truck and drew his weapon. "Stay behind me."

He approached the truck slowly and noted the magnetic sign stuck to the door. Fuller's Plumbing. He pictured its owner, Mark Fuller – tall, sandy-haired, easy-going – and shook his head. Jesus Christ. He'd played ball with Fuller in high school.

In all the years since, he'd never heard a whisper of trouble connected to Fuller. In a small town like Pine Bluffs, word got around. If Fuller had even looked at a woman strangely, had an argument or made an unwanted advance, Nathan probably would have heard of it. But Fuller had managed to stay squeaky clean.

Footprints led away from the pickup, heading further off the road, into the pine trees. "Do you hear anything from inside the cab?"

Emma shook her head. Nathan checked the truck, found it empty. A bandage, crusted with dried blood, lay crumpled on the passenger's seat.

What had Fuller thought, Nathan wondered, when the bleeding stopped so quickly? When his thumb began to heal over? Did he understand what was happening to him?

"This guy has the right smell?"

In answer, Emma put her nose to the ground, began following the footprints. They led to his place, Nathan realized, jogging beside her. Fuller must have parked here rather than risk anyone at Nathan's house seeing the truck's headlights or hearing the engine.

Nathan dialled Osborne's cell, and was putting his phone to his ear when the gunshots cracked through the night. He broke into a run. Emma streaked ahead.

He didn't slow to catch his breath when Osborne answered the phone. "Who fired?" Nathan asked.

"I did. It's Mark Fuller, hopped up on something. He took off, out of the house."

"Injuries?"

"Not me or Miss Letty, sir. I hit Fuller but it didn't slow him down."

"Did he have a weapon?"

"If he did, he didn't use it."

All right. "Hold your position. We're coming up on the house now."

Or *he* was. Nathan disconnected, searching for Emma. Her tracks followed the footprints across the wide, moonlit clearing that separated his house from the woods, but he didn't see her or Fuller.

He stopped, used the wide trunk and low branches of a pine at the clearing's edge for cover. The shadows around the house were deep; movement near the back porch caught his eye.

Fuller. Hunched over, and using an eerie, loping gait that sent prickles of dread down Nathan's spine. That gait didn't look human or wolf, but simply *in*human. Moonlight reflected in Fuller's eyes as he turned his head.

He stopped, straightened – and stared directly at Nathan.

Nathan held his breath, but his hopes that Fuller had just been searching the treeline and couldn't see him were dashed when he hunched over again and began loping towards him. An eager, hungry growl carried across the clearing.

Nathan stepped out of the trees, set his feet, steadily aimed his gun. "Drop to the ground, Fuller! Get down, or I *will* fire!"

The werewolf kept running – grinning, panting.

Nathan squeezed the trigger. Blood sprayed the snow behind Fuller's left leg. But he kept on coming.

Cold sweat trickled down the back of Nathan's neck; he fired again: an abdomen shot that twisted Fuller to the side, briefly, before the bastard righted himself. If anything, he seemed to run *faster*. Nathan had time for one more shot. The chest was a bigger target than the head. The head was a kill shot.

His next bullet ripped through Fuller's scalp, laid white bone open to the moonlight. He didn't miss a step.

Nathan stumbled back, searching for the tree branch. He'd get higher, defend himself from a better position, if he had time.

A dark form raced across the clearing and launched at Fuller. Nathan heard the impact of flesh and bone, saw the wave of snow that flew back from the two bodies hitting the ground.

Nathan sprinted towards them. Growls filled the air, yips of pain. Emma's?

No, Nathan realized with relief as their twisting battle came to a halt. Emma pinned Fuller on his back with her large forepaw pressing into his bloodied chest. Her teeth closed over his throat.

Fuller wheezed, his eyes opening wide. He flailed at Emma with his right hand. The thumb was gone, but a tiny protrusion of pink flesh had already begun to grow in its place.

Nathan aimed his weapon at Fuller's head. "Don't move, Mark. Just stay still."

Fuller obeyed, dropping his fists to the snow at his sides. His chest heaved as he tried to draw in air. His frantic gaze met Nathan's. "Can't . . . stop."

"We'll try to get you help," Nathan promised. But he had a feeling they weren't going to get Fuller out of this field. Madness filled the other man's eyes, and Nathan didn't trust that Fuller would stay down if Emma let him go.

But he was staying down now, so Nathan asked, "Did you kill those women? Rape them, and leave them off the highway?"

As if in ecstasy, Fuller's eyes rolled back into his head. He ran his tongue over the grin that stretched his lips. "They were . . . so good. Want more."

Emma's snarl echoed Nathan's own rage.

"And what were you planning to do here?"

Fuller raised his right hand. "Knew . . . you'd find . . . fingerprint. Knew . . . you'd stop me. I can't – don't – want to stop."

Nathan shook his head in disbelief. No, he wouldn't have found a match. Fuller had never been charged or booked. His prints wouldn't have been in the system.

Emma shifted her grip on his throat. Fuller's voice rose an octave, took on a sing-song rhythm. "But when I came to your house, I smelled her. Oh, Miss Letty, Letty, Letty—"

Emma tightened her jaw, cutting off the sick refrain.

"Hold still," Nathan ordered.

Fuller lowered his hand again, but his other hand moved beneath his waist, pulling out—

"Gun, Emma!" Nathan shouted. "Get back!"

Her jaws clamped around Fuller's neck as she twisted away. The rip of flesh was drowned by the roar of a gunshot.

Emma yelped. Nathan shoved her to the side, stomped his boot into the bloody cavity she'd opened in Fuller's throat. He aimed between the bastard's eyes and fired.

Nathan whipped around. Emma lay on the ground, blood spreading over and melting the snow beneath her.

"Emma, Emma, Emma." He fell to his knees, lifted her head onto his lap, stroked his hands over her fur, searching. It was a belly shot. Bad. Really bad for most wolves. "Tell me you're going to be OK."

He heard the crack, felt her ribs bulge beneath his hands. "Jesus Christ, Emma." He tore out of his coat, covered her with it, held her through the transformation. As soon as she lay panting and sweating in his arms, he said, "I just meant for you to nod your head."

She laughed breathlessly, showing him her pale stomach.

Blood stained her skin, but the wound had vanished. "Nice trick, huh?"

His relief grabbed him by his throat, and took away any response he might have had. He hauled her up, sealed her mouth with his kiss, let her feel every emotion rushing through him. She clung to him, returned everything he gave.

He stood and swung her up against his chest, her bare legs dangling over his arm. They stared down at Fuller's body for a silent moment, then Nathan began carrying her towards the house.

He took a long breath. "So, in a little while, once we've got everything settled, maybe you'll take a risk with me."

She lifted her head to look at him. "Marry you?"

His stomach dropped, but there wasn't a bit of him that didn't like the idea. "Well, that too. But I'm thinking more along the lines of you . . . biting me." He brushed his lips against her mouth which had fallen open in surprise. "I'd like to run with you."

Tears shimmered in her eyes before she buried her face against his neck. "Yes," she said. "Of course it's yes. We can be our own little pack." Her lips kissed his skin; her teeth followed it with a nip.

He laughed, pressed his lips over her hair. "Let me get you home first."

"I'm with you," she said simply, and her arms tightened around his neck. "So I'm already there."

The Dream Catcher

Allyson James

I should have listened to my mother.

Normally, Natalia Sorvenska would never have dreamed of answering an invitation to Lady Della's autumnal soiree, no matter how prettily engraved. But the invitation had borne the words: "Lady Della will display a Dream Catcher."

Natalia had never seen a Dream Catcher – mystical beings that lived in the mountainous region beyond the Eastern Rim. They were magical, mysterious, elusive. Snaring one was an astonishing feat.

To judge by the crowd filling Della's mansion on the hill, Natalia surmised that no one else could resist coming either. Della had hung her ballroom with garlands of real autumn leaves imported from the mountain forests, Dream Catchers' realms. It must have been a huge expense to have them transported hundreds of miles across the desert. Musicians had been seated throughout the balconies, and captive glow-flies swirled against the misty black ceiling.

Natalia sipped her blood-red wine and waited for something to happen. She was surprised that Lady Della had bothered to invite her, when Della made no secret that she despised Natalia and women like her. She must want to rub her acquisition of a Dream Catcher in Natalia's face. The other guests were surprised at her inclusion too, if the way faces turned away and skirts were pulled aside when Natalia passed were any indication.

At last they saw movement near the raised platform at the end of the ballroom. Skirts and silken veils rustled as the high-born ladies of Bor Narga pressed forwards to see. Natalia went with them, as shamelessly curious as the rest.

"Ladies." Della N'riss stepped onto the dais and raised her hands for silence. "And gentleman," she added as a deferential afterthought. Her guests dutifully tittered.

"I've had the greatest good fortune. After a very long search, my hunters have at last found and captured a Dream Catcher for me."

She paused, gloating under their gasps of admiration. Della had always demanded the most attention, even when she and Natalia had been childhood friends. Della always had to dance in the front, be given the most sweets, wear the prettiest dress.

Della lifted her hands again, liking her power. "I have decided to share my fortune, my friends. I will allow the Dream Catcher to choose a lady from among my guests and read her dreams." She smiled as a ripple of pleasure ran through the crowd. "And so without further ado, I bring you – the Dream Catcher."

No applause. Too many breaths were held for that. Two men in desert tunics walked onto the dais leading a third man by a rope. The rope was loosely knotted around his neck and again at his wrists, but witch rope didn't need to be tight. Just its touch would keep magical creatures confined.

Natalia froze. The Dream Catcher was a tall man, towering over his captives. He had a broad chest dusted with black hair, shoulder muscles rippling despite the bruises and burn marks on his skin. Black hair flowed like silk down his bare back, and he wore only a leather thong around his hips, a loincloth hiding his privates. The rest of his body was on display for all to see.

Natalia looked. She couldn't help herself. She had never seen so much naked male flesh in her life, not even her husband's. Especially not her husband's. The other ladies pretended to look away, to hide eyes behind veils, but how could they resist?

The Dream Catcher stood upright, not cowed by his capture. But his leg was twisted, and the marks on his body indicated they'd beaten him. He hurt. Natalia suddenly wanted to touch him, to comfort him, to reassure him.

As though he sensed her sudden stab of pity, the Dream Catcher raised his head and looked straight at her.

Natalia felt herself falling, being pulled towards his great silver eyes, larger than a normal man's, intense and magical. But no, she still stood on her two feet halfway across the ballroom. She squeezed the stem of her wine glass, unable to look away. The wine glass broke, and blood trickled down her fingers.

The Dream Catcher cocked his head, staring at her like an animal intent on its prey. The ladies between him and Natalia parted as though his gaze physically shoved them aside.

Lady Della smiled a nasty smile. "It seems he has chosen you, Natalia."

The ladies around her looked disappointed. Some pulled their gauzy veils closer over their faces so they wouldn't be caught having anything so gauche as an emotion.

Natalia turned to Della in confusion, breaking the spell of the Dream Catcher's eyes. "No," she said quickly. "Thank you."

"Don't be ridiculous. The Dream Catcher chooses the one whose desires most call to him."

Her eyes held viciousness. Natalia stared at her in shock. Della couldn't be that cruel, could she? But Della's smile told Natalia that she could. Her triumph in capturing a Dream Catcher must have gone to her head.

"No," Natalia repeated. She deposited her broken wine glass on a nearby table and turned to leave, sweeping her own crimson veil across her face.

The silk stifled her, nearly gagging her. But behind it she could let hot tears build in her eyes. Damn Della. She'd brought Natalia here for this little humiliation, nothing more. To mock Natalia's perversions, to put her in the pillory for daring to want something forbidden.

And damn Ivan Sorvenska's tattling mouth. He'd ruined Natalia when he'd bleated to his own gossipy mother what Natalia had wanted their marriage to be. *Animal lust*, Ivan had sneered when Natalia shyly asked on their wedding night if they could share a bed. *Is that what you are, Natalia, an animal? Why don't you hire a Shareem and have done?*

Shareem were males created long ago for the sole purpose of pleasuring women. They lived in the slums of Pax City, and the occasional scandalous woman went to them for carnality. Some said they'd been bred with Dream Catchers, but no one knew for sure. Natalia had never been able to bring herself to seek out a Shareem.

She'd thought that Ivan the charming, Ivan the handsome, Ivan who'd touched her hand and told her he liked her just as she was, would be amenable to doing what high-born men and women were supposed to shun – lie with each other. That was why she'd rejected the Ministry of Families' carefully chosen mate and married without their blessing.

She'd risked all to marry Ivan then discovered too late that he hadn't wanted a physical marriage after all. He'd charmed Natalia in order to gain access to her money and the Sorvenska family name, which he took upon their marriage. He wore the name like a prize he'd captured. He was disgusted by Natalia's request, and immediately moved to separate living quarters.

Natalia could have borne the humiliation of his rejection, but Ivan had repeated all to his mother. Ivan's mother, who'd never liked Natalia or the Sorvenskas, had spread the tale of her daughter-in-law's disgusting perversions far and wide.

Ivan's mother had urged Ivan to sue for divorce, citing Natalia's unacceptable predilections. Ivan could make much money from the suit as the wronged party. He'd been in the planning stages when he'd died, falling, drunk, from a balcony. People had looked at Natalia in suspicion, but fortunately Natalia had been at a meditation centre during the incident, and the speculation had to die.

Natalia had thought her hungers would disappear after her experience with Ivan. But no, her lustful thoughts continued to plague her. She'd glimpsed a Shareem once, when she'd been running an errand in the middle of the city. His physicality had nearly sent her to her knees. He hadn't even looked at her, but his tightly muscled body and beautiful face had haunted her dreams for months.

She turned back reluctantly, wanting another glimpse of the Dream Catcher. He was still watching her, his silver gaze pulling her like a magnet. She lowered her veil enough to meet his eyes again.

Don't go.

She stopped, startled, but no one else had heard him. His voice was warm, velvety and sensual, and she wanted to hear it again. *Why shouldn't I?* she stammered silently.

He didn't respond. But he couldn't read her mind, could he? Dream Catchers couldn't read actual thoughts, just fantasies, dreams.

Dreams they took and made reality. Whatever you wanted. For a little while. You could touch and hold and taste and smell whatever you wanted. Whatever you desired. For a little while.

Women spent entire fortunes to find Dream Catchers. Some became so enamoured of their dreams that they could not go back to their normal lives. Like a person who could not survive without an excess of wine, these women became addicted to Dream Catchers.

That does not need to happen, his voice whispered. *You do not live on your dreams.*

No kidding, Natalia thought bitterly.

He chuckled, the sound rough but warm. *These women need their rules and their taboos to keep from remembering they are alive. They want to forget. You, Natalia, know you are alive.*

Yes, unfortunately. Natalia's dreams, her needs, never went away. Maybe she was as disgusting as Ivan thought she was.

No, the Dream Catcher said. *You are beautiful.*

All high-born women were beautiful. They could afford to be. *You flatter me.*

Ivan had flattered her before their marriage. Natalia had resigned herself to the fact that he'd used her. Now she preferred to be left alone, far from men with honeyed tongues.

She had a sudden flash of licking honey off the Dream Catcher's tongue. The heat of the vision seared her, and she heard his laugh again.

Yes.

Natalia jerked her gaze from him, breathing hard. As soon as she looked away, his voice, his presence vanished from her head, and she was simply standing in her best gown amid a crowd of women who did not like her.

"What did you see?" Della demanded eagerly.

Natalia flushed. "Nothing."

"Oh, come now. You saw *something.*"

Natalia could feel the Dream Catcher's smile, though his mouth never moved. It gave her a warm, tickly feeling. She couldn't help but turn to him again. He stood calmly, but the witch rope held him as securely as chains.

Let me in, he whispered in her mind. *I need this as much as you do.*

How do you know what I need? she thought angrily.

I know.

Natalia pressed her hands to her hot face. She felt the weight of stares around her, of envy, curiosity, maliciousness.

These ladies wanted her to experience her deepest fantasies right there in front of them. They wanted to watch her rolling around on the floor, moaning and perhaps doing something embarrassing while they watched and laughed.

She risked a quick glance around. Dear gods, they *did* want that. They would make her a laughing stock.

Well, Mother, you did try to warn me.

The trouble was, Della was right. Natalia wanted the Dream Catcher. She wanted his voice in her head again, wanted to hear his deep-throated laugh, wanted him to say her name and tell her she was beautiful. She wanted the fantasies he could give her, wanted him to fulfil her need for passion. He could do this. She could experience it once and let him go.

But not in front of all these people. She'd die first. Nor could she stalk away in a huff as she'd begun to, letting Della win. She could hear Della's taunting laugh already. She had to bring the power back into her own hands.

Natalia resorted to the lowest trick she could think of. She'd only done it once before, the night her mother-in-law had started raving in the middle of the theatre about how disappointing Natalia was. She'd gone on and on at the top of her wine-laden lungs about how Natalia should give her money and property to Ivan absolutely and retire to a meditation centre in the desert.

Natalia's ruse had worked then like a charm. It was the only time in two years the woman had shut up.

Natalia let her eyes roll back in her head, let her body grow limp and hoped she landed on something soft. She heard the velvet laughter of the Dream Catcher over the startled gasps of the guests. *Ah, sweetling, good choice.*

Ochen watched Lady Della, the bitch who'd caught him, snap her fingers and order her servants to carry Natalia to a bed-chamber. Ochen sensed that Della wanted to toss Natalia's body out into the night but knew she could never do such a thing to a high-born woman. Instead she put on the mask of a concerned hostess.

Liar.

Natalia was far more honest. And beautiful. She wore a simple gown of brilliant red, uncluttered by ruffles and stones and the strange fripperies the other women wore. The plainness of the gown enhanced her full breasts, her long legs, the soft roundness of her hips.

Ochen wanted her. He wanted to strip off the sensible clothing and run his hands up and down her blushing body. He wanted to cup her breasts, flick his thumbs across her nipples. He wanted to spread her legs and lick between them, then he wanted to slide his wanting arousal in the place his tongue had wet.

She was starved for desire. In this sprawling desert city women had suppressed such things, making them taboo. Wives and husbands never touched each other, producing offspring by strange methods involving needles that Ochen's people didn't understand and thought barbaric.

But Natalia had desire in her foremost thoughts. She craved it; she needed it. She'd never been properly loved, had never moaned with passion as she rubbed her body over a man's.

Ochen's nature made him look deep into people's minds to pull out their fantasies, but rarely did a woman's mind intrigue him like hers did. The other women here were selfish, bent on their own amusement. Their souls were sticky, like too much sugar candy. The one who had bound him, this Lady Della, had a weak soul, dark and hungry and stupidly cruel. She hadn't even braved the wilds to find him, but had sent out men to trap him.

When he'd looked at Natalia, the small woman with red hair that looped and curled down her back, he'd seen pure, silver light. She had beauty, both outward and inward. The weak Lady Della hated her because Natalia had what she did not: the ability to feel, the ability to love.

Two servants carried Natalia away. She never once betrayed the fact that she hadn't really fainted. He smiled, amused.

Lady Della was glaring at him. Ochen dropped his eyes and refused to raise them, refused to interact with her.

He wouldn't interact with any other woman in the room either, no matter how much Lady Della had her hunters beat him. Disappointed, the guests drifted from the ballroom. Lady Della ordered her men to drag Ochen back down to the tiny room in the cellar and beat him again, just to relieve her feelings.

Natalia dreamed. She'd kept up the pretence of her fainting fit – the Dream Catcher had been too much for her delicate sensibilities, she'd whispered when her eyes fluttered open. She'd accepted a glass of cold water laced with chamomile and lay down in one of Della's spare bedchambers.

She hadn't meant to sleep, but she was exhausted. Maintaining her false front at the ball plus the heady invasion of the Dream Catcher had worn her out.

How pathetic, she thought, but drifted off to sleep anyway.

"Natalia."

He stood at the foot of the bed, his hands free of the witch rope, naked except for the loincloth. His silver eyes were luminescent in the moonlight.

Natalia gasped and sat up. The Dream Catcher stood still, straight and tall, the embodiment of desire. "What are you doing here? Did Della release you?"

"No."

She realized that he was speaking with his mouth, out loud. His voice was no longer just in her head.

Natalia's eyes narrowed in sudden suspicion. "Did she send you up here? Well, you can tell her I'll have nothing more to do with her games."

The Dream Catcher moved around the huge four-poster bed and rested one knee on the mattress. "Della did not send me. You asked me to come."

"Did I?" Natalia raised her brows at him. "Funny, I don't remember that."

"You asked me with your heart." He placed his fingertips between her breasts.

The heart in question banged fast and hard. "You aren't really here, are you?"

"I am a Dream Catcher, Natalia." He slid his hand down her breasts and splayed it across her belly. "Welcome to your dreams."

Natalia tried to make herself wake up, but nothing happened. If she were asleep, she remained stubbornly so.

The Dream Catcher moved his hand across her abdomen, gliding on the silk of her dress. "Don't send me away, Natalia, not yet."

She liked the heat of his hand. "Let me understand. A Dream Catcher is supposed to read my fantasies and let me live them. Make them seem real."

"Yes." His silver eyes warmed.

"Then why are you here? I am supposed to see my *fantasy*, not you in person."

"You know why."

Natalia swallowed, embarrassed by her own thoughts. "Because my fantasies are about you?"

He lowered himself to the bed, never taking his hand from her waist. "When you looked at me, I saw, deep inside you, what you wanted. I was so pleased, Natalia, that you wanted me."

"How mortifying."

"It is wonderful. Because when I saw you, I wanted you too." He stroked his hand through her red hair, loosening it.

"Is this a dream?" she breathed.

"In a sense."

She felt a bite of disappointment. "So whatever happens, it won't be real?"

"It will be real to you. You can do anything you want, and have anything you need, without fear. You can live out your wildest fantasies without coming to any harm, or anyone ever knowing."

"Except you."

"Except me." He grinned, a mischievous spark entering his eyes. "And I won't tell."

Natalia drew a breath. She knew what she wanted, but she suddenly realized that if she let herself have it, she'd never be able to go back to her tedious existence, the narrow confines of a woman of the Bor Nargan upper classes. She'd be too aware of what she was missing.

"I'd rather wake up," she said.

He stroked her hair, the warmth of his body covering the length of her own. "Please, stay with me."

His voice wavered slightly, as though he feared something and tried to hide it.

"Why?"

"Because I am in pain. They beat me until I fell into unconsciousness."

Natalia sat up again. "What?"

"Here, in your dream, I feel no pain. Let me stay."

Anger and worry swirled together. "How dare she? I knew Della was ill-natured, but this—"

He laid his cheek on her hair, his strong fingers finding the lacings of her gown. "I am proud that you have no fear of her."

"I will certainly say a few things to Della when I wake up."

He nuzzled her. "That's my girl. So brave."

Natalia closed her eyes at the feeling of his warm breath, of his fingers slowly unlacing the front of her gown. "No one has ever called me that before."

"Brave and beautiful." He kissed her hair. "You are all that." He spread his hand, parting the placket and finding her bare skin.

"What are my fantasies?" she murmured.

"You know," he said, his breath hot. "You tell me."

"Do you have a name?"

"You may call me Ochen, if you wish."

"Ochen." She closed her eyes, loving his fingers on her hair. "I like that. It sounds exotic."

"Where I come from it sounds ordinary. Not like you, Natalia Sorvenska. Tell me your fantasies."

"But you already know them."

"I want to hear you speak them. Out loud. No one can hear but me."

Natalia remained silent, not sure she could voice what she

wanted, even to him. *But if I can't talk to a fantasy man inside my own dreams, who can I talk to?*

"I want to be loved."

She clamped her lips shut, amazed she'd said that out loud. Bor Nargan women were above such emotions as love, need, passion. They filled their mind with higher things. *And the moons spin backwards, and the sand seas are full of water.*

"That is not a bad thing to want. You are a loving woman."

"That's not the kind of fantasy you meant."

"Yes it is." He kissed her forehead. "I need to know everything you need, and everything you want. Do you love, Natalia?"

She thought of her mother, her grandmother, women who had accepted her love. A warmth began to fill her body, chasing away her irritation at Della and the negative energy that filled Della's house.

"Think on that," Ochen said. "Think of love."

Natalia smiled, warmth filling her, relaxing her limbs.

Ochen ran his fingers up the inside of her arm. "Now. What do you want?"

"Pleasure."

"Of course."

She blushed hard. Ochen was grinning. The man was as handsome as sin, but when he smiled she didn't want to look at anything but him. Ivan was a pale shadow compared to this man.

He leaned down and licked her mouth from corner to corner. "You have the sweetest smile," he whispered.

She wanted to melt into the bed. "You must say that to all the women you pleasure."

"I do not pleasure them." He dipped his finger behind her lips. "I make their fantasies real. I am not in them as myself." He trailed his wet finger down her throat to the hollow. "But with you I am."

"Why?"

"Because it's what's in your dreams."

Natalia laced one hand behind his neck. His hair was warm and silken, feeling so real. She daringly drew his mouth down to hers, and he kissed her.

A soft kiss, no demands. Natalia explored the pads of his lips, hesitant, shy.

"This is a fantasy," Ochen whispered. "You can do whatever you want. There is no one to judge."

"Except you. Obviously."

"But I'm only a Dream Catcher. An animal. A reminder of what civilized people have lost."

Natalia slid fingers through his hair. "You don't look like any animal I've ever seen. I once had a pet sand lizard, but he was scaly and slithered everywhere."

His smile widened. "I'm not human. I can be held in place simply with a piece of bewitched rope. I am a creature of base emotion. What does it matter what I think of you?"

Natalia held his face between her hands. "It matters a great deal."

"Does it?" His hot breath scalded where he kissed the line of her hair. "But you're a great lady of Bor Narga."

"A Sorvenska. Rich, eccentric, despised."

"Shh." He stilled her lips with light kisses. "Beautiful, passionate, envied."

"Shunned."

"They all want to feel what you do. But only you are brave enough to seek it out."

Natalia pulled him close, suddenly impatient. "Make love to me. Please. Let me know what it feels like. I'm burning up for you."

He laughed again, low and throaty. "I burn for you. Can you not feel?"

He positioned his body on top of hers, his hardness pressing through the thin fabric of her gown. It was positively wicked how good that felt. She wriggled against him.

Ochen parted her gown with firm hands, lowered his head and traced her bare nipple with his tongue. Natalia arched against him, the heat of his mouth was incredible. Fire licked her body, making it tight and wonderfully loose at the same time.

"Is this orgasm?" she moaned.

"Not yet, my love. Not even close."

"I'm coming apart."

"No, you're not. You're beautifully whole."

"Do more."

"Mmm, so demanding."

"*Please.*"

Ochen nuzzled her neck, lowering his bare chest to hers. The weight of him, the heat of his body, the tickle of his hair made her wild. She lifted her hips, loving the feel of his hardness behind his loincloth. She wanted no fabric between them.

She slid her hands down his back, exploring his hard muscles. She lingered at the small of his back, then shivered as she moved to the bare mound of his backside. His eyes softened.

Natalia had never touched a man's backside before. She'd never seen one. Ochen's was tight and compact, his skin smooth. She traced circles on it while he smiled at her.

"Natalia, I want you so much."

She sighed happily. "This is a good dream."

His smile faded. A sharp sadness flickered through his eyes, then he kissed her. His tongue moved through her mouth in slow swipes, a man tasting her. His mouth was warm and velvety, wet and hot. Natalia moved her tongue to imitate his, loving the taste of him. She never knew kissing was like this, but it seemed so natural, so normal. Why shouldn't men and women drink of each other?

He pressed his body against hers, rocking into her to fit himself between her legs. The sensation burned, and she wound her arms around him.

"Please," she whispered. "Please."

He rose on his elbows, looking down into her face. His black hair hung like a curtain around them. "I want . . ."

"What? What do you want?" She was desperate for him.

He lightly traced her cheek. "I want this to be real."

"Isn't it real? It feels so real."

"I'm lying, broken, in an underground place. You are sleeping in a room far above me. The darkness, it presses me." His gaze was remote, like he saw two things at once.

"But you're here with me."

"It's illusion, all illusion. I'm very good at illusion."

"Show me what's real then."

His mouth twisted. "You don't want to see that."

"I do." Natalia touched his face. "All my life I've only had dreams. When I thought I'd found real love, real life, I was deceived."

Ochen seized her hand in his strong one. "Then come to me. Help me. I'm at the bottom of the house. They locked me in a room behind . . ." His brow puckered. "Long stems that make noise."

Pipes, Natalia thought. Della had put him behind her boiler room, the cow. "I'll come to you," she said. "Now."

His dazzling, sinful smile returned. "I will be waiting."

"I'd be more flattered if I didn't know you had no choice."

"I would wait for you if I were free in my forest or across the wildest deserts. I'd wait."

"Oh," she said. "I like that."

He gave her a slow kiss, his mouth playful and at the same time masterful. "Please come to me," he said.

He kissed her again, then his body faded, the press of his lips the last thing to go. Natalia found herself holding empty air, and then she woke with a gasp.

She sat up on the bed, her dress whole and laced. The room was darker, most of the lights burned out, and she was alone. She swung her legs out of bed, slid her feet into her shoes and quietly left the room.

Ochen lay cramped in the dark, his hands twisted behind him, the rope burning his throat. If not for the witch rope, he could transport himself instantly back home. He couldn't even wriggle free because the bewitched rope drained him of strength. He could only think and wait. Would she come?

It had been tempting to stay in her fantasy, to make love to her. But he hadn't lied when he'd said he wanted it to be real. All his life he'd searched for a female he could love, one he could take as his own. He never thought it would be a human woman, a high-born lady of the hated Bor Nargans.

The people who ruled this land took and took and took. They used Dream Catchers – when they could find them – like beasts of burden. They were used until drained of magic, and then discarded, left for dead. Dream Catchers thrived on emotion and passion, something these people had banished from their lives.

Lady Della fitted that pattern. She'd kill Ochen in the end. Natalia, on the other hand, had compassion in her. Her fantasy contained nothing brutal or selfish. She was starved for love, craving the physical satisfaction that the women of her land shunned. They thought her horrible for giving in to her true nature. Ochen found her beautiful.

He heard footsteps outside the door, light ones, not the heavy tread of Della's tame hunters. The hunters had not even bothered to stand guard, knowing Ochen couldn't possibly escape.

Something scraped at the lock on the door, then it gave a satisfactory click. Cool air flooded him as the door opened. Natalia dropped to her knees beside him.

"Ochen," she whispered. She lifted his head into her lap, ran light fingers over his hurt body. "They broke your leg. The bastards."

"Because I'm so dangerous." Ochen tried to smile then clenched his teeth over the pain.

"I'll take you to my house. My servants will help me get you out. They're loyal to me. I have healers."

"No," he croaked. "I must be freed."

He peered up at her with the eye that wasn't swollen shut. She glowed with beauty. Her red hair flowed like flame over her shoulders to be swallowed by the red of the dress. "I don't know how."

"Cut the witch ropes, take them from my skin. Then I can return to my people who will heal me."

Natalia bit her lip. "I'll never see you again."

"I will come to you. When I'm healed I'll come back for you."

She didn't believe him. Indecision warred in her brown eyes. "You're using me. You came to me and said those things so I would help you get free."

"No, my love."

"Why should you come back to me? I'm just a human who would trap you and make you fulfil her fantasies."

"I promise, Natalia."

Tears streaked down her cheeks. "Why can't my own healers help you?"

Ochen touched the rope around his neck, jerked his fingers away when it singed him. "This won't let me heal all the way. I'll weaken and die."

"You might be lying to me, so I'll set you free."

"I might be." He closed his eyes. She didn't trust him, and he was a fool to think she would. "But I'm not." His death would be proof he had told her the truth, but he wouldn't be in a position to care then.

He felt her hands on his skin again, soothing, cool. He loved her touch.

And then, unbelievably, he felt a press of cold blade and a jerk of the ropes. He opened his eyes to see Natalia busily sawing at the ropes around his throat with a tiny knife. Her face screwed up with the effort, she was a lady not used to cutting anything more difficult than an apple.

Ochen watched her, unable to help, as the knots loosened and the horrible pain lessened. At last she pulled the ropes from around his neck. She touched the burned flesh where the rope had been, tears tumbling down her cheeks.

Ochen licked away a tear, loving the salty taste of it. She moved around him so she could reach the witch rope that bound his wrists. Her dress brushed his skin, her perfume sweet.

"I can't let you die," Natalia whispered. "It doesn't matter whether I see you again. You'll be alive and safe."

Pain robbed him of too much breath to argue. His leg throbbed in agony, and it was tempting to slip back inside her fantasies to ease the pain. But too dangerous.

"What are you doing?" someone shrieked.

Lady Della stood in the doorway, still in her overly ruffled ball gown, flanked by the two hunters who'd beaten Ochen senseless.

Natalia didn't look up or stop cutting the ropes. "I'm letting him go."

Della strode in and seized Natalia's shoulder. "You have no right to. He's mine."

Natalia shook her off. "He's a living creature, not a slave."

"He's a Dream Catcher. Do you know how hard they are to find, you stupid woman?"

"He'll die if I leave him here," Natalia snapped. "Then you won't have him any more. What's the difference?"

"The difference is that he hasn't done my fantasy yet. You had your turn. Now it's mine."

"I can't help it if he connected with me first." Natalia sounded the slightest bit smug as she continued to work on the ropes.

"You really are stupid, Natalia. He 'connected' with you because I told him to. I promised I'd free him if he did. I wanted him to make a fool of you, because everyone knows what your fantasies are."

Natalia stiffened. She glanced at Ochen for confirmation and he nodded once. Della had told him to choose Natalia, to let her live her sexual fantasies while she stood in the middle of the ballroom. If he did that, she'd have her hunters untie the ropes and let him go.

Things hadn't gone according to plan. Ochen had chosen Natalia all right, but the connection had been real, deep and strong. When Natalia would not let Della humiliate her in front of the others, Della had refused to let him go. Going to Natalia in her dreams had been his choice.

The pain that flooded Natalia's face flooded him, too. He expected her to stand up and walk away, to leave Ochen to Della's mercy.

Instead she put the knife to the rope again. "It doesn't matter."

"You really are pathetic, Natalia. He is *my* property."

"Slavery is illegal on Bor Narga."

"*Human* slavery. He's not human. He's animal."

One more cut, and the ropes fell from his wrists. The burning ceased.

"He is free," Natalia said quietly.

Ochen touched her cheek. "Thank you."

Della shouted at her hunters and lunged for him, but Ochen had already formed the clear thought of his own lands in his mind. He aimed there, and Natalia, Della, her hunters and the tiny room dissolved into light. The last things he saw were Natalia's beautiful brown eyes, then he was home.

"So how was it?" Natalia's mother peered at her over breakfast the next morning in the elegant dining room. Carefully placed screens kept the desert sun from being too harsh, and the result was a room of cool shadows and splashes of light.

"Terrible." Natalia picked at her cold grouse eggs. "Della did have a Dream Catcher, but he got away."

"Good for him." Arene Sorvenska sniffed. "I'd hate to be bound to that woman."

"Yes, Della's men beat him. But he's gone now."

"Evil little witch. Best you don't have anything more to do with her, dear."

"No fear, Mama."

"Good." Arene sniffed and went back to reading her beloved newspaper.

Natalia had half-expected Ochen to come to her in the night. He hadn't, of course. He was likely back in his mountain realm, wherever it was, healing and doing his best to forget about his captivity.

It wasn't his fault he had to use me to free himself. He was desperate. It's nothing personal.

She should be used to men using her by now. But the hurt when he'd confirmed that Della had bribed him to choose her twisted like a hot knife. Of course he'd obeyed. His first concern had been to get away. If she were ever a captive, she'd be more worried about freeing herself than the feelings of her captors.

At least he'd given her a glimpse of what passion was like. She should be satisfied with that and go on.

Natalia threw down her napkin and sprang to her feet. No. She was tired of being unsatisfied, tired of making do, tired of resigning herself to disappointment. Was this what her life was to be, quietly living down her humiliation with no chance at real happiness?

Her mother looked up in surprise. "Is something wrong, dear?"

"I'm going out. A long way out. A trip into the desert. It may be a while."

"To a meditation centre? Good idea, dear. You've been restless lately."

"I'll pack and go today."

Arene smiled. "Have a good time." Natalia bent so her mother could kiss her cheek. She left the room, hearing her mother's "Dear, dear," before she turned back to her newspaper.

The Sorvenskas' hunter and gamekeeper wasn't optimistic about Natalia's chances of finding a Dream Catcher, let alone a specific one, but he agreed to take her to the mountains. After all, the Sorvenskas paid well.

He led Natalia past the Eastern Rim to an area so remote and treacherous that they had to tackle the last miles on foot. Natalia had never been in mountains, had never left the great desert around the oasis city where most of humanity dwelled.

The uplands were cool and moist, strange to her. Trees grew straight out of the cliffs so thick that the rocks could barely be seen. Even in her sturdy hunting boots and leggings, Natalia slipped and slid, cut her hands through her gloves. Exercises that kept a lady trim were not good training for climbing through mountains. The gamekeeper, Bahl, was patient with her, but she could see he worried.

Ahead of her Bahl stopped suddenly. The trail he'd been breaking the last day or so ceased abruptly at the edge of a gorge. The gorge spanned at least 1,000 feet and dropped to a misty river far below.

Bahl wiped his forehead. "We'll have to turn back, my lady. We don't have enough supplies to go much further, only enough to get back to our transport."

"You can go," Natalia said, sitting on a boulder. "Leave me here."

He looked alarmed. "No, my lady. Your mother would kill me."

Natalia sighed. "I suppose she would. And it would be my fault. The gods save me from my keen sense of responsibility."

Bahl patted her shoulder in compassion. "Not everyone's path is easy."

"Especially a gamekeeper's whose mistress wants to go on damn fool expeditions." She gave Bahl a tired smile. She wondered why she thought she could find Ochen. It had taken Della's two hunters years to find him, and he'd be doubly careful now.

"Don't worry," she said, an emptiness inside her. "We'll go back."

She stood up to turn around, and slipped on mud that sent her plunging to the edge of the gorge. Bahl grabbed at her and missed, his face terrified. Natalia scrambled for a hold then felt herself being lifted in strong, bare arms.

Her feet left the ground and she rose, high, higher still, to the very tops of the trees. Bahl grabbed a rifle and pointed it skywards, but didn't fire.

Ochen deposited Natalia on a huge platform in the trees, held by strong boughs around a mighty trunk. She whirled around and stared at him, shocked and out of breath.

Ochen's face and body were completely healed. He looked as gorgeous and whole as he had when he lay on top of her in her dream, and he was wearing just as little. The dream had been but a taste of the real Ochen. This was his solid, beautiful flesh.

But he was glaring at her, not looking pleased to see her. "What are you doing here? Having a society outing?"

"Not . . . Not exactly."

"You were hunting a Dream Catcher."

"I was looking for you."

Ochen stopped. He studied her, his silver eyes regarding her in suspicion. It unnerved her.

"I didn't know you could fly," she said.

"I can do many things." He looked her up and down, and she knew she didn't look half as good as he did. She was sunburned, bug-bitten, scratched, sweat-stained and worn out.

"Were you looking to relive your fantasy?" he asked.

"No," she said tartly. "I came to ask why you haven't come back. I remember you promising you'd come to me."

"I did," he said. He folded his arms, which did nice things to his shoulders and biceps. "I went to you, and you weren't there."

"Because I was here. Didn't you know?"

"You didn't leave a note."

"But I thought . . ." She stopped and rubbed a hand through her dirt-streaked hair. "You would know where I was."

"It doesn't work that way, Natalia. I read your fantasies and your dreams, yes, but I have to be within a certain range. I knew where you lived, but didn't know where you'd gone."

"Well, I'm here now."

"Why?"

"Because I want to be with you." She got to her feet, trying to adjust to the fact that she was hundreds of feet off the ground – in a *tree*. "I got tired of waiting."

"You didn't wait very long."

Natalia jabbed her finger into his chest. "That's not true. I've waited all my life. I've waited for someone who saw me, the real me, and didn't find me disgusting."

He stared at her. "How could anyone find you disgusting?"

"They do, my love. They think of you as a wild animal with no soul, but they see me as little better. I like emotion and feeling and desire. Ergo, there must be something wrong with me."

"No, there is something wrong with *them*."

Natalia brushed herself off and looked around the platform which, she realized, was built of woven, living tree limbs. For someone raised in the dead desert, the idea of plants having this much strength was decidedly odd.

"Well, I didn't come here to fall at your feet and beg you to take me in," Natalia said. "I just wanted to see you. To find out if you'd healed. To properly say goodbye."

He closed his large hand around her arm. He didn't hurt her, but the grip was so firm she knew she'd never break it. "Why should we say goodbye?"

"You're a Dream Catcher, I'm a city woman." She tried to sound uncaring. "Although all *this* is beautiful."

"And it's mine."

"You own the tree?"

He laughed, his velvety, throaty laugh. He released her and gestured to the end of the platform. "Everything you see from here is mine. This is my realm."

Natalia peeped over the edge, dizzy from the height. She noted that no railing ran around the platform. No need, for a being who could fly. Between the boughs, she saw a carpet of forest that ran on endlessly. Mist from the gorge rose in the middle of it.

"My family lives here too," he said, his warmth at her back. "Sisters, brothers, cousins."

"Do they fly, too?"

"Yes."

"I don't," she said.

"It doesn't matter." Ochen closed his arms around her waist. "I will hold you and not let you fall."

Natalia looked into his silver eyes. She felt herself caught, as she had in Della's ballroom, as though his eyes swallowed her. She blinked. "No. I don't want the fantasy. I want you." She had a panicked thought. "This isn't a dream, is it? I'm not hanging on the edge of the gorge unconscious, am I?"

Ochen flicked his fingers over her cheek. "You'd be cleaner in a fantasy."

"Thanks a lot."

"But I like you this way." Ochen kissed the end of her nose. "Stay with me, Natalia." His expression darkened. "Please."

"For now," she whispered.

He snatched her up in his arms and leaped from the platform. A wash of cold air robbed her of a scream, and then they were on another platform, smaller and higher, again made of living branches. This one had a bed, or at least a pallet of fresh leaves. The garlands Della had brought in for her soiree paled in comparison to this living bed. Ochen laid her down on it.

"What am I, Queen of the forest?" she asked.

In answer, he pulled off her boots, unlaced her leggings and tunic and tugged them off. Natalia instinctively grabbed at the fabric. She shouldn't be unclothed outdoors. She shouldn't be unclothed in front of another person. High-born ladies were never naked in front of anyone from two seconds after they were born until . . . well, never. Even bathing was done in absolute, strict privacy.

Ochen plucked a leaf from a nearby branch, held it between his hands, then rubbed it over her skin. She started to ask what he was doing, but she saw that her scratches, her insect bites and the swelling in her hands faded and disappeared. He was healing her.

"Is this how you healed yourself?" she asked.

He nodded. "My brother had to charge the leaves for me, but yes."

"I'm surprised Dream Catchers aren't captured for that skill instead."

"It only works with the leaves from one of the Dream Catcher's own trees. How long do you think it would be before the trees were harvested and the Dream Catchers imprisoned?"

"Not long."

"Your kind has their medicines of their own making. We have our leaves."

"I'm just surprised no one knows about it."

"They only see us as bringing their fantasies to life," Ochen said. "They've so closed themselves off to joy and pleasure that they can only see us as a way to live their dreams. That is more important than healing to them."

Natalia looked at her clean skin. "Thank you."

Ochen pushed her back into the pallet. The leaves were soft, fragrant, embracing. Ochen nuzzled her, his kisses lazy.

Natalia moved one bare foot along his leg, loving the sensation of his firm muscles. His kisses turned intense, bruising.

"Please stay with me," he whispered.

"You are very demanding. My guide must be worried about what happened to me."

"I sent one of my brothers to explain and make him comfortable."

"Very civil of you."

His smile returned. "Do you want more persuasion?"

"I wouldn't mind."

Fire shot up and down her limbs as he dropped kisses onto her mouth, her throat, her breasts. She moaned, arching to him, wanting him.

He pulled off his loincloth, and now there was nothing between them. Skin met skin, body met body, for the first time in Natalia's life.

Ochen's silver eyes were intense, watching her. "I don't want to hurt you."

"You won't." Natalia had been to the clinic, had her maidenhead removed when she went through her coming of age ceremony. Not that anyone ever expected her to actually have intercourse.

"I don't ever want to hurt you." Ochen closed his beautiful eyes, and suddenly, she was filled with him, his large arousal spreading her wide, making her catch her breath.

"All right?" he murmured.

"Very, very all right," Natalie tried to say. It came out garbled.

He still looked concerned, so she grabbed his face between her hands and kissed him hard. His face relaxed in passion, and he began to move, slowly, inside her.

This was desire. This was lovemaking. At last, at long last.

Natalia drew a breath, then her body went tight and hot, his hard, blunt arousal pressing inside her. "Ochen. I'm going to . . . I don't know. Fly apart."

"Let it happen." His eyelids were heavy. "Let it happen, my love."

Natalia wasn't sure what would happen, but black waves of sensation suddenly swamped her. She twisted and writhed, sobbing his name, her nails scrabbling for purchase on his back.

"Yes," he whispered. "Yes, love."

They climaxed together. She'd read of climax, but the scientific description fell flat. This was joy, love, power, strength. Ecstasy. It was better than she'd ever imagined it could be.

She landed on her back, Ochen heavy on top of her. His laughing mouth met hers, and they kissed and rocked and laughed some more.

"Stay with me," Ochen said when they quieted again. "I love you, Natalia."

"Yes." Natalia smiled up at him, the man who had showed her passion without judging her. He'd seen her innermost fantasies, her hopes and dreams, and they pleased him. "Do you know what my fantasy is now?"

Ochen let his gaze bore into hers. Natalia felt herself spinning, but she knew she lay under him safe and sound.

"You are naughty," he said, his smile wicked.

"Only with you."

"Yes, I know. Your fantasy is to stay with me and make love with me always."

"Pretty much."

"Then stay. Do not go back to that empty world."

Natalia looked around at the strange, green, living place that seemed to match Ochen. "I'll have to tell my mother, and pack a few things. But yes, I'll stay."

He nuzzled her neck. "What changed your mind? Our love-making?"

"My mother always told me that, when I found my heart's desire, I should hold it with both hands." Natalia gripped Ochen's shoulders. "So I am."

Ochen took her hand in his and kissed it. "Your mother is very wise."

"She is." Natalia gave him a lazy smile. "I always listen to her."

Author Biographies

C. T. Adams and Cathy Clamp
Award-winning *USA Today* bestselling authors have written
nearly a dozen paranormal romances, including the Sazi
Shapeshifter series and the Thrall Vampire trilogy.
ciecatrunpubs.com

Ilona Andrews
New York Times bestselling urban-fantasy author of the Kate
Daniels series.
ilonaland.com

Kelley Armstrong
USA Today and *New York Times* bestselling author of the
Otherworld series.
kelleyarmstrong.com

Anya Bast
National bestselling author of the Elemental Witches series.
anyabast.com

Meljean Brook
Critically-acclaimed author of the *Guardian* paranormal
romance series.
meljeanbrook.com

Rachel Caine
Award-winning author of the Weather Warden, Red Letter Days, and Morganville Vampires series.
rachelcaine.com

Alyssa Day
RITA award-winning and *USA Today* bestselling author of the Warrior of Poseidon series.
alyssaday.com

Lori Devoti
Author of the Unbound series from Silhouette Nocturne.
loridevoti.com

Jeaniene Frost
New York Times and *USA Today* bestselling author of the Night Huntress series.
jeanienefrost.com

Lynda Hilburn
Author of *The Vampire Shrink* and *Dark Harvest*, the first two books in the Kismet Knight, Vampire Psychologist series. She writes dark urban fantasy and paranormal romance.
lyndahilburnauthor.com

Allyson James
Author of the Dragon series and erotic romances, she writes as *USA Today* bestselling and RITA award-winning author Jennifer Ashley.
allysonjames.com

Dina James
Her first short story, "Play Dead" was published in *The Mammoth Book of Vampire Romance*. "Once A Demon" is her second foray into the world of the Destrati.
dinajames.com

Jean Johnson
Bestselling author of the Sons of Destiny series.
jeanjohnson.net

Sherrilyn Kenyon
#1 *New York Times* bestselling author of The Dark-Hunters series (among others). She writes the Lords of Avalon series as Kinley MacGregor.
sherrilynkenyon.com

Holly Lisle
Writes paranormal suspense and romance, fantasy, SF, and young adult fiction, and gives very unorthodox courses on writing.
hollylisle.com

Sara Mackenzie
Bestselling author of both paranormal and historical romance (under the name Sara Bennett), she has been nominated for a RITA by the RWA.
saramackenzie.com

Cheyenne McCray
New York Times and *USA Today* bestselling author of the Magic series.
cheyennemccray.com

Catherine Mulvany
Award-winning author of the *Wicked* series.
catherinemulvany.com

Mary Jo Putney
New York Times and *USA Today* bestselling author of over thirty books and counting. She writes paranormal, historical and contemporary romance, and is the recipient of two RITA awards.
maryjoputney.com

Michelle Rowen
Bestselling and award-winning author of the Immortality Bites vampire series.
michellerowen.com

Eve Silver
Bestselling, award-winning author of contemporary paranormals, historical suspense, and speculative romance (under the pseudonym Eve Kenin).
evesilver.net

Maria V. Snyde
Award-winning, *New York Times* bestselling author of *Poison Study*, *Magic Study* and *Fire Study*. Her next book, *Storm Glass* will be out in spring 2009, and *Sea Glass* follows in the autumn.
mariavsnyder.com

Carrie Vaughn
New York Times bestselling author of a series of novels about a werewolf named Kitty who hosts a talk radio show for the supernaturally disadvantaged.
carrievaughn.com

Anna Windsor
Author of the Dark Crescent Sisterhood series.
annawindsor.net